GONE TO SOLDIERS

MARGE PIERCY

Simon & Schuster Paperbacks

New York London Toronto Sydney New Delhi

Simon & Schuster Paperbacks
An Imprint of Simon & Schuster, Inc.
1230 Avenue of the Americas
New York, NY 10020

"Of Chilblains and Rotten Rutabagas" was previously published in *Lilith* 12–13, Winter-Spring 1985/5745, pp. 9–12. "Naomi/Nadine Is Only Half" was previously published in *Forum*, a Women's Studies Quarterly, vol. 12, 3/4, Spring/Summer 1986, pp. 1, 10, 11, 19.

This Simon & Schuster trade paperback edition October 2015

For information about special discounts for bulk purchases, please contact Simon & Schuster Special Sales at 1-866-506-1949 or business@simonandschuster.com.

The Simon & Schuster Speakers Bureau can bring authors to your live event. For more information or to book an event, contact the Simon & Schuster Speakers Bureau at 1-866-248-3049 or visit our website at www.simonspeakers.com.

Interior design by Leydiana Rodríguez

Manufactured in the United States of America

10 9 8 7 6 5 4 3 2 1

Library of Congress Cataloging-in-Publication Data

Piercy, Marge.
    Gone to soldiers.
  1. World War, 1939–1945—Fiction. I. Title.
  PS3566.I4G6   1987
  813'.54   86-830118

ISBN 978-1-5011-1876-0

CONTENTS

CONTENTS

The survivors have written their own books
and those who perished are too many and too hungry
for this to do more than add a pebble to the cairn

So this is for my grandmother Hannah
who was a solace to my childhood
and who was a storyteller even in the English
that never fit comfortably in her mouth

for the moment when she learned that of her
village, none and nothing remained

for her weak eyes, strong stomach and the tales
she told, her love of gossip, of legend
her incurable romantic heart
her gift for making the past
walk through the present

LOUISE 1

A Talent for Romance

Louise Kahan, aka Annette Hollander Sinclair, sorted her mail in the foyer of her apartment. An air letter from Paris. "You have something from your aunt Gloria," she called to Kay, who was curled up in her room listening to swing music, pretending to do her homework but being stickily obsessed with boys. Louise knew the symptoms but she had never learned the cure, not in her case, certainly not in her daughter's. Kay did not answer; presumably she could not hear over the thump of the radio.

Personal mail for Mrs. Louise Kahan in one pile. The family stuff, invitations. An occasional faux pas labeled Mr. and Mrs. Oscar Kahan. Where have you been for the past two years? Then the mail for Annette Hollander Sinclair in two stacks: one for business correspondence about rights, radio adaptations, a contract with Doubleday from her agent Charley for the collection of stories *Hidden from His Sight.* Speaking engagements, club visits, an interview Wednesday.

The second pile for Annette was fan mail, ninety-five percent from women. Finally a few items for plain Louise Kahan: her *Daily Worker,* reprints of a *Masses and Mainstream* article she had written on the Baltimore shipyard strike, a book on women factory workers from International Publishers for her to review, William Shirer's *Berlin Diary.*

Also in that pile were the afternoon papers. Normally she would pick them up first, but she could not bring herself to do so. Europe was occupied by the Nazis from sea to sea, an immense prison. Everywhere good people and old friends were shot against walls, tortured in basements, carted off to camps about which rumors were beginning to appear to be more than rumor.

She leaned on the wall of the foyer, gathering energy to resume her life, to walk into the emotional minefield that lately seemed to constitute her relationship with Kay. The foyer was the darkest room of the suite, for the living room, her office and Kay's bedroom enjoyed views of the Hudson River, and her own bedroom and the dining room looked down on Eighty-second Street. She had lightened the hall with a couple of cleverly placed mirrors and the big bold Miró with the spotlight on it, which she contemplated now, seeking gaiety, wit, light.

The talk she had given two hours before had bored her, if not her audience. Passing the shops hung with tinsel, she found Christmas harder to take than usual. The world was burning to ash and bone, and all her countrymen could think of was Donald Duck dressed in a Santa Claus suit. She ought to cross town to the East Side soon to get lekvar for a confection she liked to bake at Chanukah, a Hungarian-Jewish treat her mother had made, but the shop that had it was in German Yorkville. She needed a belligerent mood to brave the swastikas openly displayed, the Nazi films playing in the movie theaters, *Sieg im Westen,* Victory in the West, the German-American Bund passing out anti-Semitic tracts on the corners.

Next to the mail was a list of phone calls, scrawled when Kay had taken them: Ed from the Lecture Bureau called. Call him tomorrow A.M. He sounds bothered.

Some lunatic called about how she wants you to write her life story.

Daddy called.

The notes from her secretary Blanche or her housekeeper Mrs. Shaunessy were neater:

Mr. Charles Bannerman, 11:30. He wants to know if the contracts came.

Mr. Kahan, 2:30. He is in his office at Columbia.

Mr. Dennis Winterhaven, at 3, said he would call back.

Miss Dorothy Kilgallen called about interviewing you December 12.

Oscar had called twice. She tried to treat that as a casual occurrence, but nothing between them would ever be reduced to the affectless, she knew by now. At the simple decision that she must return his call, her heart perceptibly increased its flowthrough, damned traitorous pump. She cleaned up the business calls first, straightening out her schedule, glancing at the contracts and initialing where she was supposed to initial and signing where she was supposed to sign. She certainly could use the money.

She also decided she would talk to Kay before taking on her ex-husband. She knocked. At fifteen she had longed for privacy with a passion she could still remember. She granted Kay the sovereignty of her room, although it took restraint. Louise knew herself to be an anxious parent. She wanted to be closer to Kay again, as close as they had been when Kay was younger, even as she knew Kay needed to assert her independence. Somewhere was the right tone, the right voice, the right touch to ease that soreness.

"Gosh, that's an Annette hat!" Kay said. She was sprawled on the floor, all legs and elbows and extra joints in a pleated skirt that was rapidly losing its pleats and an oversized shirt in which her barely developed body was lost, as if dissolved. She turned down the radio automatically when Louise came in.

Louise touched the hat: a cartwheel in pink and black, with a loop of veil over the eyes. "I was addressing a literary club in Oyster Bay."

"*Literary?*" Kay screeched. "What do they want with you?"

"That's what they call themselves, but they aren't reading Thomas Mann." Unpinning the hat, she balanced it on two fingers, twirling it. She stepped out of her high heels and sank in the rocking chair to massage her tired feet. "Did your daddy say what he wanted, Kay?"

Kay giggled. "I told him about my essay and he practically wrote it for me on the phone."

"I'm sure that was very helpful," Louise said, tasting the vinegar in her voice. "Did he volunteer anything else?"

Kay shrugged. Clearly she did not care to share the riches of a private conversation with her father.

Louise remembered. "Here's a letter for you from your aunt Gloria."

Gloria, Oscar's sister, had been caught by the outbreak of war in Paris. Gloria was Kay's favorite aunt, the glamorous other she longed to be: a chic black-haired beauty who worked as a stringer reporting French fashions for stateside magazines. Gloria, like Oscar, had been born in Pittsburgh, but the only steel remaining was in her will. Louise admired her sister-in-law's willpower and her style, although Gloria had no politics besides opportunism and had married a vacuous Frenchman with more money than sense and more pride than money.

Gloria took her aunt's duties seriously. She was childless, for her French husband, some twenty years her senior, had grown children who obviously preferred that he propagate no more. As Kay knocked through a rocky adolescence, Gloria sent her inappropriate presents (either too childish—stuffed bears—or sophisticated beaded sweaters) and anecdotal letters, which Kay cherished.

Now Louise stirred herself, sighing. She brushed a cake crumb from the skirt of her rose wool suit and looked at herself in Kay's mirror. "You look elegant, Mommy. Why are you still dressed up? Are you going out again?"

"No, darling, not a step. I just wanted to check in with you." She did look reasonably soignée, her complexion rosy above the rose suit, her hair well cut, close to the sides of her oval face whose best feature was still its finely chiseled bones and whose second best feature was the big grey eyes set off by auburn hair. Louise had always taken for granted being attractive to men; it was a given, not worth much consideration, but an advantage she could count on. Now she examined her looks warily, as she did her bank account each month. Expenses were high for their fatherless establishment, and the cost of living could write itself quickly on the face of a woman of thirty-eight. Little vanity was involved. She reasoned that when an advantage was lost, it was well to take that into account. But the mirror assured her she remained attractive, if that was of any use.

When she thought of marrying again, she wondered where she would put a man. After Oscar had walked out, she and Kay and Mrs. Shaunessy and her secretary Blanche had quickly filled the space. She would not give up having an office to work in, never again satisfy herself with a dainty secretary in a corner of the bedroom behind a screen. She smiled at the reflection she was no longer seeing, thinking how that setup was a symbol of the way she had had to pursue her work in a corner while living with Oscar. Everything had been subordinated to him at all times.

"Mother! You use that mirror more than I do."

She realized Kay was sitting with Gloria's letter unopened in her lap, waiting for her to leave so that she could engorge it in private. Feeling shut out, Louise departed at once. Supper would be better. She and Kay would talk at supper, for often that was their best time. She would turn her afternoon into a string of funny stories to make Kay laugh, then ask her about school and her friends. She was always courting her daughter lately. She had to restrain herself from buying too many presents, but maybe Saturday they could go shopping together, in the afternoon. She could remember their intimacy when she had known all Kay's hopes and wishes and fears by heart, when she had held Kay and sung to her, "You Are My Sunshine," and meant it. Her precious sun child whose life would be entirely different, safer and better than her own, poor and battered, growing up.

Now she could not put off calling Oscar. She thought of questioning Mrs. Shaunessy about his exact words, but her procrastination and anxiety were not yet totally out of control. Door shut, she put her bedroom telephone on her lap, then changed her mind and decided to call him on her office phone. Desk to desk. That felt safer. Louise sat in her swivel chair looking with satisfaction on the little kingdom of work she had created and then reluctantly she dialed Oscar's number at his Columbia University office.

"Oscar? It's Louise. You called?"

"Louie! How are you. Just a moment." He spoke off-line. The voices continued for several moments while she sat grimacing with impatience. "Sorry to keep you waiting, but I wanted to pack off my assistant to the outer office."

"Assistant what?"

"I'm running an interview project on German refugees. I have a student of mine interviewing the men, and a young lady of Blumenthal's who's going to start on the females. How are you, Louie? I spoke to Kay earlier. We had a quite intelligent conversation about the meaning of democracy."

"Kay said you'd blocked out her essay for her over the phone."

"Isn't the news rotten these days? I turn on the radio expecting to hear that Moscow has fallen."

"They're fighting in the suburbs. I keep waiting for the legendary Russian winter to do its historic task and freeze out the Nazis—"

"I saw Oblonsky last week. He was in Leningrad, you know. He says they're starving."

"Not literally," Louise said acerbically. She disliked hyperbole.

"Quite literally. People are dying of hunger and the cold. He said they're dropping in the thousands with no one to bury them."

Louise was silent. She and Oscar had friends among the intellectuals and writers of Leningrad, a city they preferred to Moscow. Oscar spoke some Russian, and they had visited the Soviet Union in 1938. Finally she said, "I suppose we won't know till the war is over what's happened to everyone." She sighed and Oscar at his end sighed too. "Oh, Gloria wrote Kay."

"What did she have to say?"

"You'll have to ask your daughter."

"I'm sure Gloria is fine. She's well insulated from the Nazis, and I can't imagine why they'd take an interest in her. I do wish she'd get herself back here, but I suppose she sees little reason to pick up and leave. After all, she's a citizen of a neutral power."

"What's on your mind, Oscar? I had two messages from you."

"Sunday's our anniversary. The seventh, right?"

"It was extraordinary for you to remember it the fifteen years we were married, all my friends used to tell me, but don't you think it's superfluous to note it since we're divorced?"

"I still don't know why you wanted a divorce—"

"It's been final for a year now. Isn't that late to debate it? I found it absurd being married to a man I was no longer living with."

"Don't let's quarrel about that now. I thought it would be nice to have supper together for old time's sake. After all, we'll think about each other all evening anyhow. Why not do it together?"

"Are you asking me for a date, Oscar?" She sounded ridiculous, but she was playing for time.

"That's what I'm doing. Wouldn't it be rather sweet? We haven't sat down in a civilized way and shared a good meal and a bottle of wine in ages. I'd love to tell you what I'm doing. And hear all your news too, of course."

Oscar hated to let go of women. He tried to retain all his old girlfriends in one or another capacity, friends, colleagues, dependents, at least acquaintances. He was used to demanding his widowed mother's attention still. He could not see why he should ever let go of any woman whose attendance he had enjoyed. He also knew how to manipulate her desire for advice and commiseration on her problems with Kay. She could not imagine ceasing to be curious about Oscar; one problem she had with all other men was comparing them to him. Dennis Winterhaven said she made Oscar into a myth, but he did not know Oscar.

"Come, Louie, why not? I'll take you anyplace you want to go. But I've dis-covered a wonderful Spanish restaurant on Fourteenth, refugees of course, fine guitarist, perfect paella."

She was supposed to see Dennis that evening, but not till seven. They were having supper and then he was taking her to hear Hildegarde at the Savoy. "I have plans for Sunday evening. But I could have Sunday dinner with you."

"Pick you up at one?"

"Fine." The moment she hung up she paced her office. Why had she agreed? Because she could not resist seeing him. She would be safe, seeing Dennis just afterward. Oscar was right, of course; she would spend the evening thinking of him. She wished she had the capacity to fall in love with Dennis. The dinner was theoretically rich in possibilities. How to use her skittery feelings? Her fingers sketched circles on the pad. She could not have a divorcée as heroine. They were only the occasional villainess in the slick magazines. She herself adored the racy sound of being a divorcée. She had graduated from dull wifehood, emerging a glorious tropical butterfly, but one with a wasp sting.

Could she get away with the couple being separated? Or would it have to be a man almost married, years before? That was safer. The anniversary was of the day they had almost married, but she had decided not to. Now why? Louise glanced at the clock. She had a couple of hours before dinner. She dug for the buried fantasy that lay in the bland story. That was her power, to exploit that vein like radioactive ore in rock, the uranium Madame Curie had worked; or, more honestly, a layer of butter cream in a cake, the power of fantasizing what women really wanted to happen. Let's see, how about a widow? Widowed young? They weren't into war deaths yet, but how about an accident? No blame attached, proceed at your own pace now. A second chance at a man you'd turned down or dropped for reasons you now know were unworthy. Yes, she would work that secret fantasy in married women that their idiot husband should suddenly drop dead and the one who got away came back on the scene. This was a sure seller.

What she needed was a good hook and a good title. A bouquet of yellow roses coming suddenly to the door. A mistake, surely. The memory years before. Call her Betsy. That's a nice safe respectable-sounding name. It was a New England story, she decided, one of the ones she would set in her invented Cape Ann town of Glastonbury. A fisherman who went down in a storm? Or a commuting husband in a train accident? That would provide better class identification for her readers.

Funny how the phone call with Oscar set her off. She had often worked the effluvia of their life together for exploitable material. Growing up, Louise had never fantasized about being a novelist or a short story writer. She had wanted to be a journalist, a foreign correspondent, a Dorothy Thompson. She had written her first story when Oscar was out of work and Kay was a little girl and they had no money for rent. With the apartment they were renting in farthest Flatbush had come a shelf of *Saturday Evening Posts, Ladies' Home Journals,* issues of *McCall's* and *Redbooks.* They had not the money to buy a newspaper that winter. Oscar used to pick them up on the street after other people had read them.

That her story sold astonished her. She could still remember shopping on that money, buying chicken, lamb chops, buying Kay a real doll with hair and eyes that shut, buying Oscar a warm sweater and paying the back rent. The next one did not sell, nor did the next, but then she sold another. She began to study what worked and what didn't; she analyzed stories they printed according to sociological and psychological profiles of acceptable heroines and heroes. She laid out the plots of twenty stories each from the six highest-paying magazines. She sharpened her focus and began to sell regularly.

The pen name was the one she had signed to her first story, when she noticed no Jewish names among the writers published and that women whose names implied marriage seemed to sell well. She had invented Annette Hollander Sinclair, and later when that lady became a popular writer of women's fiction, she learned to become her for appearances. She bought Annette separate suits, hats, gloves, shoes, purses. She even had an Annette voice. Dennis, she thought, had fallen in love with Annette, which was probably why she was not in love with him. Oscar at least wanted to dine with Louise. Ashamed of herself, she began cautiously to look forward to Sunday. In the meantime she ran across the hall, changed into a comfortable smock and full peasant skirt, slipped her feet into furry bunnies and then resumed at her desk the story of Betsy whose husband died in a train wreck on the 5:15 commuter from North Station; and whose lover sent yellow roses and smiled enigmatically, whose laugh was boyish, but whose black roguish Asiatic eyes were borrowed from Oscar.

DANIEL 1

An Old China Hand

As Daniel Balaban crossed the bridge from the Harvard Business School, where he and his fellows were being housed, to the older Harvard on the Cambridge side of the Charles, he gazed at the crowds of undergraduates with as curious and wary an eye as he had the polyglot strollers in the Bund. He did not belong here. The Navy was playing a little joke on Harvard, having collected a wild assortment of sons of missionaries, naval career officers, old China hands who had been there on economic or military business over the last twenty years. Most of them had some Japanese, but others, like himself, only knew Chinese. The Navy had brought them here for a crash course in Japanese at the Yenching Institute in the yard. Daniel, the child of an immigrant Jewish family huddled in the Bronx, a student who had shown spotty ability and arrived at no particular ambition, at least none for which degrees were given, worked hard at his Japanese and looked around with surprise, pleased but also amused at his good fortune.

Daniel remembered the Depression well enough so that he was convinced he would never forget how hunger felt and how it reduced a person to nothing but itself. His father had come to the United States at fifteen from Kozienice in Poland. Gradually he had built up a small button business that prospered in the twenties. He believed in his adopted country and wanted only to do as the Americans did. He took Daniel and his older brother Haskel to see the Giants play, and he thanked his business contacts profusely for the stock market tips they passed on to him. They were doing well, very well, as in his dreams. It disappeared overnight, as if it never had been: fairy gelt. Daniel thought that neither of his parents had ever got over the shock of all that money melting into debts. Within two months, they were no longer prosperous and shortly after that, they were poor.

Uncle Nat, who had been a businessman in Germany, left as soon as Hitler

assumed power. Thriving in Shanghai, Nat sent for his brothers. Uncle Mendel
was working in France; Uncle Eli and Aunt Esther were doing very well, thank
you, in Kozienice. In the Bronx, Daniel's father received the passage money
thankfully and set off to try his brother's luck in Shanghai. Neither got rich, but
they flourished, taipans, successful businessmen. Within six months, Daniel's father sent for his family. They all went except Haskel, a brilliant if narrow student
in premed at City College.

He could still remember how he and his sister Judy and his mother had eaten
on the French boat that took them to China. They had traveled third class, but
the food had been plentiful, so plentiful they could only talk about that their first
week at sea. How much there was to eat. How often they ate. How they would
eat just as much very soon. After three weeks on board, their gauntness was replaced by tanned flesh. His mother looked ten years younger. His sister Judy at
sixteen was suddenly pretty.

Up until then, he had been an awkward child. Any ball thrown near him
would hit him in the face, as if maliciously or as if compelled by some loadstone
in his skull that called to it, so that by age fourteen, he had been wounded by
baseballs, hard and soft, footballs, soccer balls, beach balls, tennis balls, Ping-
Pong balls, basketballs; they had all in their turn attacked him and caused the
anger and mockery of his fellows.

He had been a stubborn dreamy withdrawn child, fond of books about the
dogs and cats and horses he could not have. His pets were two goldfish, Meeney
and Moe. His mother kept warning him not to overfeed them, but that was the
only thing he could do for them. One morning they floated belly up in their tiny
bowl. He did not replace them. He would rather read *Lad: A Dog* or *The Jungle
Book*. It seemed to him that wolves might be warmer, more attentive parents.
In early childhood, he had been close to his mother, but the loss of their fine
home, car, furniture, status, reduced her to apathy. She had talked to herself as
she cleaned and cleaned their tiny crowded apartment. Although she now complained incessantly about China, she had a houseboy and a cook, and every day
she went visiting with other married Jewish ladies.

Daniel's family moved into a lane house in Hongkew, a poor, crowded, but
enthralling northeastern suburb surrounded on three sides by water. They lived
there because rents and food were half the price they were in the International
Settlement or Frenchtown. Their house was one of a number of similar structures thrown up in a hurry, surrounded by a wall with a gate, chilly, heated with
small and smelly coal stoves.

Daniel was sent to a school for American children in the International District, but school hours were not long and he could wander the streets much of

the time. He bought from a street vendor some used Chinese clothes, which he hid in the wall. With his black hair, his heavy tan, his dark eyes, he did not look Chinese, but he could pass for Manchurian. If he had wandered dressed in European clothes, wearing his watch, he would have been attacked, robbed. Finding himself in an adventure of his own devising, he bloomed with new confidence. He imagined boys from the old neighborhood envying him, sorry they had not chosen him on their sandlot baseball teams, that even at stickball they had passed over him.

The streets were jammed and glittered with huge gilded signboards, flashing neon, enormous brightly colored murals advertising local products. He was growing fast and always hungry, but there was much to eat, all of it cheap: noodles, filled pao, tangtuan dumplings, sweet almond broth, sweet or salty cakes, salt fish and cabbage. He loved the races, the little Mongol ponies flashing past. He loved the steamers and sampans with painted eyes in the muddy harbor.

At the American school, no Chinese was taught. Few of their parents spoke Chinese or understood it. Uncle Nat said it was exactly the same at the other international schools and settlements. When his uncle saw that he was interested, he arranged for Daniel to have two tutors, one for conversational Mandarin and the other for reading and writing the characters. He studied with his two Chinese teachers far more avidly than with his teachers at the American school, because what he learned, he could practice at once in the streets where he always wanted to be.

"The Europeans and Americans act like fools," Uncle Nat said, pointing out that the Americans would not let Chinese into their country club. "There's no one in this world you can be sure of standing on. You come into someone's country and you have a chance to be safe, to lead a good life, then you learn their customs and you speak their language, so you don't offend more than you have to. If you spit into the wind, it comes back in your face. Understand?"

Uncle Nat was a grizzled man much like his father, but he stood differently, not stooped. He was sharply observant. Daniel felt more at ease with him than with his own father. Both his parents talked constantly of Haskel, piling up A's at City College. The firstborn, the good son.

Shanghai was crowded, four million Chinese plus a hundred thousand foreigners, with modern skyscrapers, stylish Sikhs on little cement pedestals directing traffic, five universities, numerous scholarly and scientific institutions, fancy hotels and exclusive private clubs: but for most Chinese, there was poverty and a fast or slow death. In the mornings, corpses lay in the street as he went to school. Everywhere maimed beggars shook their cans. Shanghai was seething with diseases, as well as political unrest and assassinations. He watched prisoners beheaded and garroted for political or ordinary crimes, public executions where he stood in the crowd staring astonished at how casually life ended but taking care to look as blank as everybody else, to avoid trouble.

Then he caught a strain of paratyphoid that featured intestinal cramps so powerful that he could see them rippling his belly as he lay panting in high fever. After that initial fierce attack, it came back every month; then he seemed to outgrow it. He went on eating from booths and street vendors. He shot up to six feet. At sixteen, he bought his first sexual experience in the Kiangse Road red-light district, and unlike what his reading had led him to believe, he did not find it disgusting or blasting of his sensibility, but delightful, although incomplete because in no context.

After his initial sexual experiences, Daniel looked at women with a great deal of interest. He tried to do so on the sly, but apparently the wife of a doctor from Berlin noticed his interest. She seduced him, a task without difficulty once he grasped he was being offered what he most wanted. He had promptly fallen in love with her. Oh, so that was what he had been waiting for, that was what he had been expecting. There was sex and there were crushes, but when he put them together in a particular woman, it was a compelling new game, one that lasted into his first year at Shanghai University, when he began to make friends with two Chinese boys his own age and visit their homes.

The invading Japanese army approached the city. The Chinese troops burned much of Hongkew, the Japanese bombed the rest, and the Balabans moved reluctantly into smaller far more expensive lodgings in Frenchtown until once again lane houses were rapidly thrown up. Frequent bombings shook the ground, took out blocks. The train station was bombed and the dead lay uncounted. By 1938, Shanghai was cut off from the mainland and growing less profitable. Refugees from Germany and Austria were pouring in with frightening tales. Daniel's parents grew increasingly nervous. It was time, they felt, to return to the Bronx.

He left China under protest, weeping openly. Judy was happy. She wanted the normal life of an American girl, she said loudly. Daniel had no desire for the normal life of an American boy, which he saw as a *Saturday Evening Post* cover, a freckle-faced country boy with a fishing rod. Nor did he long for fights with Italian and Polish kids on the embattled streets of the Bronx.

He attended City College. The political upheaval fascinated him as the streets of Shanghai had. He went to meetings of splinter groups, shopping the bazaar of ideas, unable to identify with any but hopeful that some ideology would ravish him into commitment. He lived at home and commuted, although he was restless with his parents, in whom he had not confided in years. He saw them as narrow, naive, sweet but parochial. Their life had been spent in survival stratagems.

He expected quite other options. He did not enjoy the company of Haskel, now in medical school, on whom their mother waited like a body servant. Each brother found the other contemptible.

Every Tuesday and Wednesday after college, he took the IRT downtown to the Upper West Side, where there was a small community of midcoastal Chinese. There he took lessons with the owner of the Shanghai Star, upstairs in a little office overlooking the restaurant. Tuesday they had conversational lessons. Pao Chi was a big man, heavyset and bald, but his voice was melodious and gentle. He liked to discuss Taoism. On Wednesday they studied the characters. Just after the American New Year, Mr. Pao permitted him to do the calligraphy on a menu.

His family disapproved of his infatuation with things Chinese. His father, his mother and his sister Judy had lived in China like a family of cats standing on a log in a brook, keeping dry, keeping out of the world flowing past. Daniel planned to rejoin his uncle Nat, who loved China as he did. That was his consuming fantasy.

He fell in love with a Trotskyist and tried very hard to be one too, because her body was silky and she had a rich sexy laugh and a good hard mind he enjoyed striking ideas against. She did not enjoy the arguing as much as he did, and gave him up for someone whose politics were stronger and whose lust appeared just as strong. He was learning that love for him was like fireworks, heat and light but little damage. His lust did not diminish, although his infatuation often did. He fell in love with trivial things, a laugh, a turn of leg, a smile; no wonder that interest dissipated quickly.

He made friends with his cousin Seymour, a year older and a Communist who tried to recruit him. "You're a dilettante," Seymour told him. "Nothing moves you or everything moves you."

Mr. Pao thought that was a reasonable way to be. "True goodness is like water. Water helps the ten thousand things without itself striving. Water flows down into the low places men despise, for water is in the Way," Pao quoted from the *Tao Te Ching*.

Daniel did not know if he truly wanted to remain so watery. He imagined wondrous passions that would obsess him for longer than two weeks. Only the wife of the doctor had sustained his interest, but she was reported to have run off with an Englishman who had been supposed to be an agent but who turned out to be a conman, leaving huge debts. Uncle Nat's letters were full of disasters of incomprehensible proportions, bodies falling like leaves to make the bloodiest of compost as the war went on and on. The Japanese now controlled Shanghai. Uncle Nat described a last contingent of a thousand Polish Jews straggling in to safety. Many refugees were stuck in Shanghai, which required no visa, no passport, no papers, no certificate of rectitude or of past or present splendor. The war was impoverishing them all, Nat reported. Soon he would only be a yang kueitze, the insulting term for a penniless foreigner.

In Hongkew, Uncle Nat wrote, amid the wrecks of bombed buildings and rubble fields, there was a chamber orchestra, several theaters and an ongoing war of cultural snobbery between the Jews of Vienna and the Jews of Berlin. Daniel was nostalgic. His parents sang the litany of how smart they had been to leave. Only his teacher Pao Chi shared Daniel's fascination with what was going on in China.

Daniel worked as an usher in a local theater. Summers he waited on tables in the Catskills. The only time his obsession encroached on his university life was when he was asked to address the Progressive Club about the situation in China. His speech was not a success, for his confidence, often leonine one on one, vanished when he saw those bland anonymous faces. After graduation, the only job he could find was serving subpoenas.

Still he felt that his rotten speech had paid off when his economics professor gave his name to someone in the Navy, who called in the spring of 1941 to ask him if he might not be interested in a special crash course in Japanese being mounted at Harvard that summer. The Navy was training Japanese-language officers. Most of the students would already know some Japanese but others, like himself, were being recruited for their knowledge of Chinese. Daniel privately thought that was an example of white stupidity, because although the written languages shared many characters, the spoken languages had not as much relationship as Norwegian and Italian. Their assumption rested on a typical American attitude that if you knew one of those funny heathen languages, what was the problem learning another?

Since he could not rejoin his uncle, this sounded more interesting than the only other option he saw, which was to go on serving subpoenas for his father's pinochle buddy. He felt as if he were personally oppressing every petty criminal and wayward spouse and luckless witness and suspected bookie on whom he served papers. Twice the servee had taken a swing at him.

So, on to Harvard. For a City College boy, it would be a look at how the top five percent lived. His parents bubbled joy. Judy was marrying a nice Jewish dentist, Haskel was finishing medical school, and now their boy was going to Harvard. He knew that a crash course at the Yenching Institute was not exactly going to Harvard, but it beat pounding the pavements of the Bronx looking for people who hoped he would not find them.

His days at Harvard were pleasant. He started in the elementary class, but once he had his teeth into Japanese, he moved up rapidly. He drove his room-mates crazy by insisting on speaking Japanese from the time he woke until he fell asleep. By October he was progressing markedly and had been moved ahead. He took long walks along the Charles, across Cambridge, into Mount Auburn cemetery. Sunday night he ate Chinese in Boston with buddies from the program, showing off by ordering from the menu in Chinese. Many of the restaurants were Cantonese, of course, which he could not speak. Someday he would learn: after the war in China, when he could return.

Still if he could not go to China, Boston would do. His roommate mocked him for preferring Boston to New York, but New York to him did not mean Manhattan, but the lower reaches of the Bronx. His attention centered on the demanding and intense classes. He worked hours too long for romance. Although he looked with sharp and frustrated interest after the Radcliffe girls on their bicycles, he found his life civilized and realized he was happy. Finally something besides an infatuation had focused him. He was no longer merely flowing water.

JACQUELINE 1

In Pursuit of the Adolescent Universal

14 mai 1939

Marie Charlotte is definitely my best and dearest friend, and the only person in the world in whom I dare confide my most secret thoughts and wishes. Suzanne has proved her perfidy, and I shall never, never be foolish enough to trust her again. I am ashamed of myself for being such an idiot as to tell her about that little conversation with Philippe in the Musée Carnavalet. Who would have imagined she would have gone straight to him and begun saying in that loud vulgar voice of hers so that everyone could hear it, I hear that Jacqueline is your dear friend, your girlfriend now.

I am the unluckiest seventeen-year-old in my entire deuxième classe at lycée Victor Hugo. Marie Charlotte has only one younger sister making her life miserable, but I have two: double trouble, twins, and completely wicked. I count my blessings that Maman is not vulgar and would never dress the twins in those disgusting identical dresses. In fact Maman is always careful to give each different clothing, but the little beasts think it is funny to try to confuse people. Today Renée went out in Nadine's sweater and skirt, and Nadine wore Renée's, and the little beasts thought it was amusing to pretend to be each other all day long. They communicate by grunts like savages or dogs and sometimes I swear by telepathy.

Maman simply refuses to understand that it is humiliating to have to haul those brats along to the park or to the cinema. They are forever pulling pranks and dashing around like the worst tomboys and skinning their knees and laughing, very loudly. In addition they call each other Rivka and Naomi, such embarrassing ghetto names I could smack them. Saturday Maman made me take them along when I went to L'Etoile with Suzanne (that slut) and my dear Marie Charlotte. During the scene where Gabrielle falls into the arms of her lover, François, those wretches smacked their lips and giggled. I was humiliated. I will not go out to the cinema if it means taking the twins along, and I am going to make that clear to Maman! Sometimes when Marie Charlotte and I sit on our special bench in the little park Georges Cain near our lycée, the little beasts sneak up on us to listen.

I believe in the universal, not the accidental particular. Being born in this house on the rue du Roi de Sicile (which name I have to admit I still derive an irrational pleasure from inscribing, for its incongruously romantic sound), in the IVe arrondissement near the Métro stop St. Paul, is simply a matter of coincidence and has no lasting importance. Similarly that I am called one thing—Jacqueline Lévy-Monot—rather than Marie Charlotte Lepellier has no real significance. I want to find what is true, lasting and universal in human life, rather than sitting in my little corner repeating to myself some few phrases of so-called popular wisdom as silly as any other superstition, as Maman does, saying, "Nor a shteyn zol zayn aleyn," only a stone should stay alone, as if we were not crammed in together. The labels we apply to one another keep us from penetrating to the truth, and we must rip them off our own eyes as well as banishing them from our view of others. The parochial mind is the greatest obstacle to progress, I believe, and I wrote an essay to that effect which won second prize, a Petit Larousse dictionary which I employ every day.

I strive with that romantic weakness in me, for instance that likes the name of our narrow street, which is after all a dingy thoroughfare of some antiquity but little architectural merit, lined with shops and businesses such as the furriers where Maman works with little overcrowded flats like ours piled above. On our ground floor is a kosher butcher. The street of the King of Sicily indeed, where the old stone entrance halls dark as little mine shafts stink of urine, where machinery roars and sewing machines whir day and night. The King of Sicily must have had run-down heels and patched his coats as Maman does ours.

How will I ever survive the desert of time that stretches out before me bleak and endless till I shall be on my own as an adult and not have to explain myself morning, noon and night to my family? A family is an accidental construct, a group of people brought together by chance and forced to cohabit in insufficient space. If it were not for my tiny room on the top floor, a floor up from our flat, I would suffocate!

15 septembre 1939

We have been at war for two weeks, but life does not seem all that different. Everywhere royal blue blackout material is going up, in case we are bombed. Maman worries that Papa will be called up. I have embarked on the première classe in my lycée, Victor Hugo. I have two students I am tutoring after school, immigrants whose French is poor, one sweet ten- and one fat eleven-year-old who can sleep with her eyes wide open. No one has ever awakened that brain, which is encased in her head like a turtle basking in the sun. I intend to open its shell! The ten-year-old is my cousin, Maman tells me as if announcing a great dessert, although I lean over backward to show no favoritism from such a quirk of randomly tossed genes. From Kozienice, Maman says, with absurd excitement: some dusty town in Poland where Maman happened to be born, a mistake she was intelligent enough to rectify by moving to France at sixteen. Aunt Batya looks older than Maman though she is the next youngest sister, dowdy as a peasant.

Sometimes I feel called to be a teacher, because I have the gift, and I believe it is as much a gift as that of acting, which I believe I also truly possess. Maman tells me that all young girls want to be actresses because they imagine it is glamorous. I know that to assume a different character is hard work. Maman imagines that I am more naive than I am. Both gifts require understanding others and both require a species of humility. Maman thinks that it is egoism that makes me want to be an actress, but I see it as a kind of self-abnegation, wherein my own personality is subsumed under the character of Bérénice, Phèdre, Juliet.

To teach literature is in a way also to enact it. Both gifts interact and complement each other, but I suspect that having two gifts is as bad as having none. Maman said something cruel to me when I spoke to her about my doubts about pursuing the vocation that I feel. She said I took being pretty far too seriously. Since then I have embarked on a discipline intended to prove at least to myself how mistaken she is in her estimate of my seriousness. I have refrained from looking in the mirror all week. When I comb my hair, I shut my eyes and do it by touch. No one in the family has noticed my new discipline, but that is perfect with me, as I am sure if I explained, I would be mocked for my efforts.

I never understand what people mean by calling me pretty, for when I look into my eyes I see despair, exaltation, joy, pity, an intense probing curiosity, compassion, an aloof questioning spirit; chaos and struggle. Marie Charlotte is pretty. Hers is a calm pure nature in which certain ideas come to rest and she is content with them, as I am content with the furniture in my little room under the eaves. But I think my face is as changeable as my soul. Perhaps only through acting can I reveal those depths and heights, those tempests that rage invisibly, shaking me profoundly. When others call me pretty, they believe they are flattering me, but I feel diminished, invisible behind the mask that they and not I create.

21 février 1940

Papa has been called up, and we are all shaken. He is very cheerful and says not
to worry, that it is just like going away to camp. It is true that being at war has
been peaceful so far and I think the sensationalistic reporting of the early weeks
has faded away before the reality of modern war, which seems mostly a matter
of arguing and sitting. The terrible icy weather continues, the harshest winter I
can remember, as if nature were mourning our idiocy in this long farcical drôle
de guerre.

I have felt estranged from Papa in recent times, but now I wish that we
communicated better. Our differences are in reality a matter of Papa choosing
to limit himself culturally, while I am trying to expand. I don't think we have
ever forgiven each other for the fight about the Farband picnic last summer. I
know I was right, but perhaps I stated the matter too baldly. After all I have
nothing in common with a bunch of gawky plain lifers simply because they're
Jewish. Being Jewish is a matter of accident too. I was born Jewish, but what
does that mean? As a religion, I find it absurd. As dietary laws, archaic! I am
told those Polish refugees the Balabans from Kozienice are my aunt, my uncle,
my cousins, but I cannot even communicate with them about the simplest
matters, about tables and chairs, let alone about my ideas, my feelings or my
aspirations.

I don't understand Papa's involvement in Poale Zion. The notion of all of
us picking up and moving to the Orient to become date farmers is a fantasy I
cannot take seriously for five minutes. Papa has always been a Socialist, but he
has been involved in the folly of Zionism for the last two years. I suspect he will
come home from the army without that baggage. He needs more contact with
intelligent Frenchmen who discuss modern ideas. His intelligence is greater
than can possibly be used in his factory work, and therefore his thinking tends
to become undisciplined.

Papa has great energy, which is sometimes wonderful and sometimes embarrassing. I still do not know if I admire him or not for what happened last fall,
when we were waiting in the crowd for the mairie to open its doors and when
it did not happen for twenty minutes, everyone was still waiting and grumbling.
And Papa just walked up to the head of the line and pushed the doors open.
They were unlocked all the time!

Nonetheless for him to talk about meeting boys "of my own kind" struck me
as vulgar and tasteless, as well as insensitive to who I really am. I do not understand what some future tractor driver can possibly want to say to me or what

Papa imagines I would have in common with him. It's one of those monomaniac obsessions. Sometimes when Papa and his copain Georges are together, all they can talk about is who is Jewish. It reminds me of that slut Suzanne after she slept with her equally vulgar boyfriend, walking down the street and speculating who's a virgin and who isn't.

Maman is very frightened and will need a great deal of soothing and comforting, I can see. The twins bawl and cling. I feel like the only one in the house with a cool head!

16 juin 1940

Really, the Germans are here and it is no massacre or bloodbath, although they have made us put the clocks forward an hour so we are on German time. It has been quiet, orderly, scarcely a shot fired and everyone feels a little stunned. I saw some well-dressed people cheering the German troops as they marched past. They seem clean and well behaved on the whole. I think our fear has been pumped up by the newspapers which have nothing else to do but try to create sensationalism. I am sure Maman is ashamed of having sent the twins south to Orléans with her boss M. Cariot.

I am committed to seeking out the universal, because only in that way can we rise rigorously out of the slough of the accidental particular. I find patriotism not only a refuge of scoundrels but of idiots and those who like to buy their thinking ready made each morning in the vacuous newspapers. Every decade or so governments create wars and whip up a frenzy, so that we will not notice the shortcomings of our own side and will not question the assumptions of our society and demand more rational institutions and laws. I am sure that the Germans aside from speaking another language will turn out to be different from us mostly as we are different from one another, as individuals. We are two countries side by side that seem to have nothing better to do than to invade one another every few years, butchering a great many young men and tearing up the countryside in the process. I suppose what we would discover if we had the courage to examine reality instead of repeating old clichés, is that the Germans are people like ourselves who are good, bad, indifferent in the same measure as we ourselves are.

If only we knew where Papa is, we would probably be quite calm. I was crossing the rue de Rivoli this afternoon and I bumped into a German soldier in the crowd, a lieutenant, I believe. He touched his cap and smiled at me and stepped back out of the way—not at all the brutes dashing out babies' brains we have been led to expect. So much for the enemy being fiends. There has been no raping or looting I have heard of. The gendarmes are back on the street and the stores are opening up again.

29 juillet 1940

Papa is back! First the twins, and then him. He escaped from the POW camp where he was being held. He said that they were beginning to sort out the Jews from the others, although I think that is just their obsession with purity and schemata. They like everybody in neat pigeonholes. He was working on the garbage detail when he escaped from the camp and threw away his uniform. I hope he does not get in trouble from his impetuousness. He wanted to come home, but they say that soon the Germans will release all the prisoners of war anyhow.

It is as if an earthquake had its epicenter right under our little apartment, since he is back. He is rushing around seeing all his copains on the old radical papers and at the Poale Zion. They even sent a delegation to talk to the Jewish Communists, who are reputed not to be going along with the Stalin-Hitler pact like the rest of the party. In the old days, Papa would not even speak to the Communists, but now he is running around Paris conferring with every hothead. He has been handing around some sort of Jewish resistance brochure called *Que Faire* copied out by hand, full of horror stories and slogans like partout présent: be everywhere, and faire face: stand up to them. I am relieved that Papa is safe, although how long he will be safe acting as he does is another question. But I must say, until the twins were returned to us, thinner and bedraggled and full of stories of burning vehicles and abandoned babies and planes strafing the roads, things here were extremely peaceful with just Maman and me. She was worried sick but I comforted her, and I think she respects me more now.

14 septembre 1940

Myself, I believe in attaining an inner tranquility. I admit it is disturbing to walk through the streets and see posters on all the walls denouncing Jews en bloc and to see all those gross new newspapers that do nothing but wish all Jews death, *Au Pilori*, for example. But I practice a discipline as I go around, saying to myself, I know I am not dirty, I am not vile, I am as French as anybody else and as thoroughly imbued with French culture as any of my teachers, so it is not me that this vileness is aimed at and I will simply not accept it. To grow angry is to give power to those who attack. To ignore such an attack is to diminish the attacker, not oneself. We give those screamers their power by taking offense.

Papa and Maman are very upset because the citizenship of the Balabans has been revoked. They have only been in France since 1935, and they have had their French citizenship taken away from them. I am sorry for them, but I cannot think it is too strange. They do not seem to have made any effort to enter French society. They speak only Yiddish or Polish among their friends and are obviously foreigners even on the street. I feel that to be so conspicuous when living in another country is almost arrogant. I feel immensely sorry for the Balabans nonetheless.

2 octobre 1940

Now we are all ordered to go to the local police station and register as if we are prostitutes or criminals, and have a big ugly JUIF stamped across our identity cards. I announced at the breakfast table that I am simply not going to do it. I thought Papa and Maman would be shocked, but instead Papa said he would try to figure out what would happen if we did not obey. He thinks it isn't a bad idea to refuse to register, if we can figure out how to avoid it. I know it's meaningless, but I find being separated out and labeled in this way simply humiliating.

Marie Charlotte has been extremely strange with me lately. The last two times we were supposed to meet, she did not show up. She simply left me sitting there waiting. Finally I had it out with her yesterday. She said that she still loved me dearly, but that she had heard that others thought she was a Jew because she was always with me, and she was afraid. She did not want to bear such a label, especially since she was born and raised a good French Catholic and her mother felt it was her own fault because she stuck to me more closely than to her own kind.

9 octobre 1940

We are all duly registered, one of the most humiliating experiences of my life. Since the defection of Marie Charlotte, I have been making friends with some young people I would have considered hoodlums last year. They are definitely not the respectable element, but they are not unintelligent and do not seem prejudiced, the way so many people one thought above that sort of thing have revealed themselves to be in the last months. They listen to jazz a great deal, especially American jazz, and affect a bohemian style of dress.

One thing that fascinates me about them is that they do not segregate themselves rigidly by age. Some of this new crowd I have been meeting are in the university, some like me in the final year of lycée, some no longer in school but not yet employed. The peculiarities of their style do not attract me, but their tolerance does. They do not seem anxiety-ridden to obey the German decrees and they do not care what I am, only who I am. For that, I respect them. They think I am too serious but they are going to set me right. I doubt that, but it soothes me to walk into the Café Le Jazz Hot where they hang out and sit down with friends and feel welcome. These days to feel welcome is rare, and their languor conceals a courtesy I value.

Every day I feel less certain what is to become of us, all of us, and whether I shall ever get a chance to be anything at all, let alone deciding between becoming instructor or actress, for doors seem to close faster than I can prepare myself to enter them. I feel the way I imagine some creature of the tropics felt when the Ice Age descended and the glaciers loomed over what had been lush and pleasant banana forests. I feel as if I no longer truly belong to my family but have no new niche or role I have created, no place to go where I am truly at home. It is therefore not to be wondered at that I now spend more and more time with my new unrespectable friends at the Café Le Jazz Hot.

ABRA 1

The Opening of Abra

For two hundred years, men in Abra's family in Bath, Maine, had gone to sea. Abra went to New York.

At twenty-three, Abra considered her real life to have begun back in September of 1938. Then, at nineteen, she transferred from Smith to Barnard and finally made it to Manhattan, the glittering Oz of her childhood where she had always known she really belonged. Last year she had been accepted in graduate school at Columbia in political science. Abra did not consider herself true scholar material and could not quite imagine teaching, but graduate school was at once sufficient in itself—politics after all was the most exciting topic in the world—and moreover there were ninety percent males in her department among the graduate students and nothing but men on the faculty. Abra, growing up with brothers, found the situation of being the only woman in a room quite natural. Among men she perked up.

She had disposed of her virginity during her nineteenth summer out on Popham Point where her family had always summered, with a sweet local boy who had settled down by now to lobstering. He had wanted to marry her, and she had understood that to put a nice face upon her apparent acquiescence, she must pretend to be considering marriage, oh, on down the pike, of course, after graduation. Abra had transferred to Barnard that very fall and she had no intention of returning to Bath except of course on vacations when John had remained for two more years her delightful summer romance. Romance for Abra included good healthy acrobatic sex.

Now here she was, twenty-three, with a lively group of friends and her own apartment in the Village, a cosy Bank Street walk-up, a good relationship with her thesis advisor Professor Blumenthal and a stimulating new research assistantship with his pal Oscar Kahan in the sociology department. Her family was appalled at her taking an advanced degree; they viewed it as unwomanly and bound to result in her remaining a thwarted and sorrowful old maid. She was compared to one Abigail of dreaded memory who had been a bluestocking and an impassioned abolitionist and who had once actually made a public speech, bringing shame on the family by this wanton act, whereupon her father had locked her up for five years. Abra, who was in the process of fielding her sixth proposal of marriage, doubted she was headed for a lonely old age. The latest was from a young man she had met playing tennis and been seeing for the last two months.

"Now, what is all this, Hank? Are you trying to make an honest woman of me, some nonsense like that?"

He was sitting on the little Windsor chair in front of her whitewashed brick fireplace, in which a couple of birch logs from home were cheerfully combusting. The chair was undersized for him, giving him a grasshoppery look. "I think you'd make a good wife for me, Scotty. Your wildness is youth and high spirits, a colt acting up. You'll settle in."

A colt that hasn't been broken yet, he means, Abra thought, smiling sweetly. "Do you think it's an appropriate time for settling down? The world is coming to pieces all around us."

"All the more reason to establish a home base. I don't for a moment believe even that madman Roosevelt is about to take us to war to pull England's chestnuts out of the fire, but nonetheless, I could be called up at any moment."

Sound the bugles, Abra thought. I'm supposed to sacrifice myself to your family notions because you may be called up as an officer? "I'd make a rotten wife. I'm involved in my own work and not about to scant it."

"Haven't you gone to school long enough? You're a real woman, Scotty, and it's time for you to live like one."

"I'm rather keen on what I'm doing." She heard herself talking in a different way with him, old inflections, old phrases. "I adore my thesis advisor Professor Blumenthal, and my topic interests me." She was well aware the thesis she was writing on the Ladies' Garment Workers Union did not interest Hank. "I have a position with Professor Kahan—"

A look of distaste crossed Hank's blond aquiline features and he flexed his right arm, then his left, a nervous gesture that seemed automatic. "Kraut Jews, Scotty. Really."

"Professor Blumenthal is a German-born Jew. So, I believe, was Marx."

"Exactly. I can't imagine why your family agrees to all this."

Abra regarded him, deciding exactly how rude she was going to permit herself to be. This was her damned fault, getting involved with somebody from her own background. She had never done so before and resolved not to bother in future. The only advantage she could discover was that she could recite the conversation that would ensue before they played through its dreary predictability. She rose and walked over to the hall door, opened it and stood aside.

Hank looked at her blankly. "Somebody in the hall?"

"You, soon, I hope. Your coat is on the peg. Do put it on yourself."

"What are you doing, Scotty? This is silly. You can't turn me down. And not like this."

"Watch me. I have no particular interest in marrying anybody. But you're the last possibility I would entertain."

"Scotty, you know we love each other."

She had a flash of anger with herself, for getting into this debacle. She must give up playing tennis. She met the wrong sort of men on the courts. The men she picked up at rallies were more her sort. "I think we both made a small mistake, easily remedied. Don't forget your hat."

Slowly he backed out, still carrying his coat and hat, staring at her. Then he ran downstairs and if the outer door had been slammable, he would have slammed it. It shut at its own leisurely pace however, with a pneumatic sigh.

Abra reflected on the ruin of her Sunday. She tested the waters of her soul and found them only tepid. It would be a good day to stay home and make an effort to do more than refer to her thesis in public. Her class work would be completed soon, but she had not really settled down to writing. She looked around her small moderately bohemian digs with the Hopi vase and the Guatemalan molah and the African gazelle carving darker than night interspersed with bright chintz pillows and eighteenth-century pieces from the family attic. Hank did not belong here. She did.

It seemed to Abra that marriage was something that would fall to her lot at a certain age, as she had inherited her little trust fund at twenty-one from her grandfather Scott and as she would someday inherit her grandmother Woolrich's ladder-back chairs and have to put them somewhere, along with a trust fund from that side, due at twenty-six. She believed that most of her women friends from college had married to acquire a place for themselves, an identity, but that she could make her own place.

She had no desire to be rich; her branch of the family had not stressed money per se, once their shipyard had gone under, unlike her uncle Frederick Woolrich, whom she had always liked, with his booming manner as if to be heard in a gale and his energy. She suspected Uncle Frederick was probably a good lay, but incest was not her particular vice. Rather the opposite. She should have told Hank politely that she had an exogamous personality. She hardly ever went for another blond and with Hank, the fire had simply not come down. A month with Hank was longer than a year with Slim, the Negro saxophone player, although in truth they had only seen each other on and off for eight months. Slim lived with a woman, who had eventually found out about Abra. Too bad. Before she had come to New York, the only nonwhites she had ever laid eyes on were two local Indian fishermen, but Abra considered she had that liberal heritage from scandalous Great-Great-Aunt Abigail to live up to.

Abra had grown up in Bath, in a family well known and well connected locally, if not nearly so well off as they had been a couple of generations back. There was a cove named for her father's family (where the defunct shipyard had been) and an island named for her mother's side. She had grown up with her two brothers in a prim white federal house on Washington Street with a cupola on top and portraits not of ancestors but of their ships, stiff formal oil paintings of the *Ebeneezer Scott*, the *General Abraham Woolrich*, in full unlikely sail upon static waves, alternating with naive local paintings of noted shipwrecks, the *Mary Frances* going down with all hands off Woolrich Island. Portraits of ancestors had not seemed necessary, since she was always being told she had Granny Abra Scott's nose and Great-Uncle Timothy's eyes. She had felt herself not so much placed as embedded in family expectations, the life before her a formal perennial bed planted with Everetts and Timothys and Toms and Mary Franceses and Abras, needing only occasional watering.

Summers had been the free and glorious times, always on the water, sailing or chugging among the elaboration of inlets and arms and bays of the Kennebec or lolling on the unusual (for Maine) sand beaches of their peninsula. Growing up they had even had a Civil War fort to play in, with spiral staircases and dungeons and parapets. They scrambled over the rocks, they clammed, they raced their cousins in catboats. The gap of two years between Everett, called Ready, and Abra which sprawled wide in Bath during the school year, closed at the summer house.

Every summer the New Yorkers came to the peninsula with their different accents, different values, different clothes and attitudes; with them came a freedom she found addictive. In Bath she was always under someone's expectant or admonitory gaze, but out in the simpler stark house on the hill at Popham, she could always escape surveillance. It was a matter of sailing off to another island or rounding the bend. The Woolriches had their family compound on an island visible from her family's wide front porch, and she could always say she was sailing over to her uncle's. If the weather precluded sailing, then there was the forest of birch, oak and fir, the marshes, the dank swamps where she could lose herself. Privacy was only one hill away. The social rules that circumscribed the depth and frequency of every contact in Bath frayed in the summer world of fir and rock, of fog drifting in magic and chilly, the sun dazzling, the wind rising till she could feel herself a real person with a will and a future as potentially tumultuous and changeable as the cold sea that quickened her. She could not go to sea, as Ready would, so she chose an island instead that seemed to her as free and rich as the sea: Manhattan.

She ate in a Nedick's, on her way to the fundraiser for Czech resistance. At the door of the rented hall, she met two friends, Djika and Karen Sue. Djika was the only other woman graduate student in her department. Karen Sue had been a bored southern belle in Memphis before contracting an inappropriate marriage her father had had annulled; an inheritance was keeping her in New York where she found life livelier. She had a big apartment on Riverside Drive where parties among the politicos they knew were often held.

It was an odd evening, the regulars the Party could call out for its fundraisers, folk singers, theater people and then a lot of Czech chorale groups and singers, many rousing speeches about the brave partisans. Up on the platform Abra contemplated hairy Jack Covington, who had once leaped upon her, satisfied himself with haste and rolled off, and then demanded to be waited on in the morning, sending her out for a bottle of orange juice, a package of Wheaties and light cream. She had spent a night with him after Hitler's invasion of the Soviet Union had reconstituted the Popular Front and she and her interventionist friends were speaking to the Communists again. She had endeavored to avoid a repeat ever since, although whenever he saw her he displayed that great toothy grin like the grille of a new truck and headed straight at her. That such a virile-looking ex-longshoreman should prove so perfunctory in bed was disappointing. She was amused to note that she found his speeches less moving than formerly. It was good that people generally knew little about the sexual habits of their politicians.

"Oh, Jack. That boy is a dundering bore," Karen Sue drawled, giving the judgment at least two diphthongs. Abra wondered if her disillusionment were similarly based, but she had no intention of discussing her sexual life with Karen Sue. Abra believed in being a complete gentleman.

"So, have you begun to work for the great man yet?" Djika asked, leaning across Karen Sue.

"Tomorrow's the first of the month, and that's when Professor Kahan is starting me."

"Seems absurd," Djika said sourly, perhaps jealous of the appointment. "You start the first of December and then you'll break off for vacation. Why not wait till the first of January?"

"Perhaps her professor doesn't take a little old vacation," Karen Sue said. "Just works his assistants to death fifty-two weeks in the year."

"I'd just as soon get on with learning the job," Abra said. "I'm curious as hell." She had been introduced to Oscar Kahan at a conference on Fascism where he had spoken, eloquently she had thought, on the tension between the petty bourgeois base of German fascism and the growing amity between the Nazi party and the German industrial elite. Her own advisor, Professor Blumenthal, was a German refugee from the Frankfurt School. Kahan had been one of the few American-born speakers at the conference to present anything sophisticated. She had been extremely pleased when Blumenthal had recommended her to Kahan.

"Is he married, honey child?" Karen Sue asked. It was always her first question.

"I never get involved with anyone in my field. I have an exogamous personality." She had got to use her line after all.

"Then what do you talk about?" Djika asked scornfully. For the last two years, she had been enjoying an unhappy but fulfilling affair with a married professor, Stanley Beaupere. Although Abra was chary with details, Djika pressed upon both of them the exact words of Stanley Beaupere, demanding full intellectual attention and analysis. As his marriage unraveled, its seamier side was picked stitch by stitch for Djika's audience of two.

Djika was a refugee from Danzig, although it was hard to think of her as such. While Djika viewed herself as living almost in squalor, she actually lived more poshly than Abra, if less poshly than Karen Sue. Djika combined fervent Catholicism and fervent socialism, the former shared, the latter unshared with her family.

Djika was bright, and Abra valued her for that hard European-educated intelligence that seemed at once more pointed and broader-based than Abra was used to among her colleagues; she also found it a great convenience to be friendly with the only other woman in her department. At least she had someone to slip off to the ladies' room with. She had met Karen Sue at political parties, gradually realizing that she was the hostess. Not only did Karen Sue seem to grasp everything about clothes, designer, cut and fabric, but she was the only woman Abra knew who read *The Wall Street Journal* every morning, speculated in stocks and bonds and seemed to understand what she was doing. The contrast between Karen Sue's fluffy belle airs and her financial acumen amused Abra, who admired expertise per se. She had even enjoyed listening to John talk about lobstering, until she had asked all the more interesting questions.

She thought several times of telling Karen Sue and Djika about her proposal, but each time she did not speak. Why? She did not care to introduce the subject of Hank's anti-Semitism. She really had to get along with Djika, and she had her suspicions about Djika's attitudes. She also did not feel as if it would be in good taste to mock Hank, who after all had meant to do her an honor, however she had perceived the proposal. On consideration, it became her to keep her Sunday to herself.

———

Abra's first impression of Oscar Kahan was that he was smaller than she remembered from the conference, that he seemed to occupy more space than he did because of his energy. As he rose to shake her hand, his palm was firm and hot to the touch, his skin ruddy, hair curling on the back of his hands.

"We're conducting a series of interviews with refugees who were active in the unions or active politically in Europe. Your German is adequate?"

"Adequate is the word for it."

"We'll try it out. What I want is someone to interview the women. Some of the questions I'm interested in having answered are personal, and I suspect we'll get further with a woman asking them."

"May I ask why you aren't hiring a refugee to do the interviews? Look, I'm delighted you're willing to give me a try . . ."

He gave much more impression of having a body than did her own Professor Blumenthal, tall, built like an umbrella bent at the end. Of medium height with a bit of a paunch, Oscar Kahan was broad shouldered. His hair was abundant, thick and curly, worn a little long. He grinned at her, shrewdly, she thought. "A good point. But any refugee who could interview them knowingly would also have a position. It's an intricate situation politically, and I don't want someone who thinks they know the answers asking the questions. I want a naive questioner—relatively, I mean. Innocent is perhaps more like it—innocent of activity and opinions in the maze of German parties before and after the onset of the Third Reich."

He wore a red tie pulled awry as if someone had begun strangling him with it. His jacket was good Irish tweed, but looked as if he were carrying half a library and his lunch in the pockets. She decided she would ask Djika for any gossip about her new employer. She found herself frankly curious, looking into the glittering dark eyes, even darker than the hair. "When shall I get started?"

"Now. Today. What I want you to do is read through these notes on interviewing procedures, and then come back to me with your questions." He pointed to his anteroom. "Read out there and bang on my door when you're ready."

Two students were sitting outside, eager young men. They gave her the baleful glare of those kept waiting for the object of their desire. Through the door of his inner office she heard the brisk cadences of his voice, deep, clear, pushed a bit as he spoke with the first. The remaining student was joined by another. They eyed her jealously from time to time, because she looked as if she belonged. The door opened, the student inside was ushered out, flushed and still jabbering earnestly over his shoulder.

As she read through the notes he had given her, clear, well organized, exciting even as guidelines to the interviews she would be doing, the students came and went, male and female, tall and short, well and poorly dressed, all passionate, avid for their hero's time. On every one he focused that beam of attention momentarily, making them feel bright, fascinating. These were his regular office hours. He gave himself to each in turn and then thrust them out into the cold boring world. They stumbled away, still engrossed in the conversation that continued in their heads, where they captured his attention not for five minutes, not for ten, but permanently. Abra understood. She was intrigued herself. It would all be more amusing than she had suspected.

NAOMI 1

Naomi/Nadine Is Only Half

The boots hit the pavement in cadence. Maman held Rivka in the doorway against the wall, so that she could not see. When she started to protest, Maman shushed her harshly, holding her pressed to the cold stone. Through a grille a concierge stared at them with hostile beady eyes, a toad in a cage waiting to be fed flies. "Get out, you don't belong here," the concierge called to them. "We don't want your kind pushing in here."

Maman ignored the concierge, still holding Rivka hard against the cold stone of the wall. Still the boots clacked by, making the pavement rattle like a kettle-drum.

When Naomi woke, she heard Ruthie stirring in her sleep in the bunk under her with soft grunts. Boston Blackie was sprawled sleeping across her feet, for she had enticed him up the past months from Ruthie's bed. She heard the furnace laboring in the basement underneath, Uncle Morris shoveling coal, the hot air rising with a whoosh as the heat began. Then she clambered down to stand over the hot air register, her icy clothes laid out last night. She would warm her underwear, her pleated plaid skirt and long socks and white blouse and red cardigan sweater, her oxfords: new clothes Aunt Rose had taken her to buy downtown at Sam's Cutrate Department Store where Ruthie worked. Different clothes than she would have worn at home.

If she woke too quickly—if there was a loud bang outside, a truck backfiring, the garbagemen clanging cans—then she woke in a panic in the dark and did not know where she was and she might cry out in French, "Maman, qui est là? Maman, tu es ici? Rivka!" But she could always feel that Rivka was not there. At home they had slept all their lives in a three-quarter bed in the alcove off the salle à manger, a bed which folded into a divan. Rivka was always curled into her side. If one of them woke in the night and padded off down the corridor to the WC, then the other would tiptoe after. Now when she woke, she clutched the cat to her.

The first nights here in the house of her aunt and uncle in Detroit back in June, she had fallen out of the upper bunk, because she had kept rolling over in the dark trying to find her twin. Everyone here, they met her and they saw only her, but she knew better. She was only half. In the night sometimes she felt her other half. She knew by now not to say that to anyone, even her good cousin Ruthie, whom she called aunt for respect and affection, who would comfort her, who would coddle her, but who would not understand. She was already too strange. She was fighting hard to fit in.

She was growing used to the sounds of the night here. It was a noisy, nervous night, a skin that could never quite form. In Paris maybe night had used to be like that, but she remembered too the quiet dangerous time when the city was emptied of traffic, which had never really returned. All the people rich enough to own autos jumped in them and drove away from the German army. All over her neighborhood you could hear dogs and pigeons. Then she and Rivka had been sent away with Maman's boss, the furrier, in his car south away from the Germans into a massive jam of cars and wagons, to be shot at by the planes.

Naomi never spoke French anymore, except to Boston Blackie when they were alone. Then he purred. She felt as if all sorts of old rags that had been good dresses and scraps of paper that had been precious books and fragments of broken crockery that had been the dishes with the yellow and blue flowers they ate on daily, all floated in her loose. They thought her slow at school. She would look at the thing she was tying on her foot and first would come the French *chaussure,* and then would come the Yiddish *shich,* and her mind would spin in emptiness and then finally if she were lucky would come the English, shoe, oxford.

At first the kids had made fun of her because the English she did speak was the wrong kind. She said ahnt for ant and bahth for bath, but not three times. She imitated. She tried hard and often missed, but she was grateful. The Siegals had taken her in, which meant less for them. Someday her papa would appear and carry her off and take her back to Maman and Rivka and her older sister Jacqueline. Papa had a motorbike, and that was how she saw him coming, roaring and sputtering through the streets of Detroit.

She had three first names now. She had always had two, Naomi at home, her Hebrew name, and Nadine at school and on her papers. The way her new family pronounced Naomi made it into a new name: Nay-oh-me, but here she could use her Hebrew name everywhere. Now she must say her last name was Siegal, rather than Lévy-Monot, for she was supposed to be adopted, but Papa had said that was just a formality to fool the immigration and she would always be his daughter. Siegal was what her papers said, just the same as Ruthie Siegal, Uncle Morris Siegal, Aunt Rose Siegal, and her other cousins, Duvey and Arty. All papers now were lies. That was how you crossed borders. If you were a Jew, you could never tell your real name except to another Jew, and often not even then. Naomi knew she must work hard every day imitating, so that no one would notice she was a refugee.

Papa was in the south—not what they meant here when Uncle Morris said rich Jews went South for the winter. That meant Florida. She did not believe there were any rich Jews. She had heard of them, but never had she met any. All the Jews of her Paris neighborhood worked in small factories, in small shops. They worked for furriers or in dress shops or as tailors or bookbinders; they sold leather goods or yard goods or fish. The closest was Papa's older brother Uncle Hercule who owned a restaurant in Alsace, until the Germans came and took it from him. The Germans had invaded and the strong French army she had learned about in school, the great Maginot Line, had gone away like a line on paper erased, and Papa had been kept a prisoner.

South really meant to Naomi the light, the scents, the heat of Provence. August they used to go to Fréjus, near the Mediterranean, where there was a little pension with bougainvillea growing over the terrace where they had their breakfast, Maman, Papa, Rivka, who in the world was called Renée, and her. Yakova, who insisted on being called Jacqueline even at home, would still be sleeping. Everyone always said first about Jacqueline that she was pretty and second that she was sensitive, but Rivka and Naomi thought she was mostly a pain. She and Rivka loved the way the bees crawled in the flowers, but toward the end of breakfast they got impatient. Maman and Papa always dawdled on vacations, les grandes vacances. Rivka said the bees sang because flowers tasted like ice cream to them. The ice cream in the south was better than the ice cream in Paris, and on vacation they always had ice cream. Even Jacqueline liked ice cream. She said love should be like ice cream, but she didn't think it would be.

Ruthie was stirring below her. Her slender legs poked out, feeling for the fuzzy battered slippers she called mules. Pulling around her the plaid flannel robe a size too small, she crossed the room and peeked around the shade to look at the weather, tucking her hands into the opposite sleeves. All Naomi could see of her was the robe pulled tight around her full high buttocks and the dark hair half hidden behind the shade. From her moan, Naomi thought the weather must displease her. "It snows?" she asked.

"Is it snowing?" Ruthie corrected patiently, smiling over her shoulder. "Anyhow, tsatskeleh, it is. Do you know how to make a snowman?"

Naomi was already wriggling down. It was darker in December back home in Paris, but here it snowed far more. Once at home the snow had been four inches deep. Papa had taken them to the park Les Buttes Chaumont and helped Rivka and her to build a fort. "Will you show me?" Thinking about the park with its artificial mountain in the middle and the high exciting bridges to it, over the water and with a view past the trees of the apartment houses around, the waterfall she and Rivka could walk under and the waffle vendors and the carousel made her want to cry.

"It'll be too dark after I get home. This weekend. If the snow sticks that long, and it looks as if it's going to this time."

Ruthie worked at Sam's downtown in better dresses, $3.98 and up, so she got clothes at discount. Ruthie had taken college preparatory in high school, hoping there would be money, and slowly she was taking evening classes at Wayne, going there on the Woodward trolley four nights a week. Ruthie had also studied typing and stenography all through high school, but she could not get an office job. Only Jewish firms would hire Jews, and there weren't many Jewish businesses looking for young secretaries. Naomi had heard Ruthie tell Arty that she considered putting down Protestant on the applications, but she figured they could tell by her name or her appearance. Besides they would figure it out when she took the holidays off.

In the kitchen Aunt Rose had made oatmeal, set over a pot of hot water to keep warm. Uncle Morris had eaten earlier and gone off to the Chevrolet plant. Duvey was still sleeping. The Great Lakes were closed now to shipping and he was laid off. He worked the ore boats. Her other cousin Arty ate breakfast in the upstairs flat with his wife and their two little children, but everybody ate supper together.

Their wooden house seemed large to Naomi, so that at first she had thought they must be rich, her American family; the apartment of the Lévy-Monot family in Paris was only three rooms, aside from the salle de bains and the WC: the tiny kitchen, the big salle à manger where the girls slept at night, which also served as a living room, and their parents' bedroom. Jacqueline had used to sleep in the salle à manger too, but Maman had arranged to rent one of the former servants' rooms on the top floor under the eaves for Jacqueline when she turned fifteen.

Here the Siegals shared a two-story wooden house with a porch out front and an additional covered stairway with little porches in the rear, onto the alley. The house had been built behind another house, wooden too and three stories tall with a little yard between, hers to play in with Sandy Rosenthal from the bottom-floor flat in the big house and Sandy's little brother Roy. A big elm tree loomed overhead like a whole forest. She had never had a tree of her own before. The nearest trees at home were in a little park near the lycée where Jacqueline had gone.

Here nothing was tall unless they went downtown, where there were very high buildings called skyscrapers, high as the Eiffel Tower but solid. At home almost every apartment building was six or seven stories tall. Here the buildings were any size at all, as if they had all grown to different heights like people, but most had only two or three stories. People seemed to build however they felt like it, different kinds of houses, of wood even, like theirs. At first Detroit had felt like a makeshift toy town, houses that might suddenly fall down.

That made her think, as she ate her oatmeal with brown sugar, about how when her parents had talked of Madrid falling she had imagined an earthquake. She had seen an earthquake in an American film, with the words in French at the bottom, that Papa had taken her to see, but he had ordered her not to read the words, so that Rivka and she could practice their English. She had thought the walls would fall, but by the time Paris had fallen, she was ten and a half and knew better. As she ate, Boston Blackie sat beside her chair hoping for a handout. He would eat anything, even oatmeal.

"Mama," Ruthie was saying, "you can't go out in the snow. You'll just make yourself sick wandering all over."

Aunt Rose was a round woman, plumper than Maman and years older, one of the four sisters from Kozienice, Poland. Her hair was still a patent leather black, but her face was seamed like a prune. Uncle Morris had come over when he was twelve and everyone said he spoke just as if he had been born in America, but Aunt Rose, who had not come to the United States till she was eighteen, spoke with an accent that gave her away. She had a low rich voice that Naomi loved, when Rose was not shouting, that made her think of rich winter desserts. Clove, chocolate, cinnamon.

"I am just going to the Farmer's Market to see what's special today. Two little rides on the trolley. It's Wednesday, the hard middle of the work week. I thought a piece beef for gedempte flaish, at least a stew."

"Mama, do me a favor. Buy the meat at the corner."

"At the corner is two cents more every pound."

"Mama, today in the snow, go to the corner. Please. For me."

"Sure," Aunt Rose said, passing her hand over the head of her only daughter. Naomi knew that Aunt Rose would wait till Ruthie had taken the Woodward Avenue trolley to work and then she would go off herself with her shopping bags to find as much as she could for what money she had. "Don't forget to take the nice lunch I packed for you."

Naomi put the very last of her oatmeal down for the cat, who ate it rapidly and quietly under her chair. They understood each other well.

Every day Ruthie ate her brown bag lunch quickly in the women's room. Then she ran to the downtown library to study. Ruthie always had a book in her purse, which she would read on the trolley, while she was stirring soup, while everybody else was listening to the radio.

Naomi wondered if Aunt Rose had remembered to make her lunch, but she felt shy about asking. Ruthie looked at her and seemed to read her mind. "Mama, did you make a lunch for Naomi?"

"Why wouldn't I make her a lunch? Just because I forgot once. At my age, can't I be forgiven and forgotten a little mistake?"

"What do I have?" Naomi asked. Maman would say she was being rude, but she was curious. Here nobody rebuked her for the question, although Uncle Morris would tease her when he heard her asking. Every morning Aunt Rose made up three lunches, in three different lunch boxes with thermos jugs.

"Today because of the snow, nice hot cabbage soup. Bread with it and a piece of cheese."

This would be borscht with only beets and cabbages, not the one with the beef. She loved it but it made her homesick, because Maman too made such a soup: a family soup, learned from their parents. She thought she could probably make it too, if she wanted. But she did not want to. She wanted it made for her, by Maman.

She put on her leggings and galoshes, buttoned up her coat, picked up her notebook and her satchel for books, her lunch box that was red and had on it a picture of Superman flying, and headed for school, six blocks away. The street was still dark and the streetlights on, but the sky was beginning to lighten.

The snow was coming down in big lazy flakes as if it had forever to cover the city. Already the parked cars were coated. Adults did not use bikes here or motorbikes, but even working people had cars. Uncle Morris had a car, from his own factory. Every month they paid money on it, like rent, although it was not new but already the fender had a dent that had been knocked out and then had rusted. Papa would have loved a car. He knew how to drive. Back before the Nazis had started all the troubles, they had gone off sometimes into the country with Georges who was a mechanic and had an ancient Renault, and his wife and fat good-natured son Razi. Her parents acted like kids then, giggling and cuddly. Everybody ate chicken and drank red wine. Papa played the mouth organ, and they sang in French and Yiddish.

She plodded off past the kosher butcher—Four Eyes Rosovsky's father—where Aunt Rose did not like to shop because she thought he was too expensive, past the fish store where Sandy's papa worked, past the hardware, past the good bread smell of Fenniman's bakery and the dark beery tunnel of bar. Here the sidewalks were slushy already. She stomped in the melted puddles. She formed walls around herself as she walked, getting ready for school, where writing and speaking and reading in English was only part of the work.

The hardest part of her task was studying how to be like the other children, who seemed to her at once older and younger than she was, who had recently turned twelve. They cared more about boys, knew about cars and sports and clothes, radio programs and comic strips. For the other kids, war was something on the radio, something distant and belonging to "Terry and the Pirates" which she too hurried home after school to listen to, followed by "Captain Midnight" and "Jack Armstrong, All-American Boy." They had never been bombed. They had never shaken with fear from planes diving on them and shooting bullets to kill. They had never seen a mother holding a headless baby. They had never seen people and cows dead together like disgusting dirty meat in the fields. They did not imagine the war as a great bonfire hiding off in the direction where the sun was rising, so that the red glare that preceded it seemed to come from the fires of distant bombing, of burning cities, of fear like smoke always on the wind.

BERNICE 1

Bernice and the Pirates

Bernice had grown up thinking her name was Bernice-Professor-Coates's-Daughter, something like Kristin Lavransdatter she realized when she read Lagerlöf's novel. By that time her name had been increased for years to Poor Bernice, Professor-Coates's-Daughter, Poor Motherless Jeff and Poor Motherless Bernice.

Mother had been a big warm frowsy woman dripping scarves and gloves, always toting an enormous cracking leather purse rotund and cylindrical as a hippopotamus and a secondary carpetbag stuffed with books and knitting, handkerchiefs and medicines not only through all of their travels in near and farther Europe every summer, but even on forays into Boston for the day, or to friends' houses for the evening. Anyone seeing The Professor, lean, prematurely greying, carrying a cane which he used mainly on the stairs, with his fleshy often bedraggled wife Viola, would have judged him as mind and her as body.

Bernice however remembered her mother reciting and discussing her way through the *Iliad* and Pindar with two of her women friends at Thursday lunches. Viola's Latin and Greek were far superior to The Professor's, and she was no slouch at his specialty, modern European languages. As The Professor escorted his charges, students or club women or retirees or schoolteachers on vacation, through a grand tour each summer to supplement the genteel penury of his faculty stipend, out of Viola's pouch came the Guides Bleues and the Baedekers, supplemented with art and political history.

Viola had been a substantial woman, with an enormous lap and a hearty amused voice, not someone expected to die in a matter of a month, one nasty never-to-be-forgotten February of double pneumonia. Bernice had been eleven, Jeff, twelve and frail for his age, bookish, shy. Bernice had begun keeping house in deep confusion, with an inner prayer that her loneliness and her burden would not be permanent. Mother would reappear as arbitrarily as she had vanished into first the sickroom, then the hospital, then the suddenly smaller body. Their father had always existed mostly behind closed doors, but their mother, although she demanded respect for her concentration, would nonetheless take them on her lap while reading or chatting.

Every morning for the next year Bernice woke hoping her mother would be in the kitchen frying bacon, making raisin cinnamon toast. She kept waiting for that smell of cinnamon and coffee.

Instead she came downstairs to a cold and empty kitchen and last night's dishes that she had or hadn't done, to make breakfast, a girl soon tall enough to reach the high shelves. For Jeff and herself she made oatmeal of one third strawberry jam, her invention. She invented many dishes in her early cooking, most of them peculiar. For her thirteenth birthday her father The Professor gave her a Fannie Farmer cookbook. She immediately hated its calm authoritative manner, its heft, its laced oxfords air, but she nonetheless mastered it. Plain sensible cooking. Why not? Wasn't that how people saw her? A plain sensible girl.

Now thirteen years later, she still made breakfast for The Professor every morning. Mondays through Fridays he liked his eggs poached on an English muffin or sunny-side up with cinnamon toast, with bacon done crisp but not blackened. He had café au lait with one teaspoon of sugar. He liked his morning *Globe* folded by his plate. Weekends he preferred pancakes with maple syrup, and breakfast was served at nine.

The Professor went off early to campus, only five blocks, but snow had fallen last night and he allowed plenty of time to navigate the walks not yet shoveled. People often assumed his slight limp must be from a war injury, for he had served in The War to End All Wars. Bernice knew that her father had spent the war in Washington translating German communiqués. His foot had been injured when a cow stepped on it at their grandfather's farm up in Putney, Vermont, when she was little.

The boar's head cane had been purchased in Cologne to replace an earlier hickory cane broken, although no one here might credit the truth, in a street brawl when he was visiting a Jewish Heine scholar with whom he had been corresponding. As they left the theater, the brown shirts had attacked his friend, who had recently been forced out of the university. Bernice considered the adventure perhaps The Professor's finest hour; certainly his physical courage had surprised and half shamed him, for he did not consider fighting civilized. Bernice kept the boar's head handle well polished. They had omitted Germany from their itinerary after that.

Bernice stood at the sink washing breakfast dishes. Holmes extends his lean sinewy arm and injects the solution of cocaine, which she imagined as a blue liquid, like cobalt. Her own drug of choice was playing adventure movies in her head. Sunday afternoon she had gone with her neighbor Mrs. Augustine to watch Errol Flynn play pirate. She had run through the movie with variations while cleaning the house, while darning The Professor's socks, while typing other professors' papers, but to imagine herself the dolled-up prize of any pirate had worn threadbare in a day, unlikely from the first moment. She had been joining the pirates since. There had been women pirates, Anne Bonney, for one.

It was swinging through the rigging and slashing away with the saber that gladdened her, although she remembered Flynn's sensual face and wiry body with approval. Bernice could handle a rapier with some facility, for she had fenced with her brother at St. Thomas, where there were always a few girls in attendance although not encouraged. Now she called up a fantasy that had lasted her three years, in which she flew into the Pacific and rescued Amelia Earhart from an unmapped island, where she had crashed. Sometimes Bernice led the expedition and sometimes stowed away and then took over in crisis, turning out to be the best pilot of the lot: that was not fantastic, anyhow. The guys at the field all respected her ability.

She trudged off to campus next with a list of books The Professor wanted. St. Thomas was not a Catholic school. To have thought so would have been to reveal inferior class origins. It was Episcopal insofar as it was anything (chapel was nominally required); however, basically St. Thomas was where rich families sent their sons who managed to flunk out elsewhere, the boys who got drunk on weekdays, the boys caught in the wrong place with the wrong sort or gender, the boys caught bribing the janitor to view the exam beforehand.

Her father had once had ambitions to leave St. Thomas for something more vital, but the combination of the Great Depression and Viola's death had grounded him permanently. She was grounded with him. "How is *he*?" the neighbors asked her. How she was, was all too obvious. Healthy, always healthy.

The postman was coming up the street with the morning mail. She waited for him, while carefully brushing snow off the rhododendrons. "How are you today, Miz Coates?" It was his delicacy to blur her name, for obviously their postman felt her spinster state a shame he did not want to insist on.

She was rewarded for her kindness to the rhododendrons by a letter from her only brother Jeff, among a handful of letters from Europe, acquaintances seeking immigration or help. Jeff might or might not have written to their father, but he knew she got the mail daily and wrote her separately.

La Colina Roja
Taos, New Mexico
November 30, 1941

Dearest Bird,

> *It's cold up here. We had a dusting of snow last week, but I miss New*
> *England most in the fall and then sharply again when the holidays*
> *approach. Sorry I couldn't get home for Thanksgiving, but frankly I can't*
> *come East twice—no $$ as usual, so thought I'd come for Christmas.*
> *(I'm half tempted not to go back, but we'll see.)*

She paused in her reading and folded the letter carefully into her small sensible shoulder bag (what had she, husbandless, childless, professionless, to carry besides her wallet, change purse and keys, with a small sensible comb to administer first aid after the wind to her short sensible hair?). Her reactions were roiled up. Jeff was about to lurch off again in some new direction. The Professor would be annoyed, sarcastic. At the same time she envied the freedom that Jeff might not use productively but always had.

The freedom to pick up one morning and shove off, clear out. He had freedom in abundance and she was starving for a crumb of it. She felt also a handsbreadth of anger, a feeling that she would have had no trouble settling herself usefully in the world and applying her energy, her intelligence, her strength to some worthy task. She could think of fifty things she would love to be able to go and do.

She should finish the typing piled up. Bernice typed papers for other faculty members, earning money which she spent promptly at the local airport. The airport was snowed in for the winter, while she was saving her money to buy a share in a light plane, a sixty-horsepower Piper Cub her friend Steve was paying off. If she could save two hundred and fifty dollars by spring, she would own a quarter of the plane and be able to fly ten times as often. Since the government had started a training program in the college the year before, often when she went to the airport, she waited all day and still could not get a plane. She was working toward a commercial license, but at the rate she had been able to afford time in the air, that would take years. Like her, Jeff had his pilot's license, but he had never bothered to go on.

As if he could read her mind, he wrote—when she opened the letter again in the overheated library with its faint serpentine hissing of radiators, waiting for the librarian to locate The Professor's requests:

I keep asking myself why I can't stick it here. The light is stark, the landscape monumental. The Tiwa call the mountain behind Taos holy, and surely they're right. Perhaps it's the ignominious grind of working for Quinlan, but this is not right for me. I can't seem to do anything original. I feel as if I'm looking through the eyes of artists who've already painted here. I can't seem to encounter the landscape freshly. For all that it's splendid and wild and compelling, I'm not compelled.

    Furthermore things with Dolores have got sticky. Speaking Spanish—and improving my Mexican Spanish which contrary to The Professor's opinion I view as a marvelously supple and electric tongue, quite superior to the lispy pansy tones of Castilian dialect—has proceeded apace, but so has Dolores's desire to view me as an incipient provider of rings, haciendas, babies.

    I could handle the Dolores situation if I felt as if I had arrived in my own proper landscape, but as much as I am moved by these handsomely colored mesas and mountains, the high painted desert, the ancient pueblos, this is not ultimately my promised land.

    Anyhow, I look forward to our time together. No doubt you will explain me to myself as usual and make all clear. I am dreaming of something more tropical. I need to follow the sun, but to something lusher, juicier. The mountains are not finally my holy places. This is not my palate. Too much ochre perhaps, too much burnt sienna. Or maybe just another social scene. Why do I feel so much more naturally and easily an artist in Europe than here?

love as ever,
Jeff

She liked earth colors, herself, the world seen from a plane. She could still remember the first time Zach had taken her up, her alone, because Jeff was painting and would not go. First he had showed her Bentham Center from above, orderly, small, soon left behind, and then they had soared toward, up and over Jumpers Mountain and then onward to the Connecticut, swollen and muddy with spring runoff. Next Zach had begun to tease her, to try to scare her, pulling into great lazy loops and then short abrupt ones, rolls, dives. Finally he had realized she was not screaming, not afraid but eager, rapt, having at least as much fun as he was. He had leaned over and ruffled her hair, pulling it. "Do you want to learn, Bernie?"

She had nodded fiercely, unable to speak, unable to admit her desire.

"Say please."

She did speak then. "Please, Zach. Please! Teach me."

He seemed to consider it at length, frowning, prolonging and enjoying her agony, making her taste the wanting and the suspense. "Maybe I'll do it and maybe I won't." But he had.

"Coming," she burst out too loudly. Mrs. Roscommon had been whispering at her. Bernice hurried to the desk, where a stack of the requested books loomed near toppling.

She was embarrassed at having plunged in that way, out in the world. Now she was back in drabness. When she remembered those times with Zach and Jeff, it was that moment in *The Wizard of Oz*—a movie she had seen three times—when Dorothy passed out of Kansas into Oz, and black and white burst into glorious and radiant technicolor. As she did not care for musicals, she had seen few technicolor movies; that transition moved her enormously. That was what it was like to pass from Bentham Center into adventure. She had gone over and over those days so many times, she was not sure exactly how events had happened, for she had freely embroidered them until they were half fantastic. She felt crazy sometimes to think she spent so much time reliving and working over events that Zach himself and Jeff must have largely forgotten, working them over until she herself was no longer sure what she remembered and what she had pretended happened.

As she plodded home to dump the books and then to the butcher for lamb chops and to the greengrocer for broccoli, if he had it, cauliflower if he did not, she thought that perhaps cavorting with Errol Flynn pirate to pirate with a saber in her teeth was a shade more bearable than returning constantly to that brief paradise of permission to follow along with her brother and Zach. Often she dreamed she was flying. She dreamed herself back at the controls of Zach's Aeronca, banking it, diving, rolling it. One night last week she had wakened crying. How could she have explained to anyone she was weeping because she knew how to fly but had no plane? The Freudians would say it had to do with sex hunger, but she knew nothing about sex, and flying was more real to her than broiling The Professor's chops.

She supposed she should hate Zach for cavalierly teaching them to fly but she could not object; it was the only taste of paradise she had ever been permitted. She had had a crush on him then, but she had been aware she had no more chance with him than a large woolly dog. He enjoyed her company. It amused him to teach Jeff's smart ungainly good-tempered sister to fly. Her loyalty and adoration were pleasing to him as to any god offered incense.

Zach was a creature from another world, exiled to St. Thomas for the same reason many of the boys arrived. Zach was not terminally stupid; he got poor grades because he had little interest in anything academic. Classes did not move through the air fast enough. Zach had cracked up a car while blind drunk. At St. Thomas he did that again, demolishing a Morgan on the hairpin turn coming down from Jumpers Mountain.

Jeff had pulled him out of the car before it burst into flames. Jeff had been bicycling home from a rendezvous in the Garfinkles' hayloft with the middle sister. Pulling the unconscious bleeding Zach from the smoking wreckage, he had then returned to the Garfinkles and borrowed or stolen a horse, on which he loaded Zach and took him to Bentham Center Hospital. Then he returned the horse and peddled home, excited and pleased with himself, to tell her the story.

That injury had pulled Zach out of the sophomore football team and toned down his drinking. It had also made the two boys friends, and Bernice had tagged along when they would have her. Zach loved sporty fast cars, sporty fast yachts, but while he was recuperating from breaking four bones, he passed the time by learning to fly. When Zach learned to fly, his friends learned to fly—at his expense, of course. Solitude was for him a temporary state, to be mended at once. Call out the troops. Bring in the companions. Summon the loyal retainers. He wanted companionship, always, in his escapades, and flying had become her passion, her center.

Why did she imagine that earning a commercial license would free her? She would still have her duty to take care of her father; winning air races, testing planes like Jacqueline Cochran was remote as joining a pirate ship.

As she peeled potatoes she glanced at the calendar. Three more days till Sunday, the seventh, her next injection of movie drug. Twenty days till Christmas. When would Jeff arrive? Tonight, after she had cleaned up, she would write, pressing him to fix a date for his homecoming. For Christmas she had already persuaded Professor Horgan, who taught art history, to pick up a tube of cadmium red and cadmium yellow in Boston for Jeff, expensive paints he loved and often could not afford. He would be delighted.

With small bribes, small promises, with endless fantasies, she made herself continue. What else was there; what else would there ever be, for Professor Coates's daughter, who had inherited the care and feeding of her father, who kept house for him and whose house kept her?—Bernice who flew in her sleep and wept only upon waking, briefly, for she was too sensible to cry long over what could not be changed or shirked.

JEFF 1

Emplumado

It had been stupid to get into a fight with Quinlan and bloody his nose. Still it got Jeff out of Taos, and he felt a sweet relief in loosing some of the anger he had been hoarding over the past months.

How surprised Quinlan had been, always assuming that because Jeff was soft-spoken and artistic, he would swallow any insult. Jeff enjoyed a fight when he could no longer stay out of it. He liked pushing himself physically. It was the same as backpacking up into the mountains, which his acquaintances in Taos regarded as bound to end in falling off a cliff or getting lost. He had first climbed in Austria, and then in Switzerland. He had found the local mountains fascinating but not overly demanding. He had found Quinlan easy to knock down.

Quinlan had acted the bully from the beginning. He was managing the dude ranch for a combine that owned it, pocketing, Jeff suspected, as much as he could get away with and taking it out of the care of the animals, the accommodations and food of the hired help and little irritating economies such as there never being toilet paper in the latrine the help used.

What Quinlan had called him was not the reason for punching him, only the excuse. Quinlan, who lacked a gift for invective, called him a pinko fag. Jeff was a pinko because he supported Roosevelt's economic policies, although he felt that the President was not pursuing them hard enough. He was a fag because he had avoided getting into bed with Mrs. Terwilligher, who was rich, as obnoxious as Quinlan and could not possibly like him any more than he could endure her. Jeff had made a practice of pretending he did not understand the help were to be sexually available to the vacationers, that sexual service was expected from the waitresses, chambermaids and trail hands, as they were called, who shepherded the overfed along careful scenic routes.

Jeff had nothing in principle against the setup. When he had accompanied his father The Professor's charges on their cultural rounds, he had viewed them as a harem from which to choose bedmates. He did not think The Professor had ever caught on, although Bernice knew. She was surprisingly broad-minded for a virgin. Poor Bernice. His Bird in a very plain cage.

He shipped the two paintings he considered the best to Bernice along with his French easel, after paying off his local debts with canvases and leaving three at the gallery just in case. If they did sell, he was sure he'd never see the money, but at least they'd display them. As a landscape painter who worked relatively small, he was definitely unfashionable, but not unsellable. Still, he had not done his best work in Taos. He kept seeing work by other painters that seized the formal essence of the landscape, as O'Keeffe or Dasburg, or the tumultuous changes of sky and mountains, as Marin had done, always the Sacred Mountain. He had not made Taos his own. Its clarity had not crystallized him. He walked out of town and hitched a ride to Denver.

He carried his few things on his back in a rucksack, easier to tote than a suitcase, but no Americans seemed to use them. In Denver he found a flop near the station. He fished a newspaper out of a trash can. The Russians were supposed to be counterattacking in the suburbs of Moscow. Zach had written from London, where he had gone with the idea of enlisting in the RAF, but they had turned him down. Too many ancient injuries? They might have considered Zach over the hill at twenty-eight. It was not that Zach hated the Nazis. His own family's run of political ideas was not dissimilar. Jeff could easily imagine Zach's father, Zachary Barrington Taylor the third—as Zach was the fourth—saying, "That Hitler is a trifle crude but he knows how to keep the workers in line," and contributing to the party coffers. Zach simply was going where things looked lively. He loved flying. He had grown up on dreams of fighter duels from the World War and he wanted to take on the Red Baron. In recent years Zach had been doing something boring in the family insurance business in Chicago; that is, the Taylors had a controlling interest in that combine as well as numerous others, not to mention the Barrington domain of textiles and sugar. Zach had done his family duties, marrying and fathering a child. Jeff had nothing to do with the respectable side of Zach's life. He would hardly be received there.

Zach urged him to come over to England, but neglected to send tickets, which meant he was not serious. Zach must know Jeff had not the money to get himself home, let alone to Europe. What had the Depression meant to Zach: more riffraff in the streets? Jeff, whose life had been chopped up by the Depression into segments of manual labor and unemployment in diverse cities and landscapes, who was sleeping in a cubicle in a fleabag hotel for the hundredth time, who had worked for the CCC and worked for the WPA and broken stone building a highway and harvested wheat, experienced a moment of resentment so strong he felt it could pierce his friend like a dagger of ice.

But Zach did not get on with his own father any better than Jeff did with The Professor; Zach had early fallen into the second son, bad son, black sheep role. He had never fitted into the life laid out like a suit of formal clothes by a valet. Had he finally escaped?

Jeff wanted to go home. Not to his father, who was a cold compulsive pre-occupied with his own work and his own comfort, and who made him feel like a bad child who played truant. For all the years The Professor had spent dragging charges through the museums of Europe, he had no understanding of a son who painted. Jeff wanted to go home to Bernice, who was and wasn't his mother. Of course she wasn't, because they had had a real mother, that creature of flesh and intellect and humor and fussiness, the best faculty cook, who loved poetry and read it to them instead of silly children's books, who read them the Pope translation of the *Iliad* and sometimes recited for them the Greek, whose lap never failed in its size and warmth.

In another sense Bernice was his mother, because she was all he had had thereafter. They had raised each other. If only she had been his twin, a boy growing into man, they would roam the world together. Bernice would have made a handsome man. As it was, she was too tall for a woman, five nine, big-boned, a woman who could pull a plow. In another era, she would have been more appreciated, he thought. Picasso's big squarish nudes of his recent classical period made Jeff think of his sister.

Now he wanted to be with her, gathered into that intelligent warmth that was never entirely without judgment but never off-putting. He wanted coddling. He wanted to share with her the adventures that since he was a kid had been almost more satisfactory in the telling than in the living. Nothing was quite real until Bird received it. Instead here he was in Denver.

If he hitched down to Boulder, he could get a ride when school let out for Christmas, but the thought of waiting that long made him shrivel with self-pity. He wanted to look at that last canvas he had completed, shipped to Bernice. He wanted to paint from the cliffs of Jumpers Mountain in the morning with a dusting of snow on the scene.

He'd either hitchhike with truckers or ride the rails, but he never asked for money from home. The Professor was paid barely sufficient to maintain the household. War had put an end to his summer excursions, which had brought in as much as his nine months of teaching. Bernice made do, but Jeff knew how carefully she managed. He himself had vastly enjoyed that bourgeois summer life, hotels, restaurants, museums, playing the artist he really was. In Taos in the local uniform of Levi's, bandanna and boots, social classes mixed, but still he was living as a ranch hand, not as a painter. That hurt.

Bernice had been allowed to attend classes, but was not granted a degree by St. Thomas. The Professor would not allow her to work, even if she had been qualified for anything. He, Jeff, would always land on his feet. He was no remittance man, adventuring on a sure monthly check. He was also free. When he went home, it was because he longed for his sister, not because he expected anything of them. Now getting there was the little problem to be solved.

Dolores had offered that haven at first, that warm place he sought with women. Women always seemed to pick him out in a crowd, at a party. One of the tedious aspects of being down and out was that the jobs he could fall into often kept him in an all-male enclave, and the truth was that most men had no idea how to live. They built no nests, they created no comfort, they made the worst out of their shortfalls. He liked to move in with a woman.

He had not actually lived with Dolores, for he had his lodging as part of the job on Quinlan's dude ranch, and Dolores was mindful of the neighbors' opinions. Still she had cooked for him frequently, and he had had the cosiness of her whitewashed adobe house to curl into. He had liked to look at her, even done a few sketches, although he knew that when he did one of his rare figure paintings, the people turned into landscapes. Her face was fascinatingly asymmetrical. Dolores herself was not aware of the way one side of her face was more angular and the other softer. Shadow playing over it had never stopped attracting him. Her body was neatly voluptuous, the flare out to the buttocks accentuated, her hips going out in a baroque curve that had two distinct waves to it. Her skin had hints of amber and of a faint green in its duskiness.

Dolores had told him he was an old tomcat, un gaton, who had got used to wandering and cadging meals. Then she had put pressure on him to settle down. Why did women do that? They picked him out for his air of being well traveled, the romantic allure of the wanderer who tomorrow would be gone, and then they attempted to enlist him in domesticity.

In ordinary times he would have been graduated from college and gone to a studio school here or abroad, come back to teach and paint, married and had children. But there had been no money and no jobs. He had begun wandering with the army of homeless men from freight train to skid row to hiring hall. By the time he had won the competition for a WPA job painting murals on post offices, he had got used to picking up and leaving a set of complications.

He would settle eventually but only when he found the right place, the proper place, his own landscape, a woman who combined Dolores's beauty with Bernice's independence and brains. He was like someone who had been put on morphine out of necessity, to kill pain, and grown addicted. Moving on had become a habit, but he dreamed constantly of a companion. Someone who would know what things had been like in the town before or the previous country, who remembered Barcelona before Franco and London before the blitz and Paris before the Nazis had occupied it. A common frame of reference. Not even fear of war was that. Most people seemed to assume it would never come. The only common culture seemed to be movies and comic strips. Everybody would talk about Gasoline Alley, Li'l Abner, Dick Tracy. Maybe that was why he needed to go home, now, immediately. Bernice was his repository. All stories ended in her mind.

Thursday morning he cleaned himself up at the train station and headed for a truck depot. He was almost immediately successful. An independent driver who was picking up a load of tires and taking them north to Cheyenne would carry him along for the work at either end. He was glad to move a step nearer. This trip was a game of chess where he was the knight who moved two steps forward and one step to the side each time. The tires turned out to be huge, for earthmoving equipment. Although the man watched him skeptically at first, Jeff did not doubt his ability to move the massive things. He was stronger than he looked, with no fat on him; and he understood balance.

As they rode north across the wastelands where he watched antelopes the color of the ground running lightly, he was considering investigating Central America or perhaps heading down to Brazil. He imagined the sharp jagged reds of the Mediterranean rocks but set against the lurid pulsing greens of a jungle. He would research points south in the library while he was feeding up on Bernice's good home cooking. They would climb Jumpers Mountain to steal a tree. They would take out the old boxes of ornaments, the Czech prisms and German globes with the gilt bites in their roundness, the wooden horses and painted drummers, the tinsel birds. He would visit his earlier paintings, ranged around Bernice's room and his own. His failure in Taos had eroded his confidence. He needed to see his best work.

What had he been sniffing after in Taos after all, the ghost of D. H. Lawrence? Everyone pointed out to him the relics, the place Lawrence had done or said this or that outrageous or meaningful, absurd or prophetic thing. *The Plumed Serpent* had been his least favorite of Lawrence's novels, yet he found himself fascinated by the imagery. A snake with feathers caught his imagination. Perhaps he had been seeking some image like that in Taos, a way to combine flight and earthiness. He had never been repelled by snakes, but had used to catch black snakes and king snakes and pretty little garters.

He had seen a Morris Graves show that had moved him immensely, but the landscapes he responded to were the opposite of those foggy seamisted visions he admired in Graves. He needed intense light, hard definitions, rock and strong shapes. Why then had he failed so in Taos?

They stopped for lunch. He bought himself a bowl of chili. The trucker stood him to coffee. The guy seemed pleased Jeff had not tried to get lunch out of him. He had an interesting face, all flat planes set against each other at different depths, a face made with a chisel, or one of Braque's cubist collages. When they were back in the rig, he asked Jeff if he knew how to drive it. When Jeff proved he did, the trucker climbed into the back of the cab and went to sleep.

It was snowing lightly. The mountains to the north were white a third of the way down. Dust mixed with the snow for a while, pocking the windshield. He remembered a dream of a woman whose thighs had been feathered. Blue and green and gold iridescent feathers blowing softly as he parted her thighs. Her hair had been jetty as Dolores's. Even thinking of her now he became partly erect. He turned the radio softly to news, half listening.

Since 1939 he had lived expecting war any moment. The Nazis were far more real to him than to most Americans he met, and far more frightening. He did not share the mirth of his acquaintances at Hitler the ex-paperhanger who made funny faces and ridiculous speeches as his legions goose-stepped and fell on their faces. He had seen them in the streets of Heidelberg and Berlin and Frankfurt. They were drunk with violence and power. They felt themselves superior be- cause they were together and together they administered pain. They had discov- ered domination under a visible god. He had attended a Nazi rally and watched crowds choreographed, manipulated, mesmerized into ecstasy and roaring blood lust and loving the transport.

He awaited the next move of the gods or his sister or his friends. He expected to be rescued from his boredom, but he did not know who would do it this time. Zach could, always. He had not been surprised to hear from Zachary Barrington Taylor, although they had not seen each other in . . . two years? Someone would make an offer, as a ride would turn up in Cheyenne.

He was not fated to be stuck in Cheyenne, Wyoming, with the snow blowing down from the Big Horns. Jeff had the sublime faith of those to whom things happen. He need only to post himself in the open, he was sure, for it had always happened, and someone would speak to him, someone would make him an offer or ask him a favor or throw themselves upon him or proposition him, for Jeff was always prepared far more seriously than the Boy Scouts. He believed the gods loved him and would surely send some interesting adventure his way, so long as he waited with empty hands and the readiness of mind and body that was his notion of grace.

He had fallen in love with landscape painting because of that element of chance and grace. He would go out to a field, to a beach, to a hill, and set himself up. As he focused on the scene before him, around him, the scene he was part of and became rooted in, it came more and more intensely alive until every leaf and every fly glinting in the sun and every dust mote demanded his attention. He felt totally open then, connected, vulnerable, better than love and more honest. In order to paint well he had to abandon control. Everything constantly changed before him and everything moved and he stood in a swirl of chaos and humbly addressed it. Whatever he put on canvas was insufficient, as love is insufficient.

If he was clear, if he was open, if he was vulnerable and strong enough in his seeing, then he would grasp some spirit present and it would animate what he painted, although his first reaction was always to hate what he had done, because it failed the vast changing thingness he had astonishingly and passionately witnessed. Studio painters could dream of control, but landscape painters knew how they stood before the gods of the place, tiny, hopeful, diddling away. All he could ever paint was a tiny flash of what truly showed itself to him, a seizure on one moment.

Thus Jeff headed East toward home and toward the next adventure that must surely save him from remaining there long.

RUTHIE 1

Ruthie's Saturday

Ruthie Siegal had dated more in high school than she did now. For one thing, she had enjoyed many more free evenings. Four nights a week she went to classes at Wayne; Friday was traditionally a family night. Although her family went to the synagogue only on holidays and although since Bubeh had died, Mama no longer kept kosher, she did bake challah and roast a chicken. Friday remained a special night with the candles in the holders Bubeh had brought from Poland and a clean tablecloth laid over the oilcloth. That left Saturday and Sunday nights only, and sometimes Mama needed her help.

Nor did she meet a great many young men eager to ask her out. The salesforce at Sam's was female and only women came in to buy dresses, unless a husband tagged unwillingly along. In her classes, many of the young men were not Jewish, and the Jews often were married or engaged.

She had gone out with Leib all through her last year of high school, but he had pushed her again and again to sleep with him. She would not. Not only did she fear the consequences, she did not want to bring more trouble into the house and betray the confidence of her mother, who trusted her far more willingly than mothers of her friends trusted them. What finally did not tip that balance was that the wish was his, not hers. She simply did not want him enough, and if she had given way, it would only have been to keep him. So finally she had not kept him.

Tonight she had her third date with Murray, who was in her Monday-Wednesday class because he too wanted to become a social worker. Ruthie had gone out with perhaps five young men since that final foot-stomping scene with Leib, when he had broken down, wept and called her names and then calmed abruptly and walked out of her life, but she had gone with none of them more than twice, and usually once was enough.

"You have to give them the benefit of the doubt," her best girlfriend Trudi said.

"You ought to wait to see what's going on with a guy." Ruthie did not have a lot of time to waste with idiots and fresh schlemiels. She would be better off home studying than killing four hours fighting off a pasty-faced gorilla or making conversation as if it were secreted out of the depth of the bone marrow one precious drop at a time. If she did not force herself through night school classes, she would never be a social worker; forever she would be stuck in a dead-end department store job. The older women who worked there liked Ruthie because she was quick to see their fatigue and offer to help; but they represented failure to her. If she was kind to them, it was part habit, for so she had been trained, part unwilling empathy and part a superstitious attempt to buy off that future she did not want by bribing it with small favors. It was not a true mitzvah.

She was nervous about tonight, because a third time seemed almost a commitment, and because she was not sure she should be going out. Mama had made her usual rounds of rummage sales for clothes, much of it needing repairs. Even though Ruthie got a discount at Sam's, they could not afford many new clothes. That afternoon she had meant to teach Naomi to build a snowman, but drizzle had melted the snow. Instead they had looked at magazines. Ruthie had not been putting enough time into improving Naomi's English.

She wished Duvey would take that on, but he was seldom home once he pried himself out of bed. He was running around with his old gang. She was not quite sure what they were up to—she knew Duvey had Trojans in his wallet and went to Negro prostitutes in the Paradise Valley section. Condoms were scattered all over the grass in the park after the weekend like punctured balloons, where Leib had shown them to her as an argument.

Duvey also had a knife that was far more of a weapon than a fishing knife, and when had he ever gone fishing anyhow? One of Ruthie's Sunday jobs was cleaning all the bedrooms. Mama was always terrified Duvey would drown in the Great Lakes. Ruthie worried more about the depths of Detroit. She saw the street life and petty crime of the neighborhood as a series of sticky traps set for each of them, to hold them fast in poverty.

Duvey played cards for money (or against money, Ruthie sometimes thought, since he so invariably lost). Still Duvey always gave Mama a wad of bills when he came home from the ore boats, before he started getting rid of his pay. Mama would put it in the bank, then draw from it when the little troubles that always came began to descend like summer hail, so many individual stones but each painful when it hit.

Their middle brother Arty had married when he was just the age Ruthie was now, nineteen. He had found only occasional jobs as delivery boy, so he and Sharon lived with the family. After Mrs. Rabinowitz upstairs was taken off to the state hospital, Mama got the landlord to let Arty and Sharon move up. The apartment had the stink of the dirt of the ages, that had taken Sharon, Mama and Ruthie a week to clean. Sharon was seven months' pregnant with Marilyn. Since then Sharon had had Clark.

The only girls Duvey ever was seen with were flashy shiksehs, usually blondes out of a bottle. Mostly when he was home, he hung out with his gang going to bars, listening to jazz and sitting up all night losing money at poker and twenty-one. He had taught Ruthie to play cards, but once she learned, she always beat him. She had been teaching Naomi the kid games, fish and war, so Naomi could play with the local children. Kids could be mean to someone a little different. She ached for Naomi sometimes. She wanted to pad the rough edges of their Detroit neighborhood for her. Naomi was a bright little thing but naive. French Jews grew up slowly. She was far more thoughtful than an American her age, but less savvy, less able to make her way socially. Her family had probably been more orthodox.

In the house of her friend Sophie everything stopped on the Sabbath. They sat in the dark and the girls could not even read or sew or listen to the radio. Even when the Siegals had kept kosher for Bubeh, they had never had that tyranny of inaction. Ruthie imagined it must turn the Sabbath from something a little special to something dreaded.

Bubeh wanted everything right in the kitchen; she really meant it when she called food trayf. She considered nonkosher food unclean, physically impure and foul, like a plate of mud or rotten fish. Otherwise Ruthie had always thought that Bubeh and Mama winged it a lot. Tata didn't care. He was a Socialist and a freethinker, and he viewed the remnants of Jewish ritual in their home as something for the womenfolks and children, nice but hardly essential.

Bubeh and Mama both thought Jewish ritual and custom important but subject to reinterpretation, a new life in a new land; their observance was strongly pragmatic. She suspected she would be that way herself. She had adored Bubeh, who shared her room until she died of stomach cancer.

Bubeh had been her special responsibility, since she was eight. When Bubeh was sick, Ruthie took care of her, even if it meant staying out of school. She could always catch up; she always did. Bubeh had said to her when Arty was talking about wanting a son, "When a boy is born, the men make a fuss. They have the bris and they pray and everybody rejoices. But when a girl is born, in her heart her mother is twice glad. Because she is born over again in her daughter, and maybe this time it will be better."

Bubeh was almost blind with cataracts. A doctor at the clinic said they were operable, but who had the money for operations? In Poland she had done fine embroidery on blouses and linens. Bubeh sewed constantly for the family, although she did it mostly by touch and occasionally she would make a mistake matching colors—then no one would tell her, so that she would not feel bad. She had been sensitive about her vision, always pretending she could see more than she was able. All day she and Mama had listened to the soaps on the radio. "Ma Perkins," "Our Gal Sunday," "The Romance of Helen Trent": Could a girl from a mining town in the West find happiness as the wife of one of England's richest titled lords? Was there romance after thirty-five? Would Stella Dallas ever give up on her rotten daughter Lolly-Baby? Since Bubeh's death, Mama never listened. Ruthie was not sure whether it was because they made her miss Bubeh, or because she had never really liked them. When she asked, Mama shrugged off the question. "Who am I, Mrs. Rockefeller, I have time to sit with my ear stuck to the radio? Who makes things stretch, if not me?"

Ruthie stood now at the window of her bedroom facing on the alley, dark already at four-thirty. A skinny cat was lurking under a box. She turned away not to see it, cold in the rain. Automatically she reached for Boston Blackie, who had been Bubeh's cat and was now especially hers. He was a big black and white tom weighing fifteen pounds and a lot of that bone and muscle. His left ear was crooked and his tail had an extra kink in the end where Tata said the vertebra was broken. When Bubeh had taken him in, he had gladly given up his alley fights and the pursuit of sex and settled down. "He's a philosopher," Bubeh used to say. "All day he thinks about G-d and the universe. You should meet a man so grateful as this cat. You give him the gizzard, he thanks you purring and rubbing. You pet him on the head, he kneels to you. Let him in your bed and he's a gentleman."

Naomi was bent over the desk working on her spelling homework. Actually it was not a desk but the bottom half of a vanity. The mirror had been broken and one handle come off a drawer, so some person with more money than sense had set it out on the street, where Ruthie had seen it. Arty and Mama and she had schlepped it home between them, where Ruthie painted it blue. Now Naomi and she had their own desk. She tousled Naomi's curly brown hair, kinkier than her own. Naomi stared up into her eyes as if in despair. "Is the homework very hard? Can I help you?" Ruthie asked.

"English doesn't make sense. There aren't any rules."

Ruthie thought about it. "There must be some."

Naomi was still staring. "Will my eyes ever turn green, like yours?"

"But your eyes are pretty, Naomi. Hazel is just as pretty."

"Will my hair ever turn black like yours, or will it always be brown?"

"Hasn't your hair gotten darker since you were born? Then maybe it'll go on getting darker. But it's a pretty color. They call that chestnut here, I don't know why. I never saw a chestnut."

"What is chestnut?"

"Look it up in your dictionary."

Naomi had a big green English-French dictionary her own father had given her. It was one of the few treasures she had carried from Europe. "Marrons! You don't know what they are? They sell them on street corners roasted, over little fires. They're ground and put in desserts. And in syrup. Marrons glacé." Naomi's little heart-shaped face took on an animation almost glittering. She vibrated energy. "There is a dessert called Mont Blanc that is cream of chestnut, tres riche. Did you never have it?"

"I don't think we have chestnuts here. We have shagbark hickories all over Michigan, and walnuts. We went out to this cottage a Russian Jew who is a friend of Tata's has and we all picked black walnuts, before you came, Naomele. I hope sometime we'll go again. They're big oily balls you have to tear off to get the inner nut, and they stain your hands dark."

Murray was taking her out to eat and then to a movie, but she helped Mama start the piroshki, making the dough for her. It was a bitter cold night. Duvey was out. Only Arty and Tata sat in the living room listening to the news. Sharon and the little ones were crowded in the kitchen with Mama and her and now Naomi too, to keep warm. They had to pay for coal, so they couldn't afford to keep the house toasty. The wind off the river tried every window and crept through the crevices in the old wooden frame. The steamy kitchen smelled good, making Ruthie reluctant to leave.

When she went to her room to dress, Naomi followed her and sat disconsolately on the bottom bunk where Ruthie slept (the privilege of being a breadwinner), watching with sad eyes. "Tsatskeleh, what are you pouting for?" Ruthie chucked Naomi under her little pointed chin.

"Who is this man? What do you want with him?"

"He's a nice young man, a scholar, from college. You'll like him."

"I won't." Naomi glared. "You're wearing my favorite dress for him."

The red taffeta. It was the only nice dress Ruthie had, although she had put a dollar down on a green velvet now in layaway. She hoped to get it paid off by January, but she still owed five dollars on it. They shouldn't hold it that long, but the woman in layaway liked Ruthie.

Murray arrived early, but Ruthie was so nervous she had gotten ready and was back in the kitchen with an apron over her dress helping Mama bake piroshki. Quickly she tore off the apron and ran into the living room. Tata was easy with Murray, shaking his hand, asking him what he thought about whether the

English would crack under the bombing, whether the Germans still meant to invade England. Ruthie liked Murray for looking embarrassed and saying he didn't know. Men often parroted what they had read in the paper, pretending they had some kind of inside knowledge.

Just as he was awkwardly helping her into her coat—the lining was ripped, for without Bubeh to mend, they got behind—Duvey came in. Mama, who was greeting Murray from the door of the kitchen scrunching her apron in her hand as if that would conceal that she was wearing it, shrieked when she saw Duvey's face. "Duvidel!" Mama cried. "What happened to you?"

"I fell on the ice," Duvey said grumpily, rubbing his nose.

Tata looked at Ruthie who looked back at him. "You should get going with your fellow before you're late," he said mildly. Tata did not believe in Duvey's fall either, but he wasn't going to scare Mama by expressing skepticism. He came home from Chevrolet bone weary, not wanting to seek any more trouble than fell on him.

"Mayn lebn, you hurt your eye, your nose." Mama was peering into Duvey's face while he grimaced his impatience, but nonetheless permitted himself to be fussed over and led off to the bathroom.

Outside in the street as they hurried toward the Woodward trolley, Murray said, "I thought it looked like your brother had been in a fight."

"Thank you for not mentioning it in front of Mama. He'll have a black eye tomorrow."

"What's it about, do you know?"

Ruthie shook her head. "I don't know if I want to know. Duvey's a little wild."

They went to a Chinese restaurant, which was new to Ruthie. That made Murray laugh. He said he thought all Jews who didn't keep kosher ate Chinese when they went out. When you got bar mitzvahed at a Reform synagogue, they told you now you were a man and you should go out and eat Chinese every Sunday with your family.

Murray was only a little bit bigger than Ruthie, unlike Leib who had loomed over her by almost a foot. She liked him being smaller, like Tata, like herself. She did not feel afraid of him, as she always had in an undercurrent with Leib. He seemed gentler.

He was telling her how after his father's Dodge-De Soto agency had gone under in 1930, his father had first tried to sell door-to-door. Then he had taken their savings and bought a chicken farm. "Why he imagined a bunch of Jews from Detroit could run a chicken farm, I don't know. Back to the land. But he kept saying, no matter what happened, we wouldn't starve."

"So what happened? Did you eat all the chickens?"

"First a dog got some, then a fox. The survivors all caught a disease. Every one of them legs up lying dead in the yard all mangy and bedraggled. Then we tried turkeys, on borrowed money. With turkeys we made it through."

"With turkeys?" Ruthie laughed. "I shouldn't laugh. I don't know why I think it's funny."

"But it was. If there's anything stupider than chickens, it's turkeys. At least they don't crow. I could never get used to that hideous racket at dawn." Murray flapped his arms and gave a creditable imitation. Everybody looked at them, but Murray did not seem to notice. He was only looking at her. Ruthie blushed. "Now he has a tenant running the turkey farm. My parents moved almost into the city. He's back selling cars for a dealer out Grand River, but with production cut back, I don't know what he'll try next."

Behind horn-rimmed glasses his eyes were a rich warm brown with glints of amber. His hair was combed straight back, a fine light brown that static made cling to the collar of his shirt and sweater, stand up on the crown of his head. They assured each other they were determined to finish college. Murray was looking for a job as a waiter so he could go to college during the day and get through faster. In the meantime he worked in a florist's.

"I have to stay in school," Ruthie said. "It's my only hope, it's what I really want. Then I can help people like my own family. I can understand them better than those people who've never been in trouble in their lives."

Murray told her his idea about the life he wanted, unwrapping it slowly as a carefully packed china plate. He would work in the city but he would not live there. "If you drive out Grand River, or Ann Arbor Trail, Plymouth Road, you come into country. You could buy a farmhouse out there and travel to work. Then when, you know, you had a family, the children wouldn't have the same problems. They'd be healthy. They'd have grass and trees and birds around them. That was good for me."

They got so involved that they were late to the movie, but only the newsreel was on. The Japanese envoy Kurusu and Ambassador Nomura were presenting what they claimed were final proposals for peace between Japan and Washington. There was a picture of the Dionne quintuplets in identical outfits playing in the snow. The Marines were evacuating Shanghai, but the voice-over said they would soon be back. Then the first feature came on, an Ellery Queen mystery with Ralph Bellamy, in which Murray guessed the murderer halfway through; and then Ann Miller in *Time Out for Rhythm*.

From the trolley, they walked toward her house very slowly in spite of the raw wind. She felt chilled through, cold and damp, but she did not want to hurry. He had taken her hand in helping her off the trolley and he still held it. His hand was warm and dry. She found it easy to walk with him, because he did not take giant steps. I like him, she thought as if astonished at herself. She looked at his face as they passed under the streetlights. His nose ran straight as if drawn with a ruler. His mouth was full and soft-looking. She imagined kissing him, but she did not think it would happen, at least not yet. Eventually she would kiss him. Maybe this time an embrace would feel right.

One Cold Sunday

Lady Hamilton was the Sunday matinee movie Bernice and Mrs. Augustine were watching, sharing a box of caramel corn, to which Mrs. Augustine was partial. Mrs. Augustine was the wife of Professor Emil Augustine, who taught chemistry. She was a short round woman who suffered from mild arthritis and terrible corns, so that she walked slowly and painfully, but she had always tried to keep an eye on the household next door since Viola died, or as Mrs. Augustine put it, passed beyond.

Mrs. Augustine believed in reincarnation, because, as she told Bernice, it was ever so much cheerier than Christian heaven and hell. That did not prevent her from attending Episcopal services with her husband, who took no interest in Mrs. Augustine's more recherché views. Mrs. Augustine clipped articles from the newspapers about people who thought they could remember previous lives. Most of those interviewed had been Egyptian princesses, the empress of Russia, Pavlova, Lord Byron, but Mrs. Augustine could recall life as a lighthouse keeper off the coast of Maine in the 1840s. She had been overly fond of the bottle and had eventually fallen to her death on the rocks of her island, but life in the interim had been pleasant and she had not ever felt lonely. Bernice considered that if she had to spend her life with the crusty Emil, a lighthouse keeper might seem a pleasant alternative.

Vivien Leigh was lovely and Laurence Olivier, handsome, but she found her attention wandering from the adultery. She recalled a portrait of Lord Nelson, was it in the Tate? One of those days they led tourists at a dogtrot through three museums, while Jeff lectured himself hoarse.

The Professor took over when they visited castles and monuments. Not always that neat a division. She remembered the summer of 1939, the last summer they had shepherded The Professor's charges across Europe. For a moment she smelled salt and heated stone. Her arms were dark under the strong sun of the Mediterranean, as she enjoyed a brief vacation from their charges' vacation, sweet stolen time to play tourist herself.

Jeff and she had sat by the harbor in Thessaloníki sipping retsina and eating the sweet little clams raw (as they always warned the tourists not to), followed by fried baby squid, kalamarakia. Their party was touring Haghia Sophia and other important churches of the lower town. The Professor had a sympathy for the solemn staring Byzantine saints his children lacked. Jeff and The Professor had studied the papers daily, for fear of being caught by the outbreak of war, but they had boarded ship and were halfway across the Atlantic when the Germans rolled into Poland. This April after the Greek army had fought off the Italians through the fall and winter, the Germans had crushed them with their massive armor and overrun the British forces on hand; would she ever see Greece again?

After the movie the lights came up and people started to rise. Bernice was zipping her rubber galoshes over her oxfords, when she saw that Mr. Berg, the portly old man who managed the movie house, was standing on the stage gripping a microphone as an usher tried to unroll the cord. "I have an announcement, ladies and gentlemen!" he bellowed, too excited to wait for the microphone to be plugged in. He stepped forward to the apron of the stage on which vaudeville used to be performed. "I have an important announcement. On the radio they told us the Navy is being attacked in Honolulu. I repeat, the U.S. Navy is being attacked."

Mrs. Augustine said, "Thank heavens Emil is too old to fight."

When she walked in, The Professor had come out of his study and was hunched over in the living room, right in front of the Westinghouse console radio with its doors open, its dial lit up and the volume turned loud.

"They made an announcement in the Bentham." Bernice sat in her accustomed chair. "Is it war?"

"War against Japan, I would assume. He'll have to declare war now."

"Has the President come on the air yet?"

"Not yet."

Bernice stared at the glow of the radio dial. She had put in a pot roast before she left, turning it low. However The Professor was looking over his glasses at her with an expectant air. "When shall we dine?"

That was not a serious question, as they always ate on Sunday at six-thirty, but she understood his question to translate as, Why are you sitting around the living room with the table not set and the finishing touches to put on my meal? She walked slowly to the kitchen, surprised to find that she was light-headed, almost dizzy. She immediately turned on the small radio that sat on the kitchen counter.

Major George Fielding Eliot, Columbia's military expert, was analyzing developments in a brisk voice. "The Japanese appear to be taking the offensive in an effort to delay American operations in the Far East. Apparently confronted with a situation in which there was no escape except war, the Japanese have attacked the main American naval base in the Pacific at Pearl Harbor in the island of Oahu in the Hawaiian Islands. This attack is by air and can only come from aircraft carriers since the Japanese do not have any bases close enough to the islands from which to launch land-based aircraft."

She remembered an evening when Zach had been visiting Jeff. He had flown his Aeronca in, and the day itself had been heaven. It had come out that Zach was separated from his wife, in spite of her having a baby. That was the month Amelia Earhart had disappeared on the leg of her round-the-world flight near the Marshall Islands. Zach had insisted the Japanese had shot her down because she had been doing reconnaissance for Roosevelt, which was why the President had had an airstrip built especially for her on Howland Island. Jeff and Zach had infuriated her, because they were rational and speculative, while she felt a personal loss. She had always been convinced she would meet her idol someday, whose photograph she had clipped from the paper and put on her wall, surrounded by Jeff's early and recent landscapes.

The radio spoke smartly into her reverie. "This is a very great risk for the Japanese to have placed aircraft carriers within reach of the very powerful naval patrol bombers and the long-range Army bombers from the island of Oahu. It is a risk that can only be assumed as a very desperate measure, one which may well result in the loss of carriers that are making the attack but which may also gain for the Japanese important time to carry out operations in the Far East, by delaying the proceeding of the Pacific Fleet to the western Pacific."

The crisp sure voice made the news partially reassuring. The major might have been describing a manager's decisions in a baseball game, or the kind of thinking she was accustomed to when she played chess with her father. She was ashamed of her light-headedness. Perhaps these events did not necessarily mean war; or perhaps war would be represented in her life by just such authoritative male voices explaining distant causes and effects: a calamity less onerous than the Depression.

Time to put on the brussels sprouts and prepare a sauce.

Oscar was right, the Spanish restaurant was good. Louise had paella and Oscar had a zarzuela de maresco: shrimp, lobster, clams and mussels in a tomato sauce flavored with garlic and saffron. She rather wished she had gotten that too, although her paella was excellent. Trust Oscar to know just what to order. He was not a food or wine snob, but seemed to assimilate the right choices through his pores, perhaps because he was curious and never shy about asking the waiter what the couple at the next table were eating. It had led them to some memorable meals over the years, most of them good, some of them simply memorable like the time they had eaten sea urchins in a Chinese restaurant.

They began with a glass of dry sherry, then shared a bottle of white rioja. Oscar talked about his project interviewing refugees. Louise had good antennae. Watching his face, she remarked, "I'd expect that a lot of this information would be useful intelligence? I presume the government has enough sense to guess we'll get involved in this war sooner or later?"

"Umm," Oscar said. "Would you like another taste of my zarzuela? I see you eyeing it with a certain interest."

"Your zarzuela, indeed. Really, Oscar." She helped herself. She had the answer, but only partially. Who was he working for?

"I wouldn't mind a taste of yours, not at all. It's been a long time."

"I'm ashamed of you, Oscar, trying to seduce me to avoid answering my question. Which does after all answer it."

"Seducing you is on the program a priori. The attempt anyhow. I used to be able to get round you." He refilled her glass. "Is your heart entirely hardened against me?" He tried to look soulful but looked only boyish, which was sufficient.

"You can't have imagined I'd go off to a hotel with my ex-husband?"

"We're too civilized and we have each a nice roomy pleasant apartment. I think of you oftener than you realize, Louie. Oftener than you'd believe."

"That's certainly true." She was quite convinced she was the one who brooded on Oscar, but she had no intention of letting that out.

"It's a cold blowy Sunday. What better way to celebrate it? I have some marvelous oloroso sherry a friend brought in for me."

"I thought you had Madeleine installed, mistress regnant."

"Louie, you always overestimated that. I was a convenience for her, an old friend in a new country. She landed something at UCLA. The psychoanalytical network to the rescue."

"Tell me something. Who got bored, you or Madeleine?"

"Louie, New York is overrun with refugee psychoanalysts. Madeleine couldn't get a foot in here. Los Angeles is no stranger to her than New York, and she was offered a lectureship. She'll establish herself there and soon she'll have a practice."

She could read not the slightest evidence of heartbreak in Oscar. He seemed to have more to conceal in whatever intelligence connection he was feeding information into, than in what remained of his relationship with Madeleine Blufeld, blond, elegant, Austrian and one of the causes of their divorce, from Louise's viewpoint. No doubt he was telling the truth, as he saw it; Madeleine needed to move West for her career and Oscar needed not to. No doubt he would expect to take up with Madeleine when she came through New York occasionally. No doubt he would expect a romantic tête-à-tête should circumstances bring him to Southern California. Oscar did not like final good-byes.

"You're looking so lovely, Louie, that even if I hadn't been thinking about you all week, seeing you across the table like a bouquet of red roses would be enough to force my mind on you." Oscar did not pay many compliments. No doubt he was aware, although he would probably never understand why, that the mention of Madeleine had dampened the mood he was trying to create. Oscar was in his offbeat way a sentimentalist, and she had to assume that for him, spending part of their old anniversary in bed seemed fitting.

The trouble was that while she could muster up indignation in the abstract, she still found him powerfully attractive. He seemed to radiate heat. His dark eyes beamed at her, he leaned his broad shoulders forward over the table and his big shapely hands on whose backs and knuckles the hair grew lushly as a well-kept black lawn, moved out onto the surface of the table, gesticulating, pouring ever more wine, passing her tidbits, claiming space, advancing. Oh, what the hell, Louise thought, why not? Madeleine's gone West and I cannot, cannot work up much lust for Dennis. I won't let myself take this seriously, I won't let myself be hurt. Not this time. I will take him the way men take women and then go home, see Dennis for a nice civilized and fairly dull evening and get to work early tomorrow. Why not? She felt pleased with herself for deciding in a properly ruthless way. Perhaps that was what being a divorcée brought with it, the freedom to make wicked abrupt decisions, decisions to enjoy and saunter off.

The waiter had been hovering over them and then departing for much of the meal. Now as Oscar signaled for the bill, he spoke rapidly and abruptly to Oscar as if he could not wait. "While you are sitting here, the radio announces you are at war. Yes, your country."

"What is it?" Louise leaned forward. "We've declared war on Germany?" She remembered suddenly that these were Spanish refugees; they had carried out their war against the forces of evil and reaction; that war that had shown her generation a people could have justice and numbers on their side and lose, that democracy too could fail in war.

"The Japanese have bombed your Honolulu. John Cameron Swayze said so on the radio while you are sitting here. They say it is still going on."

"Honolulu?" Oscar repeated. "There must be some mistake. Why would they bomb Honolulu? It's like attacking Miami Beach."

"I am sorry for your people in Honolulu. To be bombed, it makes you afraid even if you are brave. You can do nothing. They come down like rain and you cannot get out from under them." The waiter shook Oscar's hand solemnly. "I wish this country luck in its war. But you will have the money to buy tanks and planes. That was lacking us."

Oscar left an enormous tip and they stumbled into the street. He flagged a cab. "No, Oscar, I'm going uptown. I want to go home to Kay and find out what's really happening. Thanks again for a pleasant afternoon." She took his hand in a firm shake. "See you."

Oscar was too dazed to argue, although his mouth opened and closed and he reached out as if to stop her from climbing into the cab. He too was confused by the news and eager to turn on the radio. He turned to scan oncoming traffic for another cab. As hers pulled away from the curb, she saw him walking rapidly along Fourteenth Street, hastening to his apartment on West Fourth.

"It's not Honolulu, it's the Navy base at Pearl Harbor," the cabdriver said. "It's a stab in the back. But those Navy guys are real fighters, I bet they gave the Japs as good as they got. Bunch of little yellow apes. They never seen trouble like they walked into today."

Louise felt as if she had been reprieved from probable folly at the very last second, a Victorian damsel saved from the smooth villain, but she regretted her salvation. She had few illusions about what Oscar offered, although she was aware of fantasies circling deep in her, wishes like fragile tropical fish with filmy trains of tail other fish would love to nibble. Those wishes, they were mindless as guppies and she would keep them down in the darkness of her spine where they belonged. Even as she sped uptown to her daughter and the source of news and the telephone that must surely be ringing, she was sorry that the waiter had told them, instead of allowing them to discover it after they had rediscovered each other.

Murray called Ruthie in the early evening. "I can't seem to sit still," he said. "Maybe we could take a walk, a short one? I know you have homework. So do I."

Ruthie could scarcely hear him for the radio booming behind her and the equally loud radio blaring behind him, in his house. She knew she should stay home and study, but she felt roiled up. "Come over right now," she said softly. "I can't stay out long. We can go for coffee."

Naomi was carrying Boston Blackie around like a dollbaby. She asked, "These Japanese, are they like the Germans?"

"They're all part of the Axis. They're our enemies."

"But do they hate Jews too?"

Ruthie tousled her curls. "I don't think they know who Jews are, Naomi."

"Then maybe they aren't as bad."

"Shhhh!" Ruthie tapped Naomi's lips with her finger. "Don't say that to anyone else. Ever."

"I promise," Naomi said. "I know anyhow that when they drop bombs, it doesn't matter if you're Jewish or not. Even the cows get burned and lie dead by the side of the road. Even the dogs are strafed."

Murray arrived within forty minutes, having borrowed his father's old Dodge. When she saw him standing on the doorstep in his checked cap and old tweed coat, she felt that renewed sense of ease. He stood there diffident, a little hunched, smiling at her. She brought him in for the shortest time she could manage. When she started to speak, Duvey hushed her. Everybody was crowded around the living room radio.

"We have just received word that Guam may be under attack. The cable company reports its line cut. The Japanese attacked the practically defenseless city of Shanghai. They are reported to have shelled the famous waterfront section, the Bund. They are said to have sunk a British gunboat and to have taken over the American gunboat *Wake* which was acting as communications center for the American consulate. The International Settlement has been occupied by the Japanese. That means that perhaps three thousand Americans are stranded.

"From Washington the recruiting office of the U.S. Navy announces that all recruiting centers will be open at 8 A.M. tomorrow."

Outside on the street in spite of the cold drizzle, they walked slowly. Without thinking first, without turning over the decision, she gave him her hand and he tucked it with his into his side pocket so he could hold it without a glove. "I wonder if I should join the Navy?" Murray said. "My mother's against it, but I wouldn't hardly expect any mothers would be in favor. I've never been on a boat in my life. Have you?"

"Only the steamer to Bob Lo. My class went when we graduated the eighth grade and my father's union had a picnic there once."

"Do you feel scared?" He gripped her hand tighter.

"Yes. I don't know what it all means. Part of my family has been at war for two years now—"

"Relatives in Poland?"

"Some in Poland and more in France."

Murray grinned. "I never knew any French Jews."

"Two of my mother's sisters moved to Paris. My mother came here from Poland and brought my grandma over."

"My parents never talk about their family in Europe. They want so strongly to be all-American, they don't even like to answer questions I ask."

"They don't ever talk Yiddish?"

"Never. I didn't know they knew any until I heard my mother use it once in a store when she was bargaining about altering a coat."

"I think it's important to have a sense of where we come from." She would not say anything about Naomi yet, who made real and vivid to her all the relatives she had never met. Naomi had not spoken to Murray, and in the bustle and chaos of her home, he had probably missed the little girl with frizzy hair and hazel eyes and heart-shaped face like a valentine cat glaring at him.

"I don't know." Murray frowned. "I see those Hasidic guys sometimes in the curls, dressed peculiar, and I can't identify with them any more than with a bunch of Eskimo or South Sea Islanders. I feel like they're from the Middle Ages. I'm living in Detroit in 1941, and they're still living in Minsk in 1841. I feel embarrassed for them."

"But there's a connection. I'm just as much of a Jew as they are, but in my own way. That's what I learned from my grandmother and my mother, and that's what I want to pass on."

"Do you think a lot about getting married?"

Ruthie laughed sharply. "Oh, Murray, all us kids who grew up during the Depression, do you know anybody expecting to get married real young and start a family? Not those of us who want anything more than our parents have. I see it with my brother Arty and his wife Sharon, how it keeps them down to have two children already. I don't care if Arty tells me I'm going to be an old maid, I don't want to get married and have children till I'm twenty-five or maybe even thirty!"

"That's good, I mean, that's farsighted of you. I bet you'll get your degree. Ruthie, I don't know what to do. On one hand, I want to stay in school real bad. I figure it's my only chance to get ahead and be in a real profession. The kind of jobs open to me now, the moment the economy slumps, you're on the streets. I want to do work I respect. Likewise I feel I should go down and enlist. This is my country and guys are getting shot already. Besides, I'd probably get a better deal if I enlist, instead of waiting for them to draft me. What do you think?"

"I don't think I ought to tell you, but I'll respect your decision. Why don't you wait till the end of the week? All the hotheads are going to rush down there as soon as they get out of bed. Why not wait and see what President Roosevelt does? I heard a commentator say that maybe there would just be a naval blockade."

"I'll wait till I see what's really happening. I can always enlist next week. I'll hold on and keep plugging away." He stopped in the middle of the sidewalk, leaning over her. Before she had time to formulate a decision, he kissed her, then let her go. They walked on. "Would you rather have a soda or coffee? Do you want a piece of pie or ice cream?"

"In spite of the cold, I'd like an ice-cream soda." She did not bother explaining to him that coffee they always had on the stove, but that an ice-cream soda was something she had last enjoyed in August.

She felt cheated that he had kissed her so quickly, so calmly, so matter-of-factly, that she had had no time to prepare, to haggle over the decision. He was now a man she had kissed, one on a list of four, which had been a list of three till five minutes ago. It had been over too fast. From years of watching movie kisses, she expected great emotion from a kiss with a man she was attracted to. Now he might suddenly go off to war, and she would have gotten no satisfaction or substantial memories out of someone who comprised one quarter of her experience with men. She could only hope that after their sodas, when he took her back home, he would do it again, but please not on the porch under the light, where everybody in her family would spy through the window.

At the Yenching Institute, Pearl Harbor barely interrupted their studies. Daniel was rushed to the navy yard in Charlestown along with all the rest of his companions in the program who had been until this day civilians. They were given a fast induction. Clearly the doctors had received special instructions about them, because nobody was turned down, no matter what age or shape they were in. Then they were bused right back to their courses. They did not even lose a whole day entering the Navy.

He had heard enough tales of atrocities on the part of the Nazis in Europe and of the Japanese in China to make the necessity for the war real enough to him. Nonetheless he felt strange, as they were fitted for uniforms. He was a sailor whose only knowledge of ships had been gained as a passenger crossing the Pacific. Suddenly he was Ensign Balaban. He felt fraudulent in his new uniform.

What astonished him was that the Navy had allowed itself to be surprised, when surely the situation in the Pacific had been building steadily toward war. One view he sometimes held was that war had been developing since American warships had forced Japan open under Admiral Perry in 1854; a more reasonable view would maintain that the oil embargo rendered war inevitable. The Navy must have observed the Japanese army in action in China, and still they did not credit them with being a powerful modern machine of war. They just had not believed the Japanese would attack them, because they were white and the Japanese were not, and because they thought of themselves as being six feet tall and the Japanese as being short, and short men do not usually take on tall men in hand-to-hand combat. Somewhere in the mythology of defense that formed how military men thought, he had observed already, such primitive thinking had pride of place at times.

He was worried about Uncle Nat Balaban in Shanghai, with news of the Japanese shelling the city and marching into the International Settlement; but Uncle Nat had lived in Hongkew, known as Little Tokyo for years. He had always paid off whoever had to be paid off, all sides, all factions, bowing to everybody. Daniel thought his uncle's chances of survival decent. He had less idea about his own. Surely they were going to give him some kind of sea training, yet that did not seem to be in the works. He might be assigned to a ship with a very good knowledge of Japanese and unable to tell bow from stern, once again the butt of every joke, the odd man out.

———

Now this was a whole other war, Naomi thought, pointing the wrong way. She felt like hitting the radio and kicking all the adults of the world, who seemed determined to ruin everything with their wars. She had thought if they were going to have a war here that they'd have the same one her parents were caught in, but now a whole other one seemed to be starting with the Japanese, who were over that strange other ocean that used up so much of the blue on the globe.

She left the living room where the radio was booming to lie on Ruthie's bunk, which smelled of lilac perfume. She pressed her cheek into Boston Blackie's warm flank. Somewhere Maman and Rivka were listening to their little radio and hearing about this attack and worrying about her. Somewhere in the south of France Papa was listening too.

Clutching Boston Blackie, she wondered if it would start here, how it was when the Germans came. Soon when Maman went into the épicerie, the shopkeeper would not recognize her, would only wait on her last. The neighbors looked away from Naomi on the stairs as she raced up before the light turned itself off; people spat in the street; her friend Agathe would no longer play with her after school, because her father had forbidden it. At any moment the world could change toward you, and those you had always called your friends walked away from you and left you alone standing in the schoolyard. Then you moved closer to the other Jews, even tall gawky Yvette, and you and Rivka held hands and stood together with the other Jewish children, awaiting what the others would try to do to you now.

She heard steps and Ruthie's arm came gently around her shoulder. "Naomi, what's wrong? Are you frightened?"

She nodded.

Ruthie gathered her up suddenly in a fierce hug. "I'm scared too, Naomi. I'm terrified."

Naomi hugged Ruthie back and suddenly she was flooded by a fierce love for her aunt who was not really her aunt but her cousin. Something tore loose in her and for a moment she felt guilty before Maman and Papa and Rivka and Jacqueline, that she should begin to love somebody else. Would she ever see them again? Ever? She had not seen Maman and Rivka since May and she had not seen Papa since June.

All these wars cut up the world into bleeding pieces and nobody could cross over. But she would love Ruthie. Maybe after the war, if there was ever an after, she would take Ruthie back with her, and Ruthie would live with them too. "Comme elle est belle, avec ses yeux très verts, et sympathique aussi. Tu as de la chance, petite." Maman's rich lilting voice spoke in her ear, the voice that had laughter deep in it always like veins of dark swirls in light marble. She held Ruthie more tightly. She held on.

JACQUELINE 2

Of Chilblains and Rotten Rutabagas

22 août 1941

This will be a brief entry, as I have had no sleep for the last two nights. We all went into the country near Fontainebleau with Papa's old copain Georges to buy up what food we could at two farms where Georges knows the people. It was hot and Maman was off work, so we decided to make almost a vacation of it. The train was extremely crowded with others doing exactly the same thing, carrying a maximum of bags and knapsacks which we all planned to try to buy food to fill. Bean or potato trains they call them.

These days nobody but the Germans and those who cater to them and flatter them and serve them are the least bit elegant. In winter we all waddle around in as many layers of sweater and shawl and cardigans and socks as we can cram on, because we lack fuel, all increasingly shabby because of the shortage of clothing, which is rationed and mainly not available (to us; the Germans and their collaborators glitter). All times of the year we go about Paris carrying empty bags, prepared for hours in line for a handful of old beans or a jar of jam. Nobody drives except the Germans. Bicycles are the lifeline and if your tire goes, you must mend it to survive. So people stood in the mobbed train eyeing each other and wondering what edibles each of us was off to scavenge and what we were trading. We had a couple pieces of soap and a piece of somewhat ratty but still quite warm beaver that any clever housewife could make into a muff or use to trim a coat, and a pair of good wool pants of Papa's, which we feel bad about trading but we are afraid moths will eat them. Who knows when we will see Papa? In May he bought an Ausweis in a dead man's name to go into the unoccupied zone and thus get one of us to America through Marseille. I refused to go because I was studying for my bac, which I passed with flying colors. Papa took Nadine instead, and we have not laid eyes on him since, although we hear from her regularly.

When we came back today, we found utter confusion. While we were gone, the Nazis closed off the entire XIe arrondissement, shut down the Métro stations and moved in. They arrested Jews on the streets, in cafés and restaurants, waiting in line—which is all we do from one day to the next—and even in their homes. The Balabans are gone without a trace. For two days I have been running around Paris for Maman, who has been crying and crying, trying to find out what happened to them.

24 août 1941

Today I learned the Balabans are in some sort of camp at Drancy, a railroad town just a few miles outside Paris. Maman is greatly relieved to find out where they are. We must see them and ask what they need. Their apartment is a shambles, everything thrown on the floor and ripped open. Neighbors say the police did it. If they were looking for the legendary riches those sort always seem to think Jews have, they searched in vain, because the Balabans owned hardly more than the clothes on their backs and some rickety fourth-hand furniture.

26 août 1941

Things get uglier. Just a little over a week ago there was fighting between demonstrators and police—both the gendarmes and the German police—at porte Saint-Denis and porte Saint-Martin, and they arrested a lot of people even though it was no different from a hundred other demonstrations everybody who has lived in Paris through the last ten years takes for granted! Anyhow, the Germans went ahead and executed two people they had arrested. One they are making a great fuss about because he is Jewish and they list him in big letters on all the posters as THE JEW SAMUEL TYZELMAN.

Henri says it is just the Nazi madness and people will begin to laugh at them and mass disobedience will result, but I find his attitude too optimistic for me these days. He brought me a beautiful present today—five kilos of potatoes and a little piece of mutton. Maman was in ecstasy although of course her second question was, Are you sleeping with him? If I were, Maman, I said, perhaps he would have given me a bigger piece of mutton! She made as if to slap me, but then she did not, because in truth she was too happy about the mutton and the potatoes too.

His mother's brother has a farm 25 kilometers north, so he bicycled out there on Saturday and back on Sunday loaded down with parcels. We had such a feast tonight and Maman is going to stretch it over the next two nights. It is so long since we have had anything except cattle fodder and herbal extractions and a few rotten vegetables cooked for soup, beans beans beans beans beans and an occasional thin slice of cheese washed down with ersatz coffee and tisanes. Every so often one egg apiece.

Last month we had used up our bread allowance by the twelfth and even trying so hard this month, we ran out by the seventeenth. We would exhaust it sooner but we all scrounge whatever we can, and my copains, the gang at the Café Le Jazz Hot, treat me almost every day. Most of them have decent black market connections. Of course it is much easier if you aren't a Jew, but I can't complain, because they share with me.

I am writing this tonight on a full belly, and it is amazing how strong and alert I feel. Right after we ate I almost dozed off. We sat around the salle à manger, Maman, Renée and I, and beamed at each other. We felt peaceful as cows in a field, yet I could not be ashamed that my bliss was built on having for once a well-filled stomach, because I have learned how difficult it is to concentrate on an empty one.

It is also cheering to know we shall not be hungry tomorrow or the next day. I can face the problems of our lives less on my nerves, with a solider strength. I did not know if I enjoyed the lamb more or the potatoes. Even the rutabagas we loathe and eat every day tasted almost like food in the stew. Last week Céleste sold me a bag of carrots that must have weighed at least two kilos. Maman still had two of them left for our grand stew.

Most of our lives are spent standing in lines. Maman still has her job at the furrier's even though the firm has been taken away from M. Cariot. They are seizing all the Jewish businesses. The man who has taken it over did not fire the Jews, as expected, because he says how is he supposed to run a skilled business with no skilled workers? Maman says we are very lucky. Renée and I do most of the waiting in line, but I do better because I am bigger, while Renée gets pushed out of the way. I have learned to study standing and in fact that is where I do most of my reading.

Anyhow the Germans have announced that everybody arrested no matter for what—and at least over half the people arrested are merely people who get caught out after curfew—are going to be treated as hostages. You get involved and miss the last 11 P.M. Métro, and then you are out of luck if a friend is not kind enough to let you stay over, as Céleste has let me stay several times, and Henri and Albert like gentlemen once. Henri and Albert live right up the hill from the Sorbonne, in a dirty little side street but convenient. Maman hits the ceiling when I stay out. I don't do it intentionally, but occasionally everybody misses that last Métro. This decree means that if you get caught at some minor infraction, then they may take you out and shoot you one morning because some hothead has taken a potshot at a German officer. I do not understand what the Germans expect to accomplish by this brutality. Do they think when some poor dishwasher in a restaurant who misses her train is shot for an action one of the new resistance groups takes, that the Gaullists or the Communists are going to fold up and wither away?

I almost forgot, somebody else has moved into the Balabans' already. They have thrown the Balabans' pitiful things out into the street for the neighbors to pick through, but held on to their kitchen table and chairs. When the Balabans come back, I don't know what they will do. I only hope Maman is not carried away by fellow feeling into taking them in. Without Papa's income we have let go of my room on the top floor. Renée and Maman share her double bed and I sleep on the folding bed in the salle à manger.

8 septembre 1941

I was coming from my acting class when I had to pass along the boulevard des Italiens. I was wrapped up in thinking about the character of Bérénice in Racine's great tragedy, with whom in some ways I can easily identify myself, when I saw a great crowd of people ahead lined up to enter the Palais Berlitz.

"Oh, what's that? Is there an exhibition?" I asked a middle-aged woman. I am always careful to ask information on the street from women, since I would not want to give an opening to some man who might imagine I am trying to pick him up. I still remember that idiot boy who followed me all the way to Marie Charlotte's flat just because I answered his question and told him which way the Gare du Nord was. Now I understand he perfectly well knew. Henri says I am definitely naive about men, but the truth is I have other worries and do not need more.

"It's a big exhibition, everyone's going," she said, nodding at me. "It's 'The Jew and France.' You ought to go too. You aren't too young to face facts."

I thought at first she meant that as a Jew I should understand anti-Semitism, but then she went on: "You have to keep yourself pure, a young girl such as yourself, but you must understand contamination too. It's a matter of educating one's self for the New France."

I am ashamed that I was so embarrassed for her, to be so stupid and rude, that I could not say one word. I'm afraid my manners simply automatically caused me to thank her and hasten away. She was a well-dressed lady of middle age, wearing a navy suit with the new shoulder pads they are showing and a crisp white blouse with a bow tie, an oversized hat with an entire little dead bird on it.

I wish I had struck her, but that would be absurd, and actually an evil reaction to return verbal violence with physical violence. Perhaps I did the best thing. But then I took no stand. What should I have done? If I were truly a noble soul such as Antigone in Sophocles, the words would have come to me and I would have said something clear and ringing that would have shown her how foolish she was to speak that way of an entire people.

As it was I felt humiliated and simply proceeded along the broad sidewalk toward the crowd ahead. Right on the front of the Palais Berlitz between the pillars was hung an enormous four-story-high poster of an old man with a beard and long nose supposed to be a Jew and digging claws into a globe, where France was drawn in. It was ghastly. I became very hot and I did not know where to look. I was afraid I would burst into tears right on the street. As I saw all these ordinary people, my countrymen whom yesterday I might have sat beside in the cinema or said hello to at the news vendor's kiosk all waiting to cram into this Nazi display put on by a French organization L'Institut Français des Questions Juives, I felt like a cockroach they were trying to crush under their well-shod feet.

I wanted to climb a soap box and shriek at them, How dare you imagine that the ugly picture you've drawn has anything in common with me? It's your own disgusting imagination you revel in, resembling those filthy drawings the boys used to make and then try to force us to look. Tell us what that is, tell us what that is. Your own ugly mind, I told them: one time I did think up the right thing to say.

I think one of my worst flaws is that while my mind seems to work more quickly than other people's, often I see too many sides to a question, causing me to be weak in my response. I should strive to be simpler. Sometimes I think simplicity is virtue, and when I write that, I think of Maman, who always seems to go straight to the heart of a matter.

When I came home, I thought whether I should say anything about what I had seen, and then I looked at Maman, so careworn and exhausted from working all day at the furrier's and then rushing about trying to find something to make into soup for supper, and little Renée, so subdued and quiet these days I worry about her. I thought, when Papa comes home at last, I'll talk to him about it, but in the meantime, as he said to me, I must take care of Maman and Renée, because in some ways I really am cooler headed.

3 octobre 1941

Last night six of the synagogues of Paris were blown up! I went with Renée this morning and we looked at our own where we go on High Holidays and there was nothing but a shell with glass and mortar and pieces of cloth and blowing papers. Jews of the neighborhood were milling around picking through the rubble trying to save something. It made me so indignant I burn with helplessness. What a vile idiotic act. Blowing up a building of worship. What kind of fools think this is a proper political act?

All the gross newspapers are screaming that this was a spontaneous act of the French people who want us, the so-called foreign element, thrust out. Who are rejecting us as they reject a disease or a poison. I must say, it is great to have become a microbe. I walk around Paris these days and it is just as if some lout is striking me in the face every twenty paces, when I see one of those newspapers going on about how great the recent roundup is, and how France is being cleansed and purified, or when I see some truly crude and disgusting caricature supposed to represent me or Papa or Maman, or when I try to find out what is happening in the world, and in place of the newspapers that for all their partisanship at least carried the world's news, we have nothing but these rags that shriek hatred and call for death for us.

Sometimes I cannot believe it still, that all these Frenchmen run about sucking up to the Germans and flattering them and parroting their ideas. I have silly fantasies of rushing into the offices of one or another of these rags or the magazines that pretend to literary or philosophical merit. *Les Nouveaux Temps, La Gerbe, Aujourd'hui, Nouvelle Revue Française,* they all hew to the occupiers' line and none of them defends us. They are only politer forms of *L'Appel* and *Au Pilori* which shriek their diarrhea of abuse at us daily and call openly for our death. I feel as if I live in a rabid city, where every other man froths and foams in violent insanity.

I remember how even last year when I was studying for my bac, I thought I would be so happy once I had entered the Sorbonne. I would meet other students who share my interests, I would lead a life of rich intellectual ferment and austere dedication to ideas. Mostly I keep away from the other students, as I fear the shock of discovering they too are anti-Semites. The business of survival is so demanding, I take classes for granted. Often I pass the Café Dupont, which is also in the Latin Quarter, with its message, NO JEWS OR DOGS. As some converts are more Catholic than the pope, some of these imitation Nazis are passionate to outdo their masters.

29 novembre 1941

What a sad subdued birthday the 24th was for me. Then we received a message from Papa. Some callow youth in a Boy Scout uniform appeared with it, a most unlikely carrier of clandestine messages, but he made a point of telling me he is in the EIF, which stands for the Eclaireurs Israélites de France, the Jewish Boy Scouts. He shrugged off our thanks, saying it is not difficult for him, because he has his ways of crossing the border to Vichy.

He also brought a bottle of cassis to us as a present from Papa, which is certainly welcome because Maman and I particularly miss the warmth of a little wine with supper, and it has been months since we have tasted anything alcoholic. We trade our tiny wine ration to Mme Cohen for a little butter and some skim milk for Rivka. Cassis, Maman says, is particularly welcome because our stomachs are so often upset from eating rotten food or bread that has strange additives—we suspect everything from ground-up bones to plaster dust from demolition. Cassis we will measure out a tablespoon at a time after supper to warm us and soothe our poor suffering stomachs.

Papa is in Toulouse, the boy told us. He seems to admire Papa very much. He said Papa cannot cross back to Paris, but that he is a great force in resisting the Germans and the Vichy government. He almost got caught twice, but he escaped. He said Papa is a very brave man and we should be proud of him. Papa had told him to secure papers for us, which he hopes to deliver on his next trip, but that what was needed now were recent photographs for counterfeit identity papers. Then we will be able to rejoin Papa safely in Toulouse.

At that point the three of us went into the bedroom, shut the door and examined Papa's note carefully to make sure it was really from him, and this was not some Fascist youth in disguise, trying to entrap us. But the handwriting was obviously Papa's. The note was short and said only that he loved us, missed us powerfully and that we should give the young man what he needed, because he would carry it back to Papa on his next rounds, as Papa put it.

The trouble was that we had not had pictures taken of ourselves for several years, and we hardly dare pry the photos off our cards stamped with a big red JUIVE much as we hate them. We told the young man we could try to get pictures taken the coming week. We scarcely have any money. He said we should see what we could do, but that he couldn't wait, as he had something to do farther north. He would drop in on us on the way south, he said, to pick up the new photos.

Needless to say I do not intend to say a word to anyone outside the family, and I cautioned Maman, who is always sensible, and Rivka, who is not, to keep their mouths tightly shut on this visit. I have given in to my sister's desire to be called by her Hebrew name, for she has so little to make her happy these days.

Then a present arrived from Naomi in Detroit in the U.S. I was astonished that the little mischief-maker had remembered my birthday, but then I imagined that probably her aunt arranged for the package. It had been mailed two months ago, but everything was intact and we were delighted. She sent us a big kosher sausage, so I guess they make them there too, a kilo of sugar, a jar of strawberry, a jar of apricot and a jar of raspberry jam. Anything sweet makes a big hit with us. She also put in two bars of Camay soap and a jar of liver pâté.

Naomi writes regularly, but her French grammar is dreadful and growing worse. She is becoming a barbarian. I do not know if Papa did the right thing sending her off that way, by herself. We also receive letters from Rose Siegal in Yiddish, a language I cannot read, although Maman translates. Aunt Rose (Maman's oldest sister) assures us that Naomi is well and improving her English (while deproving her own language, I comment) and growing rapidly. So is Rivka, but she is too thin. If only we could get a little more food for her. At school they give the children vitamin cookies. Some of the children trade theirs, but I have ordered Rivka to eat hers every day. Aunt Rose asks about Aunt Batya, their sister, who is still in Drancy. Maman will write her what little we know, for we are not permitted to visit the prisoners.

It was thoughtful of Naomi or Aunt Rose to send us these gifts. Winter is setting in early and we are freezing. We have no heat. Maman is developing chilblains. We go to bed with a hot water bottle, but it stays warm for only an hour. We shuffle about the house wrapped up like packs of old clothes and wearing gloves except when we must take them off to wash a dish.

The soap is a particular treat, because we can institute a regular system of bathing once a week. We have had no soap since October as we have been trading it for food. Rivka must eat and so must Maman. I fare the best because I am petted by my friends who are well connected with the black market and they are always giving me tidbits and even meals. I try to slip a roll or a bite of chicken into my pocket for Rivka and Maman in secrecy whenever I can, because once Céleste caught me stuffing a half a Croque-Monsieur into my pocket and said, Well if you aren't hungry, I'll eat it, and she did.

Yes, I eat ham outside the house. I would eat a toad if someone served it to me. I would have given the ham to Rivka and told her it was corned beef. I felt miserable because I was hungry and I wanted dreadfully to eat it, but I had wanted even more to give a little to Rivka, who is so skinny and almost blue. Maman thinks she might be anemic, but what can we do about it? Henri has not been treating me to lunch this week. He has decided I have a virginity fetish, he says, and must overcome such bourgeois hang-ups.

Fine, I said, I'll go out on the Boule Mich' and stop the first pedicab to offer myself.

A stranger might have a disease, he said. I'm only thinking of you.

I know how you are thinking of me, and dream on, I said. I act very cool as it is the way to behave, but it makes me feel peculiar to sit at the table with him and have him constantly as if casually touching my knee, my elbow, my shoulder. If we did not wear so many layers of clothing, he would be able to see that sometimes I get goose bumps. Luckily for me, we are both wound up in our clothes like mummies in a museum and even when he tries to kiss me, he gets no nearer than six inches because of all our padding. Still I dream of his light brown eyes like wet sand fixed on me, wanting.

12 décembre 1941

So now Germany is at war with the U.S. Henri says the Germans have finally bitten off more than they can chew, but they seem to have digested us easily enough. I have little concrete hope except that by the time I am an old lady, I may live in a saner world. We will enjoy no more packages from Naomi and no more letters either. We are cut off from our sister as if she were on the moon! Maman cries about Naomi a great deal, and then berates herself for selfishness, since at least one of her children is safe. Rivka has never been the same since Naomi left; she is half a child, quiet, subdued and deeply lonely in spite of how much more time I spend with her.

Yesterday something simply unimaginable occurred. The Nazis rounded up one thousand French Jews, including all the lawyers who practice at the Paris bar, yes, every one of them. They took doctors, lawyers, writers and intellectuals and simply arrested them. Nobody seems to know where they have been taken, except that this time it is not Drancy, where the poor Balabans are still imprisoned. We brought them little parcels, but they would not let us in. The place stinks from a block away. It is an unfinished housing project surrounded by barbed wire and watchtowers. You would imagine the poor Balabans to be violent rapists, murderers, terrorists, instead of a family of factory workers.

Where they have taken the terribly dangerous writers, lawyers and doctors is anyone's guess. We speculate and fear, we pass on rumors and wait for the Boy Scout to return, but he has not. The excuse for this roundup—for some reason the Nazis like to have excuses, no matter how perfunctory—is punishment because somebody fired at a German air force officer. That is all.

Everyone at Café Le Jazz Hot makes jokes about how I am the last virgin in Paris. Céleste announced today they are going to have me stuffed and stuck in a case in Le Musée de l'Homme. I said that was fine with me if I could be stuffed with roast chicken and veal chops and steaks. Henri said how about his salami.

Sometimes what they say makes me blush inside but I remain very cool. I said, no thank you, your salami isn't kosher.

Then afterward when Henri was walking me to the Métro, he asked me if that was why I wouldn't sleep with him, because he isn't Jewish. He wanted to have a serious discussion on the sidewalk about what I said as a joke to shut them up. I ended having to kiss him in a doorway. Then he tried again to put his hand up under my sweater. I said, Don't you try to do things by degrees, Henri. You won't move me along that way. When I decide, I will do the whole thing, but until then, don't paw at me, I think it's vulgar. He got mad and went off, but I know the problem isn't going to go away.

RUTHIE 2

Of Rapid Pledges

Ruthie stood on a chair. Mama was pinning the hem of the skirt of a smart grey gabardine suit she had found at Goodwill, only slightly worn in the cuffs but Mama had turned them back, and under the arms, where Ruthie herself had repaired the seams. The skirt was longer than the girls were wearing them now, so Mama was turning it up. It was all having to be done in a great hurry because Leib and Trudi were getting married that afternoon in the study of a local rabbi.

Ruthie did not know what she thought of the marriage yet. Leib had been working for a place that made novelty balloons, but they could no longer procure rubber and everybody was laid off. He had got on the line at Chrysler Tank, but when his number was called by the draft, he had not been there long enough to be exempted for doing essential war work. Now he was entering the Army in three days, and he and Trudi were marrying at once. He had been seeing Trudi on and off since he had broken up with Ruthie, but Trudi had complained that she did not think he was in love.

When Trudi told her, Ruthie said, "But, I didn't think things were that good between you."

"Yeah, but it's all changed. Now he wants to marry me. Go on, Ruthie, you'd have married Leib if he'd ever asked you, and don't tell me different. Talk about tall, dark and handsome. Besides, it's patriotic." Trudi was the fourth of her girlfriends to marry since December seventh, all to men about to go into the services.

When Trudi had asked Ruthie to stand up for her, Ruthie had longed to make an excuse. She did not like to run into Leib; it still hurt. She did not think she had truly loved him. Always there had been something in him she had mistrusted. She had taken that for granted, as how it was with men—but with Murray it was not that way.

"Mama, I don't like to pressure you, but maybe I'll have to go with the hem pinned. Listen, it doesn't matter it isn't perfectly straight all the way around. It's not my wedding, nobody's going to be looking at me."

"My daughter, going to a wedding in front of Rabbi Honig with her skirt stuck up with pins? You may not dress up like a movie star, but we don't need to go out before people full of pins."

Mama had lost some weight and she wore her hair pinned up on her head now instead of pulled back in a ragged knot. She was running a little nursery for babies and toddlers of women in the neighborhood who had gone to work. Thirty-one dollars was all the allotment a husband overseas sent home. Nobody could live on that. What few nurseries existed cost a fortune.

Mama charged sixty cents a day for toddlers, fifty for babies and two meat coupons. She gave them two meals and an afternoon nap. Sharon had her own kids mixed into the pack and was helping. The house was crammed with howling babbling kiddies from seven in the morning till seven at night. Mama and Sharon were clearing about twenty a week. Art had finally been taken on at Fisher Body, working the graveyard shift, meaning they had to keep the little ones downstairs so he could catch his sleep. Arty didn't care for the project, saying they'd get in trouble with the law because they weren't licensed. Ruthie had researched the Wayne County law, and there was just no way anybody in their position could meet those requirements—or the neighborhood women could afford it if such a fancy place were set up.

"Have you heard anything from your fellow?" Mama asked, her mouth full of pins.

"Mama, you get the mail before I see it every day. I only answered his Saturday letter on Tuesday." She wished Mama wouldn't ask her about Murray's letters, for they meant too much to her. He was down South, which she pictured as an area of swamps, magnolias, live oaks, Spanish moss and night riders in sheets indistinguishable from storm troopers, who burned crosses and Jews and colored people. It was a dangerous place, almost as dangerous as wherever he might next be sent. Murray had finished out his semester; then in February he had enlisted.

"But why did you join the Marines?" she had asked him. "I thought we agreed on the Army and to try to get into the Signal Corps."

"I can't really tell you. There I am, I've just been through one of the most humiliating experiences of my life, treated like a side of beef, poked, prodded and I'm thinking what an idiot I am for my own survival to have gone into this willingly, and actually to feel relieved, to feel pleased when some bozo at a desk picks up an ACCEPTED instead of a REJECTED stamp. I'm standing there naked, Ruthie, stark naked, and these guys are sitting comfortable in their uniforms.

I think I went for the one that seemed to cover the most. The marine seemed snappier than the others. He seemed to take it more seriously. The Army and the Navy, they were officers and they were making jokes to each other and when they looked at me, I felt they had contempt. I thought to myself, that's what I want, somebody who understands this is a serious matter, fighting a war, and isn't sitting there cracking jokes."

"I never heard of a Jewish marine," Ruthie said dubiously.

"So I'll be the first."

Now he was down in Parris Island, surviving brutality and contempt as best he could. Duvey had taken his able-bodied seamen's papers and gone off to look for a berth on an oceangoing ship, although his pals in the union argued that the work on the Great Lakes was just as essential. Duvey did not think so. "Essential, what is that crap? Nobody's going to torpedo you off Toledo. I'd feel like a coward hanging around here."

"At least you won't be in the Army or the Navy fighting," Mama said.

Duvey laughed. "No, you just get shot at. You don't do much shooting."

They were all relieved nonetheless that Duvey wasn't in the Navy, having to fight in sea battles. He was just doing what he had done for years, but now in the ocean instead of the Great Lakes. Occasionally they got a packet of letters from him, mostly anecdotes of his crew, but then two months would go by and nothing would come. She felt guilty that she did not love her brother better, and she determined to love him more starting right now. Bravery he had never lacked. Maybe she just took that for granted. She had always valued gentle endurance more, but gentle endurance was not a primary virtue in wartime.

"Mama, it's twelve o'clock. I must get ready. Now!"

Mama sighed. "All right, you take off the skirt and you get ready, everything but the skirt, and I'll stitch it up. Tata will just have to wait a little while for his lunch."

"My one day off, I have to go hungry?" He was protesting pro forma.

"I never saw anybody marry themselves." Naomi sat on Ruthie's bunk watching.

"Get married. In English it's get married."

"Get married. I want to see how it's done. Can I please come?"

Ruthie paused, wriggling into her best slip. "I don't see why not, tsatskeleh. Put on your plaid dress and comb your hair." Naomi's presence might dilute her murky pain. She had wanted to bash in Leib's head when he had taken up with Trudi. With thousands of girls in Detroit and all of them making eyes at him, how could he pick out her good friend to start chasing? She had wanted Trudi to be too loyal to her to go out with the sweetheart who had just dumped her; but she had to admit that Trudi would sacrifice quite a bit to have a steady boyfriend, and now a husband. Ruthie had had to swallow her resentment or lose Trudi, and finally she had felt that she really had no right to object, because after all she had known the price of keeping Leib and had not been willing to pay it. Yes, taking Naomi would in some way shield her from the force of her own possible regret and dismay—and jealousy.

After Ruthie dressed except for the skirt, calling at the crack of their bedroom door to Mama did not produce results. She glared at the wind-up alarm on the bedside table. She'd have to take the skirt from Mama whatever shape it was in, put it on and leave. She was not going to risk being late—it would seem too calculated a gesture of disrespect or a sign she could not face the marriage. "Naomi, stop fiddling with your hair, it's fine. Just put those barrettes in. The red barrettes, one on each side." She was embarrassed, but she had to walk out in her slip bottom, dressed, including the little spring felt hat, except for her skirt.

"Mama, I have to put it on now."

"Ruthele, just another tiny minute and I'll have the hem sewn."

She took firm hold of the skirt. "Mama, there aren't any more minutes. I can't be late, and I have to walk out the door now. Right now. Let go, Mama! I mean it."

Her mother's mild milky brown eyes fixed on her questioningly. Normally Ruthie would give in. But Mama knew that when her only daughter took on a certain crisp veneer, she wasn't kidding or negotiating but announcing. "Darling, you can't wear that with pins—"

"Nobody will notice." Ruthie worked the hem loose from her mother and put the skirt on. It was sewn three quarters of the way around with a stretch on the side still pinned. "Come on, Naomi. Get your coat."

It was a cool clear day with a little moisture in the wind but none in the sky. As they hurried toward the synagogue, they passed a Catholic church that was pouring out, all the people dressed up in suits and hats and a smattering of uniforms. "It's their Easter today," she said to Naomi. "I hope it's not a bad sign for Trudi and Leib. Bubeh used to tell stories about Poland at Easter, how there would be pogroms some years. Other years the goyim would simply come and beat and kill one or two, for sport."

"In school, they made us sing Easter songs. I didn't think I should say anything, and besides, I couldn't understand the words half the time. It's much harder when they're singing."

"They shouldn't make you do that, but you're right. This is not a good time for us to single ourselves out to complain."

"I heard Sharon and Mama talking. They said Leib should have married you."

"Ketsale, who asked me? Do I want to marry Leib?"

"Do you?"

"No." She was sure about that, although as they hurried through the blocks, the lingering ice vanished, the first green shoots in the lawns and crocuses and daffodils in the bed outside the Beth Shalom temple, she knew that not wanting to marry Leib did not necessarily mean she rejoiced in his marrying another. She must find in her heart that goodwill.

Beth Shalom was a squat yellow brick building with a mogen david on its front in small panes of tinted glass above two sets of heavy doors. They headed around the rear, through the little gate. As she yanked Naomi along by the hand at a forced trot, she hoped they were not already late. She noticed suddenly that Naomi was no longer markedly shorter. "You're growing," she said in surprise.

"I grew half a centimeter last month."

"What is that in inches?"

Naomi shrugged. "I know some things in one system and some in the other, but I can't move back and forth."

The whole party was inside, but the rabbi had not appeared and only his wife was there fussing over Trudi and settling everybody till he should be ready. Leib was not yet in uniform. His black suit bought for his father's funeral two years before was now a little short, a little tight, but still became him, his high forehead under the tousled dark hair, his wide-set eyes peering commandingly from a strong bone structure of juts and caverns, his whole tall well-filled-out frame not embarrassed by the tightness of the suit but exploiting it to show off his brawn. Leib's father had been nicknamed Misha the Bear. He had been in the moving business and had wrestled furniture from one side of the Jewish ghetto to the other, most of his years on a horse-drawn cart, the horse stabled in their backyard. Leib had his strength and his temper.

Ah, he moved her through the eyes, he always had. Not enough, Ruthie thought, my eyes have easy virtue and little sense. He will make any woman happy a little while and then unhappy a long while.

Trudi wore a pale pink dress. Neither Trudi nor her mother nor Ruthie had been able to find a short white dress that would be suitable, not from one end of Detroit to the other. It was too early for a summer white and wedding dresses were out of the question on such short order—and too expensive. Trudi had cried, but the pale pink would be usable later and set off her dark brown hair and olive skin. The rabbi came in, rubbing his hands together, as Trudi's father surged to meet him. Trudi's mother lifted the veil of her old black hat with cherries on it to daub at her eyes.

Ruthie thought, we must buy a hat for Naomi, it's time, she's becoming an adolescent. Naomi had on a striped babushka. Poor lamb, what a time to begin growing up. What a time.

Then she caught Leib staring at her, the way he used to, burning hungry eyes. She dropped her gaze, then turned to Naomi and fussed with her. Naomi's eyes were huge, seeing everything including Leib's attention. When Ruthie glanced back he was still staring. She hoped nobody else would notice, but they all were gathered around Rabbi Honig. Leib's mother was doing something to Trudi's dress, a pull here, a tug there, a dusting. Then she stepped back to fix Trudi with a sharp almost baleful stare. She seemed to be asking, So what does he see in her?

Ruthie had the sickening feeling that Leib would like still to reach over and grab her the way he had used to, and drag her up to the rabbi and take her instead. Not out of love, no, but because he still wanted her in that hungry violent way that had wakened her far, far less than Murray's quiet and attentive caresses. She would not look at him again.

Ruthie stood near one corner of the chuppah. The pins kept catching on her calf. The stocking would be torn to shreds, and where would she find a replacement? She kept her gaze on Trudi, not glancing at Leib again until the ceremony was ending and he broke the glass in the napkin under his foot, stomping as he had stomped out of the room the evening he had broken off with her at last. As he smashed the glass he threw one last look at her with that same glaring intensity and then he turned away and kissed Trudi, a great film star clinch. Then everybody began shouting mazel tov and toasting the couple in sacramental wine.

Ruthie stood a little back, forgiving Leib his hungry glare, for now he was thoroughly married to Trudi and things must work their way out. She was remembering Murray's last week before he had taken the train. She had spent as much time as possible with him, and the last two days she had called in sick to work, not caring, needing to steal the time.

It had been a wet raw snowbound February with ice dripping from all the trees and rutting the side streets. They had spent a lot of time in the Art Institute, the main public library, the student lounge at Wayne. Where could they go? They saw a couple of movies. Movies were open twenty-four hours for people on the swing and graveyard shifts, and always crowded. Mostly Murray did not want to waste their time together looking at anything other than her, he said. They drifted in an intense stasis, a net of attention entangling both. They talked, on and on and on. They were giving each other their childhoods, as if playing home movies on screens in the other's head.

Unfortunately his parents had not taken to her. They had seemed panic-stricken that she and Murray might marry that week. His parents resembled each other, both oval in face and body with light brown hair turning grey so that she thought of them as uniformly beige. They were close to the same height. Both wore gold-rimmed glasses and a common expression of agitated dismay as they turned to her. Having once enjoyed a solid middle-class existence, they did not accept her. They had an idea of the girl Murray should bring home, someone with money, connections. Someone useful. His mother pursed her lips and frowned at Ruthie, but she was too ineffectual to be rude.

The day before he had to leave was the worst, sweet sour pain. Murray said, and she could see him clearly speaking as they sat in a booth in a chili joint near the college, "I have to keep fighting the urge to claim you. To tie you to me. To demand that you become mine right now, before I leave. Because I know it's wrong. It's stupid. You don't claim somebody and make them your wife and your lover before you disappear. It's selfish. It's to have a piece of somebody that belongs to you."

"I'll wait for you. I can promise that. I love you." She had said it then at the booth in the chili parlor, holding hands over cups of cold coffee. "You don't have to make any official claim." After she spoke, she was stiff with embarrassment, wondering how she could have said such a thing out loud to a man, especially a man who had not said that to her first.

"I love you, Ruthie. I think I've loved you since the first time we went out. I thought I was being romantic and making you up, but I wasn't. You're just what I want, and I wish to hell there wasn't this damned war in the way. It's a ridiculous time to fall in love. It tears me up inside to think we found each other and we may never get to live out our lives together."

Ever since she had wondered if she should have done as Leib and Trudi were doing and said, Let's get married, damn everything else. Or worse, she wondered if she should simply have offered herself to him, because he was too thoughtful and gentle to demand what he made quite clear he longed for. They had kissed until their lips were sore. She wanted him. She discovered what that felt like, and it was frightening. She wondered if the intense pain of wanting was peculiar to her, something unbalanced. Someday she would ask Trudi. But he was leaving and she was staying, and everything was still true, that they should not marry so young, that having a family would destroy them both, that if they clung too hard to each other, they would condemn each other to the desperate and grimy streets of her upbringing. Therefore she had resisted the unspoken appeal; therefore she felt guilty at Trudi's wedding.

ABRA 2

Stories to Make the Ears Bleed

"A Berliner, I was. You don't understand. It's something like being a Parisian in France, a New Yorker here, nu? You're smarter or you think you are anyhow. And if you were born there, as I was, then you think knowing everything from the inside out is your birthright." Mrs. Marlitt Speyer was thirty-five but looked younger with ash-blond hair swept up on top of her head, wearing a well-cut mannish pinstriped suit she told Abra she had made herself. She called herself a ladies' couturier. Now she had a job with some Seventh Avenue firm that she described with a twist of her firm lips as "a place that makes upholstery for women who don't know any better."

"My family had lived in Berlin for the last hundred and thirty years, and before that we lived in the Saar, in a little town where we have, where we had, a summer house. We were wine merchants. My father and my uncle had a business on Leipziger-Strasse. . . . No, not now, for on Kristallnacht, the SA, the brown shirts came. They broke the windows and looted the wine. Then they set the shop on fire. They beat the watchman and then threw him in the fire. He was a poor Jew who had already been forced out of the small town where he lived. He was uneducated, a bit simple but a good man who supported his parents. He died in hospital. My father was in the Saar country ordering the auslese, the sweet late-picked wine, you know, the expensive ones. My uncle was home and the brown shirts beat him and put him in Sachenhausen. He was there for three months and then we got him out, poor, without anything. Sometimes then you could still buy your way out. He's a cripple now, I send them a little money in Paraguay when I can."

Marlitt watched carefully, Abra felt, but without obviously staring. Abra admired that ability and resolved to perfect it herself in her questioning. She had begun to think she would probably switch her thesis subject to one gleaned from these interviews, as she had done none of her own since she'd gone to work for Oscar Kahan. It was a matter, she felt, of Marlitt snatching quick appraisals when she herself glanced at her pad.

"The Nazis wouldn't let you out till they had picked you clean and then the Americans wouldn't let you in without resources. My aunt and uncle managed to get visas to Paraguay, but we had no money left. My uncle wanted to come here, but the Americans said he had a criminal record, because of being arrested when they put thirty thousand Jews that night in the camps . . . Oh, I was working till the end. I had a special permit because I was a designer. They wanted my designs, you know, most of the German fashions are clumsy. I wanted to be an artist, but in art school, my dear, they convinced me I had no genuine talent and then I learned that I did, but not for sculpture—or maybe sculpture on the body." Marlitt sketched a shape in the air. Abra was struck by the movement. Marlitt had the habit of sitting extremely still.

"Orthodox? Oh, no, we were Liberals. Reminiscent of your Conservatives, but very, very German. We were all very German. My dear, the first Jews in Germany were settled soon after the Diaspora, in the third century A.D. I believe we were there ahead of the Germans, actually. My father and uncle were active in the CV—oh, that was the Centralverein deutscher Staatsbuerger juedischen Glaubens. It resembled your Anti-Defamation League, but not so limited. We formed a front with the central and the social democratic parties. We threw our all into those elections. Not for a moment were we blind to the problem of the Nazis, but we had not the numbers, the money, the power to stop them. Oh, no, before Hitler came to power, we thought the Zionists were silly. We were German, my dear, we couldn't even bring ourselves to identify with the Ostjuden—Jews who had emigrated from Poland because, you know, we had not had pogroms in Germany and we had economic opportunities. We found the Ostjuden foreign to us. Unsophisticated." Marlitt passed thin fingers over her chin briefly. "We were used to German pundits reviling us. We considered it as you do as a woman when you hear some man holding forth on the silliness of women. You think, oh yes, and yet one of us gave birth to you and one of us nursed you and you'll marry one of us. We were so German. My father had served in the World War. He had received an Iron Cross, that made him very proud."

Marlitt gave a quick dry laugh. "You see, we were so used to being denounced, and business as usual. Every other German was an anti-Semite accustomed to rant about the Jewish problem and the Jewish influence and the Zionist conspiracy. But they would expect you to understand, they didn't mean you personally. It was the others, the bad Jews. You grow used to thinking that they don't really mean it when they make the little jokes about Jews. You just let it pass over and wait for them to act human again. We were almost comfortably accustomed to all those little and big insults, just so we prospered and lived our individual lives."

Abra thought it a pity her written notes would never reflect Marlitt's voice, rich, resonant, mocking, spicy. Ginger ice cream, she thought, at once sweet and hot. Yet Marlitt was dry at the core, a strange detached quality to her, as if she were really much older, a nun looking back with cool disinterest on her life in the wicked world.

"No, my father and my uncle were the political ones. I was young and consumed by fashion and parties and dances and art shows. Berlin is like New York, it sucks all the arts into itself. In Berlin, the Nazis were just a handful of nuts. Nobody paid them any mind. There weren't but two or three hundred of them until that vile little weasel Goebbels arrived. He sent them around beating up the leftists. They would march into meetings in working-class areas and break them up and start riots. That got them in the newspapers, and all the thugs in town were soon queuing up to get in on the fun. Nonetheless if the rich had not gone sniffing after them, like that bitch Magda Quandt, who married him finally, they'd never have had the resources. To think I designed for her once. Oh, she didn't have two political thoughts to rub together, and I doubt she was even anti-Semitic in those days.

"My husband?" She paused a long time. Her face seemed to flatten. "No, Speyer is not really my husband, I will explain. My husband was Martin Becker. He was a handsome man, big built, over six feet tall. He had played soccer in school. He died in the camp at Buchenwald. They said of a disease. They usually said things like that. Someday I suppose we'll know. I heard typhus was endemic. . . ."

Abra recognized that a gate had closed in her informant. About her husband Marlitt did not want to speak further. Abra changed her line of questioning, intending to circle back later. "We left through France. I didn't feel comfortable in France, too many restrictions against Jewish immigrants, what you could do, what you couldn't. They resented you. We went on to Portugal. I had to work there as a dressmaker, almost a seamstress. Down in the world, no? I made fancy dresses for the ladies.

"Ah, Mr. Speyer. I met him in Portugal. Speyer is an American Jew, a widower. He married me to bring me in and we brought my father and mother also afterward. No, it was kindness. He lives with his mistress, but he can't marry her—the children of his first wife won't allow it—and I signed a paper renouncing all his property. No, my dear, not exactly a marriage blanc, let's not put that down. After all, we traveled together and I did live in his apartment when I arrived, which his friend did not care for at all. Now that my citizenship is all secure, we're having a quiet little divorce. And maybe Alfred will do it again. He's a good man, I eat with them every Sunday—Friday with my own parents. I love to think of Alfred going back and forth and marrying all these women and in truth enjoying it all and then settling us safely here. He's a very good man. You ought to interview him. . . ."

While Marlitt in that dry detached way refused to lie for the record and claim her relationship with Speyer was platonic, nonetheless she sounded as distanced about him as about anyone else. Abra asked, "But isn't it awkward, people thinking that you're married when you aren't? You're an attractive woman. You must meet men."

"It's convenient," Marlitt said briskly. "It gives no false impressions, because I was married and have no interest in being so again. . . . What? My real husband? He was a journalist, but after they fired Jews from the newspapers he became active in the Kulturbund. You see, we had these actors and musicians and singers thrown out of work and all of us who were gradually shut out of public places. He began writing little plays for the Kulturbund. That was why the Nazis went after him so early. The plays, they were very funny. Everything, you understand, was oblique. If you said anything direct, they would come right in and arrest you. You could use what we called the New Midrash, everything was in terms of stories we knew. He wrote and staged a Purim play, and we all knew who Haman was. But I think the Nazis figured that one out too."

Marlitt was easy to interview. Her English was excellent and she had insisted on speaking it. "It's harder to speak of these things in German," she said firmly. She spoke dryly, without tears. Abra began to see in her someone whose tears had been drained. "Yes, I had a son. That is no one's business who has not seen such a death. I will not speak of it.

"My father, my uncle, were both involved in the Reichsvertretung. That was the instrument through which we tried to present a unified front to the Nazis. We kept hoping this insanity could not continue. A government that was mad? Who could believe it. Business as usual, propaganda, some violence, but surely it would stop there. Surely the other powers would not permit what the Nazis said they were going to do to us. We kept expecting Hitler to begin to act like a sane government. He has the big industrial barons behind him now, we told each other, they will make him relent. The Krupps, the Farbens, they don't want to tear the country apart. If they insist, he will leave us in peace. During the Olympic Games, things seemed to be mellowing. We kept hoping. Every so often we or our friends would go and investigate emigration, but nobody would give us visas. The British wouldn't let us in Palestine and didn't want us in England and the United States didn't want Jews. But after Kristallnacht, we had no hope, no illusion. We ran. We left our dead in the earth we had lived on for centuries, and we ran."

Marlitt was suddenly and obviously exhausted. She touched her high forehead with a pale hand and stirred once in her chair. Abra took her leave, hoping that Professor Kahan would find the interview probing enough. Often as he went over her typescript he would point out areas where she should have persisted. She was learning the ground. Oftentimes even as she learned the names of the organizations these people had been involved with in Germany, she nonetheless asked each informant to explain that organization to her. Professor Kahan said there was always more to learn about an organization in another country, and that what people thought they were involved in when they joined something and what they thought the group was doing were as important as what it actually accomplished.

He would sometimes play interviewer or informant with her and show her ways of asking the same question that sounded different, or pursuing a point in the face of reticence without sounding nosy or coming across as dangerous. The most important aspect of Abra's performance—that was what he called it—was seeming naive and goodwilled and interested, but never with any deeper purpose. "A student, a good-hearted well-meaning American student, that is who you are and that is who you will show them."

"That's the sum of who I am?" she asked with some pique.

"That's not such a bad person to be, is it?" Oscar Kahan had the habit of returning a question with a question.

She was glad she didn't have to interview him, because she could imagine how he would defeat questioning. Her curiosity had been much whetted in the past months. "I'm not as politically naive as you assume—"

"Argue that with me, but don't prove it to the subjects. They need to feel a little superior in knowledge. They are refugees, remember, lost in a strange country and torn from a social web that they understood or thought they did. Nothing means the same here. Nothing is done the same way. They are children again. Allow them to make you a little the child as you conduct your interviews—not a stupid child but a willing, bright but naive child who wants to understand."

That's how he himself sees me, she thought, and was suddenly, coolly infuriated. "Professor Kahan, why do you have me ask so many questions about the street they lived on, the school they went to, the exact addresses, the names of cemeteries where their parents are buried, all that?"

He leaned across the desk toward her with a warm conspiratorial smile. "And why do you think we ask those questions, Miss Scott?"

"One possibility is that you think that when people recall specific physical details of their past life, that the other details will be more precise?"

"There. You see you have your own answer."

"If I think two and two are five, I have my own answer too."

"But we're dealing with the subjective, putting an informant and a questioner both at ease, aren't we?"

She assumed an imitation of his furrowed brow and quizzical smile. "Are we?" She waited but he simply waited also, as if for clarification. He was a subtle one, her professor, and that surprised her, for his first appearance was that of an open, curious, warm and quite unselfconscious man. All of those things he might be, but he was also singularly close. She wondered if he were more open with the women he was involved with—whoever she or they might be. "I have one more question. I notice we ask our German political refugees a set of questions about economic conditions inside Germany that we don't ask our Jewish refugees. Why?"

"We are assuming that conditions for the Jews are markedly different than for the rest of the German population, and that we can learn little about the German economy from questioning the Jews, since they're being forced out of it. We can't find out whether butter is scarce by asking a Jew."

"Professor Kahan, if we're doing a political science research project on the relationships and internal structure of German political organizations in the thirties, why do we care if butter is scarce in Germany now? And please don't ask me what I think this time."

"Do you enjoy the work?"

"Does that mean, if I like doing the work, I shouldn't ask so many questions?"

"It means, do you enjoy the work?"

"Yes."

"Good." He beamed at her. "Have you discussed this question of the scarcity of butter with your friends?"

"No."

"Why not, if it puzzles you?"

"It's nobody else's business. It's simply one of those questions that arises and then I put it aside to ask you."

"Because you have some idea of the answer?"

"Too vague to be useful."

"Let it remain that way for a while."

"For a while?"

He rose, to signal their interview was over. "One point you have made today is that you are not unobservant and will make me eat my words about your being naive. About the matter of drawing your thesis from the interviews, go see Blumenthal this week. Maybe you'd like to speed up that process a bit. We'd have to edit the interviews heavily before you take versions you can write your thesis on, but that would present no problem. Still, get on with it. Finish your thesis up as quickly as you can is my final advice of the day."

Dumped from his office with twenty more questions to ask, Abra walked home through the April rain wondering what that advice meant. He was telling her to hurry her thesis, but why? Would the project end soon? But she would still have the interviews. Was he leaving? He had an associate professorship at Columbia. Was he enlisting? He was overage, assuredly. Yet she sensed she should take his advice and curtail her social life sharply. She sighed. If he understood how little a doctorate really meant to her, he would probably lose respect and replace her as an assistant, but a doctorate remained more the excuse for her interesting life than the necessary product of it. She had intended to drag out her thesis project for years.

Normally Abra walked through the streets of New York gazing around her at the passing show, afraid to miss an event or a nuance. Today she plodded through the puddles chin tucked into her trench coat. She would follow her instinct that she should make every move he recommended and go hell-bent for her degree, if for no better reason than that Kahan had told her to, and she was convinced that he was going to be her real mentor.

Oh well, half the men she knew were going into the services, anyhow. She might as well get the damned degree. At least the interviews were interesting.

Eight days later it happened that the woman she was interviewing knew Marlitt Becker Speyer. Mrs. Hirsch had few organizational ties and little interest in politics. The only interesting part of the interview came toward the end, when she talked about Marlitt. She had known Marlitt as a little girl when she had worked for Marlitt's mother; years later Marlitt had taken her on as a seamstress in her couturier establishment. Toward the end, she said, the class lines had faded as the Jews were pushed into ghettoes and forced to live ten or twelve to a small apartment and systematically impoverished. Marlitt went on working almost to the end, because the Nazis wanted her designs even though they put a different label on them to conceal their origin, and Marlitt had kept on her own staff.

Mrs. Hirsch was fifty, a gaunt woman with white hair braided around her head and nearsighted eyes the color of weak tea behind thick glasses, a habit of bending forward as if to hear, although her hearing seemed fine. They conducted the interview in German. Abra took notes in her usual mix of German and English. Mrs. Hirsch said that shortly after Marlitt had heard of the death of her husband, whose body she was not allowed to reclaim for proper burial, her only child, a boy of four, had taken sick.

It was one of those sudden childhood fevers that shoot up and up. He grew more feverish until he was having diarrhea every fifteen minutes. Then he began to vomit blood. He was pitiful. Jews were no longer allowed in regular hospitals, and the only Jewish hospital was full beyond stretching. A doctor who could no longer prescribe medicines came, but he could not bring down the fever, and while the family hovered over him, Marlitt held her son in his suffering and his convulsions. It took the boy two days to die, Mrs. Hirsch said. Marlitt went out of the room every few minutes to weep in the hall, for fear of frightening the child when he was conscious. When her son died, she said she would pay no more tears, ever. She would get them all out of Germany, she would tear up her roots that ran to the center of this familiar earth, and she would never return, not if she lived to be two hundred. Oh yes, Mrs. Hirsch said, she brought me here. She could not save my husband, her own husband or her child, but she saved her parents and she saved me.

BERNICE 2

Bernice on Patrol

Every Monday, every Wednesday and every Friday, Bernice hopped on her Schwinn bicycle at seven-thirty A.M. and set off in rain or sun or unseasonable flurries of late snow for the local airport, hoping that the weather would permit her to take off on time. She carried with her an old leather jacket of Jeff's—the plane of course was not heated—her lunch and a small plastic bottle with a funnel, into which she urinated and which she hid in her empty lunch bucket when she landed. She had no idea how other pilots managed, for she had worked out that method herself.

Bernice had never before considered herself especially fortunate to live in central Massachusetts rather than on the coast, but now she did. Women were not allowed to fly for the Civil Air Patrol over the coastal zone, as that was considered dangerous because of U-boats. The Civil Air Patrol officially looked askance at women flying for it at all. When Bernice had joined she had been sternly informed that only auxiliary functions were open to women, running the offices. She had almost given up, during weeks of typing and filing, but the need for pilots was great and Bernice had at least as much experience as most of the pilots flying for the Civil Air Patrol. She had persisted till now she flew regularly for them.

Sometime around the end of April or the middle of May she would finally log in two hundred hours flying time. She wanted that commercial license more than ever, but she did not have the money. The Civil Air Patrol volunteers were unpaid, and now she had much less time to type faculty papers. If she could finally earn her instructor's license, she might be hired by the War Service Training Program, which taught flying to students. They had kicked women students out of the program, but they still used women instructors.

Even if flying for the Civil Air Patrol was keeping her penniless, she had three days a week of bliss, and if The Professor was cranky about his supper on those nights, she had the excuse of rationing. Moreover, he could not fault her volunteering for the war effort.

What was hard was to return when she was supposed to, after flying her route inspecting power lines against sabotage and forested areas for fires. She felt an urge strong as she supposed the mating instinct was in deer or dogs, to continue, to fly on until she reached the far unknown ocean. She had an intimate view of the little wrinkled hills of her home, of the broad Connecticut, of the hawks migrating north and the flights of small birds, of the farmlands standing under their puddles, of the rain clouds massing over the Berkshires, of the updrafts around Mount Tom. For three days every week she was ecstatic and useful, at one with the fabric body that extended her own. She did not think there had been a time since the death of her mother, when she had been happy for three days of every week.

Sometimes she was called on other days to act as a courier for documents or chemicals or plasma, to impersonate an enemy bomber in an air raid, twice to search for a downed military plane. Her life had a purpose. She begged off the Sunday movies with Mrs. Augustine, for she needed to catch up with housework and the typing that could pay for her commercial license eventually, but not at all any longer impossibly. She had the same schedule that had used to pad out seven days now crammed into the remaining four. Above all she had three days of doing what she was born to do, three days when she put on the little plane like a flimsy extended body, insectlike around her, beautiful as a dragonfly although jeweled only to her, and burst into flight.

That evening when she bicycled home from the airport, stopping to buy flounder and place the white parcel neatly in her handlebar basket, a letter from Jeff was waiting on the table in the hall. He was still stuck down in Alabama hating every moment of his life vegetating there. Bernice had expected Jeff to be placed in the Army Air Corps, as the Army was supposed to be seeking pilots desperately, for even though Jeff had not flown in years, he had his license, but instead they had focused on his unsuspected talents as an instructor of rifle practice. He had been sent for officer training and was a second lieutenant apparently stuck on the range. He claimed to be entirely covered with Spanish moss. She had felt a mixture of envy and foreboding when they packed Jeff off on the train, but he was safe unless one of his students shot wildly, and far more bored than she was.

She was serving fish oftener these days, not only because red meat was rationed, but because fish was quick to prepare. She could not reach home after her patrol before seven. Unfortunately, The Professor was thus always home well before her on her flying days, and he was not pleased with the new regimen. As she hastily dumped her gear in the hall closet and rushed through the living room toward the kitchen, carrying her parcels, he fixed her with his best admonitory "You're going to flunk this course if you don't straighten out" glare. "Is there some reason you're even later than usual this evening?"

"There was a long line in the fish store. With meat rationed, everyone's eating more fish."

"I certainly had noticed we are."

Her way of dealing with her father's ill temper was pretending, since he did not come out directly and shout at her about what angered him, that she did not understand he was annoyed. Now she gave him a brief bleak meaningless smile and bolted for the kitchen.

"You aren't going to sit down to supper looking like a mechanic, are you?"

As if he had ever noticed what she wore. As if anyone ever cared. "Supper will be ready shortly."

He snorted but said nothing more, turning the radio up. Every night she studied the war in the *Globe*, listened to the commentators and the analysts, studied the battle reports with the atlas volume of the thirteenth edition of the *Encyclopaedia Britannica* open on her lap. The Allies were clearly losing just about everyplace. On a map of the Philippines she had been following the steady erosion of the American and Philippine positions. In Africa, the battle seesawed but usually ended with the Allies in retreat.

Tonight the news was dreadful as she found herself moving ever more slowly about the large kitchen. General King had surrendered at Bataan. It sounded as if few of the forces had been successfully evacuated to Corregidor, where the Army still hoped to hold out. That fortress island was supposed to be impregnable. Something like ninety thousand Filipinos and Americans had surrendered to the Japanese. In Russia there was heavy fighting deep inside the country, with the Germans again advancing.

What would happen to them if they lost the war? The German army appeared invincible, and the Japanese had taken over Asia without difficulty. The decline of the West, she thought, but could not believe the Germans or the Japanese would really invade the United States. The first fear of invasion through California had diminished. The battles would be fought elsewhere, so what would defeat mean? Reparations? A search for scapegoats? Perhaps an American Nazi party blaming the Left or the Jews or colored people or who knows what vulnerable part of the population for the humiliation? Perhaps a return to the Great Depression?

Why did it feel so personal to lose? As if she herself were losing? She had a moment of fierce and despairing anger as she stood slicing the potatoes she had boiled that dawn into the fat rendered from Sunday's chicken, in which onions were already lightly browning. Yes, it smelled delicious and she did not give a damn. She did not want to cook potatoes lyonnaise while millions of people died and the world burned. She felt at once guilty and helpless, imprisoned. Even her flying felt absurd to her. Here she was enjoying the keenest pleasure she knew while in the Philippines emaciated soldiers were being marched to prison camps and in German-occupied Russia, partisans were hanged for daring to resist.

In the Soviet Union, women were flying in combat. Marina Reskova, the woman pilot and navigator, had formed three women's air regiments, one of fighters and two of bombers. In England, women were ferrying planes regularly. Here they wouldn't even let women fly domestically, in a support role. She longed to use her skill, her strength. She would not be afraid. She knew she could fight, if only she were given a chance.

She paused, fitting the pieces of fish dunked first in flour, then in eggy milk, then in cornmeal into the broiler pan. Could she kill? She thought so, but felt she needed evidence for her belief. She set traps for mice. She had taken part in the butchering of a pig at her paternal grandfather's farm. Her grandfather had slit the throat of the pig quickly and calmly, approaching the pig with the knife and simply passing the knife across the throat. The pig had walked away rather puzzled as the blood poured down, and then staggered to her knees. Two minutes later the pig had been dead, and Jeff and she had assisted in pouring boiling water over the carcass and scraping off the hair. The long incision and the extraction of the organs from the fat had fascinated rather than outraged her. Jeff was the more squeamish of the two, but they had both experienced the slaughter and butchering of the pig as an initiation ritual granted them rather than as a display of adult brutality.

Besides, would Jeff ever kill anyone? He was in the Army, but combat seemed at least as far from him in Alabama as from her in Bentham Center. She supposed you rarely had time in combat to philosophize. Probably you were trained to react, and you reacted. In the plane she did not stop to think about how to turn the wheel or how to step on the rudder; she read the few gauges and reacted. If she were in combat, surely the machine gun would respond when she activated it, and she would do that when threatened as automatically as dealing with the elevators or ailerons.

"A lot of the boys are enlisting at the end of this school year," her father announced at supper. "I don't know if there's any point keeping this college open. But they may be starting a governmental program here, the administration says. I don't like so much paprika on the sole."

"Sorry. I thought I'd try something different." She had been thinking about killing and not noticed what her hand was doing. "Do you believe we're going to lose this war?"

"Nonsense," The Professor thundered. "What kind of isolationist garbage have you been listening to? Despair is not productive."

He would never discuss politics with her. She could not understand why, for he had discussed everything with her mother. As a daughter, she was forever immature to him. "The fish on the second layer aren't as heavily paprikaed."

"Good. It disguises the flavor. Unless the fish were old?"

"No, no. They were perfectly fresh."

Why did she brood about combat? Because she wanted to be tested by the war, to take a real part. Jeff might not be doing anything he viewed as valuable, but it was not his choice. He was enlisted in the anti-Fascist cause, and if the use to which he was put was not what he might have chosen, nonetheless he had the peaceful mind of someone fully involved.

Even The Professor felt the weight of longing to be useful. He had written to various governmental departments about his work during the First World War (as they were calling it now, for this was beginning to be called the Second). He had received acknowledgments that looked to be form letters. Every couple of weeks he dictated a letter about his qualifications and his desire to be of service directed to some bureau, letters she sent off with his résumé to the addresses he furnished.

The Professor had put his old Austin up on blocks for the duration, a phrase local people had begun to use frequently. Closed for the duration. She realized he had pushed his plate away and was looking at her expectantly. "What do we have for dessert?"

"Dessert?" She had forgotten to make anything. "Let me start the coffee," she temporized and fled to the kitchen. Make a fast cornstarch pudding? Sugar was rationed and she was not eager to expend their month's allotment. No cookies in the cupboard. She had used to keep a supply of goodies on hand for such moments, but nowadays that was called hoarding. Then she remembered that Mrs. Augustine had given her a pint of pears canned from the tree that stood in the Augustine's yard, not yet in bloom this year but just tipping the buds open. She found the pears, dousing them liberally with the remaining rum in the last bottle.

"What's that supposed to be?" he inquired icily, staring into his dish.

"You know with sugar rationed, I can't make the same desserts I used to. It's pears Mrs. Augustine put up soaked in rum." Soaked for five minutes, but let that pass, she begged him silently.

"If you're low on sugar, I imagine the Garfinkles would let you have some maple syrup. We've always bought our syrup from them." He tasted the pears, coughed slightly. "Is that the last of the rum?"

"Afraid so," she said briskly. With little enthusiasm she spooned up her first bite of pear. She had put in more rum than she had realized. The effect was raw but not unpleasing, at least to her who had spent the day in an unheated aircraft much colder than the fields below it. Once in a while The Professor had a bottle of wine, which he stood beside his plate, and from which he occasionally poured her a sparing glass. The taste of any spirits always made her think of Zach and the days when Jeff and he had been always together and when she had been with them whenever they would endure her company. If I ever leave home, she thought, I will fly airplanes and drink whiskey. She smiled.

The Professor asked, "Do you like it?"

"Yes, I do. If it doesn't please you, I'm sorry, but just leave it and I'll eat it."

As she cleared the table, she did just that, taking the rummy syrup he had left in his dish and quaffing it from a glass as she scraped and stacked the dishes for washing. They had all gone up on Jumpers Mountain one June night in Zach's junior year and Zach had passed around a silver flask in the shape of a fish from which they had each in turn drunk gin. The gin had made her shudder, but she had felt as if she were sipping the blood of adulthood. It was a rite of passage. She had been in love with Zach and her lips touching the silver of the flask which his mouth had caressed only the moment before had made her more drunken than the alcohol.

The moon was the color of his flask and seemed to float like a fish in a light haze. In town there had been a rich and cloying scent of private but the air here smelled of balsam and spruce. Up on the open cliffs of the mountain they watched the moon just a day short of full rising and she felt as if she looked the moon in the face from the same height.

It had not been foolish to love Zach: she ought to have adored him if only out of the simplest gratitude, for he had shown her the way out of her caterpillarhood and if she still lived mostly in a cocoon, at least she knew what she wanted to be, like the moon herself, a huntress roaming free through the mountains of the clouds and the rivers of the wind.

Once or twice when she had been behind the wheel of one of Zach's sleek fast cars, she had experienced a joy of extension, of becoming one with a fine and powerful machine that carried her senses beyond herself as it responded to her decisions, her will, her skill. She was not a bad driver, but a sports car seemed inferior to the command of space in flying. The lightest, flimsiest plane with a forty-horsepower engine could penetrate a dimension the most expensive racing Ferrari in the world was denied.

No matter how meager her life at times, she was fully half owner of a plane. She had bought Steve out of his quarter when he had enlisted. The other owner, a lawyer, flew mostly for relaxation and occasionally to visit a client, when that amused him. She felt that the plane was really hers, because she was the one who flew it most of the time and she was the one who repaired it and worked on it and coddled it. Someday she would buy out the lawyer altogether. He talked of getting something fancier after the war. She could keep this one running for years. If she hurried with the dishes, she could manage to type for at least two hours, although her hands were swollen from the cold in the plane. Never mind. She would manage.

The day she got her commercial license finally she was going up on Jumpers Mountain, and she was going to find a bottle of whiskey or gin somewhere, and she was going to sit and sing songs and salute the moon. She would have her celebration. She would tell Jeff, who would rejoice with her, if only long distance. She would then have done one fine thing.

DUVEY 1

Many a Stormy Sea Will Blow

Duvey spent the first three months of 1942 on the Caribbean run, so he was damned glad to ship out on the North Atlantic convoy route instead. He had been working tankers, but no more. He had lost five friends he knew about and probably more he hadn't found out yet. All his pals had cashed in on tankers torpedoed offshore since January, hit close enough to the American shore to smell it and see the lights. Cape Hatteras was the worst, but the whole coast was deadly.

A woman he met in a bar told him that her mother lived in Vero Beach where the Dodgers wintered, and every morning on the beach arms, ears, headless torsos washed up with the twisted metal. Mostly the tanker crew went up in a great whoosh of flame and maybe that was lucky, because the guys who dived off, he had helped fish some of them out of the sea. He'd choose to go up all at once, rather than dive into a burning sea or be "saved" with burns over his whole body, to die slowly in a hospital ward or to hobble around Detroit, the local bogeyman.

The U-boats were having the war all their own way, lurking off the coast and playing shooting gallery with the tankers against the lights of Miami, Charleston, Savannah, New York. The cities weren't even blacked out. Seamen's lives were cheap. The heroes were in the Army and Navy, but the seamen were dying at much higher rates, and if anybody onshore thought the war would be won without the food, the oil, the matériel they were carrying, they were as crazy as he had always thought most people to be. If England was going to hold out and if the United States was going to get into the war effectively, the ships had to deliver their cargo.

He had made his choice. He was not going to dress up like a brass monkey and salute some asshole who happened to have gone to Annapolis. He had always been a working stiff and he would stay one. This was the real work of the war, as he understood it, and he was used to seeing cities from their ports and their bottom sides. They'd fought and pissed blood for their union, and they were going to war under union rules and union wages. The National Maritime, a CIO union like Tata's, had taken them from forty dollars a month for lying in garbage and filth to a hundred dollars a month and now they had hazardous bonus pay of another hundred. A lot of jerks behind desks wanted to cut their wages, but when the shipowners gave back the huge profits they were making, then they'd take a pay cut: that's what the union said, and that's what he said.

When he thought of it, he scrawled a letter home, because he didn't want Mama worrying. He was careful what he said, filling his letters with questions and tall tales. She thought he was safe out of the Navy because he wouldn't have to fight. Better she thought that way. He would say nothing to set her wise. He had always brought trouble home to her, but he didn't like to. As the eldest, he knew how difficult her life had been.

He was a hard case in his way, for sure, grown up in the basement of the Depression and pinched for almost everything he might have wanted. Arty couldn't see past the end of his nose. Ruthie might make something of herself. She had a streak of goody-goodyness that made him puke, but she was a straight kid and helped Mama. She might even get through college some year, the first graduate in their family, if she wasn't fool enough to get married. Marriage finished people off. Women started having babies and pretty soon they looked just like their mothers and had nothing to say but what their mothers had said. Men got that worn-down stooped look and started bulging over their belts.

It wasn't for him. He'd never even come close. He liked women he wasn't about to bring home. The only kind of girl worth the bother was one used to supporting herself, a waitress or a bar girl or a manicurist or a whore who didn't belong to a pimp, one who knew how to take care of herself so she didn't bring you a disease. The sweetest girl he'd ever had was colored, Delora with coppery skin and long fine, fine legs and an ass she only had to carry down the street to bring men to their knees. But having a colored girl was trouble. They almost couldn't go anyplace for a meal or a drink without him getting into fights with white jerks or fights with colored who didn't want him messing with their women, they said, as if any woman of the same color belonged to them as a set. He didn't mind a scrap, but not every time they left the house.

He'd grown up near colored, and he could never understand the fuss whites made. Take a Russian Jew and a Swede, or a Scotsman and a Sicilian, and they were just as different. But every time you tried to talk to a guy who was nutso on the subject, he would go on about, Would you want one to marry your sister? As if that's all those black guys were wanting all the time, to come and marry somebody's cross-eyed gimpy sister. Sure, they'd be curious to get in bed with a white woman the same as he'd been curious about a colored woman the first time, but after that it was an individual smile or way of walking or a line that made you laugh that hooked you.

Detroit had a big colored population, growing all the time because the colored came up from their dead-end lives in the South to get work in the factories. He figured that like the Jews, probably the smartest ones were those who wouldn't take it anymore in the black equivalent of the shtetl and just had to find someplace they could get ahead and make a decent life. The colored in Detroit were often smart, snappy, lively people who walked around with a load of anger for the shit they had to take.

There were six black guys on the *Montauk,* down in the engine room. They kept to themselves mostly, and while he passed the time of day with them when they came face-to-face, he didn't have much to do with them. There was one other Jew on board, the radioman, but he was an officer. If somebody asked him if he was a Jew, he said he was, but he never volunteered the information unless he knew he was talking to another Jew. You said you were a Jew, they wanted to start in on you. They thought all Jews were patsies and you had to be twice as tough.

Guys asked him about himself, he said, "I'm from Detroit, Jack, where the cars are fast and the women are faster. We're born on wheels and we burn alcohol like gas." That gave them a handle.

Duvey's nickname was Dave the Rave because of his success with women in port. Duvey had figured out while he was still in high school that the only women worth his time wanted it as much as he did, and so it was a matter of settling that you liked each other enough and when and where, and not a matter of begging and arm-twisting and promising what you hadn't the wherewithal to deliver, Christmas in July.

April 24 the convoy formed up. His ship was heavy with wheat, loaded in Montreal. They had sailed down the St. Lawrence, then waited off Halifax where this convoy was organized. Convoy HX-152 was impressive as it sailed out of the roads: thirty-four ships, escorted by an aged destroyer and three corvettes, about which sailors said they would roll their guts out on wet grass. The convoy was a handsome sight, a parade of ships out into the Atlantic with a light chop and mild sun on their faces. US-PBY Catalina patrol planes kept an eye on them from above. There was a former liner transporting Canadian troops, a tanker, a bunch of old tramps of varying registries, nationalities and degree of seaworthiness, a tidy Norwegian freighter with its own deck guns, looming freighters sprouting cargo booms.

The *Montauk* itself was the newest boat he'd ever sailed on, a Liberty ship that had only gone out twice before. All the Liberty ships were slow, but they were okay, reliable unless something hit them amidships, in which case they broke open like a loaf of sliced bread. The crew's quarters were in the deckhouse, four bunks to a room, forty-four on board including the officers. The deck machinery was steam driven and the engine was good. There were even tiled showers for the men. He'd been on ships where a bucket was all the clean you got.

Fog shrouded them on the second day, till they couldn't see their neighbors to either side or in front or back. Convoying was only beginning on the Caribbean and coastal routes, so it was new to Duvey. On the Great Lakes, you'd see another ship in the Detroit River or in the locks, but out on the lakes, you were never within hailing distance. It alarmed him to travel in such a herd of unwieldy cargo ships in a heavy fog, each ship closer to the others than he found safe or comfortable. They had no escort of planes overhead to watch for U-boats, but the day passed without an attack. The fog closed in around them thick and clammy and dank, air that felt like gaseous ice. Two of the ships suffered a near collision. One of the corvettes had to hang back to round up stragglers.

They continued without air cover for the next four days, until at midnight on April 29/30, Duvey heard an explosion. Even through the fog he could see a column of flames that meant a tanker had been hit, probably the *Fitzpatrick*. He could hear firing. The destroyer was laying depth charges on the sub, by the sound of it. Heavy smoke drifted across the water, mixed with fog. The reek of petroleum made him feel a little sick. He heard another heavy explosion. His body stiffened against the impact. Any minute now the *Montauk* might be next. Automatically he touched the buttoned pocket with his papers and his cash tied in a knotted condom. If he survived torpedoing, he would have them; if he didn't and the body washed up, he'd be identified.

The destroyer reported oil release from depth-charging a U-boat, but half an hour later, the *Belle Starr* was torpedoed. She was badly damaged and drifting. The *Montauk* had to detour around.

With no moon, no stars, no lights on any of the ships, they moved into a murk of smoke from burning ships and the damned smothering fog. All the ships were chattering to each other, for if they had tried to observe radio silence, they would have rammed each other and sailed right over the ship in front. That meant the U-boats, who were operating in one of the wolf packs he had been hearing scuttlebutt about, could home in on the signals of each ship in turn. The corvettes were bouncing around chasing after the subs like harrying dogs.

In a short while the *Montauk* began to cross debris, the bits and pieces of what had been that day a ship full of living seamen. Vaguely to the right they could see flames on the waters, the sea itself on fire, blurred by the fog. Men were screaming over there. They began seeing the little red lights of seamen in the water, the lights that bobbed on their life jackets. During an attack they were not supposed to pick up survivors, but the captain decided since they weren't under direct attack, they'd get whoever they could.

The first men they hauled in had drowned in oil, oil clogging their lungs when they went into the water, but then they got three live ones, hideously covered and blinded by the oil, one burnt all down his side and smelling like a barbecue, but alive. Duvey volunteered to help scrape the oil off the poor bastards.

On instructions then the captain swung off to the left and resumed steaming ahead. They could hear muffled underwater explosions in bursts. Depth charges. "That's the hedgehog, buddy boy," the bosun Hogan told him. "They fire it ahead in bursts. It's their new toy, and it seems to do the trick better than those damned charges they had to fire aft."

Then in the burning lurid light of a ship on fire they saw the U-boat surface in a bubbling pool of scum and oil. One of the charging corvettes rammed it. The stern stood tall in the water, tail up, like a shark upside down, and then it sank straightaway and the oil slick spread over it.

Duvey was glad he was not in the submarine service, no matter how dangerous was the merchant marine. He'd rather die up on the deck in a burst of fire or drown than be squashed like a bug in a can. He'd always had a pang of pity for the Black Gang down in the engine room. They never had a chance if a ship was hit. They were cooked right away. At least up on deck you might be able to jump for it. If you got into a lifeboat, you had a better chance, and even those poor kippered devils they'd just picked out of the water might just make it if their burns weren't too widespread and if they hadn't swallowed or breathed in too much oil.

He realized he had not heard an explosion in maybe fifteen minutes. That didn't in itself mean anything, only that the corvettes and the destroyer had lost contact with the U-boats and that the Germans were lying off waiting a better chance or a better sighting.

He had hated in his life: mostly guys who had done him in, a big Polack who had made life miserable for him on his first berth, a mate who had tried to break him, Father Coughlin who spewed out his diarrhea of the mouth against Jews from all the radios in the Catholic neighborhoods around his own back in Detroit. Never had he hated anyone or anything with the sharp steely intensity with which he hated those arrogant Nazi sharks, the U-boats. They had opened the sea war by sinking an unarmed passenger liner, the *Athenia,* and then claimed the British had blown it up themselves for propaganda. They operated against unarmed merchant ships and it was good hunting and good times, easy aces for the captains with no one to shoot back.

The next day they knew they were in the Greenland air gap, that six-hundred-mile stretch of sea where the planes based in Newfoundland could not reach them and they were not yet under the shield of the planes based in Iceland. But what use had they got from the so-called air cover when the fog had kept the planes grounded every day?

However they had their first luck. In the morning, swells were rising, looming and crashing over the decks. The wind rushed out of the north bringing snow. The visibility was actually a little better and they could catch a glimpse of the *San Martin* to their right and the *Lone Star* to their left. Then the seas grew too high to see anything but the next wave toppling. The swells were longer on the Atlantic than he was used to on the Great Lakes and the waves were even higher, but when you came down to it, they hit no harder. The water was just as fucking icy and just as bloody wet. Storms broke oreboats in half on Michigan and Superior.

They were making their way through a flotilla of icebergs, but they were safe from the U-boats, who could not surface to attack in this weather. Therefore they would outrun them. The convoy wasn't making any great speed, but the U-boats could only make four knots an hour submerged and would fall behind the convoy. They might radio ahead to another wolf pack to stand by, but no attack could take place in heavy weather. In spite of the battering they took, Duvey preferred being shaken to pieces to being attacked, so bring on the tempests.

The pack ice they moved through was nothing like he had imagined. It was irregular, wild, a Grand Canyon of weird icy shapes, not white so much as blue and purple and grey and rust-colored. He'd seen plenty of ice on the Great Lakes, but this was stranger-looking, towering cliffs, floating ice castles, nightmare jungles and fairy-tale cities of ice. When the storm finally cleared, they had lost one vessel, the *Eleftheria*, straggling on behind them with engine trouble. She ought to catch up with the convoy when they reached Iceland.

He had never seen a prettier sight than the planes roaring over them from the bases in Iceland. Now the convoy was under the air shield. When a U-boat attacked, it was immediately forced down by a bomber.

They refueled at Iceland before sailing on to Southampton. There they heard that the *Eleftheria* had been torpedoed and gone down with all hands lost. It was a good time in port for Duvey because he scored a Soviet girlfriend, who was celebrating surviving the Murmansk run. The Russians had women on their ships, and everybody else envied them. There was a lot of visiting ship to ship, partying, gossiping, gambling, bargaining. They traded canned meat and fruit to the limeys in a westbound convoy for rum, so the *Montauk* steamed off for England with morale high.

LOUISE 2

The Dark Horse

The train back from Washington was jammed beyond belief. Louise spent the trip squatting on her suitcase, wishing she had used the new leg paint Kay had shown her and not ruined one of her last pairs of stockings. Jammed in against her so closely she could smell vomit clinging to his shoes was a sailor. Exhausted, he slept standing, leaning first against her and then against the man on his other flank. It was hot for the middle of May—Washington felt subtropical already—and the train was unpleasantly rank, with servicemen sleeping even on the luggage racks.

She had been attending a meeting of the Writers' War Board. They were not part of the official government bureaucracy, although editors and publishers often assumed that they were, because they worked closely with the Office of Facts and Figures, which scuttlebutt said was about to be replaced by something more geared at putting out propaganda.

She had been tapped to help organize the Magazine Bureau. She had little to do with the Confession Committee, but she worked with the group helping to establish guidelines for the women's magazines and the magazines with a general readership: her own markets. Every three months, the board issued War Guide Supplements suggesting themes to push in magazine fiction and articles.

She hardly recognized Washington from her previous visit as a tourist with Oscar and Kay. It seemed to have five times as many people in the same space. No matter what she had done, from waiting for a taxi to waiting for supper to waiting to use the bathroom, there was a long line. Washington felt like a phone booth into which too many people had crowded all at once to shout into a mouthpiece. It remained at its core a self-satisfied segregated little southern city with restaurants and hotels off-limits to Negroes and black and white schools and facilities. Nonetheless, it was full of fascinating men, perhaps now more than ever.

Pennsylvania Station was mobbed with people in and out of uniform saying impassioned hellos and good-byes. She had sweated heavily into her suit and felt wilted and weary. She was looking for her daughter. She had asked Kay to meet her, as she had not only her suitcase but a briefcase and an extra cardboard box full of material she was toting back. She could not find a porter and dragged her load along the platform to the gate, and then peered around for Kay. Late, she supposed. She sat on her suitcase again feeling distinctly filthy, tired and unlovely. Where the hell was her damned daughter? She tried waiting for a pay phone, but the lines were simply too long to bother.

Finally after half an hour had passed, she commandeered one of the few porters remaining and got herself into a taxi and headed uptown. New York was surprisingly uncrowded for four-thirty. Even six months ago, arriving at Pennsylvania Station and embarking in a taxi at that hour would have meant sitting in traffic and fuming her way uptown. Already there were markedly fewer cars on the streets of Manhattan, and traffic moved quickly. Now what had happened to Kay?

Sensual relief flooded her as she entered the foyer of her suite. Home, home. In Washington, she had had to share a tiny room at the Mayflower that would obviously until this year have been a smallish single with Dorothy McMichaels, who under an array of pseudonyms spewed out two to four stories a month for the confession magazines. Dorothy was conservative, religious, a true believer in sexual sin and retribution, a loose-limbed loud-voiced woman who made Louise remember social workers she had known when she was an orphan being placed in foster homes in Cleveland.

Louise did not enjoy remembering her childhood, hard, bleak and unfashionably Dickensian. Because of her Christian religiosity, Dorothy recalled to Louise one particular foster home where she had been better fed and better dressed than she was used to and far more terrorized, because the father of the household tried to put his hands into her panties whenever he caught her alone. He had been a deacon of the Methodist Church. The social workers had often ignored that Louise was Jewish for, as they said to each other loudly in her presence, she did not look it. Louise knew better. She looked like a Hungarian Jew, like photos of her mother taken before disease and dismal labor had eroded her beauty. Therefore Dorothy recalled to Louise more of her frightened and powerless earlier self than she cared to dwell on. Louise liked to remember her origins in her politics rather than in her emotions. She also liked her privacy and her comfort. Traveling had ceased to be enjoyable for the duration, as they were always saying.

She made a quick review of the mail that had accumulated in an aggregation of easily toppled towers—sorted by Blanche—before hurrying back through the apartment calling, "Kay! Kay!"

Her daughter was not in her room. Mrs. Shaunessy said that Kay had told her she could not meet her mother. "It would have been nice if she had bothered to tell me that! I waited half an hour for her," Louise complained.

Mrs. Shaunessy shook her head wearily. Although they were close in years— the housekeeper, who had two married daughters, was forty-one—Mrs. Shaunessy with her grey-streaked hair pulled back in a knot always seemed to Louise grandmotherly. "Well now, missus, Kay and I had words about her comings and goings. I will tell you that she used hard language to me. And that child refused to tell me where she was going this very afternoon, when school let out."

"What do you think is up? I'll talk to her about her rudeness."

"It's not my place to say, but if you ask me, it's my opinion she's chasing around after some boy. That's how it all starts, at her age, missus. You know it."

"Kay?" She thought of her gawky long-limbed colt. "Somehow I doubt it, but I'll get right on her and find out."

Was Kay punishing her for going out of town? She would have considered taking Kay along, but that would mean pulling her out of school, Elizabeth Irwin, and in wartime Washington, the accommodations were so tight she could not simply ask for a double and install her daughter. She would have given anything for a single room.

Her own fastidiousness annoyed her. After all, sharing a room with a loud confession magazine writer was hardly on a par with the dangers European civilians and American servicemen were facing. At times she felt uncomfortable with how used to ease and comfort she had grown, how accustomed to clean fresh clothes that were in style and well made, a hot bath whenever she wished, a housekeeper to take care of Kay and herself, a secretary to handle her correspondence and type her manuscripts, clean light airy rooms well furnished and with a few good pieces of original art Oscar or she had chosen. She had grown used to all the bourgeois comforts, and she had raised Kay to expect them, a clean gracious well-lighted space in which to live and work, good and plentiful and varied food, a constant stream of stimulation in the form of concerts, books—the newest, the oldest, the best—and always intelligent and spirited conversation.

She put on her smock and slippers, casting herself into the chair that faced her walnut desk. She was extremely useful on the board, because the notion of what she wrote as propaganda was neither novel nor shocking to her. She preferred the new line to the old one: she was much closer to believing in working women as loving, responsible, even exciting citizens, than the line that had been pushed since she began publishing that the working woman was manipulative, selfish, dangerous to her family and society.

In her family the women had always worked. In Hungary her grandmother was said to have run a poultry business. Her mother had worked in a canning factory until TB had carried her from Louise to a sanatorium and finally into early death. Oscar had never desired that she remain idle or make of the work of the house her whole existence. As he frequently said, he liked intelligent women and did not want a cow. What he did want, of course, was all of that intelligent woman's full attention focused on him. Her work had been fine, so long as she would drop it as soon as he needed her to type his papers, to read and comment on them and improve his prose style, to rub his back and listen to his complaints about his colleagues.

That was the reason they had had only one child. She had realized shortly after Kay's birth that with his level of demands on her, she could barely cope. She had constantly to juggle what she knew Kay needed with what Oscar demanded. Should she talk to him about Kay's insubordination? She was avoiding Oscar these days. Almost falling into bed with him had alarmed her sufficiently so that she had managed not to see him since then, except for a few moments when he came to collect Kay or drop her off.

Kay appeared just before seven, for supper. "Where were you?" Louise followed her daughter to her room. "Why didn't you meet me? I waited in Pennsylvania Station over half an hour for you."

"Mother, I tried to call you yesterday evening until eleven-thirty, but you weren't in your room. Finally that awful woman told me not to call anymore. Didn't she tell you I'd been calling you?"

Louise had been downstairs sitting in the bar till it closed. She had been with Claude Martel, a film director whom she had met at the Office of Facts and Figures. "She was asleep when I returned—we had a late meeting working out new guidelines. Why weren't you at the station? You knew I was counting on you."

"I had an engagement. I couldn't break it."

"You can damned well break an engagement when your mother tells you to meet her train! I had tons of stuff to carry."

"Mother, I simply don't understand why you're making such a fuss! You got home all right—here you are. If you'd been in your hotel room, you'd have received my message last night."

Louise had a brief vision of Claude Martel across the little table. She had had a flirtation going with a playwright on the staff, but the first real tête-à-tête with Martel had demolished that fragile construction. Claude was the son of a Rumanian Jew who had married a French businessman; he had been brought

over to Hollywood in the late thirties and proved to be an accomplished director of talkies. Now he was with Universal. She figured his age to be forty-five.
Vigorous, magnetic, dark-haired, with light eyes, he was the first man who had
moved her since Oscar. In front of her daughter she felt slightly guilty at having
sat up so late with him, moving beyond flirtation into exploration. He had said
he would be in New York during midsummer and would see her then. Perhaps,
perhaps not. She was sure he met a great many women younger and more spectacular than herself. Nonetheless to feel that attraction was reassuring that she
was not doomed to essential fidelity to Oscar forever. That night felt dense and
heavy within her, more sensual than her couple of times in bed with Dennis
Winterhaven. Even though all that had happened was talk and hand holding,
she felt touched by Claude as not by any other man since Oscar. Therefore she
feared her daughter could read on her face that affair in words.

"Mrs. Shaunessy's calling us, Mother. She has supper on the table."

"I don't want you being rude to her, Kay. You will cooperate with her and you
will be pleasant to her."

"She's not my mother. She shouldn't try to push me around."

"She's my surrogate when I'm away, and you should treat her well. Kay, you've
always loved Mrs. Shaunessy. What's this contemptuous attitude?"

"You're talking about when I was a child. Really, she's just a servant. It's not
right for her to speak to me the way she does."

"She's a person in her own right, and she's known you since you were a little
girl. She's taken care of you. Where were you this afternoon?"

Kay flung herself into a chair in the dining room with her face twisted into
a pout. O adolescence, o bat turds, Louise thought. I never had a chance to put
on airs and throw fits. Perhaps that's a gift I'm giving her, the chance to lash
out emotionally without it costing anything. Louise loathed fights at the dinner
table, so she put off their confrontation until they had savored the roast lamb
Mrs. Shaunessy had managed to procure. Dutch irises in a blue vase. Louise
was still relieved to be home, but her bliss was mixed with irritation with her
daughter.

Having a housekeeper was a tricky business for her conscience, but once she
had made that decision, she had settled into it. Without Mrs. Shaunessy, her
efficiency would be reduced by half. They had made their accommodations long
ago. They called each other by their last names and did not chat. Mrs. Shaunessy gossiped with her friends who worked in other households in the same big
apartment building. Mrs. Shaunessy's room was off-limits to the rest of them,
and what she cooked for them, she ate in the kitchen—which was where Louise
ate when she was alone, and where Kay ate when Louise was absent. Mrs. Shau-

nessy had Wednesday afternoon and Sundays off, when she invariably took the train out to the Five Towns area of Long Island, to see one or the other of her married daughters.

Still Louise summed up the contradictions of her life in a phrase she had once heard herself say: "Just tell Mrs. Shaunessy to put the *Daily Worker* on the coffee table." She was a sympathizer who had never joined the Communist party because always she could find some part of whatever line they were adhering to at the moment with which she disagreed. Always she had scruples, reservations, issues. It had been a long flirtation but she did not think unless she or the Party changed drastically that she would ever swear to love, honor and obey. The Stalin-Hitler pact had capped her decision like a tooth sealed for good.

She made the coffee and carried it into the living room, as she always did. She felt that washing up the supper dishes ought to be Mrs. Shaunessy's last job. Kay had begun drinking coffee recently. "All right, where were you this afternoon, Kay?" She tried to sound brisk, firm.

"I had a date."

"A what?" But she had heard Kay clearly. "With whom?"

Kay flipped up the ends of her hair. She jutted her chin up and held her lashes at half mast, imitating some movie star no doubt. "His name is Andy." When Louise prolonged her stare she added, "Andy Bates."

"Do continue. Where did you meet him and who is he and why didn't you talk to me first?" Louise had the sour thought that if her adolescence had been passed in a Dickens novel, her daughter's seemed bathed in B movies.

"I'm sixteen, Mother, I'm grown up now and it's time you realized that. Girls grow up quickly during wars." Kay listened to the sound of that with some satisfaction.

"Since last week you grew up? Amazing. And who is this Andy Bates?"

"He's in the Navy—"

"Oh no! A sailor? Where in hell did you meet a sailor?"

"Outside the USO. We're too young to go inside but we meet them outside. Your attitude is unpatriotic, Mother. I'm ashamed of you."

"I'm ashamed of you, picking up a sailor in the street and trying to tell me that's part of the war effort. What did you do with him?"

"Really, Mother, you sound like a Victorian matron about to show me the door. I went on a double date with him to the Central Park Zoo and then for a row on the lake. His liberty is over. I promised to write to him, but I won't see him for months, if he doesn't get blown to pieces in the meantime."

"Kay, he may be a nice young man but you can't pick up men in the streets and expect them to act like gentlemen. You have no damned idea what you could get into. Some men are more than willing to use violence—"

"Really, Mother, everybody meets informally nowadays, and if you really think he was about to ravish me in the middle of the zoo—"

"You don't know what that word means! I do not want you hanging around outside the USO asking for trouble. If I have to go to school every day and meet you and walk you back here, I'll start doing so."

"Mother! Do you want me to die of embarrassment? I'll quit school if you treat me that way."

"I doubt that. You'd get pretty bored at home. Look, Kay, if you think you're old enough to begin dating, only on weekends and I want to meet the young men." She sounded priggish and did not care. At Kay's age she had had a honed sense of which men were dangerous and which not, a knowledge Kay had been protected from ever acquiring; nor did she wish Kay to need to walk around judging potential for brute force.

Shouldn't she consult Oscar? He might be able to reason with Kay far more effectively than she could; perhaps he could embarrass her into behaving less recklessly. She felt as if she ought to involve him, but she did not want to entangle herself in the dangerous strands of Oscar's attention. Surely she could handle Kay alone, staying free of him for good.

She was sitting up in bed with the blackout curtains drawn reading Saint-Exupéry's *Flight to Arras.* Dennis had given it to her the evening she had not been able to keep him from proposing and then retreating wounded. Suddenly the phone rang.

She frowned. Late for someone to call. It was long distance. When she heard the voice with its hint of French, her irritation vanished. "Claude! Where are you?"

"I'm still in Washington. But I have rearranged my schedule. Tomorrow I take the train to New York where I spend tomorrow night, and I see you, do you agree? Can you cancel what you are doing and see me? Because the next morning I must return to the West Coast."

"Tomorrow? Shall I meet your train?"

"No, it will be congested. I am arranging this by seeing our big money person in New York. Some lackey will meet me. I will call you in the late afternoon and tell you when we will dine. Is that good?"

"It sounds very good to me."

"I could not wait till summer, Louise, to continue our conversation. I consider it pressing. Do you agree?"

"I agree I'll see you tomorrow, Claude. Now, good night." She suspected that if Claude pushed her hard enough, she would fall into his arms. Obviously she had made an impression on him as he had on her, but would the second meeting stand up to the first? Not to worry, she ordered herself, figuring how she would work an appointment to have her hair done into her already tight schedule and what excuse could get her out of seeing Katharine Cornell in Shaw's *Candida* with her friends the Bauers after all the difficulty getting tickets. She would send Kay instead, pleading unexpected board work. The Bauers were accustomed to their friends being called to Washington and joining agencies as dollar-a-year men. They would not question her need to meet a deadline. Tomorrow morning she would have Kay help her sort the box of papers, which would impress Kay with the truth of her tale. The way was cleared for folly.

I have been faithful to Oscar not only during marriage but long afterward, even when I have occasionally dropped myself like a load of clean unsorted laundry into another man's bed. "I have been faithful to thee, Cynara, in my fashion." Louise smiled at the memory of that heavy breathing poem of her adolescence, passed around among the more literary and emancipated coeds, who had thought it sexy until they discovered Joyce and Hemingway. Claude was of Oscar's caliber, and even a brief gallop with him would be good for her sense of identity and possibilities. Louise sighed, wondering if she should have taken up writing steamy novels instead of slick fiction, because in none of her stories could her heroines experience the furnace of sexual desire that roared there at the center, fueling her life with its energy.

Louise felt too excited to sleep, but she wanted to look her best. Finally she rummaged in a drawer for a sleeping pill. She had not taken one since those months after Oscar had moved out. She could remember her misery, but tonight she had an aerial view of that hell, neat as quilted fields far below. Tonight if she needed help to sleep, it was because her life felt overly full, rather than emptied.

When she awakened, she remembered two sexual dreams. In them she had lain not with Oscar, who still seemed to control her dream life, or not with face-less youth, young anylove, who sometimes replaced Oscar. She had dreamed of lying naked body to body once and then again with Claude, so that as she rose to face her day, she found herself already thinking of him as her lover, as a man who had already twice given her pleasure.

NAOMI 2

Today You Are a Woman

It happened at school, when Naomi was outside in gym class playing baseball. They stuck her in center field, far, far from the batter, where her only terror was that the ball might suddenly fly at her. She was not used to playing baseball. She would swing at the ball when it was her turn, and once in a while by sheer luck she hit it. She had learned to run then very fast, and she understood where to run first, and where to go next.

However, when the ball suddenly chose to dive straight at her, she never could figure out what to do with it. She would stand with her arms straight up and sometimes it would veer abruptly and bounce by her, or it would hang over her head and then land right on her, or it would come to her outstretched arms and then wickedly bounce off them and hop away. Out in the grass of the outfield she prayed that the ball would not pick her to attack today.

All spring it had been raining, but today the sun shone and the sky was blue, blurred by a yellow brown haze from the factories. Dandelions were blooming in the outfield. In French they were called pissenlits, piss in beds, but they were the same flowers. She had eaten the greens in earlier, better springs. The girls rubbed dandelions under each other's chins, saying that was butter.

In right field next to her Clotilde was standing. It had seemed a perfectly ordinary name to Naomi's ears, until she had heard how the other kids teased Clotilde, who was a light-colored almost grey-skinned plump child with hair as kinky as Naomi's and only a little darker. Clotilde did not speak the way the other colored girls did. Her mother dressed her in pinafores, and she wore a little gold cross on a chain. She was Catholic, but did not go to the parochial school, she had explained to Naomi, because they were Poles there, and indeed that made sense to Naomi, since the Polish kids fought the colored kids as often as they fought the Jewish kids, and neither Jews nor colored people were welcome in Hamtramck, the Polish town enclosed by Detroit but with its own government.

Now Naomi noticed that Clotilde had drifted as if blown gradually by the wind over to her. Clotilde was not looking at her but forlornly in the direction of home plate, from which she too must wish as fervently as Naomi nothing would come at them. Clotilde was always the last chosen of the colored girls, because she had no athletic interest or ability.

"Tu es de Paris, vraiment?" Clotilde asked from the side of her mouth.

For a moment she was not sure Clotilde was speaking French, for it was a singsong French with a number of elisions and some syllables pronounced that Naomi had only heard said that way in Provence. Then Naomi began to talk to her, fervently, furiously. "How is it you speak French? Does your family speak it? Where are you from?"

"Doucement, doucement," Clotilde warned. "We are not supposed to speak in anything but English, as you know. We must be quiet. But I was born in Martinique, where I have a great deal of family and it is very beautiful with no winter and the white people are not as mean as here. I know how people here make fun of you when you do not speak English at home."

"It feels so good to speak French, to hear it, I feel like crying!"

Unfortunately the shortstop threw the next batter out, ending their conversation. Naomi was squatting among the dandelions looking for one that had made a seed head so she could blow it off, watching to see when she would have to go to bat, when she realized she felt wet between her legs.

Could she have peed on herself? She waited till she came in from the field at the end of gym class and changed out of the shorts the school had made her buy, long gym shorts in ugly navy. Big stain of red, of blood, the size of a half dollar. She remembered a story on the radio about a little girl dying of anemia and the blood rushing in her ears. Then she remembered the time Jacqueline left a napkin in the bathroom. Maman had slapped Jacqueline and called her a dirty girl, but then Maman explained to Rivka and herself how little girls became women.

Then they asked Jacqueline privately. She lay on their parents' bed reading *Wuthering Heights,* an English novel. Both Maman and Papa were at work. Jacqueline assumed an air of great importance. It was nothing, she said, although some girls made a great fuss about it and lay around all day with hot water bottles and took many aspirin. She herself thought it was merely boring. But it meant you had become a woman. It was like a private bar mitzvah and more real, because it happened when G-d chose. Then you would notice how you waxed and waned with the moon and that your time would come at a certain point in the cycle of the moon.

Naomi knew that the girls were always talking about periods and falling off the roof and that time of month, but she wasn't going to say one word. They might make fun of her or that mean Joyce might tell the boys and then she would simply die. She stuffed toilet paper into her panties and walked very carefully to her next class.

At home Aunt Rose was yelling at Sharon about changing the babies right away. Naomi stood about on one foot and then on the other waiting to talk to Aunt Rose, but when Rose noticed her, it was only to send her to the bakery for pumpernickel and to the dairy for a gallon of three percent milk.

Finally Ruthie came home for a quick supper, changing the white blouse and dark skirt she was required to wear at work. Ruthie had three such blouses and two such skirts that she was forever washing and ironing. She kept them all the way over on the right of the closet they shared, for they were never worn on any other occasion. Naomi viewed them with respect and was careful not to muss them when she looked for something in the closet. Ruthie had about an hour before she had to rush to class.

Naomi caught Ruthie in their bedroom as soon as she could. "Ruthie. Something happened to me today."

"Something good or something bad?"

"I don't know." Naomi shrugged uncomfortably. The question itself disturbed her. Was the blood a punishment or a passport to adult freedom?

"If you don't, who does?" Ruthie was digging in the back of the closet. "It's time to start wearing cottons. What a day to be stuck inside."

"There's blood inside my panties." Naomi sat miserably on the very edge of Ruthie's bunk. "It's what do you call it in English? My periods."

"Period. Is it really? Did Mama give you a napkin?"

"I didn't tell her yet."

"You need a sanitary belt and a napkin." Ruthie rummaged in her dresser. "You put my belt on for now. Tomorrow I'll buy one for you downtown." Ruthie stroked her hair, asking anxiously, "Do you understand what it means?"

"Now I can have babies."

Ruthie laughed. "Not on your own. Only by getting in bed with a boy, which you shouldn't yet think about for a hundred years." Leaving her to put on the pad, Ruthie skipped off to the kitchen, humming.

Naomi could not see why her getting blood in her panties made Ruthie feel bouncy. Maybe it was because Ruthie wanted to have babies, not for years, but she wanted babies. Naomi did not think she did. She wished she could tell Rivka that, for she had used to think they were so adorable that whenever she saw a mother pushing a pram, she would stop and make a fuss. Rivka said that was disgusting and gooey. Now since Naomi was around babies every afternoon from the time she got off school until their mothers got them, she had grown disillusioned. Mess and caca, crying and falling out of chairs, throwing their food on the floor, that was the rule.

Naomi loved the sound of the word, disillusion. She imagined a veil being ripped away. "I am disillusioned," she said out loud. After all, now she was a woman. She would never again pick her nose and put the boogers under the seat. She would master eating with the fork in the right hand the way Americans did. She would stop sneaking Murray's letters from Ruthie's underwear drawer and reading them. Now that she was a woman, she could no longer act like a child. Everything she did counted now, and she must start to behave properly and bravely and be bien rangée.

She sat on the edge of Ruthie's bunk and practiced sitting like a mature woman. The pad was uncomfortable between her legs. She wondered how she could run with it chafing her thighs. She peered at her face in the small mirror over the dresser they shared. She tried giving herself a languorous look, such as women threw at men in the movies. The words were hard for her to follow still. Then she squinched up her right eye, made her left eye big and round and bared the teeth on one side of her mouth only. That was her best witch face. Sometimes Rivka used to say maybe they would grow up and be witches. That sounded like fun.

Had Rivka started? She closed her eyes and tried to feel her twin, but she couldn't. Six o'clock. It was midnight in Paris so Rivka must be asleep. It would have been so fine if she and Rivka had each other to talk to: then she would know whether she was happy or displeased. When you have a twin, you are never lonely, unless you are separated, and then nobody ever understands what is missing but you.

She had a moment of bleak anger at her parents for separating them. It had not been supposed to be for long. Papa had got an Ausweis that enabled him to travel to the Vichy zone along with papers and a carte d'identité belonging to a man named Antoine Saligny, who had business in the south. The Ausweis included a daughter, but only one. Antoine Saligny had suffered a heart attack before his Ausweis had come through, and Papa had bought the papers. He had intended to take Jacqueline, who refused to leave with the exams for her baccalauréat just coming up. Papa had chosen Naomi as the next eldest—she had been born fifteen minutes earlier than Rivka.

Papa's idea was to get a job in the Vichy zone and then to bring down the rest of the family. That turned out to be more difficult than they had imagined. There was no telephone service between the two Frances. The only mail they could send were postcards you bought and checked off a given message. In order to go back and forth, you had to get a permit. The Vichy French were rushing to pass anti-Jewish laws to equal the Nazis. When Papa saw a chance to ship her to the United States, he had decided to move her to safety.

So Papa had stayed in the south of France while she found herself flying alone to New York where she was met by a woman from the Joint (American Jewish Joint Distribution Committee) and put alone on a train for Detroit. She had never in her life been as miserable as those five days in which she had been on the plane going from airport to airport, to Casablanca and then to Martinique and then to New York, on the plane whose roaring filled her head for two days afterward. Her English had not proved to be as good as she had always supposed it, and half the time she could not tell what people were telling her to do or asking of her.

Sometimes she felt cast out by her family. Why should she be the one to be separated? Since the new war began, she had no more letters from Rivka and Maman and Jacqueline. She had only those moments she could not demand but could only accept when she felt her twin sharply from inside her.

Aunt Rose came in and kissed her. "All right, so I won't slap you, Ruth wants me to be modern and American. But you be a good girl now." Rose pinched her cheeks between her calloused and water-worn hands, smelling of onions. "Be a good girl for us and for your own mother, my dear sister Chava, who I know is always thinking of you."

Naomi nodded awkwardly. What was all this fervent wishing that she be good? Did G-d start counting when you had your first period? Maybe G-d didn't get mad at anything you did until then, but then it counted, every thought and every deed and every mitzvah performed or failed. She felt dismayed at the prospect of having to be really good. She changed the subject intentionally. "Did my mother, Chava, start at the same age as me?"

"You're twelve, right? The same age. Chava was already pretty then, already smart. I was the sensible one, I had to take care for the little ones. Your aunt Batya was the silliest, the most boy-crazy. Esther, she was only a little baby when I left. She's the one who married well. Both Esther and Batya married Balabans, from Kozienice also, but Batya married the handsome boy with no sense, while Esther married the one with the mill, and she keeps his books."

Naomi loved to persuade Aunt Rose to talk about the sisters. It made the connections real, that she was still in the same family however scattered they were across Europe and America.

At supper when she sat down to the table, a soup of onions and potatoes served with the dark bread Aunt Rose had sent her to buy at the bakery, Uncle

Morris looked at her with such a face of sadness and worry and amusement, she knew immediately Aunt Rose had told him. She wanted to throw down her spoon and rush out of the room. What restrained her was remembering how many such stupid scenes Jacqueline had put on, accusing Maman usually but sometimes Papa of being insensitive, of not respecting her, of making fun of her ideas. Bang. Down would go the spoon and back would go the chair and Jacqueline would storm off to shut herself in the salle de bains. What she did in there was a mystery. They would hear the water running wildly. When she came out she would look as if she had received some secret message; she would act smug, withdrawn, slightly exalted. She would look at them all sideways, as if to say, You who do not understand me will understand someday after I have done great things!

Naomi resolved she would not become silly like Jacqueline. Ignoring everybody, she ate her soup. The blood was not particularly impressive. She had bled far more with a nosebleed, as had Rivka when they had been carving their names in a chestnut tree and the knife slipped. She said instead, since everybody kept glancing at her surreptitiously, "There's something I'd like to know."

"What's that?" Ruthie asked, at the same time that Uncle Morris said, "Are you sure you don't want to wait till after supper and ask your aunt?"

"Why does everybody think it's funny or wrong if you want to be friends with a colored girl? Why does anyone care?"

Everyone in her new family looked upset, as if she had asked about something even more embarrassing than periods. "Your uncle Morris will explain," Aunt Rose said, while Arty and Sharon made faces as if the soup didn't taste good. Naomi decided she was never going to understand how to be an adult, even if she did bleed now. Uncle Morris said he would talk to her after supper, as if she had asked about something dirty. She gave up and ate her soup. It occurred to her that whenever she felt Rivka lately, Rivka was always hungry.

DANIEL 2

The Great Purple Crossword Puzzle

Daniel Balaban had always been a devotee of *The New York Times* crossword puzzle. During his years at City College, he had relished a competition with his cousin Seymour to see which of them could work it faster. The one done first would call the other to crow. However, he had never imagined that he would one day be working a giant crossword puzzle day and night under intense pressure with a sense of probable doom hanging over him.

Of course cryptanalysis—deciphering codes, in this case, in Japanese—was not the same as working a crossword puzzle, yet at times it felt so, for everything in the structure they were creating was interrelated; when they discovered one tiny piece, it could change other pieces guessed at and now rendered certain or incorrect.

In the spring when men from his program of crash Japanese instruction had begun to be called to Washington, Daniel had wondered increasingly what would be done with him. He had imagined interrogating prisoners on a tropical isle. Would he be sent overseas at once? He was in the second batch called up. In college he had been a C student, rarely roused to pursue excellence. Here he had outdone classmates who had studied Japanese for several years. He had never thought of himself as stupid, but neither had he considered himself brilliant. His cousin Seymour was the intellectual and his brother Haskel, the all-A student. Now he viewed himself with a new respect for his mind.

Then came the induction all at once and over his head into the OP-20-G office, where he was put to work on cryptanalysis with dispatch and a furious pressure from above. He was reminded of Haskel teaching him to swim by tossing him off the side of a pool at the Y. He was dropped into deep and choppy waters, in the midst of a fierce storm of incomprehensible office politics. Yet somehow he learned. He could not understand the purpose of this grim activity for some weeks, but he attempted to make his way.

Daniel felt out of place when first posted to Washington, to OP-20-G. Half of the staff were Navy career men, Annapolis graduates who had spent time in Japan as part of their training. Half were civilians, men and women whose vocation and identity were bound up with Japanese language and culture. Several of them were nisei or partly Japanese, a few were married to Japanese, but he did not share the suspicion of everything Japanese-American that characterized most Americans and was, indeed, the official government position. After the roundup and internment of Japanese-Americans, the Navy had to move their own nisei from the West Coast to Colorado, to protect them. Without them, the program would have been crippled.

He moved into the first room he could find in the overcrowded city, with a family of noisy Kentuckians who drove him crazy. Finally one of the men in his section asked him if he would like to share a tiny apartment out near Maryland in the Third Alphabet of streets, a long way from the Capitol and from work, but an apartment that would be his and Rodney's only. He accepted without seeing it. That was just as well, as it was dark, tiny and hot under the third-floor roof, a walk-up with a view of the next roof suitable for anyone wishing to launch an intensive study of pigeon mating habits.

They had only two rooms and a kitchenette. Rodney, who had found the apartment, had already claimed the bedroom. Daniel got the Murphy bed in the living room. That felt just like home, for it was as lousy a bed as he'd had in the Bronx. He decided to leave the Murphy bed in its closet and sleep on a mattress on the floor. One corner of their living room thus consisted of his mattress with a heap of odd pillows on it, including the woven bamboo lion headrest he had always had on his bed since Shanghai. Over it he hung the scroll he had bargained for with a friend's help in Soochow. "Very bohemian," Rodney grumbled, but as he did not want to give up the bedroom, matters remained stalemated. Rodney scarcely spoke to Daniel unless drunk, when he would maunder on garrulously about his problems seducing women.

Washington was not a vast cosmopolitan hive like New York and Shanghai, not a center of intellectual life like Boston. It was an overgrown southern city that moved at half the pace of New York. Many of the younger men and women went bareheaded, while everyone in New York wore hats. There wasn't a skyscraper in town. Everything was segregated and marked for colored or white. It struck him as not only rude but silly, close to hysterical behavior. The colored population of Washington was large and seemed quite varied, although almost universally ill-housed, some in what were called alley houses, built behind the houses on the street in a teeming warren that made him think of the seamier parts of Shanghai.

Every day he took the streetcar to the Navy Building at Eighteenth and Constitution Avenue, went past the Marine guards up to the third deck—the first thing he had had to learn here was to call floors decks, walls bulkheads and other Navy nonsense—and checked into signals intelligence. OP-20-G was not a quiet place of intense study, not a happy family, not a place where you were welcomed in and shown your part as a jolly cog in a great operation. It was a nut farm. People who had been there before the war seemed to feel guilty that Pearl Harbor was to some large extent a Navy fuck-up and thus a naval intelligence fuck-up. They worked in a frenzy. Their boss screamed, yelled, rushed them, hovered to make sure any conversation occurring was in regard to work and work only. In one corner sat the former head of the department, with Pearl Harbor hung around his neck like the albatross about the ancient mariner. No one wanted to look at him, and he seemed to have little to do besides an endless postmortem report.

Daniel had no idea how he came to inherit being liaison, a fancy word for messenger boy, to William Friedman, but the previous contact person had been sent out to the Hypo unit in Pearl Harbor, where there was another cryptanalytic unit. Nobody explained that to him. Nobody actually explained that what they were working on were Japanese codes. The unit seemed to operate under the same assumptions with which he had noted Boston street signs were erected: as a notation to those who knew already, and with a clear suspicion of strangers, a rooted conviction that if you didn't already know where you were, you had no business being there.

William Friedman headed the Signals Intelligence Service in the Army, down one building along the Mall in another maze of rooms called the Munitions Building, up and back on the third floor there—where floors were floors. Daniel liked going over. Friedman was a paternal figure, not only to him but to his own people. He was not a jolly father but a cool, remote, omniscient father, who saw carefully to the training of his personnel. His desk and his mind appeared always in order. Daniel found the atmosphere in the Army signal intelligence unit at once bracing and soothing. They worked just as hard as the Navy, but the atmosphere was clear, rational and benign.

Friedman was a small neatly made dapper man, a wearer of spats, elegantly tailored three-piece suits, shoes that shone not brightly, for the leather was too fine and supple, but with an inner glow, like old money: but Friedman was a Jew. He had been born in Kishinev, in what was now the Soviet Union, and emigrated as an infant. He spoke with no accent other than an *o* sound Daniel associated with Pittsburgh. Friedman was a genius. The very vocabulary in which Daniel's new profession was discussed had been coined by Friedman, down to the term that described his job: cryptanalyst.

Friedman had a wife, Elizabeth, who was almost as renowned as he was, generally ranked second in that profession they had mostly invented. They had been in Washington since the twenties, setting up codes for most government departments needing them, from the Army to the Treasury and Coast Guard and Colonel Donovan's new swashbuckling intelligence operation. They had broken codes and served as witnesses in numerous trials. Friedman was reputed tight with his wife, crazy about her. No hint of scandal had ever touched their intimacy. But Friedman had been discharged from the Army before Pearl Harbor and was now a civilian. It was said that the strain of breaking the Japanese diplomatic code, called Purple, had caused him to have a nervous breakdown, and the Army had chosen that moment to punish him for his eccentricity and style. Whatever it was, there was something faintly sad about Friedman, Daniel thought, as if he had seen too much—a philosophical sadness underlying the austere and ceaseless brilliance.

Friedman had looked hard at him the first time he arrived as errand boy, a shrewd glance Daniel suspected was related to the Navy having picked one of the few available Jews to send to Friedman. Then Friedman had seemed to take several mental steps backward and judge Daniel carefully in their next few encounters. Finally he had become interested in him: not friendly, exactly, although there was a friendliness in that regard. Friedman was a man who used formality as a weapon, as in this military milieu, he must often need protection. Jew-baiting and anti-Semitism were rampant in Washington. Daniel sometimes wondered whether only the small number of Jews kept the city from establishing a third category of lavatories and schools.

It was the end of April before he began to understand what they were really doing, even as he noticed Washington changing around him, bristling with uniforms and suddenly years younger in its street crowds. Nobody read him into the large picture; it seemed to be policy not to. He had to infer the meaning of their work as he had to build up the meaning of the partially deciphered messages he must complete deciphering if he could and translate.

The Japanese used a machine to do their coding for them, a machine with many rotors. None of them had ever seen this machine. Signal intelligence consisted of plucking radio signals from the air and noting them down. Friedman's group had succeeded in building a working facsimile of the Purple machine late in the summer of 1940, and had begun to break the code. Purple was only one code. The Japanese army and navy used a multitude of other codes, which must also be broken. However, Purple was the diplomatic code, a mine of information on Japanese intentions and thought processes and observations worldwide. The Navy and the Army had been working on Purple decrypts alternate days, then sharing their results. Daniel spent his working life staring at clumps of letters that read like this:

XYBLG IRGUB NZZCU IRFLB USKLM

He was sorry when the Joint Chiefs decided the Navy should abandon Purple deciphering to the Army, because that meant he would not see Friedman regularly. He had a crush on the dapper little man with the formal manner and the air of not quite belonging. He was glad he had something good to carry to Friedman, the latest from the Baron Oshima, the Japanese ambassador in Berlin. Oshima's wires home to Tokyo were an excellent source of information on the Germans, for since the Tri-Partite Pact had been signed between Germany, Italy and Japan, the Nazis had been showing Oshima their preparations and war plans. The baron was the best agent the Americans had in Berlin. Through Oshima, they had known in advance that Hitler was planning to invade the Soviet Union, Daniel learned, but American attempts to warn the Soviets had been stymied by Stalin's absolute refusal to believe.

Friedman was sitting at his desk with his lips pursed staring into inner distance, his small fragile-looking hands playing with a pencil. When Friedman finally noticed him, he seemed almost embarrassed to have been so abstracted, but he had trained Daniel as well as his own staff not to bother him when he was working through a problem. Daniel would have stood there all day sooner than interrupt.

"When is your move scheduled?" Friedman asked, scanning the sheaf of papers rapidly. The Navy was moving to one girls' school, Mount Vernon, as Friedman's operation was moving to another, Arlington Hall. There seemed to be an excess of former finishing schools around Washington, Daniel thought idly. Perhaps all the girls had been finished off.

"We hope to move next month, if hope is the word. There aren't even screens on the windows out there."

"Then you'll have more employees than you counted on, and ninety-nine percent of them will have six legs and bite. You should equip yourself with a good entomological field guide and enjoy the swarm."

Daniel was not sure Friedman was joking, as his face remained sober, still scanning the runoff. He made some marginal notes. "I've just been thinking," he said, "that perhaps Jews are quick at learning languages, because we learn several early regardless of our place of birth."

Daniel felt a little rattled. He had been expecting a comment on the baron's wire, but Friedman's mind was running on Daniel's study of Japanese, which Friedman had told him he regretted not having the time to learn. Daniel adjusted. "Oh, you mean because of learning Hebrew. And Yiddish or Ladino or whatever is spoken at home. Then the language of the country. Within my own family, my father's four brothers and their families must speak ten languages. Maybe more." He started counting them mentally.

Friedman finished the sheaf. "This strikes me as more a wish list of Hitler's than anything real, but I presume it's gone up through channels?"

"Yes, sir, of course."

"You've been working on Purple since you arrived. Too bad we can't simply transfer you over here."

"I'd love that," Daniel said frankly. "More than anything. But I can just imagine the Navy saying, Sure, go work for the Army. We'll transfer you tomorrow because it's a rational choice."

"Sometimes they behave as if their worst enemies are the other forces." Friedman sighed. "They used to be poor relations, all the services, going to Congress cap in hand asking for fodder for their mules and paint for their old rusting ships. They've taken to power in an amazing fashion."

"Doesn't war automatically do that? Give all power to the military?"

"The British and the Soviets haven't given over ultimate power to the military, but the politicos run the show—whether for good or ill. Alone among the allies, we leave what ought to be decisions of political policy to the generals."

Dismissed, Daniel went back happy. At least Friedman would take him if he could, and that was the highest compliment he had ever received. Later that same day he saw Friedman standing with a group of the top Army brass outside the Munitions Building, three and four star generals all hefty, beefy men, with whom he had obviously just been at some quasi-historic meeting. Friedman was standing to the side with a slightly bemused half smile. He looked as if he had wandered among the generals by accident, a sleek Oriental cat, a Siamese, caught suddenly among a herd of snorting bulls, careful to avoid their hooves and not sure in what language to address them. Yet Daniel knew that when Friedman gave the military a presentation, they listened. He did in fact know how to talk to them so that they understood, for he had been educating their officers for years. He had created their whole educational system in signals and codes.

Getting rid of Purple did not lessen the pressure in OP-20-G; the tension increased until the office was shimmering with it. It was as if a high-pitched voice whined out of the ceiling, *Got to, Got to, Got to,* all the time. They must crack the Japanese naval codes yesterday; they must decipher and translate those vital messages. So much of the American fleet had been destroyed at Pearl Harbor, there was not one battleship to fight with and only four aircraft carriers. Admirals King and Nimitz had to know what the Japanese were going to do before they did it, so they could move their few pieces across the vast blue board to the right spot. Even then they would be outgunned, but without that advance knowledge, they would have no chance at all of preventing further Japanese invasions.

Therefore they worked without ceasing, shorthanded until more young officers should be discharged from the language programs in Boulder and Harvard. Therefore they worked all night. Therefore they worked a seven-day week. Therefore Daniel found himself sitting one Saturday night in a restaurant with a menu of southern cooking before him trying to decode it and unable to believe it meant what it said and unable to remember what those words that seemed to be dissolving into component letters and then into black marks might stand for.

The tension got to everyone. The normally soft-spoken Rodney threw his dictionary on the floor and swore, while the hotter tempered crypt-analysts spat insults at each other. One of the older women, Sonia, wept and Ann barricaded herself behind a wall of books in self-protection over which her sleek Oriental beauty could no longer be glimpsed. Ann never lost her temper; she merely shrank from the excesses bursting like ripe boils. Several people had requested transfers, and some of the Navy men got them, heading happily for an assignment on a ship and action.

A naval engagement was occurring, the few American ships trying to block a Japanese invasion of Port Moresby on the southern coast of New Guinea, only three hundred miles from Australia. The OP-20-G unit had broken enough of the Japanese Naval Code (nicknamed Red) to know roughly what the Japanese were planning, and had given advance warning to Admiral Nimitz. Nonetheless during the battle that the papers dubbed the Battle of the Coral Sea, they could decipher few Japanese messages. Even when the battle was over, it seemed inconclusive to people in the unit, at the same time that they realized the Japanese Navy was planning a new and bigger action. The papers called the battle a victory, but OP-20-G knew how desperately the Navy needed a victory. This did not seem to have been it, but it wasn't a disaster. The Japanese invasion was averted. Maybe they had to settle for celebrating nondisasters.

The best thing about that battle was that with so many intercepts piled up, enough evidence accumulated to break through many code groups in the next month. The atmosphere in the office was a barely controlled hysteria, because now they knew exactly what they were working toward, and they had demonstrated to the Navy brass, who tended to mistrust their work, that they were not only useful but necessary. That did not diminish the pressure, for their deadline had been set by Yamamoto himself, the great Japanese sea lord who had conceived of and led the Pearl Harbor attack.

Yamamoto was at sea on the flagship *Yamato*, and from that ultramodern battleship, he gathered two hundred other ships for a forthcoming attack intended to finish wiping out the American fleet. By mid-May, between Washington and the Hypo unit in Pearl Harbor, they could read ninety percent of the relevant signals. So far Daniel had counted five carriers, eleven battleships, sixteen cruisers and forty-nine destroyers. The Americans had three carriers, zero battleships, eight cruisers and fourteen destroyers. On the large map, colored pins marked the latest known positions of the converging Japanese forces. The Hypo unit invented a ploy that proved the Japanese were invading Midway for sure.

Slowly as the codes began to be transparent to them, so did their work make sense to Daniel. Messages went out by radio. If the Americans could read Japanese signals, they would know as soon as the Japanese officers what the Japanese were going to do. Finally the immense amount of work done round the clock in this cranky place began to have some payoff, because most of those strange five-letter clumps now meant something concrete.

June third the battle began, as OP-20-G and Hypo had told Nimitz it would, and Daniel with all the others waited in the grey room heaped with IBM run-off from the machines upstairs. They had broken so many of the codes used in battle after the Coral Sea engagement that they were able to follow the fighting from Japanese signals. After hours of disappointing decrypts, Daniel wished they couldn't. Nothing but reports of ineffective attacks, easily beaten off. One attack after the other, but no damage reports, no damage at all, besides the Japanese reports of American planes shot down. B-17s from Midway attacked the Japanese vessels and did no damage. American fighters attempting to drive off Japanese carrier bombers were decimated by the superior Zeros. B-26s roared off Midway and failed to touch the Japanese. Then the Avengers and Devastators from the two American carriers began to arrive over the Japanese ships, launch their bombs, miss and be shot down. A raid of Vindicators came over from Midway, with identical results. Daniel thought, picking up the club sandwich a yeoman had brought him and putting it down again untasted, we're going to lose this war. I'll never go back to the Orient. It will be closed to us for a generation. We're losing. We started too late with too little.

They could read the Japanese signals and tell the Americans what Yamamoto was planning, but OP-20-G could not make the American torpedoes explode, as they were failing to do; could not correct problems with the planes; could not give them more warships or pilots as experienced as the Japanese. To judge by the total wipeout of the first torpedo squads sent against the Japanese carriers, it did not look as if American pilots would survive long enough with their ineffective torpedoes and less maneuverable planes, the clumsy Devastators, to get that experience.

Then came a message from the captain of the *Akagi*, one of the Japanese carriers: his carrier had been badly hit and was burning. "We got one," Daniel cried out, and everybody cheered as if it were a baseball game coming over the radio, the Senators for once beating the Yankees. The Dauntless dive bombers had arrived from the American carriers.

They were still talking about the hit when a yeoman handed him another note. He glanced at it quickly. "I've already seen this one, Yeoman."

"Sir . . . that's not the same one." The yeoman swallowed.

Daniel looked again. One group different. This time it was the *Kaga* that was hit. Something astonishing was happening on the other side of the world, something which they, with their lists of five- and four-letter groups and constant poring over Japanese dictionaries and special lexicons of Japanese naval terms, had miraculously prepared for. The Americans had surprise on their side and for once they appeared to be winning. Daniel realized from his dazed shock that he had not expected a good outcome; perhaps they had all grown accustomed to defeat. People looked at each other across the office far more openly and frankly than they previously had, before they bent to their usual frenzied tasks.

Ann, barricaded behind books for months, removed part of the barrier. When he smiled at her, she blinked quickly and then gave him a tiny flash of smile before lowering her eyes. How delicate she was, how special and fragile. In the midst of the battle, Daniel paused wondering how he could penetrate those formidable defenses. She seemed an exquisite princess from *The Tale of Genji*.

The atmosphere of barely suppressed guilt that had hung over the office dissipated, and the humid air of a Washington June felt more breathable. Everybody was suddenly addressing each other by name and looking each other in the eye. Sonia offered him half of her roast beef sandwich, while Rodney grinned at him. Sometime in the half hour between the message of the *Soryu* being hit and the message of its having been abandoned to sink, the people in the long room began to feel less like souls condemned to hell together, Daniel thought, and more like a team. They began to be proud of their work and each other. This battle was their victory too.

The Creature from the Logey Swamp

Jeff had learned to shoot when he was fourteen. The Professor had not taught him; indeed his father had not approved. Jeff was lonely but did not always want to be hanging around with the other faculty brats. After his mother's death, he began wandering out into the surrounding countryside sometimes on his bike, sometimes hitching a ride on the running board of a rickety Model T along a gravel road, sometimes riding in the back of a farmer's pickup. He sought escape, and hanging around with kids on the hill farms had given him a ticket out from his misery. There he was no longer shy, because they did not know him as shy and bookish. He was free to assume a more adventurous spirit. He was special, the one full of ideas, a leader who could think up new adventures in an environment overfamiliar to the other boys.

He learned every side road and trail in the hills, which represented escape, adventure, companionship, which gradually he began to love with first a pencil, then watercolors, finally with oils. Perhaps his need to possess and celebrate that landscape had made him a painter.

He had learned to shoot and although it had always remained difficult for him to kill birds and animals, he did so because it was expected and the price of not being accepted was being cast out of his chosen adventure. Deer he would not hunt, but he went out with his friends for ducks and geese and shot rabbits and squirrels. He preferred skeet shooting, which he took up in college. Zach was a decent shot, but Jeff was better. Because he had borrowed so many rifles and shotguns over the years from other people, he was good at picking up the peculiarities of a weapon and allowing for them. When he was working on the dude ranch, Quinlan had him show off with a Colt .44 for the delectation of the guests and occasionally give lessons in target shooting.

It remained for the Army to punish his long flirtation with firearms, for he was stuck in Alabama bored to the intellectual level of the fungus growing between his toes and his ears, drinking far too much and feverish with some minor bug he had caught, a recurrent fever that weakened him but never quite laid him out. He was an instructor in the M-1 rifle. His classes arrived and left, but he was growing moss on his back.

The one redeeming feature had just been shipped out, his nurse Betty Jo who outranked him a full grade. She was a redhead from Tennessee who could also outdrink him, the hard-talking brown-eyed daughter of a coal miner. Betty Jo glared at the world through eyes a little slitted and lips a little sucked in until she took her shoes off, and then a ribald affectionate self emerged surprising as her soft body under the uniform. He had met Betty Jo when one of his riflery students winged his arm. The soldier had not been able to understand why Jeff had not had it in for him after the accident.

She had been lonely too. Jeff figured out why the Army made all nurses officers. She could not go out with any of the enlisted men, for regulations forbade that mixing. Therefore making them officers was a way of keeping the nurses off-limits sexually to anyone except male officers. Sometimes the Army moved in mysterious ways, but sometimes their intent was brutally clear.

Now she was gone, leaving Jeff depressed. His life appeared a series of stagnant lagoons connected by barely moving sewers. When he had first enlisted he had thought a great deal about violent death, but now he thought of perishing of boredom and inertia, rotting through like a log sunk in the swamp waters. Summer had never been his favorite season, and summer here came in April. Muggy was a permanent condition.

He was sourly amused to remember that he had told Bird he was attracted to a more verdant, more southern landscape. At first he had tried to sketch here, but paper and canvas alike wilted and rotted. His commanding officer made his life miserable, calling him Hey Rembrandt. Finally inertia overcame him and he did not think of light or color. He ceased to wake in the morning with that sense of possession, of shapes looming in the mind, of sharpening hues. He never saw paintings and he never painted. He was an animal, not even a dog or a raccoon, but low and somnolent as a salamander in rotting leaves.

He asked for a transfer and nothing happened, and indeed, the Army disposed of second lieutenants much as he dealt with used razor blades. Thus he was astonished when a letter came to him from an unknown Captain Cunningham inquiring if he wished to join the Office of Strategic Services and enclosing the usual quantity of Army application forms. He filled them out and shipped them off, wondering what they were talking about. In Army bullshit, Strategic Services could be delivering the mail or organizing recreation for the brass.

Nothing would come of this latest attempt to escape the water moccasin farm to which he had been posted.

Ten days later his commanding officer called him in. "You've weaseled your way out, Rembrandt. I don't know who you know, but this sounds like some cushy Washington job shuffling paper."

His orders read very simply that he was to report to OSS in Washington on the following Monday. In the intervening time his CO gave him the dirtiest details he could invent, marching the men into the swamps for a day of jungle warfare and then a night of camping out, which Jeff considered simply a way to feed the mosquitoes. His fever rose until his teeth chattered in the heat palpable as a smothering wet wool blanket.

Monday in Washington he learned little more, except that OSS generated as much paper as the other sections of the Army, and that from the inside it was called OSS and never The OSS. He filled out his educational background on five different forms and his next of kin on six. A Major Cod gave him a stern address of welcome, stressing that the work he would be entering upon involved intelligence gathering behind enemy lines, and was of a confidential and highly dangerous nature, and that OSS training was both strenuous and hazardous, requiring stamina of mind and endurance of body. The major liked to speak in yoked phrases. Gathering that OSS was some sort of commando group, Jeff wondered why they had picked him.

He was driven out to a compound that looked as if it had been a country club. Tents were erected on what had clearly been tennis courts. The chief instructor, a Captain Spinnaker, prematurely balding, for he could not have been more than thirty, told him he would be assigned to Special Operations and in the meantime would be developing his skills in guerrilla warfare and in clandestine intelligence gathering.

Then Captain Spinnaker handed him a sealed envelope. Inside that envelope was another, also sealed. He began to expect that inside that would be another and another, until finally in the innermost packet would be a small pill, the instruction EAT ME, and he would turn into a butterfly.

Instead inside the second envelope was a note scrawled in a handwriting quite familiar.

Old Jeff:

Hear you had a thing going with an alligator you met at a wrestling match. Sorry to interfere, but Mother needs you, and alligators are notoriously fickle.

*You should find this outfit a bit more congenial intellectually and
socially. Do get through the training. Trust no one and keep your mouth
shut unless opening it to imbibe. Assume you are never free to make an
ass out of yourself until you are out of training, when like the rest of us
you can do so with impunity and great frequency.*

Z

That large Z did not stand for Zorro. So Zach was behind the sudden letter
of inquiry from Captain Cunningham and his transfer. Jeff wondered what Zach
had gotten him into this time; but what Zach had gotten him out of was clear in
his mind and he blessed his friend, wherever he was.

This new assignment, however wrapped in mystery that had an element of old
boys' games in it, seemed the first rational decision the Army had made about
him. Everyone in his group had command of at least one European language.
He spoke French excellently and could function in Spanish, Italian, German
and Greek. In addition he knew France as well as he knew Italy and Greece.
His OSS instructors seemed uncertain whether they were teaching him to be a
spy or a guerrilla combatant, but he felt either task was likely to keep his brain
functioning and his body alert. In Alabama, he had been dying.

The intermittent fever vanished in the healthier air of Washington. They had
classes during the day and exercises at night, stumbling through the woods to
sneak up on sentries waiting for them, attempting to seize an outbuilding supposed to be an enemy command post or blowing up with dummy charges a shed
supposed to be an ammunition dump. They ambushed vehicles that passed along
the nearby road and chased each other through the woods and over the golf
course growing up in knee-high grass. They practiced laying mines in the walls
of the swimming pool.

It was not exactly an interesting landscape, the white clapboard officers'
lounge and mess, the garages and hastily thrown up Quonset huts and outbuild-
ings expanded to new uses, but he found himself sketching the oaks in front of
the verandah, the glint of sunshine on the long lolling leaves of the magnolias.
No one called him pansy when he sketched.

Of the men in his group, he preferred two. Carey had been a poet published
in little magazines, Aaron had been an engraver. Both were fluent in French, and
the engraver Aaron knew Dutch because he had been Dutch, a Jewish refugee
whom relatives had sponsored into the United States after he had managed to
escape to Sweden. He had lived in safety for one year. He was five feet six, solidly
built with carroty hair that reminded Jeff of his nurse, Betty Jo, and catlike topaz

eyes. He was a striking-looking fellow but had no casual palaver. Even in the killing exercises, he was brisk but phlegmatic.

Carey talked enough for all of them. He had taught English in a girls' school in upstate New York, which he considered the North Pole. He came from the Shenandoah Valley in Virginia, although his mother, he told them whenever possible, was a Culter from Roanoke. He had been engaged to be married to his second cousin once removed, whom he had used to ride with, but she had dumped him and eloped with a Navy flier. He was absolutely delighted to be back in civilization, which began in Maryland and ran out after North Carolina, except for Savannah, which he did consider civilized, and perhaps Charleston, although he had dreadful relatives there, very yappy, like dogs.

Jeff thought that Carey was probably what Zach had taught him to call queer, but from him Carey only wanted a brotherly attention. Jeff had had sex with men occasionally, starting with mutual jerking off in a hayloft at thirteen. The only time he had really made love with a man was with Zach. He did not find sex with a man sensually pleasing and he suspected Zach did not find him compellingly attractive. Zach liked them rough and tough. He thought Zach had seduced him as a way of explaining his preferences and as a kind of droit de seigneur. Jeff loved Zach in his own way, and that brief bout of sexual connection when he had been twenty had been part of his education. Once in a while when he was down and out and drifting, he'd had sex with a man as a way of paying for a ride or a night's lodging. Having fucked men was part of his understanding, a code he had learned that made sense of things that would otherwise have slid past him.

So almost by default he had two buddies. Many of the men in training with them he thought of as future old boys: they belonged to the same fraternity. This ex-country club had a different atmosphere than the brutality and lowest common denominator steamroller of his first enlisted experiences, or the nitpicking and nastily competitive worm wiggling of officers training. Brains were not necessarily something to be beaten out of you. Maybe this was the misfits' service, he would think, and then notice the corporation lawyers and younger sons of bankers swarming through.

He was taught to use weapons not included in basic training, to kill silently with knife, fingers and even with a folded sheet of newspaper turned into an improvised dagger and stabbed into the stomach or the jaw just under the chin. They were taught to operate radios, to communicate in code, to read maps, to observe. Where were the arsenals? The storage depots for weapons and ammunition and oil? The tank facilities? Which railway lines were in active use, and what moved on them when? The anti-aircraft emplacements? Jeff was a poor radio operator, his transmissions slow and full of errors. He hated Morse code.

He excelled however at a test they were given when photos were flashed on the screen for twenty seconds with the subject's name, age, occupation and address printed under the face. The photos were then shown again for thirty seconds in random sequence as the students wrote down everything that could be recalled about that person. Jeff did not confuse the faces. "You look, but you do not see!" their instructor berated the students, but he did not say that to Jeff.

He started working with watercolors, a halfway house. He painted along the Potomac. He wandered the countryside in Virginia and found himself beginning to think in oils again, the colors, the texture.

Jeff was gradually getting some notion of the structure of OSS. It had started out as another organization altogether, the COI—the Coordinator of the Office of Information—but because Robert Sherwood and Wild Bill Donovan had not gotten along, now there was an Office of War Information handling propaganda and there was the organization whose long arm had saved him from the swamps, the Office of Strategic Services.

OSS had a branch, SI—Secret Intelligence—that ran spies. His branch was Special Operations and he supposed he would find out soon enough exactly what they did, with whom and where. R & A was the Research and Analysis branch, full of academics. MO—Morale Operations—generated what was called black propaganda, aimed at undermining enemy spirits. X-2 was counterintelligence. Another branch worked on secret weapons, invisible inks, gadgets.

His two months of training passed swiftly. Then he was granted forty-eight hours' leave before he was scheduled to take ship to England. He had to change trains in New York, and as he was hurrying from Pennsylvania Station to Grand Central, he wondered if he wasn't being foolish. Perhaps he should spend his last weekend with the woman he was sure he could find in New York. But no, he wanted to see Bird and he even wanted to see his father.

The temperature was hovering around a hundred; sweat drenched his uniform. He had to stand most of the way to Boston, but on the bus to Bentham he finally got a seat. OSS was looser than the rest of the Army, and he had actually been able to leave early and get a jump on his weekend.

He had wired home. The Professor and Bernice were both on the platform waiting. He felt grubby and half cooked, but Bernice handed him his swimming trunks and threw his gear in the back of the truck they had borrowed. "What happened to the Austin?"

"It's up on blocks for the duration. Bernice has an absurd idée fixe you would want to go straight to the pond to swim," his father said.

"That's the only thing that would revive me. Whose truck is this?"

Bernice, who was driving, answered. She was sunburned and grinning. "It belongs to a friend of mine at the field. You don't know how good it was for him to lend it to us, gas and everything! All I have to do is work on the wing of his plane where the fabric is damaged."

"Bernice is flying for the government three days a week," his father said with intense gloom. They bounced along in the cab of the pickup, squeezed together on the bench seat.

Bernice had written him all about her flights. "I'm getting a commercial license, Jeff, I really am. But I don't have enough hours for the WAF. They're only taking the best women pilots, women with hundreds more hours than me. But I'll get a commercial license this fall."

Lying on his back in Round Pond hearing the cries of the children like a flock of bright parakeets in the shallows, he felt memories pushing in. He was used to this pond and this swim was one of an open-ended series, forming a continuity with a hundred others over the years. He was seven-year-old Jeff splashing with his mother and sister. He was thirteen-year-old Jeff diving off the pier and gashing his hand open on a broken bottle. He was sixteen-year-old Jeff making out with Hilda Garfinkle in a canoe about to tip. He was nineteen-year-old Jeff lying on a raft with Zach and two girls from Smith drinking his first martinis, mixed by Zach. He was twenty-one-year-old Jeff under a quarter moon fucking Harriet Hacker on the Fourth of July while the fireworks went off across the water. He was twenty-five-year-old Jeff home recovering from a dose of the clap and a beating.

Will I die? he asked, and then, Sure, he answered himself. Everybody does. He tried to imagine his death and all he could come up with was a feeling of sinking into deep water, managing to remain awake as he fell asleep.

He thought briefly again of getting laid, and had begun to run over the list of potential candidates in the town, when he turned and began a purposeful crawl toward the raft where Bernice was sunning herself. The Professor was sitting on the shore at a picnic table reading. It was Bird's company he needed, but he could not really talk to her here. He remembered how voices carried over the water, remembered coming out of the water to hear behind him that little redhead out on the raft telling Zach she was afraid she was pregnant.

"Let's go back," he said. "I'm hungry. You have to feed me up." What he wanted was the two of them closeted in the kitchen, so he could begin to tell her how he had almost died in Alabama, how he had been swallowed up in mindless inertia. How demoralizing it had been to lose his energy, his vision, himself. How he had first stopped painting and then stopped drawing and lastly even stopped thinking like a painter. Who else could hear him confess that he had been losing all he valued in himself, that he had come to see himself as a fragile construction over a swamp of minor urges and exceedingly minor needs and irritations?

If he ceased to paint, he lost his past, which became not the wanderings of a misunderstood and unfashionable painter but simply the empty travels of a bum. If he ceased to paint, he lost his future, for who wanted to imagine a life doing odd jobs in odd places? He had never believed he could ever stop painting, yet he had. That frightened him.

He wondered if he should ship his French easel. OSS was generous with the luggage an officer could send. Probably too bulky. He would take the more expensive colors. Talking to her, with her good mind embracing his life, truly seeing it, he would come to understand. And accept. And go on. He would again feel himself to be a child of destiny and fortune, and the luck that had plucked him out of the swamp of inertia and the slough of despond, the luck momentarily called Zach, would assume other forms and beckon him forward.

JACQUELINE 3

A Star Shaped Like Pain

31 mai 1942

They have ordered us to begin to wear a yellow star at all times. We have to trade our precious textile coupons for the stars, as if we wanted such a thing or were willing to suffer cold and wear rags to afford such a star. JUIF it says in big black ugly letters, just in case anyone is too dense to grasp the point—any of the six points. The shade of yellow is particularly strident—and I never wear yellow. All of us over the age of six have to wear them on the streets and everywhere.

I have avoided going out more than I have to, but today I am determined to resume what passes for my normal life. We are being excluded from classes at the Sorbonne, so there goes my education. A letter came. The government of France in the interest of racial purity etc. I am writing this at the breakfast table over a big mug of some weed we have brewed up with a tiny bit of skim milk added. It tastes like the grass soup the twins used to make on summer vacations, to feed their dolls. No matter how people stare in the streets, I am going to do what I must and what I decide.

Same day: I felt immensely conspicuous, as if I were wearing a sign, LEPER, and indeed, people act that way. I have never had the sense of so many people looking away from me, pretending not to see me. That isn't the worst. The worst was those who turned toward me and either swore at me, threatened me or in one case, a nasty brute of a man who pushed me off the sidewalk. If the truck coming along the street had not veered, I would have been run over, for I sprawled right in front of the wheels.

5 juin 1942

Times like these make you value your friends. Just when I accuse myself of hanging out with my zazou friends just because I don't want to be relegated to the ghetto, and they are the only ones tolerant enough to put up with a Jew, they do something that makes me feel how real is the friendship of at least Céleste and Henri. They showed up at the Café Le Jazz Hot yesterday wearing big six-pointed yellow stars with GOY on them. Then on the way home, they were caught by a bunch of those Fascist PPF youth. They tore Céleste's clothes, throwing her down in the street, kicking her and breaking two ribs. Henri they took and shaved his head and beat him until he is a mass of bruises.

They are always beating up the zazous anyhow. A lot of young people are dressing like my friends, in dark glasses, loose jackets and tight trousers with their hair long and oiled, to drive the Fascists crazy. They say zazous are the ultimate decadents and that's why France lost the war, because we are all rotten and corrupt and jazz has destroyed our minds.

I stood in line from 5 till 8 A.M. this morning for bread. I am exhausted and I have decided to take a nap after I finish my philosophy lesson. A group of us who have been forced out of our classes are meeting three days a week. A third-year student is lecturing us from her class notes and Daniela Rubin is recruiting others. Professor Moussat, who was just denounced as a Jew and kicked out of the Ecole des Etudes Orientales, is going to lecture on Buddhist thought. I am not as fascinated as I might have been a year ago, but at least it is an education in something other than how to scrounge food scraps. Daniela and I are the energy behind this attempt, setting up a little school through which we hope to circumvent the attempt to keep us ignorant! She is a year older than me and had been planning to become a doctor. Oh, Daniela told me what happened to that Jewish Boy Scout who was going to secure us new identity cards: shot. He was part of a network smuggling Jews out of France to safety elsewhere. Now I am sorry we were not nicer to him, but we were suspicious.

After I finish my lessons, I am going over to visit Henri, although I feel very strange these days as I go uphill past the Sorbonne from which I have been driven. The reaction of our "fellow" students was along the lines of, Oh, I didn't know you were Jewish. They could have shut down the school, if they cared to strike over our dismissal. I wish I could bring Henri a present, but we have long since finished the little treats Naomi sent us.

On the street yesterday I was suddenly struck by how now you can tell someone's politics by their weight. That is, those who collaborate with the Germans are all plump and healthy-looking. They are eating real food—butter, eggs, chicken, even meat sometimes—and they have soap to wash with and some even have warm water. The rest of us are getting thinner and gaunter and dirtier. We Jews are the thinnest and most raggedy of all. We would be much worse off if it were not for my black market connections through Henri and Céleste.

6 juin 1942

If I trusted Maman even a little less, I would not dare make an entry today. But she has never invaded the privacy of my diary, and I don't believe she ever would. Nonetheless, I think it a good idea to carry it with me after this, just in case.

I did go see Henri, in the rue Royer Collard. He was in bed, sitting up with a great bandage around his head, his eye black and blue and hideously swollen, and his jaw swollen too where the PPF thugs had broken a tooth.

These Fascist games of beating up people in the street in packs appeal to some like a drug. It is a license to hurt with impunity. Henri says it is a form of infantilism gone amuck, but I think it is more sinister than that. Henri maintains that nothing is more sinister than armed babies in groups who want what they want when they want it and grab for it. He says that there were many people passing in the street, and nobody intervened, and that a flic came by, but when he saw who was doing the beating and who was the beaten, he turned and discreetly strolled away.

Albert was out this afternoon, making a deal for eggs. Henri and Albert share a room paid for mostly by Henri's father. His father, who runs a nightclub and never married his mother, gives him money. Henri says the nightclub is full of Germans, not only the Wehrmacht soldiers stationed here, but soldiers who come on leave from all over Europe for what they call Paris Bei Nacht. The Nazis have changed the names of the Sarah Bernhardt theater and every street in Paris named for a Jew and persuaded (easily) every publisher in Paris to stop publishing Jewish writers and to purge their lists, and there they sit slurping champagne and stuffing themselves every night in Henri's father's club and fifty similar while Offenbach's Can Can is played again and again as they ogle the spicy dancers. They can't have a cancan without music written by a Jew, so they pretend ignorance.

Henri and I have a taste for those kind of cheap ironies, like having a weakness for too sweet but irresistible bonbons. Then he took my hand and looked into my eyes the way he does and told me he had worn the star for me. He said he could not stand it anymore and now that his head was shaved and he was disfigured, if I would not sleep with him, he might as well give up and go off to Germany like Albert, who is being drafted for labor there, but he would go as a volunteer, and at least make some money.

"You're trying to blackmail me," I said.

"It's come to that," he said. "Tell me what to do and I'll do it. I'd even marry you, except it's illegal, of course."

"You wouldn't offer unless it was, Henri, but never mind, I consider marriage about as attractive as being a prostitute, and I do not care to be paid for my favors."

"It's your romanticism and sentimentality that drive me mad," he said.

"How can you think about fucking?" I asked him, using the vulgar word intentionally. "Here you can hardly sit up, you couldn't manage to walk down the stairs to the street, and you're rabid to deflower me."

"I can do that, even if my legs were cut off. Give me a chance." He kept pulling at me.

I realized what I have known for a time, that either I have to stop seeing Henri or I have to go to bed with him. I have kept him at bay for more than a year, but he is getting more importunate. I am not in love with him (or anyone else) but I am fond of him. I suspect I am basically a cold person as far as romantic love and romanticized sex go. I think it is self-hypnosis. I watch the women around me falling in love with what might as well be large playful or small scrappy dogs, amazed at how the brain simply turns off when the hormones start pumping through the body.

Marie Charlotte, who used to be my best friend and who was once mistaken for a Jew because she always went round with me, is now in love with a German lieutenant. Because he is one of the supreme conquerors and an officer, her family are permitting him to court her. They say it is honorable. I know all this because Marie Charlotte still waits for me and motions for me to follow her to our old gossiping spot in the little park Georges Cain right by our old lycée. There we sit among the broken statuary or under the ancient fig tree, as we used to. I decide again and again I will ignore her, but when I see her, I remember how close we were, and I cannot cut her off.

I am putting off saying what I did. I extricated myself from Henri's rather tight embrace, trying not to injure him. Then I sat down on a straight chair across the room. I was trying to figure out if I should leave and never see him again, but I like Henri a great deal, and without him and my other friends, we would be much hungrier. Rivka is so thin it worries me. By her age, I had begun menstruating and so had Maman, but Rivka has not started and her breasts are tiny as strawberries. She needs the extra food I bring home. What does it matter, finally? We may all be shipped off to unknown danger. I like Henri better than any man I have met, so why not him? I will always wonder what it is like otherwise, and never know.

Sitting in that chair, I said to him in a straightforward manner: "All right, Henri, listen. I will sleep with you. But not today. Recover from your beating first."

"But I'm recovered enough, I swear it, for that I'm recovered enough."

"But I swear I could not enjoy having sex with a man whom I was terrified every instant I would injure worse than the Fascist punks have. Do you want me to enjoy this, or don't you care?" A low argument, but one I did not doubt would be effective.

He assured me he was avid for my pleasure and intended to render me delirious with joy just as soon as I place myself in his bed. I reminded him that Albert is being called up for labor service at the end of the month. I do not care to have Albert as a witness. Privacy matters to me.

"You're just putting me off."

"Henri, have I ever before promised to sleep with you?"

He agreed that I had always refused.

"Now I am promising. After Albert leaves for Germany, you'll be healthy and hairy again by then—"

"You don't love me without my hair."

"Right now you look like an onion. But then I will do what you ask."

"That's less than a month."

I knew I had persuaded him. I also felt I had given God a chance to save me if God wants to, and fate, if fate is so inclined. So, my diary, I have given my promise. It is not that a simple membrane rather inconveniently placed means anything to me. It is that I feel myself to enjoy a certain clarity which I do not encounter in most women. They are always doing or refraining from actions or believing or disbelieving or coming or going because the man they are stuck to wants it that way. If I have to start sleeping with Henri, I am going to try to remain calm and clearheaded and never to believe because we put our bodies together, that makes him more intelligent than he is or some great genius.

6 juillet 1942

Today I kept my promise to Henri. The day Albert left, and we went to see him off, I got my period. I view it as my body's last attempt to stave off the inevitable. Today I had no further excuses. As must have happened to Scheherazade eventually, I ran dry, and my moment of truth arrived, but my king Henri did not show mercy.

I was too apprehensive to feel much except discomfort and some slight pain, but I imagine I will become accustomed to the sexual act and learn to enjoy it. It would be foolish not to, since I am obliged to perform the act; I might as well acquire some skill and involvement in it. I have many questions I wish to ask Henri, but I have observed that asking intelligent questions or wanting to discuss merely points of observation during the act tends to deflate him, so I will wait till he feels more confident with me.

I wanted particularly to examine his penis carefully, but while he wanted me to handle it, he did not seem to feel comfortable about my wish to explore it as an unfamiliar object. I imagine there will be time also to satisfy my curiosity in that regard.

I felt no ecstasy and the actual intercourse was on the painful side. I am bleeding heavily, just as if my period had come back, which is what I told Maman. Our bodies are so peculiar these days, with the diet or lack of it, that we are surprised by nothing out of the ordinary in terms of aches and pains and irregularities.

I am pleased that I can detect in myself no alteration in my feelings toward Henri. I do not feel visited by love as by an angel swooping down, I do not dream of him at night (I dreamed recently of Papa and constantly of food, and last night I dreamed I was taking an enormous hot bubble bath all by myself) and I do not have any more longing than usual to see him. I enjoy his company as before. Perhaps my worst fears will prove unfounded.

I made him use a condom, although he argued that pulling out before he came was sufficient, and that he was skilled at determining that point. I remember all the stories I heard at school about girls who got pregnant because their boyfriends were supposed to practice coitus interruptus, but didn't interrupt themselves fast enough. I will not budge on this point.

14 juillet 1942

I have just had the worst fight with Maman of my life. Henri has been giving me all sorts of presents since last week, six eggs, two kilos of potatoes and a whole shopping bag of green vegetables from his uncle's farm and finally a chicken. I thought Maman and Rivka would be very pleased. I'm sure they were, but then yesterday Maman started in about why was this generosity being visited on us. I turned her off with a joke and shut myself up in my studies.

Then this morning she stood in front of me with her arms on her hips and said, "Yakova, do not lie to me. Are you sleeping with this Henri?"

"Mother," I said, "first of all, my name is Jacqueline. That is my legal name, that is the name I use and that is the only name I answer to. Calling me Yakova is simply a ploy to try to make me feel like a child.

"Second, I never lie to you. I have too much respect for both of us. When you have asked me in the past, I have always answered truthfully. I would prefer you not question me on the subject, as it is my own decision and private to me."

"Are you sleeping with him?" she repeated.

"Yes I am," I said.

She slapped me and called me a whore! She said she did not want his food and she went so far as to throw some potatoes on the floor. She told me I was confined to the flat and was never to see Henri or any of those low-life friends again. I said that was total nonsense and that I had an appointment with him that I meant to keep. He was my friend, who had been beaten out of solidarity with me, and we could use all the friends we could get. I did not tell her that Céleste and Henri and I were expecting to pick up copies of a new clandestine newspaper today as part of the illegal celebration of Bastille Day.

She slapped me again, repeatedly, and I believe she was totally out of control. We both commenced to shriek at each other like real whores in the street. Finally I locked myself in the bathroom for half an hour until I had regained control, during which time she pounded on the door until the neighbors must all have heard her. Then I packed a few things into my old knapsack and came over to rue Royer Collard, where I remain.

I am furious with her. She made absolutely no attempt to understand my point of view, thus demonstrating a complete lack of respect for my judgment and my character. Her tirade was ugly and insensitive. The simple truth is, if I did not have Rivka and Maman to worry about, I would probably never have become entangled with Henri. That reminds me that I must keep Henri from reading this diary, as I do not think he is as scrupulous in such matters as I had always supposed Maman to be. Now I wonder, frankly.

As of tomorrow, by the way, the idiots have new ideas how to torment us. We are forbidden to go into restaurants, cafés, libraries, museums, to use public telephones, and we are supposed to ride only in the last car of the Métro. We are forbidden many shops altogether and only supposed to shop between four and five, when everything is sold out anyhow, on certain days. While I am staying with Henri, I have removed my yellow star, as of course our cohabitation is forbidden, and I am not about to go home until Maman apologizes for the way she slapped me (repeatedly) and the unfeeling names she called me. I am quite firm about this. I have done nothing shameful and I am not ashamed—except of how she is treating me!

This is not a good solution, as if I stay with Henri, I must remove the yellow star, but my identification—for which we are standardly asked twenty times a day—has JUIVE stamped on it in big red letters.

I have become somewhat more accustomed to having sex with Henri. He always asks me if I have come, and I say truthfully that I don't think so, but that I don't know what it would feel like if I did. However, I have begun to enjoy the preliminaries. Kissing and caressing need not be viewed as necessarily sentimental pleasures, but taken on their own for their sensual content, I find.

Living with Henri is not comfortable, however. I have my routines with Maman and Rivka. It is easier to study at home and I could only take with me what I carried on my back. I miss my books, my easy chair, my café au lait cup with the sea gulls that Papa's copain Georges brought back from Denmark. Henri is not much of a housekeeper, and the WC in the hall is disgusting. This building is composed of tiny one- and two-room apartments, several let to prostitutes whose clients thunder down the steps all night. I am going to give Maman a day or two to cool off, and then I will appear, my own sweet reasonable self, and see if we can make peace.

The scene haunts me in its irrational ragged quality, the violence loosed in both of us—her striking me and throwing down the potatoes, and the violence of our emotions. I wonder why I could not remain calm, which had been my intention, but the more she grew excited, the more excited I grew in return, a vicious loop. Every time I think of that ugly scene, I am aghast at how we acted, how we lost our dignity and how we failed to communicate. I am resolved that we will be at peace again, but on decent terms.

16 juillet 1942

I almost cannot write. I have been weeping so long my eyes are swollen and raw and my sinuses completely blocked.

Maman and Rivka have been taken away in a bus by the police—not by themselves but with thousands and thousands of others. They sealed off five arrondissements yesterday and continuing today, the French police—apparently almost a thousand of them from what we have been able to learn—arrested huge numbers of Jews, including men, women, children, old people, little babies, pregnant women, everybody. The police forced people to leave with just what they could carry and loaded them on the old green buses. One paper says ten thousand Jews were arrested, another paper says eighteen thousand, another paper says twenty-eight thousand. All the papers think it is a wonderful idea and are full of praise of the New Europe cleansed of such lice as ourselves.

I am too sick and exhausted to write anything else.

18 juillet 1942

All of my efforts have been spent trying to find out where Maman and Rivka are being kept, and what is going to happen to them. I do not see how they can touch Rivka as she is born here, a French Jew from birth. Maman was naturalized twenty years ago. It turns out to be very dangerous to try to find out where Maman and Rivka are, because of course my name too is on whatever list they are using to pick people up, and that I escaped was only due to a quarrel. I wish I was with them, lending my level head to the circumstances and figuring out the best strategy to pursue.

It is incredibly hot this week, la canicule. Paris is not designed for fierce summer heat. Henri's room is simply too hot to sleep in. We have been getting up and going out very early, down to the river where it is a little cooler. There is danger in being on the streets when so few are about. Henri has begun working over his black market connections to get me new identification—Aryan, as they say.

But new identity cards will cost a lot. I have no money at all. I am discovering I dislike intensely being dependent on Henri, and Henri too is astonished how fast the situation developed. I do not think he wants me living with him, although he has said nothing. At first he thought it was great, but now the ramifications of the situation are beginning to impress themselves upon him. Here he is stuck with me, a Jew, in hiding, no means of support, kicked out of school, weeping constantly.

19 juillet 1942

I have discovered where Maman and Rivka are imprisoned. They took everybody with children to the Vel d'Hiv, a glass-roofed track with big grandstands where bicycle races are held in the winter. I have learned thousands of people are being confined there. Perhaps they are sorting through everybody's identity cards. Rivka was born here, and Maman was naturalized when she was eighteen, and married moreover to a native French Jew. I am counting on hearing that they are released, but so far no one seems to have been let go. I cannot learn what they are being held for.

20 juillet 1942

I ran into Daniela, so she escaped too. She said she had word via the network just before it happened, so that she and her parents fled their flat at 3 A.M. with nothing. They slipped out just ahead of the police dragnet.

She says that I could pass with good identification, and that she knows where to get it. In the meantime I must have money. Once I have non-Jewish identification, she can get me a job in a hospital, badly paid but sufficient to live on. I must come up with the money for the papers fast.

I went home and asked Henri to tell his father that he had made a young girl pregnant, and to ask him for the money for an abortion. I felt his father would give it to him, along with a lecture neither of them would believe a word of. Henri was frightened but agreed. He is feeling very out of his depth. He did not even want to have sex with me. This is not a stable situation in my estimate.

Daniela has agreed that we must try to find out what is happening to our people in the Vel d'Hiv. We have formally disbanded the school. We both believe that creating visible Jewish organizations is just lining up to be picked off. Daniela says that we must resist, but so far she has not said how. I consider that a lot of hot air, the equivalent of an angry and powerless child saying to someone who has hurt her, I'm going to get you. I'm going to show you.

21 juillet 1942

What little we have been able to learn is terrifying. They say at least one hundred thirty bodies have been carried out of there, including two pregnant women who apparently died in labor. We hear that at least fifteen thousand people, including five thousand children, are being kept without food or water. I cannot believe this, I cannot believe the French police are doing this to my mother and my sister, and yet I cannot disbelieve. I cannot eat or sleep. I am keeping a vigil.

Henri goes today to talk to his father. At this moment I do not care if I live or die. If I had not given in to Henri, I would never have quarreled with Maman and I would be with her now. I feel as guilty as the Nazis, I feel as if somehow I did this to Maman. I wish a large truck would run over me in the street.

Maman is right. I am nothing but a whore, fucking for potatoes and eggs and a few kind words in the midst of a city seething with hatred. Among all the people who were on the streets and saw whole families being carted away by the police, no one tried to help, no one tried to stop them. I have heard that some of the neighbors yelled encouragement at the police including the Laroques whose dog we always fed when they were out of town.

Six days without food or water so far, how can they survive? Maman is strong, but she is thirty-nine and made of flesh and blood. Rivka is wiry but still a child and already malnourished.

If I could give them my blood to drink, I would do it without a word.

Such a Roomy Closet

"Shall we take a walk?" Oscar Kahan said, as if it were a usual request. "It's such a beautiful day. As it were." He added the last comment with a grin because the day was hot and soggy, the sort of day when Abra remembered summers in Maine with nostalgia. Staying in New York in the heat felt sometimes as if it were masochism.

She followed him, imagining herself a character in a comic strip, a Daisy Mae with a huge question mark floating over her head in a balloon. Never before had Oscar Kahan asked her to take a walk. She had discovered herself fantasizing about him lately, and had been toying with the idea of abandoning her policy of never becoming sexually involved at work. Her policy, after all, was based on caution rather than morality. What was the use, anyhow, of throwing her own code over, when Oscar Kahan treated her with the same unfailing but nigh universal warmth he spread over all of his students? She was aware she had taken lately to arranging herself in positions designed to emphasize the line of her calf, her profile, her bosom, but if Oscar Kahan noticed, he did not act upon what he observed. Until now.

They left his office and headed westward, toward the river. As they strolled, he questioned her about recent interviews and commented on others, impressing her as always with his grasp of the large pattern and the small detail. Maybe he simply wanted some fresh air, although she did not think there was any to be had nearer than Connecticut. Perhaps the warm weather made him restless. Perhaps having grown up in Pittsburgh, he was accustomed to smog, and actually found the stinking air of Manhattan in summer bracing.

In Riverside Park, he took a bench somewhat isolated from the others, with a view of ships in the river and a couple embracing on the grass. He glanced around, taking in the scene, and then gave her a hard appraising look. "I won't be teaching in the fall."

There goes my job, she thought. "Where are you going, if you don't mind my asking?"

"Have you considered getting more involved in the war effort?"

He's managed to enlist, I bet. "I thought about the WAVES—the Navy's my family's branch of service—but I can't imagine myself marching around saluting. I'm too much of a spoiled brat for military discipline."

"Yet you take orders."

"You know that's not the same thing."

He stared intently at the tug maneuvering a stolid grey freighter upriver. "I'm planning to recruit you. But not for the WAVES."

She glanced sharply at him. He smiled. "Don't look so shocked. It doesn't become you. You know perfectly well you've been involved in intelligence work. You figured that out long ago. Now I'm officially joining OSS—the Office of Strategic Services. I'd like to take you with me."

Finally there it was in the open. "What is OSS?"

"A bit of everything, actually. Propaganda, intelligence, spying. I know mostly Research and Analysis people."

"Where would we be going?"

"For the moment, noplace but into another office. Later on, who knows? I don't want to discuss details before you make up your mind. I'll be running a little project and I have carte blanche to bring as much of my staff with me as I choose."

"Of course!" Abra said. "Of course I'll do it."

"You don't even know what you're getting into."

"Oh, but I'm sure it will be interesting. I have confidence in you."

"Did you ever finish up your degree?"

"Not exactly. I completed my class work and passed my orals, but I'm still rewriting my dissertation to Professor Blumenthal's criticisms."

"You'll have to put it aside for the duration."

"I'm not thrilled with rewriting it for the fourth time. Does it matter that I don't have my doctorate?"

"I doubt it." He stood. "This is all silly, because there's so little I can tell you before I take you there, and yet you have to decide first. I hope you aren't being romantic about this."

Did he suspect her of a crush? Perhaps she'd been a little too obvious with her leg show. "In what way?"

"It isn't a matter of cloak-and-dagger intrigues, beautiful spies and dashing heroes, just academic analysis. We'll be trying to make sense out of vast quantities of information, and the work may often be more statistical than stimulating."

"I trust your judgment that it's important. I think you have your political priorities straight, and I hope I do."

"We have a little trip to make to an office in Rockefeller Plaza that need not otherwise concern you. Sign you on, start the process." He offered her his arm off the bench with rare courtliness. "It's time I became more involved. The slowness of entry was driving me crazy," he said with a flash of anger suppressed. "Now we'll get moving."

———

In July, Ready appeared after months of absence. He had just been commissioned a lieutenant commander and was expecting to be assigned to a carrier. In the morning he was scheduled to head home by train.

Her favorite brother looked older, she thought, his skin leathery and seamed, nets of new wrinkles around his dark blue eyes, his hair even blonder than hers. He was in a good, antic mood. When she suggested various friends, he wanted all of them. After Italian food, which Ready always craved, in a local Village dive Abra favored because even before the war there had never been any pictures of Mussolini displayed, they were joined by Djika, Karen Sue and Karen Sue's new roommate, Eveline, a second cousin on her mother's side from Beaufort, North Carolina, married to an ensign on a convoy escort destroyer. Karen Sue viewed sharing her apartment as her foremost sacrifice to the war effort.

After they had drunk their way through a couple of Village spots, they went uptown to the Onyx Club and then the Famous Door, listening to swing and dancing till two in the morning. "Sweet Georgia Brown," Abra sang and did the lindy with her brother. Watching Karen Sue and Ready dance cheek to cheek to "That Old Black Magic" in the smoky ill-lit room, the mobbed floor, she suddenly imagined what it would feel like to be in love with someone and send him off to war. Falling in love was something that happened to other women, never to her, and while so far in her life she had viewed herself as able to enjoy men because she was not obsessed with them individually, now she wondered if she were incapable and if she would always avoid what others seemed passionately to seek.

Eveline was dancing with a lieutenant whom Ready had invited to their table. Karen Sue and Ready were doing a sleek flirtatious lindy. "In the Mood" was loud, the brass section standing to blare out their anthem, but Djika's low incisive voice came through clearly from her position at Abra's elbow. "Seeing you with this brother, one begins to understand the basis of your aversion to men of your own appearance and background."

"But Ready's my favorite brother. We've always been close."

"Quite so." Djika nodded, as if she were saying, Mate in two moves. "In fact you even look exceptionally like. You naturally found him attractive when you were growing up, so in fear at the incest lurking, you seek out men who could not possibly be part of your family."

"Ah, the dubious joys of Freud," Abra punned. "Prove you were in love with your father at age four, and what do you have? The same set of current problems. I certainly hope I had the good taste to lust after Ready when I was little, instead of my hideously dull brother Roger or father."

Djika told her for the thirtieth time that ignoring Freud made her naive, but Abra was sure her taste in men was motivated by curiosity, hunger, zest for life, a passion for experience far more than by the incest taboo Djika postulated. At the moment all such considerations were theoretical, as she was too busy for more than an occasional night with an old flame, and her curiosity about Oscar Kahan remained unsated.

During that dance something was exchanged, because Ready muttered to Abra as he came back to the table that he was going to spend what remained of the night with Karen Sue. The next day he told her Karen Sue made him pretend to sleep on the couch until Eveline had gone to bed. He presumed that was the southern way, but pronounced Karen Sue a woman and a half. Then Abra put him on the train north to Maine.

That Wednesday, Djika, Karen Sue, Eveline and Abra sat sharing a chicken fricassee cooked by Karen Sue's housekeeper, wine punch and honeydew melon, with their shoes off and the windows pushed high and two fans turned on them. Stanley Beaupere had gone off to the Jersey shore with his wife and children on vacation, leaving Djika to fume in the city.

The sun was setting over New Jersey and the grey ships gathered in the river. "Every evening they collect there," Karen Sue said dreamily. "In the morning they're all gone. It's got to be symbolic of something, the ships that vanish during the night."

"Out on Cape Hatteras, you wouldn't believe the mayhem," Eveline said, shaking her curls. "The beach is just dotted with wreckage and oily bodies."

"I heard you were offered an assistantship in the fall by Blumenthal and you turned it down, Abra." Djika fixed a stern gaze on her. "What's wrong with you? If we weren't at war, you'd wait forty years for such a chance."

"I'm working full time at a government information office."

"What are you doing?"

"Just researching and writing pamphlets."

"What kind?" Djika asked.

Abra pulled out of her shoulder bag a pamphlet entitled *Potatoes for Patriotism*. She handed it over to Djika, knowing exactly what her friend would read:

> *By eating potatoes instead of wheat, the people of the United States can help win the war. We have not enough wheat for the Allies and ourselves. We have an abundance of potatoes. Wheat flour is a concentrated food and therefore good for shipping; potatoes are bulky and consequently not suited for limited shipping space. . . .*

The introduction was followed by pages of simple recipes. After potatoes baked, stuffed, boiled, steamed, riced, mashed, in cakes or puffs or pies or soup or salad or codfish balls, the more desperate offerings ensued: Potato loaf with ground peanuts and canned tomatoes. Mashed potatoes as substitute for bread crumbs in fish or meat loaf. Fish and potato loaf. Fish hash with cold mashed potatoes. Potato biscuits. Potato dumplings. Potato muffins. Potato pastry. Potato drop cookies. And then the finale, potato cake.

It was Abra's experience that no curiosity about her new job survived exposure to the potato pamphlet. Amused, Oscar had sent on a memo about her ingenuity. Each of the women in turn examined the pamphlet and looked at her with a mixture of pity and dismay. The subject immediately changed.

Aside from Djika, who still dwelt in mangled fidelity in the shadow of Stanley Beaupere's apparently well-built marriage, they were all lacking the companionship of men. Their male peers were disappearing from campus. At Columbia, the space between the buildings and under the trees that had always been social territory was turned now into parade grounds for midshipmen under military discipline and far too young for them. The usual pattern of their social lives was to spend most evenings not taken up by work or volunteering with their female friends. Then when some former boyfriend or acquaintance appeared on leave, the women dropped everything, stayed out till dawn and caught up on sleep after the hectic weekend.

"Abra, come on here for one little minute." Karen Sue was beckoning to her. "I have something I want to see if it fits you, child."

What Karen Sue wanted to fit on her was a promise she would not tell Ready that Karen Sue had been married. "It wasn't a real marriage, after all. I mean, nothing happened hardly, and an annulled marriage is one that never really was."

Abra groaned. "But, Karen Sue, Ready doesn't think you were a virgin, right?"

"What he thinks in that regard need not concern us right now, Abra, and as surely as you're my true friend, I don't want you to discuss matters pertaining to my past life, which you don't know the real truth about anyhow, and therefore such talk can only cause trouble. Loose lips sink ships."

Abra went home grumpy. She did not like being forced to choose between telling a truth to Ready that might or might not interest him, and displeasing Karen Sue, whom she truly liked. Damn Karen Sue, did she have designs on becoming Abra's sister-in-law? She couldn't quite picture it, but she wondered if Karen Sue could not, with a gold frame.

If she had told her friends exactly what she was doing, they would have been as puzzled as they were bored by the potato pamphlet. At the moment Oscar and she appeared to be in the old clothes business. They were still collecting oral histories of recent immigrants, especially those whose previous addresses or places of birth had military or industrial significance. They were also collecting wristwatches, pens, razors, wallets, luggage, underwear, overcoats, shirts. They paid for everything and had a faintly plausible explanation: they were investigating the state of the German economy, and the workmanship and metals in a watch, or the type of cloth in a suit, could provide useful information. It was all bundled off to a warehouse in Washington, where this scavenged material was to outfit agents who would eventually be dropped behind enemy lines.

The information they collected, the reminiscences, also went off to Washington. The agent who had been carrying out this collection of information and rummage sale fodder before them had been transferred to London, where presumably he was engaged in something more to Oscar's liking. Every week Oscar took the train to Washington, not only to deliver the week's limp prizes, but to try to finagle or politick them into proper research and analysis work. The R & A division of OSS Washington, Oscar muttered, was rife with brilliant minds. They had to get posted to Washington.

Oscar was eating himself up. They worked long hours, attempting to do the best job they could, six, often seven days a week, but Oscar was marking time. He had not left Columbia to collect old clothes and was inclined to credit academic rivalries with what he saw as the waste of his talents. It was during his increasing frustration that he told her to call him Oscar, and indeed began to complain to her familiarly as to a wife or mistress. Abra, who was still finding the tales of the refugees fascinating, suffered less impatience. New York was her home, as it was Oscar's. Although she was resigned to a move to Washington, she was not chafing to be there.

She amused herself with watching the formality between them gradually abrade under the pressures he generated. She was Abra, he was Oscar. They ate lunch together at the deli downstairs on Madison Avenue, or she went out and brought back sandwiches. The day Oscar interviewed a Communist who had been in the merchant marine and so ready with details on German shipping that a whole dossier on him would go to OSS Washington, he took her to supper at a Spanish restaurant on Fourteenth Street. There the waiter seemed to know him and the manager came over and left a plate of tidbits as a present from the house, to nibble with their amontillado.

Oscar expanded with the food and the wine. Not that he became even slightly tipsy, he simply relaxed, and for him to relax meant to lay claim to her attention, to charm, to open up the personal as he had been careful never to do in the nine months of their proper relationship.

"There were four of us," he was saying. "I'm the oldest. My brother Ben came next, and he's still in Pittsburgh, in the dry cleaning business. Then the two girls, Bessie, who's married to a dentist and big as both of us put together, a wonderful warm mother with five kids. Then my younger sister, Gloria." He frowned at his plate of seafood.

"What is she doing?"

"I wish I knew. She's in Paris."

"Still? Why didn't she leave before the war started?"

"The war started there two years before it started here, remember. She's married to a minor French aristocrat, and she's a fashion writer. Her business is what the French couturiers put out. I don't think it occurred to her that the war had any bearing on her life. And I don't know if it really does." He rubbed his nose as if to polish it, frowning slightly.

"Do they have any children?"

"No, by agreement. He's a good deal older, and he has children by a previous marriage who stand to inherit."

"If he's rich and aristocratic, he must be in a good position to protect her, wouldn't you think?"

"I hope so. It's hard not hearing anything. We've always kept in touch, all of us. I'll go to Pittsburgh in September for the High Holidays, to my mother. Gloria used to come over every two years, and I'd see her in Paris." He tilted his head, pouring more of the coarse red wine. "What's your family like? Are you close?"

She had the sense as the dinner progressed that this was a place he had brought other women, and that part of the more personal tone of their evening was not calculation or decision on his part, but simply the fulfilling of an already established and comfortable pattern. She was amused. She suspected that both he and she were so accustomed to sitting across the table from lovers that each automatically brought that habit of warmth to the present table. Yet she was not marking time as so often she was when men talked about themselves, for her curiosity about Oscar had been honed by months of impersonal but energetic interaction.

She was pleased to tell him about Ready, about Roger, about her background, exotic to him as his was to her. He came from a family that seemed to have had little money to spare, but in which his education had come first. Perhaps the middle children had been sacrificed a bit, or perhaps they had simply lacked his brilliance or ambition. Then with Gloria, times had been easier and the others settled, so that everything that could be provided, was, and she sallied forth a beauty to conquer the world.

Yet the connections between each of them, dentist's wife, dry cleaning manager, academic and chic lady, seemed to hold in avid concern for each other. She caught spicy whiffs of emotion off that family, of tangled loves and hatreds and raised voices and tearful phone calls in the night. Yet Oscar seemed quite sure of his position, the oldest, the dearest, the distant center. His mother was alive and figured in his life. His father had died of a heart attack three years before. His mother, who must retain the family handsomeness, was considering marrying again, and all of the siblings except the exiled Gloria were passionately intriguing to further or prevent that marriage to a widower.

He spoke now of his ex-wife, but not as men usually referred to their previous spouses. "Louise is very strong, very bright, very able. You shouldn't judge her by those absurd stories she cranks out. She has a first-rate mind, and she's not shy about using it. She's very political, a progressive thinker."

If she had drunk less wine, and if she did not still feel a little off balance with him, still with the professor and student, the boss and assistant dynamic operating between them and therefore to be forcefully overcome, she might have been less forthright in her questioning. "If you admire your ex-wife as much as you say, why aren't you still married?"

"That's hard to say. The divorce wasn't my idea." Oscar rubbed his nose again. "Actually I was living with somebody else for a while, but it was nothing to make an enormous fuss about."

Abra laughed. "I doubt if that was your wife's point of view."

"It wasn't." Oscar sighed. "I don't understand why women become so obsessed with minor adventures. I fully intended to come back."

Abra felt as if she ought to reassure him that she did not expect fidelity, but after all, nothing had happened between them yet. She satisfied herself by saying simply, "I think marriage and the home are far more important to many women than they are, for instance, to me. Many younger women have a more independent stance and less rigid expectations."

"I should have realized how important it was to Louise. She grew up without that security, and when it was threatened, she just wanted to cut me off." Oscar shook his head. "I must see more of my daughter, Kay. I've been letting myself become overwhelmed. Especially if we are going off to Washington soon, that's more reason to carve out time for her."

She definitely retained the feeling, as they ate their flan and drank a Spanish brandy, that they were moving in the direction of becoming more personal. Lovers or friends? She could not even tell if there were room in the crowded field of Oscar's life for an affair with her. It would be convenient, it would have that going for it, she thought. She wondered if she was going to have to make the first move.

What struck her was a sense that she was edging into a convoy, a mass, a herd of relationships. Unlike most of the men she met who had families only as background or possible interference, Oscar seemed to come trailing a host of people with whom he was still actively involved; and she had the uneasy feeling she could not see half of his life yet. Taking him for a lover looked not so much as if she were committing her usual solitary and private act but as if she were joining a tribe. His work might be clandestine, but his relationships appeared to be all out there in the full sunlight of mutual regard, jostling each other. His wife, his daughter, his mother, his sisters and brothers, his ex-lovers, his friends, they all seemed to be looking at her and waiting to see what was going to happen. Perhaps she was drunk, but she almost felt the hot regard of many dark eyes upon their conversation.

The Jaws Close

Leib stayed in Naomi's mind, making her feel a little guilty. Since she considered him far more attractive than Murray, she could not understand why Ruthie preferred Murray. She imagined that Trudi was killed in a sudden way without pain and Leib carried her off. She had no interest in the boys in her class, who sometimes picked on her and teased her and sang about how the girls of France wore tissue paper pants and other dirty nonsense. She was now the third tallest girl in class, the tallest white girl.

She walked to school with Sandy Rosenthal, but her special secret friend was Clotilde. Black and white girls were not supposed to be friends, so they hid their secret from teachers and kids alike. What both of them watched for were moments when they could speak French together, when they could share how strange they found life here, the school, the city, the food, the weather. She saw Clotilde as beautiful, with her skin like wood and ashes at once, her grey-brown eyes enormous and luminous, her even brilliant teeth, her curly hair that was like black and red together. Clotilde was too gentle for Detroit, for the casual savageries of the school with its constant provocations, its dares, its fights in the schoolyard, its subculture of dirty jokes and gang wars and horror comics. Her father was in a submarine in the Pacific, which they agreed sounded extremely scary. He was made to be a kind of servant, but stood watches at night up in the conning tower because, Clotilde explained scornfully, the Navy thought Negroes could see better in the dark than whites.

Sometimes Naomi felt as if she had walked into an intense generations-old family quarrel in Detroit between the colored and the whites, except that they could never even see each other clearly and the whites had all the power, like the Nazis in France. They had the police, the government, the schools, the hospitals, everything. She could figure out who was getting the short end without straining her powers of observation.

When school ended for the summer, Naomi was more delighted than she ever had been before, because going to school was a test that never stopped. However, she speedily realized that her vacation wasn't going to be one, because the nursery went on in summer as in winter. Besides, as time passed, Aunt Rose and Sharon were handling more children in the same space. Naomi took over the shopping, complicated with the red points and the blue points and what points were good that week, to be used before they expired.

Sharon said that she was lucky to be learning so early all about babies, as she hadn't known one end from the other when she had Marilyn. Now Naomi would make some man a very good wife, because she would start out knowing how to feed, bathe, hold and dress her own babies. Sharon said that was much more important than anything she learned in school, and Naomi was getting a real education.

Naomi did not argue out loud, but she did not feel lucky. She felt stuck. In the early evenings she escaped to play kick the can or stickball on the corners. Both boys and girls played, as long as there was any light. One night Four Eyes Rosovsky tried to kiss her when they were all sitting on the stoop of the apartment house where Four Eyes lived, and she kicked him in the shins. Afterward she was sorry she hadn't waited till after he kissed her to kick him, so she would have found out what it was like, but she wasn't very sorry.

Naomi's hair was as kinky as ever. She talked Ruthie into cutting it short for the summer. Aunt Rose had a fit when she saw what they had done, but Naomi liked her new haircut. Aunt Rose said she looked like a poodle. Naomi said that poodles were French, and so was she. Aunt Rose said she was getting as sassy and bad-mouthed as American girls, and where was the sweet little girl who had come to them?

Naomi's breasts were growing. The nipples itched. She felt irritable and hot and bored. Sandy wanted a powder blue suit and a taffeta dress, as soon as the war was over. Sharon wanted an electric refrigerator. Naomi wanted to be twenty-one, educated already and somewhere else. When she thought how long it would be before she grew up enough to do anything on her own, she felt exhausted in advance. It would just take too long to grow up, it was hardly worth the wait. The biggest thing to look forward to were days the iceman came by with his horse-drawn cart and she could beg a piece of ice to suck. It was so hot, Boston Blackie just wanted to sleep all day under the blue hydrangea in the yard.

Maybe she would be a secretary like Ruthie. Ruthie no longer worked at a department store, but instead she had a job with the government, at the Detroit Housing Commission. She worked shorter hours for more money. Rose said that being a secretary was just as good as being a social worker, but Ruthie did not think so and still went to Wayne four nights a week.

Ruthie explained she was not really a secretary but in a typing pool. It was a lucky job for a Jew to find, working in an office, but not what she really wanted and she would not settle for it forever, she confided to Naomi. She only said that once to her mother, as Rose lost her temper. Rose grew frightened if she thought any of her children wanted what they could not have, but Ruthie said that Rose was willing to settle for too little because she did not understand how the world was changing. Things would get a lot worse, or they would get better for people like them.

Lately Naomi thought a great deal about money. When she was a little girl, she took it for granted that her parents worked. They were not rich, they were working people, like everyone in their quarter, but they ate good meals that Maman prepared after work, the girls all helped, and Sundays they would go to the cinema or the country or the Jardin des Plantes or the Musée de l'Homme. Every year they took a real vacation in August, leaving Paris for two weeks.

After Papa went to war, her family was poorer. Here since the war started, they were better off. Aunt Rose and Sharon were earning money, Ruthie had a better job, Arty was on the line at Fisher Body, and Uncle Morris worked a lot of overtime. The car was finally paid off. Their rent had gone up twice, but now with rent control, it was stabilized.

They were saving money in war bonds. Ruthie gave Naomi a quarter a week so that she could buy defense stamps at school, but Naomi often did not. She knew how the paper money the government puts out turns into just paper overnight, and she could not waste the quarters on those stamps you could not even use to mail a letter. She felt her American relatives simply did not understand how you had to hold on to metal money. She had a hiding place where one section of the baseboard was rotten in the bedroom she shared with Ruthie. There she hid the quarters till she would find out if the government was going to fall. Governments often did that.

When she heard people talk about how bad hoarders were, she felt her own hoard of Ruthie's quarters weighing her down. But if all the money Aunt Rose and Uncle Morris and Ruthie were turning into paper bonds went bad, then she would save them. Silver and gold were real. Aunt Batya had left Poland with a little gold sewn into the lining of her coat, but with that, the Balabans had been able to come to France and begin again.

At least Ruthie had more time to spend with her, for she had stopped going out with men. Sometimes Naomi went to the movies with Trudi and sometimes she went with her whole family or with Sharon (Arty worked the swing shift, so they couldn't go together) and sometimes with Ruthie alone. Small restaurants and businesses were shutting down, but the movie houses were open twenty-four hours and always crowded. They saw Alan Ladd in *This Gun for Hire*, Greer Garson in *Mrs. Miniver*, Bob Hope in *My Favorite Blonde*. They sat through *Across the Pacific, Saboteur, This Above All*, every few days another double or triple feature.

Every night they listened to the radio and read the newspapers, even Naomi whose English had improved so that she could read the papers just as good as Uncle Morris. Her favorite subject was geography, part of social studies. She loved to find the names from the radio and the newspaper on the map and to follow the movements of the armies in Egypt, in New Guinea, in the Soviet Union, even though it was a matter of the Axis always advancing. More of the map had to be colored black.

Aunt Rose encouraged her to go barefoot in the house and the yard all summer, because shoes were rationed. Her soles became so hard she boasted to Four Eyes and Sandy that she could walk on glass without cutting herself, so they broke a soda bottle. She did not want to, but she put her foot on the broken glass and hobbled across and she was right, her foot did not bleed. She won a dime from Sandy and a dime from Four Eyes, but then they made her buy them ice-cream cones with half the money.

Alvin opened a hydrant and they all ran through the water and splashed in the gutters until the cops came. Trudi said they could come to her house and run under the hose. Trudi's family lived downstairs in a two-flat house and her father liked to water the lawn. Naomi had a new bathing suit Ruthie had bought her, bright green with a halter top and a cute little skirt. She tried to decide if she looked sexy in it. Sandy was always talking about what was sexy and what wasn't. Her other word was dreamy. Sandy talked about boys too much, but because she lived so close, Naomi could play with her even when she was taking care of the nursery brats.

Sandy had honey blond hair, unusual among the Jews of their neighborhood. Her face had a rawboned look, the nose hawklike, the jaw a little jutting, but Sandy was vain about her hair and acted as if she were pretty, and so did everyone else. Sandy had to take care of her snotty little brother Roy, another bond between them.

Sandy pretended the yard between the two houses was special. Her dad had brought home a big wooden spool on which cables had been wrapped, that they used for a table, with wooden crates from the grocer's for chairs. Sometimes

Sandy or she had money for a soda, but mostly they didn't. Since both their families were always short on sugar, they made do with cold water with a slice of lemon pretending it was cocktails, while Sandy taught her the words to "Chattanooga Choo Choo," "Praise the Lord and Pass the Ammunition," "Blues in the Night" and "Jingle Jangle Jingle." Being what Sandy called a teenager seemed a great deal of work. She was supposed to know about the Red Wings, who played hockey, and the Tigers, who played baseball, and to know the names of the players, even the players who had been drafted, although she had never seen a baseball or a hockey game.

That night after it got too dark to play, they sat on the stoop of the apartment building on the corner and Alvin passed around a cigarette. He was always swiping Chesterfields from his mother's purse. Naomi could draw on it without coughing. It made her dizzy but she did not let on. One way summer was better than winter was that outside school the kids were accepting her better. The kids she was hanging around with were Jews her age from these four blocks. It was as if everything didn't count so much in the summer and everybody was easier. She was learning too. When they passed her a butt or made dirty jokes, she did not act shocked any longer and she never said Aunt Rose would not let her do something. She just went along and did it and kept her mouth shut.

"This will be our senior year," Sandy said in the same voice she used when she talked about boys being dreamy.

"So?" Naomi said.

"We get to have a senior trip and go to Bob Lo. We have a party and we sign each other's autograph books. We have a dance."

Four Eyes laughed. "And the girls have to make their own graduation dresses, ha-ha, and boy do you look stupid."

"Ugh," Naomi said. "They ought to make you sew your suits. I bet you'd look funny too. Me, I think I'll graduate in a paper bag. I'll paint it red."

"Frenchy, you'd look cute in a paper bag," Alvin said.

"The guys around here, they're always trying out a line these days," Sandy said with a sour grimace. "They think they're regular Casanovas."

Then five minutes later they were chasing each other around the big elm with their eyes shut, playing blind tag. It was fun stumbling around in the dark, but Four Eyes pinched her hard on the behind. When she cried out, he pretended he didn't know what he had done. "I had my eyes closed," he said smugly. "How do I know what I did?" Her buttock still hurt and it felt dirty to think he had touched her there.

The next day Alvin and Four Eyes went by with five guys to play ball, and they wouldn't even say hello. They pretended they didn't see Sandy and Naomi. I wonder if there really is a G-d, Naomi thought, because even though it's a sin to think that and everything counts now that I'm a woman, still I would think life could be better arranged, besides wars and Nazis even. If I were setting things up, I wouldn't make kids go through all this growing up. I'd just have people born all grown and skip this waiting and fussing and always doing and saying the wrong thing.

She wondered if it would be as hard if she were home with her family. Here she was in exile and untwinned. She would not sulk and brood and kick at things if she had Rivka always there knowing what she knew and seeing what she saw and completing her. She would not be so miserable if she were with Rivka, the way things were supposed to be.

The night was close and hot. Detroit felt like a vast low-ceilinged poorly ventilated closet full of machinery. She had a bruise on her behind. What a nasty thing to do, and why? Boys were mysterious and no good but trying to hang around with them was what girls did, and so she had to.

Whenever she asked Ruthie about boys, Ruthie talked about love, love, love. Naomi could not see what love had to do with boys. She loved Ruthie, she loved Rivka and Maman and Papa. She even loved Jacqueline. But to think of loving Four Eyes or Alvin was an unfunny joke, like falling for a large truck. Girls talked about being in love with Tyrone Power or Alan Ladd. Sandy could not decide between Harry James and Frank Sinatra. At least Jacqueline had never gushed that way. Perhaps she had not sufficiently appreciated her older sister. She looked at the years immediately ahead of her when, as Sandy kept saying, they would enter high school and go on real dates, with wary disgust at the prospect.

Finally she slept, in her bed that felt wrinkled with the heat and her own sweat. *Although the guards called the building the Vélodrome of winter, it was not winter but summer and hot. She was burning up with thirst. Her throat was parched, her tongue, blistered. She wondered how the babies crying could manage it. This morning one had died, the little girl with the big grey eyes. The young mother was still holding the baby, like a dirty limp rag doll, the head lolling.*

Rivka kept thinking she would throw up because everybody smelled filthy and shitty. Even the adults smelled like babies that had dirtied themselves. There were thousands and thousands of them packed in the arena, up on the stands or crammed onto the track in the middle under the blue glass ceiling like a mockery of sky, compressing the heat and stench downward. The guards, French like themselves but nasty now, kept screaming at them. It was as if they were at school and some cruel principal was punishing them all, but the adults were punished just like the children.

They were hungry and thirsty and lying in their own filth, jammed together so that everybody was leaning on everybody else. It was so loud and so crowded, she felt as if they all had one headache. A little boy whose mother had died two nights before had attached himself to her and Maman. He did not cry much now. He felt fiery to her fingertips. His eyelashes had matted his eyes shut and he lay across her feet with his head in Maman's lap. His name was Jules. He did not know his last name. He did not know how old he was, but Maman had said, when she was still able to speak, that she thought he was between three and four. She was Naomi-Rivka, both of them at once, her throat too burned with thirst to speak, to cry, even to ask Maman when it would stop. The air itself was dirt, and she felt her body crumbling like bad cheese. . . .

She woke in her hot dark room hearing Ruthie sighing in sleep in the bunk below her. Boston Blackie lay across her feet, snoring softly. She felt raked with fear. She felt as if she were bleeding fear onto the sheets. It was only a bad dream. But she did not believe that. She did not believe that at all.

LOUISE 3

Afternoon Sun

The sand scorched the soles of Louise's feet as Claude and she crossed the low dune among dwarf blueberries and poverty grass to the beach beyond, where bathers had already established a path through the barbed wire. The waves were rearing up to roll in smartly although the wind was only a mild breeze here. A storm had passed out to sea, distant beyond the horizon like the war, washing up seaweed, odd pieces of twisted metal, shell casings and the night before a body, Louise had heard in the village when they bicycled in to do their shopping. Louise had not been on a bicycle in years, but after a bad night of aching calves she kept to herself, her resilient muscles had adjusted and remembered.

Claude's wiry body in striped trunks was a novelty to her, still a little startling. He was thinner than Oscar, more lightly built, a nervous agility and speed to his movements. She caught herself comparing him once again to Oscar and grimaced in exasperation. Would she never stop? Since she had come away with him for this week of vacation, she kept being struck by the strangeness of being intimate with a man who was not her ex-husband. A hundred little habits and usages surprised her, that he wore pajamas, that he sang in French when he was doing some little task such as cleaning a bluefish. A local fisherman had given it to them when they had fallen into conversation watching the boats in the town harbor.

After swimming, lying side by side with salt water drying on their skin, they were both silent. She lay on her belly, the straw hat pulled over her head to protect her scalp from the sun's rays. She was grateful to be out of New York for a week. Kay was off working as a counselor in a progressive children's camp. Normally Kay would have been a year too young for the job, but the camp was short on counselors, having lost the boys to the draft. Louise found it more a relief than a pain to be separated from Kay for two months. They had been quarreling a great deal. Kay continued to pick up servicemen, claiming that all her girl-friends did the same. Louise had withheld her allowance, made scenes, reasoned, brought in a family friend, insisted on accompanying Kay to and from school, kept her in for a week at a time, but Kay was as stubborn as she was. Louise had arranged for the job in an effort to keep Kay out of trouble.

She inhaled the salty almost smoky musk of her arm. She smelled like some-thing delicious to eat. It made her think of Kay's hair when she had been playing in the sun, when they finally had enough money to take a vacation occasionally. She remembered going to Montauk Point, where there had been cheap fisher-men's cabins. The salt smell of the ocean was something Oscar had first given her. They used to dawdle along on the beach, the three of them, beachcombing, pick-ing over the shells and the rocks, popping the little bladders on the rockweed. She had been delighted to escape Brooklyn. Lying in a lumpy double bed and hearing the waves slide in had been erotic and soothing at once.

Claude stirred himself, sighing. He was lying on his back with one hand shading his pale aquamarine eyes. He flipped over suddenly. "I don't know why, but I was just thinking about St-Malo. It's in Bretagne. Have you ever been there?"

"I've never been in Brittany at all, I'm sorry to say."

"I used to spend August at a little stone house on the beach. There is sand and marsh, as here, but there is also granite. The bones of the land."

Although he said *I,* she knew he was also remembering his family in France, a wife and two sons. That was all she knew, except that his wife was not with him and she had heard him describe himself as single.

He sat up. He seemed determined to clutch the present, running a hand over her back caressingly. "You said you'd been in France, though, yes? Paris, I sup-pose?"

"Four times. My ex-husband's sister lives there. I wonder if you ever met her?"

"Paris is a large city, not a village, Lulu."

She wondered why men always gave her nicknames. She had never called Oscar poopsie or honeybunch or Ozzie. She addressed Claude as Claude. But every man she had ever been involved with invented a name for her, as if that gave him true possession. "Still, you might well have crossed paths."

"What is she called?" he asked without interest, batting at a sand flea.

"She writes under the name Gloria Ivoire, but that's just her pen name for fashion stories. She covers the Parisian designers for *Harper's Bazaar* and *McCall's.* She lives under her husband's name, as the Baronne de Montseurrat, Gloria Barthoise."

He laughed, a sharp sound of surprised delight. "In fact I have dined with her. Far more beautiful than the models she writes about, but married to a man of paralyzing dullness. He races—and resembles—a horse." Claude was smiling, alert, fascinated in a different way than he usually was—although, like Oscar, he was a man whom almost everything could interest, briefly. "I'm astonished that you should know Gloria. I knew her for half a year before I learned she was American. She has only a faint accent. A woman of formidable style and perhaps more formidable style intelligence. But you said your ex-husband came from Pittsburgh?"

"So does Gloria," Louise said, sitting up.

"Gloria Neige Noire, we called her. Oh, my." He smiled again, settling into the sand and the gossip. It was as if his American years were sloughed off and she was permitting him to talk about the people who had mattered to him in his real life. "She had something of a scandalous reputation trailing after her until she married. The sort of lovers an adventuress might choose. Then nothing. Complete rectitude. Boring fidelity. A sudden cold."

Louise was smiling attentively, but she was also thinking about that phrase, a boring fidelity. She had never found fidelity boring. She had given it absolutely to Oscar, and she had vainly expected it back. If Oscar had used that phrase, she would have begun an argument at once, but she was obviously going to let it pass by. She had much to learn about Claude.

"How did you ever meet her?"

"When I was seeking backers for *La Tête du Bonhomme,* we were brought together at a producer's house. But I like going to the races at Longchamp. I like to watch the crowds even more than the horses. To make little bets and care passionately if a nag wins or loses, to drink champagne and watch the most beautiful and fashionable women of Paris. There's nothing like it here. Nothing at all." He looked tired.

She had a moment's sense of them as curiously mismatched. She would not care for the races at Longchamp, and what did someone who adored the most beautiful and fashionable women of Paris want with her?

He looked up frowning. "But surely Gloria Ivoire isn't Jewish?"

"Sure she is. Her husband isn't, of course. She stays in close touch with her family. Or did till December of forty-one. We haven't had word from her since then. I know Oscar's extremely worried."

"I'd imagine she'd be safe enough. The Nazis and the French Right are going after the Jews, but she's well protected, married to that nothing of impeccable family. We never did get any money out of him, by the way."

"I suppose she's safe, but it would be a relief to know. I have no idea how Gloria would respond to living in an occupied country. She has an iron will and detests being ordered to do anything."

"I might be able to find out for you," he said casually. "If you really want to know."

"I do." She did not take the offer seriously. He was showing off, assuming she would forget.

That evening he found a grill in the old barn beside the house, and decided he would broil the bluefish they had been given. This was his idea of roughing it, staying in the well-equipped house of a friend with hired help lurking and broiling a fish over an open fire. A good breeze whipped off the marshy inlet at the foot of the knoll on which the house stood, a grey weathered double Cape with many small rooms upstairs that opened into each other. All along the edge of the crabgrass lawn where Claude had built his fire, rosa rugosa, the wild beach roses that made enormous orange hips, were flowering in pink and cherry red.

The house belonged to an actor who used it only in August, a man who usually played crusty country doctors or crazy old scientists or mellow old lawyers. The house was beautifully sited and well built, with wide eighteenth-century flooring, a beehive fireplace, but the rooms were small and had been built without halls. Bathrooms had been stuck in, one in an old birthing room. To get to any of them, she walked through other bedrooms, fine with only the two of them in the house, but unimaginable to her when it was fully stocked with children and adults.

With the house came a local carpenter who turned on the plumbing and electricity, whenever a telegram came to do so, stacked firewood, repaired what needed it, and a widow, who cooked. This was her night off. It was a new ambiance to Louise, but one to which she felt she could easily become accustomed. Claude, who had never been there before, was full of anecdotes about the house, the town and now the fish he was cooking.

"Bluefish are tigers," he announced. "They go into a feeding frenzy like sharks, until they drive their prey up on the beach. They will even take a sizable bite out of a swimmer."

I am learning about myself as well as about him, Louise thought. She observed similarities between Oscar and Claude, as well as the obvious differences. She seemed passionately drawn to men who felt the necessity of charming everyone they met, whereas she was a person who mostly went about keeping to herself. She did not start up conversations on the bus or in the post office. But Oscar did. And Claude did. Both were constantly picking up strangers and turning them inside out like pockets full of curious odds and ends of information. Both sat down in a restaurant wanting their waiter or waitress to like them. Louise wanted her waiter or waitress to be decently paid, to provide good service, to have a happy and fulfilling life outside the restaurant, but never would it have occurred to her to wonder whether or not the person liked her, or to try to seduce their liking.

In many ways, they were different, she reminded herself quickly, because a fear came on her occasionally that she was trying to repeat what could not be repeated. Oscar was an intellectual. He dreamed in ideas. He was an unusually physical and sensual man for an intellectual, but he loved to argue, to explore, to clunk ideas hard against facts and other theories to see how they rang when challenged.

Claude noticed light on the weathered wood, the slant of the mullions across the wide floorboards, the way the carpenter who took care of the house favored his right leg when he walked up- or downhill. He loved gossip and anecdote and speculation about why someone had done or not done something. If something was alien to him and he could not penetrate its behavior, like the swallows who darted at them if they went around the far side of the old barn and who streaked through the twilight air, he invented stories about it. The swallows were the ghosts of people who had been too busy to enjoy living, he said, who had never in the midst of ten thousand things to do, taken a week and run off with a beautiful lover, and so Venus was punishing them in the afterlife by making them fly aimlessly to and fro always in a terrible hurry. Oscar would have read a book about swallows and then closely observed their behavior.

"Actually I think they're catching insects." Louise sat on a bench watching his labors. They were drinking white wine he had brought with him. In the midst of the war, Claude always had wine.

"Exactly. What greater punishment than to spend your next lifetime eating mosquitoes, flies and gnats? Would you like that? No? Then you must always be prepared to interrupt your life when Venus bids you. Or she will have the last laugh."

Louise very much doubted that Claude had become a successful director by always dropping his projects to run off with a lover, but then she doubted he had ever needed to go farther than a convenient and almost adjacent bedroom. The heat wave was slowing everything in New York, he had a little time, and he had spent last week in New York and must spend next week in Washington. She did not doubt he wanted to see her, but she also recognized that the timing was not dictated by passion but convenience. She must keep a level head. Not to want more than he would easily offer; to enjoy what was possible, then to turn away when he did, or if she were truly lucky, to let go the instant before Claude.

Each time she saw him, she found him more attractive, his eyes of aquamarine, like the earrings she had once been given because aquamarine was her birthstone, his agile wiry body that tennis and his own energy level kept trim in spite of the quantities of rich food and wine he took in. Another similarity, she warned herself: both good trenchermen, avid and adventuresome about food, querulous if not sufficiently and promptly fed. If he thought he was in danger of missing a meal, Oscar could throw a tantrum that other men might reserve for infidelity.

Claude's brows ran straight across with no arch to them, not thick on the brow ridges but thin brown lines as if drawn with a fast pencil. His mouth was full, the upper lip dominating the lower. He shaved daily, but his body sported little hair, a few coppery wires under his arms and curling around the base of his short thick penis. His skin was tanning a golden olive. His dark brown hair glinted with brass highlights under the sun. She had begun to experience that melting between her hipbones when she looked at him. Her body wanted to trot after him wagging its tail and pushing a wet nose into his palm. Her body was enormously pleased and lacking in dignity.

He liked to make love in the mornings and again when they came back from the beach. He talked as he made love, up to the point where he entered her, which took some getting used to. He would praise her breasts and thighs, call her sweet names, tell her what he was going to do to her, tell her what she was going to do to him. He spoke in French and in English and occasionally in a language she finally asked about, Rumanian. He was not talking to her but to himself, she decided, exciting himself, proving to himself what he was doing, making it more vivid, with his running commentary.

"Voici, le petit bouton rose, comme il se gonfle. Now you're going to beg me for my man, and he's going to push hard between your little lips."

She liked making love with him, mostly just tuning out what he said, as if it were a sound track or background music. She could not suddenly become someone who talked about making love while she did it. Her few attempts to imitate him simply made her feel awkward. She saw no reason she should not remain silent and allow him to bathe them in a puddle of sexual and semisexual words. He did not like her to mount him, preferring missionary position or entering from behind. He muttered, he moaned, he bit her shoulders. He had several different rhythms. Her body opened up wide for him and took him deep in, turning molten, improvident and vibrantly ripe.

In bed Oscar did not talk much, so perhaps he had created her reticence, or perhaps it was native to her. Never had Oscar called her by any other woman's name in bed. However, one of the early warnings that he was involved with somebody was when he began to do some new little thing. Suddenly he was flicking his tongue against the corner of her mouth, he was rubbing her round and round on the belly. These new tricks were delightful in their way, but they also chilled her, because she learned to ask herself, Now where did he pick that up? It was generous of him to want to carry home to her every pleasure he encountered, but she would just as soon he had read a sex manual or a dirty book instead.

When would she stop remembering, comparing, gesture by gesture? Yet she could tell that Claude also disappeared regularly into his mind and his past. After all, she thought, we are not virgins, we are not twenty-year-olds. We are each formed by a full and busy and loving life, so why be surprised that neither of us has totally discarded that past?

By silent collusion, both avoided discussing the war. Compulsively after supper they listened to the day's news. Then Claude went for a walk alone and Louise straightened the house, while the widow did the dishes. The British were holding at El Alamein against Rommel, but for how long? German forces were pouring across Russia, toward the oil fields of the south. The Japanese had invaded British New Guinea. All sorts of ugly rumors floated around about what the Germans were doing in occupied Poland, where they were reportedly imprisoning millions of Jews, along with Gypsies, the Catholic Left, Communists, Socialists, homosexuals and resistants, millions of people uprooted and shipped off with only what they could carry, probably to the primitive conditions of work camps where disease and poor nutrition would be prevalent. Still, the worst rumors sounded like the sort of virulent propaganda that had been spread about German soldiers bayoneting babies during World War I. Everyone was leery of horror stories, not wanting to be fooled as the public had been in that war to end all wars.

Only on the train back did they talk about the war. "If the Soviet Union doesn't stop them, nobody will," Claude said. "The Americans are totally unprepared and the British seem to have lost the knack of winning on the ground. Once Hitler seizes the Caucasian oil fields, he'll be twice as strong." As they were gliding across Connecticut, he asked, "What does your ex-husband do now? Is he in the service or still teaching?"

"He's in Donovan's newly reorganized bureau, OSS. That's—"

Claude sat up, stripped to alert nerves as when she had identified Gloria for him. "What branch?"

"He's doing research for them, that's all I know. Among German exiles."

"R & A, probably." He picked up *The Times*, his interest vanished.

Louise felt a small nerve in her neck squeeze a signal. She looked sideways

at him but asked no questions. She did not even experience a moment's para-
noia, because Claude was a Jew and thus would not suddenly unmask as a Nazi
spy, but she felt that same area of opacity she had with Oscar in the Spanish
restaurant. Somewhere in that little frisson of the nervous system was a story,
Louise thought: the good wife who knows far more than she ought and sees
far more and puts it all together like a first-rate detective, but is so clever, in
women's magazine terms, that her own husband goes on believing she is naive
and accepting of his cover stories. She made a few notes on the margin of "The
Week in Review."

Walking into her New York apartment—hot, rather dusty, large and empty,
with Kay off in camp and Mrs. Shaunessy on vacation with one of her married
daughters, Louise experienced several moments of devastating sadness, a Great
Plains of loneliness which this week only set into relief. Her body had wakened
and was howling already in the empty apartment like a dog tied up and abandoned. She wanted Claude back. She wanted him with her. She had just been
beginning to know him. She felt as if she had spent the whole week in a vain
effort to defend herself against what was inevitable. She would fall in love with
his quick nervous grace, his quirky lovemaking, his anecdotal mind in a way like
her own, and be forced to realize the affair was only an anecdote to him.

She could not even plunge into her mail, sorted by Blanche into towers. It
represented a hundred demands, two hundred duties, and zero love, zero joy. The
guidelines she had been working on with her group at the Office of War Information's (OWI) Magazine Bureau lay on top of one pile, the Magazine War
Guide for fiction writers. It laid out the propaganda goals as well as the themes
the government wanted stressed, and would be updated every three months. It
would go to the editors of several hundred magazines and to over a thousand
free-lance writers. She supposed all that propaganda ought to do some good,
but at the moment it felt remote. She took a bath, washed her hair, made herself
a pot of coffee and sat down to write a story that would pay the rent, about the
clever wife who kept her mouth shut. Outside, the streets of the city were as dim
as her mood, all neon signs shut off, the streetlights at quarter power. She might
as well work.

JEFF 3

High Tea and Low Tricks

Jeff pushed away what had been called blackberry trifle, a pasty oblong innocent of knowledge of the blackberry although intimate with cornstarch, and examined his friend. Zach was signaling the waiter. "You should have had the gooseberry," he said reprovingly. "Always take Mother's advice. She has your welfare at heart."

"I do thank you for the rescue from the Slough of Alabama. That place was rotting me through."

"This is the way to live," Zach said, ordering cognac with specificity that made Jeff smile. Zach looked well. In the two and a half years since Jeff had last seen him, Zach had taken off most of the weight he had put on during his marriage. He looked hard and amazingly for the English summer, tanned. He always tanned red as moroccan leather.

"By the way, are you still married?" Jeff asked.

"Why not? No reason not to be, unless something arises that makes it inconvenient, like an invitation to marry the heiress to a throne. As it stands, I'm not married unless I wish to be. Ideal state. No interference and all the excuses in the world." Zach's ash blond hair was worn a little longer than regulations would permit, but regulations around OSS were loose. When Zach had dropped in on him in the small hotel where he was billeted, Zach had been wearing a major's uniform, but now he sported an elegantly tailored pale grey suit.

"Do they give us a Savile Row allowance?" Jeff asked. "Never have I seen such sartorial splendor as hangs around Grosvenor Square HQ."

"Most of the HQ lads, they could pay OSS a pension and not miss it. We'll take you to be fitted. Can't bring you around looking like a Salvation Army reject. Of course the uniform covers a multitude of social lapses. All officers are supposed to be gentlemen."

He didn't inquire how he would pay for the suit. If Zach had reason to pass him off as a rich man's son, he would accept the disguise. In the meantime, as Zach had remarked, the uniform would do. The cognac was smooth, with oaky depths. He felt it easing the knot at the top of his spine. Tonight was the first alcohol he had had in weeks, for the troop ship had been dry.

They were in a club to which Zach belonged. Except for the sticky dessert, the meal had been excellent and the service, smart, although he supposed the linen was less snowy than it would have been formerly. The windows were covered with blackout curtains. Uniforms were everywhere, but nobody seemed to glare at the many men not in uniform. Here, as in Washington, everybody seemed to assume anyone not in uniform was in the government or in some important clandestine or propaganda work. He had been astonished to see women enlisted personnel and officers—not just nurses, but women in military uniforms. The bigger shock had been the extent of destruction. Half of London seemed reduced to plaster dust, broken bricks, stains on the shattered pavement. The hotel The Professor had used with their charges was a smashed facade and a rubble field.

"I can't quite get used to the bombing."

Zach laughed, sharply. "In one sense, you never do get used. In another, you become pleasantly numb and blasé about climbing over the rubble. Half the time you don't bother to take cover, it's just too big a bore. You learn to affect a cool demeanor. Finally you sleep through a raid, and then you know you've arrived." Zach lit a cigar, proffering one.

He declined with a shake of his head. "People tell me it was much worse the last two years."

Zach grimaced. "There were nights when London was simply on fire, the whole damn vast plain of the city going up in a thousand separate and uncontrollable fires, the pressure down, the power out, the fire fighters helpless. You'd hear people screaming and you were at a loss to help. It went on like that night after night after night. I wanted to rip the bombers down from the sky with my own hands. I wanted to kill." Zach smiled, leaning back and drawing on his cigar. "I presume you think they taught you how to do that in the States? We are babes in arms compared to the ancient and Byzantine deviousness of the British MI-6. They have taught us everything we know, which they consider about enough to qualify us for kindergarten. Prepare to be patronized."

Zach had changed the subject. Jeff deduced it was considered bad form to express consternation at the bomb damage, or even to appear to notice it unless one had a specific reason. ("Oh, rats, Jerry got my flat last night. Now I'll have to find somewhere to sleep tonight," Jeff had heard one young man remark in the hall at SO.) "Do we deal with them a lot?"

"Rather a lot," Zach said with a lengthy sigh. "Who is the enemy?"

"The Axis?"

"They too. But we have other enemies. There is J. Edgar Whoopdedoo—J stands for, Just wait till you see my file on you, will you give me whatever I want or do I leak it to the press? He envisioned an international FBI and our existence affronts him. In Washington at one point the FBI was putting more effort into shadowing us than the Nazis, and they fucked up one of our operations at an embassy because they considered we were poaching on their turf. Plus they kill to keep us out of Latin America—but then Nelson the Rock wants us out of there too."

"Tell me, do we have any time left to fight the war?"

"Which war is that? Then we have enemies in the State Department, those narrow-minded tight assholes. They fight us every step of the war. At one point the lady in charge of issuing passports would only give us ours with OSS in big letters. Talk about stamping a passport, ARREST THIS SPY. In Spain this year the American embassy almost blew our operation. We *were* running a sloppy team. I was over there twice, and I thought it was a bit of The Marx Brothers Hit Madrid—no wonder Madrid hit back."

Jeff was realizing that Zach seemed happier than he had been since college, certainly since his family had forced him to marry, settle down, take an active role in the insurance business and fulfill his full range of dynastic obligations. Zach was free again. Now he looked older in some respects—his skin had aged, his forehead had faint but always present lines, the grey of his eyes had more iron in them.

He looked younger in other aspects. He did not look as if he were drinking too much, which meant he was enjoying his life. When Zach was fully engaged, he drank but he could go off it when he should. When Zach felt confined, he needed alcohol to get through his days and nights. He could be mean then. Zach had a sadistic streak, but when he liked his life, he controlled it. He had an equally generous side to him. Many virtues, many vices, all a yard wide.

Zach ordered two more cognacs and Jeff sipped his. "In spite of what I take are your efforts to sophisticate me, to tarnish the fine glow of my organizational innocence, I want to repeat my gratitude for getting me out of Alabama—and essentially out of the Army. It's not my favorite pastime, being a soldier. I don't know what the hell we're supposed to be, spies or backdoor fighters, but it's easier on my psyche."

"Look around you. You'll see a lot of fine old names and you'll see the rising cream of the best banks and investment houses in New York, the snazziest law firms, the boys who'll be judges and senators and sit on the boards of the big corporations. You can be bloody sure that they have picked one of the best berths in the war. But field officers are another matter, my dear. That's what I have briefly been, in Greece for the Brits, and once the bloody Brits stop squatting on us and trying to keep us from getting our hands dirty, that's what I shall be again. That's the real fun and games." Zach leaned forward over the table, his grey eyes glittering. "Then it's you against everything, and you're down to your nerve, your guts, your smarts. It's life, says Mother, on the cutting edge."

"Sounds better than Alabama," Jeff said, wondering when he had finished that second snifter of cognac and when he had begun a third. They had killed a bottle of Margaux over supper. He wondered lazily if he would have the guts Zach was talking about. He tried to remember anything dangerous he had ever done, but at the moment his previous life appeared tame in retrospect. He thought of rattlesnakes, fistfights, riding the rails, getting mugged in an alley in Kansas City. But somehow he had walked through all of it. Perhaps as Zach suggested, this would challenge something so far unused, unawakened in him. He hoped so.

Zach gave that short choppy laugh as if reading him. "How the boy cottons up to it, how the boy shines in anticipation. One of the best stimulants—the nerves' own fine high overwound keening. Feeding and watering oneself at a decent table is lovely now and then, but nothing beats fucking and fighting for keeping the whole man fit."

"I gather the fighting is mostly infighting at the moment. What are you fucking?"

"Anything that moves, dear boy. I remain totally without prejudice and ever ready. My cock knows no frontiers he cannot penetrate." Zach grinned, wriggling his thumb in a gesture that had since adolescence meant sex to him and thus to Jeff. "Wartime London is a great place for all kinds of ginch. You always did have to fight it off, but here you'll have to wield a club."

As Jeff observed over the next weeks, Zach seemed to be dividing his sexual favors between ladies and navvies. The ladies were the well-born daughters of country houses, war widows of distinction, cultured and emancipated ladies vaguely connected with SIS or SOE, the branches of British intelligence they had the most contact with. The low-born lads were the rough trade Zach always seemed to find without looking hard.

Neither scene appealed to Jeff, who was sent to a country estate in Sussex for a course in special operations (over here they seemed to assume nothing he had learned in Washington was sufficient) and when he got back to London, Zach was not around. You did not ask, he learned, when someone was suddenly missing.

Jeff was marking time in London. Unless he had a bomb dropped on him or was run over by an emergency vehicle while stumbling home looped from one of the constant OSS parties or a friendly bash in a pub, he was safe while people were dying in great bloody piles everywhere across Europe and Asia. He began to think of painting. One Sunday he went out with his oils and a canvas and worked in a frenzy all day. He turned it to the wall and did not look at it again for a week. Then he turned it back. Yes, yes, it was a jump painting. Something had happened in/to him.

At eighteen, he had begun by imitating the Impressionists and then worked his way into something of his own, harder edged, a passion for the shadows and pits in a landscape where dark hid and welled up, where light bled into darkness, lanced across it. Lately Turner had been on his mind, but Turner celebrated masses of light, light almost as wind, and he felt some different approach working like yeast in him.

Oddly he began sketching the ducks in St. James's Park. He had seldom used animals in his landscapes—occasionally a gull high overhead stylized to a flattened W, except for a dead coyote he had painted at Taos. He began painting water, the ponds, the Thames, and then rain. There was nothing Turneresque in his studies of the grey England damp, yet he knew he was being moved in some new direction and yielded to it. This was real work at last, but slow going except for that first jump painting.

Zach reappeared on a Friday night and invited him to move into his flat, the upper floor in a smallish brick house in Chelsea. It managed to suggest itself as a cottage, in spite of being one of a row of partially bombed houses in a U-shaped street a couple of blocks from the Embankment and Cheyne Walk. Zach had been sharing it with a captain just posted to Stockholm.

The flat consisted of two small bedrooms, a pretty sitting room with a view of a fine old plane tree dropping its leaves without turning any particular color except the brown of paper bags, and a peculiar narrow kitchen. A cleaning lady came in to complain and to clean up the mess Zach mostly created. The flat gave Jeff a peculiar settled feeling, as if he had come to the war and to London in order to find a place he could call home at least temporarily. His bedroom would do as a studio.

Out front a low brick wall set them off from the quiet street. On both sides of the walk to their house were pedestals, with the gate hung between them, and a cement ball balanced on each side. Zach in giving directions always referred to their house as the one with the blue balls, or the cement balls, or he would say, "We have a shopkeeper's sign out front, two big balls, so you can find us."

Jeff could not remember the last place he had actually moved in, fixed up and lived in for any length of time. Zach relied on him for any nest building that was to occur. Zach had found the captain who had gone off to Stockholm too similar to himself in his bachelor habits, and seemed to expect Jeff to make things nice. Zach's women were no more domestic than Zach and cleaned up by ringing for a maid.

Jeff hung around SO, being given occasional minor assignments, assisting some officer in tasks needing little assistance. In October he was sent off to parachute school for a week, to learn British style. English parachutes opened differently than American and he had learned to jump out the side of a plane, rather than through the bottom. Carey and Aaron from his Washington group turned up to train with him.

As time passed he found himself feeling slightly guilty. Here he was fulfilling his dream, studying art in London—rather than Florence or Paris, unfortunately, but that was a relatively minor complaint—on a government subsidy, with a nice flat in a pleasant part of London, even if it was under siege. He finished two more paintings and enough time passed for the first to begin to look good to him. He took his pay and bought real linen, the last the art supply store had. He had been painting on cotton for years.

Occasionally he ran into someone he had known from before the war, one of The Professor's cronies from the University of Grenoble or Cologne, involved in the research operations for which his side of OSS had such scorn. He wondered. They seemed busy, useful, engaged. He had been prepared and prepared and now lay, a too sharp knife in a drawer quietly oxidizing. At other times he thought, why not? He had lost his youth in poverty and working-stiff jobs. Why not reclaim what the Depression had robbed from him? Why not taste a little of the ample freedom and comfort for which he had envied Zach? If there was anything that war was, besides organized murder, it was organized waste. Let him not waste his time here.

Therefore he painted, fiercely, compulsively. He began what might be a series of rubble paintings, across the river in the industrial, working-class sections always heavily bombed. He had begun to paint rubble in morning light. The tentative period of the water studies was behind him. Painting on the street in his uniform, nobody bothered him. They assumed, perhaps, it was official work, a record for some government office. Sometimes people on the streets would crowd up behind him to look over his shoulder and see what he was getting down and then they'd make some comment he frequently could not decipher, but which sounded friendly, and walk on. He was obsessed with the partially destroyed buildings, what was pulverized and what remained, the rooms blasted open, the tree with half its branches splintered, torn open to the light, the shadow of a chimney standing alone, the tawdry pathos of rooms opened like stage settings to the passerby.

"Don't think we'll be hanging around forever," Zach said. "We'll be shipping out sooner than you think."

"I've heard that one before. How was Turkey?"

"I'll take a load of grandmothers with me if I'm sent again. It's certainly the place to sell them. Double agents are a drug on the market. Triple agents, quadruple agents, agents selling back at extravagant prices to the people who first floated the rumors, the rumors they floated. I found it rather smarmy. They say Switzerland is the same scene on a cleaner scale. But you have to rank higher than I do and have more top honchos for your friends to pull that service."

"Someone said to me last week that Istanbul is where we flirt with the Germans who want to carry on an affair with us."

"So is Switzerland. There you don't have to worry about bugs in the bed. I thought Istanbul would be exciting, reeking of wild unbridled sexuality and spices. Instead I got a dreadful case of body lice. Don't gape at me—I got rid of them."

"My dear Zachary," Jeff imitated his friend's lordly tone, "if you think any parasites you caught would find me a virgin to their teeth or claws, you don't understand how I passed the last few years. I've fed enough lice to populate Istanbul." Jeff sighed. "I wish I'd gone with you. We never went farther east than Thessaloníki, a city Bernice and I always enjoyed."

"There are other, more imminent fleshpots," Zach said with a tantalizing smirk.

He was painting so fiercely he simply drifted socially in Zach's wake until one night the gaunt blonde who had gone to bed with Zach wakened him by climbing on top. "He's too drunk to get it up," she said in a cold, precise voice, unaffected by the gin she had consumed. "How about you?" She had her hand on his prick as he sat up.

In the morning Zach was annoyed. "Someone is going to wring that tramp's neck," he announced. "That was sneaky of you."

"Zach, I was had. I was taken without permission and used like a dildo."

"You don't adore me enough," Zach said darkly. "You lack appreciation."

"I appreciate you all day. At night I sleep. What do you want?"

"More love." Zach grinned sourly. "Everybody should love me. But you love no one. Not even your inestimable sister. You merely permit those of us adjacent to love you. You take it for granted, like water out of the faucet or the postal service. Your beauty makes you cold and passive."

That decided him he needed some anchor other than Zach. Jeff accompanied Zach to about half the parties he attended and some of the houses he visited, but when he settled on a steady lover, he chose a fresh-faced art student from Wales who was working in a munitions factory. All English women between eighteen and sixty had been conscripted for factory work, for nursing or the armed forces. Mary Llewellyn had translucent pale rosy skin like fine china and dark brown curls that popped out from under her turban. She was a hefty bottom-heavy girl with well-muscled and magnificently turned and rounded arms and legs. She liked to laugh, in and out of bed, and she could put away a quart of beer without pausing. Zach found her plebeian.

"Really, Jeff, when I consider what Mother has introduced you to. You can lead a horse to champagne but he'd rather drink warm beer."

"She takes good care of me," Jeff said honestly. He did not tell Zach the most important attraction, that he could talk art with her. He had not been able to do that with anyone since the group of painters he had met in Taos. She knew about shows and trends and galleries and who was doing what and where. She understood his problems finding the supplies he needed. She was close friends with a one-legged muralist named Tom Knacker and gradually through the two of them, Jeff met painters, now working for the British government. To Zach he said only, "I like her body. And she likes sex."

"They all do," Zach said mournfully. "Where are the fainting frigid virgins of yesteryear whose maidenheads could only be stormed by a battering ram? Gone, all gone. War is the most reliable aphrodisiac." He tossed a letter on the coffee table. "Your fair sister writes. News of the hearthside, apple pie put on hold for those of us fighting for our lives in the wilderness of Mayfair and Knightsbridge."

Jeff tore open the letter and scanned it quickly. "Bird is trying to fly the coop."

"About time, poor lass. She's been your father's keeper too many years. Off to a factory job in the wicked city?"

"No. She's trying to join some women's air service."

"They've had the WAAF over here for three years. Does she really still re- member how to fly?"

"Drop that patronizing tone. She has a commercial license. But The Professor doesn't want her to go. She wants me to intervene."

Zach shook his head. "Poor Bernice. She'll never cut loose. She has too tender a conscience."

"I suspect so," Jeff said, feeling the peculiar sense of comfort mingled with guilt his sister aroused in him. "I'll write The Professor, but he has never yet listened to me."

In the meantime he spent more and more time painting and more and more time with Mary Llewellyn. He liked her crowd, women art students and their boyfriends, Tom Knacker, young painters. Tom had lost his leg in an auto accident before the war, but everyone assumed it was a war injury, he said. Never been a better time for a one-legged man in London. They were in and out of each other's studios and even when they were eating stew on a rickety old table and dancing to a phonograph, wherever he turned, he saw paintings and thought about them. They looked at his work as he looked at theirs, and they saw him as one of them.

I could live like this permanently, Jeff thought. For the first time in his life he could locate no urge to move on. The better he got to know Mary, the more there was to her. Her friends were more suited to him than Zach's friends. He had liked the crowd around the galleries in Taos, but with a ranch job, he could not hang out with them. Mary's friends became his friends. He was part of a couple. He painted and he hung out with painters, as if he had finally grown up to the life he had always wanted.

DUVEY 2

The Maltese Crossing

Duvey had sworn he was going to stay off tankers, but he ended up shipping on the *Ohio* out of Clyde because he ran into his old buddy Ziggy from Detroit, who used to work the ore boats with him. It was too much to pass up, a chance to be with an old friend who was full of gossip about home. Ziggy had just returned from the Murmansk run, in a convoy that had lost half its ships to planes, subs and the weather, and he swore he'd go to hell before he'd go back to Murmansk. Duvey had known Ziggy since high school, a tall gangling basketball player whose hair looked black in the winter and ruddy brown under the sun, with a sharp nose that had a bump midway down it. They'd covered each other's backs endless times. They'd spent a lot of happy nights drinking beer and listening to jazz.

They signed up on the *Ohio* before they knew where it was headed, which turned out to be Malta. That didn't mean much to either, for Malta was a limey run, but the Mediterranean sounded inviting after the waters off Greenland and Iceland. They could see the escort they were getting: no couple of corvettes and one ancient dowager destroyer. When they sailed out, they were accompanied by two British battleships, the *Nelson* and the *Rodney,* four aircraft carriers, six cruisers, a special cruiser bristling with antiaircraft batteries, twenty-four destroyers, four corvettes and four minesweepers—all for their fourteen merchant ships. "Piece of cake," Duvey said. "Why don't they give us this kind of cover all the time?"

Cal, an Aussie who was hanging around with them, laughed at Duvey's optimism. "Listen, mate, there aint been a convoy got through there since June, and then only two ships. It's running the bloody fucking gamut with them pounding from all sides. It aint the bloody big Atlantic, you know. You can't play no hide-and-seek in the Med, it's just a bathtub full of seamen's bones."

Duvey figured that Aussie just didn't know what he was talking about, because he'd been on the Pacific till recently. Duvey had heard that Australia and

New Zealand were milk runs. Cal had no idea how dangerous the coastal shipping had been, or how many ships the U-boats picked off in the North Atlantic. Duvey'd been a sitting duck on merchantmen. Here they were finally getting some protection, and he figured with the fighting ships around them, they could steam through the jaws of hell.

He'd heard there were U-boats in the Med, but not the raging packs of them like hungry laughing sharks that surrounded the Atlantic convoys. Besides, he'd always liked it hot. In Scotland it had been damp and dreary, and for the last week it had rained, not his idea of August.

Cal hung with them because he was a self-taught politico like Ziggy and the two of them were always arguing about Trotsky and Prince Kropotkin. Ziggy was a highbrow and should have gone to college, but there hadn't been money and his mother needed his paycheck, so like Duvey, Ziggy had been working since he turned sixteen. He was always reading and always ready to argue. Duvey didn't know how Ziggy stayed alive when he wasn't around to watch out for him and the trouble his mouth could get him in. Ziggy had a long reach and he was well coordinated, but he didn't react fast enough in a fight. Somebody was always getting to his soft belly and doubling him over.

Cal said Yanks were easier for him to understand than limeys. Limeys had their brains twisted around from being moldy all the time. He said men from countries with a lot of room to spread out in and swing yourself around were naturally looser and didn't get mental bloody piles.

During the night of August 9/10, the convoy passed Gibraltar safely, because a dense fog lay in the straits. The coast of Spain was not blacked out, and even through the fog they could see some lights. In the dawn, the mountains of Spain looked grand. Duvey and Ziggy spent a lot of time reminiscing about Detroit, till Duvey began to feel a little homesick. Ziggy said Detroit was jammed with immigrants up from the South to work in the factories. "They recruit them with big promises. Housing's so tight, people are sleeping in the same bed in shifts. Man, I'm not kidding you. You rent a bed for so many hours, and then it belongs to some other bozo. Guys are working sixty hours a week, really racking it up. Everybody's got cash in their pockets, but man, half the restaurants in town are closed cause they got nobody to wait tables or work in the kitchen."

"Even my old lady's working," Duvey said. "She's running some kind of baby-sitting deal."

"My old girlfriend Francine got a job on a streetcar, do you believe it? They'll be hiring old ladies to drive hack."

Just before midday on the eleventh, they saw a small Heinkel following the convoy. One of the aircraft carriers turned to launch but the plane was a scout and withdrew. The maneuvering of the carrier cost everyone some speed, so the next time the scout (or another like it) appeared, although one of the cruisers fired some shells, they mostly ignored it.

The weather cleared. It was warm with a brisk dry breeze that had a different smell to it, besides the salt. There was a good chop but nothing to set the ship rolling. They were chipping and painting when suddenly the *Eagle,* the aircraft carrier that had swung around in the morning to launch its planes after the Heinkel, belched fire with a big explosion aft and while everybody was turning to stare, another explosion smote the air, then another, another and finally the whole ship was engulfed in flames within five minutes. Duvey just stood and gaped with the general quarters shrieking. It was a big heavily armed ship, its deck the size of his old high school, and in five minutes it was a mass of flames and twenty minutes later, it was listing. It reminded him of a tanker going up. Then he realized, sure, with all those planes on board, it must be carrying a hell of a lot of fuel. Seeing the carrier burn with those huge black clouds did not make him feel cosy, with tons of aviation fuel slopping under his feet.

The destroyers were rushing about dropping depth charges. But the sub was gone. No oil slick appeared. It had surfaced only to fire its torpedoes. Unless someone on the *Eagle* had seen it too late to take evasive action, no one had observed its arrival. All that firepower, and a damned U-boat could sneak up on them. What was the use of that radar stuff? He had never been on a ship equipped with it, but the aircraft carriers and the cruisers and even the destroyers all had those funny screens like open cages turning back and forth. That sub had slipped in and slipped out, leaving the aircraft carrier burning with an enormous black plume of smoke that must be visible for fifty miles.

Another of the aircraft carriers let off its Spitfires. He and Ziggy thought they were hunting the sub, but the Aussie Cal said they were on their way to Malta and that carrier and the destroyers with her were going back now. "Guess they'll get there before we will," Ziggy said, watching the slender planes going east.

"If we get there at all," the Aussie said. "One down and one leaving us."

That evening the first wave of Italian bombers came over, from Sardinia the crew speculated. They came in low and dropped their torpedoes while the anti-aircraft batteries filled the air with noise and smoke. One bomber came down just off their bow, splashing water and oil up and jolting the ship. A few feet closer, and they all would have croaked. It sank like the big piece of metal it was and nobody crawled out.

When the bombing was over, all the ships reported to each other, a chatter of relief and lively joking, because except for a couple of casualties on one merchantman from the concussion of a near miss, they were uninjured. "Those wop pilots can't hit their grandmother," Ziggy said. They were all feeling more cheerful. Another squadron came over in the morning of the next day, but again, damage was slight. Duvey had never been bombed before. It seemed to him not half as scary as the U-boats. You could see the fuckers coming at you and nine tenths of the time they missed. Some of their torpedoes were duds and others just streaked off for the horizon.

They heard the scuttlebutt that one of the destroyers in the returning carrier's screen had rammed and sunk an Italian sub off Gibraltar. Duvey hoped it was the one that had burned the *Eagle*.

It was early afternoon when they heard the drone of more planes. This time flights were coming in from several angles, dive bombers, fighter bombers, torpedo bombers, all coming in at once. They were not in the sloppy formations of the last two attacks but peeled off one after the other like trained acrobats. These guys were pros. Glancing up, Duvey could see the planes were being choreographed like dancers in a big show.

"Holy Tomoley," Ziggy said in a soft voice. "There must be a hundred of the bastards."

The dive bombers were the worst. Duvey felt as if they were aiming right for his head. It was hard not to panic, to remain upright and at his post. They made such a screaming roar as they came down, it seemed to press right on all the panic buttons in the spine. It was raining bombs in clouds of smoke so dark and choking they could not see the next ship on either side, but they could hear that somebody had been hit, from the explosions.

When the planes finally dropped what they had to drop and left and the acrid smoke cleared, the cruiser *Manchester* was sinking and the freighter *Cormorant* had been hit and was taking on water. As the afternoon wore on, she fell farther and farther behind. They could not wait for her, as they were all too vulnerable.

Now the subs were at them, worrying them, closing in, firing torpedoes. The *Ohio* was constantly turning at a sharp angle, taking evasive action, crossing her own wake and almost plowing into the freighter beside them, which was turning and twisting on its own crazy way. Duvey saw the destroyers hunting off the port side of the convoy, after something. This time they were lucky or better at the pattern of their depth charges, because an oil slick came up. Dead and stunned fish floated up, surrounded by a pack of screaming gulls. Then the sub surfaced. It was not one of the German U-boats he had seen in the Atlantic, but Italian. Its conning tower was much bigger and enclosed, unlike the open tower of the German subs. While he was watching, one of the destroyers rammed her and she went down.

Dead ahead of them lay the straits between Sicily and Tunisia, the Skerki

Channel. "Still standing? Good on you, mate." Cal came ambling up. "Guess what. This is the end of the line for the big boys."

"What are you talking about? We're two days from Malta, still."

"They're going back to Gibraltar in another couple of hours, that's what I hear. The Navy's saving their hides and leaving us to our own devices."

"You're crazy," Duvey said. "They see what's happening. For the last twenty-four hours we've been peppered. Every bastard with something to shoot or drop in the whole Med is having a go at us. If they dump us here, we'll never make it."

"I been telling you that since we passed the Rock, mate."

"Shit," Ziggy said in that soft voice the day had been wringing out of him, as if all the hardness hammered on the streets they had roamed together had been shaken into fragments. "Here come more of the kraut bastards. They must have two hundred planes."

The men moved sluggishly to their stations. They were getting plain exhausted. Duvey had had a headache for hours from the explosions and the smoke. His eyes burned. His throat felt sanded raw. Even if he saw a bomb dropping on his head, he couldn't move fast enough to clear out of the way. This time, however, the planes concentrated their fire on the escorting vessels. The carrier *Indomitable* was hit right on the flight deck three separate times, and one of the destroyers disabled. While Duvey was watching the wounded destroyer, he realized that Cal was right: except for a few cruisers and destroyers, the big stuff was leaving them and sailing back toward Gibraltar at full speed.

For the next two hours while they steamed on through the Skerki Channel, all hell broke loose. They were glad to see long-range fighters, Mustangs from Malta, arrive to form an umbrella over them, because the U-boats were swarming. There was little room to maneuver in the narrow waters of the channel. Duvey had had enough trouble getting used to how close the Atlantic convoys steamed along, but they had been distant neighbors compared to the cosy logjam they were causing here. One of the U-boats got the antiaircraft cruiser right off and crippled another of their remaining cruiser escort. That left two goddamned cruisers and two only of all those that had sailed out of Clyde, and ten destroyers.

Right after that Duvey was near the bow when the *Ohio* caught it aft. It was a sharp blow, like an enormous crunch, and everything loose fell, including Duvey. He thought he was gone. This is what I get for shipping on a tanker, and Ruthie always said I was going to catch trouble for hanging around with bad company. Although Duvey had never been religious, he found the Shma Yisroel going in his head. He guessed he was ready to die a Jew. Then he was rushing aft to help with the hoses. Amazingly the torpedo had not penetrated the oil. They were burning but not yet exploding. He was too busy to notice when the fighters from Malta headed back to refuel.

They hadn't been gone half an hour when twenty German Messerschmitts made their attack. They ignored the *Ohio* blessedly, which was putting out its own smoke screen, but the captain had the engines up and was steaming ahead, taking what evasive action he could with a fire on deck and freighters packed in all around them. The torpedo had taken their steering gear, and they were hand-steering from aft. The convoy was like a river full of smelts struggling to make it upstream to mate and being had by every hungry gull, every fisherman with a line or net, every bigger fish that could get at them. The *Clan Ferguson* bought it and went up like a fireball, so close to them that Duvey's cheek was gashed by a bit of flying debris. He was bleeding all over himself, but it wasn't serious and the fire was.

At last the damned bloody sun was going down and soon the Germans would have to stop bombing them. Cal called out that another ship had been hit repeatedly and was sinking, one of the merchantmen behind them, but in the smoke nobody could see which one. Finally the Germans ran out of stuff to throw at them and left, but they hadn't been gone a few minutes when the U-boats were back. This time they got a torpedo into one of the two remaining cruisers, but she stayed afloat and dragged along with them.

It was clear the *Ohio* wasn't going to explode or sink. They had the fire under control and they were still proceeding at seven knots, although they had fallen toward the back of the convoy. Not a great place to be but if they managed to stay with it, they had some kind of a chance. Scuttlebutt had it that the *Cormorant*, dragging along miles behind the rest of the convoy, had got clobbered while they were under attack and gone down. A boat alone was dead in the water, everyone's leisurely prey.

Even though nighttime was the right time to the U-boats, at least it kept the bombers off them. They hoped that they would be less visible against the dark shore as they passed near Tunis. Maybe the U-boats did have trouble seeing them, for they were left alone. Duvey had been awake now for forty-eight hours. Early in the night he slept for a while in his clothes till general quarters sounded. This time they were under attack by torpedo boats from Pantelleria Island, where the Italians had a base. They were small but they were fast and nasty. Again, they too were new to Duvey. He felt if he survived, he would find the North Atlantic run peaceful by comparison, with only the U-boats and the fierce storms to menace them.

The first ship to be knocked out was the remaining intact cruiser. After that the torpedo boats seemed to pick off ships at random. The attack went on and on and on and on. When Duvey looked at his watch, he could see it by natural light and it was dawn, just before six. Four of the merchant ships had gone down. They picked up what survivors they could. At least the poor bastards had a chance in these warm waters. They wouldn't die of exposure, anyhow.

They had company at the straggling end of the convoy now, because another ship loaded with food supplies and machinery had taken two torpedoes but was staying afloat and steaming along with them. They should be within a day of Malta now, one more bleeding day, as Cal said with feeling. Duvey stared at the sun rising in the direction where safety must lie. If they did make it, how in hell would he get back? He decided he was going to love Malta if he got there, he was going to jump ship and shack up with a Maltese girl. Maybe if Maltese cats did not have tails, the girls would, he said to Ziggy. Ziggy said that was Manx cats he was thinking of, not Maltese.

Cal said, "I hear it's no vacation being there. They get bombed twice a day on the off days, four times on Sunday."

Ziggy said, "Me, all I care about is Maltese pussy. That's my kind of tail. I bet they're dark and zaftig. Did I ever tell you about the longshoremen in Murmansk? They're babes, everyone of them. . . ."

There were only seven ships left afloat, and two of them, including theirs, were barely moving. It wasn't long after daylight that the German bombers and dive bombers found them. The Jerries got the *Ply* three hits in a row and she went up in a shattering blast of pungent yellow smoke. Explosives, must have been. One dive bomber came roaring down at them, dropped his bomb close enough so that the deck was drenched and then lost control of his dive, or else he was hit. "Oh my God!" Cal screamed.

Ziggy cried, "Down!" and threw himself on Duvey. Duvey found himself thrown forward and slammed into something hard and metal.

He came to without attention sometime later. His head ached as if it were cracked open, and his left wrist was broken. Something heavy and wet was lying on top of him. He could not move at first. He could hardly breathe. He was covered with blood, sticky, cooling. Finally he crawled out from under. The something heavy and wet was Ziggy. Duvey could not take it in. He looked around, calling for help. Nobody heard him.

Every man who could was fighting the fires where the kraut bomber had crashed into them. Half its wreckage was still on the deck and so was what remained of Cal. He recognized Cal from the snake tattoo on his remaining arm, or he wouldn't have known because he was mostly pulp and smashed bones. Ziggy was drenched in blood and charred, intact except for the top of his head sliced off. His dark hair ended abruptly in a semicircle of smashed bone. He knelt over Ziggy thinking he should touch him, somehow lay him to rest, as a small explosion shook the deck. He heard himself calling Ziggy. If Ziggy hadn't responded so fast, he'd be dead too. Why should he be alive? He thought he was going to pass out as he tried to walk the deck toward the fire, tying up his broken wrist roughly. It was his left, which was lucky anyhow. They had to get the fires out before anybody could look to get treated.

Once again they got the fire under control. Duvey didn't know whether he was on the unluckiest ship or the luckiest. They had been hit twice and they had lost by now a quarter of the crew, with maybe another quarter wounded or badly burned. But a tanker hardly ever survived one hit.

The German bombers were back. They blasted one ship and then they torpedoed the *Ohio* and Duvey, who was being patched up, found himself on the floor with the medic on top of him. This time the Jerries had got them where it really hurt, in the engine room, and they were standing still like a fucking dead duck in the middle of a pond just waiting for the planes to come back. They had a lot of company. Two other ships were cripples too and they were all going to die together. The engineer swore he could get them going again, but he couldn't say when. The captain lined them up and told them they were going to make it because they had to, and he expected everybody wounded or not to pitch in, because they were going to reach Malta and nobody was going to stop them.

Duvey felt like crying as he watched the three ships that could still make speed draw away and then fade over the horizon. Duvey thought of the brave parade that had steamed out of Clyde, and now what was left around him? Three cripples waiting for the hunters to come back and finish them off.

By afternoon the engines were going again, although they were slow as a river barge. Then he saw ships coming, and he was damned scared. He'd heard Italian warships were steaming around out here. When Duvey saw it was the four destroyers coming back for them, he wanted to kiss the stiffs in monkey suits on board them.

Sparks passed the word that the three ships had made it into Valletta, the harbor of Malta, escorted by minesweepers and motor launches. Here they were still at sea and the Jerries were back with more planes. The bombs were falling all around them, but in spite of the *Ohio*'s slowness, the Jerries kept missing. The sun set lurid and beautiful and the Jerries kept coming. It was hardly light when the dive bombers set at them one after the other, peeling off and coming and coming and coming, till the *Pride of Portsmouth* was hit and hit and turned in a helpless circle, bombed apart as if with a massive hammer, stroke after stroke. Then the *Ohio* caught it again right in the engine room.

This time they had killed the engineer and the guys in the Black Gang, and the engines were scrap metal. Still the *Ohio,* sloshing full with aviation fuel, did not explode. They were once more adrift, this time without hope of fixing the engines. Nothing would ever fix those engines again. Furthermore the ship was cut almost in two, a great hole separating forward and aft and leaving only a thin net of metal to hold the ship together.

One of the destroyers was signaling them. She came up alongside and then actually bashed against them, as if nuzzling. The little destroyer was going to try to move them toward Malta by being lashed to the side of the *Ohio.* Duvey had never heard of such a maneuver, but he wasn't about to complain. It was nice to feel somebody besides him wanted him to get to Malta. He had never wanted to be anyplace so bad in his life. Two minesweepers came out from Malta to meet them and attached towlines to the smashed bow. Still with all the tiny boats tugging at them, their progress—a heavy tanker loaded with aviation fuel and riding low in the water—was barely visible. The ship with its two sections trying to swing apart and in different directions kept breaking the towlines and almost smashing into the destroyer and the minesweepers. Low in the water, listing, drifting, taking on water, the *Ohio* or what was left of it was dragged onward.

The other remaining cripple had got up steam again and was proceeding, escorted by two of the surviving destroyers. Soon she left them behind. All night they crawled forward. There was a strange calm. Duvey slid into a dreamless overheated bog of sleep, suffocating, sweating cold. He woke with his head and wrist throbbing and the bruises he had not noticed black and blue all over his swollen legs and battered shoulders. He could not raise his left arm at all. When he shat, his stool was bloody. It was the first time he had had a moment to take a crap in three days. He found himself weeping and pretended to be barfing to cover his noise.

He kept seeing Ziggy lying on his face with the top of his head sheared off. He could not mourn him yet. He had a sheared-off feeling himself, something ripped out, missing. He could not mourn Ziggy yet, because the odds were he'd be joining him any moment. For years he'd thought of himself as looking out for Ziggy, then Ziggy had thrown himself on top of him.

They were wallowing along, barely moving, as the fourteenth dawned. The fighters from Malta came out, but they were told that Malta was so low on fuel for the fighters, that they could barely put up twenty of them. Those twenty acted like eighty. All day the *Ohio* dawdled forward, almost stationary under a massy brazen sun, as the dogfights swirled over them. The destroyer was still lashed to them, to share their fate, and the minesweepers tugged them forward. All day the planes came at them and all day the Spitfires from Malta fought them off, always outnumbered but always there. Bombs never stopped bracketing them as they lumbered along, big as a factory and almost as stationary, yet nothing hit them.

All through the night they stayed at their stations. Duvey was seeing and hearing things by now. He saw land. He saw flashes of light out in the sea. He heard Ziggy calling, "Hey, Duvey. Look what I got." He heard his girlfriend Delora singing a song about, Come on in my kitchen. He heard Mama talking just behind him. He kept smelling something burnt but after a while he figured out that was no hallucination. It was his own hair burnt all off his arms and the back of his head he was smelling. He had a scorched bald spot on the back of his head the size of a grapefruit. He had to doze with his head turned sideways. When he did doze, he kept seeing Ziggy with the top of his head cut off, like a soft-boiled egg. Acid rushed up his throat and he puked, briefly. He was too exhausted even to throw up at length.

At dawn the minesweepers led them forward still, and the island was visible, finally, Malta with its mountains and its cliffs gleaming darkly out of the blue, blue sea so bright it hurt his sore eyes, with another island to the side. As they made their endless approach, he could see that the narrow entrance to Valletta harbor was defended by an ancient fort with tall stone ramparts, crowded with people as if they had come to see a parade. It was the *Ohio* they had come to greet and they cheered and waved and called to them, some in English, but some in a language he had never heard. They were throwing things at them, hats, flowers, pieces of paper. They were crying, some of them, with joy to see the half-gutted, blasted, crippled hulk of the tanker dragged into port with its bloody charred decks and its crippled crew.

Duvey tasted his exhaustion like an industrial poison in his mouth, like lead thickening and tainting his blood. This place looked incredibly old, it looked like the most ancient place he had ever seen, the way he had always imagined Palestine. It looked hot, dusty, dry, sunbaked, poverty-stricken and beautiful climbing up its rocks and tumbling over them and burrowing into them, swarming up the mountain. Everywhere in the port, bomb damage was visible, the wrecks of boats at their moorings, hulls upturned, twisted cranes, smashed walls, roofless buildings. Yet people crowded the quays and brightly painted little boats and passenger ferries crisscrossed the harbor and headed out to sea. He felt in his exhaustion as if Ziggy were looking too, out through his eyes.

When he disembarked, he was going to get down and kiss the poor stones of Malta. He was going to settle here. Anyplace that looked this old, the people must know a lot about survival. Here they greeted a tanker and the poor slobs aboard like conquering heroes. They must know a thing or two about peace and war and living. Now that he had reached this port, he just wanted to stay. Forever.

RUTHIE 3

Of Good Girls and Bad Girls

Early in August Ruthie got a postcard from the government. The United States Employment Service asked her whether she was interested in factory work, whether she had any experience and when she was available. Ruthie not only filled out the card with her best printing, she brought it to the office and asked to be referred to a factory job. Nothing happened.

Still she decided to go around to the plants and fill out applications, in case they suddenly did decide to hire women. A number of the employment officers were nasty, and the men there stared as if she were naked and prancing out of a cake. Nonetheless long before Labor Day, Ruthie had a job at Briggs. Morris grew alarmed and treated her to a lecture about how many more factory workers had been maimed and killed the previous year than troops in combat. Ruthie told him he hadn't given a speech like that to Arty, and that she did not plan to be careless.

She would be working the graveyard shift, so she immediately switched to day school at Wayne. She would try to take close to a normal load of daytime classes, go home to sleep, then get up to work all night. Women did not like the graveyard shift, because with the dimouts, the streets felt dangerous. However, Ruthie rode to Briggs with Vivian, who had been taken on at the same time. Vivian drove her husband's 1938 Nash (he was in the Army), picking up three women every night and taking them home at dawn, for sixty cents a week from each.

Ruthie started out at thirty-eight a week, twice what she'd been making a year ago. She could go to school on that and save for later on and still help her family, who needed the help less than ever because Morris was working overtime and so was Arty, and Mama and Sharon were bringing in money from the nursery. For the first time in Ruthie's life, everything they owned was paid off. Her parents were actually saving in a bank account, although Rose always kept cash in an old teapot up in the cupboard, in case the bank failed. Also hidden in the teapot were Rose's amber necklace that had been Bubeh's, a gold bracelet that had been Morris's engagement present to her, and eleven silver dollars.

"If we ever have a fire, if a bomb falls, that's what you should grab first," Rose told Ruthie.

She would grab Naomi first and Boston Blackie, she thought to herself. Then she'd worry about the teapot. They had buckets of sand and buckets of water in the attic and the basement. Everybody was supposed to do that, but only they did, because Morris was the block air raid warden. Morris liked being air raid warden, for it gave him an excuse to go around to shmooz with the neighbors, and he liked reading through the official notices that came to him. He felt a part of the war effort and a genuine citizen.

Rose also took the various campaigns seriously, eager to be American and patriotic. She washed empty cans and once a week, Naomi and Ruthie stomped them flat. Rose saved fat and newspapers. Ruthie heard her explaining to Naomi what milkweed looked like, so Naomi could collect pods. The kids insisted that the milkweed silk was used to manufacture parachutes. Even Naomi believed that.

Ruthie knew better, because her shop steward had told her. Up in Petoskey, a plant was making flight jackets lined with milkweed silk instead of kapok, whose supply had been cut off by the Japanese. He had a brother employed there. He was a big burly Finn and not half so bad as most of the men she worked with. If it wasn't for the combination of the money and the time to go to school, she would have quit after the first day. She was pinched, she was handled, she was stared at until she felt as if she were a mass of raw bloody tissue. She still could not cross the floor without forty men making lowing noises like besotted cattle or whistling. Some men were always trying to sabotage the women's work. They seemed terrified women would take jobs permanently.

"They really know they've got a good thing going," Ruthie said to Vivian on the way to work. "Before the war we worked at those crummy jobs that pay half as much. Of course they don't want us coming into the factories, because we work harder than they do. We don't jack off."

"I'm just working till my husband comes home," Mary Lou said, but Vivian said she liked getting out of the house and she sure liked the money.

"Not that there's much to buy with it nowadays. But for the first time in my life, I can go buy myself a dress without asking Can I? Honey, can I?" Short and broad-shouldered, Vivian wore the first slacks Ruthie had seen on a woman, except in the movies. Now she herself was wearing overalls. At first they felt odd, stiff fabric rubbing against the inside of her thighs, but the pockets were great. Best of all she liked the way she could run along the catwalks without guys looking up her skirt.

People on the street were still touchy about women wearing slacks and often called out insults or obscenities. Just last week, Joyce had been sent home for wearing red slacks, as if the men were bulls and would charge her. The foreman called her red slacks indecent, provocative. The women all agreed it was a hoot, but Joyce lost a day's pay and had that put on her record. They had not even been tight slacks, but loose and pleated.

Ruthie got off the Woodward streetcar and slowly walked toward her house. It had been a wet summer and now, two weeks after Labor Day, it was hot, as if to make up for the rainy August. She was exhausted, for she had worked eight hours, then spent nine to two at school.

She noticed a bunch of the local kids in the alley entrance as she crossed to her own block, two of the guys with fags hanging out of the corner of their mouths and the girls smoking too. Some of the younger girls had started wearing slacks, probably their brother's pants, with oversized men's shirts pulled down to cover the fly. She was dismayed to realize that one of the girls leaning on the side of the building flirting with the scuzzy-looking boys was Naomi. With a hand on her outflung hip and an expression of smiling disdain, her lips daubed with bright pink grease probably borrowed from the other girls, she looked mean and cheap.

Ruthie was embarrassed as she called to Naomi, not wanting Naomi to think she was spying, but truly dismayed. Naomi looked completely assimilated, one of the street kids, tough, scrawny, flip. Ruthie herself had never belonged to a gang or even the sort of protogang she could see forming there. Why not? Ruthie walked on more slowly. She had duties at home. She had always felt a strong identification with her mother, her mother's troubles, the difficulty of making things stretch for the family.

Then too she had feared the seductions of that street world, had feared being stuck here, married too young, pregnant too young, forever poor and just one step off the dole. Arty and Duvey were not going anyplace. She had always been the best at school. She had not thrown in her lot with the tougher kids but with those who meant to go to college, whose families pushed them successfully to excel, to study, who saw in classes and exams and grades a personal salvation, who found books a passport to elsewhere.

Rose was more harried with Naomi than she had been with Ruthie, and Bubeh had also overseen her, taught her, comforted her for the small and bigger abrasions of life as a poor Jewish girl. Naomi was not Rose's child, but they owed her more care and attention. Yet Ruthie herself had little enough time. She was always tired, always rushed. Between the noise and confusion and harrying, almost intolerable pace of the line, and the world of lectures and library, exams and the imaginary case studies of school, there seemed no overlap. Sometimes she felt crazy, as if she belonged in neither place and ought always to be in the place where she was not.

Here she was studying to be a social worker, and there was her own charge, her cousin, hanging out with a gang of scruffy kids smoking butts they must steal someplace and who knew what else they were getting into? She sighed as she plodded along the driveway past the Rosenthals' house to their own. Washing hung in the yard, sheets drooping in the humid heat. The last coals of summer, she thought, feeling the air stain her with its weight of sulphur and smoke until her skin had the smell of river bottom mud. Rose met her at the door, hefting a squalling baby on one hip.

"Your young man is coming, Ruthie mine. Your young man is coming this Saturday to see his mother and father and you. Pick up your head and give me a smile, you look so tired, tsatskeleh."

"Murray? He's coming? How do you know, Mama? Who told you?"

Rose smoothed a telegram out of her apron pocket and handed it to Ruthie. "This came for you. I was so scared, I thought something happened with our Duvey. For once it's good news, we should always be glad when it happens and it should happen more often."

The telegram, addressed to her, said simply that Murray had forty-eight hours' leave and he would call her as soon as he got in Saturday.

She had to take off work. She had never yet been absent, but she would call in sick on Saturday. Sunday she had off anyhow. She kept reading the telegram again and again, hoping for more information. Love, Murray. Love. She would see him Saturday. She could not speak. She could not eat the soup steaming for her. She chewed a piece of rye bread she could scarcely choke down and then went upstairs. Because of the noise from the children, Ruthie, like Arty, slept upstairs.

Arty was snoring in the bedroom, but when Ruthie lay down on the couch that Rose had already made up for her, she could not sleep. She was parched for sleep, but she could not quiet the excitement that rattled and tore in her like a fan with sharpened blades. They would have such a short time. She had to share him with his own family. She could already feel past this brief respite in her longing for him how desolate it was going to be when he was gone again.

Why did they give them so little time? It wasn't right, it wasn't right. She understood why Trudi had traveled down to Tennessee to stay in a dismal town where she was overcharged and treated like an outcast, just to be near Leib all of August. Now Trudi was back, perhaps pregnant, and Leib was somewhere in Scotland.

When she woke, Sharon was asleep and Arty was in the bathroom. She went downstairs to bathe and dress. On the table, the candles from supper had burnt out but the old Sabbath candleholder from Poland was still in the center of the table with the layers of colored wax dripped down its tarnished silver sides. A year ago, it would have been freshly polished every week, but Rose was too overworked. Ruthie decided she preferred it dimmed and festooned with multi-colored wax. What she didn't like was missing Sabbath dinner.

Rose was waiting for her at the table, with her supper heating. "I wish you wouldn't wait up, Mama. Your day starts too early."

"It's my pleasure," Rose said, sweeping crumbs from the table with the side of her hand. "I sleep better knowing you had a good meal."

It was odd to eat supper upon waking, in the middle of the night, but nothing was normal. Rose brought her a plate on which was set out slices of roast chicken, stuffing, applesauce, potatoes and salad from their victory garden. Across the table from her Rose sat nibbling a slice of challah to keep her company, trying to hide her yawns as she played with the bread.

"Tomorrow I'm going to stay out of work, Mama," Ruthie said.

Rose looked down, her face puckering with worry. "You had such a hard time getting this job, shainele. You need to take such chances with it?"

"I haven't even been late once yet. Everybody misses sometimes and I'll go in Monday. I can't help it, Mama, we have almost no time."

"After the war, you'll have lots of time."

"When will that be, Mama? When I'm fifty? That's assuming Murray will come back to me."

Rose spat into her hand. "Kine-ahora, don't say such a thing, don't even think such a thing to yourself."

"Murray's a marine, Mama, he's not just on a ship. He's going to be fighting. I'm convinced that they're sending him overseas, and that's why he has this leave. That's what happened with Leib and every guy we know, Mama. They give them a little leave and then they go."

"He'll go and then he'll come back. Then you can talk about all the time you need and be serious. The radio sings all day about love, love, love, no wonder young people go crazy."

"Mama, I'm worried about Naomi. She's hanging around street corners with some tough-looking kids—"

"Naomi's a good girl. She doesn't help me as willingly as you used to, but she does as good as she can in a strange country away from her own mama. She tries. So she speaks like the other kids and of course she tries to look like them too. When you go into another country, it's so hard, Ruthenyu, I remember, everything is hard. They all look like zhlobs nowadays, it doesn't mean they're no good. It's the times."

When she got home from work Ruthie went straight to bed. She was always short on sleep by the weekend, ready to fall into it and let it wash through her. Only women with six-day-a-week factory jobs left their kids with Rose and Sharon on Saturday. Ruthie could sleep in her own bed and wake in her own room. That was better for her, better for Naomi, who seemed to miss her presence. That was one of the few days she woke feeling as if she had sunk all the way down into sleep and been rebuilt.

Today she would have supper with her family and then Murray would call. If he could not see her tonight, she could always go in anyhow. She had till ten to make up her mind, and now it was daylight when she woke up, a luxury she loved, and only five-thirty. Boston Blackie lay against her purring softly. He missed her too, but he had taken to sleeping with Naomi. That seemed to comfort both of them.

Lying in her bunk peaceful with the rare feeling of being rested and refreshed and trying to keep her mind off Murray, hearing the sounds of cooking and the clatter of dishes from the kitchen, work which she ought to go and help with but did not, she wondered if she were doing the wrong thing by working in a factory. Going to school four evenings a week, taking two classes, she had in a year finished the equivalent of one semester. At the rate at which she had been able to take classes, she would have needed eight years to get her degree, eight years of deferring marriage, family, personal joy, to arrive finally in her profession handicapped by her late start.

Now going to school days, she would be done in two and a half years. When Murray came home, she would be able to offer him more than labor for an aging bride, as Jacob had waited for Rachel, who then had all that trouble with childbearing, probably from being overage. Perhaps she would be almost finished or even have her degree and be working. Instead of liabilities and the promise of joy deferred, she could help Murray, and they could begin a life together.

With that hope she finally got herself out of bed.

At eight Murray called. Ruthie had intentionally not been answering the phone, because she could not stand to answer it and have it be someone else. Knowing that Ruthie was waiting for that call, Naomi came running. "The chassen is on the phone," she said wryly, coming to a halt.

Ruthie rushed to the phone through air thick as honey. After the brief conversation it seemed to her she had not spoken at all and had scarcely been able to listen. He was on his way over. He had his father's very old but still functional Dodge.

She ran to dress. She could think of nothing to put on except the pink chiffon Rose had bought at a rummage sale. "Are you going to a fancy party?" Rose said to her, tsking her tongue.

"Seeing him is the only party I care about. What's more important than to look good to him before he goes?"

She stared at him as he came through the door, a little dismayed, for he looked different in the uniform. His fine light brown hair was cut so short he looked bald, his ears sticking out like handles on a sugar bowl. His eyes were the same rich warm brown with flecks of sun in them; that reassured her. She did not know how she got him out of the house, but she did. Tata wanted to talk with him, Arty was waiting around, Sharon and Rose were avid with curiosity.

What got them out was that they both wanted desperately to be alone together, and politeness simply failed and the urge to bolt into the night won out.

"Where are we going?" she asked, in his car.

"How about Belle Isle? At least it will be cooler there."

Rose had been right; the pink chiffon dress was silly. But he was saying, "You look so beautiful, I can't believe it. I can't believe we're together and I can't believe I have to leave you in less than twenty-four hours. . . . Don't you ever wish we'd gotten married before I joined up?"

"Sometimes. But it doesn't make sense. At least, maybe by the time you get out, we can do it without losing everything we want."

"Right now all I want is the right to walk into a room with you and close the door on everybody else in the world."

"You sound like you wish we'd got married?"

"We were stupid not to. At least you'd get the allotment checks."

In the pavilion on Belle Isle, a band was playing. Murray was not the world's best dancer and neither was she. The female singer was belting out, "One Dozen Roses." The dance floor was so crowded that they could do no more than embrace where they stood and sway back and forth with little steps. Half of Detroit seemed crowded into the river park tonight.

He held her very close. She kept having trouble catching her breath, not because he was hurting her but because of their bodies pressed thigh to thigh and belly to belly. She could feel his erection against her. Through the flimsy chiffon, her skin burned. The dance floor was hot, reeking of beer, sweat, perfume, hair tonic. Fights kept breaking out on the fringes. They simply stood in place swaying, taking mincing little steps and holding each other.

When the band started a fast jitterbug, "Pennsylvania Six Five Thousand," they sat down. The floor cleared out some. They drank soda and looked at each other. She kept feeling as if she were on the edge of bursting into tears. "It was hard for you at Parris Island, wasn't it?"

"The Marines must recruit the worst bullies and the most prejudiced foul-mouthed goys in the whole country."

That was a word he had used to object to, a ghetto word, he had said. Now it came to his lips with feeling. What you send away, you don't get back the same, she thought, but felt no less close to him.

He handed her a check for one hundred ten dollars made out to her. "I've been saving. You open a new account for us. I have to feel we're getting some-place. This'll start us off, when the war's over. We'll both save what we can. I don't want to live with your parents or move in with mine. I have to know if I come back, and I'm going to come back, I swear it, that I'm coming back to you. That you're waiting for me—"

"Murray, you must know that. I haven't looked at another man since the first time we went out together. I don't want anybody else."

"But it's hard on you too. I want you to know we're homing in on what we want together. That we will make it happen. I won't give up any part of it. I won't let go of you, and that's going to bring me back."

"You're going overseas?"

"I'm sure of it. The guys are guessing New Zealand."

How could they be together at this table tonight and tomorrow separated, perhaps for years? "We could make a code to get by the censors, for all the places we can think of." They made up phrases for New Zealand, Australia, New Guinea, Samoa.

"It's like a shvitz bath in here, let's get a breeze," he said, leading her out to the old Dodge. He drove toward the downriver end of the island and parked on a loop with several other cars, dark and occupied. As soon as he shut off the engine, he reached for her.

She knew almost as soon as he touched her that he was not going to hold back. He was not trying to restrain himself, as he always had, as she had always trusted him to. He wanted. "Murray, I'm afraid. Don't!"

"Ruthie, if not now, when? When will we have a chance together? I have a rubber, I'll take care. Don't be frightened of me."

"You are so sure of me, you bring one of those things?"

"I'm sure what I want, and that it's you I want. Aren't you sure yet?" He did not wait for her answer but started kissing her again, slipping his hand down inside the V neck of the dress and into her brassiere. His hand felt hot against her breast, engulfing. No one had ever touched her naked breast before and she felt as if she were turning to warm jelly, the calves' foot jelly Bubeh made for invalids.

She tried to twist away from him but he held her. "Ruthie, you want me too. Don't make us both suffer any longer. You are mine. Or aren't you?"

She felt the slither of despair cold and dry on her back. Fighting off Leib had been one thing, discouraging Murray another. She had let him too far in. She loved him. She could find no words to raise between them that would refuse him without pain. She thought of her mother. Rose would be furious. She was caught between them, pulled to each. But Rose had her husband and she must have hers, the only man she had ever found herself wanting all through her body and her mind.

She could not wrestle with him or strike him as she had more than once given Leib a smart slap across the face. She was going to give in. Rose would have many names for a girl who was that foolish, but Rose had never had to send Morris off to be shot at. The worst danger he had ever faced had been beatings on a picket line, and at least they had been married then.

Murray could read her body language, her sighs, her sudden passivity in his arms. "You will. Come on, take off your dress. We can get that undressed."

"Suppose the police come."

"They won't. They're scared to come in here when so many servicemen are parked. They know they'd start a riot."

They got into the backseat. Ruthie was shaking slightly as he slipped the dress off. She insisted on keeping on her bra and her slip. She was not wearing stockings. She was rigid with fear.

"Ruthie, my love, my baby, you're so stiff I'll hurt you. Relax to me. When we were dancing, you wanted me. Can't you want me now?"

"I'm so scared I can't stop shaking. You should just go ahead and do it anyhow."

"Put your hand on me. There. Is that so frightening? It's just flesh like your flesh. It stands up, it lies down. You can make it do anything you want just by touching it. It's not as big as your foot or as hard as your elbow, right?"

She laughed. "I'm touching it. Don't think I'm an idiot. I've seen my brother Duvey's, when he was asleep on top of the covers and I was sent in to wake him, but it was just hanging there, little."

"Haven't you ever touched yourself, kitten?"

"You shouldn't ask me that." She felt herself blushing. Her hand tightened around his thing.

"Haven't you? Of course you have."

"Just since I met you! Before that, I didn't have to!"

"The fire I lit, I will put out," he said softly in her ear, her hair, and put his hand between her legs. "That's better. That's good. Tell me you like me to do that."

"Murray!"

"Ruthie!" He kissed her. His finger slid up into her. "It doesn't have to be grim. We'll do this thousands of times before we die, thousands and thousands and thousands. We'll do it till we're ninety. Does that hurt?" He slowly slid another finger and then another into her.

"Yes, it hurts." She had her hand on his penis, so she knew it was only fingers. Still, "Hadn't we better put that cover on you?"

"Okay. Now." He took his hand away from her. Her body still ached where he had touched her, the sting of the stretching but also an ache that was wanting. He tore open the foil and fitted the rubber over himself. "You put him in." He drew her slip up away from her hips and put his handkerchief under her buttocks.

"Me?"

"If it hurts too much, stop." He lay down half on her and pressed his penis against her. Slowly he moved it back and forth, back and forth, until suddenly he slid in, as his finger had done, just a little. It did hurt but she thought, I must do this, I must, and she lunged forward, with a sharp tearing pain that brought tears to her eyes. Slowly the tears trickled over his shoulder.

"There," she said.

"We did it." He moved slowly in her at first and then suddenly faster. "Am I hurting you?" he gasped, as if he too was in pain.

She did not answer, not wanting to lie. Then he groaned and stopped. After a few minutes, he slowly drew out of her. The condom hung heavy on him with fluid, and his penis was smaller again.

They had to go back soon after that. "I'm going to say we went out and drank coffee down by Wayne and then went to a movie," Ruthie said.

"If they believe that, they'll believe anything."

"You better hope they believe it. I'm praying."

When she got in, Sharon was crying because she had just had a fight with Arty as he was leaving for work, and Rose was holding her and saying, he didn't mean it, he didn't mean it. Arty had lost his temper because Sharon always fell asleep before he left. He said his mother would sit up to see him out of the house, but his own wife was too lazy.

Ruthie felt profoundly relieved. She was safe from Rose's attention. In the bathroom she carefully sponged dried blood from her thighs and washed the stained panty. She could not sleep, because she had slept during the day. This was the time of night she usually worked and she was wide awake. However, she played at going to bed until the house was dark and quiet and she could be sure everyone else was sleeping.

Then she sat at the kitchen table trying to make peace with herself over what she had done. Now she had to marry him. But she wanted to anyhow. At least they had had that much. Finally she took out her schoolbooks and studied, making notes for a paper she had to write. Homework was something that took up any spare moments she had. Was she a fool or had she done the right thing? There was no one to ask. She had put Murray's desire in between herself and her mother.

Tomorrow they had only the hours until noon, so Murray would be coming over at nine. That would be their last three hours for nobody knew how long. Then she would eat a quick lunch with his parents and Murray and then they would take him to the station. She would try even harder than before to make them like her, for it counted more now.

She would say they were going on a picnic and take a blanket. They could go to a park and walk into the woods. Back to Belle Isle or to Rouge Park, which was farther but much bigger. She was a bad woman to plan so, but she did not care. He must carry off with him the knowledge of her love, even if she couldn't give him anything else to take away. The check meant he was serious about their future. They would have a joint account like married people, long before they could have a house or a bed or a name in common. Every week she would put some of her paycheck in, toward that future that might never come.

Bird on a Wire

Bernice was using her electric cake mixer to beat the spot of orange dye into the viscid white oleo. Butter was not only rationed, it had virtually disappeared. At least The Professor was busy again. After a period in which everyone had been afraid the college was about to be closed down, St. Thomas had let women in and secured government contracts to train Army and Navy personnel. The Professor was teaching German, but he also had to fill in with French, Spanish and an algebra course, as the school had lost over half its faculty.

Propped against the tiles of the kitchen wall just behind the mixer was a letter addressed to Bernice. It was back in its envelope, already limp with handling, but she knew by heart what it said. It advised her that she had an appointment with Jacqueline Cochran in Boston at the Ritz Carlton next Monday at 1:00 P.M.

Pinned to the wall of her room was the first news item, that Nancy Love was organizing a service of women pilots to ferry planes. Bernice had not qualified for that; Love was taking only the most experienced women pilots in the country, women with four, five, six hundred hours, women who had been flying professionally for years. Her hope had been humbled, and then she had been grounded. The coastal strip for one hundred fifty miles inland had been closed to civilian patrols. Now she could not fly at all, and her life pressed in on her, narrow as a typewriter ribbon.

Then an article had appeared saying that Jacqueline Cochran was organizing another ferrying service. She had written at once, but she had not heard for two months. Down in Houston, Texas, the first class of WFTDs were training. Bernice had her chance at the interview Monday to persuade Cochran to let her fly for the Women's Flying Training Detachment. Enough literature had come for her to know she was well within the weight requirements, high for women's bodies, and thus suitable for her big-boned frame.

Since that initial response she had been walking miles every day. She had joined a calisthenics class at the college; she studied her old manuals and read library books on aeronautics. What she had not done was tell The Professor about the interview. He had already dismissed the idea of her going anyplace. She only wished that the WFTD had the power to draft her.

Monday morning she got up before her father, made his breakfast, wrote a note about the interview and fled, running through the lightly falling snow to the little bus station behind the post office. She was in time for the 6:45 bus, crowded already by the time it reached Bentham Center. She stood near the back, all the way to Boston, arriving there two hours early.

She walked into a coffee shop filled with sailors, but she saw no place to sit and realized she was too excited to eat. She got a coffee to go and drank it sitting in the Public Garden. Boston was not as cold as Bentham Center, but had it been below zero, she would not have cared. Couples huddled earnestly talking or desperately necking on the benches, sailors and their girls. Thanksgiving was coming soon and she had ordered a turkey from the Garfinkles, who raised them. She wondered how Jeff was managing in London. She did not think the English celebrated Thanksgiving.

She tried to imagine what might impress Jacqueline Cochran, but she could think of nothing special about herself, except that she had managed to get her commercial license. If Cochran knew how many boring papers she had typed on how many late nights and through how many dreary afternoons, she would be moved a little. Perhaps.

Her heroine had been Amelia Earhart, but that did not mean she did not admire Jacqueline Cochran, who had come up from poverty, who had won the Bendix Air Race in 1938, the only woman in the race, Los Angeles to Cleveland in eight hours, ten minutes and thirty-one seconds, landing with less than three gallons of gas left in her tank. Climbing over a ferocious storm, to twenty-two thousand feet in an unpressurized cockpit—that was how she had won that famous race. The next plane did not arrive for an hour. After that Bernice had put up her photo next to Amelia Earhart.

At twelve-thirty Bernice could wait no longer, for fear of being late. She headed for the Ritz where she huddled in the lobby waiting till she could persuade herself it was all right to go up. In her old grey coat, she felt conspicuously dowdy. She kept imagining she would be asked to leave. Finally at five to one she had herself announced and took the elevator.

Cochran had the room partially set up as an office, a big desk and chairs, files, a secretary in the next room, but it was still and obviously a well-appointed suite. Bernice had not expected the woman she saw at that walnut desk, an exquisite woman whose mink coat was tossed artfully over the back of her chair, made up like a model, with blond hair in gentle ringlets and brown eyes set off by mascara. In short, Cochran was stunning and dressed like someone Bernice would see in a movie, in a pale mauve suit with a watered silk blouse. Bernice had a momentary urge to weep. Cochran was never going to accept her. Bernice tried to remember that this was the woman who had set a record climbing to thirty-three thousand feet in an unpressurized plane, sucking oxygen from a tube with the temperature in the unheated cockpit sixty degrees below zero. This was the woman who would test anything, new types of oxygen masks, engine superchargers, spark plugs, airplane fuel and wing designs, who was absolutely fearless in taking risks and trying out whatever the inventors could produce.

Cochran had her file on the desk. "You were flying for the Civil Air Patrol?"

"Yes, but they've grounded us now."

"When did you start flying?"

The first questions were obvious but the later ones, not so. Cochran asked about relationships with men. She seemed pleased that Bernice lived with her father, a respectable professor. "Will he object to your going?"

Bernice spoke carefully. "He's very eager to contribute to the war effort. My brother's in the Office of Strategic Services overseas. My father has been trying to get a war post in Washington. I feel sure he'd be excited if I could join the WFTD." Bernice felt proud of her wording. The Professor would certainly be excited: she had not lied.

"Some of the questions I've asked I know have surprised you, but we have to be very careful with our girls. The public suspects women who fly planes of being racy and fast, chasing around a man's world, as if the skies could be anyone's monopoly. I'm as interested in the character of my girls as I am in their flying experience. Any breath of scandal and we'll lose an irreplaceable opportunity for women."

"All I want to do is fly," Bernice said with complete honesty. "It's the thing I do best, and the only time I feel completely happy is when I'm up there. It's the best work and the best play in the world to me. Nothing competes with it. All I ask is the chance to do it. I'll work hard and I'll learn anything we have to learn."

Cochran smiled at her. "I think that might be arranged, Miss Coates. Good day. You'll be hearing from us."

Bernice did not arrive home in time to fix The Professor's supper, but she had arranged with Mrs. Augustine next door to invite him over, confessing where she was going. She gathered that he went and ate heartily.

"She's a better cook than you are," The Professor said, glowering out of his favorite chair by the Westinghouse console.

"Then you enjoyed your supper, and no problem," Bernice said in that falsely cheerful tone she was always adopting with him.

"I don't want to eat at the Augustines' table. He smokes a stinking pipe with his coffee. I want to eat at my own table."

"That summons was important. If the government needs me, I must go."

"Your duty is here. You don't have to run off looking for useful work."

"I have a skill that few women have had a chance to acquire. Now suddenly it's worth something."

"They aren't looking for a girl like you. If they write you again, I will answer them. You're needed at home. They'll understand." The Professor erected the fence of *Christian Science Monitor* before his face. He read the *Globe* in the morning and the *Christian Science Monitor* every evening. A few moments later his voice issued from behind the paper. "Imitating your brother is a ridiculous thing for a big sensible girl like you to indulge in. The house has been better managed since you left off chasing out to the airport." When she still did not reply, he actually put the paper down to look at her. "They don't need a silly overgrown girl running around airports, and this woman, whoever she is, is just a flash in the pan."

She would not engage him. She saw no use in arguing. She merely had to collect the mail every day before he saw it.

The trouble was as the weeks went by, she could not be sure that a letter had not come and been answered by The Professor. She did not dare ask her father or write Cochran's office. She baked some cookies from a recipe that used potatoes. They came out better than most such efforts, and she presented some to the postman and then told him exactly what the envelope would say. She begged him to give her the letter personally.

This postman was not the same one, for he had been in the reserves, but an old man who pulled the mail around in a child's wagon. She did not know if he would do as she asked, but five days before Christmas, the letter came. It told her to report to Westover Air Force Base on January third for a physical examination, Form 64, the same rigorous physical that combat pilots received. If she passed, she was in.

She read the letter standing on the walk she had shoveled yesterday, while the old mailman pulled his grandson's wagon down the block delivering Christmas cards in large bundles. Then she ran next door, just as she was in her slippers, old jumper and no coat, to Mrs. Augustine's kitchen.

Mrs. Augustine looked for her glasses until Bernice found them for her on the windowsill between the begonia and the Dutchman's breeches. Mrs. Augustine read through the letter twice before handing it respectfully back to Bernice.

"Your mother Viola would be very proud of you. What's The Professor going to say?"

"He'll try to forbid me to go."

"Will you let him?"

"I'll feel guilty, but if they want me, I'm going. I could sound really patriotic, but the truth is, I love to fly and this is my chance. If I fly for this outfit all through the war, then afterward I have to have a crack at commercial aviation. I do want to help win the war, and I'm not doing a thing here, but above all, I want to fly."

"You've given him your youth, Bernice. Get out while you can."

Bernice wanted to embrace Mrs. Augustine, but it was too many years since she had embraced anyone. The only person in the world she ever hugged was her brother. She could not think of anything to say except to repeat to Mrs. Augustine her thanks for the understanding. Mrs. Augustine looked so drab, a plump middle-aged woman with greying brown hair up in an untidy bun, a woman who put up twenty different kinds of preserves, conserves, relishes, chutneys, canned fruit, the best cook on the block, that no one would expect her to entertain wild fantasies or encourage them.

Mrs. Augustine saw her to the door. "Your father can eat with us. He's not the most agreeable man, but I don't mind. Or I can take his supper over in a covered dish. You go fly your planes. I know a lady who'll clean for him and do the laundry. She talks too much, but he won't be around when she's working. Between us, Bernice, we'll figure it out."

Christmas was a sour time. This was the first year Jeff had not come home for the holidays, nor had they had word from him in a while. All she could think about was her physical on January third. She continued calisthenics, although her class at the college was suspended for vacation. She cooked, she baked, she scavenged. They had a tree with real candles, as they always did, dangerous but beautiful. They exchanged their few presents and the radio alternated carols with news. The invasion of North Africa seemed to be proceeding less smoothly, with the British and Americans bogged down attacking Tunis. On the Eastern Front, desperate fighting continued at Stalingrad. In the Pacific, desperate fighting continued on Guadalcanal. Some right-wing general had been assassinated in Algiers, but the killer, a young French student, had already been captured.

A Form 64 physical exam took all day, with her running from lab to lab with two other women in hospital coats, while the Army closed off the hospital section by section presumably to protect them. It was a big flap, but she was doing all right. She was certainly healthy: big and strong and healthy. That had always sounded like a curse, but today it was a blessing.

Two weeks later the notice came that she was to report in Texas to Class 43-4 at Houston Municipal Airport on February 1, 1943. She would have to pay her own way there. That was a problem.

She had borrowed two hundred dollars from Mrs. Augustine when she was getting her commercial license. Since she had been forcibly grounded in September, she had been doing a lot of typing, although half of her regular customers had left. She finally repaid Mrs. Augustine just before Christmas. Now she had only two weeks in which to earn the money to get herself to Texas. She had sixteen dollars. Today she would learn exactly what the fare was, and she would get that money, if she had to rob a bank. After all, Jeff had ridden the rails. If that's what she had to do, that's what she would do. She was off to Texas in two weeks, no matter what.

She began making arrangements long before she broke the news to her father. The Professor simply did not believe her. "You're not going."

"But I am." She heard her own cheerful voice and thought she would have hated to be talked to in that empty vacuous way, but there was no intimacy between them. They simply could not communicate in any other way than by his issuing commands de haut en bas and by her replying in that fake cheerful tone as if totally unaware of his anger. They were caught in a bad family game that might change if their lives changed, not otherwise. She was not so much his daughter as his servant: the poor replacement for the wife he had loved, the only human being with whom he had been able to be intimate and affectionate. She should not have stayed home with him, she said to herself; perhaps that had not been filial duty but laziness. If she had gone off, he would have married again. Now he was too set in his ways.

"I forbid it," he said loudly. "I mean this."

"Father, I'm way overage. This time it's not my duty to stay, but to go." The clichés of wartime dripped from her tongue grey and fatty as melted lard, but she would not be shamed into dispensing with them.

On January 31 she left. The Professor had stopped speaking to her and did not see her off. Mrs. Augustine drove her to the station. Bernice had written last week to Jeff at his military code address, but judging from the letter that had arrived Saturday, he had not got hers yet, although he had received the cookies and the woolen muffler she had knit for him: a useless gift as he was obviously in North Africa from hints in his letters. Well, she would write him from Houston and she would have plenty to tell him, for a change, something more exciting than the chrysanthemums have been killed by the frost, or the last red-winged blackbirds have gone south. Something more than nature notes and the sardonic comments on her life she could never resist.

Mrs. Augustine kept beaming at her. "Have a good time, dear Bernice, and be proud of yourself." The day before there had been a storm, but the tracks had been cleared and the morning glittered like freshly washed cut crystal, the Waterford goblets she was leaving behind. Ahead of her was Texas, land of the six-gun and the Women's Flying Training Detachment, and planes, planes, planes. Mrs. Augustine stood on tiptoes to give her a brief but firm kiss on the lips, handing her her lunch in a tea towel. "Good luck!"

One More River to Cross

Murray was shipped to Samoa to reinforce the 7th Marines, who were supposed to be transferred to New Zealand. On September 14 they sailed out of Espíritu Santo on five transports accompanied by two supply ships and a cruiser and destroyer escort. Soon afterward they came under attack from submarines and bombers.

They arrived at dawn four days later on a long island that rose to a jagged ridge. The shores—studded with twisted metal wrecks of ships and planes—offered spacious, elegant groves of coconut palms, but the breeze off the land was sour, fetid. It smelled like the icebox when his family came back from vacation and discovered they'd left food inside to spoil. They landed without difficulty and were marched inland. The men who greeted them or more often did not bother to acknowledge their arrival were another matter. Murray did not want to stare, but he could feel the reaction of the men around him, and it was no different from his own: horror. Are we going to look like that? The marines who had been holding the beachhead on the island were filthy skeletons. They were hairy, skinny, stinking: the gutted hulks of young men. The island was called Guadalcanal.

The perimeter of the airfield, cratered with shell holes, was littered with the burnt-out planes, smashed palms, wreckage that had rotted so fast it could no longer be identified. The ground was deeply pitted by nightly bombardments. There was no back to the lines, no rear, no rest area. Wounded and brought back out of the line, a marine was as likely to die of a violent attack in his hospital bed as back in his foxhole. They held a small area and held it hard. Every day and every night they were attacked. Usually the Japanese destroyers came down the slot between the islands and shelled them at leisure; during the day, Bettys, the Japanese bombers, came over and dropped on them. After the first night of casualties, they became grim and businesslike fast.

There was no such thing as a night's sleep. If there was noplace to go on the island to get away from the war, and anyplace he stood might be the subject of attack at any moment, neither was he safe in his waterlogged foxhole by night. Every night Louie the Louse came over to drop green flares and an occasional bomb. Every night Maytag Charlie came over to toss impact bombs from his twin-engined flying boat, circling around above them. There was no method to the bombing, completely random in the dark. It meant he never slept through half a night.

The Japanese usually attacked at night, anyhow, and that was the commonest time for shelling. In addition a sub called Oscar lay off the shore and waited for the little Higgins boats they used to cross to the installations on the offlying islands of Tulagi, Savo and Gavutu, where marines were garrisoned. Occasionally Oscar lobbed a few shells at the field too.

At breakfast on the third day they were given Atabrine and also issued three condoms, which caused a lot of bitter mirth because none of the marines had seen a woman on the island. Most of the men would not take the yellow pills of Atabrine, because rumor insisted it made a man impotent. Murray figured that from what he could see of malaria, endemic in the marines there, it would be smarter to risk the Atabrine, so he took it, although his buddy Manella told him it would make his prick shrink to a baby's. There were so many walking malaria cases, no one could be excused from combat unless he was running a temperature above one hundred three.

They were always wet. Everything was always wet. Water seeped into the foxholes. It rained every five minutes anyhow. The local skies could drop a foot of rain in two hours. Everything he touched was spongy, rotten, moldy. They all stank. Because of the constant shelling and bombing, there was never a time he could take all his clothes off and dry them out, so by the end of the first week, he had the crud, a fungus infection that they all shared. His balls, his ass, his feet were raw. He was learning to shake out whatever he had put down, because scorpions and centipedes liked to crawl into anything dark, a shoe or a pocket or a pant leg.

Even the ground stank. He lived in a constant cloud of mosquitoes, and soon he had a fever like everybody else: not malaria but one of the hundred diseases the mosquitoes pumped into him when they sucked his blood. The medic gave him pills but admitted no one knew what it was. Murray shook in the late afternoons as his fever shot up, leaving him weak.

At least they had enough food. Besides the raging dysentery, the reason the marines who'd been here since early August were so skinny was that they'd been hungry. If they hadn't scored Jap supplies, they would have starved. They had been living on Jap rice, dried fish heads and beer. With the Japanese navy controlling the waters around the island and sending in fresh troops and supplies, and with the Japanese air force attacking with more planes every day, Murray foresaw with a fatalistic chill how easily they could be sealed off and starved.

They were sent across a local river to attack. The Lever Brothers coconut plantations that lined the coast gave way to jungle. Murray's images of jungles came from Tarzan movies, or featured Dorothy Lamour in a sarong under some scenic palms with a nice sandy beach where gentle rollers coasted in. Here the trees, vast edifices of eucalyptus, ipil, banyan, towered a hundred feet or more, but he quickly learned not to lean on one without testing it first. Trees as big through as trucks could suddenly keel over in a strong wind, in spite of how the monsters were surrounded by outlying suburbs of knees and roots that made going treacherous. Everything was rotten and the soil itself felt spongy except where coral outcroppings slashed at them or where jungle gave way to openings like miniature prairies, golden in the distance, where kunai grass with blades sharp as cutlasses loomed over the heads of patrols.

Climbing over the trees were vines, creepers, lianas, strung crazily and intertwined between hummocks of fiercely competing vegetation. Everything was wet, because this was true rain forest. There was a rainy season, and the rest of the year for a change, it rained. They hacked their way through a labyrinth of creepers, brush, ferns taller than his head. They couldn't see past the impenetrable green veil they were attacking. Whatever they touched bit or stung. There were wasps as big as his palm. Leeches dropped on them from the trees and sucked their thin feverish blood. Spiders crawled up their dungarees to leave bites swollen to the size of golf balls. Everywhere white ants swarmed whose acid bite burned like hot coals. The only mammals they saw were rats, who infested the base and were reputed to eat the corpses. Out here life was lush but alien and hungry. He could understand becoming an ascetic, he could understand wanting to leave the sick, scabby, fearful dysentery-racked body behind.

The war was already changing him, although he hoped the changes were temporary because he did not like them. He had always had contempt for fatalists, but he had become one almost immediately on the Canal. If your number came up, if the bullet had your name on it, if your luck ran out; they were all fatalists in the ranks. Everyone had personal superstitions, a few buddies. Everything else belonged to the other place. Home. Back there.

They hadn't penetrated far into the jungle, although that little way had taken them hours, when they hit the first enemy outpost. Pinned down by fire, he couldn't tell what to shoot at. It felt to him as if they were surrounded, but he lay on his belly and did what everybody else did. Often in training Murray had doubted he could actually kill another human being, but if this was going to be combat, firing into green chaos, he was unlikely to damage anybody and wouldn't find out if he did. In the first two engagements, Murray never saw a live Jap, although as they moved forward over the captured outposts, he saw plenty of dead ones. At first he stared at the bodies, trying to comprehend death. Most of them were just kids, thrown down and savaged randomly. One gaunt kid who looked sixteen was bleeding from a severed artery in his groin. The corpsman with them tried to save him but couldn't, while they all stood around. Murray felt cramped by pity as the blood spurted out. But after one of the corpses rose up and knocked off two marines with a grenade, and another corpse tried to shoot him with a pistol, Murray lost interest in the philosophical side of death, and they all began routinely to bayonet the fallen men, dead or wounded. Their officers told them to take prisoners, but the Japs didn't, so why should they? It was hard enough to look out for yourself.

By the third day they finally reached the stream they were supposed to cross, the Matanikau, and tried to take the ford. The Japanese were well entrenched there and they could not force it. In three days of heavy labor, of exhausting dawn to dark traveling, he figured they might have advanced two miles. This time he could see what he was shooting at and what was shooting at them. There were lots of Japanese dug in on the west side of the stream with light but effective artillery in well-concealed positions.

The commander called in an air strike, but after it was over, there seemed to be just as many Japanese and just as many shells and bullets coming at them. He kept thinking, Suppose they drop one of those bombs on us instead, as guys told him had happened in early fighting. Instead of being killed off by the bombing, the Japs seemed stronger than ever when the planes left. They started their own attack.

A shell landed so close to him he was covered with hot mud and clouted in the head with a rotten log that dumped stinging ants all over his back, although he did not dare move to deal with them. The man to his left was hit in the chest and taken off coughing blood. Murray felt sick. He found he had wet himself in the impact, but they were all so stinking, covered with the foul mud, he didn't think anybody else could tell. To wet himself like a baby. He felt ashamed. He wondered if he would crack apart under this strain. Maybe he was just no good when it came down to it.

Then the Japanese came at them over the river. Murray wondered again if he

could really kill anybody, but as the enemy came slogging through the sluggish
waters of the river screaming like cats in heat and tossing grenades, their bayonets fixed, Murray shot as true as he could and the man he had in his sights fell
before he could get his grenade off. He felt weak with a combination of relief and
the ebbing of adrenaline rush, but then another wave started across, leaving him
no time to congratulate himself. If he got somebody in his sights, he shot. It was
like paying his money and taking a turn to hit the moving ducks at the state fair,
except that these ducks were blasting holes in men all around him.

Finally they were ordered to withdraw. He could not feel bad that they had
failed to take their objective. He could only be glad they were turning back. As
they followed the narrow trail along the river, the Japs hit them again and again
with mortars. He hadn't slept in three days. They had eaten little and that filthy
and foul tasting. They all had dysentery. His fever was up and raging. All the time
he was thirsty, with the sluggish brown river just to their west. He couldn't even
fantasize trying to drink that turgid stuff. Besides, he'd seen the crocodile that
had carried off a wounded Jap at the ford. "Why the fuck do we want this place?"
he asked Manella, who was the friendliest to him of the men in his company.

"Hell's too crowded," Manella said. "That's why."

"They don't know what the fuck they're doing, sending us in here," Fats said.
None of them knew each other well, because the new men like Murray had been
added to an established regiment to bring it up to strength. "The brass don't give
a shit. It's Bataan all over again. We're going to die here."

"The guys say it won't be like Bataan. They say if the Japs take the field, we're
all going up in the hills and live like guerrillas," Manella said.

Murray had his doubts they were equipped to live off this land. He thought
that only a lizard would try. He tried to stand away from Fats, because he reeked
of shit. Whenever he could, Murray smoked, because it deadened his nose. In
the Marines he didn't want a nose. When they sank onto the spongy rotten earth
to rest, sometimes he thought of Ruthie and sometimes he thought of a long hot
bath. He had lived over that time in the car and the next day in the park so many
times, he was no longer sure exactly what had happened, like a photo fingered
and folded until the image began to disappear.

Manella poked him. "Sucker on my stacking swivel." He had a leech on the
nape of his neck. The men lay in a sodden heap under a banyan tree on the edge
of a nasty mangrove swamp that would be even harder going, and like a troop
of monkeys picked leeches and lice and spiders off each other. Their intimacy
was that of shared pain, shared danger, shared discomfort. Men he would not
have spoken to twice at home were his life now, his family; he was growing to
sound just like them and to look just like them. They were a filthy, motley crew,

although it would be a few weeks before they looked as wild, as skeletal and as mangy as the marines who had come to the Canal in the first wave.

Murray took out his cigarettes. The condoms had turned out to be useful issue; they were the only thing that kept matches and cigarettes dry, and when he was lucky enough to have a chocolate bar, that was where he kept it safe. Now Manella was grooming him for leeches. The sergeant spoke to them flatly, with his usual contempt, and they shuffled to their feet. "Saddle up, boneheads. Into the boondocks."

Murray carefully pinched out his cigarette so that he could finish it later. As he stood, his sight riddled through with black spots and he swayed on his feet. Without waiting for his sight to clear or his nausea to pass, he fixed himself behind Manella and stumbled forward. It was a long way yet back to the perimeter, where instead of dying one by one strung out along the riverbank, they could die in the company of hundreds. At least there would be warm food, even if only the canned Vienna sausages and beans his body could no longer digest.

DANIEL 3

Daniel's War

Daniel's focus was Guadalcanal and the Japanese headquarters at Rabaul. Deciphering was fast now, not only because they had made excellent progress on the Japanese naval codes, but because when the Marines had achieved surprise capturing the half-built air base they named Henderson Field, they had overrun the Japanese positions so rapidly that a codebook had been pulled from a fire unburned. Daniel now had the same book the Japanese used, where he had only to look up the code groups to translate messages.

Not that the Navy seemed able to grasp the situation presented them. The sea off Guadalcanal was now called Ironbottom Sound because of the huge number of ships sunk there. Many were Japanese, but a great many more were American and Australian. The Japanese still owned the night. Even with the aid of the codebook, Daniel could not always tell what the Japanese were talking about. When they began to discuss rat operations, he had no idea what they meant, but soon it became evident that was the Japanese cover name for the night runs up the slot between the islands to deliver troops, weapons, supplies: fast in, fast out, stealthy under the cover of the night but armed with teeth.

Every morning Daniel rose from his mattress heaped with pillows in the corner of the living room of the apartment he shared with Rodney Everly and took the first of his buses to work. Then he entered a different universe. The former girls' school at the corner of Massachusetts and Nebraska avenues lacked screens on the tall windows, so insect life in semitropical abundance poured in to swarm around them. Daniel kept a bottle of citronella in his desk drawer.

The real world he entered at work was that of intimate contact with the Japanese naval mind. He saw the war backwards from the way most Americans did. He had learned of the desperate improvised American invasion of Guadalcanal from surprised Japanese reports to headquarters. He learned of the sinking of

American ships from the triumphant claims after battles, although they were learning that the Japanese, like the Americans, claimed far more than were really knocked out, always. They could check the American claims of ships torpedoed and sunk against the Japanese damage reports, and they could check the Japanese crowing against actual U.S. losses. Every pilot always thought he hit his target, but few did.

His knowledge of Japanese continued to grow, which gave him a schizophrenic feeling of entering the enemy culture. He had to see the world as they did, or try to; it was deeply alienating and yet fascinating. He found himself not infrequently thinking in Japanese. The two cultures had extremely different premises, what they took for granted, what they thought you could and could not do in any given situation.

For the first time in his life, he felt useful. Enrolled. Engaged. People lived or died, ships with a thousand men on them survived or went down because they did or didn't decipher and translate a Japanese message correctly. They could not teach the American brass how to fight night battles or how to use their radar or how to respond aggressively and fast to the chance to fire on a Japanese vessel. One of the admirals in the Pacific was always withdrawing to refuel his forces whenever an engagement loomed. Intelligence could only offer opportunities. They could warn the Marine pilots of impending raids, for those pilots were scrappers who took advantage of any chance they were given. Daniel felt a controlled importance, a fine passionate honing of his attention and intellect that made him impatient with his whole previous life.

He was like a man who has lost forty pounds and taken up systematic exercise looking at photographs of his former flabby self: he felt disgust. How could he have drifted along weakwilled and passive? He had been a child until he arrived here.

At night he went home to the tiny apartment on the third floor. The pressure was less extreme this fall, except during battles. Enough new people had arrived so that they were divided into three watches, covering the entire twenty-four hours. Nonetheless, their hours of work reflected the level of crisis in the waters off Guadalcanal. When the fleets steamed off to refuel and repair and regroup, he went home at normal suppertime. During periods of heavy naval engagements, he worked through the night. Half a world away, day was night and night was day, but the volume of traffic overwhelmed them and they slogged on.

Rodney was not the roommate of Daniel's dreams. He was a tolerable-looking man who thought of himself as handsome, as he had been raised to believe everything about himself was perfect. He was tall and blond, his complexion pasty or beet red with the sun; he had rabbit teeth and watery eyes.

Daniel found the observation of Rodney shaving almost more than he could take in the morning without cracking up. Rodney ogled himself. He drew up his chin and threw himself glances of arrogant hauteur, of smoldering passion, of frank approval.

Rodney smoked a meerschaum pipe. During the week, he never drank, but when Saturday night arrived, he seemed to have the policy of continuing until he was maudlin. Daniel had never heard an opinion out of his mouth that he found interesting.

Downstairs an apartment of girls moved in. One was dark, willowy and engaged, flashing a diamond the size of a pecan. One was a short brown-haired southern-sounding girl who made eyes at him on the stairs, but disappeared permanently before he had made serious contact. The third was a tall blond with a down-east twang who went swinging along the street with a walk he appreciated, fast, sexy, covering ground. She was not around much, but she had a charming wide-eyed smile. She told him her favorite brother was Navy too.

"What happened to Dixie?" he asked her.

"Gone abroad," she said and did not pause to elaborate. She was off down the street running because she saw a cab stopping and if you had a need for a cab and a chance at one in Washington, you did not dally or stop to say your farewells.

He expected a third roommate but none appeared. He learned when Down East went to work, contriving to walk to the bus with her. "Are you looking for someone else to move in?"

"We wouldn't have to look hard around here, would we? No. It's a tiny place for two people—just like yours, I imagine—"

"Why imagine? Come up and visit us. Borrow a cup of something."

"I don't know," said Down East with a flash of her cornflower blue eyes, "that you have anything that I need, Ensign."

"My name is Daniel. Daniel Balaban. What does the A. in front of Scott stand for?"

"Abra. You're from New York?" She waited for his nod. "I lived there. Actually I've only sublet my apartment, because after the war, I'm going back. It's the only vital place."

"I liked Boston better. Boston and Shanghai."

That intrigued her. She raised a single eyebrow at him. Then the bus arrived, ending their conversation. On the overcrowded bus, Daniel thought, staring into the blond head tucked below his nose, sodomy would be easy but conversation impossible.

———

Many new people arrived in the OP-20-G office from the two language schools and from other far reaches of the Navy, the universities and civilian life. Daniel, now made a lieutenant junior grade, supervised three yeomen and began a tentative affair with Ann Korobuso, hedged around with her prohibitions. She would not come to his apartment. With the anti-Japanese feeling endemic in Washington as well as the rest of the country, she did not like going out. She would only permit him to visit her at her apartment observing a list of precautions when her aunt, with whom she was living, was safely and surely out. She was always a little nervous.

Ann was the offspring of a nisei father and a woman of Norwegian ancestry from Seattle, now divorced. Her father had been put in a camp in Missoula, Montana. Ann lived with her mother's sister, who had a civil service job in the accounting office at State. Her aunt Elinor was kind to her, she said without conviction.

He found her beautiful but reserved. Sadness clung to her like the sandalwood perfume she used. He enjoyed her company, yet he enjoyed leaving her and escaping the sighs, the veiled glances, the enigmatic retreats. He knew that he either had to save her or offer her little indeed, and he opted for the latter. Her enthusiasms were those of an American woman her age, so that at times she reminded him of a blighted Judy. Only her exotic appearance and her knowledge of Japanese redeemed her from boring him, that and their ability to talk shop together. They tended to be on the same schedule and did not have to field questions from each other on what they were doing. Rodney was always having to break dates with women when a crisis arose, and his lame explanations never seemed to make amends.

Ann read movie magazines, ladies' magazines, serials about plucky women who made do. Her favorite author was one he had never heard of, a fluffhead named Annette Sinclair. Once he arrived to find Ann in tears. He was terrified that something had happened to injure or frighten her, that some new menace had stretched out to touch her father in the camp, her mother who was remarried with small children in Nome. All that had happened was that she had read one of Annette Sinclair's dopey stories in which the man deeply wounded the woman who loved him, accusing her wrongfully of infidelity when she had only been trying to save his job.

It was a very partial romance, perhaps encompassing two or three evenings of intimacy a month, then another couple of teatimes or polite suppers under the maiden aunt's suspicious glances, lunches at a table in the cafeteria with other decoders and translators. If anyone else guessed their affair, they paid no attention. Ann never cast him obvious glances. She was too polite, too reserved, too shy to transgress against proper office demeanor. Often he forgot she was there. His work absorbed him.

In the hall, on the way to the bus, he flirted with Abra Scott. He tried to figure out why she fascinated him. She was moderately pretty; Washington was jammed with girls just as pretty. Her features were too angular, her face a little too long for beauty.

It was the way she held herself, the way she moved, that raised his temperature. She was what they called spirited, with a racy air that intrigued him. She seemed to be involved in her own adventure. He did not think of her as innocent, the way he thought of Ann as victim. Neither was she sultry or sluttish. He had the feeling that she did what she wanted, when she was sure she wanted it. Obviously she liked his company. If he was not downstairs when she arrived, she loitered to wait for him. Although she flirted with him and let him take her arm as they strolled to the bus, she would not see him. She would not come upstairs and only invited him in when her roommate needed help carrying a trunk.

Several times when she was off to a party in a dress that left her arms bare, he noticed her smallpox vaccination scar, a rosy star in the flesh of her upper arm. Each time he wanted to touch it, to bring his mouth to it. Whenever he imagined being in bed with her, he remembered that scar on the honey gold skin of her arm. All through the fall he associated a light ferny odor with her body, but one day she changed her perfume, and after that she wore a more distinctive musky floral.

A number of mornings she did not show up at all. He learned not to wait, because he would be late, and she would not appear. He decided she had something going, although he could not figure out who the lucky guy was. The Army uniform, the sergeant, belonged to Susannah, the dark-haired roommate with the rock. Otherwise many young people came and went. They had occasional noisy farewell parties to which he and Rodney were sometimes invited.

Both girls were working for the government, but he could not figure out who or what they were involved with. Like him, they volunteered no information. Some of the men who came to their parties were in uniform, but many were not. A lot of them seemed to be ex-academics. Sometimes Abra came home from wherever she worked at suppertime, and sometimes, like himself, she arrived much later or even in the middle of the night—and the same with the engaged woman, Susannah.

Naval engagements and the Japanese buildup on Guadalcanal took them over completely at work. Even with all the new people, they could barely keep up with the flood of intelligence. It was crazy, he thought, how in this room in a former girls' school in Washington they read messages from half a world away and told Marine pilots at Henderson Field when and where to bomb and warned the Navy that the Japanese were preparing to send a force against Guadalcanal and knew more accurately than the ships slugging it out in Ironbottom Sound with incredible losses exactly which Japanese ships had been hit badly enough to hurt them and which were only scratched. He felt sometimes as if he were up in the tower of an immense battleship. He liked that image. They were obsessed with the fighting, but they viewed it from the reverse side. He could still remember when Martins, who was following transmissions from the *Shugai* cried out, "Damn, they got us." Then realized what he was saying. Because them was us, and us was the enemy. Daniel simply pretended not to hear, as had everyone else around them, because they understood. Watching the war through Japanese eyes, sometimes they passed over.

Over in Africa, Allied forces had landed in Casablanca, but that fighting was unreal to Daniel, because he was not a part of it. He made a faint effort at following the rest of the war, but the fighting that engrossed him was Guadalcanal; there was little in the papers, intentionally he was sure, because of the high risk of failure, and yet he felt that was where the war was being won or lost and that the issue was up for grabs.

One of the men who had requested a transfer out of the cryptanalysis division into field intelligence had been killed on Guadalcanal. He had been left wounded on a sandbar, where a fleeing marine had seen the Japanese bayonet him. Suddenly policy in the department changed because it occurred to the brass that guys like Daniel knew secrets that could change the war. If the Japanese had interrogated Cory instead of bayoneting him, would they now know about Purple and the other decrypts? Wouldn't they have found out that the Americans were reading the naval codes? Wouldn't they change all the ciphers to a completely different system?

No one from the cryptanalysis section was to go into the front lines again, that was the new ruling. If Daniel had sometimes fantasized about what he would do in combat, now he knew his combat was to remain mental. What he carried in his head was a weapon the Navy was finally learning to value, knowledge worth a carrier or two.

As he had learned in the Yenching Institute at Harvard that he had a brain, so he was learning here that he could be useful. He was beginning to trust himself. Now his earlier enthusiasms and attempts to escape the tedium of what was expected could be perceived, if he chose, as apprenticeship for what he was doing. And that was in the fullest and most honest use of that word, intelligence.

JACQUELINE 4

Roads of Paper

11 novembre 1942

Today the Germans poured across the border to the unoccupied zone, and now we are one country again, united miserably under total Nazi control. I wonder how Papa is—if he is well or ill, if he is free, if he has been caught, if he has been deported. Daniela and I sat up late tonight discussing the news. Now I am writing this in bed under the covers.

We have two rooms in the XIe arrondissement, some blocks from the Jewish quarter. This is a French-born working-class sector, many Communists here and supposedly some resistance, although we have seen few signs of it aside from an occasional slogan on a wall or a creative defacement of one of the endless posters telling us of executions, reprisals and new laws hemming us about ever more tightly.

Maman and Rivka are in Drancy, reachable by train if I was permitted in through the Gare du Nord nearby. I can sometimes get a food package to them and we are able occasionally to pass messages in and out with M. Tiefelbrun of the General Union of French Jews, the GFIU, who tries to act as liaison between those inside and those outside.

Daniela and I both have good false identification. I was easy to outfit, because as they say, I can pass. I took on the identity of a young woman who died in a bus accident. Her name was Jacqueline, which makes it easy for me. I am now Jacqueline Porell. She is a year older than I am—or than I was, perhaps I should say.

Daniela's papers say Paula Guerlain. If we keep her hair very short, it does not curl as much. Daniela is very dear to me. Without her friendship and her guidance, I would never have survived this long. I think after Maman and Rivka were arrested, I would have given up and walked into a dragnet. For a Jew to survive, you have to want to all of the time; that is not sufficient, because you also need papers and money and friends and luck, above all, luck. But without that hard-glinting, ever-wary willpower, we have no hope of survival. Eyes in the back of the head, Daniela says. Eyes on stalks. Ears perked forward and back.

Daniela is shorter than I am and much darker. I took after Papa more than Maman, which right now is lucky. Daniela's hair is naturally kinky, dark brown. She has enormous wide-set very dark eyes with lashes she could paint with, a strong nose, a strong chin and a large sensual mouth. Her figure is much fuller than mine, although she is not at all plump. She is strong as a little horse. Even on our dreadful rations, she can run up the six flights to our room and barely be out of breath at the top, while I am dragging myself up and puffing. She was studying to be a doctor and is now working as a nurse.

We work in a hospital ten blocks away. There we have managed to disappear a number of Jews by pronouncing them dead. We have a little conspiracy of a doctor, several nurses and orderlies. We kill people on paper and then bring them to life under new names. We use the hospital facilities to counterfeit papers. Antoine Moussat—who used to be a professor at the Ecole des Etudes Orientales and was involved in our short-lived school—does the counterfeiting.

Besides our occasional work passing people through the hospital, the other task Daniela and I have taken on is to distribute some of the beautifully fabricated papers Moussat produces. We change the identities of up to three people a week. Some are rare individuals who escaped from a camp; others are simply Jews or Resistance people needing to be somebody else. We can hand out a complete sheaf of identity cards: birth certificates, work permits, certificates for repatriated prisoners, baptismal records.

The hard cases are when we need papers that will cover people obviously not French-born, and then we have to search the prewar issues of the Journal Official for names of naturalized non-Jews. My friend Céleste, who is not even Jewish, does this work. She is forever in the libraries doing research for us so that we have good identities. Then if the police call a mairie to check on a suspect's identity, the records confirm it. Since her beating, Céleste has been committed to defying the Nazis.

Handing over the cards is always touchy, because that is the likeliest time for us to get caught. One of us goes and the other watches from a safe distance. We take turns, Daniela and I. Are we scared? Of course. But we are illegal beings anyhow. We might as well do what we can, because our chances are not good even if we sit still. At least this way we feel we are striking back.

I do ask myself why I do this, and the answer is, to make amends to Maman and Rivka. I often wish I could see just one member of my family again, although best would be all of them. I wonder how Naomi is doing in the U.S. I hope they do not mock her because she speaks English so poorly. I'll bet now that she wishes she had studied and not played around so much when she should have been practicing grammar and conversation. Neither of the twins were scholars. I always enjoyed excelling at school, but they never cared, although I think they are probably bright, or perhaps I just expect them to be bright because they are my sisters. I don't care anymore if they are bright or stupid, I only wish I had them back.

My own English is kept up because Daniela has a little radio we listen to under the quilts every night. Of course it is illegal—illegal for us to have a radio at all, for they insisted all Jews turn in our radios months ago, and illegal to listen to the BBC at any time—but just about everybody who has a functioning radio does it. We huddle under all the quilts and listen to the broadcasts in French but also to those in English. Daniela and I live in a state of anxiety that a tube will burn out and we will be cut off from our oxygen supply, real news of what is happening outside France—and even inside, sometimes.

I love Daniela the way, I believe, the twins loved each other, as if she is my sister, my other self. Without her, I would have given up and perished. When she is the one to make the delivery of false IDs, I hate it. I cannot lose anybody else. I prefer when I am the one. I am not as terrified then, although my heart beats fast. I have imagined being arrested so many times that it feels almost boring. At first I could think of nothing else but the danger. A roaring filled my head till I could scarcely catch my breath. Now except for the accelerated heartbeat in my throat, my wrists, my chest, I remain cool and observant.

We keep varying the place where we carry out our drop, so that we minimize the danger of somebody noticing the pattern. Today I was the one. After work, Daniela stood across the street while I sauntered into a greasy-looking bistro. I ignored the men at the zinc counter, thinking how often our drops lead me into places I would never willingly enter with any lesser motive. Will I ever get over feeling self-conscious walking into such a place alone? Sometimes my face heats up with embarrassment.

I had a ghastly newspaper *Paris Soir* which I opened and pretended to scan. I looked over the men in the bar obliquely, in a series of sideways blinks so that I would not make eye contact with anybody. I try to guess if any of them are Gestapo or French police. None of them give me any prickles of fear or hostility. At times like these when I am making a drop, I feel as if time slows down and I have a great many moments in which to examine every detail of the tabletop and the clothing of the men.

When a man sat down at my table and tried to pick me up, I did not know at first if he was my contact or only a local wolf. He was maybe thirty-five, with pale sad brown eyes and a shy, droopy look, puppyish. Then he said the magic sentence, "With the weather so cold, how about something hot to drink?"

I said, "I'm waiting for a friend. But I see he is not coming, so I am leaving." Under the table he put the tightly wound roll of bills in my lap. I jumped up as if pestered to death by him, leaving my paper on the table. As if idly, he picked it up saying to the room at large how stuck up I was and how some women didn't know what they wanted. In the newspaper were the identity cards, glued in an envelope to the page, so they would not fall out if he took up the paper awkwardly. We try to anticipate these problems. Then we went home to our supper of cabbage soup.

12 novembre 1942

I was writing about food yesterday, when my hands got too cold to continue. At noon we eat at the hospital, so we have one filling meal. Every three days we cook up a stew or a soup and then eat it until it is gone, that anonymous soup that Daniela calls potage de rien. Still, life is not terrible, because we laugh all the time. Daniela has taught me the Hebrew alphabet and a few words. She wants to go to Palestine after the war. I hope she will change her mind. I would not like to be without her company.

Daniela's parents left Paris shortly after the Vel d'Hiv raid in which Maman and Rivka were taken away. They were passed over the border into Vichy France and have been living in Nice, which has been a pretty safe spot for Jews. Now Daniela is extremely worried about them, with the Germans occupying the south too.

Her brother Nathan is living in the western suburb of Neuilly, where he has a factory job under a false name. He is also involved in the Jewish Resistance, but we do not know what he is doing. All the Jewish groups that remain pass on information from one group to the other with the speed at which mouths can work and feet run, but only the news we must hear. We do not ask each other unnecessary questions, for fear we may inadvertently betray each other if we are captured and tortured. Our cell deals mostly with young adults and sometimes with adolescents, but there are other groups that exclusively help children. Then there are groups that do acts of reprisal or attempt sabotage.

Personally I am pleased with what Daniela and I can accomplish, with the help of Marcel, Céleste, Dr. Lefèvre, Professor Moussat and the nurses and orderlies in our little cell. We are ten altogether, all Jews except for Céleste and Dr.

Lefèvre, who has a Jewish wife he fears for. We hold firm. Every week we save as many lives in our clandestine work as we do in our hospital work.

As a result of my work as a nurse's aide, I am no longer physically squeamish. Maman, who used to make fun of me because I did not like to handle dirty laundry or anything rotten, would be pleased with my iron stomach and my iron will. If only I could see her. I have learned a fair amount of nursing, since the hospital is shorthanded and I am called upon to do tasks that would normally be carried out by trained nurses. I give injections and change dressings. It makes me laugh to think that after the war perhaps I will end up as a nurse, if I survive, because that is the only training I am being permitted—a long way from being an actress in the Comédie Française or a teacher in a good lycée.

Now it is time to sleep. We have to get up early for work and the apartment is bitter cold already. We have stuffed rags and papers in the cracks, but still the wind slips in. We call our little apartment Bald Mountain, as in Night on. Daniela used to study the violin.

15 novembre 1942

Daniela is pleased because we have learned it is the Italians who have occupied Nice, and that things are easy under them. Her parents have nothing to worry about, so Daniela has been singing all day.

This weekend there was a deportation to the east of a thousand from the camp at Drancy. They say there is to be a thousand a week transported from now on. We have been unable to find out where they are being sent. The BBC announced a tremendous British victory in Africa, at a place called Tobruk. We drank a little wine to celebrate, sharing a glass. It is so cold we are both huddled in bed, so I will make this entry brief, as I am keeping Daniela awake.

20 novembre 1942

We have heard something terrifying. There is a special courier in Paris right now named Jan Karski who has been in the ghetto in Warsaw and witnessed camps where Jews are sent. He says that most of the Jews sent east are not resettled but killed at once. The others are worked to death. It is planned to smuggle him out of the country via Spain and Portugal, so that news of what is happening to Jews will cause England and the U.S. to open their borders to Jews who do manage to escape, and to bomb the railroads to the camps as they are now said to be bombing inside Germany.

I have heard rumors before, but it is said that this man has testimony and papers with him. I do not want to believe this, but after the Vel d'Hiv raid, I can credit almost anything.

I must go and talk to whomever I can reach about whether it is possible to bribe anybody out of Drancy. I have heard of no one managing it, and my resources are slight. Escape is what haunts me. How can I get them out? I can save them once I have them, because I can provide false ID and I know whom to contact to whisk them out of Paris. I believe I could arrange for them to be secreted in a village with farmers. But how to get them out?

1ier décembre 1942

M. Tiefelbrun said that Maman should have had an Ausweis to say that she was a Wirtschaftswertvoller Jude, an economically useful Jew, since she was working in the fur trade. He said it was stupid that she did not have that, and maybe it was not too late to try to get it for her. He is hopeful anyhow and is beginning the paperwork. When I see him, of course I use my old name but do not ever tell him where I live or work. In general more people tell me I might be able to get Rivka out than extend hope I may be able to free Maman, but I am determined and working very hard on every person I can get hold of who may be able to help at all.

We have heard of a mass deportation of very young children, many of whom had already lost their parents. In many cases, rumor has it, the French police rounding them up in the stockade at Drancy and marching them to the railroad tracks do not even know who they are. The Germans simply demand a fixed number.

10 décembre 1942

Yesterday I had a very encouraging meeting with an official who is working on getting Maman the economically useful status. Her old boss has written very strong letters saying that she is wanted back on the job and that the work is slowed down because of her lack. I really appreciate what he is doing for her. I'm going to get them out, I'm determined!

We had an emergency at the hospital today just as we were about to leave.

People try to heat with all kinds of ancient apparatus now that the weather has turned bitter cold. We had to handle a whole family whose little wood stove, in which they were attempting to burn rubble and sawdust, exploded. Dr. Lefèvre handles the difficult burn cases, on which he has published several important papers, and Daniela is his right hand. The condition of the two little boys was pitiful. We were tied up for hours. Thus Daniela, who was to make the evening's drop in a seedy little café near Gare du Lyon, was a full hour late.

When we got there we heard that the Gestapo had picked up the man we were to meet. Apparently he made the mistake of approaching every woman who entered the café, in desperation, and somebody turned him in for the reward. We came home feeling guilty, but what could we have done? At least we hope that his desperation gave him away, as the other possibility, even more frightening, is that they were already watching. I talked over with Daniela the possibility of returning to that café perhaps in a few days and sitting around to pick up local gossip. That way we would probably hear if somebody local got a reward for tipping off the Gestapo that night, or if the Gestapo already had the drop under surveillance.

Every night we get under the pile of covers and listen to the BBC news of Stalingrad. The war in Africa does not seem to be going well, although it is exciting to hear that French troops are fighting again on the Allied side, and to realize there is French territory where we would be safe if we could reach it. The Mediterranean is wide, but not so wide as the Atlantic. We live off these little fantasies. Daniela and I have worked out a system whereby we trade off certain fantasies, equal time for each. She plans our life together with her fiancé Ari in Palestine on a kibbutz that will raise apricots. Then I get my turn to plan our life together in Paris attending the Sorbonne.

She asked me tonight if I ever miss Henri, and I said, honestly, no. I feel he dealt honorably with me in borrowing the money from his father for a fictitious abortion, which paid for my identity cards, and in sheltering me for a month and a week. By the time I moved out, he only wanted to be free again; he was terrified he would end up in prison because of me. He did not talk of love again after the first week of my having to move in; that was actually a relief, since I could not lie. I harbor no anger, no malice toward him, some gratitude but not a lot, frankly.

Daniela asked me if I ever missed sex, and I said, again honestly for that is our policy with each other, not really. I had begun to enjoy aspects of the act, but I believe I never had an orgasm, and Daniela too says that if I had one I would know it. She misses Ari. She is glad that they began to make love together before he left Paris six months ago to try to go over the border into Spain, where he fought during the Civil War. He intended to make it to Palestine to join the Jewish Brigade, but we wonder now if he may have gone to North Africa instead, to join up there. At least he is free—probably. People disappear every day and it is unusual luck if you happen to find out what happened to them. She intends to remain faithful to him the rest of her life. I consider that a little quixotic considering she doesn't even know what country or indeed what continent Ari is on, but it is all theoretical anyhow. I think it makes Daniela feel secure to think one aspect of her life is firmly fixed. She carries his picture with her, a full-faced boyish but stubborn-looking young man posed with a rifle under a too hot sun that makes him squint. She insists that when we finally meet, we will like each other and be friends also. I look at the photo skeptically but who can tell? Will she ever see him again? Will I ever see anybody from my family? Nowadays you can count only on seeing those whom your eyes rest on at that moment. It is interesting that both Daniela and I have had one lover, but she seems to have thought more of the experience. I wonder what makes the difference?

18 décembre 1942

We heard via the network that a deportation was scheduled today, and that Maman might be in it. I got off work yesterday faking a toothache and went racing all over, but to no avail. The Ausweis is in the works, but always in the works and never real.

I took the train to Drancy this morning, to stand with a group of others on the bridge over the railroad yards, where we can watch. They will not let us nearer. It is flat and drab there, a scraggly railroad suburb around the marshalling yards. Somewhat after dawn the first pale raggedy tottering ghosts were marched double time beneath us. I almost did not recognize Rivka, because Rivka has grown as tall as Maman and is so lean and stooped she looked like an old lady at first. I saw Maman at once. She looked bone thin but she walked with a very determined step, looking around and grasping tight to Rivka. Many of the others just hung their heads, but she saw me at once and we stared at each other as hard as we could, hungry for the fragile contact. She blew a kiss to me and had Rivka do the same. The moment was over much too quickly and then they were gone in the crowd being driven along like starving sheep to the cars. I had to rush off to work, as being absent again would not be at all wise.

I did not cry all day but now I cannot stop. The tears keep leaking slowly down my face. I wonder if what the Pole told us is true, and I fear it is. I hope Maman and Rivka do not know where they are going. I hope I am wrong. Hope is the feeblest emotion.

If we were not engaged in our little counterfeiting action, I would go mad. What saves me is the hard work we do daily in the hospital, and our lifesaving work afterward. Only lately it all feels too little. Daniela and I used to talk about the violent Resistance as something almost criminal, becoming like the Nazis, but I no longer think so. I begin to respect that work. Now that Maman and Rivka are transported, should I stay in Paris or try to find Papa? I do not want to be separated from Daniela, but her parents are also in the south. Our best information is that the Gestapo were waiting for the drop to be made in that bistro near Gare du Lyon, so we don't know where the weak link was and how much danger we are in.

I try to sleep but I keep seeing Maman marching forward so firmly and so much herself in spite of her pallor, gripping Rivka by the hand, who has shot up taller than Maman but thin as a seedling hatched in the dark. To see them and not to be able to speak, to touch them, to hold Maman just for one moment to say I want to be forgiven and I love her! At least she saw me. At least they saw me. At least I saw her. That is a little more than nothing.

JEFF 4

A Few Early Deaths

Jeff and Zach spent a few weeks in Casablanca before they were ordered on to Algiers, where OSS headquarters for North Africa was located, in the sumptuous Villa Magnol with a view of the harbor. The head of Algiers OSS, Colonel Eddy, trusted only the OSS Secret Intelligence people who had suffered through the long spring and summer of discontent when the Joint Chiefs could not decide whether they would listen to his agents in North Africa, whether they would support the French Resistance there, whether they would send any weapons or supplies whatsoever to conduct the sabotage they ordered but did not back up. Eddy had watched his French operatives gradually arrested as he made promises he could not keep because Allied Headquarters would not let him.

The French the Allies had put in power or left in power after the successful Operation Torch invasion of Northwest Africa, Jeff considered an unsavory crew, many of them Fascists who had either supported the Vichy government in southern France or cooperated, as did that government, most enthusiastically with the Nazis. Some were simply slimy opportunists. They were a different breed than the Free French he had met in London, who were touchy, vainglorious but thoroughly anti-Fascist. The local OSS brass were anti-Gaullist. The pro-Gaullist element in OSS had been purged or rendered powerless.

The Allies had made a fast alliance with Admiral Darlan, who had been a high Vichy official and so far to the right he considered the Bourbon pretender to the throne, who was also hanging around Algiers plotting, insufficiently reactionary to back. It was some liberation, Jeff thought. The local Jews were still being persecuted under Vichy decrees, still had to wear their yellow stars, Resistance fighters were still in concentration camps, the Fascist supporters of Vichy retained their positions and flourished. Allied Headquarters had run to embrace Admiral Darlan, who had extolled cooperation with the Nazis under Marshal Pétain.

When the French laid down their arms a couple of days after the Allied landing, the Germans rushed fresh troops to Africa. Now fighting was fierce in Tunisia. Although OSS had been in Africa before the Torch invasion, they were shut out of Eisenhower's headquarters, for he preferred British intelligence. OSS was orphaned, hanging around the outside trying to wriggle in.

"Eisenhower's got a British girlfriend, and he leans toward them. He thinks they know everything he doesn't. All the American brass cling together and bitch about it," Zach reported. He had a cousin in headquarters who was bitter indeed.

Zach and Jeff were kept in Algiers, partly because of Jeff's idiomatic and excellent French, and partly because Zach was one of the few people in SO who had actually had any experience with irregular warfare, acquired as he said from assisting in British disasters in 1941. An OSS faction still supporting the old Resistance commandeered them. The controlling powers in OSS were support- ing the Darlan regime, but there was a younger element in rebellion who wanted to protect the local liberals and the Resistance people.

Since the Americans had not told their French agents when the invasions were to take place until immediately before, the sabotage and uprising had been abortive and costly, leaving a number of Resistance people behind barbed wire. With Eisenhower's decision to work with the old Vichy officials, getting their people out was proving difficult. Jeff, as a Special Operations person of no ex- perience (in which he resembled just about every other SO person in North Africa), was handed part of the problem to solve, clandestinely. The first job was to prevent more of their people from being arrested, as was happening weekly.

"It goes without saying we'll spring them somehow," Zach said. "In the mean- time, can't we find a more comely Fatima?" That was what the Yanks called the Moslem women they hired to clean their rooms, do their laundry, all the dirty little jobs which they no longer had to do for themselves.

They certainly ate better than in London. There seemed no shortage of food here, and the local cooking—both the French and the Algerian—was excellent. Wine was coarse, strong and bountiful. "After the war, I could imagine retiring here," Zach said. "I mean for a month or two. It compares quite favorably with Palm Springs or Palm Beach. Cheaper. Better food. Hash. Tea. Vin du pays. Arab boys and French girls. Who could ask for more?"

"It would help if Eddy didn't view us as so obviously expendable." Jeff found Algiers less enticing than Zach did. He missed the London art scene. He did not like the French colonials. His Parisian friends had been artists, bohemians, leftists. Here he enjoyed none of the intellectual fervor or play he associated with speaking French. He was also unaccustomed to the colonial position, to being one of a small minority comfortably squatting on a large impoverished population. He was not used to being in a city, large areas of which were hostile and closed to him. The weather was iffy. The rain laid the sticky heat and the dust by making mud. The frequent bombing made every cock in Algiers crow all night, in competition. He remembered Renoir's paintings of the local landscape, but he was not moved to try his hand. When he felt most open to the land, he thought rather of Cézanne. But he was not painting, only sketching desultorily.

Zach plunged into the Casbah with zest, the narrow streets jammed with robed men, veiled women, begging children, the streets of prostitutes each in a cubicle open to the passerby behind a curtain that would fall after a customer entered. "Ah, the stench of the stews!" Zach flung back his head. It stank certainly, with open sewers running down both sides of the tiny winding, always climbing streets, tobacco, incense, hash, the baking smell of strong sun on stucco and stone, the aroma of little cups of sweet Arabic coffee that came on brass trays as they sat cross-legged in sidewalk dens. Jeff reflected that it stank no worse than the flophouses and shantytowns he had slept in, and he had seen child prostitutes in Chicago and El Paso. Here, however, there were more and larger flies. It was a subject for a Mediterranean Hogarth. Zach and he were spending almost all their time together. Jeff felt overwhelmed at times, crowded emotionally.

He desperately missed his Welsh art student, Mary Llewellyn. He missed the yellow London fog and the bomb ruins in the rain. He missed their neat apartment in Chelsea near the embankment. He missed seeing paintings two or three times a week, staring at them, going back to look again, talking over what he had seen and what he was trying to do and what others were attempting. In London he had felt himself fully a painter. It was a royal gift, the milieu he should have had in his early twenties that the Depression had robbed him of. He had hated to leave it. He missed it daily.

Nonetheless he was aware that it was war that had brought him to London, and he was here to pay for that beautiful time that had been granted him, the taste of the life he, with more money or born in less interesting times, might have led, and might conceivably live after the war. That remained his fantasy: that he would survive, return to London, perhaps even marry Mary Llewellyn, share a studio and paint forever. She was the first painter he had ever been involved with, and the relationship had felt much fuller, much richer, than he was used to. They never ran out of something to talk about.

When word came that a French liberal was in trouble, one of their jobs was to hide him or her, temporarily, if that would do the trick; if not, they had to spirit their protégé over a border to safety, or install him or her in the back country somewhere, just so they could keep them away from the Darlan government and keep them out of prison. It was a war against Allied Headquarters, who found this worrying about Communists and Jews, as they put it, ridiculous. Finally it was war against the old Vichy establishment.

Zach managed to visit one of the prison camps, which had made him keener on what they were doing. He described it as a hell hole run by sadists who wanted to be Nazis. Jeff felt satisfied with their work, but he minded strongly that it was necessary. Some war. The wrong allies, the wrong enemies here. At least in Tunisia everybody was fighting the Germans.

However with their new assignment, he began to like the French better. Instead of gouty right-wing generals, dealers in vegetable oil and financial manipulators trying to convert worthless francs into dollars, all of whom talked about the native problem, sneered at Roosevelt and held anti-Semitism as a passionate faith, they were dealing with younger officers, petty merchants, the little punks who had stuck their necks out, mechanics, refugees who had fled here to get away from the Nazis. They were dealing with people who had trusted the Americans and still wanted to like them.

"The British, they don't like us and we don't like them," a dealer in second-hand furniture told them. "Fire and water. We don't mix."

"They don't think much of us either," Jeff said. "They think we're children."

"You are," the merchant said. "But soon in this war, you'll ripen or rot."

The furniture seller had become a friend. Many nights they sat in the back of his shop drinking wine. "Before I got into the war," Jeff said, in French, as all their conversations were conducted, "I had a sense of it as a crusade of good versus evil. But now that I see our side in action, I don't know. I see fortunes being made. I see business as usual. I see us shoring up the corrupt and the rich."

"To fight evil you do not have to be good. If you are simply a little less brutal, that too is an improvement. You don't have to believe your side is just to recognize the Nazis are the shit of the earth."

Jeff felt responsible to these people, even though he had been happily in London when OSS had gotten them in trouble, recruiting them into the local Resistance. When OSS received word that the French police were searching for weapons and arresting everyone who had them, Zach and Jeff scrambled to collect the weapons that had been smuggled in so charily and doled out to the resistants. Most of them were World War I issue, but would serve as a ticket to a camp. One room in their office gradually filled with aged weapons. Then an acquaintance of Zach's who was recruiting agents in Spanish Morocco to function in Franco's Spain said he could find a use for old rifles, so Jeff and Zach smuggled a truckload over the border the day before Christmas.

When they got back to Algiers, OSS was buzzing. Admiral Darlan had been shot by a young royalist student. Who had put him up to it was anybody's good guess, but the youth was marched out and shot at dawn on the twenty-sixth. "Just in case he might get conversational," Zach muttered. "A good job well done, whoever organized it. It might even be us."

"We aren't that smart."

"Some of us are, my dear, some of us are."

"Zach, don't pretend you know more about this than I do."

"Where is that dear naive boy of yesterday who didn't know his cock from a teething ring? The pity of it. You're right, dear thing, I know nothing. But I have suspicions as ripe as the smell of the Casbah."

"Now will they let de Gaulle come over?"

"Never. Now it will be General Giraud."

"At least he fought the Germans."

"Escaped from a prison camp, he did, no mean feat. He's not neanderthal—merely neolithic. A slow improvement I would guess."

Not so they could notice it. As fast as warrants were drawn up to seize those out of favor with the still repressive and still proto-Fascist government, Jeff and Zach tried to get there first. However, the police chief of Algiers, who had been helping them, was arrested himself and accused of conspiracy in the murder of Darlan. They were able to get a few of their people on every British boat that left for London. There the British would quarantine them and give them a bad month or two, but then they could join the Free French. Jeff felt as if they were scooping up sand in a bucket by the seaside; moreover their activities did not give him a glowing faith in the results of an Allied victory for the oppressed peoples of Europe and Africa. Nonetheless under OSS aegis, there was room for their clandestine liberation work, as well as the sweetheart relationship SI enjoyed with Giraud's intelligence network. One of Jeff's unsettling discoveries about intelligence and irregular warfare was how much room existed for improvisation, for the chosen vendetta or crusade. It made for a quite personal war.

In January came the Casablanca conference, when Churchill and Roosevelt decided to bring de Gaulle to North Africa and force a shotgun marriage of convenience with Giraud, because of the rising clamor about Allied cooperation with French Fascists. Gradually the de Gaulle supporters began to gain some power inside OSS, and in Algiers itself Jeff noticed people wearing the cross of Lorraine or scrawling it on walls.

Their little contingent celebrated the Soviet victory at Stalingrad on February first, when they heard of it, by drinking everything they could get. A French auto mechanic swayed on a table singing "The International." Jeff sang it with him, although in English. Zach said it was one of the silliest songs he had ever heard and it would never take off, lacking catchy words and a catchy tune. However it had been a smashing victory and they would all be likelier to live longer because of it.

February came and with it the disaster at Kasserine Pass, when green American troops were overrun and surrendered en masse, panicked. After that the whole command was shaken up, and OSS came out a little higher up the mountain, because they at least could not be blamed—and British intelligence could. More OSS men poured into North Africa.

Jeff got a letter from his father, an unusual occurrence. The Professor had a small neat engraved-looking hand, capitals with flourishes. The letter itself was full of self-pity, gloom and foreboding. He did not know what would become of either himself or Western civilization. He saw the time as a twilight of the gods, an end of the world he had known. So much the better, Jeff thought, remembering soup kitchens, lying flat on top of freight cars in twenty-below weather, hungry children with dead eyes and sores on their legs.

Jeff also heard from Bernice, who was in Texas. She enclosed a photo. "This is me in my zoot suit. That's my buddy Flo." Two beings ensconced in vast and ill-fitting GI flying overalls, flight caps and goggles posed in front of a flimsy-looking plane that Zach, fascinated by the photo, identified as a PT-19—a standard light trainer. Her letter did not keep to neat lines but ran up the margins of the little blue V-mail. She was living in a tourist court with several other women. Army trucks picked them up before dawn to take them to Howard Hughes Field. She gushed about their drill instructor. In the photo she bore an immense grin. It was hard to tell her age or sex, only that she looked enormous and joyful. She was determined not to wash out. All the women were great. Some of their instructors were out to get them, but some were sweet and helpful. They were going to show everybody. She hoped Jeff was safe and well. She herself had never been better in her life.

Jeff put the photo in his wallet, from which every couple of days her face shone out at him with that wide glowing grin, incandescent with unselfconscious satisfaction. He had not seen her look that happy since she had turned twenty-one and finished with school.

Letters from Mary came in clumps. She missed him as much as he missed her. She was faithful, she assured him, and had painted his portrait from memory. She was sketching some but they were working a sixty-hour week in the munitions factory and she was a bit overtired. She hoped he would be posted back to London soon. Everyone was seeing a movie called *Mrs. Miniver* with

Greer Garson, a bit soupy. It was a hard winter and she had a dreadful cold she could not shake. Their mutual friend Tom Knacker had got a commission to paint a mural in a new officers' club up near York.

Rumors were that Sicily was next, if they ever succeeded in finishing off the Germans in Tunisia. Zach caught the clap and got rid of it, without having to go into the camp where regular army personnel with VD were cured and punished at the same time. Zach went to a private doctor who did not report his problem.

Guadalcanal was being proclaimed a great American victory. Casualties in Tunisia continued high. They were soon to be moved up to an OSS detachment there, they learned in March. All negotiations having failed, they decided to effect a last remedy before departing Algeria. One moonless night, they broke ten of their people out of a camp near Bou Saada. Zach had planned out the operation thoroughly and it went as he had envisioned, except for a guard who was tardy making his rounds. Zach slit his throat in thirty seconds.

Two years and three months after he had entered the military, the scrawny balding guard was the first person Jeff had seen killed. It sat uneasily on him. He decided, driving the truck at dead heat over the brutal mountainous road, that it would perhaps be easier to kill than to witness killing. They slipped their men into a Free French unit, no questions asked. Jeff kept wondering if Zach had needed to kill the guard. Would not rendering him unconscious have permitted the escape as easily?

During the raid itself he had not been particularly frightened. He had been calm, at times almost bored, efficient in what he was supposed to do. It had oddly resembled some of the pranks Zach used to dream up and Jeff to carry out with him, when they were both at St. Thomas. It had scared him no more than those adventures, whose worst outcome could have been only expulsion and his father's wrath. He had always had the same dreamy detached sense of seeing himself acting during those escapades.

Zach too was remembering St. Thomas. He squeezed Jeff's knee, as they bounced over the goat trail that passed for a highway. "Remember the time we bombed the provost's house with horseshit, old dear? And when the three of us played bullfight with your fair sister's red skirt? Though the bull was real and mad enough. Ah, Hemingway, what nonsense is committed in thy name."

When they were finally back in their quarters, shortly after Jeff had gone to bed, Zach came into his room, whispering his name as he let himself down on the side of the bed. Jeff faked sleeping. He thought at once that Zach wanted him, yet could not believe it. Zach slid his hand under the blanket and caressed his penis. Jeff groaned as if in sleep and twisted away, curling into the fetal position. He was simultaneously convinced that Zach knew he was awake and that he had fooled Zach, who remained sitting on the bed's edge another few minutes, and then left. A few minutes later, Jeff heard the outer door slam.

He began to brood over the idea of switching to SI. After all, in spy work behind enemy lines he would be endangering only himself. He felt the urge he had in London, suddenly acute again, to distance himself from Zach. Yet he blamed himself for his response. War was killing, what had he supposed when he volunteered? Zach did it well, that was all; and he would probably do it badly. That momentary fumbling after the raid was meaningless. Zach had felt horny and nobody else was handy. He did not want to have sex with Zach. He did not want to feel that much within Zach's power. He did not want to embrace Zach or have Zach embrace him.

Just before they left for Tunisia, a letter came from London in an unfamiliar hand. It was from Tom Knacker, Mary's one-legged painter friend. He wrote that he was sorry to be the one to tell Jeff, but Mary had been killed in an accident in the factory where she worked, the evening of the previous Thursday.

Two and a half weeks ago, Jeff counted numbly. She had been dead already for two and a half weeks, dead before they got their orders, dead before they pulled off their raid at the prison camp. Tom wrote that Mary had been taken to hospital and had died there the next morning, without regaining consciousness. Tom had taken some of her things for Jeff, because he knew Mary had really loved him. Her family had not objected. The funeral had been held in Wales. When Jeff came back through London, he should ring up Tom. Until then Tom would hold on to Mary's things for Jeff. They were all dreadfully sorry.

He felt a futile raging anger as strong as his grief. How could this happen? He had been ready to commit to her. She was a civilian. It was not right. He felt the same smothering anger he had felt as an adolescent toward his father, when The Professor emerged from his study to interfere suddenly in their lives, to promulgate some edict from Olympus. If there was a god, he was probably an egoistic self-involved dogmatist like his father, and any changes he made would be for the worst.

He could not accept Mary's death, bizarre, accidental. His fantasies were smashed like a cheap tenement bombed. He had lost not only the first woman he had shared more than a bed with, he had lost his imagined future. His after-the-war had vanished.

ABRA 4

Hands-on Experience

Research and Analysis Washington felt to Abra like a continuation of academia. They were housed in the annex of the Library of Congress, a stately white marble building connected by tunnel with the library across the street. There were the professors and the graduate students, in essence, and she of course was a graduate student. Given the minimal level of her ambition, that suited her just fine, although she considered herself fortunate as she had at Columbia that she did not depend on her stipend to live. Here the academic hierarchy flourished. Oscar was Oscar to sociologist Franz Widerman, with whom he had studied in Frankfurt, while his old professor remained formal Dr. Widerman to him. She was calling him Oscar and he was calling her Abra. That far she had gotten with him, but no further.

One difference with academia was that they were all organized in teams and had to work together. Another was that every time the big chief of OSS, Wild Bill Donovan, came through, everything got turned topsy-turvy. Charging in with Langer, the boss of R & A, kowtowing to him, Donovan would decide they should study how to infiltrate the Tibetan monasteries or how to use rabid bats against the Japanese in the South Pacific, and there went somebody's time wasted for six months.

One of the big team projects at the moment was developing an accurate estimate of the military manpower pool available to the Germans. Another was centered on harbor conditions in Sicilian and Italian ports. Another team worked with the Office of Economic Warfare on selection of bombing targets, also a big project in London R & A. Some reports were for internal use, some for other sections of OSS, such as Special Operations (SO) or Secret Intelligence (SI). Others were done for the military or the State Department. Some projects were requested and some originated in R & A and were then peddled to likely customers in other departments or agencies.

Nonetheless, standards for scholarship and objectivity of presentation were high. They were something new under the sun, because while a few economists had infiltrated New Deal programs, never had such a large number of university people come to Washington to work on very much their own terms. The contact with the center of things—the sense of being involved in a highly important and momentous enterprise—was exciting to almost all and addictive to some. Many saw themselves as men of destiny, finally consulted as wise by those with power, Plato's Republic come at last. If a certain contempt for the more clandestine parts of OSS was endemic, most tended to take on the swashbuckling airs that came with the ground.

Another academic characteristic was the incessant plotting, counterplotting, the faction fighting, the backbiting, the war of the committees. Oscar did not relish the infighting, but he was better at it than she would have guessed him to be. He had a sharp eye on the way he wanted to go, and he waited for advantages to open up. He formed alliances warily. He made others court him. From a newcomer he had risen rapidly to a position of some visibility. The truth was, she thought, he was smarter than a good many of them and more genuine in his respect for the materials they dealt with. She had not made a mistake in deciding to work for him and to move on with him. If Oscar often waited for others to approach him, he was by no means passive in the face of the main chance and struck hard when he had decided to take something over or start something new. As a Jew, he had been one of two in the social sciences at Columbia, Blumenthal and himself, which made Columbia more liberal than most schools of its caliber. But in R & A, the old boys of the Ivy League schools and DAR surnames mingled with refugees like Widerman and native born Jews like Oscar and even an occasional immensely overqualified Negro like Cora DuBois.

As an expert on Fascism in Germany, Oscar had ended up working on a team effort on unions which had nothing to do with his past work, although oddly enough it did relate to hers. She was treated as Oscar's property, although that did not prevent several of the younger men from pursuing her.

Abra was not given to being pursued. She tended to decide quickly to try or not to try whatever flavor adventure a man represented, but she was not acting normally. She was surprised at herself and half pleased, half displeased. She was fascinated by Oscar, stuck as if up to her waist in warm mud, and unable to go backward or forward. This stasis could continue for years, obviously.

He was friendly, courtly, warm and yet it never seemed to occur to him to take her to bed. She understood he had long-ingrained principles against involvement with his students; but she had never been his student formally. She figured out that in New York he had been sleeping with an actress appearing in a Maxwell Anderson play, a stately redhead who had showed up at their office several times to Oscar's obvious annoyance. That affair had presumably sputtered out with Oscar's removal to Washington, although the actress had taken the train down at least once to see him. A Viennese psychoanalyst had also come through town and spent a weekend with him. Abra was reasonably sure he had not yet become seriously entangled with anyone in Washington.

Sometimes she felt like a young girl with him, but not primarily because he was older. No, it was that she had to remember back to age fourteen yearning after Leslie Howard and Clark Gable, to identify the sexual malaise known as frustrated desire. There had been a lot of lust in Abra's life, but it had been lust easily satiated. If her roving eye lit on a man who turned out to be unavailable, she had never been apt to sit and brood on what she could not have, but to move on to what was enjoyable. She had not endured this stifled, congested wanting since early adolescence.

If they had worked less hard, her frustration would have bothered her more. She sometimes considered letting the curly-headed cherub-faced naval lieutenant upstairs inveigle her into bed. She would not take up with anyone in OSS, because she wanted to leave a clear path to Oscar. But she did not accept the invitations to a genuine Chinese feast upstairs, because in part she was enjoying her state. Is this love? Abra wondered; it was certainly something novel. Anyhow, the lieutenant was probably better employed as a friend and confidant than as a stopgap lover.

She spent her spare moments—in the bathtub, washing her hair, riding the overcrowded trolleys, proofreading, waiting for books they needed to come out of the stacks—staging scenes in which Oscar finally succumbed to the attraction that she knew, she knew, she knew was mutual. She wondered sometimes if any actual consummation would not be anticlimactic, but she never doubted she would prefer to find out. Hanging in steamy self-heated limbo did not suit her self-image or her real needs.

She felt his gaze upon her often when he thought she was not aware. He liked to touch her, although his caress was light, almost fleshless. He took care for her and of her. All of that, but no cigar. Abra cursed his control. Somehow she had to get through it. She also respected the quality of the work they were doing. They were writing an internal report at the moment on the Socialist unions of Germany and of Austria, their history of opposition to Fascism, their economic role in the greater Reich, and their interconnections to unions in other countries occupied by the Nazis.

Oscar believed that the Socialist unions were a potential intelligence resource, but of course the report would have to suggest that conclusion indirectly, in proper pseudoobjective style. One of the advantages of the new project was that she frequently had to run up to New York to conduct an interview with some exile who sounded promising. Thus she kept up with her New York friends, staying with Karen Sue on Riverside Drive. Karen Sue had a photograph of Ready in his lieutenant commander's uniform on her table. Abra did not consider it a flattering photo, as it made him look horsefaced, but Karen Sue was proud of it. Karen Sue dropped several broad hints about how she would love to spend Christmas in Maine with Abra, but Abra put her off, saying she had no idea if she would be able to take Christmas leave long enough to travel to Bath. Ready would have to make up his own mind if he wanted to take Karen Sue home to meet their parents. It would not prove an easy introduction.

Sitting in Karen Sue's living room gazing at the ships gathered in the Hudson River, Abra smiled to think how her parents would protest that Karen Sue was too exotic, and what graver shock they would experience should she bring Oscar to Bath. That thought startled her. She had never before considered bringing any man along home. Her brain was being addled by sexual repression.

She openly asked Karen Sue and Djika's advice. They were flattered, because Abra had never talked about her sex life. Djika had no useful formula. She had been a virgin until Stanley Beaupere had seduced her, and he had entertained no qualms about an affair with his graduate student.

Karen Sue was more practical. "Sit on him. If a man has been so nasty and unfair as to rule you out of bounds, you don't hang about looking sickly and lovelorn, dangling yourself like some overripe bunch of grapes. You just put your little hands on him and introduce yourself directly. Sit on his lap and throw your arms around his neck. He'll cotton to the idea then. Especially if you're sitting on you know what. You have to figure men are generally a little dense."

Abra decided this advice was worth attempting, if she could arrange the occasion. A party? Could she get him drunk? He did not tend to drink hard liquor, preferring wine, and she had never seen him drink more than he could handle. The rest of November sped by without her seeing much of Oscar. She had been given a piece of the project to pursue on her own through the archives and the German-language periodicals, and she was producing her own report due in mid-December.

Thanksgiving Abra went home to Bath, while Oscar spent it with his ex-wife and his daughter. On Kay's several visits to Washington, Abra had done her best to charm, without success. She considered Kay spoiled and shallow. Kay was clearly hung up on her daddy and acting out resentment that he had left her by punishing her mother and him. Abra kept these opinions to herself.

She laid her plans. She was not intimate with Susannah, with whom she shared the tiny glum apartment, but it was impossible to avoid knowing each other's business. She knew Susannah was sleeping with her sergeant, and Susannah knew she longed to get her hands on Oscar. Susannah's boyfriend from the Quartermaster Corps procured Abra a steak for her birthday. She was working closely with Oscar that day, because she had presented him with a draft of her report and they were going over it word by word, note by note, table by table. Late in the day as he was expressing satisfaction with her work, she sighed repeatedly with a lugubrious intonation not altogether feigned. She let Oscar wheedle out of her that it was her birthday, that she had a steak but no one to eat it with, that she was longing for company, a bottle of wine and a little celebration. The steak was part of the bait, since Oscar had often taken her out to dinner, and that was a dead end. She had to infiltrate his apartment or lure him to hers.

They brought the steak to the wine. Oscar had sublet the apartment of an OSS official now in Stockholm, the second floor of a shuttered brick town house in Georgetown. It had come furnished in French provincial and well equipped, although Oscar remarked he had removed the dismal paintings of hunt scenes and slaughtered pheasants to a guestroom. He had also removed the owners' library to that room, in boxes along one wall. It ran heavily to genealogical works, laudatory biographies of minor nineteenth-century judges, college presidents, naval officers, and morocco-bound uncut volumes of Thackeray, Tennyson, Longfellow and Emerson.

Oscar watched her in the kitchen for only a couple of minutes before he said kindly, "It's your birthday. You sit down with a glass of wine and I'll make supper."

Abra wondered if perhaps she should have learned to cook. It had always struck her as a drab, unnecessary skill: What were restaurants for? "Was your ex-wife a good cook?"

"Actually she is. I learned out of cookery books—that's their raison d'être, right?" He was in fact competent in the kitchen. The meal was simple enough: broiled steak, mashed potatoes, a salad and a little cake they had bought on the way to his apartment—but it was more sumptuous than Abra usually enjoyed. She would have enjoyed it far more if she had not been engaged in working up her nerve for the pass she intended. If he rejected her, would she have ruined their work relationship? It was even riskier close up than it had appeared when she had first contemplated direct action. So much could go so thoroughly wrong.

They had espresso afterward from a little stovetop pot. Oscar traded sugar coupons for coffee, since he had almost no sweet tooth and was addicted to coffee. Abra's hands burned cold in her lap. She must do something soon. Sit on him, Karen Sue had said. At least that was some kind of action. Hot flashes and icy cramps possessed her.

She had to act or the evening would slip away, tomorrow would dawn as bleak and frustrated as the day before, and she would have to wait another year before she could cook up a second birthday scheme. She wished she could down a good belt of whiskey to give her liquid courage. All her previous conquests seemed pitifully easy. She had only had to smile, to show a little leg or bosom, to lean forward in a doorway, to linger behind the others in the street and take a man's arm, to put a little english on a party kiss.

"Oscar," she said as meaningfully as she could across the table.

"Ummm? That steak was good. I wonder if Susannah's boyfriend could be suborned into providing another?"

She stood. "I'll do the dishes . . . a little later." My, that was a great come-on line. It practically ought to give him an orgasm. She had lost her touch. She had lost her marbles. She had regained her virginity. She was a blathering idiot and he ought to laugh at her. She marched around the table for the next several hours, approaching, approaching, approaching. Finally she arrived in front of Oscar to carry out what she had decided: sat down in his lap, put her arms around his neck and kissed him. Although it seemed to her no man could be surprised, she could sense that he in fact was. His lips against hers were warm but inert. She pressed harder against him, and finally his arms came tentatively around her, and he began kissing her back.

When she let his mouth go, his hands went up to her arms. Before he could disengage her, if that was his intention, she said against his neck, "Oscar, I am not drunk. I am not your student, nor ever have been. Guess what I want for my birthday? Come to bed with me." By the end of her little speech, she could feel his erection against her hip as she leaned into him.

He chuckled, taking her face between his hands. "I'm being seduced, am I?"

"That's the intention."

His right hand slid down her back to her overhanging buttock. "You have the sweetest heart-shaped ass I've ever watched. It's delighted me for a year now that you never wear a girdle."

"I didn't think you'd noticed."

His black olive eyes looked into hers, his hand moving on her thigh, over the wool of her skirt and then under it. "Don't tell even little lies. Abra, you want me, you've got me, but on my terms. We will play no games."

She was not sure what he meant but she would ask later. She was burning. They stood heavily together, kissing, and then he turned her to the right. "Let's go."

It certainly had not proved to be a lengthy seduction. Abra lay under him five minutes later quite convinced that the attraction had been mutual and was intense. It all happened almost too quickly for her to fully respond, but the second time they made love that night, she came in a long inrushing series of towering toppling waves. The first time was fierce, the second time, sensual.

Afterwards she lay spent but quite pleased with herself beside Oscar, who had fallen asleep. She owed Karen Sue something. Not a family Christmas, for she was not sure she was primed for one this year herself, but she would never tell Ready Karen Sue's past. She had anticipated lengthy arguments, gradual acquiescence, but Karen Sue had been on the mark. Oscar's defenses were all out in front, defenses of head and habit. His flesh was on her side. A sleeping lion, she thought, looking at the hair on his arms in the little light of the bedside clock.

She felt none of the urge she had often experienced after sex to get up and slip out, to go home to her own neat bed. The wanting was only a little abraded; rising up beneath it was an enormous new construct of desire, to know what Oscar was thinking, had thought, was about to think, to know everything he imagined and had done and wanted to do, to understand, to examine, to perceive, to relish, to discuss. This might not be love as other women used the term, Abra thought, stroking lightly the hip of the man sound asleep beside her, sprawled as if he had fallen from a height, but it sure was more than curiosity.

Having him sexually was fully as satisfying as she had fantasized, and now at last she was out of that limbo of shadow fucking. She worried briefly about the next day. He had assumed they would spend the night together. That was already something, for she knew well that urge to clear the other out, as she knew the urge to move on out herself. His body was on her side. She had faith that once the barriers were lowered, they would stay down. If the first time had been like a dam breaking, the second had been far more conscious. He did not tend to ask if something pleased, but to watch, to feel for reactions. He had been exploring her. She was astonished that she could not sleep. Something had hooked her and hooked her hard.

Home Is the Sailor

"It's a rotten time to get born and grow up," Four Eyes Rosovsky said meaningfully, drawing on a fag he rolled from discards in his parents' ashtrays. He could roll cigarettes with one hand.

Naomi agreed, sighing. "It's not fair." Lately she had been feeling that her family, her own real family, had thrown her away in sending her off. She never got letters from them any longer, and she could not even feel as if they cared about her. Maman had always preferred Rivka, now she was sure of that. Why hadn't they insisted Jacqueline go? Naomi no longer really belonged to anybody. The only one in the world who adored her was Boston Blackie and he was just a cat.

It was their senior year and her friends swaggered around the halls of the grade school. There were paper drives or scrap drives every couple of weeks, when they got to escape classes to collect flattened tin cans, bundles of newspapers and magazines, old machinery and pans from basements and garages all over the neighborhood. There was always time to sneak a smoke with the gang and hang out watching the freights or if anybody had the money, to go arm and arm into the drugstore and have a milk shake or a double chocolate soda. That was the best part of senior year. But what Sandy had warned her was true, they had to make their own graduation dresses.

"Don't fret, little one," Rose said, although Naomi was now three centimeters taller than her aunt. "If your dress doesn't come out good, you bring it home and I'll fix it for you."

To Sandy, Naomi announced, "When I grow up, I will live in a tent in the summer and in a hotel in the winter. I will never sweep from the floor every day the dirt of that day and I will never stand and scrub diapers stinky with baby shit."

"We'll be in the movies together. I'll be like Lana Turner or Betty Grable, and you'll be like Hedy Lamarr or Dorothy Lamour. They always have a blond actress and a brunette. We'll have mansions with lots of servants, and they'll do all the things our mothers make us do. I mean my mother and your aunt," Sandy corrected herself condescendingly.

"I have a real mother too." She did not think Sandy believed her. Naomi and Sandy acted parts from movies they had seen. They put on Ruthie's dress that was too frayed in the seams to repair. They dressed in old lace curtains that had belonged to Sandy's mother. They did sexy dances in Sandy's bedroom and watched themselves in the mirror, swinging their hips and giggling. They practiced jitterbugging and doing the rumba and the samba to the radio. Mostly Naomi was the boy and led, because Sandy did not like to be the boy, although she knew the dances better. One time when they had Sandy's flat to themselves, when her mother took little Roy to the doctor for his adenoids, they played Fred Astaire and Ginger Rogers, and Naomi made up a tap dance on Mrs. Rosenthal's dining room table.

But those dress-up games were only for the days when Sandy did not have to drag Roy with her. Fortunately he was finally beginning to hang out with other kids his age and could not spy on them all the time. "I'm never going to have babies. I hate babies," Naomi said. "If I was ever that loud and that dirty, I don't want to know it."

"I intend to have four children, two boys and two girls," Sandy said. "Blond like me and darling, in little suits and pretty little dresses. But I'll be rich, so I'll have a nursemaid for them." Sandy extended her head on its long neck, as if she were practicing to be a giraffe. "If they do it in their pants, it will be *her* problem."

Sandy insisted that Naomi had to have a movie star to be in love with, so she picked Errol Flynn. She did think he was handsome and he seemed as if he could save you, if you needed that. Then Errol Flynn in real life was all over the papers because he was accused of statutory rape. Sandy and Naomi spent a whole afternoon in the branch library with the *Encyclopaedia Britannica* trying to figure out what was statutory rape. It made Naomi nervous. She switched her affection to John Garfield. At least he was Jewish, while seeming to be someone who could fight if he had to.

Every day they walked to school together; every afternoon they came home together. It was not like walking with Rivka, who shared all thoughts, reactions and wishes; who fed on hers and built on them and turned them about so that they gleamed with polish; but it was better than being alone. People who had had a twin knew what love was and everybody else made do, she decided. They were best friends, Sandy said, and Naomi quickly agreed, because Sandy was popular and protected her in her spiky strangeness that still remained, no matter how she tried to keep her elbows in and appear like everybody else.

When she had a chance to talk with Clotilde at school, they spoke often of their favorite fantasies, When I go back to Martinique, When I go home to my family in Paris. Lately she did not want to talk about that fantasy, because instead of making her feel better, she felt more abandoned. Instead she asked Clotilde about Martinique, about her grandma, who remembered a volcano erupting, and her big family back there on the beautiful island. Clotilde came from Trois-Îlets, "comme la belle Joséphine, l'empresse." Twice Naomi dreamed she was on a tropical island with Clotilde. Each time it was peaceful and then something terrifying would happen. Once it was a blue jellyfish that exploded, stinging them. Another night it was a mob of people chasing them down the beach, armed with clubs and torches.

She loved Ruthie, but Ruthie hung out with Trudi when she had time off or with Vivian from the factory. Naomi knew now that Ruthie did not always tell her the truth. Ruthie had a period that came two weeks late. Naomi knew because her period always came the same day as Ruthie's. It had become that way slowly and now they were synchronized. When Ruthie's period was two weeks late, so was Naomi's. When she mentioned that to Ruthie, Ruthie became agitated and pretended that she had already had her period. Naomi did not say anything to Sandy or Aunt Rose, but she decided that Ruthie had done it with Murray and was going to have a baby.

Finally both their periods did start and Ruthie was cheerful and sang "I've Got a Gal in Kalamazoo" in the bathroom. That had been five months ago, but Naomi did not forget. She was becoming sly and secretive. She had always told everything to Rivka, whatever she thought and felt. Now she was twisting round inside like a corkscrew.

Trudi and Ruthie shared secrets. Naomi felt jealous, but sometimes Ruthie took her over to Trudi's. Then she felt as if she had leaped over her awkward sticky painful growing and emerged into adulthood. Trudi was living in her parents' house, but at least she had a room all to herself, a big sunny room that faced the backyard. Trudi's mother threw stale bread, leftover noodles and oatmeal out on the snow for the birds. Naomi had not realized how many birds lived in Detroit. Looking at them made her feel good. At first she wished she could have a bird, but then she looked at the canary Alvin's mother had, and it did not make her feel nearly as glad. A cage was a cage. It made her remember the bad dreams she had been having, about Maman and Rivka. Better to go over to Trudi's and ask her mother if she could help feed the birds. Trudi had learned to knit and was teaching Ruthie and Naomi.

As the winter deepened, sometimes Naomi went over to Trudi's alone. She brought with her the mittens she was knitting. Then she tried a scarf. She did not take Sandy. If she took Sandy, she would feel like two little girls hanging around an adult. No, she went over as a friend visiting a friend. She could go to Trudi's oftener than Ruthie, because Ruthie could only go on weekends. When only Naomi was there with her, Trudi would put sad romantic ballads on the phonograph, like "As Time Goes By," "Smoke Gets in Your Eyes," "I'll Never Smile Again."

Trudi worked four evenings a week at a local clinic, as a receptionist; but then she quit. Naomi thought it was funny for an adult not to work unless he or she were going to school; then she finally noticed what was happening to Trudi. She was getting fat in the middle.

"Trudi's going to have a baby in May," Ruthie said.

"Does she want to?"

Ruthie nodded. "I think she hopes it will tie Leib to her more firmly. Me, I don't say anything. It's too late to say anything. She knows him better than I do. Maybe she's right." Ruthie shrugged.

Naomi liked the way Ruthie shrugged; it was a fast motion, as if she were flipping something away into limbo. She practiced it, but when she tried it out, Sandy asked if she were itchy and offered to scratch her back.

Children were running all over the frozen rutted soil of the yard. It was a dismal yard, the buildings around it unfinished but jammed full of people who were yelling and lamenting. Looking down from a window without glass, Rivka could see what was going on, if she clung to the sash. She was locked into the building with the other adults and the big kids. The little children were crying loudly. They were being called by name, but most of them didn't know their names. They knew what their Mamans called them, but they were too little to have learned their last names or their formal first names. Many were called a Hebrew name at home, not the French names on their papers.

Finally the officials just numbered them. They had to have a thousand children. Little ones were running all about and some officials began to beat them. But that did not help. The children would just lie down and weep. They did not march in neat lines the way the guards wanted them to, into the buses to take them to the train station where the cars were waiting.

French policemen were lined up along the way to make sure they did not escape. Children would run up to guards and beg them to take them to the bathroom so they would not wet themselves, ask them to tie their shoes.

Rivka was watching from above, locked in with the adults. She was watching so that she would remember and tell. The little ones were being shipped east. The French officials had decided the Jewish children must go. What else could they do, they asked, with all those little Jewish children? Someday there would be a chance to remember and tell how the little children had been beaten and marched to buses to go to the railway cars and then the buses were shut up and went off with the hands still reaching out to wave, little fluttering hands still trying to please, to entreat, all she could see as the children were taken away.

In late January Duvey arrived on two weeks' leave. He liked to lie late in bed. One day he wasn't even awake when Naomi came home from school. Rose said he was run down and needed building up again.

Then Naomi was home on break between semesters, when she would go from 8B to 8A and finally graduate. The American system was confusing, but she had learned not to comment on how differently things were done in France. Nobody here cared and they would just make fun of her. She grew used to silently commenting on the absurdities she saw about her, as if to the twin from whom she had been taken.

Duvey gave her a nickel every morning, if when he woke up around eleven, she would bring him a big cup of café au lait made the right way, the French way, with the milk heated. They had little coffee, but everybody agreed that Duvey should have his big morning cup. He would lie in bed and wait for her to bring it to him on a tray. Then he would tell her to hand him his pants and he would give her a nickel and a big kiss. She did not like being kissed that way, but she liked making the coffee—it was one thing she knew how to do right—and she liked being given the nickels.

By the fifth day, he began putting his tongue in her mouth, the way Alvin tried to do. She told Duvey she didn't like that. He said she would like it soon, and gave her a dime instead. She felt funny about what went on in Duvey's room, because every day he held her a little tighter. He told her to shut the door, but she wouldn't. On the other hand, Rose beamed at her and told her she was a good girl to take care of Duvey's breakfast.

Saturday morning they were going through their daily push and shove when Ruthie said, "What do you think you're doing, Duvey?" She stood in the doorway in her old plaid bathrobe, holding the doorjamb in one hand.

Naomi jumped off the bed's edge and went to stand by Ruthie. She did not know if she should be ashamed. It was confusing, because uncles had a right to kiss her, even if she did not want to, but not with the tongue the way Alvin and Four Eyes tried to. They called it French kissing but nobody in Paris had kissed her that way.

"Aw, go on, Ruthie. What are you doing up? I was just fooling around with her."

"You're damned right you were." Ruthie was vibrating with anger. Her fists clenched and unclenched.

"I wasn't doing anything. I just kissed her."

"She's a little girl, you pig!"

"She is not. She's pretty now. She's growing up. She knows what she's doing. She's a little flirt."

"Duvey, you're crazy." Ruthie put her hand on Naomi's shoulder and propelled her out of the room. "I'll see you in a moment."

"Are you going to drive Mama wild with this nonsense?" Duvey said, sitting up in bed.

"You leave Naomi alone and I won't tell Mama. But I mean what I'm saying: Leave Naomi alone. She'll tell me if I ask her, Duvey." Ruthie shut the door.

Naomi stood outside trying to listen. She could hear their voices, but with a Saturday baby bawling in the next room, she could only make out the anger in their voices.

When Ruthie came into their room, she asked Naomi to tell her exactly what Duvey had done. Naomi answered all her questions, still trying to tell if Ruthie was mad at her. "You were only trying to help Mama and make a little money," Ruthie said sadly. "When an older person tells you to do something, it's hard not to. You feel in the wrong. But Duvey was taking advantage of you. If Duvey or any other man does anything like that to you again, you tell me. I'll break their neck for you." Ruthie stood at the bureau brushing her hair with smart savage strokes. "Now I'm too mad to sleep. I don't think he'll bother you again. Monday you go back to school, right? Good. I will take him his damned coffee tomorrow morning. And I'll spit in it."

Still the whole thing made Naomi feel as if she had done something bad. The only thing she liked was that she had fifty cents to spend on makeup at the dimestore with Sandy. She could pick out a Cutex lipstick and a matching fingernail polish and polish remover—to take off the polish before she went home. Then she wouldn't have to borrow Sandy's stupid Passionate Pink lipstick all the time. She could get a red one.

Maybe she was not alone. Maybe she did belong to Ruthie, because Ruthie worried about her. In the house crammed with squalling babies and sleeping men, only Ruthie thought about her. She loved Ruthie more than anybody except Maman and Papa and Rivka. More than Jacqueline, maybe.

Ruthie suggested that Naomi go over to Trudi's for the day. Rose objected. "I need her to help me today. What are you doing out of bed?"

"Let her have a little fun. She deserves to get out of the house. It's not fair to demand too much of her."

Indeed the next morning Ruthie set her alarm and got up only two hours after she went to bed, grimly made Duvey's breakfast, took it in to him and then went back to sleep. Naomi still felt what happened must be partly her fault, but mostly she felt that Ruthie loved her and would take care of her. She suspected that Ruthie had said something to Trudi, because Trudi insisted she stay to dinner there Sunday night. Monday morning Naomi went back to school. When she got home, she worried that Duvey would be angry with her.

He didn't seem angry. Instead he kept saying she was his favorite. He winked at her and cuffed her lightly. He told her all about Iceland, with volcanoes, and Malta, with cliffs and ruins and strange deep ruts in the rock so old nobody knew who had made them, and Scotland where men wore skirts when they got dressed up. He gave her a handful of foreign coins.

Naomi was careful not to go into his room. That was easy, because he was still asleep when she went to school in the morning, and when she came home in the late afternoon, he was sitting around the living room with the *Detroit Free Press* or out, if the kiddies had got on his nerves. He came home for supper, then went out and stayed out late.

"That Ruthie," Duvey said to her. "She sticks her nose in where she isn't wanted. She's a ballbuster."

Naomi turned her face away. She would not say a word against Ruthie. Ruthie was the one who cared about her.

Sometimes she remembered that Duvey had said she was pretty now. She stared into the little mirror in their bedroom to see if she had changed, but the same Naomi looked back. If she wore her new red lipstick, Satan, she would look better. Still she did not want Duvey to push himself against her again or to make his mouth hard against hers and stick his fat tongue in her mouth. She had just wanted to hear him talk about being a sailor and to tell her she made coffee just right, the way it should be—because the way she knew how to do things, everyone kept telling her was the wrong way. She could not imagine wanting to do secret dirty things with Duvey. He was just an uncle, but she could not help enjoying his stories and that he had called her pretty, even if he hadn't meant it.

Nonetheless although she lined up with Rose and Sharon and Ruthie to kiss him good-bye and waved and waved as he went off down the block with his duffle bag, she was glad he was gone. Now the babies would nap in his room and she would not have to worry about whether she was guilty because of what Duvey wanted to do after his coffee. She could relax and go on with her knitting. None of her projects had been a success—lumpy mittens, a shapeless scarf—but this one would be different, a warm hat for Ruthie. She had not told anyone what it was, although Trudi teased her to know. It was green like Ruthie's eyes, and it would be beautiful.

LOUISE 4

Something Old and Something New

"Mrs. Shaunessy's youngest daughter just had a baby, and the father's overseas, so I let her take the week off." Louise stood on a chair to put the roasting pan away. "I still think we should have had Kay help clean up. She does as little as she can get away with." Her images of how the evening would go after the Thanksgiving afternoon dinner had been exploded by Oscar already. She had hoped they would all three talk about Kay's rising intrasigence and her recently discovered pregnancy, for Louise was ready to admit she needed help from Oscar.

"Why not let her see the movie with her girlfriend? I thought we needed to talk." Oscar let the dirty dishwater out of the sink and dried his hands. "Here's the cover." He passed it up to her.

When she turned to get off the chair, he put his hands on her waist to assist her down and instead pulled her against him. As he kissed her and his familiar body engulfed hers, she felt herself turning butter-soft. It was an ongoing return of the sexuality that had been the core of her life, this man with whom she had made love for fifteen years almost every day. The solidity of his body was familiar, its heft, its heat, as if he had a natural temperature above the human. Then her anger came scalding back. She yanked away from him. "You've never been much of a parent, Oscar, but you might at least pretend to take an interest in Kay's problems. I need help."

"And I need you. And maybe Kay needs both of us."

"You can't need me. You'll have a live-in lover in Washington soon, if you haven't had time to find one already." She tossed her apron away and marched into the living room, flinging herself in an armchair.

"Oh, come on, Louise. You always did like Washington. You'd have a ball there. OWI is after you. Why not go back to Washington together?"

She wanted to kill him, she wanted to kick him right in the balls. All she could see in her mind were those evenings he had spent with Madeleine, Madeleine says, Madeleine believes, Madeleine interprets Freud to mean such and so. Him coming home to kiss her with that scent clinging to him, damned Parma violets. Madeleine was tall, blond, wore lavender and grey and smelled, discreetly, of violets. Her voice was low, husky. It was said Jung had been in love with her. Oscar certainly was, so besotted he could not keep from talking about her. Now that Madeleine had left him for the money-rich pastures of Hollywood, he wanted Louise back. How dare he?

"Oscar, I thought you had taken that attractive helper of yours with you. Won't she oblige?"

Oscar grinned. "In about five minutes. You know that I don't get involved with students. I have some scruples, even if you never thought I had enough."

"Because it might prove professionally inconvenient. Right?" Louise tossed back her hair. It made her furious that she was insulting him and he was looking at her breasts. The way he looked at her made her feel as if he were touching her. It was unfair. It had nothing to do with what she wanted from Oscar. She wanted to call him a pig bastard and break a dish on his head, but if she did that, they would end up in bed. They had had some rare fights in the old days and they always finished in bed. That was one reason her rising temper was making Oscar smile. Damn him. "If you've been too busy to find someone yet, someone will find you. Women always do, Oscar. You attract women like a garbage truck draws flies."

He laughed. "Then it's not my fault, is it? I have always been true to you in my fashion, and that's what's real. You're the only wife I want."

"I was always true to you, Oscar, but did you think I would sit for the next forty years being true to a man who left me? I'm true still—but not to you. I am not about to be unfaithful to the man in my life with you—or anybody else. I don't break my own rules."

Oscar wasn't smiling now. His eyes closed to slits. His skin got redder. He spoke in a silky soft voice. "And who is this lucky man? You're not making this kind of fuss about that wizened little prick, Dennis Winterbottom? You can't be faithful to a lapdog."

She had actually got through to him. Now she felt good. She felt like giggling. "No, I am not talking about Dennis Winterhaven."

"Who is it?"

"None of your business, Oscar."

"How do I know it wasn't this man who got Kay pregnant?"

"Oscar, don't be vile. Kay doesn't know him, as a matter of fact."

"Oh. You're supposed to be involved with this jerk, and he doesn't even care enough about you to deal with problems in your life?"

"Why should he, when you don't, and Kay is your flesh and blood daughter?"

Oscar knelt at the liquor cabinet rooting around, came out with a bottle of bourbon—which he never drank—and poured a healthy splash into his wineglass. He asked, as if conversationally, "An old friend of ours, no doubt? Half the men we know would have done anything to get you into bed. Fred Bauer. I bet it's Fred. He was always trying to get his hands on you. He used to kiss you hello, he used to kiss you good-bye. I used to wonder how he could bear to go off to the john without kissing you."

"Oscar, remember all the lectures you gave me about jealousy, how ignoble and unnecessary and primitive an emotion it is?"

"Damn it, Louie, I never asked you to live like a nun. But I want you. So you've had an affair. So it's not finished. Neither are we finished."

"No, because we have unfinished business, the daughter we made."

"Charley! It's your agent Charley. He's been in love with you for ten years."

"Oscar! Charley is homosexual. You don't know my friend. Now listen! Kay has to have an abortion, but she's evolved a romantic masochistic fantasy in which she brings the baby into the world and the father is dead—while in truth she may not be sure which of several men is the father—and she suffers gloriously in her own melodrama, without thinking she actually then has to raise the child for the next eighteen to twenty-two years."

"I'll talk to her. Tonight when she comes home from the movies, I'll deal with it. I can arrange it with a doctor who's very good."

"He'll use an anesthetic? I couldn't bear for her to go through that pain." She had thought Oscar would know a good abortionist.

"I'll go with her if she wants me to. Are you sure I don't know the man?"

"Will you really do that? She won't listen to me. Somehow I got off on the wrong foot with her when I found it out. I was shocked. I dealt with my shock by becoming very practical, and I accidentally oversold her on the difficulties and gave her that intoxicating whiff of martyrdom."

"Kay's at a difficult age, Louie, and nothing you do with her comes out right. This too will pass. She'll love you again, because we both know you've been a good mother."

Louise felt tears briefly heat the inside of her eyes. "I don't know that, really. I keep thinking of things I did badly."

Oscar knelt in front of her, taking her hands in his. "We both did many things well and many things badly. But the worst thing we ever did was to let go."

"What's past is gone, Oscar. I'm sorry through and through that you didn't think this way three years ago, but our lives have diverged."

"He must not live in New York, if he's never met Kay."

"Oscar, there's something I have to tell you. He has some connections left that reach into France. I asked him to find out about Gloria."

"Is she all right?"

"She's on their country estate. Her husband, the baron, is doing business with the Nazis. So long as he doesn't divorce her, she's probably safe, but it's not a comfortable situation."

"That mildewed weasel. What's he doing?"

"Promoting the new German culture, the New Europe. Everything masculine, heroic, squared off, men are men and women stay home pregnant, and Jews are dogs. He puts on displays of muscle-bound sculpture and patriotic paintings. He's become a cultural impresario."

Oscar rose, paced. He drank off his bourbon and paced more. "I wonder if there's any way to get her out?"

"I don't see how. Probably she's in little danger, unless the baron chooses to get rid of her."

"He married her because she's beautiful and was notorious in that little beau monde. Now she's a liability. I don't trust him to hang on. After all, she doesn't have her own money." He strode from one end of the living room to the other, absently running his hand along the back of the couch they had selected together when they moved here, when he got the job at Columbia in 1935. "I hate to think of her vulnerable."

"Do you want me to try to find out more?"

"Is he in OSS too?"

"No. He's connected with OWI—"

"As you are."

"Not officially. They want me to take on a more active role. I've been working on the writers' board, but they want me actually producing propaganda, and I have to brood on that longer—"

"Why would someone in OWI have links into France?"

"I said he was connected with OWI, not that he works for them. He has connections in French intelligence. De Gaulle's people, I suspect."

"He's French, uh?" Oscar frowned, for the first time a little daunted.

"Oscar, what is the point of this? It's no secret, but I haven't been running around making a fuss about it mostly for Kay's sake."

"I'm worried about Gloria," Oscar said, coming to stand before her with melting eyes and soft anxious voice.

"Oscar, if you try to use your concern over Gloria to move me, I'll break a lamp over your head, I'm not kidding. I do not fool around. You will not, will not seduce me. I'm a woman of principle, remember?"

"The reason you write those damned gooey stories so successfully is because you really do believe in all that romantic stuff, deep down, Louise. As a left-wing Socialist, aren't you ashamed not to be more liberated?"

"No," Louise said. "Now I am going to bed and I am locking my door and I am leaving you to wait for Kay. And damn it, you better do something to save her, or I'll never forgive you as long as I live."

Oscar did arrange for Kay's abortion, but it was Louise who went with her the following Thursday. Louise's own period started in the doctor's office, with fierce cramps that she could not remember having since her own troubled adolescence. Please don't let it hurt her, please, she begged the air. Hurt me instead. Why didn't I get pregnant, instead of her? I could survive another abortion.

Afterward she brought Kay home in a taxi and put her to bed. Louise found herself shaking. Kay looked wan, drained, an injured child. She held Kay as long as her daughter would let herself be held. Soon Kay pushed her away, turning to the wall. "Now nobody will ever want me. Now I'll never be able to have a baby. That's what happens."

She tried to take Kay's hand, nervously plucking at the sheet. "That's not true, baby. It's only the end of this trouble."

"That's horseshit, Mother. I know the score."

"Kay, when I was your age, I had an abortion. I had been raped. I went to a woman who did it for me. Afterward I got very ill, I ran a fever and almost died. That won't happen to you. But I had a life afterward. I had you. I wanted you, and I had you."

"You had an abortion when you were seventeen?"

Louise nodded.

"Does Daddy know?"

"Of course he knows."

"Why didn't he tell me?"

"He probably didn't think of it. He was worried about you, kitten. Why would he tell you old stories about me?"

"Because it matters."

"How does it matter?"

"Why did you make me feel so bad when you did it too?" Kay began to sob.

"I didn't mean to make you feel bad." She stroked Kay's dark hair back from her damp forehead. "You frightened me. Your life has been out of control. You've been self-destructive."

"Only because I got caught," Kay said sullenly. "Now leave me alone. I'm tired, I hurt, and I want to sleep."

While no miracles of communication occurred, it was as if a fever had reached crisis and abated. Kay would talk to her now. Kay acted like a convalescent, unwilling to hurry back to her classes, her friends. The school had been given a doctor's excuse about pneumonia. Kay was doing schoolwork at home, tutored regularly. Louise was determined to be patient and not to rush her back into her school life.

Kay opted to spend Christmas with her father in Washington. Louise visited Claude in California, perturbed beforehand because she imagined the company of glamorous empty-headed actresses. Claude, however, lived in little France, a community of directors, writers, intellectuals who had wangled jobs at UCLA or one of the smaller colleges, all passionately involved in exile politics and living for the day they would go home.

From there she took a train north to cover Henry Kaiser's four-day building of a Liberty ship at Richmond, California. It began at midnight Saturday in an empty way and twenty-four hours later a complete hull stood there. Louise had been commissioned to write on the romance of shipbuilding and the miracles of prefabricated technology for *The New York Times Magazine,* and a piece on women who were swarming to work in the shipyards for *Redbook.* The government wanted as many articles and stories about women working as could be ground out, for they had made a decision not to go to the English system of drafting women for essential jobs, but to rely on advertising, propaganda, the magazines. Women were to be depicted enjoying work, taking on new roles, becoming stronger and more confident in blue-collar jobs.

The ways bristled with scaffolding above the concrete foundations with a raised speakers' platform where the ship's prow faced the yard. Louise was sitting with perhaps a hundred reporters, many of whom she was beginning to know as they turned up at various staged occasions such as this one. Workers swarmed over the crossbeams. On either side of the way two sets of railroad tracks ran down to the water, the narrow set for railroad cars and the wider set for the spider cranes high as six-story buildings squatting over the cars to reach out their long arms into the bowels of the growing ship. Three cranes poked into the ship, bells jangling as they eased by on their high wheels. Riveters, welders, shipfitters, riggers, chippers and caulkers, burners and shipwrights ran busy as ants over the hull.

The flat keel, the bottom of the ship, had been laid first, let down in sections onto the keel blocks. Then the outer hull plating began to be fitted in, starting at the keel. Tanks were dropped into place. Then the frames of both sides began to shape. She watched the bow swing into place as *The Times* photographer snapped away. She could not help feeling pride in the spectacle. It was not that the ship was gorgeous, for the Liberty ships were slow clumsy cargo tubs, but the hard work, the efficiency, the solid workmanship involved in turning out ships as standardized as Chevys or Fords pleased her. A well-paid unionized work force that knew it was getting value back for its work and was motivated could do incredible wonders: that was what she would like to stress, but could not.

Kay came home from Washington ready to return to school. She announced, "Daddy's having an affair with that Abra who works for him. She's twenty-four. That's young, isn't it? For Daddy? How old is Daddy, anyway?"

"He's forty. No, forty-one. Yes, I would say there's a little discrepancy in their ages." At least she had not succumbed to Oscar's blandishments at Thanksgiving. How stung she would feel if she had believed him.

"Aren't you jealous?"

"Not particularly. If he were living down the block and I saw them together or feared I might run into them, I might be jealous. But, Kay, he's in Washington, and by the time he moves back here after the war, he'll be with someone else."

"Do you think Daddy is a rat?"

"No. He's attractive to women, and he doesn't see why he should resist. You ought to know that that was one of the big issues between your father and me."

"If you aren't jealous now about him having an affair with that twenty-four-year-old Abra, why couldn't you put up with whoever he was shacked up with when you were married?"

"He isn't mine now, so nothing is being taken from me. Right?"

"If you think so," Kay said sullenly and slammed out of the room. Nevertheless, Louise rejoiced, because now they talked of matters Kay considered important, however unsatisfactory might be the outcome of individual chats.

Kay's adoration of Oscar annoyed Louise because Oscar had been a rather indifferent father. He loved Kay. He was a deeply affectionate man, warm, charming, giving, but much of the time he was off being warm, charming and giving to somebody else's nubile daughter or winsome mother. He found paternity boring. He always said Kay would find her own way, rationalizing his lack of direct involvement as modern childraising. It was not fair for Kay to idolize the father who had smiled at her often and worried about her little, and to struggle so unendingly with the mother to whom she had been precious daily and hourly, whose care had surrounded her like a shimmering net of extra sensors wherever she went.

The last week of January, Claude came for the opening of his new picture, *Angels of Glory*, which he described as straight Air Corps propaganda. He would be staying at the Plaza for a week. Having a big romantic affair was quite different from being married to someone she loved passionately. Louise studied it personally and as grist for Annette. There was more anxiety involved in an affair, because each time might be the last if things did not go—not smoothly, so much as excitingly. On the other hand, during the long intervals between meetings, she had her apartment, her work, her daughter, her mind to herself. She did not expect help that did not prove forthcoming.

Louise worried about losing Claude because she felt she had become involved with a man perhaps a shade too sophisticated, too worldly, for her, but the week went well—so well that the week after Claude left, Louise came down with what her gynecologist leeringly told her was honeymoon cystitis, so that whenever she urinated, her urethra burned until she doubled over. She had to drink two gallons of acidulated water every day.

Still, she was content. Claude had brought her a dozen pairs of nylons, an antique emerald ring and enough eating and drinking and lovemaking to last her awhile. She had resisted entrapment in Oscar's old patterns and she had continued to create her own new ones. Claude thought of her when he was away from her, wrote her, called at least twice a week, brought presents to please her and gradually, gradually, took over her sexual imagination so that now when she created heroes for her heroines, they had Claude's nervous agility, his speed of reaction, his tight neat wiry body, his full slightly pouting mouth, his seawater eyes.

The steely taboos of the magazines she wrote for were such that she had to pack all the energy of lovemaking, all the knowledge of passionately moving and intersected bodies, all the ecstasy of orgasm into descriptions of kisses, as Claude for the American market must suggest as much from a movie embrace. But under the fervid steamy descriptions of kisses mouth on mouth, Claude's sexual sensibility was active in her fiction as in her own imagination. She was, as she had told Oscar, faithful to the man she was with. That man had finally ceased even in her dreams to be Oscar.

Thus Louise worried about losing Kay and worried about losing Claude, but the one she lost was Mrs. Shaunessy, who took a job at Grumman Aircraft on Long Island and moved in with her daughter.

"But, Mrs. Shaunessy, we've always thought of you as family."

"Thirty-five dollars a week I'll be starting at, and that's without overtime. My own family can use the help."

Louise found herself without a housekeeper, and the disturbance in her life was at least as great as when Oscar had moved in with Madeleine. Louise called all her friends. "I need a housekeeper!"

"Who doesn't?" her friends replied.

To Kay she said, "You'll just have to pitch in. We're both going to have to manage everything Mrs. Shaunessy did."

They made lists. Sweeping, dusting, shopping, laundry, ironing, cooking, dishes, bathrooms. Kay was appalled. "You should have paid her more."

"I paid her what the job goes for, Kay."

"You should have paid her more."

To herself Louise said, I don't need a lover, I don't need a husband. In fact, I couldn't manage at all if I had to deal with a live-in man as well. If I can't have a housekeeper, what I need is a wife.

JACQUELINE 5

Of Common Wives and Thoroughbred Horses

29 mai 1943

Daniela and I are in hiding, out in the suburbs in Maisons-Laffitte. We are staying in servants' quarters over stables, where there are actually a number of sleek and well-fed horses, better fed than most people nowadays. When the groom comes to feed or water the horses, we have to be absolutely still. We do not speak or move. Fortunately most of the day the horses are outside being exercised. The woman who is hiding us says that we should never wear our shoes upstairs, but remove them at the bottom of the steps. My last pair of leather shoes wore out this spring, just before we had to run for it, and now both Daniela and I are wearing the wooden shoes that have become so common.

This hiding place is less safe than it might seem, because the woman's husband is a collaborator, whom we are to avoid at all costs. She has warned us about him. However, he is living in town with his mistress, she says, and pretty much leaves her alone. The house is a large rambling, partly XVIe, partly XVIIIe century sandstone pile, mostly closed off. The only men here are the grooms, others having been taken for labor in Germany. She is running the house with an old cook and a young maid, working in the gardens herself.

Last night, she had us in the house to supper, saying that she was sure he was not going to show up suddenly. We sat in the kitchen and ate a large leek and potato soup and a salad from her garden. "You can't trust the grooms. You mustn't let them catch sight of you or hear you."

Daniela cast a look at the old cook, who was beating eggs at the other end of the vast kitchen. The woman noticed the look. "Oh, Denise lost a son to the Germans. She hates them. You're safe with her."

"And the girl, Jeanne?"

"Her mother is Jewish," the woman said. "As am I."

She is probably in her midthirties, with that crow-black hair you read about more than you see, a fine clear creamy complexion, dark almond eyes, high cheekbones. She seems a woman accustomed to being admired, to being stared at, although she wears old clothes. In the daytime often her skirt is draggled with mud. Her hands are covered with small scratches and cuts and her nails are short. Daniela asked her, "Madame, are you, were you, an actress?"

"Never. Until this war." She laughed, softly. "You may call me Gloria. We ought to be on a first-name basis."

"Did you grow up speaking French?" Daniela asked.

"I was born in the United States. I still have dual citizenship, for whatever good that may do me, which is nil."

"Oh, madame, I mean, Gloria, why didn't you leave when you had the chance?" Daniela asked, her eyes wide. I could see her thinking that if she had had that option for escape, she would have seized it. Daniela's family had tried very hard to emigrate, but they lacked the credentials or funds to get into the few countries that would take Jews.

Gloria laughed sharply. "To tell you the truth, it never occurred to me until several weeks after the Germans had arrived. After all, I had a French family, my life had been here for many years."

"You didn't think of yourself as Jewish?"

Gloria smiled wryly. "Not really."

"Do you now?"

"It has become a fact. Only fools ignore facts. But what do I think of myself as, most? Angry, my dear, very angry."

I was not saying much, but I was thinking a great deal as we sat at the table. It was seductively comfortable in the big old kitchen. Since the raids that caught at least half our little cell, we have been running and hiding, running and hiding. Here we are relatively safe. We hope to receive new identification papers soon. We had three nasty terrifying weeks of sleeping in garbage bins, in an abandoned warehouse overrun by rats, before we were able to make contact with another group.

When she speaks about not identifying as a Jew, I hear myself. I do not think that has really changed for this woman, but for me it has. Daniela feels thoroughly and proudly Jewish. It is part of her bones and also something she has affirmed, claimed, while for me it is something I have backed into, something I had thrust upon me. It is the same way I used to feel when I was discussing philosophy or literature with some fellow student, and suddenly he would put his hand on my knee, or put his arm around me. I would be saying, I, I think, I am a thinking spirit, and he would be saying, you, you body, you female body. It is not that I dislike my body, female as it is, but that was not how I was experiencing myself. Similarly, I considered being born in a Jewish family as a contingent peripheral part of my being, not part of my essence. Now it defines me. How can I come to master, to own, that definition?

Hearing Gloria speak, I felt I was learning something troubling to me. If I am to be myself, entire, authentic, I must find a way of being Jewish that is mine. I must find an affirmation in this identity, as Papa and Daniela have. Now I understand his obsession. I understand him better and I understand Maman also, as I never did. If only I could tell each of them how much more fully I could love them now. I could give them, not the dutiful, selfish and perfunctory love of an adolescent, but an understanding love that would lighten their terrible burdens.

I saw that both Daniela and Gloria were looking at me. Gloria smiled, that slight smile with the eyes burning she has, and touched my arm very lightly. "You're exhausted, aren't you? It must be monstrous to have to pick up one day and run, leaving your life, leaving everything you possess."

Then the phone rang and she was called. I kept thinking about what she had said, and at first I pondered class differences, how little I had to leave in the way of possessions. I do not even dare carry photographs of my family, for fear if I am taken, reprisal might be made. Then I started to think about our old flat on the rue du Roi de Sicile, and suddenly I was swept by fierce nostalgia for my little room up under the eaves, for the old teapot from Poland, for the dishes with their nosegays in blue on which we ate every day, for the sea gull café au lait bowls.

When she came back, she looked imperturbable but said firmly, "Tomorrow my husband is coming. You'll have to stay upstairs in the stables all the time he's here and remain very, very quiet."

"You can depend on us," Daniela said, and I nodded.

"I don't expect him to spend the night, but I can never be sure. If he didn't stable his racehorses here when they're not off at Longchamp or some other track, he probably wouldn't bother visiting at all. But we must put up with him."

"It's thoughtful of him to call before he comes."

"He must, if he wants dinner prepared and the house ready. We live simply here. He wants a luncheon for twelve tomorrow, so it suits him to let me know." She smiled again, that faint quiver of the lips. "If he doesn't call, someone else lets me know, so don't trouble yourselves that he may suddenly descend."

The servants address her as Madame, but the grooms called her Madame la Baronne. We do not think we are the first people who have hidden here. Everything is too practiced, too prepared. The floor of our room over the stables is muffled with piles of old blankets and mattresses. The windows are blacked out. Ropes hang from the ceiling so that if you walk around in the dark, you know when you are approaching the stairs, and do not fall noisily and painfully down the open well.

Also I heard the girl Jeanne giggling about a flier, till cook shushed her. The second night we slept here, I said to Daniela when we lay in the dark on the bed made up for us with a goosedown comforter, that I thought this was a stop on some underground railroad, and she agreed at once.

Gloria and maid Jeanne came out to the stables with us when we went up to bed, carrying a jug of water, a bottle of wine, bread, fruit and cheese for tomorrow. Gloria showed us a hole where we can kneel on the bed and look out facing the house, while once again warning us to be absolutely still until we are told that he and his party have gone. Fervently we promised we would even breathe softly.

"I wonder if anybody else got away," I said, as one of us asks daily.

"We may not know for years. That's what it's like nowadays," Daniela said. "One day you see a friend and the next day they're gone, as if they never had been. You don't know if they were killed, if they went underground, if they were picked up and are being tortured. Unless you see that face again, you never know."

"I had so many plans, ambitions, ideas, Daniela. I thought that was what I was. Now my ambition is to survive."

"We have done better than that. We will again."

We stayed up talking, as we had so often in our old flat. Why do I feel safe? I just figured out it has to do with the feather bed in which we are sleeping. In our family flat, I always slept in a feather bed. Maman had three big beautiful ones from her own mother. I am told when I was very little, I met Maman's mother, on her way from Poland to the U.S. I have tried lately to remember her. The year the war began here, she died in that distant country, in the house where my sister Naomi now lives.

Daniela knows a great deal about her family on both sides, telling me long tales as we hide about great-grandparents and aunts and uncles. I can barely list my mother Chava's three sisters: her older sister Rose, who has taken Naomi in; her younger sister Batya Balaban, who was arrested in Paris with her entire family; the youngest sister Esther, only seven years older than me, who married another Balaban brother, the one with the mill, and lives still in Kozienice. Of my father's family, from Alsace, I have some early memories, but they perished in a fire when I was ten and only Uncle Hercule survived, who had a restaurant till the Germans confiscated it. It strikes me how little interested in my family I was. Maman told tales, but the twins listened, not me.

When we were hiding in the warehouse full of rats with the rain dripping on us, I felt glad for Naomi in that far, safe city. The more that comes to us down the pipeline about what is going on in the east, the less I can genuinely hope for

Maman and Rivka. Sometimes I think that they cannot really kill the children. But I know better. Many people who did not raise their voices to object to anything done to Jews did seem a tiny bit upset at the deportation of the little ones, but Pierre Laval, who cannot stoop low enough to please himself when it comes to satisfying the Germans, said that he wanted the Jewish children out.

As for Papa, I have not had word of him in a year. I do not know if he is alive, dead, in a camp or in prison. As for me, my chances are those of the others who run. Taking an active role, I have already survived dozens of those sweeps we call raffles, in which thousands of others have been taken, and survived even the arrest of my cell. I would prefer to be shot rather than perish in one of those camps, if I had a choice which I won't. When I am realistic, when I am silent and talking only to myself and this journal, I say that my family will go on, but only because Naomi is safe.

30 mai 1943

After I had got in bed and was half asleep last night, suddenly Daniela whispered, "Do you trust her?"

"Gloria, la baronne? Yes," I said. "She doesn't have to do this. She isn't doing it for the money. She isn't taking any, from them or from us."

"I find her cold."

"I think she runs on anger, now."

"A rich lady like that, she must have thought the war could not touch her. Married to a rich aristocrat."

"But, Daniela, none of us expected the war to land on us the way it has. We expected some trouble, but it's beyond imagining. At your most paranoid, did you conceive we would be treated like cockroaches to be exterminated? Squashed underfoot? I don't think I ever considered the power and the force of hatred as something that could wipe out the whole world, before these past few years."

Daniela was quiet for so long I almost fell asleep, before she said, "I used to think about love all the time, never about hatred. I detested those who were rude or nasty to me, I despised those I thought bigoted. But I never hated anyone, and I never imagined anyone would hate me."

"Nobody hates us as ourselves. In their minds we're not human. We're not Daniela and Jacqueline. They don't hate us because we did something or said something. They make us stand for an evil they invent and then they want to kill it in us."

"If it's not a personal hate, it'll do. It kills us just as dead."

1^{ier} juin 1943

Early yesterday morning, we heard the grooms downstairs. Late in the morning, many voices, some speaking French, some speaking German, rose. We did not dare whisper or move. In such situations, inevitably some part of my body begins to itch until that is all I can think about, an itch of my nose or my scalp or my foot or my behind that fills my entire consciousness. They were laughing and jolly, admiring the horses and teasing about some horse on which two of them had placed bets. That was all in French.

I know minimal German, but Daniela can understand some of it, from knowing Yiddish. She said later that in German they were joking about Gloria and some other woman—probably the mistress.

After the stables emptied and we could look out the window, for a long time we did not see anything. In the afternoon, however, Gloria came out of the house with the party. She wore a black and white wasp-waist dress cut fashionably, I suppose. At any rate, it was elaborate and she looked distant and beautiful. If I had not heard her voice and seen her black hair, I would not have known her for the same woman. She looked like a high-fashion model, a creature molded of ivory and jet and marble. I could not really associate that image with the woman digging spring turnips and hoeing weeds, the woman who sat in the kitchen with us.

The Germans were all in uniform. One man wore a Waffen SS uniform, but when he spoke, we knew he was French. That chilled me to the bone. Imagine a Frenchman, who might have been my neighbor, my teacher or my dentist, wearing the uniform of death. I kept fearing they could look up and see us at the peephole, but no one glanced in our direction. I knew we were not visible if they did, but I could not help but feel vulnerable. All day we kept to our featherbed, with the chamberpot beside us and the bread and fruit in bed. We would like to place the chamberpot farther away, as by now it has a bad smell, but we do not dare walk about. We have neither of us managed to get used to the stench, and that it is ours does not make it any easier, frankly.

Toward evening they left for Paris, followed by a truck carrying one of the horses and a groom. Everything quieted. We got up cautiously and stretched our legs. We didn't hear from Gloria. After a while we heard a car arriving and quickly we lay down again and were still. Much later we heard the car leave.

In the morning still no one came to us. We saw Gloria, the cook, the maid and the other two grooms go off moderately dressed up. They drove an old-fashioned open carriage pulled by two of the horses who work on the farm, not the racehorses. They pull the manure wagon, and now, I guess, they serve as local transportation.

We had eaten all the food, so we were very hungry by the time that Gloria and the other women came back. The grooms did not return with them, and the girl Jeanne came skipping to the stable to tell us we could come to the big house to eat.

"We always go to church," Gloria said, "all of us. It's a good idea and we learn the local gossip. It's a convenient way to communicate. Here are your new papers. I have by policy not examined them, so you should check them yourselves."

"Are we to move on soon?" Daniela asked.

"Unless I hear otherwise, Tuesday night you are to walk out of here down to the main road and there a car will pick you up."

They know I want to go south, where Papa was last heard from, that we both want to be active and useful again. We don't want only to hide but to join some other cell or network. We've been here long enough, both Daniela and I agree on that. We have recovered our strength. We are well fed and rested and ready to be on our way. This is only being in storage.

"It must be hard on you, dealing with those German officers and the Waffen SS man," I said. "Isn't it dangerous too?"

"They never consider this other than a pleasant place to visit, admire the horses and eat well-prepared French country cooking. They think they are liberal to eat at the table of a French-Jewish baroness, very liberal. They are amused, and my husband is extremely useful to them. The ones who will not sit at the table with me don't visit him here. He has a blond mistress in the city who speaks German with the most charming lisp, I am told."

"How can you control yourself around them?" Daniela asked.

"If I don't, I won't last a week. I am servile and silent. I set a sumptuous table and keep the wine flowing and stay out of the way—when they let me. They don't always."

We both wanted to ask who returned last night, but we did not dare. It is none of our business, just as the condition of the papers she has just handed over to us is none of hers. She will not learn our new names any more than she learned our old names. This precaution protects everyone.

7 juin 1943

I am writing this by flashlight in a shed we share with farm implements, many mice and one overworked grey cat, who is asleep beside me.

Tuesday midnight we stood on the road carrying our small bundles of a change of underwear, our identity papers and bread and cheese. When we heard the engine, we hid in the bushes until the darkened car stopped and from inside came a whistle, the first bars of Beethoven's Fifth. We scrambled out of the ditch into the car, whose inside light had also been turned off.

"So, so," said a male voice from the front seat once we were huddled in back, "hello, ladies. You're bound for Limoges, eh? We can't get that far tonight. We'll drive till morning and then you have to pedal. We give you the routes, but you provide the muscles, eh, ladies? Good, good. Now, you know what I have for you? Chocolate. Real chocolate. A little piece for each of you."

Each of us carefully hid our chocolate away. We were not hungry Tuesday night, but soon we will be again, we know that. We thanked the cheerful man's voice fervently. We never saw his face. We slept in the back of the car. Just after dawn, he left us at a crossroads, with a hand-drawn map we were to memorize and then destroy. We found the bicycles leaning against the fence of the last house in the town, just as he had told us we would. Daniela got on one and I got on the other and we set off.

Shortly after noon, it began to rain. It rained on us for the next three days. Soon we were sneezing and running low-grade fevers, but we were making the distance each day we have to make from safe house to safe house. Finally Saturday the rain diminished and we were able to dry out a little.

Then today we had a disaster. The old tire on Daniela's bicycle split completely. There was no way to repair it. We were devastated. We walked both bicycles into the village, but when we found a shed where a man was said to repair bicycles, he laughed at us.

I sent Daniela ahead to the edge of town. Then I made my way back with her bicycle. It was market day and I bought some strawberries and a roasted chicken, at exorbitant prices. Then I casually took a bicycle I had noticed, leaving Daniela's in its place, and pedaled off rapidly. But we had to sleep in this shed tonight because we could not reach our day's destination.

It is raining again. I will not write about how our bodies ache. The first night we wept in each other's arms for the pain. Uphill is the worst. Often we just walk the bicycles up. Finally my legs have stopped waking me with cramps so painful I would have to bite my sweater not to cry out. We are always hungry. Our bodies are simply long hard pains.

12 juin 1943

We are at last in Limoges where we have reported in. Our identities here are invented, but we will not need to use them long. Soon we hope to get good identities (based on real people). We will be working with a group moving children into safety, either over the border into Switzerland or into Spain or into homes where they will be given new identities, with Gentile families. We will have to work with others until we learn the ropes, but then they promise that we will be able to work together again, once we arrive in Toulouse.

M. Blot, the man in whose flat we are staying in a shabby steep little street looking down at the river, knows my papa and admires him greatly. He says the Milice—the new French political police—and the Gestapo have put a price on Papa's head, and that he is involved in something M. Blot calls Armand-Jules, but refuses to explain. M. Blot is a chemist, classified as having an essential war job. His boss had his papers altered so that they do not say he is Jewish.

He says that Papa was operating out of Toulouse, but that his cell was arrested. He knows that Papa escaped, and thinks he may be up in the mountains now. For the meantime, I will content myself with asking about him. We were not brought this far to relax, but to do some useful work.

The mountains are clear of snow now and all passes open. I am to go on the road next week to start learning the routes south, through the Dordogne, through the Midi and over the Pyrénées. I will get a head start on Daniela, because she is sick in bed with a flu she cannot yet shake. I think it is the continued strain of our flight, sleeping in sheds, in barns or in open fields or abandoned buildings. We have often been hungry. We have pushed ourselves to exhaustion. I myself am lean and sinuous with new muscles.

I am to work with a young man whom everyone calls Larousse, because he knows every route through every landscape. He is a year younger than me and two inches shorter, but he has already established he is the expert and I am one with the little children we will be shepherding, until I prove otherwise.

He reminds me a little of that Boy Scout who came to see Maman, who was to provide us with new identity cards, except that he was shot. Larousse is a rabid Zionist, like Daniela. They are becoming friends but that is all. I do not find him a figure of romance, any more than Daniela does, for she is faithful to her lover Ari, whose picture she still lugs about.

I look forward to my first journey with Larousse, who has a reputation for taking no unnecessary chances, but being quick in response to danger. I want to do something useful, to resume a life that is more than a headlong flight. I hope when finally I meet Papa again, he will have reason to be proud of me. Besides, when we move on to Toulouse, I will be in a city where Papa was living and fighting. Probably he is not far distant. When we reach Toulouse, Daniela and I will get better papers and settle in—or what passes for it these days. At least we hope to have a base of operations that we can call home and names and identities we can keep long enough to be able to remember in an emergency. We hear Toulouse has a big and active Jewish Resistance movement, of which we hope soon to be part.

DANIEL 4

Their Mail and Ours

Alan Turing, who, as far as Daniel could figure out, seemed to be the British equivalent of William Friedman, was visiting America from the cryptanalytic stronghold of Bletchley. The first time Daniel heard that name, he thought his boss was making a joke. Surely no place could actually be called Bletchley. But his superior was not joking and spoke of Bletchley with a blend of reverence, jealousy and suspicion. It was the center where the British did their decoding of the German ciphers. The Allies were supposed to be trading information, but cooperation was spotty.

The British were using machines called bombes to crack the German Enigma codes, apparently more complicated than the imitation Purple machines Friedman's crew had built. Turing had a theory about a machine that could do logic that Daniel found too arcane to follow. Machines that could think?

The cryptanalytic world in Washington had been reorganized for the seventeenth time since Daniel had been working there. Sonia had heard this arrangement was based on the British. The British seemed able not only to generate signal intelligence, which after all they did well enough in Washington, but to get it out to where it could be used speedily and securely. They did not slop the decrypts all over the landscape, as the Navy had permitted at Midway, when the *Chicago Tribune*—anti-Roosevelt forever—had published a report about how the Navy had known about Japanese plans from reading their codes. Then there had been terror and cold sweat at OP-20-G. Daniel had been convinced they were going to be starting from zero again. The Japanese would realize from the *Tribune* report that their codes were being read, and would scrap the old system. By some sweet typhoon of luck, it seemed the Japanese had not read the newspaper article. Either none of their agents had sent it along, or they simply had not believed it—thought it was a clever plant to deceive them.

Nor did the British sit on their decrypts as if on marble eggs waiting for them to hatch dodo birds. When Daniel had arrived, he had heard stories of how few people in the U.S. government had been allowed to view the decrypts before Pearl Harbor, and then only for a moment. It seemed to Daniel that the military apparatus had been so security conscious, they had only permitted the decrypts out as if a flasher had run through the White House flapping his raincoat and then vanishing. Finally now a joint committee was coordinating all intelligence from radio interception and cryptanalysis. Now they could have some sense their work was going out to where it could best be used.

Daniel went on liking his work, but some aspects of his life he liked less well. Careful not to promise too much to Ann, for fear of falling into the potentially bottomless pit of her dependency, he found himself locked into the extremely limited relationship permitted by her propriety. Even when she bought herself a new blouse or hat, if he did not praise it sufficiently, she returned it at once. Yet she told him she thought he had little taste in clothes. If he did not praise something, she could not take pleasure in it, simply because he was her man.

He was tired of his roommate. He fantasized living with a woman instead of a creature who left the bowl hairy as a chin after shaving, let the trash pile up until the kitchenette was wall-to-wall garbage and dropped his dirty socks under every chair.

Intent on seducing Abra, he had become her friend instead. Now he knew far more than he wished to about her affair with Oscar Kahan. On evenings when neither of them was working—not frequent but more than occasional—when Ann did not require his company nor Oscar permit Abra to enjoy his, they went out together, to movies, to hear jazz, to sit and talk. They were increasingly frank, for it intrigued each to confide in the other. It had a touch of flirtation about it, a hint of risk.

Snow that week brought Washington to a halt. Four inches of snow here were treated like four feet elsewhere. They thought they'd had a blizzard and government offices shut down. Public transportation did not run. He had a late breakfast with Abra in her apartment before they went for a walk. Abra considered the snowfall ridiculous. Bath, Maine, had this much snow in an hour, she said.

The snow was wet and made good snowballs, which they threw at trees and then each other. They could both suddenly become children, he thought, without embarrassment, without faking it. She was rosy and breathless, leaping to throw at him, hard, underhand, the tomboy showing. He wanted to seize her and roll in the snow. How could she not see that this was the way to be, playful, spontaneous, instead of that crippling affair with a man almost old enough to be her father?

They sat on a bench watching kids clumsy in the unfamiliar snow. "If only he could open up. I don't know what he fears in me. I'd never try to possess him the way his wife did."

To him it seemed simple. He wanted to say that to her. This morning in the clean frothy snow he decided to do so, with a sense of daring. "You love him. Fine. But obviously he doesn't love you. He likes you, he likes to sleep with you, but he doesn't love you." He thought Abra might be struck dumb and run from him, might erupt into tears. There was the whole truth, finally out.

But she scarcely noticed he had said anything conclusive. "Don't be silly, Daniel. Of course he loves me. Why would he be with me, otherwise? You don't understand how attractive he is to women. He doesn't know *how* to love me. I'm too different from the other women he's been with."

Sometimes he wanted to shake her until her teeth flew out. Was he in love with her? Perhaps. He would love her if he could get her, he was sure of that, but he could not get her. To love a woman who treated you like a girlfriend was lacking in dignity. At the same time, he enjoyed the friendship. He enjoyed walking with her. He enjoyed sharing an occasional bottle of red plonk or South African brandy or an informal supper in her apartment or his. When he forgot his lust, he had a good time.

What he did not choose was to go to bed with her some evening she was furious with Oscar. He sensed once or twice he could have that, but he also knew that if he took that, he would never get anything more. He would be relegated to a role that was quite minor, a walk-on and a walk-off.

His best times with Ann were those times in bed when she did relax, when she did not fear her aunt might surprise them. They had a good weekend in February, when her aunt went to New York for an operation on her sinuses. Beds in Washington hospitals were notoriously unreliable. Not only were there far too few, but a patient could wait a month and be bumped by brass or the relatives of brass at the last moment. Everybody told stories about women who had just made it to New York on the train in time to have their babies in a New York maternity ward. Ann's aunt, an old Washington hand, knew better than to trust a local hospital for minor surgery.

Saturday after work they returned to Ann's apartment to eat an improvised meal out of cans and go straight to bed. Ann was far more talkative than usual and willing to prolong their caresses. They made love leisurely and far more sensuously than he had come to expect. He felt loving toward her. She seemed to him as warm tonight as she was attractive, a radiance of pleasure animating her delicate features. They made cocoa and had it in bed, a rare treat; the aunt had put some Dutch chocolate away. "A war makes you appreciate little pleasures. A steak. A glass of scotch. A cup of cocoa. The smell of a new car. A train that isn't crowded. Being able to order a phone installed," he mused.

"Getting the radio fixed when it breaks. Being able to wear stockings without fearing that they'll run and you won't be able to get any more. Being able to buy real French perfume, instead of this sandalwood essence I have to make do with."

He was startled, for he associated the soft curves of her body, its slightly flattened hips, the purplish beige nipples, with the scent of sandalwood. He could not imagine her smelling differently, whereas she considered her scent temporary. For the duration.

Some of their best times were talking shop. The light from the bedside lamp she had for once not turned off while they made love shone on her black hair, loose on the shoulders of her kimono. It dipped low at her shoulder as she sipped the last of the chocolate, exposing her fine skin. He could not understand why Japanese were popularly supposed to be yellow. He thought of her skin as dark ivory. It had little pink in it, but no yellow either. Her face in repose had always an air of sadness, but now it was animated.

". . . and so I had to go to the Pentagon, which they have just opened, and I could not believe it. It goes and goes and goes and goes. I thought I'd never find my way in and then I thought I'd never find my way out." She giggled behind her hand. "After the war, what will they do with it? They could use it for a prison. No one could get out without help."

"After the war. We all keep saying that, as if things will slip back as they were, automatically. Do you really expect that?"

"You mean, you think my father won't get his nursery business back?"

"Do you believe the people who have been running it will let go?"

"But it's not fair."

He put his arms around her. "No. It's not fair. But I was thinking more along the lines of the Pentagon and Washington itself. Sometimes I suspect that those who are running things might grow addicted to power. Secrecy's essential in wartime, but once in place, will it ever be removed?"

"Why not? Who would we be hiding anything from? Besides, nobody's going to be willing to spend all this money on the Army in peacetime."

"I don't know if what we called normal before the war will ever seem normal again. This town is full of men growing used to the sensations of power. When someone has wielded power, especially self-righteously, especially with a sense of necessity, will he ever relinquish? In 1940, when the Dutch army surrendered to the Germans, our Army moved up to seventeenth worldwide in size. Do you think we'll ever again be willing to be ranked seventeenth in weapons?"

"I worry more whether all my life I'll be stigmatized. Belonging nowhere.

Nowhere accepted. Each half of me at war with the other half. I never used to feel this way. Now I wonder if it's permanent. I can't stand to think of my whole life like this, a war without, a war within."

He held her and for a moment he thought she would weep, but she rubbed her eyes, sniffling, and asked him to make more cocoa. Tonight she reminded him of a Chinese garden. He realized, as he tried to verbalize his appreciation to her, that he was thinking of Soochow, a beauty spot west of Shanghai, a city of canals lined with willows, of whitewashed houses and famous gardens, where rocks and water and structures were as important as the plants, everything arranged and soothing. That led him to describe excursions out of the city, before the Japanese had surrounded it, with his uncle Nat or Chinese friends. In mid-reminiscence, he looked into her eyes and saw them glazed over with boredom. His China ramblings alienated her.

"Do you ever imagine our counterparts?" she asked him. "Somewhere in Tokyo, somewhere in Berlin, a couple is sipping saki or beer and gossiping, and when they go to work, they deal with our codes."

"I don't think the Japanese are reading our codes. They certainly have been running traffic analyses on us, but I don't see evidence of more."

She laughed. "Remember the Japanese embassy reassuring Tokyo that they saw no evidence we were reading their codes, back when we were reading the Purple code regularly?"

He did not remind her he had not yet been in the office in the pre-Pearl Harbor days, when she had first come. "On the other hand, I'd be surprised if the German B-Dienst, our German counterparts, were not reading some of our mail. You could make a case they're reading naval or merchant marine codes, because they seem to know exactly where our ships are going to be in the Atlantic, for instance."

"I thought your friend Friedman had set up impervious codes."

"He isn't my friend. That's like talking to the last violinist and asking him about his friend Toscanini. He never set up naval codes. A lot of naval operations use old codes."

"Battles in the Pacific are going better than what they call the Battle of the Atlantic, aren't they? It seems to me every day I read about a bunch more vessels down."

She was inviting him to explain the war to her, her dark gaze expectant. She considered it appropriate he should act as the expert, although in truth he knew no more than she did. With her aunt employed at State, she might conceivably know more. Still she waited for him to structure the world.

"The Japanese and the British are in the same position, essentially, overpopulated highly industrialized islands that depend on shipping for survival. We're starving the Japanese of oil and the Germans are starving the British of oil, food, weapons, everything."

"Doesn't it seem crazy to you sometimes? Each side hiding meanings that the other side ferrets out? I wonder if our counterparts are talking about us and trying to guess which of their mail we read, the way we're trying to guess about them."

"An infinite series of mirrors," Daniel said. "Can we be truly bold? Your aunt can't possibly get back before Monday. Can I spend the night?"

DUVEY 3

The Black Pit

"The worst winter in fifty years," Mike said to Duvey. Mike was Boston Irish, a wizened scrappy runt of a man but quick-witted, fast-talking. "The weather's been putting down as many ships as the Heinies. My last crossing, there was only one soul on the whole scow not puking his guts out, and that was the bosun because he was dead already. Of a burst appendix."

"I like shipping out of New York—it's a great liberty town," Duvey said. "All those sweet-assed liberty girls shuffling along giving you the eye. Lots of good jazz. You can always find a bar with something hot to listen to." Seamen weren't wanted at the USO, but he could find his own good times, no problem.

"Well now, I don't care about that myself. My mother says I have a wooden ear. But the ginch, that is something else. Let me tell you what happen to me . . ."

Duvey never got to hear the end of the story until two days later, because at that moment they cleared the headland and the full force of the storm hit them. This has got to blow itself out soon, Duvey thought, but twenty-four hours later it was worse. The sea would stand above them, fifty feet it had to be, a cliff of boiling water. They were somewhat south and two days east of Newfoundland heading into the storm. At four-thirty it was night.

On March 8 when their ship the *William Eustis,* with a load of tanks, trucks, jeeps and half-tracks, had left New York, there had been a hint of spring in the air, a damp southern wind breathing off the Gulf Stream. The twilight had been lavender, a word, a color, he associated with his mother, to whom he had scrawled a brief note before sailing, stuck in a birthday card embossed with heavy paper roses. He had also sent her a bottle of lavender cologne a buddy claimed was the real French stuff. He hoped he had wrapped it okay. He also sent a postcard to Arty and one to the kid, with the Statue of Liberty on it. "I see this coming and going," he had written on the back. "It looks prettiest when I'm heading into port."

In the submarine command post, the makeshift operations room of the Hotel am Steinplatz in Berlin where Admiral Doenitz controlled the tactics of the U-boats, the message came in, the list of boats, their cargoes, their route across the Atlantic. B-Dienst (German intelligence) was on the job reading the BAMS code (British and Allied Merchant Ship code), which they had deciphered years before. Doenitz ordered the twenty-one U-boats of the Raubgraf picket line to meet the two convoys, the slow and the fast. Three hundred and fifty miles ahead of that wolf pack, the twenty-eight submarines of the Stuermer and Draenger groups began to advance west.

Now the sky was black although the sea was visible enough, a frothy mass that shone from within in its whiteness, alive, a maw of fangs. How the hell were they supposed to see icebergs? The ship would rise on a steep hill of water, hang there on the crest of a wave with icy churning water pouring past and over them and the screws rotating in air, the ship almost shaking apart with the force of the disengaged propeller. Then they would pitch into the trough, landing with a thud that shook his bones loose from their sockets, that slammed the segments of his spine together. Then they would resume that sickening swell up and over, to hang in air and come crashing down. The tanks were the worst, always breaking loose and starting to roll. They had to keep lashing them down and one colored guy had his leg crushed. Deck cargo was a bloody nuisance in a storm.

The convoy straggled out for miles. There was another ahead of them, a slow convoy. The slow convoys usually made about six knots, and the fast convoys like this one made about nine, although as far as he could tell they could be standing still on the same bloody wave just banging to and fro. Although their convoy was made up of thirty-eight merchant ships and their escort, they could have been alone in the sea gone foul and crazy. They could not see another ship. The merchant ships lacked radar anyhow, but Duvey knew that the escorts who had it couldn't get any use out of it in this weather because the aerials froze over and sometimes they just broke.

They had some escort. The other half of his convoy, which had been split into two parts, had got the best of the available defenders. Their own defense was patched together out of what was available, because the escort ships had been taking the same pounding as the merchant ships. Whenever they finished a crossing, they turned right around and shepherded another convoy across. With so many ships broken up in the winter storms, they were using boats that should have been junked. They had two destroyers, *Volunteer* and *Beverley,* two little corvettes *Anemone* and *Pennywort,* and two ancient class S destroyers that should have been decently retired, *The Witherington* and *The Mansfield.*

He thought whoever in the British Admiralty decided to name corvettes for flowers had a slimy sense of humor. They were rugged little boats that rolled in any sea, even a light one. On his last voyage, he'd seen a Free French corvette ram a sub on the surface and send it down. That time he'd been torpedoed. They hadn't exploded but had sunk with enough time to lower the boats that hadn't been stove in. The rescue ship picked them up maybe twenty minutes later. Almost two thirds of the men from his ship had been saved. When the rescue ship had its act together and when it wasn't torpedoed itself, then a seaman had a chance. But they had no rescue ship in this convoy.

In Bletchley at Hut 8 the Triton codes of the German Enigma machines used by the U-boats were deciphered, as the code had finally been broken in December. From Bletchley the deciphered messages were transmitted by teletype into the Operational Intelligence Centre and the submarine tracking room. From this charting of the movements of the U-boats, warnings flashed to convoys and their escorts and the headquarters of the antisubmarine services. Every morning there was a conference on a three-way telephone link enabling the staff of the Operational Intelligence Centre, Coastal Command and Western Approaches to devise defense strategies for the convoys.

On 8 March, a signal was decoded at Bletchley indicating that the Triton code (the Enigma code for submarines) was about to change to one involving a fourth rotor, thus multiplying the possibilities astronomically. By March 11, Bletchley had no ears into the U-boats and submarine tracking was blind.

They imagined that the wolf pack Raubgraf was still located four hundred miles north of where Doenitz, whose eyes and ears of intelligence were still working, had relocated it.

Finally the seas began to settle to a thumping swell. Snow squalls swept down on them. The superstructure of the ship was thick with ice they had to hack away as best they could. Their elderly escorts were buzzing around the convoy trying to shepherd the stragglers back in. They called it falling out of bed when a ship got left behind; the life of a lone ship was not long. An occasional merchantman might have a gun fitted in her bow, but most had nothing on board but a casual assortment of small arms. They passed into the Black Pit—that's what the seamen had begun to call the Greenland air gap.

March 15. During the storm the convoy passed right through the Raubgraf line without being sighted. They were now between one line of U-boats and the next. There would have been no air gap had there been long-range bombers in Newfoundland, the famous Liberators the seamen loved to see coming over, but Admiral King would release none to protect the convoys. His eyes were on the Pacific. Europe was the Army's war. Churchill's scientific advisor reported to the British War Cabinet that they were consuming three quarters of a million tons more of essential war supplies than they were importing and in two months would run far, far short. The Navy looked westward, but in the Pacific the Japanese submarines did not attack merchant ships, for they held there was no glory in such easy prey, and warships should fight warships.

March 15 they sailed under a low grey sky. Twice the sun lanced out and blindingly lit the icebergs they passed among. The bergs looked grizzled, ancient. He knew they were mostly underwater, but he could never quite imagine it. Some looked like dirty islands, but one they passed near, too near, Duvey thought, was blue and pocked with caves. Seen from their stinking ship, those caves of ice looked almost inviting, clean and private.

The fuel below had sloshed around so much in the heavy weather that the food reeked and even tasted of oil; the air itself belowdecks felt oily. Everything had got sodden with the seas churning in and over. Now at least they could get warm when they came off watch. They could begin to dry out their clothes. The convoy re-formed neatly and was moving off at a good pace. In spite of the storm, they were signaled they had made good progress. They were right on schedule, closing on the slower convoy still some hundred miles in advance. Duvey mended his sweater, torn on a half-track in the storm.

By the third day in the Black Pit, Duvey was feeling brisk. After heavy seas and being pounded like that, he was glad just to stand upright with a deck under his feet. This ship was a sturdy one. Some of the others had reported damage, and *The Witherington* had to hove to with low fuel and storm damage. A newer destroyer was on the way to catching them, out of St. John's, where it had been worked on after the last crossing and the last storm. Tanks and half-tracks were safer cargo than all those tons of fuel in a tanker just waiting to mount into a torch. He had always managed to stay off the ammo ships; they scared him worse than the tankers. If oil exploded, it was by accident, but what was ammunition for but to blow up everybody in sight?

No, this was the berth to get, a middle-aged ship built in the twenties and decently kept up, with a smart skipper and officers who knew what they were doing. Sometimes he signed on a ship and knew in the first two hours it was going to be a hellhole, the food rotten, the discipline nervous or too lax to run the ship. He could smell disaster like rat turds. A dirty ship was often a dangerous ship. A guy he knew died when some bozo set off a snowflake rocket by accident, tipping off a U-boat to the convoy's passage, and that was the end of all of them, bye-bye, just because it was a sloppy ship and nothing tidied away in its place.

He went over his gear and dried his socks, worked on a too-stiff zipper. He hadn't sent a postcard to Ruthie because he was still pissed at her. He hadn't meant any harm with the kid. Naomi was too young to fuck and in his mother's house? Did Ruthie think his brains were fried? He was just fooling around with the kid, and why not, when it felt kind of sweet to do it. She was just that age when they ripen weekly and he knew he was the first ever to put a hand on her. She wasn't going to be a beauty, exactly, but she was going to be something special. She had a nice body already and a heart-shaped face like a kitten, big green-brown eyes and that air of being easy and tough at once that only working-class women ever genuinely have, in her cheap and slightly outgrown sweaters and skirts. She wasn't Mama's little girl, the way Ruthie had been.

Okay, she was too young now, and Ruthie was an asshole not to figure out he knew that too. It had been a cute game, playing with her when she came in in the morning, her a little scared but wanting to please too. When he jerked off, he didn't remember the girl he'd met in a bar on Canal Street and shacked up with for two days and the way she'd blown him. What he remembered was how much fun it had been to push the kid a little further, never knowing just how far she would go or what would happen, knowing nothing could or should, but still enjoying that funny power. The way she would look at him, as if puzzled at what he was doing.

U-653 was on its way back to France for engine repairs, away from the rest of its pack and picket line. The convoy had changed course northwards. U-653 was traveling on the surface, since subs could only make way slowly underwater on batteries. The lookout was posted on the conning tower, watching for enemy boats, since in the air gap they expected no planes. The lookout saw the masts of the convoy. U-653 signaled its sighting report home, "Beta Beta BD1491 Geleitzug Kurs 70." The sighting signals were special short messages in a highly compressed code, always beginning with Greek letters. Back in the operations room in the Hotel am Steinplatz, the U-boat command was pleased to alert the nearest Raubgraf boats and those of the Stuermer Group. By early that afternoon they were shadowing the convoy, waiting for dark to attack.

It was a cold night with the moon laying down a wake of light on the wave crests when it skipped out of the clouds. Duvey came off duty and had a cup of coffee, even though he meant to go right to bed, because he was so cold he wanted something hot and he figured he was too tired for anything to keep him awake. He was standing there with the cup in his mitt when he felt the thud, not in their own boat, but nearby. He followed the others on deck. It was a Norwegian freighter, the *Elin K.* She went down in a matter of minutes, while the snowflake rockets tried to illuminate the U-boats, who had to be on the surface to attack.

The poor old destroyers and the little corvettes went dashing out on contacts, either from their radar or their huffduff—the radio direction-finding equipment they used to pinpoint the position of subs when they radioed sighting or other reports. The U-boat commanders were, fortunately, a talkative lot. Tonight the escorts seemed unable to catch any of the U-boats. They were out there, but nobody knew where. The captain ordered them to sleep in their life preservers.

Mike told him a story about being sunk in the Pacific, attacked by a Jap plane, and floating in an open boat for ten days among basking sharks. The Germans called the coordinated attack of the subs a wolf pack, but he thought of it as a feeding frenzy of sharks. The U-boats looked like sharks to him when he saw them, usually when they were under attack. Otherwise you never saw the sub that got you. Once he caught sight of a periscope and reported it. Then he was not sure whether he had really seen anything, or only a trick of the moonlight and the water.

The moon was setting, two hours later, when he felt that same impact through the water and the ship next to theirs burst into flame. It was maybe two thousand yards away but he could feel the heat on his face when suddenly he fell to his knees. He felt as if a great fist had just slammed him into a wall. His eardrums screeched with pain and his body felt half smashed, as if he had fallen a long ways. Then everything went pitching sharply, violently forward. He grasped the bulkhead in front of him and turned to see that the ship had broken in two. The aft section was upended. No point trying to get to his boat station, no time. He was scrambling up the bow section hand over hand trying to get high enough to jump. They were being sucked under fast. He realized he could not get any higher and so he clambered over the rail and tried to thrust himself through the air as far from the ship as he could.

The breath was knocked out of him as he hit the water, but he kept his life jacket. The little light went on okay. He swam as hard as he could toward the sound of the next ship, to get himself beyond the suction of his own. He could not see over the waves, swimming hand over hand in a rough crawl in the icy, oily water. God, it was cold, it was cold. *Let me make it, let me make it,* he begged. He could feel another explosion in the water and it got bright. The waters pulled him around and down but he fought free. He was still afloat.

He could feel the boilers explode behind and beneath him as his ship sank. Ahead of him he could hear somebody softly cursing and splashing. It was so fucking cold he already couldn't feel his feet. His legs were heavy and pulling him down. He kept struggling forward. Somebody should be launching a boat to pick them up soon, they had to come. The sea was full of drowning men. He bumped against a body buoyed up by its jacket. A keg was floating near him and he held on to it for a moment to rest, but it kept rolling over and thrusting him beneath the waves, so he let it go. Come on, you bastards, come on. Where are you? Are you going to let us die? The fucking ships looked like they were all changing course, and he thought one of them was going to cut right over him. It didn't, it veered off. Still they didn't pick him up. He screamed, swallowing icy salt water, but he knew they couldn't hear him over the propellers.

Where were the boats? His mouth filled with water and he choked and coughed his lungs clear and tried to begin swimming again, but his legs weren't working and he was getting covered with oil. Everything was heavy, heavy and he was cold all through.

A boat from the destroyer Volunteer *put out, rowing among the wreckage. At first they collected all the bodies, but then they had too many. They could hardly row and had no room for survivors.*

Finally the ensign who had taken out the boat decided they should collect every body, look into each face and try to see if the man looked alive. His men's hands were too numb with the cold and rowing to feel for a pulse, so they had to go by the look of the seaman's face, if his eyes seemed to see them. What else could they do? If he seemed to be alive, they kept him; if he seemed dead, they looked for his papers and then tossed him back over. When they found David Siegal, he was in shock and in a state of hypothermia. When they let his body slide back in, he landed face in the water.

Dark in here. Must be in bed. Warmer now. Mama, I can't get my breath. Can anybody hear me? Mama, did you like the cologne? Mama nodded, reaching out for him. She was speaking but at first he could not hear her. She was saying that he should have sent Ruthie a postcard too.

RUTHIE 4

Everybody Needs Somebody to Hate

When Mama let out that geshrei and fell to the floor, Ruthie was sleeping. At first she had no idea what had disturbed her. Then she heard her mother's voice rising again and Sharon's voice beating around her mother's like a little dog, helpless, circling a disaster.

As she stumbled out of bed, her first thought was that something had happened to one of the little ones, and now Mama and Sharon would be in trouble. That was not the tenor of her mother's voice as she homed in on it, following that keening to the living room. It was a cry of grief. Something had happened to Tata? With everybody working six days a week and overtime, with so many inexperienced workers, with the speedup and pressure always growing, accidents happened every day. Ruthie ran.

Rose lay on the floor clutching a telegram. "Who is it?" Ruthie asked, not of her mother but of Sharon. She did not step into the living room, afraid to press forward.

"It's Duvey," Sharon said, shaking her head as if ridding herself of something loose. "They say it's Duvey," she repeated, turning to Mama, who lay on the floor pale and gasping. Her eyes stared. She was not weeping but once a minute one of those noises tore from her, the cry of a huge bird, an eagle in extremis. Boston Blackie lay belly to the floor having crept near Mama, terrified. All the little children began to cry.

Ruthie knelt over her mother and tried to hold her, but Rose could not see her, could not respond. In the meantime the children cried louder. Ruthie got up to deal with them. She was still half asleep and stepped on a box of animal crackers Sharon had put down.

Ruthie never got back to bed, which meant that when she finished work, she was dangerously exhausted and had to cut classes. At home, Mama wanted to sit shivah but Sharon and Arty persuaded her they could not suspend the nursery for all the little ones whose mothers couldn't stay home until the period of mourning was past. In truth, as Sharon said privately, it was better for Mama to keep busy with the children or she might collapse.

Three days after Mama had opened the telegram, the bottle of cologne arrived, a birthday present from Duvey.

Ruthie felt confused in her grief. She had not been close to Duvey; she was not sure they could be said to have loved each other since she had turned twelve. She had had trouble seeing Duvey's virtues because, first, Mama had always favored him, and second, he represented the choices that most frightened Ruthie. He had turned to male pals, the quick pleasures, the fast fuse, an edge that needed constant sharpening, toughness and street smarts, women who fell for a Cagney style.

Then too she had not forgiven him for tampering with Naomi. Her anger for that trespass remained like a splinter worked into her palm. She prayed, Let me mourn Duvey. Let me find in myself sorrow for my brother so that I may honestly grieve with Mama. Please, let me find it.

She prayed as she had not prayed since she had feared herself pregnant. She judged herself harshly because she could not achieve an honest mourning for her brother. She could imagine herself devastated by such dreadful news about Murray, and from that she pumped some hypocritical tears, imitation offerings to Mama. Ah, she condemned herself: Ruthie who cried when a stray cat was run over in the street had trouble mourning her own brother.

Morris came to her. "Your mother is keeping that room like a shrine. She goes in there and weeps. Sunday when she goes out to the market, we have to clear it out. For her own good. Give to the poor and clear it out. Three weeks, and every day she cries in there."

"What will we do with an empty room?"

"Give it to Naomi," Morris said. "Isn't it time you had your own room? First you shared with Bubeh, now with Naomi. Don't I see how hard you work? You fill in all the cracks, you always have." He tousled her hair.

Sunday Sharon, Ruthie and Naomi cleaned out Duvey's room. He did not possess a great wardrobe—none of them ever had much to spend on clothes. Here was his blue serge suit, for weddings, bar mitzvahs, graduations and funerals. A drawer full of well-worn shirts and mended underwear. Handling the darned socks released Ruthie's tears. Duvey had large feet for his size and he was always forgetting to cut his toenails. She could see his big toe sticking through his socks.

Marbles, aggies, a penknife, bubble gum wrappers with comics on them, a couple of packages of Trojans, a scrip dollar in which the state had paid teachers during the Depression, a circus program shared a drawer with perhaps forty snapshots of women. Most were taken against somebody's car or against a stoop or the wall of a house, squinting into the sun in a bathing suit on Belle Isle, posed with straw hat in hand in a little Detroit yard by some dusty-looking irises. Most of them were women Ruthie and Sharon had never seen. Some were colored women. The prettiest of all was a woman who had signed a studio portrait of herself in a fancy dress, Love to Duvey my heart of hearts from his Delora.

Sharon was squinting at the photo. Naomi looked over her shoulder. "I think maybe Naomi should leave the room," Sharon said.

"If I do, you won't get done before Aunt Rose comes home," Naomi said.

"We need her help," Ruthie said firmly. She was younger than Sharon, but Sharon always let her make decisions. Married women, Ruthie noticed, sometimes got into that habit until they couldn't decide even minor things. Ruthie considered that Naomi had the right to learn what there was to be learned about Duvey.

"Well, is she a shvartzer? I can't tell, this Delora."

Ruthie took the photo. "I think she's part Negro."

"Ruthie! You can't be part Negro."

"Like you can't be part Jewish. People want to know which you are so they can hate you right." Ruthie sighed. "We'll just throw these away."

"Can I have the marbles?" Naomi asked.

"Do girls your age play marbles?" Sharon frowned, arms akimbo.

"Girls don't play marbles at all. I just think they're pretty. Like eyes."

Ruthie grimaced, handing the marbles over as they dumped the rest of Duvey's memorabilia in a box, saving pictures of Duvey with Ziggy, and one of Ziggy with a grinning blonde. Ziggy's mother might want them. Naomi volunteered to burn the things in the trash can. She was careful burning, so it was often her job. Ruthie left Naomi standing in the shadows of the alley with a book of kitchen matches. The rats never bothered anybody when there was a fire going. She did not want to watch the photos burn.

His ties, his ties. There were the worn silk and woolen conservative pindots and solid colors Mama bought at rummage sales, never worn by Duvey or worn perhaps once, and then the wide rayon ties with hula dancers and desert sunsets he bought himself. Handling the seedy remnants of her brother moved her more than her three weeks of yanking on her own conscience had done. A woven sweetgrass basket from Sault Ste. Marie stood on the night table. He had probably bought it for Mama, but ended up emptying his pockets into it at night. It still held a handful of pennies, some Canadian. Ruthie worked with tears running down her face, until Sharon exploded at her: "Now you're carrying on like Rose. It's not good for the children, all this weeping and moaning."

There was a hip flask with a high-kicking chorus girl embossed on the pewter. The glass liner was broken. She discarded it. Old shoes were molding in the closet with a baseball bat. Sharon said, "I'll save it for Clark." Something from the uncle he would never remember. At last the room was stripped of Duvey.

On the job, Ruthie did not know if she would ever become accustomed to the noise, the roar of machinery, the staccato machine-gun din of riveting, the throb of the metal presses that she could feel in her thighs, in her spine, even as she walked out of the plant. A full quarter of the work force in the Briggs plant were women now. The men could still be ugly but it wasn't full uproar when she had to cross the floor, and she wasn't dependent on any of them to break her in. The first of April she was transferred to the swing shift. She was making $44.52 spot-welding on airplane subassemblies.

Now her days made more sense. She got up just in time to grab breakfast on the run and race to Wayne. After her last class she went home to change fast, and then Vivian, who had been moved to the swing shift with her, picked her up at two-thirty. That meant she had to take all her classes in the morning. She would finish out the term with her afternoon class by buying the notes from a fellow student and missing work the day of the final. By eleven-thirty P.M., she was home. She got to bed by one and slept six hours, then caught up on the weekend. At least she could go to bed in the room now hers alone, when everyone else slept. It was easier to study in her room on weekends, about the only opportunity except for time on the trolley. She could read standing in a dense pack of people; she had become expert at turning pages with the slightest pressure of her finger to avoid poking anyone.

When Mama was not running the nursery, she was off pursuing scarce food or clothing around Detroit. Morris dug a patch in a vacant lot where eight families were staking out little victory gardens. Morris loved being out there. He tried to get Arty interested, without success. With Tata on the day shift and Arty and Ruthie on the swing shift, the house settled into a better routine. Ruthie felt less like a vampire, a weird creature of the night on a schedule against the grain of her body and her family. She was always, always tired, but she was getting used to that, and it kept her from brooding incessantly about Murray.

He had been in a New Zealand hospital with a fever. Now he was released, although he still felt weak in the late afternoon. Maybe if he stayed just a little sick, they wouldn't send him back into combat. Her prayer was that he keep on having something just debilitating enough to keep him safe.

Sundays she tried to spend time with Naomi and Trudi. She felt close to Trudi, who was pregnant while Leib was overseas. Trudi kept drawing plans of houses. She knew exactly where she wanted the baby's room and where she wanted a screened porch. Ruthie would bring Naomi over to Trudi's, encouraging Trudi to take an interest in Naomi to keep her from that gang of street urchins. Naomi took to Trudi and was learning to knit. Ruthie only wished she could persuade Naomi to take more of an interest in books and school.

Now they knitted for their men, Trudi for her husband and her approaching baby, Ruthie for her lover. She had confessed to Trudi, for the comfort of telling somebody when she had been frightened. Sometimes she wished she had married Murray; it would feel less tenuous and fragile. Trudi asked her, "Aren't you scared he'll marry some girl in New Zealand? I bet they're all over the marines."

She worried that she had no official claim, if he were wounded. Only their bank account proclaimed their involvement in a mutual future. She wrote him about its progress. He answered that he regretted nothing except that they had been too sensible to marry when they had a chance.

Trudi welcomed her to the ranks of the fallen, for she had slept with Leib before marriage, but being wedded, she was now safe, cashed in, and Ruthie who had been so good and so sensible was still in doubt. It enabled Trudi to patronize her, but Ruthie did not mind for the companionship and because she would rather be Murray's lover than Leib's wife.

Before Pesach, she called Murray's mother and asked her if they would like to come to her family for the holiday, either the first or second nights. "Oh, no," his mother said. "We wouldn't be comfortable with strangers. It's a family holiday." They had never invited her over.

The letters on pale blue onionskin went out regularly and came in bunches, often hacked up by the censor. Sometimes Ruthie awoke frightened, wondering if she had not made him up, wondering if their connection could hold across thousands of miles through the fragile censored letters.

In the car that Monday afternoon, Mary Lou was rhapsodizing over her preacher at the Temple Baptist Church. This time she mentioned his name, Reverend J. Frank Norris. Ruthie froze. She had heard him on the radio, denouncing promiscuous racial mixing in factories, trains and housing in one rant and the international godless Jewish conspiracy in the next. Father Coughlin had finally been forced to stop raging over the radio last year, but dozens had sprung up to sell the same anger, linking rationing, always unpopular, and shortages to Jews and colored, stirring up the discontent that seemed endemic to the streets.

The buses and trolleys were overloaded with people jammed into each other, after waiting half an hour or longer. The whites said the colored belonged to bump clubs and sought opportunities to jostle whites. Mary Lou swore that was true. Somebody's maid was supposed to have confessed it, as if any woman in the factory ever had a maid. There had been hate strikes in several of the plants, when Negroes were hired or when they were let into any positions but the lowest. Just recently a few colored women had been hired at Briggs, and some of the white women wanted to walk off in protest. They said all colored women had syphilis.

Vivian was saying, "Listen, honey, you got your religion and I got mine. But you leave the Reverend Norris out of this car, or you get to work on your own trotters, understand?"

"He's a man of God," Mary Lou said indignantly. "He comes back and forth from Texas to Detroit just to be saving our souls every week."

"Look, honey, we're Jews, Ruthie and me, and proud of it, so you keep him to yourself or you walk."

Ruthie wished she had thought of something to say like that, but it was Vivian's car, not hers. There was a long silence. Joyce was still on the graveyard shift, probably because of the episode of the infamous red slacks, and now they were riding with an older woman Joann who never said anything but hello and thank you kindly.

Finally Mary Lou said, "Well, how was I supposed to know? You all don't look Jewish."

That broke Vivian up and Ruthie joined in, but Ruthie was never comfortable with Mary Lou again. In two weeks Mary Lou began riding with a man who lived near her. As soon as Mary Lou was no longer riding with them, Joann opened up. "I can't stand them hillbillies," she said. "They never have a good word for anybody, but they're dirty as bedbugs. They talk down the colored all the time, but the colored around me, they keep up their houses fine. They aren't like the colored down in Paradise Valley. They own their houses and they keep their yards nice. They were all born up here and they belong. But those hillbillies, they never saw an inside toilet before. They throw their slops out in the yard to stink."

Everybody hates somebody, Ruthie thought. You'd think that during a war, people could be satisfied hating the enemy, but no, the enemy is too far away. You want someone to hate right on the next block. Joann was unusual in her targets. Anti-Semitism was as common as general bitching in the factories, and everybody took for granted you despised colored and had a right to do so at full volume. It turned out Joann knew one of the colored women who had just been hired, and after a lot of preliminary twittering, asked Vivian if Rena could ride with them. Ruthie felt sorry for Rena, because she was the only colored woman in the whole plant on the swing shift. Ruthie and Vivian conferred and said okay.

Rena turned out to be in her late twenties, both children in grade school and her husband in the Army in England. He was a skilled draftsman, but the Army made him a mess boy. She was about the color of Delora in Duvey's photo but wore her hair severely back. She was Joann's next-door neighbor, shy with them the first few weeks as they were with her. Ruthie had never had a colored friend. Rena was getting a lot of trouble on the line. She had it worse than Ruthie when she first hired on, with the women giving her as hard a time as the men.

Morris said, "Some of the management are backing those hate preachers because they not only denounce Jews and Negroes, but they attack the union too. It's divide and conquer. The union may not be great always—I don't go along with this wage freeze and no-strike pledge—but they let everybody in and that's right."

"It makes me sick to hear, all the insults about Jews, Tata. I don't know if I should keep arguing with them or keep quiet."

"You can always say something, but say it softly, and maybe be heard better. Don't let it eat at you, Ruthie. Half those loudmouths ranting about Jews, they don't know they're working next to one. They think we got tails."

Now that the war was going better, she did not think as she sometimes had that maybe the Nazis would conquer. But sometimes she wondered if what made Nazis out of Germans wasn't something she felt and saw around her here. There were days when it seemed to her every other piece of paper around the factory was a hate tract from some preacher or priest or secular maniac or little Ku Klux Klan grouping, the Silver Shirts, the Dixie Voters for Southern Society, the Mothers of America, the Committee of a Million. She felt weary before it all and sore.

She longed for Murray to talk to, but he had enough to worry about without having shipped to him homefront squabbles. People would grow used to each other as they worked together, perhaps. Her policy was to identify herself always as a Jew when she heard one of those nasty remarks, but to try to avoid a fight. She did not know if her policy was brave or cowardly, but gradually the women and men around her stopped making the remarks so often, at least in her hearing. She supposed that was some kind of improvement. Each occasion left her raw with silent anger. She was not as friendly as she had been.

BERNICE 4

Up, Up and Away

Bernice was living in The Yellow Rose of Texas tourist court, sharing a room with Helen and Flo. Every morning an Army truck hauled them to the field, where they had calisthenics in the mud. After breakfast in the mess hall she marched with the rest of them to the flight line. Houston Municipal Airport was enormous and consisted of several different fields. Well away from the women, Ellington Field trained combat pilots. The women used a hangar and shed complex near the commercial airlines.

That very week, she had passed her flight check, avoiding the dreaded pink slip that could wash a trainee out of the program. Pink seemed somehow appropriate. Strip off your flying gear and slink back to kitchen and parlor duties. In a PT-19 trainer, she had gone up with a military check pilot—not her regular instructor—and performed all the fancy maneuvers he commanded, the rolls, the stalls, the spins and dives. Now instead of the PT-19, she was flying a BT-13 basic trainer, a great improvement. Instead of the open cockpit, it had a canopy. It even had a radio. Above all, the BT-13 had a 450-horsepower motor, vastly more powerful than anything she had flown. It was hard to handle in a dive and it shook like an old Model T bumping over a corduroy road, but she did not care, she did not care at all.

In the afternoon they had classes in aerodynamics, engine operation and maintenance, mathematics, navigation and meteorology. Then they marched out for more calisthenics, supper in the mess hall and return by Army semi to The Yellow Rose of Texas for studying and gossiping until ten o'clock lights out and an early beginning the next morning.

Bernice had never been as happy in her life. She discovered she was not a person who needed to be alone as much as she had thought, which was lucky, because in fact she was never alone except when she was ordered to solo in a plane. She liked these women far better than she had liked the few friends she had had at home. Home? She was far more at home here than she had ever felt in The Professor's house, after Viola died.

She no longer felt oversized. They all looked enormous in their gear, the bulky fleece-lined leather jackets, the high-waisted, fleece-lined leather pants which zipped along the leg and needed suspenders to stay up, worn over woolly long johns. They were less ridiculous on Bernice than on smaller boned women. That was their winter gear.

The things that mattered here she was good at. They were actually paying her a hundred fifty dollars a month to learn the most exciting job she could imagine. She might have been living a fantasy, but her aching body told her otherwise. After she had stalled and spun her trainer, the bones of her neck felt wrenched out of place. Their physical program was designed to keep their sexuality in check, or so the women speculated; it certainly wore them out.

In March a directive had come down that the women were not to fly for one day before and two days after their periods. All the women had been quietly furious at the idea of being grounded for a week out of every month. Not only did none of them obey the directive, they soon realized that neither their instructors nor their officers were about to enforce it, the women because it infuriated them also, and the men, because they were too embarrassed to try to compel observance. It seemed to Bernice that since she had been enrolled in the program, her periods were shorter anyhow, but she did not ask anyone else if that were the case with them. Since the directive had come down, the women were engaged in a conspiracy of silence about menstruation. The only time anybody ever mentioned it was if she had to borrow a pad.

Winter in Houston passed, chillier and rawer than Bernice had expected. Many times the airport was fogged in. She had been caught up in the air when the airport closed, with no choice after a while but to land anyhow, with the tower yelling at her.

In the meantime, Jacqueline Cochran had opened the first all-female airfield at Sweetwater, Texas, Avenger Field, so that the class that had entered after Bernice had started there. Now Bernice's class was to fly to Avenger, cross-country, ferrying their own training planes from Houston just as if they were graduates already and delivering planes around the country, the way she would be doing in another three months, she hoped. She was enormously excited as April fifth approached. Bernice expected the Air Forces to think up some stupid reason why women couldn't be allowed to transport themselves and their planes, but the day dawned, the weather just fine—springlike and sunny—and no last-minute order from the male hierarchy on high had come to countermand their flight.

As they rode to the airport in the Army truck for the last time, Helen asked her if she would miss Houston.

"I like it here," Bernice admitted. "But why shouldn't we like it even better where we have our own field?"

Not everybody was going. The class ahead of them, class of 43-3, would stay in Houston till graduation, then fly to Avenger for the ceremony. Flo said, "Besides, we got to try out different fields—different flying conditions. We'll be all over the country once we start ferrying."

Flo was a year younger than Bernice and two inches shorter. She had strawberry blond hair and freckles, pale grey eyes that squinted against the sun, a big grin that showed bad teeth. The oldest girl of a family of ten, she had run off with a man in a barnstorming troop of stunt pilots who had played her hometown of Carbondale, Illinois, where all her male relatives had been coal miners. She had started out wing walking and then learned to fly. She was a good pilot, but the aeronautics courses were hard for her. Often she took a flashlight under the blanket and went on studying after Bernice and Helen had gone to sleep.

Helen, the daughter of a Nebraska newspaper publisher, had taken the civilian pilot training program in college and come in tops in her class, one of the only three women in the program at her university. Flying had seized her imagination, as it had Bernice's. After initially trying to dissuade her, her father had settled for being proud and buying her advanced lessons and her own plane, in which she had flown him around the state. At first Bernice had resented Helen, feeling that everything had been too easy for her; but no one thought of their civilian lives any longer.

Bernice, zipped into her baggy overalls they called zoot suits, climbed into the BT-13 assigned to her for the day. Two of their instructors were to act as flight leaders. They were divided into two flights. Helen took off in the first group, Bernice and Flo in the second.

Once they were up, they formed into two big squares, flying close as they had been taught and keeping in formation. They were heading north. It was a clear day, a tinge of dust in the air, a bit of a headwind but not enough to slow them down. Bernice felt like singing at the top of her lungs. She had had the same dream last night that had recurred since her second week in Houston. She was crawling down a long tunnel. Sometimes it was a drainpipe or a sewage pipe; other times it appeared to be a culvert for runoff. Sometimes it was one of the steam tunnels that connected the older buildings at St. Thomas. Suddenly she reached an exit and struggled out. The dream always ended with her standing at her full height in a field and feeling as if she were soaring, free.

Their flight leaders had them set down for lunch in San Angelo, at the regular

Air Force base. Then they all marched double time into the base cafeteria, where they took over half a dozen tables. Flo was grinning. Shaking her strawberry blond hair out of her hairnet, she began whistling at every passing cadet. About half the other women began doing the same thing: wolf whistles, catcalls, everything they'd always had passed out at them. Bernice did not join in, although she was surprised to notice that Helen did, with a big amazed smile. Nobody had ever pestered Bernice with those animal noises, and she had little hostility built up toward men in general.

Her best friend had been her brother. She had never had a really close girlfriend. Often she had been the only girl, sitting in on classes at St. Thomas, where the ticket to survival was remaining inconspicuous. Until Jacqueline Cochran had picked her to try out for the Women's Flying Training Detachment, the only help in flying had come from men, starting with Zach.

Feeling happy, feeling a part of a group for the first time in her adult life, Bernice ate her chicken potpie and drank her coffee and thought about herself with a cool detached acceptance. She did not feel female; she did not feel male either, certainly not. What was she?

Flo had a streak of sexual pain through her like a raw welt. She had loved and been dumped; she felt used and abused. Helen had a side of frank sexual curiosity. She hinted in their gossip sessions after dark that she had had a lover, a man she had been engaged to but had decided not to marry. When finally forced by the curiosity of her female friends to dredge up some male in her past, Bernice produced Zach. He sat well for the part of one loved and lost. It was almost ladies' magazine stuff: the playboy from the rich family who had taken enough of an interest in her to teach her to fly.

Bernice admitted openly to being a virgin. She felt she could not fake knowledge not only unpossessed but not imagined. She talked about Jeff to her friends. They studied his photograph and both pronounced him handsome. He had written about his English girl and then her death; that too she shared with them.

Once every two weeks she wrote home, a brief letter, factual, full of her training and the weather. The Professor did not answer. She also wrote occasionally to Mrs. Augustine, who did. Mrs. Augustine informed her The Professor was just fine, eating at her house, driving his new housekeeper crazy, and that she soon might have to find him another. He had gained weight. Her husband Emil and Bernice's father were both overworked, for campus was crowded with military personnel in V-5 and V-12 programs to train officers for the services.

They took off again and flew the last sixty miles to Avenger Field in their two tight squares. The earth was red under them and flat, obscured at times by rolling dust. The roads ran straight for miles, then took an occasional dogleg and continued as straight as before. The grey green of mesquite dotted the brown land. The place called Cochran's Convent was on the horizon. Soon she picked out the tiny X of gravel runways. From the air, it looked just like the field they'd lunched at earlier. When she landed, the heat closed around her like a fist.

As she found out immediately, here they lived in barracks. She enjoyed even less privacy than in the tourist court in Houston, and they had to make their beds Army style so that a dime would bounce. Every barracks was divided into two bays, each with six bunks, with a bathroom between the bays. In addition to Flo and Helen, three others who had shared a cabin in Houston moved into Bernice's bay.

There were already more than a hundred women at the base, for the class that had started after theirs, 43-5, had come directly here. Sometimes fifty planes at a time were trying to take off and land on the two small gravel runways, with the wind blowing the red soil in gusts or dust devils or lifting it as a solid wall of bricklike swirling mess, the loose bales of tumbleweed threatening to tangle in the propellers.

A great deal of Bernice's time was spent learning to fly blind, first in the hot-box Link Trainer on the ground, with the sweat running down her in rivulets and plastering her hair to her skull under the regulation hairnet, then under the hood in the air. She flew for hours under a black curtain while her instructor bellowed instructions through the headset. She was supposed to judge everything by watching the altimeter, the ball with the needle and the air-speed indicator to judge position and correct herself.

She was also learning to fly at night. Avenger Field lacked lights, but burning pots of oil were set out to mark the runways. The first time Bernice flew in the dark, she landed so hard she knocked the wind out of herself. After hundreds of smooth landings, she almost pancaked. After that, she trusted the instruments over her eyes in the dark.

One hot day in May—when every day was hot and the temperature never seemed to sink below one hundred between dawn and dusk—the class of 43-2 roared in with their advanced trainers for graduation. Jacqueline Cochran arrived for the ceremony. She had just removed the previous command at Avenger and put in her own, men that the women were already finding more sympathetic, less interested in washing them out and proving women incompetent, more interested in developing good ferry pilots. From the distance of the ready room, where women waited for planes, Bernice looked at the glamorous figure with respect and gratitude. She did not think she would ever understand the woman who strutted like an actress across the field from her own plane, followed by her personal maid, but she would have done anything required for Cochran. Had she been religious, she would have prayed each night for the welfare and happiness of Jacqueline Cochran.

As the summer deepened, the heat thickened. The only time she was ever comfortable was aloft, where the wind and altitude provided natural air-conditioning. All the women were varying shades of mahogany. Bernice had not been as tanned since she was little, when Viola had taken them to the lake every day, where she sat under an umbrella reading Sophocles in Greek.

She had a letter from Jeff. They had ways of informing each other the censor would remove if he understood. Jeff had only to refer to incidents in their past to identify his location. He was telling her that he had returned from Tunis to London, but that he had hopes of getting into France.

One day during instrument training, Bernice was confronted with a dilemma. All the women had to choose a buddy to go up with alone—no instructor. Instead the buddy was to act as the instructor while the pilot flew on instruments, under the hood. Bernice realized that both Flo and Helen were expecting her to go up with them, but that she could only choose one. She waited, hoping they would pick each other. She would rather go up with somebody she knew less well, than hurt either's feelings. Still they waited, both expectant. Bernice wanted to hide. She could not bear to give pain. Finally she thought to ask herself which she would rather depend on up there, to be her eyes and ears in an emergency. Flo. Flo was the more desperately serious flier. Flo was also essentially orphaned, as she was. Her family was hostile. She could never go home.

As she walked out to the flight line with Flo, she felt Helen's reproachful gaze on her like a burden, which made her walk slowly and clumsily. In the air, she forgot everything except what they must do. They were utterly dependent on each other.

How serious the results of inattention could be, or how final the results of engine or other failure, was brought home to them when a student and an instructor were killed in a night crash in the class coming along behind them. I could die at this, Bernice realized. The thought kept occurring to her for the next four days after the crash, at odd times, when receiving the food in runny piles on her plate with its metal dividers; sitting Saturday night in the canteen in Sweet-water drinking local moonshine from a bottle in a bag under the table and soft drinks on top. As the moonshine burned the back of her throat but warmed her stomach, again she thought about the charred bodies in the crumpled wreckage. Finally she said to herself, Not a bad way to go, after all. What was I doing before this? Could you call it living?

The next day when she was up alone in the AT-6 Texan working on cross-country navigation, the image came back for the last time. This time Bernice, sighting along a railroad track that was to guide her, simply smiled. The AT-6 was that plane she had watched the previous graduating class landing that day they had flown into Avenger for their ceremony. It was sleek, wicked-looking, powerful. It went faster than anything she had flown—145 miles per hour—with a 600-horsepower engine and a rakish line to it she loved. She thought that now she could feel what Zach had about his racing cars. Such pleasures were keen enough to be worth the risk.

In two weeks she would be graduating, a working pilot. That was living; her twenties had previously been a slow death. Better to take her chances and be, fully, what she had dreamed. Bernice had never been one for looking in the mirror. Now sometimes when she was wearing her outsized flying gear, she would catch a glimpse of herself, and she would almost blush with pleasure. She looked powerful. She looked bigger than life. She looked like a pilot.

What Women Want

The wife was in town. Why did Abra think of Louise that way? She was the ex-wife but somehow still reigned. Bringing the daughter, Kay, Louise had come on OWI business rather than to connect with Oscar. Kay was installed in Oscar's flat, while Louise was staying with some bureaucrat from OWI. At first Abra was banished for the duration. Then she was summoned for supper, on Louise's instigation. Louise must be curious about her. She was certainly curious back, but she felt powerless.

The four of them went out for seafood. They had to wait an hour for a table, making disjointed conversation. Only Oscar seemed at ease. She suspected he found nothing unusual in being surrounded by ex-wife, girlfriend and daughter. He has the mentality of an Oriental potentate, she told her crab. Abra was used to feeling on top of awkward situations, but this time she felt outclassed, barely older than Kay, sulking across the table. She almost liked Kay tonight, because at least she also wished to be elsewhere.

Louise was extremely well preserved, Abra thought, much more attractive than her daughter, who had a sullen inturned expression and slumped over her food, picking at it. Louise's hair was shoulder length and shining auburn, her skin rosy, her eyes a light luminous grey above high marked cheekbones, like Oscar's. Her features were fine, set in chiseled bones, but she gave no impression of delicacy. Her voice was throaty and carrying. Before she said something she considered amusing, her mouth would give an odd little quirky contraction, as if bidding herself not to laugh. Often her laugh when it did bark out bordered on the vulgar, surprising in a woman who kept herself so well turned out. Any daughter of the two of them should have been gorgeous. She had to think that Kay screwed up perfectly decent features by pouting ninety percent of the time.

Louise was wearing a jade voile dress artfully draped. As Oscar and Louise

discussed the follies of various acquaintances unknown to Abra and uninterest-
ing to Kay, Louise grew animated. She began to use her hands, causing a green
ring to flash.

"Where did that come from?" Oscar caught Louise's hand.

"A present." Louise freed her hand none too smoothly. She turned at once to
Abra. "It's dull for you, all these ancient people. What do you think of Washington?"

Abra did wonder who had given that to Louise; Oscar had glowered as he
permitted the subject to be changed.

Abra could not satisfactorily complain about her relationship with Oscar to
her roommate Susannah, because Susannah's immediate comment was that she
should not have got involved with a man so much older. Susannah thought
every young woman should marry, or at least sport an engagement ring as big as
Louise's emerald.

Abra found one person who would listen to her dissatisfactions, and that was
curly-headed Daniel upstairs. He was involved with a woman in his office too.
She found his apartment amusing. At first it had almost shocked her, a mattress
on the floor, a bookcase full of Japanese and Chinese books, a strong Oriental
motif in the decorating: a Chinese vase, a scroll, a carved box. "I'm a translator
for the government," he explained. "They need translators now who can read and
write Japanese and Chinese." Sometimes he worked as long hours as she did.
She felt sorry for him, as translating technical material, as he explained he did,
sounded crashingly dull.

He was attractive, but compared to Oscar, terribly young. She was relieved
that he had a girlfriend, because she felt that she could talk to him without
leading him on unfairly. "I feel as if *he* absolutely controls the relationship," she
complained to Daniel, sitting on his mat with her knees drawn up, drinking
cheap rum. "He chooses when we see each other and when we don't. He defines
what we do and what we don't do and when. He sets the boundaries."

"What are they?" He had already told her that he felt that Ann, his friend,
did the same to him.

"No possessiveness at all. Be ready to clear out of the way when any of his old
girlfriends or his ex-wife hits town. Ask no questions about tomorrow or the
next day."

"Do you think he loves you?"

"He says so often enough. He's warm and affectionate, Daniel, he really is, or
I wouldn't put up with his games. But I feel as if somehow he has me classified

as inessential—not in his work life, but in his emotional life. I'm disgustingly convenient."

"Maybe because he's so much older, he can't take you seriously."

"Certainly he's mostly been involved with women his age. But I think of myself as unusually mature and experienced for my age—"

Daniel grinned, waggling a long forefinger. "Have you ever, ever heard any of our contemporaries say, 'I consider myself unusually immature and callow for my age?'"

"Point for you. . . . You don't think I am?" She was just thinking how they were both almost exactly the same age, born within two weeks of each other, and she thought of herself as far more mature.

"To tell you the truth, no." Daniel beamed cherubically, pouring them more rum. "Tastes like hair tonic, doesn't it?"

Abra was stingingly insulted, yet to show it would be to prove him right. She wished he would make a pass at her so that she could reject him coldly, but he had not done that in months. He was much too smart, unfortunately, to bother as long as she was crazy about Oscar. She probably needed Daniel more than he needed her, because while he enjoyed chewing over his relationship with Ann, he was not obsessed with Ann. She lay awake at night analyzing Oscar. Daniel was the only sharer of all that cogitating.

"When I think how simple my life used to be!" she burst out. "What we call love in this society can expand to fill any amount of time and brain cells. It's a cancer! When I was wanting him and not having him yet, I thought when I had leapt that hurdle, life would be straightforward again."

"Sometimes it works that way," Daniel said. "If what you want is just a body or some entity you've invented to fit that face or body. But if you come to know the person and then you want them, I don't think going to bed does more than increase the fascination. Or so I would suppose."

"You've never really been in love." Now it was her turn to attack. "Do you think you're capable?"

"I think I was in love once, back in Shanghai. Mostly I've been a virtuoso of infatuation. I've fallen in love with a scent, a way of wearing a scarf. I've fallen for characters in novels or in films. Sometimes I think I could become infatuated with a bowl of ripe fruit."

"Isn't it fascinating how discussion of one's faults can be a vehicle for flirtation and self-aggrandizement, Daniel dear."

"That was the old days. Then I used to have a problem focusing on anything. Now that I have work I find passionately involving, I believe I can focus my mind and energy when I locate the right woman."

"Translation is that interesting?"

His gaze broke away. He tugged at his hair. "Well, the kind of translating I'm doing is demanding. Oriental languages are so foreign in their construction, they cause you to organize the world quite differently."

"I'm surprised. At one time I did a fair amount of translation from German speech . . ." She stopped. She had to give some explanation. "I was doing some interviews for my thesis in New York. I had to interview a few refugees in German." She hoped that had not sounded lame. She must watch such references. She had recently had her clearance raised, but she imagined that someone like Daniel had probably never been vetted at all. She must watch what she talked about more cunningly; lately R & A had been madly stamping documents SECRET, TOP SECRET.

The next evening she had a conversation with Oscar about the new security measures in R & A. "Do you really think it's necessary?"

"No, but I think it's irresistible." He was sitting propped up in bed. The daughter and the ex-wife had finally left town, and she was spending the first night that week with him.

"Irresistible to whom?" She brooded on his strongly cut profile.

His eyes, facing ahead as he thought about his answer, were chips of anthracite. "Irresistible because, A, we cannot resist it because such messages come de haut en bas and overwhelm us academic peasants. B, Irresistible to those on high because security measures make them feel important, that they're playing poker with the big boys."

She liked about Oscar that if he said "A" there was always a "B." If he said there were three things wrong, he would not forget after two or go on to four. She liked that orderliness. She was more intuitive herself. She might say she loved three things, but then she would always think of a fourth to add to the list. He finished his survey before he spoke.

He was saying almost dreamily, hands crossed on his belly, "Most of our research is based on facts out there for anyone to use. Only putting them together and analyzing them makes us unique. Most of the so-called secret intelligence we get down the pipeline from SI is bullshit, just rumor mongering, social, political and ethnic prejudices passing for hard data."

"Oscar, what did Langer want with you today?" William Langer was the head of R & A. "Can you tell me?"

"I not only can, I must. Langer is sending me to London to head up a little project in the Labor Branch there."

"Oh . . ." She thought her heart had stopped. She thought she could not speak out of fear of the answer. She must keep her voice light, if she had any strength and any dignity remaining. "Will I be going also?"

"I put in for you."

"We work so well together," Abra said sweetly, curling up against his side. "Wouldn't you miss me a little?" Now keep it light, she ordered herself. He asked for me. He is trying to take me along. If I show any violence of feelings, it simply will not go as well for me.

Oscar turned to face her. "I missed your soft self this week. However, that was not one of the arguments I used to Langer."

"You can't just say to him, See here, old boy, she's my bedmate, don't you see? Work much better that way, don't you know."

"One always suspects that in the true old boys' network, they can get away with that. But while R and A is a lot looser than the ruling class Ivy League network that began it—for one thing, there are Jews like me in it—I can't presume. They're always sticky about moving women overseas, but I think I'll succeed. I'm one of his favorites since we rang so many bells with that last report."

"What did you say on my behalf?" Did you argue hard and effectively enough? Or are your feelings mixed about taking me? How could what went on in one man's head be so important to her?

"I called his attention to your sections in our last two reports. I described you as highly efficient and most objective in your analyses. They eat that up. I made yard-wide promises about the wonders we would perform in London for R and A Washington and how we would never, as some have been reputed to do, allow trying to help with the war effort to deflect us from our primary duty to feed R and A Washington useful goodies. I depicted us as loyal to the end to our bread and butter." He took her chin in his large hot hand. "Trust me, Abra. I'll get you over . . . one way or the other. Now remind me why I want to." He guided her head down toward his prick.

Oscar had taught her oral sex. Most of her sexual encounters had occurred with graduate students, suitors from her own background or New York politicos, the best of whom had been rough and ready fuckers. Oscar liked oral sex as a prologue to intercourse. Sometimes she had a preliminary orgasm with his mouth on her; sometimes she just grew very excited. She felt connected with his body in a more intimate and compelling way than she had to any of her previous bedfellows. Not infrequently she had multiple orgasms, sometimes of an intensity that came close to frightening her.

She did not see him after work the next night. They worked late and then he got tied up in a consultation with two other researchers. Since he had tipped her no sign, she gave up and left with Susannah at eleven. She was exhausted but could not sleep, worrying about London. What would she do with herself if he could not take her along? She felt as if she had been grafted into Oscar; she could not conceive of her life without him.

The next days were gutted by her inability to think about anything else. She was afraid to bring it up again with him, yet she was convinced he knew exactly what was on her mind, and even to what extent it obliterated logic. They worked all day Saturday. Traditionally Saturday night was OSS party night and Sunday they took off. Sunday it rained, hot and rusty. Oscar was at home working. She went for a walk in the rain with Daniel.

"Disgusting leakage," she snarled at the thick dirty dripping air.

> " 'With my eyes looking skyward
> I wait for heaven's water
> Eager as a baby hungry for milk . . .'
> As they always say, it's good for the gardens."

"Is that poem yours?"

"Otomo Yakamochi. My translation. It's good practice."

"For what?" She kicked a cardboard container lying in the street. "I'd write about the sky as a big grey stallion pissing all over Washington."

"What a charming image. I perceive you're in a fine uplifted mood and will prove great company today."

"Up yours, Balaban, up yours with a flowering cherry bough."

"By the way, did you notice this spring those poor trees had become known as Korean cherries?"

"Be glad they didn't ax them. I'll ax you something. My lover is going off to a posting overseas, and I still don't know whether or not he can take me along. If he doesn't, the mood I'm in today is sweet Nesselrode pudding compared to how I'm going to be feeling if he goes and I stay. What am I going to do with myself?"

"London, Stockholm, Algiers, Lisbon, Madrid or Istanbul?"

"Does that about cover it?"

"I try to be thorough."

"You try to be a smart ass, and commonly you succeed. If I do go with him, I'll miss you."

"You're missing me now," Daniel said, taking her arm companionably.

———

On May 22, 1943, Oscar and Abra sailed out of New York on the *Queen Mary*, turned into a troop ship. They were not in the same cabin; rather they were each sharing a cabin with numerous others. Three other OSS women and eight nurses shared an eight-by-eight cabin with Abra, makeshift bunks thrown up with barely room to fit herself into her slot. The *Queen* being a fast ship, they did not travel in convoy but charged on alone. Abra was out to sea two days before it occurred to her they could actually be torpedoed. She was horrified to note that her first thought was how she and Oscar could end up in the same lifeboat.

Yet lined up at the railing watching the water break and sky alter, she enjoyed the time in limbo, talking, endlessly talking. Oscar admitted to her that one reason he had intrigued for the London posting—the first time he had not pretended it had emerged from the blue heavens like an angel descending—was that he nurtured vague hopes that once near Europe, he could get some word of his sister Gloria in occupied France. Through Louise he had learned something that led him to believe that surely there were ways in and ways out that he could exploit at least to learn her situation and at best to help her.

Every day was livened or rendered obnoxious, depending on what was interrupted, by lifeboat, fire, collision, enemy air and enemy sea attack drills. As many people as possible hid in the bathrooms after the first day. The boat was jammed. Except for the dining rooms, all the large rooms were dormitories. They were among the only civilians on board, along with half a dozen other OSS people. There were fourteen of them altogether, but the others had been given noncommissioned or commissioned officer status, and wore nondescript uniforms. They tended to keep together, as they had to tell other people cover stories. Meals occurred in four sittings, the last for the colored personnel. The *Queen* was segregated all ways.

She actually began to feel that she was approaching the war zone. She had been so muddled about whether Oscar was going to take her, whether he genuinely wanted to take her, that she had not focused on where she was headed. Evenings tended to be dull. A strict blackout was observed. No one was allowed on deck after dark. Sailors were stationed to block any conceivable area of privacy where the few women on board might copulate with the many men. They managed to make love exactly once by skipping their sitting at lunch, but there was time to think and time to talk.

"I was in Europe in thirty-eight during the summer. Ready—my middle brother—had just graduated from Annapolis, and my parents took us abroad to celebrate. I remember we came into Le Havre on the *Normandy*—my mother swore by French boats as having the best food. I know we spent time in Paris, Florence and Rome, where it was unbearably hot. I remember Nice and someplace with a Roman amphitheater where my parents had a dreadful row. Then we visited third cousins in Northumberland and in Edinburgh. My father had a prejudice against London, the same as he did against New York."

"I've been in London, but not long enough to know it. I spent a good part of a year in Frankfurt, with Louise. We had no money, but we thumbed rides and rode third class on the slow trains. At the end we wandered around Italy. Later on we came back every couple of years. Besides Frankfurt, Paris is the European city I know best."

"I can't say I got much out of the trip. I gawked at a mess of paintings and churches and ate great quantities of veal and pastries. Every single day I fought with my father or my mother."

"What did you fight about in those days? Not politics?"

"I was a flaming radical, or so I imagined, for I'd never met any. I thought saying that I was a Socialist was rather risqué. It certainly exercised my father."

"I've always enjoyed traveling, but it's better when you don't drag a child along. . . . Sometimes I wonder if Louise and I should ever have had Kay. Only children get too much attention or none."

"Why did you, then? Just because that's what married people do?"

He grinned. "Exactly. At least on my part. I think Louise wanted a baby, although I never could grasp why. It wasn't as if her life was empty and needed filling."

She waited to see if he was going to ask her if she ever wanted to have a child, but he did not. That was rude. Involved as they were, he ought to at least pretend to be interested in what she wanted long-term. Or was he afraid to leave an opening? Watching a squall blow up, she thought that perhaps he defended himself so well because he feared their intimacy. She had won to a relationship with him; she would win through to a fuller love.

They had to clear off the deck as it was time for the twice daily drill of the antiaircraft crews, shooting into space. Once and once only on their sixth day they saw the smoke of another ship. Oscar was feeling the frustration of prolonged chastity also. The way he took her arm had become quite desperate. He explored the ship incessantly without success. Even the lifeboats had guards posted to keep them from use as improvised bedrooms. "When we get to London," Oscar said in her ear, "the first thing I'm going to find is a nice double bed. And a door that shuts."

She worried too much, she decided, because love had come to her comparatively late. He told her he loved her; he showed his attraction every desirable way; he had taken her off to London with him. What more did she want? She tried to pack herself tight the way she had packed her trunk, everything folded or rolled in its place and the lid locked on. In London he would be far away from his ex-wife, his ex-girlfriends, his daughter, his mother, his brother and sisters. He would be with her and a handful of Americans, and they would become much closer.

LOUISE 5

Of the Essential and the Tangential

Louise swore at her alarm, but hauled herself up. She was determined to rise every morning before Kay, to prepare a proper hearty breakfast and present it with appropriate motherly behavior. She was not at her best upon waking, but she summoned up images of warm, understanding, efficient film mothers. She had been seeing too many movies lately, because it was something she and Kay could do together without friction. In addition, there were always films she ought to see because she knew someone who had had a hand in making them, Claude or an acquaintance she had met in Hollywood.

She had visited Claude several times, because Billy Wilder was filming one of her novelettes. Claude satisfied her on many levels, but they did not share a life or even a common context. With him she learned the pleasures of tangential relationships, but she knew quietly and without it being something she would find appropriate to convey to anyone else, how hollow that left a place that had once been well filled.

Claude thought in French; he dreamed in French landscapes. He lived in an exile world whose true coordinates were streets in another city, on another continent. There were women who would seek the exotic to love, who would follow a man willingly into another set of customs and expectations to achieve not only abnegation but a personal liberation in the abandonment of what they had been. Louise could imagine Kay doing that, escaping from her obsession with her father by running off with a sheik or a gaucho.

She prodded her melancholy warily, mistrustful that any good could come of pitying introspection. Her situation seemed obvious and neither ideal nor sad, a life to be lived, rich in friends, rich in work. No writer had financial security and no mother alone ever felt secure, but she made a good living. What would she change, if she could? She wished she had a better relationship with Kay. She wished Kay were—more responsible? less sullen? less self-pitying? more affectionate? All of the above, perhaps.

"Mommy, ugh, here I am." Kay stumbled in, rumpled from sleep. Lately Kay had been calling her "Mommy" as she had not since she was ten. It was not so much a sign of Kay's dependence as of her willful sojourn in childhood. Kay one day dragged out her favorite doll (last seen in 1938) and placed it on her bed, where it sat in a pink organza dress. She reread her old favorites, *Anne of Green Gables*, *The Wind in the Willows*. She began braiding her hair, but girls at school teased her out of that affectation.

Louise bore with the regression, because it could not last past September when Kay would be going to Mount Holyoke College. This was an easy time to choose a college, because they all wanted students, although traveling was rough. Louise and Kay had visited a dozen colleges up and down the Eastern seaboard, from the University of Virginia to the University of Maine, but Kay had liked South Hadley, a pretty, placid New England town. "It seems very safe here," Kay had said approvingly. They saw few young men, although many young women passed them on bicycles and on foot.

Louise had been almost sorry when Kay had chosen, because she had been enjoying their trips. Each college was a new experience providing them a topic of conversation. They could compare colleges in endless discussion; not endless, for the idyll had run out.

Louise had been pleased that she could offer this benign educational experience to her daughter. She had gone to night school herself and never managed to get her degree. She had hoped that Kay might attend Wellesley or Radcliffe, but Kay wanted a small college town.

It was not that Kay was less critical of her, as now poking her English muffin. "But why don't we have butter? Other people get it all the time. What's the use of being so thick with the government and all the time running off to Washington, if we can't do a little better with rationing?"

No, Kay was just as critical as before, but obviously enjoyed absorbing Louise's time and energy. In truth Louise sometimes enjoyed her daughter's company, but often did not. Kay was self-absorbed, and her conversation never strayed far from what she wanted or did not want, liked or did not like, what she thought this one or that one thought about her, or might do to or for her. Louise liked a greater degree of intellectual content and a higher degree of abstraction in discourse. Nonetheless, she gave and gave to Kay, aware that Kay would be leaving home in September and aware too how her sexual misadventures had left her even more insecure than she had been.

Louise was still in her bathrobe when Kay left for school. Glancing at the clock, she hastened to bathe and dress. With Oscar home, she would never have appeared at breakfast in deshabille. When the phone rang at ten to nine, she was sure it was Blanche with a problem. With her twins in school, Blanche worked from nine to three. But the voice that queried, "Louise?" was Oscar's familiar rumble.

"Oh, hello, Oscar," she said, seeking as always an appropriate tone to use with him, neither artifically chilly nor encouraging. "How are you? Are you calling from Washington?"

"I'm at Grand Central Station in a booth. I'm off to London—"

"Can you tell me when, or is that a military secret?"

"I'm in New York for the next eight hours. I thought I'd come right up."

She felt a cold panic. "Where is Abra, by the way?"

"Visiting her family." He cleared his throat. "I thought I'd come by now and see you."

"Oh, not right now, Oscar, I have an appointment." She lied in a panic. She had not prepared herself to meet him. She could not face him at once, without armoring her nervous system.

"Oh." He allowed himself to sound disappointed, forlorn. "An important appointment?"

"Professional." After all, he was off to the war zone. She could not refuse to see him. "Kay just left for school. I'll try to reach her."

"Oh, you shouldn't call her out of school."

"I'll meet you for lunch." She was not going to let him come to the apartment. "Twelve. That Spanish place you like?"

"Let's eat uptown. I haven't had decent Chinese in ages. What about the Harbin Inn?"

"Fine," she said. "Then we can meet Kay at school."

She really had considerable work. She had been writing less fiction and more journalism. Her present state of mind was better suited to the latter. That had been her original ambition, and the war was giving her an opening. She could exploit her name to write features on all aspects of women's work and lives.

She was off in two weeks to zigzag around the country for a piece on women fliers for *Collier's*. In the meantime, she owed *The Saturday Evening Post* a story, and she had to finish a rewrite on a *Times* magazine feature on children of working mothers. She had been quarreling with her editor, as he wanted something far more negative than she felt the material warranted. Psychologists she had interviewed had been gloomy and prognosticated doom for children not supervised by their mothers all of the time for all of their childhood, but her own observations of good nurseries and her interviews with families had persuaded

"Louise," he began meaningfully, when she glanced at her watch, saying, "Get the check, or we'll be late meeting Kay."

What she most hated about Oscar was that he had not valued their marriage enough to preserve it. She felt still a harsh cold anger at that thought, as if he had taken something precious, something irreplaceable, the beautiful but daily used Ming bowl of their marriage and carelessly let it fall to the floor and crack irrevocably apart.

Why had he not seen that having fifteen years of common history was precious and could not be replaced? A decade and a half of common politics, growing knowledge, error and success, a decade and a half of passionate conversation. She loved discussions with him as obviously he did with her, but it had meant so little to him that he had let it all go with a carelessness for which she would always feel contempt.

They met Kay on time and the afternoon passed swiftly and then Oscar was gone in a taxi, to London, to the war, and Louise was left to wish she could get thoroughly drunk.

———

Traveling was full of delays. She might be bumped from any plane at any time and left to sit in the drafty cold waiting room of an airport for the rest of the night. After hours in a DC-3, her bones felt jarred loose. Her head ached from the noise. The inadequate pressurization meant piercing headaches. Trains were crowded to the point of nausea, dirty, late, without the barest amenities, people even jammed traveling in the bathrooms.

In Texas she visited Cochran's Convent, as some referred to Avenger Field, the only all-female air base. She liked the women and their spirit, and she enjoyed the graduating ceremonies. Now, a month later, she was following up on some graduates, to see what had become of the skills learned at Avenger and how they were aiding the war effort. General Hap Arnold needed many more female pilots, so she was to promote the effort. There was talk of a film, but for the moment, she was producing a *Collier's* piece.

She flew to Detroit, then was taken to Romulus Field, in an industrial suburb. There she met a group of WASP ferry pilots from the class she had watched graduate. She sat with them in their mess: Flo, the redhead who had barnstormed before the war; Helen the lady, daughter of a newspaper publisher; Lorraine, whose father was a commercial pilot; and Bernice, a big intelligent woman whom all the others seemed to depend on to get them through hard times. She was a tall rawboned woman, articulate in the accent of New England, a professor's daughter.

Bernice was reluctant to act as spokeswoman, constantly glancing at the others for approval of what she said. She was a woman, Louise thought, who had not realized yet she was a natural leader and that others turned to her. She had low self-esteem, perhaps because she was not conventionally pretty—or even unconventionally pretty, Louise admitted to herself.

Yet Bernice moved confidently, with evident strength and with a natural grace that was more animal than human—the grace of a horse or a lioness. She had soft straight brown hair she kept short, a pert nose, a warm smile. Her hands and feet were in balance with her body but large for a woman. Except when she was doing something mechanical, Bernice tended to keep still, her hands folded as if to keep them out of sight. What wounds were inflicted on women who did not meet society's standards of prettiness.

The Army had granted special permission for Louise to accompany the pilots as they ferried planes. She had a photographer at Romulus for an afternoon, who interrupted everything with his insistence on posing the women in unlikely positions on random planes, complaining about their tan gabardine pants and white shirts as nondescript. He wanted uniforms.

"Gee, so do we," Flo said.

"If they'd put us in uniform, it would make life easier," Bernice said gently. "Oftentimes people don't know who we are. We have trouble with the military at some fields. We have such an in-between status."

She accompanied Bernice in the backseat of a training aircraft to an air base in Tennessee. It was not a comfortable journey, and she decided that once was quite enough to get a feel for the difficulties. At dark, Bernice landed at a field in Ohio. Then they hitchhiked into town to try to find lodging, ending up in a sleazy rooming house, where the bathroom down the hall smelled of men who had pissed in the dark and missed. Everyone treated them with the utmost suspicion, as if they were traveling whores. At dawn they were back at the tiny airport ready to take off for the final leg of the delivery.

"You have no military status—no privileges, no protection, no insurance," Louise pointed out. "Don't you feel as if you're being taken advantage of, because you're women?"

Bernice looked at her without comprehension. "But it's wonderful. It's heaven," she said, as they sat in a hot airless room at the field in Tennessee, waiting for a ride into town so they could take a bus toward civilization.

"Heaven?" Louise repeated. She looked around at the bleak room. Bernice expected to travel all night back toward Detroit. Louise was accompanying her as far as Nashville, from which she was returning to New York. She felt as if she hadn't bathed in a week. The food at Romulus had been plentiful, if not inspired, but they had been living on chili and hot dogs since. She disliked peeing through a funnel into a soda bottle. When Bernice finally reached Romulus, she would start out again with another small plane to deliver and then the endless trek back. The women ferry pilots were not allowed to thumb rides on military aircraft.

"Almost every day we fly," Bernice said simply. "There's always a plane waiting. And we arrive on time. We don't get lost. We deliver the planes safely. Please tell people that: We're good at what we do. And we fly—all of the time, we fly!"

Friends Best Know How to Wound

"It's nothing but bitchy impatience. Why go off into France by yourself?"

"I'm not going by myself. I'll have a radio operator."

"Don't give me technical answers. It's an absurd choice. You're an SO man. Why are you switching to SI?" As deeply angry as Zach was, he spoke plaintively rather than aggressively, his head hanging over a chair arm.

"I think I'm better suited to intelligence than to action. Besides, I'm sick of London."

"You're sick of me."

"Zach, don't be an egomaniac. You aren't London. We'll work together again."

"Do you have any rudimentary idea, you idiot, how many agents have been lost in France just this year?" Zach sat up to glare, his eyes glittering and blood-shot. "The Gestapo is eating them up entire, whole chains of agents. They penetrate with ease. I don't think the British have one intact ring in Paris."

"But I'm not being sent to Paris. If in fact they ever do get it together to send me anyplace. This is a highly theoretical discussion."

"Why are you doing this?" Zach was more agitated than Jeff had ever seen him. He was coldly furious and worried at once.

Jeff felt flattered, but far more strongly he felt the urge that had been growing in him to get into France, into the war, into another set of problems; he also felt defensive, because it was Zach he was trying to escape. "London depresses me."

"London depresses him." Zach addressed the plane tree outside, lush in fiery green leaves. "One of the most fascinating cities in the world and it depresses him. Heaven would depresses this lout."

"At the moment, it probably would."

"Does London depress you, or do I depress you?"

"Zach, not everything in my life is you. Being here reminds me of Mary—"

"That milkmaid. You only fuss over her because she's in forty fragments and you can't have her. Otherwise you'd be bored by now. You've never stuck to a woman longer than six months without being bored out of your skull. You no sooner tumble into bed with someone than you want to seduce him, her into loving you. You like that love, you eat it like bonbons, but then it grows passé. Adoration is so predictable. You've always wanted to lose someone—"

"I've lost people before. My mother, for one."

"Think you wouldn't have broken Mummy's heart too?"

"I doubt it. She was a tough cookie. She had many interests."

"As do we all. You're just bored because you had a little social scene going with those bearded frauds, and now it's dissipated. You can't play at being an artist in London."

"I wasn't playing."

"Ruins in the rain. Really, my dear! Don't you find that a wee bit too sentimental and rather done? It doesn't matter that they aren't crumbling Roman walls. It's the same genre brought up to date. Fuzzy walls in the luminescent rain. Yawn."

Jeff found himself on his feet bearing down on Zach, who lay in an easy chair with his long legs over the far arm. He realized as he stopped himself just over Zach that he had been about to smash his friend right in the face. Zach was intentionally provoking him, but he would not play. He did not want the scene of them pummeling each other. The idea disgusted him. Instead he turned on his heel and strode out, slamming the door.

What Zach had said about his painting made him furious. It was bad enough to be an unfashionable landscape painter in 1943, but to be accused of sentimentality or romanticism was unbearable. Did Zach really think so little of his work? He might never again be sure. Zach had wanted to hurt him and had succeeded. He wished sharply for Mary, as he had almost on the hour since he had returned. He wished for his previous life in London, for the woman and the circle of friends now scattered. He could hardly remember her face, although sometimes he fancied he heard her voice. She was vanishing into his frustration. Yes, he was tired of hanging around after Zach. Zach had his own ends to pursue, but they were not Jeff's.

He walked down to the Thames through the light his eyes identified as late afternoon, although it was past supper. The long pearlescent twilight would soon wash the sky across. The light was dull and orangey, beaten copper, a bowl in which his mother stood before him whisking egg whites for a meringue. It was winter and hot in the kitchen. Bernice was cutting lemons with intense concentration.

He would like to go straight to Bernice now. He would like to run to her and throw himself down with his head in her ample lap and pour out his anger against Zach. She would make him feel how silly it was to allow Zach's anger to touch him. He wanted soothing. How chaste he had been. Since Mary, he had been with no woman besides a few whores in Algiers. Without his sister, he needed a lover to comfort him. He had been stupidly withholding himself from any entanglement, as if that would bring Mary back.

Yet his wanting was far too specific to be satisfied. If he only wanted a woman, he could find one easily enough. London was full of lonely women looking for company. Many of them were curious about Americans, who projected a certain glamour. What he really wanted was to complain to his sister or his lover; his sister was thousands of miles away at an airfield; his lover was dead. He had never collected those mementoes Tom Knacker had promised him. He needed nothing to jog his memory. London was studded with little time delay fuses that evoked specific walks, meals, conversations about Constable or Whistler or Blake.

He did not know if Zach were right to accuse him of nurturing his grief to make it grow. Was he mourning Mary or was he mourning the life as an artist he had experienced with her or was he mourning that fantasy briefly fulfilled of his stunted youth? Did it matter? His grief was genuine enough. He wanted what he could no longer have. He compared himself to the refugees he encountered around OSS London and their governments in exile. The present was only a stratagem to find a way back: back where anyone else could see they would never go. Warsaw of 1937. Paris of 1938. Berlin of 1932. He, who only wanted London of 1942, was out of luck too.

Now London was an irritant, representing what he couldn't have while constantly reminding him of what he had lost. He was painting some, without passion. He cursed Zach freshly, turning on Royal Hospital Road heading for the tube. When he had returned and looked at his paintings of the previous fall, he had been excited and almost dismayed by them. They were better than anything he had previously done, with a power he had never before attained. Now Zach was telling him his best was third-rate.

There were restaurants, there were pubs where intelligence people went, like those in any other profession—convenient to the offices and likely to shelter acquaintances. After a sketchy Greek supper he washed up in an OSS pub and looked around for company. Friends of Zach he did not wish to deal with. He imagined them sneering at him: thinks he's a painter, isn't that a rip. He thought of joining a group of R & A scholars, but they were a closed company, involved in some esoteric political discussion.

A young blond woman from Labor Branch was sitting with a couple from R & A, involved with each other and ignoring her. He had met her, he knew, at a recent party. Zach had danced with her before disappearing with somebody's younger brother. She had been with a man, yes, Oscar Kahan, who was running a project. The girl was here without anyone to pay her attention, drinking with a fixed broody expression.

Usually women picked him up, as Mary had at an exhibit. After fending off the gentle approaches of women for two months, he could hardly complain none were standing around waiting for him to change his mind. On those occasions when he had to make an approach, he sought a woman who looked as if she wanted or needed something, because he might be it. The problem was he could not think of her name. Catching his eye, she waved perfunctorily back, then returned her gaze to the far wall, over the heads of the men at the bar. He remembered her eyes, because of the unusual darkness and brilliance of their blue. Name, name?

He strolled to the table, nodding at the couple. "That party in Knightsbridge two weeks ago, I believe. You're in Labor Branch, aren't you? Barbara?"

"Good try. I can tell I impressed you. No, the name is Abra. Don't apologize. I don't remember yours at all."

"Jeff. Jeff Coates."

"SO?"

"Had been. I transferred to SI." Recapture initiative. "How long have you been in London, Abra?" See, I have it right this time.

An hour later when he suggested a pub that he was sure she would find amusing, so different from the London she had seen so far, she acquiesced but remarked as they walked into the dark street, "Frankly, I'm spending time with you because my lover is out with an old flame, but I have no intention of carrying revenge too far. So I'm a waste of your time."

"Not if it makes it pass," he said. Her bluntness pleased him. "I'm trying to forget a dead woman, who's a lot more real to me than you are."

"That sounds like a story you might want to tell me."

"When we get to my pub. It's on the river. Do you know Chelsea?"

"I don't think I've been there yet. That's where the writers used to live, isn't it? Carlyle? Rossetti? Oscar Wilde."

"Painters too. You should let me show you London. What's left of it." He laughed, taking her arm. "I used to be a professional tourist guide, summers. We shepherded students and teachers through Europe, explaining the difference between Romanesque and Gothic, moving them through customs, finding clean toilets, dealing with their stomach- and heartaches."

"Which is worse?" Abra laughed sharply, letting him keep her arm.

"Surely that depends on how bad each is? Watch your footing." The street was pocked with bomb craters. It was strange to walk across a city in the rosy grey twilight of late evening, among buildings hiding behind blackout curtains that made them appear deserted, like Mediterranean villages in the afternoon, starkly shuttered. "If we have a bad stomach, we fear dying of food poisoning. If we have a heartache, we think of suicide." Actually he had never considered suicide in his life.

"Not me. I think of murder."

"Then your grief is less than the wound to your self-esteem."

"Tell that to Othello, why don't you?"

Her voice was merry, crisp, with the roughness of country honey. He was suddenly aroused. Her hair looked silver in the etiolated twilight as they stumbled through the broken streets. He could feel her against him, her cotton dress flimsy and the flesh beneath spare but sufficient. He stopped and pulled her into his arms to kiss her. He judged that she had drunk a fair amount, but not enough not to blur her awareness of what she was doing. She was surprised, standing stiffly in his embrace for a moment, then leisurely kissing him back. After a few moments, she gave him a little push and stepped away.

"Now, now. That indicates you have hopes I don't share."

"A kiss is always in order at this time of night."

"You're an accomplished picker-upper, aren't you?" She peered at him, cocking her head. "You're used to women adoring you. So's Oscar."

"I thought this was a vacation from him. Voilà, my pub." His local, as opposed to the pub where he met OSS personnel, was right on the Thames a few blocks from his flat. The King's Head and Eight Bells had windows upstairs overlooking the river and a paneled bar downstairs, a far cry from the bars he had wasted evenings in back home.

She liked it, as he had bet she would, and they settled down to observe the scene and chat. He told her what he felt like divulging, mostly about being a painter and the deaths with a bit of the hard times for decorative relief. She was not as sympathetic as the women he liked best. She tended to view things critically and with amusement. Listening to her story, he considered her spoiled, the darling of an old New England family and accustomed to getting what she wanted when she wanted it, from toys to boats to men.

Still, he continued to find her attractive, even the abrasive quality of her mind serving to distract him. She had done whatever she pleased, he thought, going to school because that amused her, dabbling in radical politics when that was exciting, exercising a good appetite, joining OSS. Not quite rich, of a lesser rank than Zach. He had learned not to confuse choice with power. In the old days of family tours, he had met occasional women with that streak of fresh-faced adventurism, and often he had enjoyed their company and their beds.

When he finally steered her out of the pub, he headed her toward his flat. Night had finally fallen, a night darker than any city night he had known, a plush black that filled the eyes. She was not accustomed to it and had to trust him for guidance. Yet she was not completely disoriented, as she said, nodding toward the river, grey wavering silk in the night, "We didn't come from this direction."

"Would you like tea or a nightcap? I'm close at hand. I'm afraid the last train may have passed the station."

"Don't assume I am drunker or stupider than I am. I am trying to decide if exercising my freedom actually creates that freedom, or only makes clear to me I no longer have it."

"Wouldn't it be nice to find out?" He would prefer to go home with her, but probably she was sharing a flat with other OSS girls. He must take her with him, because he wanted her presence to release him from the obligation of dealing with Zach. The anger and pain were there in a tight coil, tension unreleased. "Do you want to be alone? I don't. The lack of what you want is more boring—"

"More boring than taking what you don't want in lieu of what you do?"

"But you do want it more than a little. You're tempted. Curious."

"In the old days, I wouldn't have hesitated to act on mild curiosity," she said with a broad yawn. "Love is a hobble, that's clear."

"Good, I'm glad you decided in my favor."

She laughed but did not argue further. She went along, as he had been sure she would. The momentum was useful. A scent of peonies in the front yard, ghostly white plump smears. She admired the flat, said a passing hello to Zach and was ushered at once into Jeff's room.

The sex itself was pleasant but of no great excitement. They were both tired and the spark of compulsion was missing. He liked her trim athletic body nonetheless, and her sexual confidence, her gaiety in bed, her smile of relaxation afterward. They slept. He appreciated the insulation from Zach.

In the morning he had a message to report to SI. They were shipping him off to Kent for intensive French language review, the latest radio techniques, the most recent information on Gestapo, Abwehr and collaborative French police procedures. He was to be infiltrated into the south of France by summer's end.

That was what they said. He knew of course the same problem remained: how? SI lacked planes. The American Army wasn't about to give them any. British intelligence didn't want American agents entering France, and thus denied them transport. SI had had good agents trained and ready to go, sitting about twiddling and twitching for at least a month.

When he saw the plane to take him to France, he'd believe he was going. Until then, he was glad to get out of London, but he suspected in two months, he'd be back again, a tremendously well-trained agent trekking from office to pub to flat. Maybe by that time, he would be able to stand the sight of Zach's slightly ravaged handsome face again, but at the moment he doubted that softening of his anger.

NAOMI 5

One Hot Week

Naomi thought that Paris had never gotten as hot as Detroit. School was still in session. Today was June 21 and the air felt like a pool of hot oil. She dragged herself to school through streets that felt crazy. Cars were gunning their engines and peeling off with a screech of rubber. Broken glass lay on the sidewalk and Mr. Weinstein was boarding up what had been his store window. Obscenities leered from every wall.

She was a little late, and so she didn't notice how weird everybody was till she got into class. Graduation was this week and her classmates had been strutting around lording it over the lower grades and generally doing no work at all. They had rehearsal today; last night with Aunt Rose's help, she had put the finishing touches to her yellow graduation dress. Ruthie and Aunt Rose had sat around the kitchen table with her, all their feet on a cake of ice in a washbasin with a towel folded on top.

Now the colored kids were gathered on the near side of the classroom. The Poles were together muttering, the kids from Appalachia in one corner, the Jews against the back wall. Their teacher Miss Cahootie was not even in the room. She was out in the hall with a knot of teachers talking in loud whispers about Belle Isle and Them. *They* were coming with guns.

She wondered if this was an invasion. She felt dizzy with fear. The papers all said that the Allies were winning, finally. The Russians were fighting back and the classroom map had turned from black to red on the eastern side. The Allies had conquered all of North Africa, turning the map blue. But papers lied. She still remembered the invincible Maginot Line.

Why did she keep thinking about Paris in 1940? Because Detroit felt like that to her today, the adults gathered discussing in low hysterical voices what they thought the children did not know, while the children passed misinformation to each other. She spoke first to Clotilde, who was standing a little apart from the colored kids gathered whispering. "Clotilde, qu'est-ce qui se passe? Est-ce finalement la guerre?"

"It's some kind of war. The whites threw a colored mother and her baby off the Belle Isle Bridge last night. Thousands of people were fighting, colored and white, on the bridge, and then a mob came to Paradise Valley." Smoothing her skirt, Clotilde frowned. "What did you hear?"

"Nothing. Our radio is broken, and my uncle Morris is still trying to find a tube so he can fix it."

Sandy was motioning frantically for her to join the group of Jewish children. Now they'll come to take us away, she thought. They'll separate us out the way they took Maman and Rivka. They were no longer in the last place she had dreamed about. The new place gave her worse dreams.

"Don't talk to them!" Sandy hissed at her. "They all have knives."

"Who?" Naomi looked around quickly. She did not see any police or men with knives.

"The shvartzers. They all have knives."

Naomi looked over her shoulder at the ten colored children huddled against the wall, Clotilde in her white pinafore holding herself across the chest. Their teacher Miss Cahootie was still gossiping with the other teachers. From down the hall she could hear the sounds of other classrooms, more subdued than the glad roar which usually rose when teachers stepped out. "Knives? No more than you do."

"The Negroes are beating up on the whites. It started last night at Belle Isle—"

"When the Negro mother was thrown in the river with her baby?"

"What are you talking about? It was a white woman who had it done to her, you know?" Sandy whispered, "Like what we looked up the library that time, you know, before you took down Errol's picture."

"Some nigger sailor raped a white woman," Four Eyes Rosovsky said loudly. "That's what started it."

"Started what?" Naomi felt completely lost. If it wasn't the war, what was it? Everybody was scared, for she could smell that familiar ammoniac tang that she had first registered just before the Germans entered Paris.

"The Negroes and the whites are fighting each other downtown and every-place," Sandy said breathlessly. "They're beating up on each other and shooting and knifing each other. Mayor Jeffries called for everybody to stay home and be quiet if they don't have to go to work, but gangs are roaming all over the city beating up on each other and looking for trouble."

Miss Cahootie came charging into the room, red-faced and wringing her hands. "Now, what is this, class? What are you doing all up out of your seats?

Don't think because you're supposed to graduate this Friday that I can't control you. Anybody who gets too big for his britches will miss his graduation, do you hear me? If you think I'm fooling, just try me. You'll be the sorry one."

"She wouldn't dare," Sandy said out of the corner of her mouth.

"I don't care. Then I don't have to wear my lousy yellow dress."

"Do you have something to say to the class, Naomi? Because you can just stand up and say it to everyone."

"No, ma'am."

"Then you can keep your mouth shut. We'll start with attendance. Ralph, you can take the attendance for me today." Shoving the attendance book at a boy in the first row, Miss Cahootie suddenly bolted into the hall again. As Ralph was calling each name, making faces, she reappeared. "All right," she said, grabbing the attendance book from Ralph, "if that's the way you want it. We'll start with our reading lesson."

In homeroom, they always had math and then spelling before reading. It was just another sign that the adults had lost their nerve. Miss Cahootie didn't even tell them where to begin. When she called on Four Eyes and he started back two pages, so that they all knew what it said anyhow, she didn't even notice.

Sandy passed her a note. "Alvin says the shvartzers broke into his uncle's store and stole all the furniture they could carry."

Why were these people acting as if they were in a city without government? Suppose the Germans or the Japanese really were coming? If it was the Japanese, maybe they wouldn't pick her out to take away. She only followed the war in the Pacific because Ruthie did. Murray was always on some small island that was only a dot in the expanse of blue. She worried more about Europe, which reached much closer to Detroit and where Maman, Papa, Rivka and Jacqueline were lost. Leib was in Tunisia, in the infantry. Trudi thought that maybe he would be coming home, now that they had captured North Africa. That was the rumor, and in his last letter, Leib seemed to believe it too.

The glass in the street made her think of Kristallnacht, one of the only German words she knew because Papa had explained what that meant, a word that sounded like fairyland but meant only people beating up on Jews and breaking their windows. Would that start here? Or were colored people the local Jews, the ones they picked out to beat up when they got excited and started running around in the streets?

She was impatient to ask Ruthie, who would explain everything, but she would not see Ruthie until very early tomorrow morning, unless she snuck out of bed when Ruthie came in at eleven-thirty. Sandy just repeated rumors. Four Eyes was taking advantage of the fear to say dirty things. She wished she could talk some more to Clotilde who, being a foreigner like herself, looked at things with different eyes.

When it was Naomi's turn to read, she could hardly focus on the words. She became aware she had been thinking in French again, and she could not remember how to pronounce the squiggles on the page. As she was struggling to read, suddenly she became aware of a murmur around her and that Miss Cahootie had stopped frowning at her.

She peeked cautiously from behind the book. In the doorway a woman stood whom she identified without hesitation as Clotilde's mother, because she did not look like any of the other colored women Naomi had seen. Like Clotilde she was tall and straight and wore a little gold cross, with her hair up in a bright kerchief. She was wearing a white blouse and a black skirt, like Ruthie had worn at the department store, and she was standing diffidently just inside the classroom door, motioning to Clotilde. "I've come to take my daughter home."

Miss Cahootie did not ask her if there were a family emergency or how she could take her daughter out of school. She simply stood aside as Clotilde's mama took her arm and then motioned to Lizzie White to come along too. "I told your mama I'd bring you along home till she can get off work, my child."

The other colored children forlornly watched Lizzie and Clotilde prepare to leave. Then little Janie McDougall, who was the tiniest girl in the whole eighth grade class, ran after Clotilde's mother. "Mrs. Dumoullet, can I go with you too? Please? My mama's in the foundry working. She gets off at four, and I wouldn't need no lunch."

Clotilde's mother motioned her along. "You come along too. We don't want to worry your mother."

"Naomi, you were reading. Why did you stop?" Miss Cahootie glared. Not five minutes passed when Four Eyes Rosovsky's father loomed at the door, still with his butcher's apron on. "I need my son today."

By ten o'clock half the class was gone. When Sandy's mother appeared, Sandy whispered to Naomi, "Don't be afraid. I'll take you too."

She felt unreal leaving school at fifteen after ten with Mrs. Rosenthal, carrying the lunch not eaten and the homework not handed in. As they walked, a car full of white youths passed them and screamed at them to get off the streets, because the niggers were coming. Then a car with a colored couple passed, and some older kids on the corner began throwing rocks. One of them broke the side window into streamers of glass. They could hear sirens, sirens, and the air smelled of smoke.

Morris did not get home at three-twenty, the way he always did. Aunt Rose was pacing, praying aloud in Yiddish. She had tried to keep Ruthie from going to work, but Ruthie had insisted she had to go. She said nothing was wrong down at Wayne, the white and colored students in class today as always, and no incidents. Now they were both out there, in the sea of smoke and violence.

Uncle Morris finally walked in at five-thirty. He cut short Rose's passionate upbraiding. "We had a meeting to discuss what the union can do. Then the police put up a roadblock we had to drive around."

"I was worried sick!"

"We have to respond. There was that Packard hate strike not ten days ago. All those worker preachers are stirring up the men. There's been fighting in Inkster."

"And at the Edgewood," Naomi chimed in. Alvin had told her about goyim and black gangs fighting over control of the amusement park.

"We voted not to close the plant. We can't let it happen. Most of our Negroes stayed out today. They're scared, and I understand. White hoodlums are beating up Negroes all over the city."

"Why not close it down?" Rose wrung her hands. "Stay home with us till it's all over."

"We don't want to make it worse than it is. Better those rednecks should go to work and do something useful, than run around the city looking for people they can abuse. Down in the crowds on Woodward, Gerald L. K. Smith's *Cross and Sword* is being sold with their Jewish conspiracy headlines and some of the local Klan offshoots are handing out down-with-the-Jews leaflets."

Naomi felt as if she were pretending to help with supper, pretending to iron the yellow dress, pretending to help take down the wash from the backyard lines. She was huddled far into her body with her hands drawn up to hide her face so that she would not see. She said to herself, it does not concern me. It is the special madness of the goyim and the colored of this place, who tear at each other. All people want to be blaming someone, for the weather, for the war, for the lack of money, for the Black Death, as Papa had told her, killing Jews because of germs that rats spread. Somewhere people must be safe. Which people?

She envied Clotilde her mother who rushed to carry her home to safety. Everyone in the school could see who was really loved. If it were not for Mrs. Rosenthal, she would have stayed in school all day. At the end of the day she was sure a handful of kids were still there whom no one had cared enough to fetch. She would have been among them.

When Aunt Rose sent her to the bakery to get a loaf of rye bread, she met Alvin and he told her that they had had an easy day. At one the principal had decided to close the school. Those who wanted to stay till their parents came to fetch them could wait in the girls' gym. The gym teacher offered to stay till the last kid was safely picked up.

Alvin was embarrassed because nobody had come for him, but she felt as if she was just as abandoned, because if Sandy had not spoken to her mother, she would have sat there herself. Alvin explained his mother had been working and then she had been too scared to come out, but they both knew his mother was pretty useless, acting like a kid herself chasing after soldiers and partying with them.

They were standing on the corner talking when they saw a bunch of guys chasing a colored man down the sidewalk. "That's Mr. Bates," Naomi said, grabbing Alvin's arm. "From school."

"No sir." Then Alvin craned for a better view. "Shit, you're right."

They did not know the young men, high school age or older, who were chasing Mr. Bates. Then they caught him. One tripped him. He caught hold of the lamppost to keep from falling. Then he turned to face the pack, holding up his hands in a show of harmlessness, but they closed around him. One hit him in the belly and another started bashing his head against the lamppost. Mrs. Fenniman in the bakery began to scream that she was calling the police, but the boys did not run off until Mr. Bates lay on the sidewalk with blood all over his head. Even then one turned back to give him a final kick in the ribs.

Naomi made herself walk forward. Alvin followed her. "Is he dead? Did they kill him?"

Mr. Bates was always carrying out the trash at school to the incinerator and cutting the weeds in the schoolyard. He would whistle hymns while he was working. He called all the girls Missy and all the boys Bo. Now he lay on the sidewalk looking broken, fearfully hurt and bleeding. Naomi was terrified but she knelt to examine him. "He's breathing."

People had made a detour around the gang and now around the body. Mrs. Fenniman from the bakery came out. "The police don't pay any attention or help. The poor man. I'll call an ambulance. Help me pick him up."

Alvin said, "If somebody's knocked out, I don't think you're supposed to move him."

"Bubkes," the woman snorted. "We should leave him in the street to be stepped on?" She spat, glaring at the passersby. "If I dropped dead in the street, I know who would step on me. Come on, you're a starker, you can help me get him up."

Mr. Bates was groaning now. Blood ran all over his face and his hair was matted with blood and dirt. Between them, they carried him into the bakery, where the bakery woman brought him a chair to sit in. His lids fluttered. When he opened his eyes, he winced back when he saw white faces. "Mr. Bates," Naomi said hesitantly, "you know me from school. Mrs. Fenniman is calling an ambulance."

"They won't take us at the hospital. How bad am I hurt, Missy?" He pawed at his face, stirred but could not rise.

Mr. Fenniman came to the door of the salesroom from the back. Naomi got him to show her where the sink was and a clean dishtowel. She wiped the blood off Mr. Bates's face. He was badly beaten, but the worst wound was in his scalp. Alvin, who was hanging back warily, peered at the cut. "You're going to need stitches."

Mrs. Fenniman said, "I haven't been able to get an ambulance. They're all out, but they took the address. Can we call anyone for you?"

Then Naomi remembered. "Please, a loaf dark rye, my aunt Mrs. Rose Siegal sent me to get." She counted the coins out of her pocket.

When she left the bakery, Alvin was waiting for her in the next doorway. He took the loaf to carry it. "Everybody's crazy. Wow! We better not even tell anybody we helped a shvartzer, even Mr. Bates."

"I don't care," she said. "He's a nice man and he works hard."

"Have you ever seen anything like that? Them just beating on him?"

"Yes." Naomi walked more slowly. "But it wasn't colored people they were beating."

———

That night she could not sleep for a long time. The air was hot and filthy and damp. She imagined lying underwater. She imagined being a fish. But fish were always being eaten. She imagined being a tree, a tall strong tree, but trees were chopped down. She imagined being a polar bear. That was good. She was alone in a wilderness of ice. She did not mind being hungry, because she was huge, strong and alone.

The hunger was the worst. She thought about food all the time except when she was in pain from a beating or dreaming about escape, through the electrified fence where the bodies hung, past the towers, across the plain. They were never alone, always with hundreds of others standing, running, picking up rocks and running more, pushing to get at the ditch latrine, pushing to get the watery soup, pushing for space on a dirty wooden slab. To be alone with Maman was the only pleasure, sometimes accomplished on a Sunday afternoon briefly behind their barracks. She was standing outside. On her arm, a spindly grey twig covered with sores, dirty and disgusting as a run-over alley cat dying in the gutter, the ash came down, the black oily ash she hated to smell and feel, that soaked into their skin and their lungs and lay on them always like the shadow of death. She shivered in the wind waiting because it was very early morning and they were standing all in a row while their numbers were called and they stood until some of them fainted and were beaten or taken off to where the pillar of black smoke rose, from which the black ashes fell like deadly snow.

JACQUELINE 6

Catch a Falling Star

6 juillet 1943

Daniela and I are settled in Toulouse now. We are living over a garage where we share a room that gives on a side street, with a view of a plumbing supply warehouse, all built of the red brick they use so much here. We live with M. and Mme Faurier, both naturalized Jews born in Galicia, but who have good false French identities and no accents. That is, they do not sound Polish or Yiddish but speak with a thick Toulouse accent, which to my ears is quite pleasant although Daniela finds it coarse.

Both Fauriers work in the garage, where besides cars he has taken to repairing appliances, bicycles, anything with moving parts. I saw him repairing a wagon the other day, whose axle had broken. She keeps the books and runs all over looking for parts, which are harder and harder to find. They have two girls, eight and eleven.

Daniela's chest has not quite cleared and she stays in Toulouse doing our local counterfeiting. She made mayoral seals for various towns out of dried potato, but now she has linoleum to work with. She has become very proficient. The local Resistance has good contacts in some mairies, so we can get the blanks right from them, but for others, we have to acquire them more roundabout.

Daniela is also busy as a nurse, since many refugees arrive sick, and often the escapees are wounded or have been tortured and maimed. People we spring from the camps generally have deficiency diseases, parasites, such ills as paratyphoid and the various strains of typhoid that come from desperately poor sanitation. The inmates organize the camps as best they can, but the physical conditions defeat them.

Me, I do not stay in Toulouse. With you, dear diary, in my blouse I go trekking the paths through the mountains. I will confess to you alone how my heart stopped when I first saw the Pyrénées. I was imagining mountains as in the Dordogne, green, steep but comfortable mountains with red ochre or limestone cliffs here and there. I saw before me a wall of rock, going up from a few conical foothills, up and up and up into permanent snowcapped peaks with glaciers hanging there, snow in June and forever. How can I go over those myself, I thought in terror of what I had blandly promised, let alone take children—children!—over? Impossible. But it is precisely the impossible we have to accomplish to save lives. So we do it.

Right now I am with my seven children camping without a fire near the town of Ustou. We take them as far as we can safely by train and in what vehicles are available; then we walk over the mountains into Spain. There is no easier way, as the roads are all patrolled by the Germans and they shoot on sight. They have guardhouses and patrols but the border is long and wild and many trails cross. The regular guides who take escaped prisoners, refugees and downed pilots across are Basques around here, or nearer the coast, Catalans.

Lately the way I have been working is to take the children over alone and meet my Spanish Basque guide just the other side of their border, where he takes over. We try to walk twenty kilometers a day, but in rough country, often we cannot manage anything like it. I carry the smallest as much as I can, but she is five and not a feather on my shoulder. The others in this flock, fortunately, range in age from nine to fourteen and are far better able to march along. Friday I must bring my children over the border to Spain, where I expect to meet the Basque guide who takes them on and a representative of the Joint (the American Joint Distribution Committee from which comes, illegally, much of our funds), who will see that my children go on safely and survive.

Some I forget, some I will always remember. They are all my charges. If I daydream, if I doze, if I become distracted, they will die. It is the future, the reluctant whimpering, weeping future I carry on my shoulder as I go panting along the rocky trail that always seems to climb far more than it descends. The smallest cries for her mother. Her mother is already dead, shot in Gestapo headquarters in Lyon. Her father has been deported. I lie and promise her that her mother is waiting on the far side of the mountains. If she is quiet and we all climb the mountains like good children, then she will find her mother on the other side of the Pyrénées.

I feel guilty lying to her, but it is the only way to save her, to keep her from crying and calling out. She knows about being caught. All the children understand that, even this little five-year-old. Sometimes she makes me think of the twins, because she has tight brown curls, but her eyes are blue and she seldom smiles although today the flowers beside the path made her smile. She still grips a Pyrénées geranium as she sleeps with her head in my lap. I am ashamed how grubby all the children are, but I have no way to keep them clean or to dry them properly. One of the reasons I cross them here rather than nearer to the sea where the way is often less steep is that the rivers up here are cold and swift but narrow and can often be crossed from rock to rock. Downstream it is necessary to swim, and too many of the children cannot. They suffer from the cold and the wet clothes afterwards, and they look at me so pitifully, but I must rush them on, always pushing them harder than they believe they can endure. Every hour I let them rest for five minutes, but then they do not want to rise again. Their little feet bleed. I carry a supply of bandages and plasters, but that helps only feebly. Parts of the route we can travel in the daytime, but others, like the frontier itself, must be crossed at night, unless clouds make fog on the mountains, some but not too much to find my way. At least there is no problem with water, until we climb above the tree line.

As I walk, I repeat that old litany of Daniela's, eyes on stalks, ears perked forward and back, listen to the inner voices too and trust your gut. My children, stolen from the death's-head legions. Shall I too one day have a child? Could I trust the world that much? Sometimes I feel as if I am a child too as I trot over the hills with them, hardly more capable than they are of what is demanded of us. Not that I should give you the impression I am dreaming of marriage and family. Only that being around the little ones makes me think, on the contrary, how casually people bring babies into this world, how often a birth is celebrated, when perhaps it should be mourned. Yet I grow attached to these grubby morsels of flesh, even when they are wicked and punch each other and steal each other's bread.

When I look at Gitel, a girl just turned fourteen, I realize how out of date is my picture of my sister, Naomi. I saw Rivka only for that moment at the viaduct as she and Maman were being marched to the railroad cars, but even then I noticed how tall she is. I am sure that she was taller than Maman. Gitel already has little breasts and a wariness with men not that of a child. She watches the other children for me and moves with a sadness which is different and more thoughtful and more permanent than theirs.

Gitel makes me think of the years passing with Naomi far from me. I am going to write her a letter tonight after this entry. Then when I have brought the children safely over, I am going to ask the Joint representative if he could mail it for me from Madrid. I will be very careful what I say, but I need to make that contact with my sister.

7 juillet 1943

Tomorrow I should meet my contacts and deliver this brood. Unfortunately, it is raining—drizzle, but cold, making the little ones shiver. I do not dare make fire this close to the border. Instead I gather them together to tell stories. While I write this, Gitel, the fourteen-year-old, describes a movie she saw.

When we got to Toulouse, things picked up for Daniela and for me. I am still trying to understand why, in spite of Daniela's continued weakness and our fears about those we left in Paris, we are much more cheerful here. I like the south. Also I feel as if the Resistance is all around us here. I know many Resistance groups are active in Paris, but the collaboration is so visible, the power of the Nazis so manifest, swastikas everywhere, that we felt a small minority struggling to die with dignity.

It isn't that everything seems to be turning from shit into flowers, as Lev, our local chief, says. In fact, the Gestapo and the Milice hit the Resistance hard this summer. I never met Jean Moulin, who was de Gaulle's emissary to the different Resistance groups, but Lev admired him. In a series of raids, the Gestapo arrested the heads of a number of the groups and tortured Moulin to death and executed many others.

But for Daniela and me, it is moving from feeling a member of a tiny cell to being a member of a movement that feels large. No matter how bleak our lives and how vulnerable we are one by one to arrest, torture, deportation, execution, there always seem to be people to replace those lost. More come in than the Germans catch. News of the war is better these days, the Allied armies fighting their way up Sicily (although why they wanted to attack there mystifies us), the Soviets pushing the Germans back across the map. We know that if we can last, victory will come, and that is a new sensation. Here instead of working in a little cell with only tentative contacts with other isolated cells, the whole Jewish underground is interrelated and connected to the rest of the Resistance.

Furthermore, I feel at home in Toulouse, maybe because the countryside where the maquis rule is much closer here than in Paris. Maquis is a local word for the scrub vegetation of the mountains, but people use it lately to mean the guerrillas that have set up armed camps there. Or maybe I feel good because I am away from Nazi flags and among rocks and trees often, maybe because where we live is pleasant, near the canal with its little bridges and plane trees, with other Jews who have a family still. Our life flows now as swiftly as the mighty Garonne through this rosy brick city.

14 juillet 1943

I delivered my charges safely to our regular guide and to the Joint representative. He agreed to mail my letter, but not until he is in Lisbon. At first, I was devastated, but then I agreed. What does it matter whether she receives the letter in one month or in two, after such a long silence? She cannot reply to me. She can only know I am thinking of her.

Today is Bastille Day. Last Bastille Day I had that lacerating quarrel with Maman. I saw my first underground paper that day, *Libération*. Publishing papers is a riskier business than counterfeiting identity cards or shepherding refugees, for everyone in the Resistance I have known who has worked on a clandestine paper has been caught and deported or executed. It is hard to hide a printing press, and the noise they make seems to tip off the police eventually. Some right-winger turns them in for the reward.

I have a young man with me, a British agent who is on his way to Lyon with money and a fancy new type of radio, only the size of a brick, for the underground Combat organization there. They could use such a radio in Toulouse too. They never had enough of anything: not of money, not of arms, not of safe houses, not of radios or information.

The young man, whom I am to call Girard, speaks good French, although a little bookish. He seems afraid of me. I was extremely unwashed when he met me. If I have to touch him, he shrinks a little. It is amusing how much confidence his timidity gives me. When I saw I was to cross the mountains with a young man alone, I was frankly not overjoyed. I anticipated problems which have not developed. The shier he is, the more expansive and confident I feel in his company. I am no longer afraid of him, and I have gotten him to tell me about the blitz in London and about what is happening in North Africa, which is even worse than we had heard.

The Americans are still clutching hard to the Vichy Fascists there and sustaining them in power. Many resistants are *still* in camps, and Jews were only allowed to leave off the yellow star months after the Americans came. We cannot allow that to happen here. The only thing that will prevent that kind of degrading replacement of one foul regime with another version of the same is if we have a strong Resistance the Allies cannot ignore, so they won't be able to leave French Fascists in power after the Germans go home.

Girard, who worked in a cheese import firm before the war, shared a flask of whiskey with me and we toasted liberation and Bastille Day, watching the sunset steal over the snowfields across the defile and then descending to a place I like to camp beside a spring that gushes from a cliff. It was still except for the sound of the copper bells on goats and sheep below in the pastures. It was getting dark and I almost lost my way, whether because of the whiskey or because of the lurid purplish light. We actually went past the little path to the spring before I realized it, and had to turn back, because here is where we are to spend a few hours till the moon rises. The night is chilly in spite of it being the middle of July, and the warmth of the whiskey is appealing, a pocket of calming heat right in my belly. Still, today of all days I would like to be down in Toulouse, where I know a major demonstration is planned, with the forbidden tricolor and distribution of clandestine papers.

22 juillet 1943

Now I know what Armand-Jules is, that Papa used to be involved in and probably still is: it is the never spoken name of the Jewish army, l'Armée Juive. In Toulouse Papa was active in a sabotage group, but when his group was broken, he escaped and went into the mountains with the maquis. Many of them like Papa have had to flee arrest. Some are refugees; some, determined anti-Fascists; some, young men fleeing forced labor.

Again last night I dreamed of Papa. I was with a group of children. As I led them around a huge boulder, Papa was there in the path waiting, his arms opening to hug me. I realized when I woke that I am disturbed he has not got in touch with me yet. Surely he could send for me, if he cannot come, or at least send a messenger.

Today I had a huge fight with Lev about a drop to be made to the Resistance here. I am always alert when traveling for places that might be safe for drops, so I suggested a plateau near Castres where horse carts could be brought in but the drop could not be observed. London has agreed that a load of weapons and another radio are to be dropped this Saturday on the site I scouted. I assumed I would be there to help, but Lev vetoed my presence. He said it was no place for a woman, that it was too dangerous.

I blew up. I said that I do whatever is asked of me, and if he thought watching for a couple of parachutes was more dangerous than trying to travel with up to ten children in the mountains for sixty-five kilometers, then he is crazy. I also said that if I couldn't take part in the drops, I would not scout any more sites.

I have been angry at Lev ever since he made a remark when he first learned that I am my father's daughter, about how it was a pity my father had no sons. I have not forgiven him for that remark and I don't think I ever will. He said that without a son, there is no one to say Kaddish for you. I said I was perfectly capable of praying for my own dead to my own God, and that I consider Lev a living fossil.

Lev is twenty-seven and was in the regular army in artillery. He knows a lot about weapons and explosives and incites a hot loyalty from the men. They know he will not let them down. He is good at making quick plans and then refining them so that they work and we do not lose people because of a lack of foresight.

He is also not a bad orator. Even I who often detest him get very excited when
he gives us a pep talk, and then I am ready to take on the world. He is of medium height, darkly complected and has a beard like a spade that sticks straight
out. Everyone says he must shave it, but so far he has resisted. Lev has actually
worked in Palestine. He was in the Zionist Youth movement. Daniela asked him
why he came back from Palestine, and he said it was to marry his girlfriend,
Vera, who is a doctor. They were working to save the money to go back when war
started. The Milice picked up his wife a year ago. He organized her escape from
the camp at Gurs, but they picked her up in a dragnet in December and he has
not been able to trace her since.

Lev has a hoarse voice and smokes so incessantly his hands are yellow. He is
incredibly brave and fierce, but he has rocks for brains. However, I got the best
of him. I am to be at the site for the drop. Lev has given me my nom de guerre,
by the way, Gingembre. He says it suits my character.

24 juillet 1943

When I read over my last entry, I took out several pages and burned them. I
decided if others think it is too dangerous ever to use those words, I should not
so blithely write them down. So what I wrote, I have now censored. I have re-
written everything since arriving here in a code I have worked out, private to me.
Mostly I write ordinary words in French, but names and places I call by a physical code mapped out on our old Paris apartment. I realized that if I am taken
suddenly or shot in the mountains, the French Milice or the German Gestapo
would surely read my diary.

Last night the drop did not happen because of poor weather. Now it is put off
until the next full moon. From the BBC message tonight, we gather that someone
is coming with the radio so long promised to us. We all have mixed feelings about
that. We found our recent British visitor more a difficulty than an asset, and the
poor boy has already been picked up by Klaus Barbie's men in Lyon, we hear. I am
a little nervous, because if he talks, he knows the route I have been using. I must
set up a new route and new meeting point with my Basque guide immediately.

3 août 1943

Well, I am back and safe and that is a wonder, because in fact I almost walked
into an ambush.

They had set two for me. I feel like a person of some importance, all those French police and German Gestapo tied up just to wring my neck. Fortunately I met Larousse two stations down the line, where he was not expecting me, and we took the children off early. We heard about the Milice boarding the train in Toulouse and looking everywhere, asking about children. They were waiting for us, but we were gone.

Then I took the route I scouted last week, that my Basque guide showed me. Thus I avoided the ambush at the border. The Gestapo was on the French side and the Spanish Guardia on the Spanish side, but although they arrested my Basque friend and the Joint representative, they let them go again because I never arrived with the children.

What happened is, when I approached the border, I left the children, making them promise they would keep together and quiet, and I went ahead alone. As I skulked up, I heard the clink of metal. I lay there and after a while I heard voices. So I crept back and took the children down the valley and around, bushwhacking through. I did not admit to them I did not know exactly where I was but bulled ahead as if I knew. I was not sure for a long time that I had actually got them into Spain.

I have learned a little Basque so once again I hid the children. For a long time I lay in the scrub watching a farmhouse. Then I took a chance. I did not know what else to do. I told the peasants frankly who I am, although I did not say the children are Jewish. I gave them the Spanish money I always carry on the crossing, in case. The children were exhausted and very hungry, and one of them was running a fever by the time I could deliver them. It was a nightmare, clumping around in a strange country not sure exactly where the border was, but that Basque family let us sleep in the barn the first night and on the third day I managed to get back in contact through the drop near the border we use as backup, and they sent somebody to meet the children. Then I crossed back into France.

14 août 1943

Two nights ago was the full moon and fine clear flying weather. We waited at the drop with our bonfires ready to be lit and our flashlights ready and when we heard the engine of the Halifax, which reminded me of an old motorboat, we moved onto the field, lit the triangle of fires and started flashing our signal in Morse. The Halifax signaled back.

It was exhilarating. We were terrified, as I imagine one always is. You must make yourself visible, but there is no way of knowing which plane is coming. It might well be the Germans, as most planes that pass over are. We could not see markings as it crossed the moon. The pilot slowed the engine, and first a package came down on its parachute, and then another, and then another, and then another. Then came a parachute that seemed to open more slowly with a man hanging there, imagine how vulnerable. Then a second man, dangling after him. It would be easy to shoot a man parachuting down, I kept thinking, as they were followed by more packages. You have such a long clear shot at him and he can do nothing but hang there in his harness, waiting. At that moment too, I kept imagining we would hear the bark of a gun or the lights would suddenly come on from the surrounding Gestapo. But the only sounds were those of the plane climbing, and our people searching to retrieve the precious matériel. The first man came down in the clearing, rolled and rather gracefully rose, staring around him. The second man had more trouble. They released him a little too late and he drifted while we watched toward the trees.

We were all running around to pick up the packages that had been dropped, Sten guns in one, ammunition, plastique (I confess, I still don't understand why it doesn't explode on impact), fuses, the radio and then the second man who missed the trees after all but who landed so awkwardly that he injured his ankle. I should not sound scornful, as I am sure I would break my neck jumping from a plane, but nonetheless, it was a problem as he had to be helped away, leaning on Lev's shoulders in pain, while the horse carts carried off the matériel.

Therefore after we brought both men to a safe house near the big cemetery in Toulouse, I ran off to wake Daniela and fetch her, so that she could look at the American's ankle. It is broken all right, for she set it for him. Daniela is as good as a doctor, and she has to perform most of the functions of one. That was what she wanted to be, originally, back in our distant youth when we wanted more than to survive to fight another day, when we had ambitions and dreams and plans, those fragile constructions we imagine to be as real as guns and trees.

The radio landed far more safely than the man. His being American, by the way, made everybody happy as we think of the Americans as having less of a game of their own to play here, and also as being far more generous with their money, although certainly so far they have done little for anyone in the Resistance and they are enamored always with old Fascist farts they exhume and try to foist on us as leaders. For some reason, they hate de Gaulle. He seems dangerously right wing to me, but he is the leader of the Resistance and at least he includes everybody, including Jews, including the unions, the Socialists, the Communists, the middle, everybody.

The American's code name is Vendôme. He speaks good Parisian French, quite idiomatic. I was shocked, as I did not think any Americans spoke French beyond, "Combien coûte cela." My Joint representative cannot speak French in spite of all his time abroad, so we use English together.

The radio operator is French, from Toulon originally. He was recruited in Algeria for this mission. His name is to be Raymond. We have moved him at once out of the safe house and up to a village near Lacaune. Radio operators too, they say, are highly vulnerable because the Germans have such accurate signal-finding equipment. That makes it dangerous to transmit more than a short message, and the radio should keep moving every day or two.

With his ankle in a cast, Vendôme is a great nuisance, frankly. We are terrified that since he lacks any power to move, he may be caught. Daniela and I are delegated to see to his needs, and Larousse is taking my next herd of children across. I am furious, because I have no particular talent for making chicken soup for clumsy American spies. Once again Lev assigns to me whatever nobody else wants to do. Vendôme is supposed to scout around the local industry and to establish a network of informants about German military movements and strength in this entire region. How he is going to do this encased in a cast is beyond me. Furthermore he does not observe the precautions we ask of him.

For instance, this morning when I arrived, he was sitting in the window drawing on a piece of paper. I know he had been told not to appear at the window. He has a good identity, but we do not want to be answering questions about how he broke his ankle and where he came from and why he is not in the forced labor draft working in Germany. I scolded him, but I made a bet with myself that he would not listen. Indeed, after I left, I walked back around the corner, and there he was at the window sketching again. I bolted upstairs and this time I did not mince words.

"You're going to endanger us all, you idiot!" I shouted, a soft shout, you understand. We never really raise our voices, haven't in years. Shouting to us means hissing loudly and with scornful inflection (unless we are putting on some sort of public scene for a purpose, as the time Daniela and I staged a fight of two jealous women to distract the police, while Lev and Lazare took up their positions to shoot the traitor who had been responsible for breaking up the sabotage ring Papa was in).

"Come on, sketching a cemetery is not likely to be construed as potential espionage. Only my ankle is broken, not my back or my head. You have to let me enjoy myself a little. Or do you think of drawing in the same category as smoking opium?" From his window you can look over the wall into a huge cemetery, which I admit to my northern eyes too is quite ornate, a crowded apartment house row of the dead with no space between, no grass, family mausoleums built of pale stone and decorated with ceramic flowers in bright colors, with a horizon of the tall black formal shapes of the cypress.

"It means you don't pay attention to what you're doing."

"I'm paying attention to drawing. I have to keep up my practice, or how will I draw quickly what I have to?"

"You think this is a game. The only joker here is you." Putting up with him is the price we pay for getting a good radio. Moreover, he brought in three hundred thousand francs. He is a goose, but he lays golden eggs, as I said to Daniela. I could see when it dawned on him he was with the Jewish Resistance. He seemed to consider it amusing.

Lev scolded me for leaving him, but I reminded him about the refugees that need new identities locally, and he backed off. "All right," I said as I was getting ready to brief Larousse on the new route. "I will baby-sit the clumsy American until he can dance on his ankle again, but I want to learn to use the weapons that arrived. Daniela and I want to learn how to shoot. That's our price."

I thought Lev was going to spit blood, but Larousse said to him, "Come on, old man, the maquisards on Montagne Noire have women with them too, and the best shot in the whole corps franc is the woman called Dalia."

Lev blew out his lips. "Dalia is forty-four and tough as a Camargue horse. With Daniela's temper, she'll probably shoot me. Jacqueline here could blow her foot off. Then I'll be lynched by the lovelorn men of Toulouse."

"If you think that's flattery, you're mistaken. It's disgusting," I said.

Larousse, who is my defender since I kept him from walking into that trap in the station, said, "The best spy system the British still have running is headed by a woman. Young and pretty too, and you can believe me, because I met her in Marseille when I sent those plans of the base out."

"What do you know about young and pretty, Boy Scout?" Lev sneered, but he has arranged for Daniela and me to begin our training next week. We have to train without live ammunition, as we have none to waste.

16 août 1943

I forgot to say Vendôme draws well. He told me today he is an artist. "Was," I said bluntly. "In another life. In this life, if you don't want to die quickly, remember you are nobody you were. What you wanted then, you can't have now, so you'd better forget it to survive. Remember when you fail here, you bring others down too."

Daniela thinks it is funny how I talk to Vendôme, but to me, he is just a large clumsy walking wallet. We needed what the plane dropped—all except for him. But the men feel differently. I notice that Lev worried that maybe this man would take over, and he likes the fact that the American broke his ankle. He is very sympathetic because it means the man is no rival for power.

Some of the other men hang around him begging for news, as if he were an oracle on the war. Why do they think one American spy knows the real inside dope on the war? I'd just as soon listen to the BBC. What I missed most in the intervening months Daniela and I were hiding and wandering was that old radio we had to leave in Paris. Now we listen with the Fauriers.

Finally at supper tonight, Vendôme decided to be charming and thank Daniela and me for taking care of him. After the business with the sketching at the window, I was in no mood to be charmed. "That's all right," I said. "We're being paid. We're going to learn to use those guns you brought us, along with the men."

"Oh." He twisted his mouth as if words were sour. "The romance of the gun."

"No romance. I used to pride myself on being philosophically nonviolent."

"It just didn't survive a war, did it?" He is looking at me as if he is amused, trying to put me in my place, as younger than him in years but, dear diary, never in experience.

"I saw my mother and my little sister marched off to the killing camps like cattle into a cattle car. What I have learned is simple. When somebody wants to kill you, they do it—unless you can stop them."

"So you kill them first?"

"First? First was ten years ago. Sometimes to be able to act is enough to save yourself." By that time I was too angry to talk further. All Americans are naive, I think. They always fight their wars over here, which keeps them from understanding what war is. It's just something they drop in to, like this amateur. Afterwards they go home, as from a job, and for them everything is like it was, the house, the garden, the car, the bank, the family. We are stuck with the consequences.

RUTHIE 5

Candles Burn Out

During the race riot, Trudi had been caught and buffeted in a street brawl. "I'm glad my baby was born, or I'm sure he would have been marked!"

"My bubeh used to say that was nonsense, Trudi," Ruthie said, knitting away madly on the sweater she was making for Morris. If she worked hard in the little time she had to spend with Trudi, she might have it done by fall. "She saw my grandfather, her husband, beaten to death before her eyes in Kozienice. Not only did she not lose her baby, but Esther, the last daughter, was smart and pretty and certainly the only one who ended up with money. Think of that!" Ruthie laughed, although the story was of pain, because she was imitating her bubeh's manner, whom Trudi had known, and that made her feel good, almost as if her grandmother were in the room.

"If I'd known what giving birth is like, I don't know that I would have agreed to it." Trudi, who knitted much better than Ruthie, was turning out a roll of blue wool in a flutter of clicking needles. "When I say that to my mother, she gets mad and calls me wicked, but I went through the wringer."

"But you're glad to have baby David."

"Of course! And I'm glad to be able to wear a dress not made for a hippo. It's great to walk around the house without steering myself like a zeppelin. Leib is kvelling because it's a boy. My mother knew because he was so active inside."

"A girl sleeps more? Not in this life. My father gets to take an occasional nap. My mother hardly gets five, six hours sleep a night."

"Aren't you sorry you didn't get married when you had the chance?"

"So I can have a baby too?" Ruthie smiled.

"Ruthie, what you did with Murray, you don't have to be married to have a baby."

Ruthie knitted awhile in silence. "Trudi, do you ever have trouble feeling that Leib still exists, that he's real?"

Trudi gave the cradle where David was sleeping a push with her foot. "Are you kidding? The Christians may do this all by their lonesomes, but among us, it takes two."

"I'm serious. How often do you really think about Leib?"

"Ruthie, I knew Leib for practically my whole life. I know him in a way you don't know Murray. And you don't forget your husband the way you forget a boyfriend. You're one flesh." Her hand rested on her belly.

"I haven't forgotten Murray one bit!" Ruthie said defensively, yanking at her knitting. "I haven't looked at another man since I met him, and that's the truth."

Ruthie was always exhausted, but that did not mean her sleep was sound or sweet. Sometimes the factory noise vibrated through her bones still. Sometimes her mind seemed to move like an assembly line from thought to thought, blurred and anxious. Sometimes she lay staring at the dim light reflected off the ceiling and worried about her life.

She was losing her sense of Murray. The letters helped some, but a month or two months could go by without a letter. She wrote him every other day, but often she pieced words into banal empty notes, nothing but what Naomi had said or the gossip at work. She wrote again and again that she loved him and he wrote again and again how much he loved her, but she did not feel as she read his letters that they were any longer particularly addressed to her. They were to a woman. Some woman. Any woman. His letters stressed his sexual longing, but her sexuality was disconnected.

It was not that she was attracted to other men, although men at work had tried to start something with her. Her body was turned off. A large switch had been thrown and the machinery of attraction would not engage. She was only polite with those men. She had no time for them.

"Do you ever have any trouble feeling connected to your husband?" she asked of Vivian and of Rena. Joann's husband was a streetcar conductor, overage to be drafted.

"Jake writes real good letters," Vivian said. "It's like him coming home from work and talking to me. I always loved suppertime, because that man can make a story out of buying a paper. It's the same way with his letters. Always a joke, some character he met, some place he's been."

"Bobby's not much of a letter writer," Rena said, "but Joey is the spitting image of his daddy. Every time I look in his eyes, it's his daddy looking back.

And Nancy has her daddy's smile. Besides, when you live with your old man's family camping on your doorstep, they don't let you forget a thing about him. They're a close-knit family, and they took me in. That's why I never worry about my children. I got seven baby-sitters free."

If Murray's parents did not insist on pretending she would go away if ignored, maybe she would feel a stronger connection. Even Murray had stopped urging her to spend holidays with them, for she had finally written that they never invited her and would not respond to her invitations.

She had no interest in going bowling or dancing. If she had any unbudgeted moments, she wanted to be with her family. At twenty-one, her youth felt far behind her. If she asked herself if she was happy, she hardly knew what the question meant. She was often afraid. Afraid for Murray. Afraid for Naomi.

Since Duvey died, and she had not been able to mourn him, death hovered on the edge of her field of vision. The city seemed nothing but sharp edges, explosive traps, pits, minefields, quicksand. Typhus was reported epidemic in Willow Run, from the poor sewage. Diphtheria and TB were rising in the city. Syphilis was supposed to be rampant. Even the activities that seemed the healthiest, like going swimming, held the threat of polio.

She knew she was not living in a plague city, but perceived dangers licked at the hot dirty air. She knew that those in danger were people who faced the enemy, who tried to find shelter from bombs in a shattered city, who fled down roads and were strafed, who were herded into concentration camps. Yet she never felt safe. Never.

She could sense the same uneasiness in Naomi, and that made them draw closer. The race riots might have alarmed Trudi briefly, but they had deeply terrified Naomi. Naomi confided in Ruthie about a Negro friend she had, and how dangerous the city was for her friend. Naomi seemed to feel that most people were violent and mean when they dared to be. Instead of looking forward to high school in the fall, she seemed to dread it. Alvin was always hanging around now, but Naomi and he did not seem crazy about each other. Alvin was quieter too these days.

Morris was home less, for he had become involved in agitation trying to rescue Jews from Europe. He was less active in the union, because he felt that all they worried about were hourly wages and a closed shop, instead of being willing to deal with issues of power and control. "They loved us Socialists when they were organizing, but now that they're established, they don't like us asking questions."

He kept bringing home articles about what was happening abroad. He said that every Jew in Europe, every Jew, was in danger of being killed. He said there

might be no Jews left at all if someone did not act. Mama tried to calm him, but
he was obsessed, as he used to be with the union. He wanted Ruthie to go to
the meetings with him, but she could not. He tried to get Arty to go, but Arty
worked swing shift and didn't want to get involved. "Tata, you're an American.
You should act like one. You couldn't even talk to half the people you're worrying
about. You got more in common with a Polack or a hillbilly who works on the
line with you than some ignorant shtetl Jew who never saw a car in his life."

Ruthie glanced at Naomi, as often listening to everything but silent, standing
in the doorway.

"That's who I was born from, Arty. That's where what brains you got come
from. Don't judge by the dirty black clothes. They can't afford better, and they
wouldn't spend their money on their backs anyhow."

"What do you think you're going to do at these meetings? Change government policy? Turn Congress around? I read the papers the same as you. Every
time a bill is introduced to bring in refugees, little Jewish kids even, the same
senators and congressmen threaten to close the door altogether. Better to leave
well enough alone. If you have the will, if you have the green stuff, you find a way.
Didn't we get Naomi in?"

"They closed that loophole afterward. Few get out and fewer get in here."
Morris sighed.

"Besides, you come back from meetings and half the time it's Jews fighting
each other."

"We got seven organizations and each one hates the other worse than Hitler.
Some international Jewish conspiracy. We can't even agree to meet in the same
room. That's what gives me the sharpest pain."

It was Sunday afternoon. Morris was about to go out to yet another meeting.
Naomi leaned against Ruthie on the couch, where Ruthie was studying. Ruthie
kept her left arm around Naomi while she took notes with her right. Naomi was
taller than Ruthie but she hunched herself up as if she could become a baby by
willing it and thus entitled to Ruthie's lap.

Ruthie closed her eyes to rest them and concentrated hard, trying to call up
Murray's face. She kept seeing the photo beside her bed, the one she had taken
the last day with Morris's Brownie box camera. In it he looked dwarfed in his
uniform standing next to a picnic table. In one photo the shadow of his cap fell
over his face, but in her favorite, he had taken his cap off and held it to his chest,
smiling over it at her.

I say I love him, she thought, but I hardly know him. I was embarrassed before Trudi. I thought my love superior to hers, more intelligent, more profound,
but she loves Leib just as she did, while I'm lost in doubt. Murray is in danger,

while I who am comfortable and able to get the education we both dreamed of, I forget him from a kind of mental laziness.

Real loving must be a hard discipline that I have yet to learn. From somewhere in myself, I must find the energy. I owe him a love that is living and whole and vivid. That is made every day fresh like bread. That is what I must render to him.

Her arm tightened around Naomi, who snuggled closer. The house felt vast and quiet around them, huge without the children and babies. Sunday afternoon was boring for some people, but Ruthie could have wished it to last all week, just so she could sit quietly and study and spend time with her family. Then she could try to locate her feelings, her own thoughts, her own self that the incessant battering noise, the frenetic rush, the nagging exhaustion of the week buried and dulled in her. Maybe she could not remember Murray because she hardly had time to be Ruthie.

She was still sitting there with her arm around Naomi when the phone rang. It was Trudi. The baby was sick with a high fever and she was standing in the emergency ward of Henry Ford, waiting to see a doctor. Could Ruthie run over to her house, take the key from under the flowerpot and turn off the oven her mother had left with a meat loaf roasting in it? "And think of me here and pray for baby David, he looks so miserable!"

Ruthie had no trouble shutting off the oven, but the prayer she doubted would mean much from her. Sometimes she felt as if G-d had died with Bubeh, leaving her to manage as best she could, with merely human help. Baby David was well by the next morning, the fever departing as suddenly as it had come, but Ruthie assumed that was the nature of the germ. She no longer felt on intimate terms with G-d.

The Crooked Desires of the Heart Fulfilled

Bernice had grown used to the ferrying life, picking up new planes to be delivered wherever they were needed from San Diego to Hansen Air Force Base near Concord, Massachusetts. Her navigation skills were excellent; she had only gotten lost once, then found her way again after the storm had passed. Her group of ferry pilots had a home base at the field in Romulus, Michigan, and sometimes when several of them were there at once, they went into Detroit for a night out. Most of the time, Bernice was on the road, flying, seeking lodging and a meal, or slogging her way back to Romulus on overcrowded public transportation.

In some small towns, some small airports, people were friendly, but in others, they were deeply suspicious of a woman flying a military plane. Some air bases welcomed a WASP as they were now called, but others treated her as if she were a tramp. When she had walked into one mess and sat down at a table with the local officers, the colonel in charge ordered her to sit elsewhere.

Perhaps they were right, she thought, gazing down on the flat rectangles of Michigan, pale green and dark green and blue green, puddled with lakes like little tears in the fabric. Perhaps women flying planes were necessarily subversive. She felt a sense of power that few men would ever experience. She felt strong, independent, free—in spite of working in a military context with orders given, a schedule to keep to, irrational rules hemming her round.

The week before, she had had a peculiar experience at a South Carolina field. When she had landed in the rain, they had taken her for a man. She had not quite realized what had happened, except that she was being treated more respectfully than she was used to. When one of the mechanics slapped her across the back she realized their mistake; and had not corrected it. Had stood taller. Had lowered her voice in reply as she swung off the field. She had remained a man at that field the next morning. She kept waiting for them to guess, but they never had. She had not told any of the other WASPs about it, maybe because Lorraine was always teasing her about being too big and masculine.

She stopped envying Jeff. She felt that her love for him had cleared like a stream no longer contaminated, without the taint of envy for his freedom, his opportunities. No, having what she wanted made her more generous. Her father might not think she was a better person, but that was because he was concerned only with his convenience.

In his last letter, Jeff had written that he might not be in touch for a while, but that she was not to worry. He too was going to do what he most wanted. She knew he could not explain, but he sounded glad. His letter was scrawled in an uncharacteristic hurry, some words unclear.

Back at Romulus, rumors were flying in the mess. Helen learned that women from the class just after theirs were working at Camp Davis, on the edge of the Dismal Swamp, towing targets for gunnery practice—towing a muslin sleeve behind the plane so that artillery students could practice with live ammunition, or diving at the students as if to strafe or bomb them. Helen had also heard the women were having a hard time of it, lots of trouble from base personnel and planes that threatened to disintegrate.

"What it means," Bernice said, "is that Cochran is pushing on the Army for us. That we're going to get to do more interesting things than deliver trainers. Not that I'm complaining about what we're doing, but maybe they're going to let us take over more noncombat functions. There's no limit to what we could do even if they won't let us fly overseas."

"I met a woman," Flo said, "who said she'd flown for the British, ferrying planes around England, long before they let us start here. I don't see why they won't let us deliver the planes overseas. They won't even let us take them up to Alaska. It's silly."

"Hey, girls, you got your picture in *Collier's*." One of their mechanics tossed a magazine on the table.

"Let me see!" Flo grabbed it and flipped the pages.

Helen said, "I wish she'd given us some warning. My hair looks as if I'd combed it with a propeller."

Bernice had never seen many pictures of herself. She was the tallest of the women and the broadest shouldered. The picture seemed to center around her and the plane behind them, a Douglas Dauntless that happened to be sitting there. "It's too bad you're not a man, Bernice," Lorraine said, tossing her pert head. "You'd be so good-looking."

"Like my brother," Bernice said, but she felt herself turning red. She kept thinking of South Carolina.

"Lorraine, has anybody ever told you you're an asshole?" Flo said loudly. "Bernice looks fine. Some like them big and some like them small, but I don't know nobody who likes them as mean as you."

The others were giggling that night as she was trying to go to sleep about something called The Mile High Club, which consisted of women who had screwed while aloft in a plane. You couldn't do it in the small planes of course. That such a rumor was going around meant to Bernice just one interesting thing: Somewhere women were being allowed to fly bombers, where they probably had male navigators. If women were flying big planes, she wanted to be one of them.

One Friday she returned from a trip, hitched a ride to the camp and found a message waiting for her, along with several copies of *Collier's* that had come in her absence. The message said that Major Zachary Taylor was in town, staying at the Book Cadillac Hotel in Detroit, and would like her to call as soon as she arrived.

It was actually the next morning before they managed to get on the phone together. "Zach! I thought you were in England. Is Jeff with you?"

"Not this time, Bernie. He's wandered off on his own, the ungrateful little tramp. I'll give you all the news over supper. Have you something you can wear here? Or will you arrive in your overalls, and we can have room service?"

"I have a dress. It isn't too fancy. . . ."

"I'm indifferent. We simply want to glide by the management. I'll pick you up from the sticks at six."

"How?" she asked bluntly. "Surely you don't have a car?"

"They hire out, even in such frontier outposts. You see them on the streets painted yellow or green with little lights."

Until she told Flo and Helen about her evening plans, she forgot that she had made use of Zach to give her a man in her past.

"Zachary Barrington Taylor. Where does his family live?" Helen asked.

"Chicago."

"*In* the city?"

"No, north. On the lake."

"What town?"

"Lake Forest."

"That's all right. Their money is from . . . ?"

"How do I know? Zach worked in insurance for a while. My goodness, Helen, he can pay for the cab even if it would be a small fortune to me, don't worry about it. He's not living off his military pay."

"Is he commissioned?"

"The note says major."

"Better and better. He hasn't been able to forget you . . ."

"Helen, he's in a strange town and bored. I'm one of the few people he knows around here. If he knew you, he'd call you up."

"You can use my Arpège," Flo said. "And I'll do your hair. I'll paint your nails too. Now what are you going to wear?"

"He said I had to wear a dress, so we can eat in the restaurant."

"Well, of course you'll wear a dress! We're not all crazy." Flo gave her behind a swat.

"I prefer the tan gabardine pants and a white shirt."

"Not on a date, silly!" Flo seized her by the arm. "We'll get started right now."

That was the day's activity: fixing up Bernice. She was so sorry she had told anybody she was seeing Zach that she could have kicked herself twice around the field. She had not spent a more uncomfortable day since she had graduated from the hotbox where they learned instrument flying at Avenger. She felt entrapped in her own lies about the nature of her relationship with Zach. He would find her gussied-up appearance peculiar and might even think she was interested in him. She had never been sure she had managed to conceal her long crush. If only she had kept her mouth shut and simply vanished at six o'clock!

Oh well, it would shut Lorraine up. In all the primping and fussing, she almost forgot to anticipate actually seeing her old friend. She would have news of Jeff. Zach would tell her whether or not he was supposed to, she was sure of that.

The thing that made her really unhappy as she waited for him, already half an hour late, was that she could not meet him on the field in her flying gear. What she longed to do was take him up and show him how she handled a plane now. She wanted to show off to him. Instead here she was stuffed into her only good dress, which was fortunately simple and lacking even one flounce or ruffle or sequin—an absence mourned all afternoon by Flo—with her hair distributed unnaturally about her head, drenched in Arpège and wearing Helen's pearls and Flo's earrings, tripping along on wedgies with bows borrowed from the only other woman on the base with close to her size feet. She had no silk stockings, and while nobody would go quite far enough to lend her any, Flo had carefully painted Bernice's legs.

It was close to seven when Zach arrived in a checker cab to fetch her. Flo and Helen managed to be on hand, so she had to introduce them. Zach was polite but perfunctory, hurrying her into the cab. She had remembered his height but not his breadth. As he gave her a quick buss hello, he surrounded her. His ash blond hair was worn long for the military.

He had seen the *Collier's* piece. "I come back and find you famous. I bet The Professor is furious."

"He won't even write me."

"I've seen his letters to Jeff. You're better off without."

"Why are you wearing that black armband?"

"Oh, let me remove it." He did, examining it as if to read something from it, before he opened the cab window and tossed it out into the brisk September evening air. "That's why I'm back in the States. My father and my older brother were hit by a train at a grade crossing in Kansas where they were off inspecting a plant we own."

"That's horrible, Zach. They were killed outright?"

"Immediately. In fact there wasn't much intact, if you see what I mean. They gave me compassionate leave."

"What a shock, losing your brother and your father at once."

"Come on, Bernie, you know bloody well I detested my father, and he had nothing but contempt for me. I'm the black sheep. My brother was the good son and I was the bad son, and now I'm the whole show. The one I feel sorry for is Mother. She's collapsed and under sedation. She's going to have a hard time, because whether she actually loved the old man or was just used to having him squatting on her head, she feels lost. I've done what I can, stuck my thumb in the business, but it should run itself just fine."

"I know your history with your father, but those things can get you. I never thought I'd feel guilty leaving home after being a live-in servant for years, but I did."

"Ah, but you're softhearted, while mine has been hardened by the slings and arrows of this world, till it resembles a granite monolith."

"It'll probably hit you after the war. . . . How is Jeff?"

"And where is he? I'll tell you later." He gestured toward the cabbie who was obviously listening.

He waited to resume the conversation about Jeff until they were seated at a table in the Hawaiian Room, with paper leis around their necks and tall fruity drinks sprouting parasols before them, eating a sweet pork dish. "He's in France. Gone off on his lonesome and become a spy."

"Jeff?" She stared into the plate before her, trying to imagine what it must feel like to be alone in enemy territory. "They shoot spies, don't they? If they catch them?"

"Hitler's orders. Special operations, guerrillas, partisans, parachutists, all of us are shot. But it was a damned fool thing to do. Our branch is just getting into high gear. He's too impatient."

"I wish he hadn't done that, Zach. It frightens me."

"As well it should. It frightens me." He took her hand for a moment and squeezed hard. "Buck up. You had better believe that I tried every argument and every trick in the book to get him to change his stubborn, foolish, arrogant little mind. And I failed."

"He didn't write anything about it to me. Only that he was going to do something he really wanted to. But why?"

"I don't know." Zach frowned. "But I feel we owe it to him to figure it out together."

"I know he was upset about the English girl who died."

"Oh, her." He waved off the memory of Mary Llewellyn like a pesky fly. "The only reason he made such a fuss was because she talked up his painting and because she did die, which made her unique, you see. He didn't leave her. She left him, and irrevocably. Like your mother."

Drinking the tall pineapply drink he had ordered she shuddered. "I'm sorry. I feel as if we're in this garish place surrounded by death."

"Drink up and we'll go. I've had enough of this fruit salad decor and those whining musicians. I have some nice scotch, and we can talk where it's quieter."

"What was in those drinks?" she asked as they rode up in the elevator. "I thought they were like Shirley Temples, at first."

"Rum, by gum. But you always could hold your liquor like a little trouper."

"Little?" she laughed. "Who else on earth would call me little?"

"All things are relative." He loomed over her, taking her arm. "Come along, this way. I have the corner suite."

There were two rooms. The living room had a sofa that faced the windows on the corner of the building. He turned out the light and opened the draperies. Detroit was dimmed out, but not as dark as the coastal cities, and the moon was bright. He sat beside her on the couch pouring scotch into two tumblers. "You've turned out nicely, don't you think?"

"Me?"

"I wasn't speaking of Eleanor Roosevelt."

"I am proud of myself. You were the one who taught me to fly, and for years, I wasn't sure you'd done me a favor. I felt I'd been given a door into freedom and then denied entrance."

"Why didn't you leave home years ago? Look at Amelia Earhart. Wasn't she a heroine of yours?"

"I had to take care of my father. I worked part time and I spent what I made on lessons. It took me years to get my commercial license—eight of them."

"Oh, if it was money, you should have asked me."

"Zach, how could I have done that?"

"By phone I would suppose, by letter, by cable at last resort."

"Zach, come on! Both Jeff and I have been on the short end of things for years. He wanted to go to art school abroad. The last thing he wanted was to spend years of his life harvesting wheat and building roads and planting trees."

"Oh, I rather think he liked being on the road." Zach sniffed at his scotch appreciatively. "He liked loving them and leaving them. He liked walking or hitching away from whatever messes he created or blundered into. Freedom can be an addiction, potent as any other."

"Perhaps. But I'd guess he was making the best of second best."

"He's always been a hero to you, hasn't he?"

"Not at all. I'm just close to him. We were all each other had after our mother died. I see his faults, Zach, how could I not? I got stuck and he could walk out. But that doesn't mean I don't also understand his disappointments and frustrations."

"Closer than to anyone else. I suspect that's always been true, au fond."

"Of course." Surreptitiously she kicked off the borrowed shoes, wriggling her numb toes.

"Siblings don't automatically adore each other. I was never close to my older brother. I found him a pompous and nasty bore, who tried, unsuccessfully once I caught up to him in size, to bully me. Your closeness was unusual and fascinating. It seemed at times to border on incest. But you never did consummate it, did you?"

"Don't be absurd."

"You think those things never happen?"

"Not with Jeff! How can you even imagine that?" She felt as if Zach might have seen some flaw in her she had overlooked.

"I see things other people may be too banal to imagine. And I act on them. I taught you to fly. That gives me a kind of permanent interest in what you do with it, and I'm very pleased right now."

"If I could take you up! I'd love that."

"It can be arranged."

"Oh, you can't guess the number of regulations that hem us in . . ."

"I have a few friends and more than a few acquaintances. I have certain powers." His arm that lay along the back of the couch fell hard on her shoulder and he turned her to face him. "I have one theory about Jeff's flight into spydom. That he was getting away from me. He found me too demanding."

"Jeff finds everybody too demanding."

"Except you."

She shrugged under his hand. "What do I demand?"

"That's it, exactly. Did you ever happen to guess, when the three of us were playing musketeers together, that Jeff and I were lovers?"

"No."

"You never guessed. Yet you don't seem shocked. You should be fainting."

"I don't know how to say this, but perhaps I don't know enough about the subject to be shocked by what other people do. I knew you had some special kind of intimacy, but probably I wouldn't have put the label lovers on two men."

He smiled wryly, his hand still heavy on her shoulder. "I seduced him, of course. Now it's your turn."

She heard her breath exhale. I am drunk and this is not happening. She said that aloud. "I am drunk. This is not real."

"You are not drunk. You shouldn't tell yourself such nonsense. You have a pleasantly relaxed buzz and nothing more. I would under no circumstances get you drunk before laying you. And what in hell else do you suppose I came to Detroit to do? I have a nice official cover, but that's my aim."

"This is insane! Are you playing an elaborate joke?"

"I'd like you better in your flying gear, as you like yourself better, but I couldn't think how to arrange things that way tonight. Come." He pulled her to her feet. "You always did want to do this. It's time." With the one hand still gripping her shoulder, he zipped her dress down.

She stood there in her slip, with her dress around her bare feet, and could not move. She felt as if all her gears had locked, her rudder unresponsive. She was frozen with fear and she simply did not believe what was happening. "Zach, this is a bad mistake! It's ridiculous. What do you want with me? Yes, I had a crush on you. I always hoped you hadn't noticed. But that was when I was a kid!"

"Then you were green, and now you are ripe." He kissed her, his hand sliding down to her buttocks. When he stopped, he gripped her, saying, "I don't believe it, but you're a virgin, aren't you?"

"Do you see, it's ridiculous! A virgin at my age. I don't even know what to do. You could find a million women who would know exactly how to do it and how to please you."

"Bernice, little buttercup, I can please myself very well, thank you. Now come along. I'll teach you a different way to fly. Are you afraid?"

"Yes."

"Of what?"

"Wanting what other women want. Wanting what I'm not fit for. Settling for what other women settle for."

"But I am nothing to be settled for, I'm the caviar of lovers, Bernice. I made you what you are today, and I am very very well satisfied. Come along." Vigorously he pulled her toward the bedroom. "You owe me a little return, and your virginity while admirable is about to meet its just desserts."

Reluctantly she dragged along but as she saw the bed, she dug in her heels and grasped the lintel. "No. This isn't what I want."

"Bernie, it is, you simply don't know yet." He stroked her back as if she were a large cat. "The kingdom of touch awaits us. Isn't it time? Besides, I'm done arguing. You're a great big strong woman, but I am stronger than you and I know lots of nasty tricks. It'd be very undignified to flop about on the floor making ugly noises, and end up the same way with bruises that will need explaining."

She let go of the lintel and stood dumbly, flat-footed. Zach laughed and picked her up in a fireman's carry, dropping her gently on the bed, and then undressed methodically, placing his clothes over a chair. It felt unreal, lying in a hotel bed waiting for him. Then she thought, maybe he was right. Maybe this was the best way for her if she was ever to know what sex was. No awkward dating, no making lame conversation, no trying to act feminine as if it were a duty to make a fool of herself. No. She was Bernice and he knew her and he wanted her and she would try to see what it was all about.

She should have been more shocked at what he had told her about Jeff and himself, but she had always known Jeff to fall into bed with almost anyone. With his flippant comment about incest he had struck a sore within her. She had observed for years that when Jeff and she were together, they were interested in nobody else. They felt complete. She had so frequently been called mannish, she had brooded on what gender meant and found it murky and implausible, where others seemed to find it simple as a light switch that was on or off. No, she was not affronted or disgusted. She was more shocked that Zach suddenly wanted her.

He knelt over her, grinning. "Resigned to her fate. Ah, Bernice, give me a little smile. That's right. You can leave the slip on for the moment." He lay down beside her and began to explore her body with his hands, large, warm, competent as her own. After a moment she touched his back tentatively. He felt enormous under her hands and well muscled. She had imagined men's skin would be as prickly as their beards, but his face was smooth from recent shaving and his back was satiny and hot.

"Will you get undressed now?" he asked her, and she obliged.

"Can I touch you there?" she asked him, her voice sounding oddly polite against their heavy breathing. "Am I holding too tight?"

"No, sweet, no. Move your hand. Yes."

When he reached between her legs searching for her clitoris, she put his hand on it. "Around is better," she said simply.

He laughed, softly, against her ear. "I believe you have been guilty of self-abuse, my child."

She smiled. "What do you think I have been doing all these years?"

"You'd be surprised how many married ladies don't know how to press their own buttons. Like this? You can tell me what you like. I'm never too proud to learn a new trick."

It was strangely familiar and strangely different, for no one else had ever touched her except herself. She felt embarrassed to be huffing and puffing and making little noises in the company of someone else, yet it also felt exciting. When she came, she stopped the movement of his hand.

Then he let his body down on top of hers and pressed the cock she had held earlier against her flesh. It hurt and an involuntary cry escaped her. He said nothing but pulled back, then thrust harder. She turned her face aside. She knew he would not stop and she could imagine that amused grimace he had some-times when he was causing pain that she would bet was on his face now. He thrust and thrust until she felt herself tearing. She bit the inside of her cheek open. She bit her lip until it bled. At least he was inside her now and the tearing was done, although the pounding hurt too.

Afterwards there was little blood on the sheets: a blob about the size of a clenched fist, bright red. When he returned her to the barracks, she had stopped bleeding. Her thighs were sore, the tendons stretched from his weight.

Flo and Helen were sitting up for her, and when she came in, they murmured and cooed about her, avid with curiosity. She saw herself in the tiny mirror of the shared bathroom, hair mussed and loose, makeup long gone, her dress rumpled where it had fallen to the floor.

"What happened?" Flo asked.

"Did you have a nice evening?" Helen asked more cautiously.

"What happened? What was supposed to happen? Don't women get tricked up like that to attract men? So he was attracted. So he made me go to bed with him. That's what happened."

She had silenced them both. She took a shower and went to sleep.

The next day orders came that she was to pilot Major Zachary Taylor to Washington, leaving immediately. Zach wanted to see more of her, and he had so arranged things. She felt a little encumbered by his will, his power. She also felt deeply confused. The sexual connection was interesting to her, but in a way she did not approve of. Down, it led, into murky depths of wanting and needing and being caught.

She did not worry about pregnancy. Zach told her he had failed during five years of marriage to impregnate his wife, who had finally borne him a son that was not his, whom he had acknowledged because it got him off the hook to produce an heir. He believed he was sterile, as none of the women he had slept with had ever gotten pregnant, and for the last three years he had not bothered taking precautions.

She could not find in herself any different feeling toward Zach than she had before. It was only that he had suddenly grown from a distant cloud to an overarching sky. She did not usually think of herself as object rather than as subject, but that was how she experienced herself with Zach.

In Washington Zach spent half his time on the telephone and most of the rest in meetings, so that she saw comparatively little of him in the thirty-two hours they spent there. "I'm getting into the war when I return," he said. "Probably Italy. Lots of fun and games there. I rather fancy Rome or Florence where the underground is hopping. I'm not even passing through London, so I won't get stuck this time. I'd love to take you with me. Think you could pass for a man?"

She told him the story of her impersonation in South Carolina, and he was amused. "Someday, we'll give it a try. Put on my uniform and let's see. . . . A little big on you. Baggy as it is, however, it's true catnip. Come here."

When she boarded a train in Washington, the roomette arranged and paid for by Zach, she could not decide whether she hoped the affair would end as abruptly as it had begun, or if it would, at least as an occasional aside in both their lives, continue. Her cheek against the dirty pane of the railroad car, she thought of him much as the Greek maidens so violently chosen must have experienced Zeus or Apollo. The god descended and choice vanished. Then the god went about his business, and you resumed your own forward motion at your own pace. She was neither altogether sorry nor altogether pleased. What she looked forward to was the regular run of ferrying, her solitude in the plane that was hers for the ride.

The End of a Condition
Requiring Illusions

Louise awoke too early in the apartment that suddenly felt too large. She had set the alarm for eight, but again she woke at six and could not coax her way back down into the warm pool of oblivion. A few years ago, four people had lived in these rooms. Now with Kay at college, only she remained. Perhaps if she were home more, she would not feel the air of disuse that seemed to taint the apartment. Disuse? Louise smiled. Maybe it was only dust, without Mrs. Shaunessy to keep the rooms spotless. Louise had once been a diligent housekeeper, ten years before, but she did not think she was about to be one again.

That particular joy, of keeping a clean apartment, had belonged to the golden stage of her marriage before and for several years after her pregnancy. She had not felt trapped with her young child in farthest Flatbush in those penniless years, but safe, shining, fortunate. She had a home. In her orphan's bones she believed her family could vanish, and therefore her housework held an element of magic play: here is Louise pretending to be a good balabusteh, washing windows and making stew of chicken gizzards and backs; here is Louise playing mommy with her kitten-doll K-K-K-Katie. Nor had she ever found Kay a burden in traveling, even the months they had spent in Germany while Oscar was studying with Franz Widerman.

Until the day Kay left for college, this apartment had felt barely adequate. Kay could expand to fill any space with magazines, rumpled sweaters, sneakers, tennis racquets, hair curlers. Then all at once it was too big. Louise was traveling a great deal. What she missed most was a person at home when she returned, someone who had prepared a welcome.

When she was thirteen, this would have been her idea of paradise: room upon room to herself with no one to intrude. Yet while she had enjoyed little privacy in her days as a foster child, she had also been lonely all of the time like an ache in the bottom of her belly. Now she shook herself roughly: dwelling in the past again.

Grumpily she made herself breakfast, the radio on. When she had poached her eggs, toasted her English muffin and sat down with a cup of dark coffee before beginning her morning's work, *The Times* arrived, permitting her to kill an hour and cover the drinking of still more coffee, to make up for the sleep she had not enjoyed. The Soviets were attacking along the Dnieper. The Germans had taken Kos in the Aegean, wiping out the British garrison. In Italy, American forces had reached the Volturno.

Suddenly she glanced at the clock and ran for her bedroom. She made it a point of professional pride to be dressed before Blanche arrived; now she had exactly seven minutes. At nine o'clock Louise sat at her desk, going over the day's work. Nonetheless she felt bleak: a tree whose leaves had fallen. She disliked feeling sorry for herself. In the middle of a world war, she had little to complain about.

A decision began forming in her. Why not take up OWI on its constant attempts to woo her to Washington? Blanche could take care of her mail until she got back. Don't moon about, don't hesitate, she instructed herself: act. They say you will be useful. Give it a try. As soon as she had finished dictation, she reached for the phone.

———

By the end of October, Louise was glad she had decided to move temporarily to Washington, because she was too busy and overworked to brood. However, living in hotels was untenable. The law said no one could stay more than five days in a Washington hotel, so on the last morning, she had to hike to another hotel, followed by a bellboy carrying her suitcases and her portable typewriter, and meeting a stream of other Washington visitors, trekking to her hotel with their luggage. It was absurd and exhausting, and the night she went home in a rare taxi at one A.M. to the wrong hotel made her swear to solve her housing problem at once.

At once was not quite what happened. She asked every acquaintance, but mostly she heard bad jokes about the scarcity of housing. Ramsay in her office said he had always believed in polygamy, and she could move in and be wife number two. It was through Franz Widerman, whom Louise suspected of recruiting his old student Oscar for OSS, that Louise finally heard of an apartment. Something about it did not quite sound on the up and up. Louise thought she detected suppressed amusement in Widerman's voice.

She tried to guess what was wrong as she questioned the woman who was living there now. Louise would have to share the apartment with Susannah for some weeks, but then it would be hers, free and clear. Was the woman an alcoholic? dipsomaniac? round heeled? Susannah seemed normal, although obviously well into the fourth or fifth month of pregnancy. She had married recently and was leaving Washington at the end of November.

The joker materialized as soon as she talked to the super, for this apartment had been occupied by Oscar's girlfriend Abra, now in London. Thus Franz knew of the apartment. He thought it was amusing to install the ex-wife in the current girlfriend's abode. Louise almost gave up.

She walked around the block trying to decide if it was injurious to her dignity to move in. She had not found any other apartment whatsoever. She had seen rooms in private homes, exorbitantly priced and offering accommodations much worse than the hotels. This would be all hers by the beginning of December. There would even be room for Kay when she came home on her periodic visits.

She imagined dragging through the winter moving every five days from hotel to hotel, never able to make herself breakfast or a late supper, never able to have her books, her desk, her privacy. From the end of the block she came trotting back at a clip that left her breathless, to tell Susannah and the super that she was extremely pleased to take over the lease.

Her office was in the limestone and brick new Social Security building on Independence Avenue in the heart of governmental Washington facing the Mall, right near the Botanic Garden and the Capitol. She had a cubicle with a window onto one of the courtyards, which indicated her middling rank. This Monday she was lunching with a New York–based radio and print journalist who was the chief writer for "Now It Can Be Told." That was a show designed to whip up enthusiasm for the war by telling stale secrets, no longer classified tales of derring-do and danger. He felt he wasn't getting what he needed out of the OWI, and she was there to hold his hand and soothe his irritation. Louise wanted to help him prepare a program on concentration camps, but her bosses had strictly forbidden that. OWI had a policy she disliked of putting out no information on what was known about the camps and the fate of the Jews in Europe.

By midafternoon, Louise was feeling mildly rebellious herself. She had gone directly from lunch to a meeting on the campaign that was supposedly in high gear already, to recruit more women into war work. Survey after survey showed that women worked primarily for economic motives, but they were not allowed to gear any propaganda toward women's desires to make money. Their propaganda assumed all women were housewives who had never worked before, married to middle-class men.

All the ads prepared for the campaign stressed emotions she thought far less compelling. Some were based on guilt. The bullet she didn't make was not there to save her husband. "You know, most men in the armed forces are not at the front, and their wives know it. I frankly don't think this kind of approach will work as well as stressing the money she'll make and what her family can do with it—after the war, if that's more patriotic."

"We want to appeal to them as mothers, as wives." Ramsay sucked on his corncob pipe, wreaths of smoke around his head and floating toward her.

"Why? Why not appeal to her as herself?"

The guidelines were going to maintain an emphasis on women's nurturance supporting husbands, boyfriends, brothers and sons overseas or stressing glamour, showing beautiful young models working on assembly lines. OWI had launched a big campaign in September to get women into factories, targeting areas of severest labor shortages, but they would only sell the war to women on terms that did not alarm men. The slogans Louise had worked up were going to be ignored.

Well, at least they were recruiting. Louise had seen a recent intelligence study released to key people in OWI—and to her because she was a resident expert on women—that indicated that although there was a far more acute shortage of laborers in Nazi Germany than in the United States, the Germans were using foreign workers, slave labor, anything rather than their women. There was a perfunctory effort to get women into factories, but it was hampered by the Nazi party's dogma on women's place. Fascinating. Even in wartime, maintaining sex roles could be felt as more important than victory.

Moved into her new apartment, Louise asked herself, Do I feel emanations from Oscar's affair? She could not imagine him crawling into Abra's bed with Susannah in the living room. She had seen his Washington digs, and they were far more sumptuous than this place. No, she doubted Oscar had spent much time here. Visiting her New York apartment on a weekend Kay wanted to be home, Louise felt as if the deserted rooms were reproaching her. Kay was on the phone half the weekend to old friends, telling them about her new classes, her professors, her roommate, practicing her elementary French and giggling.

Louise brought back to Washington a load of books, papers, some cooking utensils and a few accents, a vase, a Klee print, a Ukrainian bowl. Her major decorating, such as it would be, must await Susannah's departure. Neither Abra nor Susannah seemed to have done much to the place. It was graduate student scruffy.

She and Susannah were ill-suited as roommates. Susannah was a young twenty-three, mainly concerned to create the illusion that she and her master sergeant had been married for months instead of weeks. She related to Louise as a surrogate mama upon whom to dump her troubles, who would surely love to take care of her. Louise marked the days until her departure.

Thus when the young man upstairs began hanging around on Sundays, although Susannah seemed used to him and saved up little tasks—putting things on the high shelves or getting them down, carrying out the heavier trash—Louise decided to make her position clear. "Look, Daniel, that's your name? I don't mean to be unfriendly, but I don't like being appointed anybody's part-time mother. I have a daughter seventeen at college, and if I'd craved more children, I would have had them."

"Susannah has been leaning on you." He grinned. "She does that. Don't worry. I'm just curious about you."

"About me? Why?"

"I was Abra Scott's confidant. She claimed your ex-husband was still in love with you. You were the looming figure in her romance. How could I not be curious?"

"With a little self-discipline." She looked him over carefully. A young man with a pleasant-looking open face and black curls. "Were you involved with Miss Scott?"

"Only in the line of friendship. She needed a shoulder to cry on."

He was a friendly type, not at all threatening. Accent of the Bronx toned down by time away. She wondered idly if he were homosexual, like her agent Charley; perhaps that was why he gave that impression of relaxation with women. What she must do was restrain her sudden curiosity about Abra. The less she brooded about Oscar, the better for her. A translator: one who put off queries about his work and put in long hours. She said, "I suppose it seems absurd, even masochistic, that I'm living here."

"I've been around Washington too long. I know couples who don't break up because they can't. After the war, they'll divorce. In the meantime, who would get the apartment?"

Claude had not sounded pleased when she told him she was taking the position in Washington. After Thanksgiving she learned why. She phoned the hotel where he always stayed. He was out. When she finally went to bed at one in the morning, he was still out. The next day, he called her. They had supper together. She was appalled how frightened she felt as she went out on his arm in her perennial mink and her best black dress. She wanted, she needed, the relationship with him, but suddenly it was not there.

He was impersonally ebullient. "This will be my chef d'oeuvre. I'll bet you've never heard of Marshal Zhukov. There's a big move on to explain Russia to the American public, and we're going to make a battle epic about Kursk. Do you know that was the greatest, the most decisive battle of the war, and nobody here has heard of it? Thousands of tanks, hundreds of thousands of soldiers, cavalry— yes, believe me, they use horses! The Russian horses in their thousands beat the German horses in their thousands, because they bear cold better. This is a movie Eisenstein could make, but I'm in charge, and it's going to be brutally beautiful, realistic and epic at once."

She marked time through his description of his Marshal Zhukov epic until she could find out exactly what was going on. She found out.

"Louise, my precious, we all have many commitments. We have lived long and full lives, both of us, and we have old friends. I wish you had talked to me before you decided to pick up and transplant yourself. . . . But as adults, we can work things out to everyone's mutual benefit. Trust me. . . ."

It turned out that in Washington, Claude had another friend, a French singer in a local supper club. Claude was in the habit of seeing Monique in Washington, as he saw Louise in New York. Now he would have to divide his Washington time between them.

Sitting there, growing chilled at the table in the restaurant of his hotel, where they had eaten together that first evening a year and a half before, she knew she could not oblige him. Why had she thought the relationship more serious than it was? Nobody had given her an emerald before. She was not used to expensive presents, so she had thought that meant more than it did to Claude.

"But you do mean a great deal to me, Louise. I value your company. I adore you. Surely you know that." Across the table he was as handsome, as charming, as ever. With the same gesture that had so often warmed her, he swept up her hand and pressed it against his heart. "You can't doubt my love for you?"

"Love is a word too widely used nowadays," Louise said, freeing her hand. "I don't think in this case, it quite applies."

"Darling, I know you never thought you were the only woman in my entire life. After all, we live three thousand miles apart. I'm a married man, even if I don't know where my wife is."

"What I thought seems to have been largely wish fulfillment. That would be the most charitable view."

"Louise, when we're together, you're happy, I'm happy. That isn't real? It's real, it's beautiful, and it's something we can give each other again and again."

"Not me, Claude. I need a few illusions. Now that I don't have them, the frost is on the pumpkin with a vengeance." As he looked puzzled, she added, "Monique is an older commitment, and I bow out in her favor."

———————

When Susannah finally left, the landlord gave Louise permission to paint and actually presented her with a couple of prewar gallons, for which of course he charged exorbitantly. Daniel helped her do the living room ceiling. When they stopped, they were both speckled with white, and had to help each other turpentine off the spots.

"I'm trying to figure it out, how it feels to you," he said. "The equivalent is if I found out Ann was sleeping with another guy two or three nights a month. My relationship with her was just as partial and just as distant as yours with Claude. I'd feel betrayed, even though I didn't love her and I didn't give her what she wanted."

"I did love Claude. In a minor way, but real enough. I understand why Abra confided in you."

"Because I'm here. That is, when I am."

"First, you have a reciprocal nature. You understand if you want to be listened to, you should put in time listening. Frankly, that's unusual in a man. Reason two: you take an interest in relationships."

"My work is so . . . analytical, so devoid of personalities and faces, that I crave gossip as an antidote."

"Your work." Louise smiled at him. "It doesn't scan. It's interesting how every time there's a major battle in the Pacific, you work round the clock. And when I brought up the idea of doing a piece on your kind of translation work, the Navy stonewalled us dead. It's none of my business."

"Right." Daniel was startled. She had observed he was efficient at discouraging interest in what he did with a barrage of technical details about translating captured Japanese material that could put acquaintances to sleep in five minutes.

With the sense of herself as an alcoholic deciding that one little drinkie wouldn't do any harm, Louise gave in and asked, "Have you heard from your friend Abra? How is she doing?"

"She likes London. Your ex-husband continues to drive her crazy. She's forever convinced that he's about to open up, to give her what she thinks she wants from him."

"You're a little in love with her, aren't you?"

"In lust. Oscar Kahan must be an interesting man. I find that he and I have absolutely the same taste in women. I'd be quite happy with either of you. And like him, I think I prefer you."

"That's very sweet of you. I'm only fifteen years older than you are."

"I'm mature for my age."

"Guess what, Daniel? So am I. Go home now. I thank you for the painting and I'll make you supper after the paint smell wears off."

"Sleeping here will be unpleasant. There are no paint fumes upstairs."

"I'll open a window. Good night, Daniel."

"In France, relationships of younger men and older women are taken for granted. If we were in France, you wouldn't hesitate."

"You mistake me. I'd hesitate in Tahiti. And if we were spiders, I'd eat you. And if we were cranes, you'd do a dance. And if we were oaks, you'd forget about the whole thing, which is the best advice I can give you." She suspected he was trying to cheer her up. Some men assumed that a pass was always flattering, but she would just as soon skip all the bowing and dancing around and resume their friendly chatter.

"I never made a pass at Abra, although I admit I was attracted to her. Because she was in love with Oscar, why bother? But I suggest to you that we're inevitable. We're both busy and lonely, we're right in the same building and we get along well. We'd be kind and affectionate to each other. What's the point wasting time deferring what will be very nice when it finally works out?"

She took Daniel's elbow, steering him to the door. "A word of advice. In future, don't tell any woman it's inevitable you'll become involved. Nothing could sound more boring! Thank you again, and good night."

But she was smiling. She smiled still as she opened windows and got into bed. She had lost something real from her life, but his little farce had distracted her, and of that she was appreciative. A hint of ersatz romance was cheering. Would that work as a plot? Better if the man being used as a distraction turned out to be more interesting than the lost one: but that was magazine fiction, not Louise's life.

Love's Labor

When Abra first arrived in London, she was shocked. London had always conjured up images of ceremony and status to her. They arrived at midnight in a city without lights, a vast plain of murk and rubble where an unbroken row of buildings appeared unusual. It resembled an elegant antique sofa whose springs were broken and whose stuffing was leaking out. Few shops had windows and in those few, empty boxes were displayed. Streets were interrupted by pits and hills of broken stone. Outside of every shop long lines seemed a permanent fixture, women carrying old shopping bags wherever they went in hopes of coming on some food.

She was almost run down four times during her first week, on the worst occasion glancingly bruised by what she had learned by then to call a goods lorry. She continued to experience a sense of confusion about stepping off the curb for another couple of weeks, looking frantically in all directions including up, but finally she adjusted to British traffic patterns and was only in the same danger now as the rest of the populace.

R & A Labor Branch operated out of a town house on Brook Street, just past Grosvenor Square where the American embassy and several of the components of OSS were located, around a pretty park full of plane trees, occupied by an all-female barrage balloon unit. The balloons were put up to discourage dive bombers and low bombing runs. What they most resembled were large shiny bath toys, silver duckies, vast padded toy fish.

Both she and Oscar had found lodgings within walking distance of work. She was surprised that they both could live in Mayfair near each other and the office. In Washington, people pursued a place to live the way they might have pursued conquest, glory, passion, a killing in the stock market in peacetime. If an apartment was found, one did not let it go casually.

Here because of the blitz fancy flats went begging, although there was a shortage of housing for the working poor. Those who could afford to move to the country homes they also had, had long since done so. The estate agent had shown her six possibilities right off, and had she time to waste, could have shown her ten more. She was living in Culross Street, just off Hyde Park in a cottagey row that had probably been a mews, now apartments over garages. The garage below her housed a Bentley up on blocks; she lived above in four light and airy rooms. She removed the more froufrou decorations of the couple whose pied-à-terre it was in peacetime and put some effort into making it comfortable and mildly bohemian. Furniture was unavailable, since so much had been lost in the blitz, but London was secondhand heaven and she could find anything in the way of decorative bric-a-brac. She mixed art deco and Victoriana, both out of style and cheap, for exactly the effect she wanted. She would have repainted, but paint was unobtainable, as were most objects of daily life she had taken for granted: soap, curlers, pencils, matches, cups with handles, spoons, towels, sanitary napkins. She sent off a list to Karen Sue and one to her mother, deciding she would let them compete to assist her. Karen Sue won hands down with the bigger and earlier bundle. Oscar's goodies arrived, she noted, from old girlfriends in L.A. and New York as well as from his mother and his sister Bessie. The arrival of a family parcel for Oscar always meant a feast.

It was a pale gold October Friday and Oscar was making supper out of a parcel just arrived. On the way to his flat she bought yellow roses from a street vendor near the antiaircraft emplacements in Hyde Park. They reminded her of the old-fashioned roses that grew at the Scott summer home near Fort Popham. She experienced a moment of keen homesickness, not so much for her family as for that beautiful clean landscape of sharply etched firs, jutting rocks and cold surging water.

He put his arm around her, affectionate as he often was. "What sexy-looking yellow roses. Like you."

She enjoyed bringing him flowers sometimes, courting him. In their relationship, he was the beloved and she, the lover, so she might as well act it out. Occupying the third floor of a Georgian town house on Chesterfield Hill, Oscar's London digs were darker, too much mahogany and tall glowering furniture that looked as if it might topple on you out of dour spite. She particularly disliked a sinister eight-foot-high clock in the hall that occasionally missed a beat, like a failing heart, and rang quarter hours constantly. But the cleaning lady who had come with the flat insisted on winding it.

He had traded candy bars from his mother's parcel for fresh eggs Sergeant Farrell in R & A brought back from the country. Out of those precious eggs he was making an omelette, with unidentifiable cheese the color of aged erasers, to be relished with the coarse but tasty Sicilian red wine from the office. A shipment of local wine about to be loaded in Palermo had been commandeered and had arrived providentially in London from a researcher following the Allied forces into Sicily and now Italy. Their first course was real sardines from a tin his mother had sent, more precious than caviar in peacetime. With it they had one half tomato each, withered but real and red. One advantage of austerity was that he seldom now remarked he had tried to do a sauce the way Louise used to and failed.

"Shall we celebrate the first loser out of the war?" He tilted his glass toward her. "We've been too rushed for the last month to pause and enjoy the victory."

"Oh, that's why the Italian dinner. Here's to the speedy exit of the other two."

"I know neither of us thinks it will be speedy. Scuttlebutt has it we hit Fortress Europa in the spring. May, probably." He shrugged. "Anyhow, one down. We never got to celebrate."

"Because the brass never ask for the information they want in advance, but always just after they need it."

The phone rang. Wilhelm back at the office had turned up something interesting. When would Oscar be back in? Soon, soon.

Labor Branch was the poor stepchild of the London espionage community, a far more glamorous mise-en-scène than that centered around the old National Institutes of Health building in Washington. Abra recognized the names: a board of directors for any university, corporation, bank or a fine old law firm could be whipped together out of the men's room of any of the Grosvenor Square buildings that housed OSS. There was a younger, more liberal, often grubbier junior echelon, but they tended to be out in the field, exposed to fire and danger. A number of them had been in North Africa, and a great many of the types who got their hands dirty in actual fieldwork were either already in Italy or on their way.

Espionage, or at least directing it, was obviously in the British view the work of gentlemen, and the Americans were pleased to taste that heady mixture of cynicism, noblesse oblige and international manipulation like the cocaine she had tried once in Harlem that went straight to her brain and lit it up till it crackled. The Labor Branch dealt with shabby anarchist metal-workers, with Schachtmanite bricklayers, with Communist railroad workers. Instead of the scions of the Mellons or the Du Ponts who flocked into the other addresses on Grosvenor Square, refugees in baggy patched jackets and the faded blue of the French working class, in Basque shearling coats redolent of sheep dip met with the representatives of the Labor Branch in East End pubs and dingy restaurants, when they were not trekking in and out of the Brook Street offices.

Much of their work was tedious and minute, going over economic information, sometimes as obscure as bills of lading for ships and barges, for railroad
freight cars passing from France to Germany. Some information went to the
strategic bombing clearinghouse, because it revealed the movement of troops,
the siting of hidden factories, ammunition dumps or oil storage facilities. One
analyst could tell by the price of oranges in the Paris market when the Germans had the railroad freight system working, so that it was time to bomb
again.

One of their unwelcome recent conclusions was that bombing was not nearly
as effective as internal sabotage. The French Resistance was not popular in London. For one thing, dealing with it meant dealing with General de Gaulle, who
was perhaps only slightly less unappreciated than Hitler among the Allied brass.
Neither Abra nor Oscar really understood why, although certainly he took himself seriously; but so did numerous little kinglets the British sheltered and fussed
over, who did nothing whatsoever but fret when they could move back into their
palaces and resume the good life chez lui.

Perhaps the whole complexion of the Resistance made the Americans nervous. While there was a right-wing resistance, sometimes openly anti-Semitic,
the bulk of the Resistance was well left of center and a large and very active part
of it was Communist. Every so often they would be asked to assess the prob-
ability of a French Communist takeover during or after Liberation. So far the
analysis of London R & A gave that little chance, but the brass did not seem to
believe them.

Everything Oscar and she had been able to piece together suggested that
the Résistance-Fer, the organization of railway men, or cheminots, did a far
better job than the air forces of stopping the trains by specific acts of sabotage,
ranging from blowing up exact sections of train as the right cars went over the
dynamite, to putting sand and gravel in gearboxes, or removing sections of tracks
just before a troop train went through. Resistance workers were eager to provide
this service, because they kept saying that the so-called precision bombing was
killing far more of their people than it was hurting the Germans, and might turn
the population against the Allies.

Oscar raised his glass again. "To our report. May it rest in peace, because the
brass are surely not going to believe it."

"But wouldn't they just as soon use the planes elsewhere?"

"If you're a surgeon, you don't want to hear about a great faith healer. If you're
an organization that bombs, you don't want to hear about the great work of a
bunch of amateurs with a few sticks of dynamite."

"What's the use of working so hard on it, then?" She flung out her arms melodramatically. She was not discouraged. The idiocy of bureaucracies amazed but did not daunt her. She just wanted to hear what he would say.

"Once information exists, there's a chance some political reason to use it may arise. You know, the Labor Branch is about the only source on conditions inside Germany, but they pay little attention to what we tell them. Even R & A exaggerates the effects of bombing."

"R & A Washington, you mean." The London people felt unappreciated by Washington. Here everybody tended to connect a lot more—a life typified by interdepartmental, interagency organizations.

"The brass keep thinking if they just dump more and more bigger bombs, it'll win the war. But as far as we can tell from our labor sources, German factories are still producing not less, but more war matériel. We seemed to be locked into the kind of thinking—if you can call it that—that says a bomber is necessarily better than two guys with a crowbar and a screwdriver, because it's technologically advanced and it costs more."

Maybe I'm in love with him because I find him always interesting to talk to, she thought. He was an excellent lover, but she wanted to make love more often than he did. He carried home the burdens of the job. She would have made love with him every night or every morning or both, but she was lucky to get him three or four times a week, and during stretches when they never stumbled out of the office till after midnight, they might only make love twice in a week.

She tried not to put pressure on him. Still, the question of whether they would or would not make love any given evening was a drone oscillating under the rhythm and the melodies of the day. Perhaps if they lived together, the opportunities would naturally present themselves. That would not quite do. They could not live openly together, though they need not conceal their relationship.

Love, she thought, sponging up the last of the egg with the dreadful bread—I was better off without it. It's the ultimate boring obsession. But when she imagined a life without Oscar, it was a sepia landscape, devoid of color, drained of intense light and consuming shadow. No, her obsession might bore her, but he did not, and that in her experience of men was new.

"I've been reading the Naples reports." Oscar leaned back in his chair. "In enjoying this food as we do, we must never forget what real, honest food tastes like. It's important not to confuse the imitation with the reality."

"Is that some sort of comment on Naples?"

"Lord, no. Only on the food."

She was brooding whether he was implying some comment on their relationship so that she missed the first part of what he said. ". . . a city without water, without lights, without electricity, without gas, without food, without a functioning public transportation system, without railways, without phone communications—all blown up by the retreating Germans, but a city that freed itself. There's the first full-fledged uprising of a resistance movement anyplace, and it's impressive. It hasn't changed any of the brass's thinking yet—they hate armed civilians—but I consider it significant."

"OSS is pouring a lot of people into Italy. It's the first real chance for the cloak and dagger boys to cut loose."

"There's the same tug-of-war between the Right and the Left going on there that happened in North Africa, except that the Left has more going for it—far more militants, organizations, arms." Oscar sighed. "I wish I had learned Italian. I'm sure I could pick it up quickly. But they aren't going to send us. They're already concentrating on the Channel crossing." He rose. "Back to work now. I have a treat for us Sunday. I procured tickets to Barbirolli conducting all Beethoven at the Albert Hall."

Oscar always scouted tickets for the finest music he could find. She thought of it as a habit left over from his marriage, for she had never had the courage to tell him she would rather go to the movies or dancing, and that her kind of music had a backbeat. She sat through the concerts watching the audience and brooding. Would she ever have the stomach to suggest that concerts were wasted on her? No, better she sat beside him than somebody else did. When he remarked that Louise particularly liked Toscanini's Seventh, it was only by accident she finally figured out Toscanini had not written it, but rather Beethoven. She felt she was condemned to sitting in the presence of loud boring music because Louise loved it. Always coming after her, always.

Two weeks later, Oscar finally had word of his sister, Gloria. It came in the debriefing report of an American flier who had been shot down and then passed along the ratlines over the Pyrenees to freedom. After the military was done with them, Oscar's section went over those debriefings to gather economic information. This one was a month old before he saw it, but Gloria was unmistakable. "That's her house in Maisons-Laffitte, and that's Gloria, absolutely," he said, showing her the description.

"Is she tall?" Oscar, after all, wasn't.

"She can seem taller than she is."

Gloria was a stop on the underground railway that sent downed pilots and escaped prisoners south to the Pyrenees. The flier had thought her a Frenchwoman who spoke unusually clear English, and she had not corrected his impression. He had also taken her to be a widow.

"That's funny," Oscar said. "I wonder where the baron is? She does wear a lot of black, always. She looks stunning in black."

It was the first concrete news he had been able to gather of her. Here was a flier who had actually met her. Oscar would have liked to look up the fellow but he was flying again. Abra was pleased to be taken into his confidence, to share in his family news. She had still to meet any of them, except for Kay at college, whose letters came irregularly but amply. Perhaps Gloria would be the first.

———————

Daniel and Abra wrote to each other, letters marked more by wit or attempts at it than by hard news. However, in mid-November Abra got a letter from Daniel mentioning with obvious glee that Oscar's ex-wife had moved into Abra's old apartment in Washington, sharing it with Susannah until December. Abra was both angered and, in a totally irrational spirit, felt invaded, spied upon, crowded. It was true she had let the apartment go. The lease was in Susannah's name, and she was posted to London indefinitely, possibly for the duration; nor was she particularly attached to those tiny, drab rooms which she had never taken the trouble to make hers.

Nonetheless, she was not amused, as Daniel seemed to be. She thought it tacky of Louise. She was further displeased to learn that Oscar knew about the move already, from their former team leader in Washington. Dr. Widerman had never warmed to her—she was not the type of woman he approved of—and she was sure he had told Louise about the apartment as a dirty trick.

Oscar also seemed to consider it mildly amusing. Daniel and Franz Widerman and Oscar should get together and giggle in their beer. Abra would have liked to be able to tell Louise what she thought of her lack of tact.

Finally she felt most annoyed at Daniel, who seemed to view Louise as a fine stand-in for herself as a handy downstairs flirtation and walking and drinking companion. Abra felt not only invaded but replaced. She was piqued by Daniel's defection. Even her flirtations at home were forgetting her. She did not feel invincible these days.

DANIEL 5

Working in Darkness

For much of the fall and early winter, Daniel was on night watch and did what sleeping he could in the daytime. Rodney, his roommate, and his lover Ann were still on an earlier watch, so the change affected his life more than he would have supposed beforehand.

He scarcely saw Ann. No more circumspect lunches on the cafeteria deck of the building, and the occasional evenings of lovemaking were hard to arrange. Sunday afternoon, her aunt was always home. Gradually the relationship was lapsing, and although he fancied a tone of reproach in Ann's voice when they did manage to speak, it was less marked than he would have expected. He wondered if she too had grown bored with the small beer of their extremely partial intimacy.

Yet at odd moments he missed her keenly. His desire for her had always been partially sexual, partially aesthetic, for he had never grown tired of looking at her. Her least gesture had a casual grace—putting on a wrap, lifting a cup, turning to answer the phone. He missed the frank gossip about their department. He did not miss the tedious recitals of her feelings, her wan ambitions; he did not miss the constant evidence of her passivity. Sometimes he had felt she approached life with the avidity of a bathroom waiting to be remodeled. Yet he knew his impatience was unjust. She lived like a silverfish in cracks, the interstices of a society actively hostile to her. She wished for normality as for Oz or Shangri-la. Perhaps his prizing of her exotic beauty and grace was equally unjust as his impatience. She would have given them up in a moment for common acceptance.

If he missed Ann more than he would have anticipated, he did not miss Rodney at all. He slept while Rodney was at work; while Rodney slept, he worked. Downstairs a very attractive older woman had moved in, who turned out to be Abra's bugaboo, Oscar Kahan's ex-wife. At first he thought there were two new roommates, because two names appeared on the mailbox, L. Kahan and A. H. Sinclair. After a week of seeing only Susannah, who was quite pregnant and about to move out, and the new woman with the auburn hair and rosy skin and the figure that even Rodney had noticed right off, he inquired.

She laughed. It was a deep laugh that seemed to well up from her full breasts. "It's all me." She was carrying up her mail in both arms. She seemed to get more than the rest of the building put together, letters of all shapes and sizes, big manila envelopes, packages of books. "I work under both names."

Briefly he entertained the fantasy that she was in some kind of show business, because she was attractive enough and she had the easy presence of a woman used to talking in public.

Then one day she dropped half her mail. There were too many slick magazines wedged into the tottering pile. The letters slid to the floor. As he stooped to pick them up, he read the name on one, Annette Hollander Sinclair. He was following her long full classic ass up the stairs with his arms full of what she had dropped. "Why does this name sound so familiar?"

"Do you read much magazine fiction?"

"Oh my God," he said. Ann's favorite writer. "You write that stuff? I mean . . ." He shut up.

"I do write that stuff." She grinned at him, slightly irregular teeth under her large grey eyes. "But I bet you've never read any of it. My ex-husband never could. It was better if he didn't try."

"Should I? I'm curious enough."

"No, you shouldn't. If you want to read something, read this." She handed him a *New York Times Magazine* off the coffee table, at the same time that she steered him firmly, as she always did, out the door.

He read it in the bathroom, three interviews joined together by commentary that set them off in ways that were complementary to each other, a much decorated woman sharpshooter from the Soviet Union, a woman who was flying B-17s for the WASP, a woman who had just escaped from France where she had been active in the Resistance. He remained intrigued by Louise, although he lacked time to pursue his curiosity. She clearly did not take him seriously because of his age, so much younger than she must be, an attitude he was sure he could get around. She was more vulnerable than she realized.

He would not be on night watch forever. Louise was at least as busy as he was. She had just ended an affair with a French movie director—a hard act to follow, but Daniel considered that his absolute contrast might be a strength in disguise. It was a drifting off to sleep fantasy, a Sunday afternoon indulgence. The rest of the time his mind was on his work.

Even at night sometimes he dreamed in code, and more than once, in Japanese. One night he woke from an erotic dream all in Japanese in which he was making love to Ann, except that when she spoke to him, she was Louise. It seemed unpatriotic to dream in Japanese and to have erotic fantasies set in Japan, but he could not help himself.

Naval transmissions had less personality than the old Purple decrypts. The Japanese diplomatic corps often sent messages that were longer than the naval codes and far more redolent of wit, snobbery, ego, acute observation. The Baron Oshima in Berlin had been a fascinating correspondent, a shrewd and artful observer whose cables could have formed the basis of a fascinating book on Nazi Germany. Various diplomats would throw snits when they felt themselves undervalued, a common occurrence in that world of self-importance. They took all queries personally and threw tantrums when their security was questioned. The world of Purple was quite human.

In the naval signals, the drama was intuited rather than acted out. Yet they came to know the admirals, the captains of that fleet. He knew he was not the only officer who had had mixed feelings about the American assassination of Admiral Yamamoto. Their decoding had enabled him to be shot down when he was inspecting forward outposts.

The office had been processing a great many messages from the garrisons in the Gilbert and the Marshall islands. The Gilberts were obviously the next step in trying to pierce the ring of formidable Japanese defenses. Daniel had been handling as high priority transmissions from the Japanese installations on Makin and Tarawa after an American carrier force had gone in to deliver a fast strike. On Betio Island eight out of sixteen planes had been caught on the ground and demolished.

All the garrisons reported their effective strength regularly, including combat ready, wounded, ill, giving a rough inventory of stores, fuel, planes, ammunition. The decoders tried to keep track of refueling and the marus—Japanese merchant marine ships—that replenished the supplies of the various islands. The maru code had been broken by the naval code breakers in Hawaii. The maru code was one of those tasks that had lacked excitement. Then when somebody accomplished the brute work, suddenly vast amounts of information appeared that changed the nature of one aspect of the war.

The maru codes gave departures and destinations of cargo ships and tankers and sometimes what was on board them. Most importantly for the American submarines that had had trouble sinking any ships the first year of the war, the codes gave the position where the convoy would be each day at noon. In a vast ocean dotted with tiny islands, such information made all the difference. Suddenly like the German U-boats, the American submarines were in the right place at the right time.

Daniel was on night duty when the amphibious invasion at Tarawa began— dawn in the central Pacific. The mood among the men on the night watch was excited optimism. This ought to be a walkover. All that intelligence could hand to the command, they had: the cryptanalysts had even identified the four biggest guns as eight-inch coastal guns taken by the Japanese from the British defenses at Singapore, where they had pointed the wrong way to help when the Japanese attacked from inland.

The command knew the strength and the location of individual Japanese units, even the officer in charge. The decoders in Washington and in Hawaii had passed on details of the fortifications, the weaponry available to the Japanese, estimates of ammunition and of food on hand. This was no improvised slap-bang operation like Guadalcanal. Daniel expected, along with everybody else in the office, that the invasion would be over, if not by the time they went off duty, surely before they came on again.

Yet it became clear, before the night was half through, that nothing was working out right. It was harder for them to follow than a battle at sea, but progress was simply not happening. When Daniel returned the next day, a disaster for the Marines was coming down on the other side of the world. The casualty figures were bad. Japanese sub I175 reported that it sank a carrier, *Liscombe Bay*. In the ensuing explosion, the seven hundred men on board were all lost. The Marines had casualties of about one man in four. It was the third day before the Japanese garrison sent out their last message. "Our weapons are gone and now everyone will attempt a final charge. May His Majesty the Emperor and may Japan live ten thousand years!"

As near as Daniel could piece it together, the Navy had used nineteenth-century maps and expected the amphibious assault to go in on high tides that never came. Moreover, reporting on numbers and types of weapons turned out to be useless when they were carefully concealed and dug in.

As for the Japanese casualties, they were total. All died except for one officer and sixteen enlisted men. Tarawa was taken, but hideously. It daunted them all. Daniel imagined the war slogging toward Japan with enormous casualties on each tiny isle. There was no celebration among the signals intelligence people. It felt as much a disaster as a victory.

At Thanksgiving Daniel went home briefly to his parents in the Bronx. Haskel brought a woman he had been seeing, extremely nervous in the full family presence. Judy was there with her baby on her lap. Her husband was in the Italian campaign. Judy kept asking Daniel what he was doing hanging around

Washington, while he attempted to deflect her questioning and pass her off with bland answers and little jokes. "I think it's a disgrace," she said. "You've got an office job, a cushy office job, while other men are out there fighting."

"Why should you wish your own brother to be in danger?" their mother asked, kneading her hands.

"If he wasn't a coward, he'd want to be out there too."

Nobody suggested Haskel should go overseas. Daniel kept his mouth shut, but his appetite was poor. That night he must return. The war would not wait. Still he found himself depressed. His parents' apartment felt claustrophobic to him, overfurnished, overstuffed, overheated. His parents seemed to feel more secure, with his father managing a small blanket factory, and they mentioned plans for postwar acquisitions. He wondered if he would still feel close to his Shanghai uncle as he could not to his own parents. They asked him about nice Jewish girls; he passed them off with the promise, after the war. After the war, they would buy a refrigerator and a couch and he would shop for a wife. He felt suffocated, guilty for his alienation.

When he returned to Washington, Operation Flintlock was in preparation, the attack on the Marshalls. It was early December before he realized he had not heard from Abra in a while. In wartime, many events could impede correspondence, but he guessed that she was annoyed with his last letter, in which he had mentioned Louise favorably. He knocked off a quick funny letter to her about wartime Washington and the jokes going around. Just before Christmas he got a reply, friendly and flirtatious. He was apparently forgiven.

Louise confided in him that she had not decided what to do about Christmas. She had never cared for it herself, but Oscar had thought they should celebrate it for Kay's sake, so that she would not feel deprived. Louise would just as soon let it lapse, but she felt with Oscar abroad, she ought to make up for his absence. Kay was annoyed about coming home to Washington instead of New York, where she could see her old friends from Elizabeth Irwin, but Louise had sublet her New York apartment to a couple in OWI New York.

"How come you feel so guilty in front of your daughter?"

"I suppose no mother ever feels she did an adequate job. And if your marriage has come apart, part of you thinks you failed, even if the rest of you thinks it was probably all to the good."

He was curious about the daughter. He expected her to be a young version of the mother, but he was disappointed. She wasn't bad looking, sleek dark brown hair curled on her shoulders, pleasant enough features in repose, but she was awkward and sullen with him. When he first presented himself at the door to have Sunday dinner with them, with a gift of a quarter pound of real butter and half a dozen fresh eggs, she said, "Who's that?" in a loud and rude voice, in spite of what he was sure had been her mother's briefing.

He could see that Louise was disappointed too. She hoped that he would be drawn to Kay, he suspected. Perhaps she thought he would be good for her daughter, but neither he nor Kay liked each other. They both addressed almost all remarks to Louise. He found Kay self-engrossed and pedantic, as if a few weeks of college had given her insight into every subject raised. My professor says, was her constant outcry. She had none of her mother's charm, none of her warmth or her wit.

Once his Shanghai uncle had told him, when he was flirting with the daughter of a Turkish attaché, to look at the mother to see how the daughter would turn out in a few years. Kay should be so lucky. Now he understood Louise's guilt over her daughter. Whatever Louise had done, she must judge insufficient, because look at the results.

After that, although Louise invited him to the movies with them, on walks, skating at an indoor rink and out to supper, he begged off until he saw Kay shipped back to school. The operation known as Flintlock was fast approaching and he would be in for another bout of crisis at OP-20-G. Before then, he persuaded Louise to come up for a genuine Shanghai feast. He bribed Rodney into disappearing for the rest of Sunday by taking out all their mutual garbage and cleaning up the kitchen and bathroom.

Louise came, Louise ate and enjoyed but was not conquered. All he could get off were her shoes, but persuading her upstairs alone with him was a great step forward, he told himself. It was only a matter of time. She liked his company, and he had as yet no rival. Gentle persistence would win her. A lust as great as his had to prove catching.

MURRAY 2

A Little Miscalculation of the Tides

In the hospital, the doctors decided that Murray had hepatitis—not apparently the worst kind, but bad enough. Still it was curable and not a million-dollar wound. They would not send him home, assuring him he would be fine in two or three months.

He was sick and feverish and weakened. He turned out to have parasites as well as the fungal infection. Nonetheless, he liked being in the hospital, where he refound himself, as if he were waking and discovering he had dreamed himself to be someone entirely other. He read; he enjoyed reading; he could prefer one book to another, judging, comparing. He began to have ideas again, thoughts focused beyond the moment, beyond anxiety. He could contemplate something more than filling his belly, discharging his ragged bowels and trying to catch a safe snooze. He could think of Ruthie without reaching for his cock. He could be silent when the other men would let him be.

Unfortunately, the doctors decided all too soon he was sufficiently recovered. He did not feel well. He could scarcely remember what it had felt like to be entirely without pain, to walk easily, to run up a flight of steps without dizziness, without nausea.

In the mysterious ways of the Marines, he was not returned to his old outfit, but posted to the 2d Division, 8th Marines, who were almost all San Diego boot camp marines, not Parris Island like his old outfit. He felt mistreated, shoved among a lot of guys who knew each other. The 2d Division was based out of Wellington, New Zealand, where he'd been in the hospital, so maybe they had just decided not to bother shipping him any farther. He reported to Camp McKay and his quiet time was over. A lot of the men had been in New Zealand awhile, so it felt like home to them. They had friends, they had girlfriends, they had taken up the local slang and called each other cobby. He felt as much an outsider as he had in boot camp.

He was assigned to a tarpaper hut heated by a kerosene stove. He still became easily chilled. Some men here had been on the Canal too, and still had malaria. At least he had been spared that, thanks to the Atabrine that gave him a yellowish cast and had probably masked the hepatitis from the corpsmen—what the Marines called medics—on the Canal.

The major in command of his new outfit believed in hiking. They went on sixty mile and eighty mile hikes in the mountains. The first time, Murray couldn't make it. His feet had softened up in the hospital and soon began to bleed. In the Marines, nobody was ever supposed to be weak, even two days out of the hospital, and he was punished like a goldbricker. Still, a lot of men dropped out, because so many had been sick.

The scuttlebutt was that they were going to retake Wake Island, where marines had been captured. Murray's strength was seeping back. At least the climate in New Zealand was bracing and healthy. He made friends, one of the other Parris Islanders who had ended up in this outfit, Jack Robelet from Maine, and the only other Jew, Harvey Meyerhoff from San Diego, who had joined up because he thought of the Marines as a local service, with the boot camp only a few miles from his parents' gas station.

Harvey had sandy wavy hair, light brown eyes and a nose that swerved slightly left from an accident in a high school wrestling match. He spoke in a nasal voice with a slightly melancholy air, a spaniel who had learned to mistrust but found it against the grain of his good nature.

Jack was short and sleek, otterlike. His hair was dark, his eyes dark, his complexion ruddy. He was brighter than Harvey but less educated. He had grown up bilingual, his parents speaking French at home but school conducted entirely in English, in a town where the lower classes were solidly French. He had expected to go to work in the paper mill where his father worked, but what he loved to do was play the fiddle. He could also whittle dogs, cats, a mermaid, a man in the moon with Harvey's leftward leaning nose. Jack was the youngest of the three, as Murray at twenty-two was the oldest, but Jack seemed older than Harvey.

Jack had married a girl named Gisele who looked enough like him in photos to have been a sister or cousin. They corresponded in French. Gisele had a job in a shoe factory, making boots for the Army.

Murray had worked hard to establish those two friendships fast, because he couldn't survive without buddies. As a Jew, as some kind of intellectual, he would be the butt of every sadistic joke if he stayed aloof. Jack for all his small size had a reputation for being fast and hard in a fight and for attracting girls without apparent effort. At the local dances, women always found him. Murray had only to stand with Jack and pretty soon women were flirting with him too.

The first time he had to make a decision was after a dance near Camp McKay. He kept thinking he would just let the evening drift a little longer, because it felt good to be with a woman, even a plain young woman who laughed too much. He ended up in bed with her. It was fast and furtive, in her friend's house. He had to be back at camp by curfew. The next day, he waited to see if he would feel guilty, but he felt nothing in particular, except that he had had a mildly good time. He saw her a few times more and then they were shipped out. They were taken to the New Hebrides to practice amphibious landings. Except for that time hitting the beaches, they spent eighteen days on the transports, jammed in.

He had a dream one night that he came home, and Ruthie was an old, old woman, skinny as a bag of bones with long stringy white hair. It scared him more than his nightmares of combat. Some of the guys in his outfit had got married in New Zealand, including Sergeant Reardon, but none of those women touched Ruthie's hem. Then he had that nightmare.

He believed she was faithful to him, but every time a guy in his outfit got a Dear John letter, he'd wonder if he was taking too much for granted. He also wondered if he should have pressed her to have sex with him, considering that if she did it with him, maybe she would then do it with somebody else. In the hospital, he had felt confident, but now he felt less sure of her, less sure of his judgment in choosing her.

The campaign sounded straightforward. It was not to be Wake Island, but some little bitty island Betio that was part of an atoll called Tarawa, wherever that was. The brass was always picking some dot on the map to jump on. Every one of them seemed to be boiling with Japs, so it didn't seem to matter. This one was supposed to be a healthier climate than the Canal, but hell had a better climate than the Canal. It was described as two miles long and half a mile wide, an island that they could swarm over and clean up in one day.

The Navy was blasting the shit out of the Japs, a bombardment that wouldn't leave a structure standing, and then they would just waltz in and mop up. No jungle here. It sounded almost too good to be true. For three days the ships and the carrier based bombers had been pounding the hunk of dirt and coral rock. Their mission was described to them in their briefing as a police action. They were wakened in the night for a breakfast of steak, potatoes and eggs. Then before five A.M. came the signal, "Land the landing force." Murray followed Harvey and Jack over the side into a Higgins boat. Then they transferred into an amphtrac, an amphibious tractor.

For what felt like hours they circled in dim choppy water. There was a wave ahead of them. They were the second wave, if they ever got going. The Japs were shelling heavily, so another round of bombardment and another run of the dive bombers off the carriers sent shock waves through the air.

In the dim light, they stared at the long low shore. A long pier and a shorter one stuck out. Coconut palms bent in the blast from the bombs. Most of them had already been broken. Murray could not see one intact building. It looked as if the Navy had done its job. As the amphtracs finally started in, however, it became clear plenty of Japs were still dug in, somewhere below that bomb- and shell-pocked surface.

The first trouble was that the tide was supposed to be high, but it wasn't. They couldn't float over the coral reef that stuck up like fangs. The amphtracs crept through the water and then crawled over the reefs, awkwardly lumbering under the increasing but still spotty fire from shore. Whatever the Navy had hit, there were intact emplacements gunning for them. As time passed, as the cumbersome amphtracs dawdled along awkwardly, the Japanese fire grew fierce, concentrated, accurate. Shells were landing in the water around them, close enough to soak them, close enough so that the lieutenant took a piece of coral in his cheek that bled like a gusher. With the shells bracketing them, they all figured the Japs could improve their aim and get the next one on them. In the little boat, the smell of shit was strong. Scared shitless was no empty phrase in battle. His stomach burned as if he had drunk acid. Why couldn't the damned amphtrac move faster?

This was his first landing under fire. He wished they were back in the pack that would come later in the boats, once they'd cleared the way. He figured being in the second wave, they'd get it bad.

A couple of destroyers were laying down a smoke screen but it was blowing away and smoke from shelling hung in the air instead. The lagoon was choppy, eighty-eights landing all around them. About half a mile out, the shore artillery opened up, and as they came farther in, they came under the machine guns. As they came closer yet, the amphtracs waddling like ducks in slow motion over the sharp angles and abrupt drops of the reef, everything began to hit around them including mortars. Ahead of them the first wave of amphtracs was going aground. Behind them came another wave. He couldn't make out anything in the smoke, the water exploding, coral hunks flying, and he wasn't about to stick his head up to see anyhow, but the shells rattled his bones.

The man between him and Jack had his head blown half off. He lay between them with his blood soaking into their boondockers, while someone wedged in just behind in the twenty-man boat was screaming in pain or terror, who could tell in the deafening noise and the smoke haze and the pounding of the guns? They were soaked from the seawater and soaked with blood too. The driver had been killed and his replacement was wounded.

As their amphtrac finally grounded, they were ordered out and went into the crotch-deep water. They headed for the pier that stuck out from the beach on coconut legs, not much shelter but all that he could see as he dove for it. Someone landed right behind him: Jack. They huddled, stealing glances toward shore, but the Japs were well protected. Now that they had landed, what in hell were they supposed to do? Harvey was clinging to the next post with Rinso, a corporal. The water all around them was riffled with the crisscross of machine-gun bullets.

Amphtracs were blowing up or grinding to a disabled halt on the reefs or in the shallows. Each wave was getting more concentrated fire. As he lay beside Jack in the slender protection of the coconut column, they saw that the marines in the Higgins boats were really catching it. The boats struck bottom on the coral, wedged there vulnerable to fire. The men had to clamber out, eight hundred yards from the beach in water up to their chins and go wading without cover into the increasing fire. Men kept dropping. As each boat wedged or foundered, men jumped out and were shot.

Maybe he was lucky to have been in the early wave, where at least they had been brought in most of the way to shore. If anything, the Japanese fire was hotter now. The air zinged with metal. Some boats landing out there on the reef were being wiped out to a man, whole boatloads killed within minutes. He wondered why they didn't all sit down, start weeping and refuse to move. He saw his bed in his mother's house vividly, the dark blue blanket, the bird's-eye maple headboard. He wanted to crawl into that bed, right now.

The shallows were a red clay color from blood. Things hit him in the water, nudging like fish, and he shoved them away furiously, a bled white ragged arm, a lower leg, a haunch. Right off the end of the pier an amphtrac went up in flames, probably hit in the fuel tank, and the men leaped into the sea with their clothes and hair burning. The hideous smell of roasting flesh and charred hair blew over him and Jack. The lieutenant and Sergeant Miller were yelling at them to start advancing.

"Come on," Sergeant Miller yelled. "No use standing here and getting shot. Let's get ashore." About a third of their men were down already. Harvey and Rinso were still huddled nearby, but another man who had taken shelter with them had been picked off. A shell would finish them all. Murray looked at Jack. Jack, whose face was still streaked with blood from the dying man in the amphtrac, shrugged at him. They flung themselves forward at the next column of coconut.

They had been supposed to be landed on the beach itself. They had been supposed to be landed at high tide, when the boats could pass over the coral easily. There had been supposed to be air bombardment from the Army. There had been supposed to be such heavy big gun pounding that scarcely a Jap was left alive. Instead here they were landing wave after wave of marines to be cut down in water too deep to run through, too shallow for the boats to cross the reefs. It was a stupid fucking massacre and he was going to die right where he was. Except he might as well die drying off on the beach as wading in the bloody water.

He was right behind the lieutenant when the looey got it in the chest and went down. The sun stood overhead like a crab on fire before they made it to the damned beach. It was hot. Oh, they'd been right about one thing: there was no jungle here. There wasn't anything except a rain of metal death. No jungle, no swamp, no trees, no houses, no hills, nothing except flat death coming at him from everyplace. Not a scrap of shade or shelter except for a four-foot seawall where sixty other terrified marines lay and where Murray hurled himself to join them, Jack right at his side. Murray turned back shouting to Harvey who waved back and ran toward them. Murray was still facing Harvey when the shell hit. He saw Harvey come apart like a busted bag of groceries. He stared. Then he turned to the wall. His bowels gave way but there was nothing left in him.

They were passing around what water they had. It tasted like paint. Some of the men were puking it back up, but he managed to keep it down. His mouth felt blistered with thirst. Something had cut his elbow. It hurt now, the wound inflamed by salt water. At first some guys always told you to wash out minor wounds with salt water, it would cleanse them, but after you'd been out here awhile, you knew better. A wound washed in seawater would get infected. The water was a soup of microorganisms, all of which seemed to like living in the blood. A coral cut could be particularly nasty, because coral could just take up residence in you.

For a moment he grinned, lying there against a four-foot wall pinned down by fire with the bodies of the dead washing up like a bad fish kill in a river. He was doomed. They were low on ammunition already. The Japs were dug into concealed and buried emplacements and pillboxes. His group had little water, and he was lying there worrying about would his elbow get infected. He'd be luckier than Harvey if he left an elbow to be sent home in a body bag. It was just another grand fuck-up that some bunch of generals and admirals had thought up in a haze of ego stoking. When he looked out to sea, he tried to avoid the smashed carcass that was Harvey. The lieutenant bobbed facedown in the choppy water, his body gradually working its way to shore. Sergeant Miller lay groaning on the beach. Two men tried to pull him to the wall. Both fell dead across him.

The amphtracs that hadn't been hit on the way in were taking back wounded and returning for another trip. By early afternoon, there wasn't one left. They had all been wrecked. The tide was falling even farther now, ten hours after it had been supposed to come in. It had never really risen and now it was going out. The fourth wave had never landed. Nobody new was arriving. Murray whispered to Jack, "Looks like they're calling it off. Are they going to dump us here?"

"They dumped us here already. Shit, I suppose they're waiting for dark. Or would that be too smart? Do you suppose that was high tide? If it was, we're fucking screwed, because they'll never get the heavy stuff in."

There was no way they could take those gun emplacements and dug-in pillboxes with rifles and a few grenades. It was a raw bad joke. They huddled there, the three men left from the twenty who had embarked in the amphtrac, Rinso who was a regular marine, Jack and Murray. The officers were dead. Sergeant Reardon had been taken back wounded and Sergeant Miller lay on the beach with his belly open.

Rinso was the one to take command, being a corporal, but Murray was damned if he was going to stand up and charge. Onward the Light Brigade. They could stuff it. As the shadows lengthened, they had more water because several men died of their wounds. In a couple of places surviving officers led charges through or over the seawall and were cut down.

Suddenly Rinso grunted. "They got a tank there, trying to go through. Let's go, lads." He rose. Jack and Murray looked at each other and slowly, slowly keeping low went after him. At some point an amphtrac had made a hole in the seawall and then been blown up on the far side, offering some shelter. A Sherman tank that had managed to get ashore was going into the breach with a sergeant whipping a motley group of marines on after the tank. It was dusk now. Murray stumbled and fell over a half buried leg. Jack grabbed at him suddenly and pulled him down flat. As he lay on his face, on the other side of the seawall the tank was struck dead-on by a shell. The men who could make it scrambled back, but they could hear the crew screaming inside the burning tank. Jack and Murray crawled back to the foxhole they had dug. Rinso didn't come back. When it began to be dark, they ate some of their rations.

"I'm not hungry," Murray said, "but I got the great-grandfather headache of the world."

"Eat anyhow," Jack urged, chewing methodically, staring up at the red-streaked sky. "Sometimes that helps a headache. Who knows when we'll get to eat again?"

They curled up together in their little foxhole behind the wall and in all the chaos and noise, they slept. Lying against Jack, Murray called up his old bedroom at home, his bed, his blanket, his blue flowered curtains. Jack was there with him, in the safe room of his childhood, not even the real room in the house where his parents now lived. He and Jack were in his old room in the country, the turkeys gobbling in their run outside.

In the middle of the night, they woke to machine-gun fire from the sea, the sea, damn it, raking the beaches. Some of the Jap marines had swum out to the wreckage of a maru that lay in the lagoon and to the blasted amphtracs that littered the shallows. Still the attack Murray and Jack expected never came. The air remained heavy and hot, thick with fumes from burning fuel.

The next day was hotter. The fucking tide finally rose and boats hit the beach. Tanks landed, flamethrowers, heavier guns, reinforcements, ammunition, water, rations. Wounded were taken off. They formed up and began crawling inland.

He was past exhaustion into the nightmare state when everything felt at once raw, vivid and numb. Jack and he had come upon the remains of their platoon, the guys who had landed if that's what you'd call it in adjacent amphtracs, minus the guys in the squad whose amphtrac had blown up in the shallows. They were commanded by the one surviving and functional sergeant, Zeeland, a grizzled tubby man who always seemed to know what to do. They lay in the scrub beside an airstrip firing at enemy positions as a tank knocked off the pillboxes one at a time. The fighting was fierce and casualties were high, but they were no longer pinned down on the beach. At least what they did made more sense than simply to stand and die.

"Poor bastard," Murray said suddenly, thinking of Harvey and not even realizing he had spoken.

Jack nodded, understanding at once. "At least he went like that. Miller was dying for two hours."

So? Dead was dead. Dead was the majority and didn't matter. Living was what was temporary.

The Japs were really dug in, so it was a matter of blasting each emplacement, each dugout, each pillbox one at a time. If they couldn't blast them open, they'd try to seal them, get up on top, toss in some grenades or TNT or pour gasoline in the vents and set it off.

So it went. Hardly anything vertical stood and the stench of burning bodies hung in the air. Jack heard they had taken only seventeen prisoners and eighty Korean laborers. Marines vs. marines. The Japanese marines wore chrysanthemums on their helmets. He picked up one of their helmets but then he threw it away. Who cared? Jack nodded, saying, "Just one more piece of shit to haul around."

By Tuesday afternoon Betio was taken and Tarawa was secured. For what? In five years, he thought, there'll be nothing here but rusting machines, a few bones and some unexploded shells. To have survived this place was something. He had never felt closer to anyone in his life than he felt to Jack. Harvey was gone, but the two of them were still together. He couldn't count the number of times they had saved each other in the last three days. They would get each other through. If I live to be a hundred, Murray thought, and grinned sourly because the odds were so slim, I'll never know anybody by blood or marriage, no mother, no son, not even Ruthie, the way I know this guy, my buddy I share my foxhole with.

JEFF 6

A Leader of Men and a Would-be Leader of Women

He fell from heaven into a dense net of lives, Jeff thought, but crouching in the unpressurized rattletrap Halifax on a pile of explosives and weapons being delivered with him, expecting to be shot down any moment, was not his idea of heaven. No, heaven was what he arrived at, crashing painfully through the branches of a tree. He had been dropped too late and had landed badly, all his hard learned lessons from his two courses in parachuting, the American way and the British, deserting him in midair as the dark air rushed past him. He was embraced like a victorious hero, patched up, fed a duck and bean soup, plied with wine and marc.

He had forgotten how much he loved southern France, although this was not an area he had visited, as Toulouse was off the standard tourist routes. The nearest they had brought their charges was Carcassonne, to the restored ramparts. At once he began to notice the skies over the brick city, which seemed to breed huge dramatic-looking clouds and splendid lighting effects. Now he was supposed to establish himself and set up an intelligence network, making contact with a previous agent sent in by submarine from Algiers.

It did not take Jeff long to learn what had happened. "The Gestapo got him the first week," Lev told him. Lev had a bold swarthy bearded face, a hawklike nose and sharply amused dark eyes that judged quickly what they saw.

Nothing Jeff had been told about what he was to do seemed to gibe with reality, now that he was in Toulouse. "But he's been sending back reports."

"Not him." Lev grinned, his black beard sticking straight out as he flung his head back in silent amusement. A Daumier, Jeff thought.

"Long detailed messages on German troop positions."

"Of course the Gestapo can send long messages. They aren't in danger of being caught when they're transmitting." Lev put his arm around Jeff's shoulder.

"I'm telling you, that little man walked right into them. You guys waltz in and they grab you right off. You don't know how to make it here. It's tough." Lev squeezed his shoulder till Jeff winced and only then let go. They had improved on his papers, so that he was identified now as working for a local wine merchant who gave them money; that would cover much traveling in the countryside. "Lucky for you that you're with us."

He wasn't supposed to be. He was to fade into the population, set up his agent network, transmit through his radio operator and keep a low profile. According to the British model followed by OSS, escape nets were one department, intelligence another, sabotage another and preparation for armed combat yet another. Here he could not locate those fine distinctions.

He had fallen into a group of Jewish hotheads, some of whom had been at war since Spain, some of whom had never surrendered their weapons when the French army was defeated. The few arms he had brought in had increased their arsenal by fifty percent. They didn't have a rifle per soldier. They didn't have one weapon for every three. Most of what they used had been taken by force or stealth from Wehrmacht soldiers or the Milice, the French terror squads set up to fight the Resistance.

Lev was a roughneck, almost a corsair type, Jeff thought. He did not know why he liked him as much as he did. At times Lev tried to lean on him to see if he could be pushed. Perhaps he worried Jeff would threaten his position of dominance. Jeff, who had never before thought of himself as a potential leader of men, was amused. But his prestige stood high in spite of his mending ankle. He had brought them weapons and plastique, keeping secret what an afterthought the drop had been. Somebody in OSS had had the idea that since Jeff was being dropped to a local Resistance group for help in getting started, although it had not been foreseen he would work with them, a present of what they were clamoring for would grease the wheels.

Further he was American. By and large, these resistants mistrusted the British. Lev had actually fought against the British in Palestine and expected to do so again. "We should tell them this is the Jewish Resistance? You've got to be crazy. They'd probably bomb us." Lev shook his head over Jeff's folly.

His prestige as American officer, purveyor of weapons, official emissary to these ragtag Jews, did not dim the contempt for him shown by the girl Gingembre—Ginger, in English—aka Jacqueline, who had been assigned, over her loud protests, to take care of him. Lev had bribed her by promising her lessons in shooting the rifle and Sten gun.

Her friend Daniela was shorter, plumper, with dark curly hair and a serious maternal air. Her dark eyes brooded on Lev with an air of furtive concern.

She treated Jeff with impersonal kindness, after setting his ankle. He had been shocked to learn she was only a nurse. Obviously she should be a doctor. She was smart, observant, cautious. He thought she was in love with Lev but for some reason suppressing those feelings.

Jacqueline's hair, which she wore sometimes in braids, sometimes pinned up in a French knot on top of her head, sometimes loose in bristling waves, was a subtle light brown that in the sun had glints of gold and even of green. Sometimes it looked metallic. Sometimes it looked soft as cat's fur. Her eyes were large and hazel, her cheekbones high, her brows arched as if in perpetual surprise at the folly and stupidity of those around her. She was tall for a Frenchwoman, small-boned, long-legged and slender but with an ample bosom for the amount of flesh she carried and with a pronounced arch to her hips. She moved fast and well with a surprising authority, as if she had more confidence in her body than was common in a woman.

He found her first oddly attractive, then pretty and finally maddeningly beautiful, while remaining quite sure she did not give a damn—neither about her beauty nor about him. She dressed totally helter-skelter, in whatever clothes she found at hand. She and her friend Daniela seemed to share a common pool of old clothes—outsized shirts, baggy wool sweaters, sensible dark dresses—that they wore in turn, fitting neither of them. Yet when he saw her on her bicycle pedaling hell-bent down the twisting brick street in a mended black skirt and sloppy maroon sweater with an emblem of some sporting club on the back, a cap crooked on her head, her braids flying out, she looked outrageously smart and captivating.

If he had brought many images in his head of what his life would be like as a spy in occupied France, he had never imagined that the mainstay of activity would be the bicycle. Oh, they had access to two gazogène trucks (trucks modified to burn kerosene), an ancient Citroën and one fast Renault whose engine had been rebuilt. But seventy percent of their business was conducted by bicycle and most of the rest on foot. He remembered the moment he had realized that the weapons and explosives were being loaded in farm carts drawn by horses. Horse-drawn plastique. No, nothing here was the way they had laid it out in London or the way he had imagined.

She was just a kid, he told himself, self-righteous, dogmatic, naive: a kid who thought it would be chic or exciting to play with guns. But kids, he learned, grew up fast here. The Boy Scout Larousse, who would be nineteen at the very outside, had personally led at least one hundred children over the Alps or the Pyrénées to safety. A thin gnarled quiet-spoken boy, he had walked over most of France. He knew the railway system as well as the cheminots who worked on it. He knew the passes and byways and mountain shelters. His parents had been deported with his baby sister. His little brother he had hidden in Le Chambon, the Protestant village of refuge in the Alps.

Larousse startled him by speaking of Jacqueline with marked respect. "She keeps her head. She calls it eyes on stalks. She and Daniela have worked together since '42. Everyone else in their cell in Paris was caught. She saved my skin once when I was herding children into a trap and she has never lost a child. But the Milice have her description all over the border towns now, so it's better she stays here for a while."

Daniela was not only a nurse but a counterfeiter. Daniela and Jacqueline had both taken part in violent actions, including one in which a local collaborator who had fingered a number of Jews and resistants, had been gunned down right in the Place Capitole in the middle of downtown Toulouse, to make an example.

Then he began to see that fierceness in her, a catlike capacity to strike; instead of being repulsed, he imagined its expression in sexuality. Did he have an answering courage? That was the question. He had begun his spy work, which turned out to consist of telling the local people what he wanted and waiting for them to provide it. Plans of the chemical company? The airplane factories? Munitions dumps? The Waffen SS chain of command? Railroad schedules? Troop concentrations? It came to him and he had his operator Raymond transmit it to London. Raymond was in the Lacaune Mountains near the end of a railroad spur. While in a cast, Jeff had to rely on couriers who were almost always women. London seemed pleased with the information he was sending, but he felt like a fraud. Other people were taking all the chances.

Then came the Friday when Daniela announced that his cast could come off. Neatly she broke it and there was his ankle, dead white and extremely hairy, with a kind of dandruff of the skin and a sour smell. When he tried to stand on it, he toppled. Daniela prescribed a regime of exercise, but he was determined to get back on his feet at once. Here he could show some energy to Jacqueline, who treated him as an overgrown and underbrained baby.

London did not understand the situation in the field. They wanted an underground army created without bothering to send weapons, an army that would function only when called into action, presumably just before the Allies invaded. He knew that was scheduled for spring, but he wasn't vetted to know more. Now he saw that he could not expect recruits to sit about waiting for some future miraculous date of Allied arrival, when every day they were in danger from the Germans and the French collaborators, when every day they lost people they knew, when their very existence was against the Nazi and Vichy laws.

Up in the mountains he was told maquisards were encamped. Now it was fall but soon it would be winter in the mountains, and most men had arrived in light summer clothing without coats or boots against the snow that would come sooner than any of them wished.

There was much to be done to equip and train this local assortment of hot-heads and politicos, refugees and petty criminals, teachers and professionals and factory workers and a surprising number of women who fell into all the categories. His arrival had given them hope and plunged them into action he thought precipitous. He must get involved, whatever London thought. He was responsible, whether he wished to be or not, a new sensation. Did he feel trapped? No, surprisingly. He monitored his emotional state as if it were a bum heart, but heard no murmurs of discontent. He had felt far more trapped in London, with Zach.

He began to see that as ill assorted and disorganized as they appeared at first, they were connected into a large organization. They had close communication with the railroad workers, the cheminots, so that they always knew exactly when trains with troops aboard or essential war materials were going through. Sunday night a train laden with high explosives and artillery shells was departing the Toulouse yards at midnight.

He had lectured on the use of plastique, but he thought the best pedagogy would be to use it on that train. Gilles, a Jewish cheminot, let the other workers know that they were blowing that train, after the engine had passed. Gilles would tell Lev the order of cars out of the yard, so that they had the maximum opportunity to blow the high explosives. Because of the large blast they might set off, they had to pick a spot where the tracks were not bordered by houses.

Jeff knew he was exceeding his orders, but he had been trained to work with guerrilla and sabotage groups long before he had trained as a spy. And he turned out to be useless in collecting information. He was merely a coordinator of the work done by dozens of ordinary people who had jobs in sensitive areas—clerical and factory workers, scientists, engineers, even Thibaud, a spy in the mairie, and Margot, a secretary in the Milice headquarters. He sat down with Lev and they planned Sunday night's attack.

The train would move out on the line that headed toward Gaillac. They would hit it near Gemil, where they had people. Lev, his lieutenant Roger, Gilles and Jeff would travel Sunday to Gemil, where they would stay in the countryside with a family whose sons would take part in the attack on the train. Gilles had the day off. He worked in the yard at Toulouse, where his usual method of sabotage, he told Jeff as they lay in the back of a truck under a tarpaulin, was to drain oil from a gearbox. Sand and gravel could be effective too and impossible to trace.

They rode in a gazogène truck delivering wood, their bicycles hidden under the logs, but the last twelve kilometers, they had to pedal. Jeff's ankle pained him sharply before long, and he had to beg them to stop frequently and rest. He hated to appear weak, but Gilles was sympathetic. He said that the first thing he wanted after the war besides a new suit of clothes and shoes with rubber soles was a motorbike.

Jeff, who had never owned or used a motorbike, could not follow the heated discussion that followed between Lev, Roger and Gilles about the merits and faults of the different makes and models. It was like Americans arguing about cars, a subject from which he had always been alienated as it featured in the animated talk to his male peers, since he'd never owned one. Instead he sketched the plane trees along the white dusty road, dark gold leaves against the mottled bark. Sometimes the French attacked the beautiful plane trees, chopping off their crowns so they looked maimed, dismembered; then they sprouted to huge lollipops, phalli anointed with green pubic hair. Fortunately these had not been attacked. This direction was not particularly interesting countryside, but south from Toulouse lay the plains and then the Pyrénées. He longed to explore every direction, but he had not yet even got to the mountains of Lacaune or those of Montagne Noire, where maquis were holed up.

None of the men seemed to find his sketching odd. As they were mounting their bicycles, Roger said, "I think you should keep your limp. A limp explains why you haven't been taken for the work draft."

Gilles was quieter spoken than Lev, a married man with four children. He had been born in Lithuania, but had arrived young enough for his French to pass as native. His wife was a more recent immigrant. Roger was tall, hunched over, with a round head with oversized spectacles, a shock of prematurely greying hair. He had been a teacher but had lost his job when all the Jews were fired and had worked in a tannery since. His hands were stained dark. He talked less than the other two. Although he was older, he deferred to Lev, whom he obviously worshiped.

Lev produced sandwiches of goose pâté on thick bread, a bottle of dark red wine. A golden October light made bluish shadows under the plane trees. A wind had knocked some of the seedballs loose and they too cast little blue comma shadows. Grass in the meadow beyond was the color of wheat, but plumier, airier. Doves were gurgling and cooing nearby. They heard a train whistling on the tracks beyond the trees, perhaps a mile away. He accepted the pain in his ankle without rancor. Crickets chirped in the grass; the air was crisp and the light, languid.

They finished with a pear apiece, female bodies, sweet. He thought of her hair brushing him as she had bound his ankle for support. Luckily his pants were loose and baggy. Her hair carried a scent from his childhood, of newly washed laundry dried in the sun.

The farmhouse was built of grey stone under a red tiled roof, with a barn set at right angles and open on three sides, walled with hay. The sons were sixteen and eighteen. Only the eighteen-year-old Theo looked like the parents. The sixteen-year-old Alain had a slight accent and was smaller boned than any of the others. A black draped photograph of a young man stood on the mantel: the older brother, who had been taken prisoner and was reported as shot escaping. His widow lived with them and did the cooking, as the mother was crippled with arthritis. They were peasants, hardworking, ham-handed, extremely curious and personal in their questioning (How is it you never married? And your sister never married either? What does your father say? Will he marry again?), looking sixty at forty and forty at twenty-five, but setting a table that would have shamed a four-star restaurant at home.

They ate, drank, lay down, although Jeff was far too excited to sleep. He sat by the dying fire, a cat slowly approaching, black with yellow eyes, and then leaning on his leg and then climbing in his lap. She was pregnant and purred loudly, rubbing her cheek against the side of his hand until he agreed to pet her. Would they blow up the train? Would he die this night? He felt nervous in a fine-tuned way, the same as when he was going to bed for the first time with a woman he really wanted or on a hot streak painting and knew he had it. His fingers wandered the cat's fur in compulsive jerky caresses as he went over the steps of their simple plan. He checked his Browning .38, his knife sheathed against his right leg, the fuses.

Roger, who probably had not slept either, came down just as Jeff decided it was time to get his party moving. They set off through the wan moonlight. Theo faded away to stand guard down the tracks with a Sten gun. Alain they placed on the nearby road to watch and signal any trouble. They did not arm him, as he was only to give warning if necessary, then hide in the brush. With a shotgun, Gilles went up the tracks to guard them from that end. Lev and Roger squatted to watch as Jeff placed the plastique and set the fuse.

They had allowed half an hour, but Jeff was done long before that and whistled the others in. They marched single file toward the farm, but then Theo led them up a rough track, difficult for all of them but Theo who bounded ahead like a goat who could see in the dark. They came out on a little ledge from which they could watch the lights of the train down below, the curve of tracks. Jeff remembered traveling all night with Bernice, sitting up in a darkened couchette staring at the night landscape of southern France, north from Marseille, and realizing how like a Van Gogh it looked. The train was coming fast. The engine passed, the first few cars must now be over the explosives, but nothing happened.

Jeff wondered if they would ever trust him again if the plastique did not work.

He was still wondering when the sky lit up, first a burst of fire followed by the sharp whack of an explosion, and then explosion after explosion made the hillside shudder and loose rocks rattle down.

"Come, we must get home now before the patrols come," Theo said and led them precipitously downhill, leaping from boulder to root before them in the stifling dark.

"It was so beautiful," Alain murmured. "Better than any fireworks. Once in Cologne I saw a fireworks on the river—"

"You're not to mention that," Theo said sharply.

"I know. I'm sorry. But it was so beautiful. Flowers of fire and waterfalls," Alain said dreamily. "I would like to do this often."

Another peasant came to warn that the Milice were checking identity cards and stories on the highway, but Theo led them before dawn by dusty and unpaved country roads into Gemil, where they climbed back into the truck and headed for Toulouse. Jeff felt satisfied. Gilles would soon know the exact extent of the damage, but they could guess it had been considerable. He would be at work on time.

They lay in the back of the truck, the logs pressing down on them as the truck huffed and lurched and swayed. "A little while longer and they would have married you off to the widow," Lev said to Jeff.

"The younger kid Alain isn't theirs, is he?"

"German Jew," Gilles explained. "Larousse placed him there two years ago. He escaped on his own from a transport after his mother died. Larousse noticed him in Marseille going through garbage."

"You'll be wanting a woman soon," Lev said. "There are two whores, Bibi and Paulette by the station, who are good to us. They pass us information and give us money. You'll like Paulette, she's young."

"I'll wait awhile."

Lev laughed sharply. "For what you have your eye on, you'll wait longer than awhile."

"It's that obvious?"

"Don't worry, she probably hasn't noticed. You'd have to take your pants down and wave it at her. Then she'd just turn up her nose and hand you a blanket."

"She's not involved with anyone?"

"She's involved with everyone," Roger said, "but not as you mean." He sounded as if he were delivering a rebuke to a dunce of a student.

"She's a nice Jewish girl," Lev added. "Go see Paulette. She'll take care of you."

He felt as if he had suddenly banged against a large No Trespassing sign. He did not bother saying that it was after all up to Jacqueline, as so far she had shown no signs of responding. The mannerisms, the little charades and poses other women had found irresistible, she simply walked through as if they were white noise. He was going to have to woo her in some totally new way.

Gossip about the big train wreck was all over Toulouse and pressure came down. A meeting scheduled with a representative of the regional coordination of the Resistance, the FFI—Forces Françaises de l'Intérieur—was put off and moved to a suburb south of Toulouse, near a big bend of the Garonne where the wine merchant, Jeff's putative employer, had a house on a hill with a magnificent view of the river, the railroad, the highway and all approaches. A week later, Jeff along with Lev, Roger, Jacqueline, Daniela and six others met with Captain Robert, the FFI representative. He told them about a deal over the border in Spain where some Basques had got hold of guns they could buy. Lev memorized the details. They would figure out who should go and how. Captain Robert was a short, stout fast-talking man who had been a captain in World War I, then a Renault salesman. The captain had procured the Renault rebuilt by M. Faurier, who ran the garage where Jacqueline and Daniela lived. Captain Robert said he had come in part to meet the new Commandant Américain, for whom he had many questions, which Jeff fielded as best he could. He had no idea when OSS would send more arms and could only promise he would keep asking.

As the meeting was breaking up, Captain Robert guided Jeff out onto the terrace. "You're to go to meet the maquisards. Lapin sent for you. And he wants to see you too," he said to Jacqueline.

"Is that my father?" Jacqueline asked brusquely, her face going white and rigid.

Captain Robert seemed embarrassed. He nodded. "Lev will make arrangements for transportation. I have the meeting coordinates."

"Does that mean the place and time?" Jacqueline's usually fine speaking voice was acidic. Jeff watched closely. "He has taken his sweet time arranging this."

"Both the Boches and the Vichy rats have a price on his head. They have been chasing him since forty-one. Lapin, he moves fast and he goes to ground well, but no one would say that meeting with him is easy or safe. Probably he didn't want to endanger you."

"He protected my mother and sister so well." Jacqueline turned away, leaning on the low parapet where the last full-bosomed pink roses—flat, crammed with petals, the way Redouté had painted them—were blooming. Below, the river shone like a bronze scythe, full of soil from the day before's storm, riffled with rapids. The land was a green plain stretching to the wall of mountains, an enormous busy sky like one of Turner's stacked above, the sun setting ruddy against clouds stained with green and violet. Daniela seized her hands and said something softly. Jacqueline shook her off. Daniela again went after her, as the men drifted back in, ignoring Jacqueline, discussing the means of buying the Basque arms. Some of Jeff's money would go for that, it was assumed, and he saw no reason why not.

He moved in on Jacqueline, who sat on the parapet with her arms folded tight against her breasts. "This man, Lapin, is your father?"

"You heard."

"You haven't seen him in a long time?"

"In forty-one he sent one of my sisters to America to relatives. He never came back to Paris. I haven't seen him since."

"If he'd been with you, do you think he could have kept your mother and sister from being deported?"

"Yes! How do I know? He was an escaped prisoner of war. And he was active in the Resistance already. He got involved in his war and left us to survive as we could."

Daniela had her arm around Jacqueline, pulling her head against her shoulder so that Jacqueline was off balance, her neck stretched and her shoulder lowered to the shorter woman's height. Both their legs dangled off the wall side by side. Jeff sat on Jacqueline's left, taking her cold hand between his. "Were you close to your father?"

"When I was little. Later we fought. I thought his Zionism provincial and naive. I was wrong. He was prescient. But I'm still angry."

"Angry because he didn't save your mother, whom you couldn't save either? Or angry because you've been waiting in Toulouse for four or five months, and he only just has sent for you?"

Daniela, surprisingly, winked at him, but Jacqueline glared. Then she frowned and considered. "Perhaps it is both," she said with fury and almost pedantically exact pronunciation. "Perhaps it is both vanity and pain. But it hurts."

"I've had such a sore relationship with my own father, I can sympathize. But I must say, yours sounds more interesting than mine."

"Interesting! Who wants an interesting father?" Jacqueline snorted. She shook back her hair. "Of course I will go."

He hoped it would be a long and slow journey. Daniela and she sat embraced while his body imagined the impress of hers, his hands clenched on his knees. He must ask the wine merchant if he could return here with his paints, which had been produced for him as he had requested, from some hidden local supply. In all respects but one, he was well taken care of. In middle air the swallows turned and twisted and shot themselves like arrows across the gathering clouds: as fast as she was, as fierce in their concentration, as difficult to attract.

A Few Words in the Mother Tongue

In September, Naomi entered Central High, mixed racially as her grade school had been and with a reputation for being rough. She saw the first day that there were local styles. The tough girls had a shuffle. They slouched along swinging their hips and hardly lifting their feet off the floor. Naomi could do that. They wore dark or blood red lipstick, bobby socks, saddle shoes, sloppy jo sweaters, and the ones who went out with servicemen boasted of it. They picked the soldiers and sailors up in bus and train stations, but had to watch out for the policewomen who were on guard to arrest the girls on morals charges.

Alvin was in her algebra class. They were both taking college prep: Latin 1, Algebra 1, English 1, Social Studies 1, Biology 1, boys or girls gym, first aid for her and a military prep course for him. In Algebra the desks were set up in doubles, and Alvin sat right down next to her, glaring around daring anybody to speak. Two Polish girls from their graduating class started passing notes calling her Mrs. Sobolov, but it was nothing to the rest of the class, who didn't know them yet.

Naomi looked sideways at Alvin, trying to figure out why he had picked her. It was extremely bold. Boys never came right out in public and indicated an interest in a girl, except to tease or mock. She did not know if she wanted to be claimed, but Alvin was a big boy, even taller than she was growing to be, and broad-shouldered. His hands and feet no longer seemed to belong to somebody else. She remembered Aunt Rose saying about Alvin, when he had started hanging around that summer, "You can tell how big a puppy will be when you look at the size of his paws. This one, he'll be a shtarker, a moose like Leib."

Suppose the Germans did come and they were running away. Alvin was big enough to hit somebody. She imagined them hiding together. The landscape was France. She had never seen the countryside here. She did not know if there were mountains. The papers talked about harvests and labor shortages on the farms, so she had to believe there were real farms, although as far as she could tell, Detroit stretched horizon to horizon.

What she treasured about Alvin was that he didn't like fighting. He fought when he had to, for no guy could get through school otherwise, but he didn't seek it out. She decided that if Alvin could be so forward, so could she, so in Latin, she sat with Clotilde in the double seat, where they could whisper and pass notes in French.

Not only did he sit with her in Algebra, but far more blatantly, he waited for her after school to go home on the bus. They did not get off together because he lived three blocks farther, and he had to get home too. So Alvin stood with her on the bus, and then Sandy caught up with her as she got off, and they walked home together. Sandy called Alvin, your boyfriend.

Naomi tried fantasizing about Alvin in those nightly secret stories she made up to try to stave off the images that came to her from her twin. She had the habit now of lying in bed for an hour or more making up exciting stories about Leib and herself. They were spies together, they were partisans, they were underground. She experimented with replacing Leib with Alvin, but Alvin did not arouse in her any of the scary intense guilty out-of-control feelings that Leib did. Alvin was hers because they had helped the colored man Mr. Bates together, and because they both felt neglected and abandoned. He was comfortable as the cat who waited on her bed for her.

Alvin's father was in Sicily, which made for a neat explanation if you didn't know he wouldn't be home anyhow. He had left Alvin's mother and they had been arguing about a divorce when Mr. Sobolov's reserve unit was called up. They had married when they were seventeen and eighteen, respectively, and Mrs. Sobolov had not finished high school. She looked in her twenties and acted even younger, constantly dating soldiers on leave, while Alvin stayed home listening to the radio, doing his homework and the dishes and feeling sorry for himself, or out with the gang.

Four Eyes had named their gang several times, but none of the names stuck. People would respect them more if they had a name, Four Eyes said. Four Eyes tried out The Dukes of Second. Then because of the Purple Gang, criminals who were mostly Jews, he called them the Orange Gang. He picked orange because black and red and yellow and green all seemed taken, pink and white had their problems, and blue lacked zing. But when the Polish gang nearby started calling them the Lemons, he dropped that name fast.

Petty shoplifting was a group activity. They would go in together and Alvin and Four Eyes would attract attention by being their loud selves, while Sandy or

Naomi would swipe what was wanted, potato chips or candy bars or flashlight batteries, but often there wasn't much in the stores. Sometimes they swiped a movie magazine or a comic book. Naomi never let herself be frightened. It was as if her hands belonged to somebody else. Once in Woolworth's, Sandy got caught but cried her way out of trouble.

All the older kids in high school had jobs, and many of them fell asleep in class and in study hall. There was a sense in the air that everybody ought to be making money, a kind of itch they felt. The streets of Detroit were crowded day and night with servicemen mingling with men and women out of the factories, lines in front of anyplace a person could get food or a drink or dance or bowl or see a movie or hear music.

Naomi still liked to go visit Trudi on her own, as well as on Sunday with Ruthie. Naomi enjoyed feeling like a lady visiting her friend Trudi with baby David. Leib's grandfather had been David, but Naomi thought of Duvey and his nickels, the coffee she had made for him. When she thought of the times he had stuck his tongue in her mouth, she shrugged. Alvin kissed her like that every time he had a chance. She did not like it any better than she had, but it was his right, as her boyfriend, so she did not object. She felt that Ruthie had made too much fuss about Duvey putting his tongue in her mouth. She had been a baby to get scared. She was an adult, tough, able to take care of herself. She did not see much difference between David and the babies who filled their house, but she imitated Ruthie and crowed over him. She learned she had to do that before Trudi would talk about real things, what Leib had written, what scandalous things Mrs. Sobolov had been seen doing, about Alvin, about houses and how they should be fixed up.

Trudi regularly withdrew books from the library with house plans and sketches to pore over, constantly altering the ideal house she was building in her head. Naomi loved playing that game with Trudi. The house was as important to her as it was to Trudi, but not as a real house in the future. It was an absorbing game that kept bad dreams away. Ruthie was not interested in houses and tended to make practical objections, raising issues of cost and financing, which made her a killjoy. Trudi's mother saw no reason why Leib and Trudi should not continue living in Trudi's old room after the war. Only Naomi wanted to play house plans with Trudi. Often she forgot that Trudi was years older than her and a mother besides.

Sandy talked about clothes the way Trudi talked about houses. Sandy could draw pretty girls comic book style, like the paper dolls they had both played with till recently, putting on and taking off elaborate costumes. Sandy still had a Deanna Durbin paper doll. Now Sandy preferred to draw two cartoon ladies, one labeled Sandy with blond hair and one labeled Naomi with curly brown hair, and dress them in imagined outfits. She drew Naomi to resemble Ritzi in the Sunday papers.

Naomi found clothes less interesting than houses, but she did not allow Sandy to know that. She did not imagine putting on and taking off elaborate garments when she was trying to stave off those bad dreams of the bleak nasty place far away, as she sometimes imagined herself moving through one of Trudi's elegant and comfortable houses. Houses felt more protective than fancy dresses. If she was always having to pretend to be interested in things she was not, and keeping to herself things she wanted to say, it was because she was in someone else's country and someone else's house.

Sandy still shared her daydreams about boys with Naomi, who could tell that Sandy had none of the murky feelings she suffered, the fear, the dark fascination of Leib, the fevered imaginings. It occurred to Naomi that unlike Ruthie she was probably going to be a bad woman. Perhaps she would be a jewel thief or a bank robber. She would die in a swarm of police bullets, like Alan Ladd in *This Gun for Hire.*

One Wednesday when she got home from high school, early because the overcrowded school was in double sessions and she was home by one-thirty, Aunt Rose met her at the door waving a thin blue letter. "It's from your sister, I think, but she wrote it in French."

Naomi experienced a moment of fury at her aunt for having opened her letter. How could Aunt Rose do that to her, open the only letter she had received since the day after Pearl Harbor from anyone in her family! She looked swiftly at the end, but she could tell from the handwriting that it was from Jacqueline, not from Maman or Rivka.

At first she could not read the letter, could not read the French, and she felt a sharp panic. She was no longer French. Soon she would no longer speak or read French, and she would belong noplace and to nobody, ever. She ran to her room and slammed the door, leaving Rose and Sharon staring after her. She turned and opened the door a second time and slammed it again, so they would know she meant it.

Ma chère petite soeur Naomi, the letter began, which was a surprise in itself, as Jacqueline had always, always insisted on using their French and not their Jewish names. The handwriting was extremely tiny, as if Jacqueline, who had always had a delicate handwriting, now could inscribe letters on the head of a pin. Jacqueline said she thought of her sister often and missed her and wondered how she was doing far away in America where none of them had ever gone before. They were all so scattered, their whole family, sometimes she felt frightened that they would never be together again. She did not think she had been much good before at being a big sister, but she loved Naomi dearly and missed her constantly and wanted to do better if she were ever given the chance. Maman and Rivka had been captured and deported to the east. Papa was a hero, and she, Jacqueline, was not doing a bad job either. She could not write more, but Naomi could know that they loved her. She had not seen Papa, but she had had news of him very recently. She had hoped to see him long before this, but she supposed it was perhaps too dangerous for him.

Dangerous? Naomi flattened the tissue paper letter on the bed and tried to understand these phrases. Papa a hero. Jacqueline not doing a bad job either. Too dangerous. Maman and Rivka deported. She realized she was thinking in French again. Deported meant that her bad dreams were true. She felt a rush of bad smells and loud noises, the constant fear and hunger, the cold that gnawed the bones covered by scabby skin. The place she saw did not come from her subconscious, as Ruthie said about bad dreams, but was a place that existed there in the east, where the black smoke rose as if from a volcano and hung greasy and potent in the air.

The letter continued, I am in the south but not the south you and Rivka used to love so much. I hope that your aunt and uncle and their family are good to you. At least you will continue, whatever happens, and you will carry on our family and remember all of us. I love you and I mean to bring you home as soon as France is free again. Many Jewish children here have to be hidden in Christian homes to save their lives. They too cannot see their families, even though they are still in France.

My dear, if you feel lonely there, you must tell yourself that even if Papa had not been smart enough to send you to safety, we could not be together here. You would have to be sent to Switzerland or Spain or hidden in France, with a Christian family probably, and you would have to act Christian to survive, go to Mass, say their prayers, pretend constantly. Where you are, you are free to be a Jew and you should be proud. Know you are loved and that if we all survive, we will be together. Someday soon the war will be won and our people will come from the shadows. Someone will mail this from a safe place. Je t'embrasse bien fort, ta soeur Jacqueline.

She read the letter and read it again and read it again and again. She understood some of it, and some sounded strange. She had trouble believing her irritable snotty sister had written to her like that, so loving and saying she was free to be a Jew and should be proud. She wondered briefly if Jacqueline had really written it. Perhaps Jacqueline too had bad dreams and saw the place where the dead walked, the skeletons in striped rags with the eyes as big as moons and the bones all knobbly.

Then she lay down on the bed and cried into her pillow until she could no longer breathe through her nose and until her eyes were raw with salt, the lids swollen, clutching Boston Blackie like a pillow. Then she sat up and read the letter again, pausing over every sentence to try to understand. What was the danger? That both Papa and Jacqueline would be caught and sent to the place of cold and pain and unending hunger and fear?

Almost she wished the letter had not come. The letter said she was not sent away because she was unloved, she was not sent into exile, but saved. That she was special. That she alone was protected. Perhaps she did not feel that way because she was bad.

What she understood was that they were all separated, not only her, and that they might never come together again. Maman and Rivka must be sent as far to the east as she was sent to the west. In the middle somewhere were Jacqueline and Papa, but even they were separated, unable to find each other. Her loneliness was not unique but shared among her family. Only Rivka and Maman were together, in the place of death.

She stayed in her room until Aunt Rose came to knock on her door, quite politely, and ask her to come to supper. She started to follow her aunt, then turned and, folding the letter carefully, tucked it into the pocket of her corduroy skirt. As she sat down at the table, it made a little noise, as if it whispered to her.

Everyone was waiting to hear what the letter said. They ate quickly, and then Uncle Morris and Aunt Rose sat there, elbows on the table and hands cradled over their coffee cups, waiting. Reluctantly Naomi brought out the letter and smoothed it on the table. She was passionately glad it was in French, so that no one but she could read it word by word. She would simply tell them some of what it said and keep the rest to herself.

"My sister Jacqueline says that she is in the south of France but not in the part of Provence where we used to go for vacations. She doesn't say where she is. She says that my mother and Rivka have been deported."

Aunt Rose cried out sharply and Uncle Morris groaned. Then he said, "But we really don't know conditions in all the camps, if they're similar, what's going on. It's all rumors and counterrumors." He looked grim.

Naomi said nothing. She knew the conditions from her dreams.

Morris raised his head. "Well, does she say how she has managed not to be deported yet? Is she hiding?"

"She doesn't say. She says that Papa is a hero and he is in danger. She says that she is not doing a bad job either. I don't know what she means."

"Let me see the letter."

Slowly Naomi unclenched her hand and let Morris take the thin sheet.

"Ach. It's French. I forgot." He handed it back. "Translate for me, exactly."

Reluctantly Naomi did, taking the letter back and smoothing it over and over, to erase the touch of anyone else.

Morris rubbed his bald spot. "It has to be the Resistance she's talking about. They must both be underground. That's how she could get the letter out. It was mailed in London, but obviously she's still in France. She's in touch with some network outside of France."

"Poor girl," Aunt Rose murmured, "separated from her family and alone, in danger. What will become of her? Her father has a duty to find her."

Morris shrugged. "In wartime, the primary duty is to fight."

"Nu, so you'd go and leave us to fend for ourselves, in trouble?"

"I'm an old man. Nobody's handing me a gun and saying, Kill Nazis. But there is something we can do."

"We can take care of their daughter," Aunt Rose said, "the way we're doing."

"The Joint is raising money. They take it as a loan. You give them money now, and after the war, they give it back. Why not? We can't buy anything with our savings. Maybe the money will find its way to help."

"Morris, are we Rothschilds to be giving money away? Are we so rich?"

"For the first time in our lives, we're doing okay. What's the use handing it over to the banks? Jews give to everybody's charities. I see you give silver to the nuns when they come around. Who gives to the Joint but Jews? And now, it's more important than ever." When he said that, he glanced toward Naomi, and Aunt Rose gave him a quick frown of warning. Something he wasn't to say.

Naomi was thinking about killing Nazis with a gun. That's what Morris meant that Papa did, and that was why he was in danger. Uncle Morris knew that was what the letter meant. She remembered Papa in his uniform going off to the army, looking handsome and serious. He could protect himself. He would survive. He would come and find Naomi, just as she had dreamed at first, riding his motorbike but in uniform. Even if she was not a good girl, he would not mind, but be glad anyhow because he had been shooting and killing and would not be so fussy about what she had been doing.

Maybe they would stay in Detroit, and Ruthie would live with them. Maybe they would go to Paris. Jacqueline would apologize for calling her Nadine all those years. Then there would be a loud ringing at the door, and Maman and Rivka, thin and pale, would stand there and Maman would say, I forgot my keys but here I am home and hungry.

Several times in the next few days she caught her aunt and uncle talking about the camps. When she entered the room, they changed the subject right away, so she took to being very quiet and waiting outside. Uncle Morris said that she would find out anyhow, because he was always bringing home pamphlets and Jewish newspapers. Aunt Rose said that most of the newspapers were in Yiddish. Uncle Morris said there was plenty in English around the house by now. That made Naomi smile, although the smile hurt as if her face were tearing, because both Rivka and she could read a little Yiddish. Papa had taught them the Hebrew alphabet years ago, and Maman used to get a Yiddish weekly. She could make out what the papers said, the gist of it, and sometimes there were photographs that had been smuggled out of German-occupied countries, of bodies machine-gunned in a ditch or Jews being pushed into freight cars. She was at once angry with her uncle and her aunt for thinking she did not know as much as they did about the camps, and grateful, for unlike G-d, at least they tried to keep the pain from her. At least they tried.

RUTHIE 6

What Is Given and What Is Taken Away

It was a fall of crisp nearly clear days and days of scudding granite grey clouds. The first frost had just ended the tomato canning when Arty was drafted. It happened almost too fast for them to register what was happening. Then the Army had taken him and he was gone, looking as ill at ease in his uniform as Murray had a year and a half before.

Ruthie had always had a sparring relationship with Duvey and a more workable one with Arty. Arty had been the good boy, not ambitious, not overly bright but diligent. He had married so young she could scarcely remember his days of dating. He seemed to have gone directly from boyish pastimes of baseball and street hockey to a man's responsibilities of marriage and family, while Duvey had remained the perennial adolescent. Arty never left home, only moving upstairs, and scarcely a day had passed in her life without seeing him.

Sharon lay in bed the day after he left and would not get up, although her own children were crying and Rose was distraught and overwhelmed. When Ruthie got home from the factory at eleven-thirty, Rose was waiting up to complain about Sharon.

Ruthie privately thought they should let Sharon collapse for a few days after which she would surely get up on her own. The volume of work, however, was more than Rose could handle. More importantly, she was furious with Sharon for taking to her bed over Arty's being drafted, when Rose had not left Sharon to manage alone when Duvey had been killed. Morris refused to get involved, insisting it was a matter for the women to settle. Rose said she couldn't manage one more day, and if Sharon didn't get up tomorrow, she would have to keep Naomi home from school to help her.

"But, Mama, I can't march upstairs now and talk to her. It's midnight."

"*She's* not sleeping. Besides, who needs to sleep twenty-four hours a day?

That's not a woman, that's a piece of furniture, a chair, a stuffed owl. Who needs a stuffed owl for a daughter-in-law? Oy, oy, my man is gone, so I'm going to bed like a princess?" Rose grabbed her by the elbow and took her into the bedroom where Morris softly snored. "Listen," she whispered, poking Ruthie in the ribs.

Through the ceiling came the sound of a radio. Glenn Miller's "In the Mood." Sharon wanted to deny reality. Ruthie could understand. She could imagine, as she climbed the steps reluctantly, pausing on the landing to make sour faces, that it would be heaven itself to go to bed and sleep for a week, a month, to snooze the war away. Maybe instead of routing Sharon out as she had been instructed, she would climb in beside her and give up at last: relinquish her ambitions, her hopes, her insane and exhausting schedule attending school, starting early for one full workday, and then going to the factory and working another full shift.

Still she could not let Rose keep Naomi out of school. Naomi was doing all right, but the language barrier remained. She might never be the student in English she could be in French. Naomi needed more schooling, not less. Ruthie could not let her be sacrificed to Sharon's indulgent grief.

Long ago Morris had put a stout lock on the outer door, so that the upstairs and downstairs apartments need not be locked from the stairwell. She followed the sound of Jimmy Dorsey's band to the master bedroom over her parents. Sharon was propped up in bed with her high school yearbooks, wedding photographs, summer snapshots and dance programs spread around her. Her face was red and swollen as if she had toothache. Wadded up handkerchiefs had been tossed into corners. "This is your make-believe ballroom bringing you cheek to cheek music to dance to, to dream by, to bring back stardust memories. . . ."

"Sharon!" Ruthie cleared her throat, sitting on the bench of Sharon's vanity. "Mama's very upset. She can't handle the nursery without you. It's too much work for her."

"How could they take him? A father doing essential war work? It's not right. It's not fair. There's thousands of useless no-good men they could have taken. I could send them a list of twenty right in this neighborhood nobody would miss and a lot of women would thank them from the bottoms of their hearts."

I'm too weary for this, Ruthie thought, words have left me. What went through her mind sitting there was that Sharon had a lot of room to herself and that it would be nice to have a vanity, if she ever got dressed up again. "Sharon, I can tell you from my own experience, it's better to keep busy, or you just can't stand it."

"You're talking about some boyfriend. Maybe you'll marry him and maybe you won't. It's not the same thing, not one tenth the same thing!" Sharon sat up, clutching their formal wedding picture in its leather frame to her breasts.

"Think of Trudi, who had Leib go away two days after they were married, and he's not even home to see his baby. Come on. You helped get Mama into this. And you're going to need the money."

Sharon put down the photo. "The Army pays less a month than he was making every week! What am I going to do? How can I live on an allotment?"

"You won't make it at all if you don't get out of bed and help Mama. I'm telling you, she can't manage. She'll have to find another woman from the neighborhood to work with her and split the money. She'll have to find someone right away."

Sharon snapped off the radio. She pulled her mouth out thin. "All right. I hear you. But it isn't fair!"

Ruthie lay in bed, her joints aching as if she had fallen from a height. Long after she had come home, she could still feel the vibration of the line resonating through her. We do what we can, each of us, she said to the ceiling and to the distant and increasingly unreal Murray, we do what we can.

Maybe she was as unreal to Murray as he had become to her. Maybe he had stopped loving her. He did not have to marry her. Maybe he would not view her getting her college degree as contributing to their common future, but would be resentful of a woman who had acquired the education to which they both aspired. Maybe he would want a younger or more glamorous woman. What would become of her? She would have thrown away her virginity and would remain alone. One of her professors at Wayne had lectured the women in his course that they were a lost generation, doomed to spinsterhood. He had orated over them in a mixture of pity and scorn as they sat taking notes.

Two fat tears slid from the corners of her eyes. Then she saw herself as silly as Sharon, clutching old dance programs. If Murray did not want her, she would still have her degree. She would be a professional. She would move into a little apartment of her own and she would take Naomi, yes, and she would save for Naomi to go to college at Wayne too. If Murray no longer wanted her, she would have her own life. She would not be robbed of her ability to support herself, to do good work in the world, justly, compassionately. If she lived just with Naomi, she could sleep late on weekends. She could sleep as late as she pleased.

The alarm was ringing beside the bed like a buzz saw biting into her head before she knew she had been asleep, and then it was time to rush again, again to rush and rush and rush.

Sundays she liked to go for an hour with Morris to the garden as a break from studying and because except for a hurried breakfast, she scarcely saw him Monday through Saturday. The victory gardens for their block were in vacant lots where three houses owned by the same brothers had been burned for insurance during the Depression. The steps for each house were still in place but the foundations had been filled in years before. One of the lots was an outdoor skating rink, a built-up rim of earth flooded every November when the weather turned cold enough to freeze hard. The other two were divided into many small vegetable plots.

Morris wanted to dig the carrots, the beets, the rutabagas, the parsnips. The week before, November had opened with the first snow, although it had melted by ten o'clock. Still it was a sign that winter was coming soon. She helped him and for a reward they got to talk.

"We know something about the deportations to the camps, how many Jews die there. I don't think Aunt Chava or Naomi's sister are still alive. If the rest of her family is in the Resistance, she's likely to be an orphan. I think, Ruthele, we have her for life and we better face that."

"I'm sorry for her family, but I'm more than willing to keep Naomi."

"Yeah, we'll keep her, don't worry. She's a good girl. We lost Duvey, we got her. Somewhere in G-d's mind, does it balance? I don't see how, but never mind." Morris sighed.

"You miss Arty, don't you?" In his letters, Arty sounded unhappy. Most of the draftees were kids. He longed for his family. The food upset his stomach.

"We did the same kind of work, on the line. We're in different locals of the same union. I never had that with Duvey, just to be able to talk about what happens. Arty and I talked the same language."

She wanted to say that she too worked on the line. "I always had trouble talking to Duvey too."

"I wish they hadn't taken Arty. I don't think they should take fathers." Morris shook his head. "War goes on long enough, they'll start on old guys like me. Hand us a gun and point us at the enemy."

"Tata, you sound so discouraged, you scare me."

"I need something to hope on." He leaned on his spade. "The world is more evil than I gave it credit for when I was a young man. I thought, all we need is to get more civilized. But Germany's a cultured country, as cultured as any. I find myself thinking about the darkness in people, and I wonder how any good happens."

"Tata, whatever the world is like, you're a good man. You try to be just. I try to be like you."

"Like me." He rubbed his bald spot. "*Arty* is like me, he won't make much of a soldier. They should have left him home. It isn't right for them to take one son and then put the last one in danger."

A son, a son. As if she did not count. It was time for her to go back to her schoolwork. Morris would putter in the garden for hours. He talked about getting a little place in the country when he retired, where he could raise cabbages and tomatoes. Ruthie didn't believe him, because he had his organizations. Since the letter had come on thin paper for Naomi, he was even more insistent that American Jews must lobby the Roosevelt administration into saving European Jews. They must make the administration let in more than the tiny legal trickle which the State Department as a policy attempted to stop at the source in Europe. They must push for bombing of the railroads leading to the camps and bombing of the camps themselves. The Allies must denounce the killing of Jews. Now Morris had three meetings every week.

Thanksgiving came dismally. Tarawa was taken in the Pacific. Arty was still in Louisiana training. Heavy fighting, town by town, house by house, went on in Italy. An old atlas lay permanently on the kitchen counter so they could look up the places in the news. All week a freezing rain fell, sleet, wet snow changing back to sleet. Ice formed on the trees and branches cracked. First Sharon got a cold and then Rose, then Naomi, then Ruthie and Morris. It brought a middling fever and a sore throat.

Ruthie was in bed with a fever of 101.4 and a splitting headache when Trudi appeared with a telegram. Leib had been wounded in action at someplace called Monte Pantano. He was in the hospital in Naples, but he would be coming home. Trudi was weeping. She did not know whether to celebrate or mourn. "They don't say if he'll live, if he's okay, if he's half dead. What's the use of this? They don't even say when he's coming. How can I live, not knowing?"

Ruthie croaked, "Be glad he's alive. He's hurt enough to get out of the war, so be glad. He's alive and coming home."

Would she receive such a telegram? No, if it happened, his parents would hear. Did she wish for a wound that would save his life? Who wouldn't wish for it? But what price would she pay for his life: a leg, an arm, paralysis? She could not sweet-talk Trudi into calm. Trudi had plenty to fear.

She slept and dreamed that all that came home of Murray was a head in a cage, a talking head that watched her with sad eyes as she rushed to and fro in the house. She woke sweating. Her fever was breaking. If she was not too weak, if she could crawl out of bed, in the morning she must return to school and to the factory.

Toward a True Appreciation
of Chinese Food

In the drab middle of sleety January, Louise flew out to the West Coast on assignment. This time there would be no gossipy vacation in Claude's little expatriate world, and she found herself depressed and resentful of the interminable delays, bumped off planes in Chicago, again in Kansas City to spend the night huddled in drafty waiting rooms hungry, cold, exhausted and fending off attentions of bored and overfed businessmen who seemed to be doing very well indeed out of the war. Taking three days to get across the country was nothing to complain at length about; nonetheless she felt dirty, messy, with a sore stomach and tired eyes.

Lonesome and impinged upon at once, it was not any of her fellow travelers for whose company she longed, but she attempted to keep up a facade of conviviality. Finally she pretended to suffer a bad cold and was left alone to her reading. She had T. S. Eliot's *Four Quartets*. The ideas seemed to her willfully medieval but the music of the lines sang in her ears. She was also reading the former drama critic of the *Partisan Review*, who had come out with a book that was somewhere between short stories and novel, *The Company She Keeps*. The author, Mary McCarthy, wrote with a matter-of-factness about sex in ways that intrigued and fascinated Louise as a new level of discourse about women's lives.

Huddled in her mink in the Kansas City airport, she had a vision of women writing about sex as openly as male writers, but quite, quite differently. Some women would treat sex much as men did, as conquest, as adventure—in a way as McCarthy had. Other women would treat female sexuality far less romantically than men who did not consider themselves romantics, like Hemingway, were wont to. The earth would not move, no, there would be more biology and less theatrics. Women had less ego involvement in sex than men did, but far more at stake economically.

She had a brief fantasy of writing about her own childhood, honestly, of writing about anti-Semitism and sexual abuse in foster families, but she grimaced, lowering her head to her book. It would not be permitted. It would be seen as too depressing. As a woman there were still far more things that could not be said than could be said; if they were said, they could not be heard. Madness lay that way. Forget it.

She finally arrived at Portland, where she was taken to the Bentley, an extremely civilized hotel that still kept up a passable grade of service in spite of the war. She had a bath, a good supper and a night's sleep followed by an ample breakfast and a second bath. Then she was picked up and taken to Vanport.

Vanport was the largest of the instant cities that had been put up overnight, four miles west of Portland. A car from the Kaiser shipyards drove her, while she scanned the press release. Nothing could have prepared her for the utter bleakness. Thirty-five thousand people were living in mud, out of which rose identical pale one-story wooden houses up on concrete blocks which were sinking or sunken in the primordial ooze. The Portland Housing Authority had thrown up the houses the year before, making this Oregon's second biggest city. Thrown up seemed the right word.

Vanport even had its own suburb, East Vanport, which stood on a swamp formerly a shabby golf course on a peninsula sticking into the Columbia River. That was perhaps the saving grace: the river was vast and handsome. The other saving grace was the rent: $7 a week for a studio and $11.55 for four rooms. Plenty of shack stores sold whatever the merchants could lay hands on to sell.

In the hospital she saw badly burned children. Many of the renters were not used to electric heat and electric stoves. They had had wood stoves all their lives, and they never thought to turn heaters or stoves off. Fires broke out in the little wooden houses that went up in minutes. Yet the inhabitants were cheerful. Most were earning what they called top dollar, with everybody in the family bringing home money, and they all had plans to live differently after the war. They were hardworking, likable people with heady ideas about what they would buy and what they would own and where they would live. Something began to strike Louise as she conducted her interviews, an observation that would never enter her articles. She had interviewed enough refugees to know what they thought they were fighting for: they were defeating Fascism or liberating their homeland or fighting for their own freedom to be whatever they were that had become illegal or dangerous, Jews or Masons or Communists or Socialists or Seventh-Day Adventists, avant-garde painters, surrealist writers. Or they were simply fighting like the Russians for survival, because the Germans planned to annihilate them.

But Americans were fighting for a higher standard of living. They were fighting their way out of the Depression. They were fighting for the goods they saw in advertisements and in movies about how the middle class lived. What these people saw in their future was not a new brotherhood of man (and certainly not of woman), but the wife back at home, a new car in the new garage of the new house in the new tract with grass this time. They saw themselves moving into an advertisement full of objects they had coveted, but never owned and seldom even touched. They were fighting for what they had not had before the war, a want list of specific objects with plenty of room to add more.

On the way back, she stopped in Detroit to visit another instant town, Willow Run. Snow was coming down hard, falling on the uncollected trash and rutted mud. It was even more dismal and undergoing a hushed-up typhoid epidemic, because of poor sewage facilities. Out in Washtenaw County, the workers who had poured in for the Ford Willow Run bomber facility were facing hostility from the farmers and townspeople around them, who viewed them as an army of occupation. The school was overcrowded and desperately understaffed. The women who did not work were going stir-crazy in their trailers or tiny huts. It was not instant city that had been created at Willow Run, but more obviously and strongly than at Vanport, instant slum. That she was going to say, as strongly as she knew how. These people had come to do a job and were being treated like cattle. She had seen German prisoners of war in the South better housed than these families.

They had fires here too, but a woman was being carted off bleeding copiously from between her legs because of a badly done or self-inflicted abortion. Remembering Kay, Louise wrung her hands unconsciously as she watched the woman carried on a stretcher along the street as the ambulance bearers talked about her as if she were a criminal, while her little children ran after them and the neighbors watched.

She decided since she was stuck in Detroit with a snowstorm delaying flying that she would call on the WASPs she had written about. Perhaps she could extract a follow-up piece from this visit.

She found Bernice and her sidekick Flo jubilant, for they had just received notice they were being transferred to another base, where they would be delivering not trainers but fighters, the top line of the best planes being produced. They would be among the first women ever to fly fighters; in fact, they would be the first pilots after the test pilots, and they had heard that an increasing number of women were being used for testing new as well as repaired planes. They were celebrating with gusto and some local moonshine, and they invited her to join them. The photos from the article she had written about them were on the barracks wall.

The raw whiskey shocked her mouth, but she drank it anyhow, trying to quiet voices in her head that warned of blindness from treated alcohol. Imagine putting poison in alcohol just so people couldn't use it to get drunk: the society that did that had a screw loose. Helen had a phonograph in the barracks—the daughter of the Republican newspaper publisher from Nebraska, was it?—that was playing Tommy Dorsey and the Andrews Sisters. Flo was trying to show Bernice how to do the lindy, but Bernice obviously did not want to learn. Finally Louise got up and danced with Flo. She used to dance at rent parties and fundraisers. Oscar had been a good dancer. Perhaps he still was. Claude waltzed and fox-trotted well, but could not lindy. Idly she wondered if anybody had ever taught Daniel how to dance.

She was a big hit. When she finally plunked down out of breath, she felt sober again and hastened to drink more of the white lightning, as they called it. Her feet were sore from the splintery boards of the barracks—she had kicked off her shoes long before—and her blouse was damp with sweat, but she had enjoyed doing something physical. She never seemed to lately.

Watching the young women at play, she brooded on her daughter. This year, Kay was her own person, even if that person found someone new to imitate every six weeks. She was currently in love with her French professor, who must be fifty and had a white beard like Santa Claus. She reported his opinions as holy writ. At Daniel she had turned up her nose. He was too young: this from an eighteen-year-old. In fact, Daniel had not put himself out to be charming to Kay, either. That tentative matchmaking had been a flop over Christmas vacation.

"He has a crush on you, Mother!" Kay had said as if reporting leprosy.

"Oh well," Louise said. "He's much too young. Don't worry about it."

"You knew!" Kay sounded shocked. She pulled on her hair, the way she had done since she was little when she was nervous or annoyed.

"Well, you do notice those things, dear. It's of no importance."

"I think it's tacky. . . . Is Daddy going to marry that girl he has? Abra the horseface?"

"I have no idea, Kay. Actually I doubt it."

"Abra—what kind of a jerkwater name is that? And why did he take her to England, if he isn't going to marry her?"

"He didn't take her, honey. The OSS sent them both. I suppose they need her too." Actually she was sure Oscar had put in to have Abra Scott transferred with him, and why not? He never let go of anyone. He could hold on to Abra till she was forty-five and never marry her and never permit her to move in with him. Louise shuddered. "I believe she explained to you that Abra is a family name."

"Why do you stick up for her? I think that's tacky too."

"Abra tried very hard with me and I appreciate the effort. She never did me harm, and she found me a nice apartment in Washington, inadvertently."

"What are you talking about?" Kay had looked aghast.

Louise realized at once that she had not told Kay the apartment had been Abra's, and that she could not. "A friend of hers knew about this."

Kay turned away. "I hate it. Why don't you move back to New York, to our home?"

Remembering that conversation in a roomful of women midway between her age and her daughter's, she doubted Kay would ever return to live with her. Kay would marry young, she suspected. She would like that not to be true, because she considered Kay far too immature and far too silly around men to choose well; but she did not imagine she would be consulted. Let go as you must, she told herself, you have no other choice.

The vaunted romance society was selling was instant passion. The great romance happened all at once; it swept a woman off her feet. A true woman couldn't resist. You hardly knew who he was but you saw the uniform and the message was, LOVE NOW. Every man in uniform was entitled. Every woman was carried away.

It ended in real life with the woman carried away all right, bleeding on a stretcher. It ended up in those squalid maternity homes she had visited where sullen and overweight sixteen-year-olds were treated like ax murderers and read appropriate passages from the Bible by squinting evil-minded men and vindictive overstarched women. It had ended for Kay more safely but painfully enough in the offices of a Park Avenue physician. Yes, and her own stories were one more way of selling that hypnotism to women, love as a drug, a cure-all, a religion.

One outstanding thing about these WASPs was that they were engaged in their own romance. The country might know little and care less, but they were heroines in *their* story, and they shone with that confidence and that energy. Here in their barracks, they did not have to play at primness. They told the raunchy jokes she usually heard from men. They laughed, they drank, they danced with each other and they seemed for the most part pleased with themselves. Louise was surprised how relaxed she felt. Bernice sat beside her. They were among the two people the least drunk in the room, although both of them had been drinking steadily all evening.

"Do you like Washington?" Bernice asked her. "I've only been there once."

"It's a younger town now. Everybody used to idle along in the southern way, two-hour lunches, gracious living, servants at your elbow. Now it's a short-tempered town in a hurry. I'll never really like it. Too much manners and power hunger, too little art and intellect."

Helen stood in front of them, her face flushed, her hair tousled. She had been dancing with Mary Lou. "If you could stay any age forever, what age would you choose?"

"Right now plus a couple of months," Bernice said. "Once we get into the cockpit of those fighters."

"Twenty-five, twenty-six, I think," Louise said.

"That's sad." Bernice looked her in the eyes. "To want to go back. I can't think of anything I want to go back to. I want to hurry on forward."

"But that's as sad in its way," Louise said defensively. "I'd not like to feel my life as I'd lived it wasn't full and rich."

Waiting in the stuffy terminal at Detroit City Airport and then on the windy field to board, and then in the plane to take off, and then looking out into grey nothingness on the long trip to Washington, she pondered that judgment. Perhaps Bernice was right, and she was ruining her own life by looking back to what had been. It could not be taken from her, but it also would never be given back.

Kay was an adult, Oscar had gone and she was alone with another thirty to forty years. She had better arrive at some way of living that did not involve telling herself lies about what was going on, as she had with Claude. She was a victim of romance, as much as those girls falling for uniforms and imagining heroes and saviors, marrying men they had known for a total of twenty hours and knew less about than they did their milkman or dentist.

Why couldn't she take Daniel seriously? He had been courting her since she moved in. He was charming, bright, helpful. That he was almost as much younger than she as Abra was younger than Oscar need not deter her any more than it had Oscar. Why couldn't she accept a sexual friendship, without needing talk of Love? She was a creature of romantic myths and expectations, those manufactured dreams. The war had given her a chance to work in the journalism she had always longed for, while revealing to her its shortcomings, but she had not escaped from the suppositions of her fiction.

She would try to make herself more pragmatic. Oscar was again too much on her mind of late. Claude had disappeared from her consciousness, except as a measure of how thoroughly she could delude herself when she so desired. If Daniel represented only a short-term solution to a problem that would always remain, that did not mean she should refuse to consider him.

Pragmatism: to appreciate a room that remained stationary, a comfortable chair, a good bowl of soup, a hot bath and a clean bed. To appreciate, perhaps, a young man who cooked her Chinese dinner upstairs. There was something in that: some threat, an approaching danger, provoking an appreciation of small domestic joys hitherto taken for granted. Bracing herself as the plane bounced like a square ball down a long stairway of clouds, she began to imagine a short story that would chart such a transformation.

She would call it "A Bowl of Soup." Chicken soup, or was that too ethnic? A bowl of vegetable soup? Alphabet soup? Her mother used to make a potato soup she had loved, but that was ethnic too. What soup did Americans eat? Transformation stories always grabbed people. Inspiring, they would call it, and they would be right. She must change her life.

JACQUELINE 7

The Chosen

8 décembre 1943

Larousse has been caught. I thought I was hardened, but I have wept all night and I find myself unable to think of anything else. We are trying to find out where he has been taken, but he does not seem to be in any of the places we have infiltrated. So far, no news from Margot except that the Milice ambushed him, that they beat him, that he did not talk and that the Gestapo came and took him away in a van.

Seven children are waiting in Limoges, brought in on that two A.M. train we use. Of that batch of twenty, seven have been placed in homes, in friendly convents, on farms. Six were taken to Le Chambon, the Protestant village of refuge in the mountains near the Swiss border that Larousse has often talked about. But the seven remaining cannot be passed off as French and were scheduled to go out through Spain. I must take them. They are in danger where they are hidden and bring danger to everyone around them. How can you explain away seven Jewish children?

The day after tomorrow I leave to pick them up and deliver them all the way through. Lev is huffy about it. He says with my picture all over the border, it is dangerous and I have to change my appearance. I said I will grow a mustache, but he did not find that amusing. Vendôme wants to go with me, but I said he would be a bigger nuisance than any of the children.

9 décembre 1943

What a day. Lev insisted I had to go to a hairdresser near Place Capitole at dawn before she opened for business to change my appearance. She was a fast-talking lady with a cigarette pasted on her lower lip, her own hair plastered up in a ridiculously elaborate pompadour with a wilted-looking silk camellia aloft, but she was no nonsense I will admit when she looked at my hair. She said that making me a straight blond would not look natural, with my hazel eyes; she decided on what she called ash blonde and a look she said was a pageboy bob.

When I turned to the mirror, I was extremely annoyed, but then I said to myself, Larousse is probably being tortured and I am put out because this woman has made me look like a tart. Daniela says that is not true, but she is kind. I said to myself, if I had become an actress, I would have had to assume many appearances and no doubt dye my hair, so why the fuss? This is simply a role. Besides, the woman told me it would begin to grow out soon.

Lev and Vendôme stared at me when I came in to the garage, where they were amusing themselves while M. Faurier worked on the gazogène truck which lost its clutch. "She's a problem," Lev said to Vendôme, shaking his head as if I were not there and could be talked about like a faulty engine. "She's too beautiful and it calls attention. Now it's worse than before."

"Not worse," Vendôme said. "But the same. It would be the same if she wore a paper bag."

I marched over to Mme Faurier's desk. "Fine. I will solve that problem now." I took out her scissors and headed for the bathroom.

Lev caught my arm. "What do you think you're doing?"

"I'm going to give myself a useful scar."

He twisted the scissors out of my hand and threw it to Vendôme, who came scowling. "You're an idiot," Vendôme said. "Nothing makes someone easier to identify than a scar. It can't be hidden. Hair can. So can beauty. Rub dirt in your face, rub ashes in your hair, put on a dirty babushka and a filthy rag of a coat and look down and sullen."

"I will," I said, and thanked him. He actually came through with the best advice yet, and I took it at once. I am much better pleased with my appearance. I walked along rue Columbette for two blocks and no one looked at me. Vendôme is not stupid, for his mind is less conventional than Lev's and his ideas can surprise. I feel almost invisible. I should have asked Vendôme how to disguise myself before I let that hairdresser mess with me.

He was waiting in the garage tonight when I got in from my errands. "If you need to disguise yourself further, put a few wads of cotton batting up between your gums and your teeth. It will distort your face. Also, redden your nose a little. It brings it forward."

"Why are you dressed like that?"

He was wearing baggy much-mended pants, a ratty beret with oil stains, a chewed-looking scarf and a filthy and ragged shirt. He walked with a more pronounced limp than usual and leaned on a stick of the rough kind you see shepherds use. On his feet he did not wear his good boots but sabots, those wooden clogs I always wear now. He grinned. "I'm sleeping down here tonight, in the garage." There's an old divan against the far wall, and it wouldn't be the first night one of our people spent there.

"Why?"

"Why not?"

I said nothing, but I am determined to slip out in the morning silently. If he is hanging around with the intention of accompanying me, that is not going to happen.

Upstairs Daniela was sitting up in bed in her nightgown waiting for me, the candle still lit in its saucer. "If they can catch Larousse, they can catch anyone," she said, her dark eyes strained in her worried face.

"So what else is new? I have imagined so many times being caught, I cannot become more afraid or more careful."

"For you to go is reckless."

"For me not to go is selfish."

There was nothing more to say. We kissed each other good night. I am writing briefly, and now will blow out the candle.

11 décembre 1943

Before dawn I slipped down the outside staircase but he was waiting just inside the big doors of the garage and came after me. "No!" I stopped.

"Yes," he said cheerfully and took my arm. "We are to go together and then to visit your father on the way back."

"I don't like having decisions made over my head."

"We are all soldiers in the same army, taking orders," he said as if he did not plot this with Lev.

"*Why* do you want to go with me? Getting seven children across the mountains in winter, it's no fun. Not exciting men's stuff. A lot of blowing noses and pushing them along and lying up in the brush waiting for dark."

"If anything happened to you and I wasn't there, I'd blame myself for the rest of my life."

"The rest of both our lives are likely to be short and busy. I think of Larousse unceasingly, but I don't wish I'd been along when he was caught."

"While I see you, I know what's happening to you. You've never felt that way about anyone?"

Daniela, I thought at once.

We walked briskly out of town to board the local train in the outskirts, intending to get off outside Limoges and proceed by bicycle from there. That way
we can avoid the serious identity checks. We rode third class, in a carriage with a
little stove at one end and wooden seats back to back in the middle. All the seats
were taken, and the places near the stove, so we stood together at the far end.

It seems to be a custom when women of the Resistance are escorting escapees
and downed fliers, to pretend to be lovers with them, but this has never been my
habit. I believe that acting as lovers in public actually draws people's attention
and they look at you more carefully than they might otherwise. The women look
at the man to see whether they find him attractive and at the woman to judge
what he sees in her. Whereas if you act as if you are a bored and sullen couple
with little to say, nobody pays attention. That is my theory.

Therefore we talked little on the train. It stank in the compartment. When
the doors opened a cold wind blew in, but the air at least was fresh. It was fatigu-
ing standing for hours. He put his hand over mine on the bar and occasionally
supported me with his other arm. I was hungry, as I had eaten only a piece of dry
bread in the kitchen, not wanting to wake anyone, but I had a good lunch Mme
Faurier had packed for me. Shortly after eleven, when there was a long delay
because of damage to the tracks from bombing, we sat on the embankment and
ate the cheese picnicking in the snow.

"What do you dream of?" he asked. "What do you imagine if you could have
anything?"

"My mother, my sisters. Daniela and me safe. All of us together eating a big
feast at our own table. Roast chicken stuffed the way Maman used to do. The
special soup she would make of eggs without shells from inside the chicken.
Her cabbage soup with the shinbone. My own bed, my books, my old diaries,
my little treasures." I stood, shaking the snow off. "But of course none of that is
possible. Nothing shall be as it was. To tell you the truth, I didn't appreciate my
life when I had it."

"Maybe you still don't."

"Appreciate my life? Oh, I have an immense will to live. Fierce."

"Appreciate what the people around you offer you."

"I love Daniela more than you seem to think I do."

"I wasn't speaking for Daniela."

When he approaches mushiness, I always change the subject. Men seem to
feel an obligation to talk a certain amount of nonsense with a woman, although
he would not dream of boring Lev or Roger with such moonshine. "You must
dream of home too."

"I don't want to go back to the life I had. No, I see before me here the life I want." His eyes were glittering. He fits in with the crowd in the train better than I expected him to. Unlike the British agent, whom we dressed in appropriate clothes but who wore them as if they were somebody else's, Vendôme is at ease among the peasants and workers in third class. Like a woman, like the poor, he is used to being uncomfortable, to standing and waiting, to taking what he can get. I never thought Americans were like that. Yet he is a painter and went to college. He says that was free because his father was a professor, the father he feels totally estranged from. He is close only to his sister.

"Will you not tell me I remind you of her? Men always say that."

"Not at all. My sister is a big strong woman who loves to fly planes. I only wished you would adore me the way she does."

"Come, we're to get on again." The train was preparing to move. "Oh, you want to be adored? Why, I wonder? What do people get out of that fixated attention? It seems that once you had it, it would be boring."

"Of course. What I really want is a love of equals." With that he got on and left me to follow.

I will admit I was almost sorry that the conversation broke there, because it was growing interesting. I had a moment of worrying whether he was going to try to make me sleep with him, as every time men have talked about love, that is what they meant. In the presence of seven children, it should not be difficult to avoid his importuning, but afterward, it may be a problem. Still, he is more engaging to talk with than Henri was. Daniela remarked that he was interested in me that first week, to which I replied, nothing could be more boring than his interest. Daniela said, Besides, he is impossible because he is Gentile.

Henri wasn't Jewish either. Does it matter to me? I don't want to get involved with anyone that way, but he is working with us. The Nazis would treat him just like a Jew if they caught him. So that would not matter, finally, if I were interested, which I am not, not at all. He is always drawing me, which feels odd. He does not draw anybody else, but draws the cemetery, the canal, the river, the vineyards and hills. In one recent painting he has painted himself and me in a vineyard, small figures, me looking off to the mountains and him behind looking at me.

Anyhow, we reached Limoges by nightfall and I left him talking to the local Resistance and hurried off to organize my children for tomorrow morning.

16 décembre 1943

This crossing has been extremely difficult. The rivers are frozen solid, so I am crossing them lower in the mountains than usual. Also I fear trying to take one of the high routes, with the snow already deep and storms coming daily.

Vendôme has made himself useful. He is one of those people who talks to children very much as he talks to adults, and as he generally speaks gently to adults, this seems to work fine. Children sense right away when adults are putting on an act.

We have two adolescent boys, twelve and fourteen, a girl fourteen, a girl ten, a boy nine, a boy of seven and a girl of eight. This afternoon as we lay up in a thicket waiting to cross on the ice after dark, I had them play with a dreidel I have along, because Chanukah is coming and I never know how long storms may delay us. But when the eight-year-old, Raizel, was playing and she got Shin, where you lose and pay, she began to cry. Pearl, the fourteen-year-old who mothers her, immediately began soothing her, but I worry about Raizel. She is weightless as a dried leaf, colorless, of a stupefied sadness. Pearl says Raizel saw her family killed before her eyes, then was left for dead in a pile of bodies. She has a bad scar on her shoulder and another on her ribs, which are easy to count, believe me. She never plays, so I was happy when she was drawn to the dreidel. Bad luck.

We sleep in piles with the children to keep them warm, and thus far Vendôme has not given me any trouble. He is a pleasant traveling companion because he does not complain of the weather or the short rations or the cold wind, and he always notices the landscape carefully, which is important. "He is so handsome," Pearl said to me. "You must love him."

"Why must I? Why should a face be that important in anyone's life?"

"Because you're pretty, you can be fussy." Pearl touched my hair. "I want to be loved, I don't care why. I just want someone to love me and tell me to stay."

I think at fourteen she has already had an unhappy affair. War is an absolute disrupter. At fourteen she is a century older than the two boys or than I was at her age. Nobody can give her her childhood back. But she has immense will to live; if I bring them through safely, she will make it. She tags after Vendôme, who accepts her adoration tactfully. I worried when I saw her press herself against him, but he just put his arm around her and turned her to look up at a hawk circling high overhead. Up in the mountains frequently I have to go ahead to scout the way, and I must leave him alone with them. He dislikes that intensely, but I point out to him again and again, the children are the priority. We are here to save them.

He obeys me, which Lev would never do, and for that too I am grateful. I also know that whatever mandate he was given, it surely did not include shepherding Jewish children illegally into Spain. His government has been opposed to this project all along, and their State Department puts every obstacle in our way. He is doing this on his own, I know, and as it turns out, he has been useful. I never like leaving the children alone as I go forward. Still, I am often exhausted because I walk parts of the route three times, while everybody else has enough trouble tramping it once. Sometimes I lack the extra energy for carrying a large exhausted child, which is another place he steps in.

17 décembre 1943

Raizel is dead. We had to scratch out a shallow grave and lay her in it and leave her to the wild animals. When I awoke at dusk, she was not with us. She had gotten up and wandered away and lain down by herself, and she was dead. Dead of the cold? I have never lost a child before.

I find grief in myself, perhaps even something as tainted as spoiled pride that I should lose one of my children and also something just as rotten: anger. Why did she wander away? I accuse her in my heart of giving up on life and of choosing to die. Choosing to join her mother, her father, her grandfather and grandmother, her brothers and sisters and the baby, her whole village. Turning and slipping into death. Shin. I will have Gimel, everything! At least Hey, half, but I am aiming for Gimel. And Gimel I want for these children, whose world has burned.

It is getting harder and harder to pass the children through. The Germans and their accomplices are crazy, simply. If they want to win a war, you would think that would be their priority, but they care more to tie up huge numbers of men trying to keep a few children from escaping. Those children have no military importance, alive or dead. Now the ratlines which move downed fliers out, I can understand their passion to unravel those, because it takes money and time to train a pilot. None of these children represent a second's danger to the Third Reich.

The tracks we leave in winter are dangerous. We will have to return a different way and we must keep moving. They can rest only while I scout ahead and I must sleep no more until we have crossed into Spain. We can take five minutes rest on each hour and that will have to do all of us.

18 décembre 1943

The six children are safe. Jeff and I are rapidly descending the Pyrénées, making much better time. We scout carefully as we go. Now we are on the way to a rendezvous with Papa. He is in the Montagne Noire, mountains less than half the size of these but noble enough, to the east of Toulouse. It is extremely cold and this will be a very short entry as I can scarcely write. We sit by a tiny fire. When we stop, we lie in each other's arms to keep warm. There is no choice. We would freeze, apart. I thanked him for not taking advantage of the situation, and that made him laugh. "How could I?" he asked me. "I'd probably get frostbite on the part that matters."

I liked his being able to laugh about it. He asked me to call him Jeff, which is his real name, and I promised to do so when we are alone.

The first night of Chanukah 1943

We are in Arfons, in the Montagne Noire, where we are to meet Papa whenever he in fact appears. Tonight is the longest night of the year. I cannot imagine why I am extremely nervous about seeing my own father. Perhaps it is simply the length of time. Nevertheless I am nervous, perhaps because in some way I expect him to judge me. Now that the day approaches, I am glad that Jeff is with me, because it dilutes the intensity of the meeting. This is a small grey village built around a square, the same fish-scale slate roofs I see when I am crossing the Pyrénées. The local people say the Germans seldom come here, unless raiding for food.

We are put up in rooms over a restaurant. The food is plentiful anyhow, as they also traffic in the black market here. Some patriots sneer at the black marketeers, but in truth, many Resistance people are involved, because it is a sector of the economy which the Germans cannot control. Whatever food is on the black market is not available to them, who ship out of the country three quarters of what is grown here for themselves and leave us hungry, and the money made there is invisible money and can go directly to support the Resistance.

I have the back room which opens onto the fields of snowy stubble, while Jeff has one immediately next to me. Two of the waitresses have doubled up in the next room. Normally one of them lives in my room, and Jeff's room is the spare room, for guests and often now for Resistance people passing through. Both the waitresses have been making a big play for Jeff, not even bothering to ask if we are together or not. What opportunists!

They eat well here. Even though my stomach is shrunken, I find it is easy to stretch it again. We eat and eat. We help in the kitchen and make ourselves useful. The kitchen is run by a stout woman with a peppery temper and a strong right arm, and we both attempt to stay on the lee side of her.

Perhaps there are no Jews in Arfons, yet even if I were back in my old apartment on the rue du Roi de Sicile, I know there would be no proud candles proclaiming our identity tonight. The first candle unlit tonight. All across this deep dark night, I think of all the candles of lives blown out.

22 décembre 1943

I hardly know how to describe what I did last night, but I will go on being honest. I think as long as I live, I will always wonder if Maman read my diary about Henri, if that precipitated that dreadful quarrel. I only wish there were a chance of her reading this, but I am writing in code now anyhow. I would give anything to see her!

I have become lovers with the American, Jeff. It was I who made it happen; shamelessly I got up half an hour after we had gone to bed in our respective rooms and I went tiptoeing along the hall to his room. It was noisy downstairs, someone singing and the cook shouting in the kitchen and banging of pots and cutlery. Fortunately his door was unlocked and although his candle was out, when I said his name softly and ready to bolt, he sat up. I was astonished at myself as I went to him and kept thinking that I could not really be doing this, and knowing perfectly well that I have been coming to this decision for days.

He got out of bed at once. "Is something wrong?" He lit his candle and took his automatic from the bedside table.

"No. You don't need that with me," I said, beginning to laugh.

I thought that I would have to explain, after putting him off for so long, but he came right to me and began to kiss me, so I did not have to make clumsy overtures. I thought I had better say something, so I remarked, once we were undressed and in bed, "I am not a virgin, by the way."

"By the way, good."

I was startled. "I didn't think that was supposed to be good."

"Did you find your first time ecstatic?"

"Of course not. It was painful, to say the least."

"This won't be," he promised, and it wasn't. In fact I found myself forgetting how awkward I always found placement of the bodies and instead of permitting, I was wanting. That was new and more interesting. My body seemed to take on a life of its own. I begin to understand what the poetry and the moaning and fussing arise from. It was as if my body were growing from within and taking over and demanding. I actually wanted to put him inside me. He had a condom, which was convenient. After we had finished, I decided I did not care whether the whole house knew we are lovers or not, so I stayed and slept there. It was cosy and warmer. He sleeps like a kitten, curled up. Sometimes he seems very young, the way Americans are, and other times like a wizened old man who has given up on what he had wanted. But not now.

I thought it might be strained in the morning. I woke first and I got up to pee and that woke him. When I came back to bed, he sat up and held out his arms to me. Then it was as if a fist clenched and unclenched in my belly, my womb perhaps, as in the Bible it says her womb moved? Anyhow, I wanted to also and we made love again. Then I went down and brewed us café au lait and found some bread in the kitchen and butter and strawberry jam made without sugar, because nobody has any, but it is still good.

I brought it all up on a tray and crawled into bed with him and we talked and talked. We are telling each other our lives. His hands are like a woman's hands, not like a man's. I mean they feel what they touch. They don't grab but caress. He says he has eyes in his fingers. He lost his mother at twelve. There is sadness in him at the core, sweetness and then sadness. I cannot believe I have done this, but I have chosen him.

On the other hand, maybe I just want to dilute things more. Maybe I want another man who has a claim on me standing there when I see Papa. I always view myself with a somewhat jaundiced eye, ever since the quarrel that sent me from Maman's house. I also think that losing Larousse makes me more needy. Whatever my motives, I chose wisely. It is not sex that gives the pleasure, but the lover, if he knows how—at least that is my conclusion.

The oddest thing is that from that first moment I experienced orgasm with Jeff, I thought to myself, oh, this, yes, and it felt terribly familiar. It felt at once strong and completely familiar, although with Henri I never had anything of the sort, as if the body knew all along.

I told him I do not love him, but I like him strongly and I chose him. He says he also chose me. He says women have been telling him since he was fifteen that they love him, and he has never been quite sure what they meant except that they usually wanted him to set up housekeeping with them. He says that he wants us to be together and I should not tell him anything I don't mean. I liked that. I told him the same.

24 décembre 1943

They all went out to midnight Mass, but we stayed in the kitchen by the fire. The door opened and first a boy with a Sten gun came in. He was about sixteen and big as a polar bear standing on its hind legs and just as shaggy. Jeff said, "I recognize that gun. That's one of the load I brought in, isn't it? Don't wave it about, you'll scare the mice."

"Lapin is here," the enormous boy announced, after he had searched the house. That's what they call Papa, because he has escaped the Germans so many times. Then the boy/bear whistled and Papa came in.

He has a beard, dark curly blond. He looked the same and different. He had a German rifle on his back which he leaned against his chair and came to peer at me and then hug me. He felt very cold and bumpy, his jacket on, with an ammunition belt and a canteen and all kinds of hardware clanking and sticking into me.

"You've grown like a weed, you're almost as tall as I am! You've grown up, Jacqueline."

"Rivka is tall too," I said. "I saw her when they were marching into the cattle cars to be deported to the camps."

He sat down abruptly. "Your mother?"

"Her also."

"At least they didn't get you."

"Not yet."

"When were they deported?"

"Last year at this time."

He rubbed his chin and said nothing for a while. Jeff was standing by the fireplace looking ill at ease so I decided to make matters worse and introduce them. "Papa, this is Vendôme—"

"The American commandant." Papa leaped out of the chair to shake hands with Jeff. "We are overjoyed to have you with us, but we need more arms. We need them desperately. They must drop mortars. We have nothing heavier than a machine gun, and only seven of those. We have nothing to use against armor."

"I can only pass messages on. I have no authority to command weapons for you, or believe me, I would. It's dangerous for you to be so lightly armed, I understand. But back in London, they don't understand."

"Vendôme just helped me take a group of children to Spain, Papa—"

"In this weather?"

"One of our best people was caught, and the children could not stay where they were. They endangered everyone. I have been taking children over the Pyrénées for months." I suppose I was sounding rather stilted, but I was boiling inside. "Vendôme is also my lover."

That dropped like a bomb that falls and does not go off and you wait to see is it on a time delay, so that if you raise your head it will kill you. I believe both Jeff and Papa were far more embarrassed than I was. Jeff startled babbling, "She really shouldn't be still taking the children through because her description is all over the border and they have a price on her head. But we had no serious problems."

No serious problems. Only my first dead child. I said nothing, as I knew his nervousness was speaking. For all he knew, perhaps Papa would pick up his rifle and shoot him to avenge the family honor. I was quite sure Papa would do nothing of the sort, although clearly he himself did not know quite how to behave.

Instead Papa said to me, "I am proud of you, the work you're doing. You have to judge when it is too hot for you to stay down. When it gets dangerous, you should come into the mountains with us. It's a hard life, but I think you would manage just fine."

"She's tough and fit," Jeff said. "I should say I am not married and that I am very serious about your daughter."

Papa laughed, wiping his eyes. "She has a hard head. You don't look Jewish?"

"People always say I don't, Papa, but he isn't, and don't start on me again about that."

"Have I said anything? After the war, we'll straighten everything out. You're in the Jewish underground and not Jewish?" Papa motioned for him to sit at the table. I was still standing. The boy with the Sten gun was on guard by the door. It was not embarrassing to talk in front of him any more than it would have been to talk in front of a large dog.

"I don't think they knew what they were sending me into, but it doesn't matter. We all fight the same war."

I pulled out the third chair and sat. Papa opened the cupboard as if he knew where to look and brought out some armagnac and two glasses. Then he looked at me and brought a third. "Are you Catholic?"

"I'm nothing. I'm not even a Christian," Jeff said.

"L'chaim." We all clinked glasses. Papa said, "If the mother is Jewish, the children are Jewish. What would you think of that?"

"I have no tradition I want to hand on to them, except that they should want to be free and use their eyes."

I have slept with this man two times and we have children already. Suddenly I felt compassion for both of them, trying to deal with each other and with me, who am not easy. "He's a painter, Papa. A real one."

"What do you paint?"

"Landscapes." He grinned. "And your daughter."

I knew it was all right. Papa was focused on Jeff and not on me, and I have forgiven him, and punished him a little too, I know that. Now I could look from one face to the other and feel warmth in me that was not of the armagnac, but of my heart and my joy. With just the light of the little lamp burning and the fireplace, they both looked fine enough to melt anyone's bones.

Papa was thin under his heavy leather jacket and his clanking hardware. His beard makes his eyes burn from his face. We have the same coloring and the same nose. We have the same stubbornness too. I was sure he would have to like Jeff because I want him. I almost thought Papa would marry us off while he was here tonight, but he restrained himself. Perhaps he still hopes for a Jewish son-in-law. Perhaps he only hopes we will all survive. Perhaps like me he dreams of a different society afterward. Next time I see him, I will ask him. All too soon another armed man knocked on the door, a code knock, Beethoven's Fifth, and the boy with the Sten gun and Papa prepared to leave. I went to the door with them but they just melted into the night and were gone into silence before I could speak again. Then and only then I began to cry.

BERNICE 6

In Pursuit

The P-47 felt all engine to Bernice. The monstrous engine with its huge gleaming propeller blades blocked her view forward, so she had to maneuver in S-curves down the runway to see for takeoff. The first time she had flown at P-47, during a training course for pursuit aircraft at Brownsville, Texas, she had felt overwhelmed, frightened. She was given no time to get used to the power of the beast, because there was room in the little canopy for only one. Her first flight had been alone as all afterward would be.

The P-47 was a descendant of the plane in which Jacqueline Cochran had won races and set records before the war. The fighters were the fastest planes of all, the most advanced aircraft available, and she was flying them all the way from Long Beach, California, to Newark, New Jersey.

She was glad to be out of Romulus, where the local commander had mistrusted the WASPs and tried to keep them from flying anything but trainers. Actually, Lorraine and Helen back at Romulus were flying fighters now too. However in Great Falls, Montana, they had to hand them over to men. There the commander had dictated that women could not be trusted in Alaska, because there were too few women there and too many men who had not seen a woman in years. Alaska was forbidden to WASPs, and at the Canadian border, the women had to get out of the fighters.

Bernice was glad she had been reassigned, although she missed the tight group that had been her family for months. Flo had been transferred to Long Beach with her, but often they did not see each other for a week at a time.

February in Long Beach was perennial summer, but she flew into winter as she made her way east. She could not believe how fast the flight was in the pursuit plane. Commercial flights took two or three days to get from coast to coast, but she could reach Newark in one long day, weather permitting. Weather forbidding, it once took her five days. Gradually the white would overspread the landscape beneath her. If she took a more southerly route, she would fly for hours over areas that were white and then areas that were clear, browns, greys, sepia tones, the dark green of pine. She felt enormous power and clarity as she sped above the landscape that from a plane always appeared orderly, arranged, even the wilderness neatly sculptured and mowed. Then the clouds moved toward her in their serried rows and she was alone in a world of sunlight above, or tossed and bounced and shaken in high columns of swirling grey.

The first time she had climbed into the cockpit of a fighter, she had felt an immediate urge to pry herself back out. She had wanted to bolt. She could not possibly learn the use or the meaning of all those dials and switches, those levers and gauges, those buttons and knobs. Then she thought that fighters were flown by men who had to react in split seconds or die in flames, so she could surely learn to master the instruments' apparent complexity with no one shooting at her. She would not let herself be daunted and she would act at all times as if she felt complete confidence.

Bernice barely fit into the cockpit. Flo was more comfortable physically. Bernice imagined that the ideal fighter pilot ought to be small in stature: in fact, a woman rather lighter boned than herself, but she kept such heresies to share only with the other women pilots. She was extremely lucky to be stationed at Long Beach, for here they seemed to go less by the book and more by ability.

With many different airplane manufacturers located in the area, she would eventually get to fly every single fighter in production. Sometimes they did not return directly but might be given a trainer or other plane to deliver anywhere else in the continental United States, and might end up flying four or five different planes to destinations thousands of miles apart before reappearing at Long Beach to claim the next fighter for ferrying to Newark, whence the planes would be sent on to the war itself.

Mrs. Augustine reported that The Professor had solved his problems with a live-in housekeeper, a German refugee, "not a Jewish lady as I understand it, but the wife of a Socialist professor who was fired and came to the United States." He had died of cancer, leaving his widow destitute. Her English, Mrs. Augustine reported, was patchy. "Sometimes I understand her, sometimes I don't. Your father talks German with her."

Some of the neighbors would not speak to her, because of her being German. They thought she might be a spy. Her name was Mrs. Gertrud Ansheimer, and she had moved in with a little dog.

Bernice had some trouble imagining her father living with a dog, big or little, as he had nothing but contempt for pets. Jeff and she had been forbidden them as dirty and unnecessary.

Bernice soon received a note from her father, the first since she had left home. He did not say he forgave her, but he commenced as if he had been writing regularly. He complained about having to teach classes in which he could only be a step ahead of his students. He was teaching all the languages, from French to German to Italian (and you know, he wrote, how faulty my Italian remains), Spanish, and also navigation and algebra. He had taken brief courses in order to bone up on those subjects, but he still felt like an impostor.

"We have a pooch now, named Der Meistersinger because of the droll noises he produces when he wishes to go out or demands to be fed or given his doggy bone. He is a terrier of sorts and has been catching rats in the woodpile. Not your brown rats, but the local wood rats who seem to hang around the house in the winter. Very useful animal, this Meistersinger."

Bernice hastened to write back an equally bland and factual letter about her work. She sent along a photograph of herself with Flo in front of a P-38 Flo had been about to ferry east.

"Notice my suntan," she wrote on the back. "Today it's 92 here. My poor body must be horribly confused about the season. Ninety-two here this afternoon and in two days I'll be in a blizzard."

Crisscrossing the United States seemed to confuse their bodies in other ways too. She missed a period entirely. If that had happened right after she had slept with Zach, she would have been convinced, in spite of his pronouncements of infertility, that she was pregnant. However, she doubted she could carry a sperm around hidden in some crevice for months, and when she finally brought up the subject, she discovered the other women pilots experienced the same dislocation. "Too close to the moon," Flo hazarded.

Zach wrote occasionally. Sometimes he would send off an amusing account of some activity safe to describe, such as a rock-climbing expedition—presumably in some partisan context—when he was attacked by an irate nesting eagle. Twice he wrote her sexually explicit letters in French. Her French was excellent—her mother Viola had made sure of that from early childhood, as next to ancient Greek that had been her favorite language—but she lacked the precise vocabulary for sexual parts and action, and had to guess his meaning. Zach wrote that he liked to give the censors a workout and a little fun. He could not contemplate anything more boring than reading the average person's mail, unless it was being forced to listen to his phone conversations, or his sins in a confessional. Once he had had to pose as a priest and it seemed to him a lousy way to make a living.

He felt there were few original sins, although he planned to see what he could manage in that line when next they got together.

He wrote, "I hear that your brother is alive and functioning, that's all I know. I still would like to kick him from here to Sunday. If he survives, you and I should gang up on him and beat him to a pulp for putting us through all this. My opinion is that you have the real brains of the family, and turn out to be surprisingly more fun to hump."

Flo referred to them when they came as Bernice's love letters. Bernice found that an amusingly inaccurate label. Sometimes they were funny, sometimes petulant, often obscene, but never did they speak of love, which was just fine with her. She could still not quite believe what had happened between them, but her memories were strong.

For years she had masturbated by imagining herself in various movies which slowly brought her into a state of excitement. Now her masturbation was more efficient, relaxing her to sleep in fifteen minutes. She focused on one of the scenes with Zach. His body was as vivid and real to her as the dials on the instrument panel of the fighters she flew. Zach's blatant control and his streak of sadism made her feel flown. That was somehow potent. It was the ignition spark. No more vague glories of melting flesh.

Except when his occasional letters came or when she masturbated, she seldom thought of Zach. Her life was absorbing. She thought oftener of Jeff, with a rootless anxiety. Having no idea where he was or what he was doing, it was as if he had vanished. She presumed that any news would be bad news, and that it was better to exist without information, but daily she thought of him and hoped he was safe and thriving.

In the meantime, she was learning to shoot. They were required to carry a .45 sidearm, not to protect themselves but rather the extremely valuable planes equipped for combat, with a number of secret devices and instruments on board. Aside from delivering the plane promptly and safely, their other prime directive was to keep it from being stolen or examined by anyone unauthorized.

Helen wrote that she hated the ugly object and always took the bullets out and stored the .45 in the bottom of her suitcase. Flo already knew how to use a rifle. She liked to practice at a local range, where Bernice began going with her. Although Bernice considered the .45 inelegant, it was still an impressive piece of hardware, and she did not want to be excluded from its mastery.

Weapons had always been Jeff's prerogative. Learning to shoot had been one of his private pleasures, those jaunts into the countryside when he explored the male world and then the world of sex open to him but not to her, at the same time managing to denounce wordlessly The Professor's values. It had never occurred to Jeff to teach her to shoot, just as it had never occurred to her to ask to be taught.

Carrying the pistol, she felt stronger. Why was a swagger built into it? Was it the myth of the West? Was it an artificial penis? Was it going against the grain of her upbringing? It can't hurt to know how to use it, even if I never need it, she told herself, and besides, it's a lot quicker than poison and surer than sleeping pills if I ever decide to check out in a hurry.

Death was never far away. One of the women test pilots had cashed it in two weeks before, at another California base. A woman who towed targets in the South had crashed, not from being hit by the live ammunition she faced daily but, scuttlebutt said, from sugar in the gas tank put in by one of the men at that base who hated the WASPs. They felt the WASPs were taking their safe or semisafe jobs and sending them into battle overseas—which was the point. Sometimes they just felt women couldn't be allowed to do what they did. That woman had died in flames for the right to fly.

No weapon could defend against sabotage by maintenance personnel or somebody else with a grudge and access to the hangar, but only the pursuit pilots had sidearms. It was one more way in which they felt chosen, special. When she came in for a pursuit-style landing at a hundred and twenty miles an hour dead-on and then climbed out of the plane, she could not help enjoying the shock, the whistles, the moans, when the pilots at the base saw that it was a woman flying a plane they might not be checked out to touch. Once again in Texas, that did not happen, because that time too she was taken for a man. Expectations were powerful and often controlled what people saw.

Nights in run-down tourist homes and seedy hotels were not amusing, but she could always read. Sometimes she read mysteries to relax, because there was nothing like a good locked room puzzle to engage her mind and make her forget a drab and often hostile little town. Sometimes she read Proust, a squat red Modern Library book. Other times she worked on a mail-order accountancy course she was taking.

With Flo, she talked about what they would do after the war. Bernice would not return to Bentham Center. "The only way I'm going back there is in a pine box," she told Flo. "And then only if you don't heed my dying wishes. I want to be cremated and scattered from a plane over Long Beach. I like it here."

Actually the perennial summer bored her, but she loved the work she was doing. They chatted about starting a back country airline, about teaching flying, about running an air circus. What they were sure of was that they were going to stay in flying. Maybe they'd get jobs as test pilots. Maybe they'd get jobs as commercial pilots. Everybody said that the aviation industry was going to take off after the war. Their base commander said every middle-class family would have a plane, just as they had a family car, and they would use it for long trips instead of driving. "Say you have to go from San Diego to San Francisco. Instead of a drive that would take two days, you'll hop in the family plane," he explained to the group of WASPs.

"Whatever happens, we'll be in on the ground floor," Flo said softly to Bernice. "We'll keep on flying."

"No matter what," Bernice agreed. "We'll keep on together."

ABRA 7

The Loudest Rain

The Labor Branch was buzzing with energy these days, in preparation for the invasion in the late spring. Almost every night they worked late. Oscar was off at a meeting. Abra left work at nine with Wilhelm and one of the secretaries, Beverly, to drop in on a party for an R & A man back from Algiers. Beverly was a broad-faced drawling Idaho girl. Wilhelm had been a pipefitter in Cologne, a stooped but burly man with a great scar on his face, from a fight with the brown shirts.

She had left the party in a mews in Belgravia for home, when the sirens went off. Must be a practice air raid, she thought. Bombing in London was a thing of the past, just an occasional nuisance raid everybody ignored. Abra was used to rubble, to walking down a street and seeing a gap between buildings like a missing front tooth, to seeing facades with nothing but rapidly sprouting weeds behind the gaping orifices that had been windows, to buildings sliced in two with the rooms open to the cold rain.

She walked a little faster wondering idly what she was supposed to do, reflecting how much at home she had become in London, used to warm beer and cold bedrooms. Probably she should head for the Underground.

Oscar had not volunteered any information about tonight's meeting, some sort of inter-Allied intelligence huddle. He always hoped to learn more about his sister, Gloria. She seemed to be part of MI9 which kept aloof from the other agent networks, specializing in the retrieval of downed pilots and escaped military personnel. A great many women worked in and even ran the MI9 networks. The Germans and their French collaborators were zealously trying to roll them up. All of the time Oscar was a little worried about his sister, a sort of whine in the walls of his mind like a piece of machinery left running, a tension she could sense. He slowly collected what information he could and dreamed of crossing into France to find Gloria, but he was not trained for espionage or liaison work, and OSS had no intention of so training him. They needed him where he was. He was too valuable to be risked on personal odysseys.

Planes overhead, many. She heard a loud thud and the pavement beneath her shook. Suddenly she realized it was not a practice drill. London was being bombed. She felt quite unbelieving, staring up at the skies in which searchlights were crisscrossing and ack-ack guns were roaring into life. She watched the shells bursting. It was better than fireworks, really. The barrage balloons turned like silver dolphins among the lights. A big four-engine plane was caught in the beam of a searchlight and then another fixed on it, so it was trapped in their crossbeams. Rocket shells went off but it continued, unscathed. The plane dived but the lights stayed on it. Its belly opened and out tumbled an amazing number of objects like great seeds turning and falling lazily. A man grabbed her by the elbow.

"Come on, love, we'll hop it to the tube. Jerry's at it again. Come on, briskly."

They ran down the street together, as the big guns in Hyde Park began barking. The pavement quivered as if a train were running beneath them. A bomb dropped extremely close. "Almost on us," Abra gasped, running faster.

"Ah, no, love, don't think so. Half a mile maybe. There we are."

They piled into the entrance of the Bond Street Underground station and ran down the steps into the crowd of people settling themselves, men, women, children, dogs, cats, a bird or two in a covered cage, babies squalling in arms and one nursing contentedly. The man who had run down the street with her sat down with friends who were saving him a place on a blanket. He gave her a wave and paid no more attention. She was grateful to him. Americans were not used to being bombed. They thought bombs were for other people.

The bombs came nearer. It was like something vast walking over houses, shaking the earth. Moloch the metal with feet of fire. It began to feel more personal, that someone up there was trying to kill them all. How safe really were the underground stations?

"Where're the Spitfires?" one man asked querulously. "Where's the Air Defense?"

"All over Germany doing the same to them, wouldn't you wager?" came a woman's nasal clipped tones.

"How long does it usually go on?" Abra asked.

"A Yank," the woman said. "It's new to you, isn't it? Oh, sometimes it's over in forty-five minutes and sometimes it goes on all night."

"The worst is," the man said in his quavering voice, "when the all clear sounds and you go out, and then it starts again. That's the worst."

Abra looked around, but she saw no one she recognized except her hairdresser and the newspaper vendor from the kiosk where she always bought her morning paper. He was playing checkers with a woman who must be his wife. Both of them had the loose skin of fat people who have lost a great deal of weight. It would be hard to remain really fat in London these days, Abra thought. She herself had lost weight, but it was hard to figure out how much. The British measured their weight in stones, and she always gave up before she figured hers out. She only knew her skirts had grown loose. She tried to think about stones and skirts and the interesting faces of people, quite a mix of social classes, but the bombs kept walking nearer, nearer. She could not think of anything else but the one that was going to fall next, here, on her. Bombs were shaking the walls. "Hitting Westminster hard. Tonight he's letting go a hogshead of the big ones."

"Yes, tonight Jerry means it. He thought we forgot him."

"Sounds like the ack-ack blokes got one."

"Anybody for pinochle?"

"Harry, sit down straightaway and stop tormenting your sister. I'll box your ears if you don't behave."

"Ooooh, that was a loud one."

The ground shifted under her. The ceiling would split open, the girders descend in a fall of rock and masonry, burying them, crushing them. She had to use the bathroom. There was already a queue of thirty. She joined it. I would not like to die among strangers, she thought. I want to be with him. It occurred to her that Oscar could die, wherever he was out in London. After all, if that man hadn't grabbed her arm, she might have stood in the street watching the fireworks until one of them landed on her head. She tried to remember the splendid spectacle of the bombs turning in the air, but her throat closed. She could not swallow her saliva.

A man came stumbling down the steps bleeding from cuts on his scalp, his left cheek and his left arm. "Flying tigers," she heard someone say as people gathered around him. She asked and was told that meant fragments of glass blown at you.

"Make way, I'm a doctor." A woman left the queue and pushed her way through the crowd.

The noise was the worst, she thought. It made her feel claustrophobic. She felt as if her head would burst with the bombs. If only it would be quiet for a few minutes, just quiet enough to catch her breath and think again, just quiet enough so her head would stop ringing, she would feel restored. She kept imagining that the next bomb would drop directly on the Underground station and they would be buried under tons of rubble.

A woman who had joined the queue behind Abra was saying, "And one of the first bombs dropped on that cinema in Curzon Street full of people watching that new movie with Laurence Olivier and it was dreadful, the ceiling fallen and people screaming and trapped. . . ."

She wished for Oscar, his presence, the solidity and warmth of his body and the power and mercurial zest of his mind, to talk to her, to distract her, to comfort her. She did not want to die separated from him, in ignorance of his safety or danger. As she finally pressed forward into the overburdened toilet stall to relieve herself, she stared at the door scrawled with the names of fifty different couples.

It was two when the all clear sounded and she followed the crowd up into the street thick with smoke and all the varied burning smells of a hundred different materials and compounds ablaze, the stench of sewage from a burst main, the wail of fire sirens, of ambulances. Flames licked at the sky toward Hyde Park, where the antiaircraft batteries were still at last. She walked along Gilbert Street, but Weighhouse Street was roped off. A bomb had fallen right at the corner and sheared off part of a building. They were digging in the rubble looking for bodies. On the pavement lay something dark and sticky she did not want to see more closely. The street ahead was impassable with fallen masonry and a burning car. What a mess it makes, she thought and laughed at herself. She would have to go back to Oxford Street and round the long way.

At her corner, the sidewalk was covered with glass, glittering dully out into the middle of the road. She picked her way carefully. No bombs had dropped here, but the shock wave of one close by had broken windows. She was relieved to see her own building standing secure, dark behind its blackout curtains.

In her flat, one of her pictures had fallen from the wall and its glass broken. She was exhausted but not sleepy and went over the flat to check for other damage, turning on the electric fire in the sealed fireplace. The ivory walls were growing shabby, painted last probably in thirty-nine, as was the wan pastel floral chintz of the armchairs and sofa. One cushion had leaped to the middle of the floor. A vase that had belonged to the flat's owners, white china studded with raised roses, had broken, to her relief. Items of bric-a-brac had fallen. She supposed that interior decorating in a bombed city must take such problems into account. Was it really safe to go to bed? Perhaps it would all start again. Would she dream of the bombing? She was still righting the fallen objects and realigning the pictures that had lurched crooked on the walls when her phone rang.

"You're there, good. I was worried. I called the office and learned you'd left a couple of hours before the raid started."

She was pleased that he worried. "I'd just dropped into a party and I was starting home. I was a bit naive. I stood in the street when the sirens went off gawking at the show. Where were you?"

"Quite safe. Don't worry. I wouldn't think anybody would mind if we came in a bit late tomorrow. How about ten?"

She agreed, wishing he would offer to come over, but it was, after all, three in the morning.

Abra began to notice the enormous number of Americans running around London, especially in Mayfair, outnumbering the native English and overwhelming them. She was suddenly not the exception she was used to being, but one of a herd trotting along. Even American women were no longer rarities, for she saw WACs and nurses everyplace.

After growing accustomed to British behavior, she shared certain amusements with the native Londoners, one being how often the Americans saluted each other. It could be dangerous on the streets, elbows always flying out. The Americans were louder, heftier, well-fed looking. Suddenly indeed there was more food in London. In the massive brick Grosvenor Hotel nearby, overlooking Hyde Park, a vast mess was established, the size of a dancehall serving a thousand at a time for fifty cents a meal cafeteria style, American pork chops, fried chicken, ice cream. She had not had ice cream since Washington. The regulars named it "Willow Run" after an aircraft plant outside Detroit, because of the assembly line approach to meals. Soon Abra would be able to take what meals she chose there, since Oscar had become a captain finally and she was in the process of being militarized and would get her rank in a week or two.

In the halls of OSS she heard the good old boys complaining loudly about how bitter cold it was in their club since the windows had been blown out by Jerry that night. The fresh damage shocked her eyes. On Brook Street, where R & A was housed, a building in the next block had been hit and cracked open like a brick egg. She could not help thinking of the people she saw going in and out of all these buildings every day. The rubble she had got used to had seemed as ancient as Roman ruins: part of the landscape, overgrown with weeds and wild flowers in the spring and summer, purple rosebay, the home of stray hungry cats and rats that never seemed to lack for food. But these new blast sites had been buildings she had passed daily, places she stopped in for tea, her own greengrocer, the shop where she had her hair cut, bringing a towel along as one did to the hairdresser's nowadays in London. To have one's regular shop bombed was a disaster, because she could not divorce a shopkeeper who had her ration book. The butcher or the grocer were not choices lightly made nor easily changed.

Oscar and she were lucky to have rented their flats when they had, for many Londoners had returned during the bombing lull. Lodgings were in short supply; hotels were crowded; restaurants, mobbed. Now London felt more like Washington, overflowing with thousands of headquarters personnel who would never see a battle, and with an empty apartment worth a hefty bribe.

People seemed cranky in the wake of the bombing, as if they couldn't bear the thought of the whole thing starting again; as if having survived the immense ordeal of the blitz, they really shouldn't have to survive what was already being called the little blitz. In general she thought the British were wearing thin on nerves, getting angrier, bitter. When she had first come, she had never seen an antigovernmental slogan, but the working class who composed most of the homeless who slept in the tubes were getting tired of Churchill and the Conservatives. It was rumored that the miners were about to go out on strike.

On the eighteenth, another raid hit while Oscar and Abra were still at work. They could not suddenly run downstairs, as there were classified documents scattered all over the desks and cabinet tops. There was a great crash, while they were still making their papers secure. The building rocked and all the lights went out. Abra remembered a flashlight and fumbled it out of a drawer and they made their way with other stumbling and joking workers down to the shelter in the basement. "The phones are out too," someone making his way downstairs by the flare of his Zippo was complaining. The steps were slippery with fallen plaster. By the time they reached the basement, the auxiliary generator was up and working and the lights came on dimly.

Oscar found a seat on a pile of barrels and pulled her up. He leaned over to sniff them suspiciously. "For all I know the SO boys could be storing gunpowder here."

The lights went out again. Everyone groaned. Someone made loud kissing noises and somebody else was whistling "When the Lights Go On Again All Over the World."

"Last night I dined with some of our British colleagues," Oscar said. "I wish I could have brought you along, not only for company but for the food. They don't live badly. Salmon and plover. It felt inappropriate to eat a plover, whatever that is. I wouldn't even know one if I met one."

"They're mostly shorebirds," Abra said. "Although there are upland plovers. I wouldn't think they'd make a meal."

"They served several. Were you a bird-watcher once?"

"Had a boyfriend who was. It's inevitable to learn a little."

"What have you learned from me?"

Too much, she thought. "To keep my mouth shut." She winced against him as another bomb landed close by. The trouble was she could not tell the difference in sound between the big antiaircraft guns in the park launching their rockets at the planes and the sound of the bombs coming down. She clutched at him.

He held her close to his chest, until the lights came on. Then he held her more circumspectly, an arm around her shoulders.

"After all," he said in her ear, "there's no use being frightened. You should wince whenever you hear a car engine. Your odds of being struck by a car are much higher than of dying in a direct hit by a bomb." His own pulse was steady.

She realized she had been wrong. It wasn't better with him. Oh, it was an improvement to keep an eye on him and know he was safe, but she could not display her fear. If only the bombs would be less noisy. She could not think, could not find a clear silent place inside her skull to collect herself, to hide from the loud disasters that rattled her bones. She found her mouth fallen open, panting. She felt like an instrument the bombs were playing and she could not escape.

Fear was so tedious, so incredibly tedious. She knew that her fear of the bombs made the raid stretch out to eternity. She anticipated from moment to moment the shock, the blast, the flames, the concussion. It was as if she lived every moment three times over. Oh, she was bored with her fear, but that did not lessen its grip on her bowels. Once again she had to apologize her way stepping over the people sprawled on the floor and look for a bathroom. Please can I be excused from the war: bombing gives me diarrhea. She saw before her an endless series of air raids to be endured in silent asphyxiating terror with her bowels turned to cold churning liquid, her heart racing, her palms clammy. It was worse here, much louder than in the subway. Dust filled the air and objects kept toppling.

She must not let Oscar despise her. She must conceal her fear and manage conversation, when with every bomb that fell she wanted more and more to start screaming, to cover her eyes, her ears and crouch in embryo position and pray to the bombs not to hurt her.

"Something I ate," she said to Oscar, who was chatting with Wilhelm and blunt stalwart Sergeant Farrell. "I'm fine now."

"Wonder what Goering has in mind, wasting his bombers on London?" Wilhelm mused.

The man who answered, lounging nearby, was a tall beefy blond major not in their section. "I suppose they must have busywork while waiting for us to invade. He's stripped the Balkans and the Eastern Front of what air power they can peel off. What are they going to do while we keep them waiting? But they don't have the pilots they had in forty." He spoke in an affected drawl, the halfway-to-British accent many rich Americans adopted.

She recognized him. He had been the roommate of that young American she had picked up in the OSS pub one night when she was pissed at Oscar. The major had struck her then and struck her now as vain, arrogant, the type of her richer cousins. She did not feel a great urge to remind him where he had seen her, although he nodded a vague greeting in her direction. That young man could have been her twin, both of them used to getting what they wanted from others with a modest display of charm. She had never bothered telling Oscar about the night, because it would not make him jealous. What would be the point of cheapening her fidelity that had not been diminished by that act? The dismal revelation of that evening was how little pleasure she could now abstract from the sexual adventures that had been her forte. That young man had been a more than competent lover, experienced, attuned to a woman's responses, yet the pleasure had meant little. She had not been able to escape the feeling of being in the wrong place with the wrong person.

The egoistic major had been in Italy with SO; he had been in Yugoslavia and seen Tito's army in action. He pronounced on all subjects oracularly but with an undertone of amusement, as if he was playing at arrogance. He was too much like her cousins to attract or interest her, and she stayed back in the shadows, waiting for Oscar to finish with him.

She was annoyed with Oscar because he felt no fear during the raids, and ashamed before him because she did. She was not accustomed to fear. She had learned to ride, been thrown and hopped back on before her injuries healed. She had been in a car crash with a drunken boyfriend and made jokes about her black eye and her broken wrist and the tooth that had to be capped. She had been sailing since she was old enough to grasp a rope, out in rough weather, and loved the rising wind and the scudding foam and even the heavy lurch of a ship the waves were pounding. She had listened to music in Harlem and danced in bars her friends were frightened to enter. She had marched in demonstrations with the police breaking heads and throwing tear gas grenades into the crowd, and never thought of missing a May Day because of the danger.

She was ashamed of herself, yet she thought that the vast majority of humans were of the same mind during air raids. In the shelters no matter how cheerful or stolid people tried to sound, she could smell their fear. She resented having to lie to Oscar. Why wasn't he afraid? Did he lack imagination? That night she worked up the nerve to ask him.

He was lying on his back, arm cocked behind his head, other arm still around her. They had just made love at length. "To be buried alive would be a crying shame. But to die at once in blast, not bad as dying goes, and there's plenty of it around. It's not that I don't have enough to live for. But in some ways I have fucked up my life." With that he turned on his side and went to sleep or pretended to.

DANIEL 6

Under the Weeping Willow Tree

Daniel was back on early watch, rising in the morning and getting home at a reasonable time, periods of crisis aside. Due to the heart attack of a commander who had worked in a little cubicle, Daniel had a new job. Also a new rank. He had been promoted to lieutenant commander. He did not suppose this was so much because of the excellence of his work, as because the job had previously been done by a commander. Therefore it could not be done by a lieutenant. The Navy thought that way, and no doubt, his promotion had followed as the day the night, or as the indigestion the overeating. So he told Louise as they celebrated over crabs.

His boss had told him privately and in a serious tone that he should remember that in the Navy, there was no advance to a grade higher than captain without sea experience. His boss sounded somber, depressed. He was talking about himself, obviously; they were rooted firmly in Washington and in OP-20-G. To Daniel, for whom a promotion was a pleasantry, a little more pay and a couple more privileges seldom exercisable at OP-20-G, the Navy's intransigence meant little; but for the career men, much.

Spring was sneaking up on Washington, the loveliest time. Sometimes he felt it was the only attractive season, in between the sleety winter and the steam-room of the summer. After New England, fall was a disappointment. But spring was early, lush and flowery. Dogs were already copulating near the reflecting pool. The soldiers at attention had a dreamy look. Daffodils bloomed. Secretaries brought their lunches outside to eat while the fat squirrels begged. He had heard rumors that during the meat shortage, local people had been trapping them.

Suddenly women emerged from their winter huddle willowy in pastel flowered dresses. Pale aqua, pink and robin's egg blue suits, unlikely hats under silk flowers or ceramic cherries bloomed on the sidewalks and in the restaurants.

What would spring be without falling in love? Ann was seeing somebody else, although he did not know who. Then he saw her at lunch, her face animated with the urge to please, staring across the table at a translator who had been a professor at Berkeley and who had a wife and family back in California. He tried, tardily, to have an avuncular conversation with her at lunch next day, but only made her angry. He had not realized he had done so, until she rose and left him at the cafeteria table alone.

Once he had mastered his new duties, Daniel promised himself he would be free to pursue Louise. He had not been in just this state of aroused infatuation since the first two weeks with Ann. It was a good spring tonic. It actually gave him increased energy to devote to his new situation, for the infatuation was not yet real enough to interfere. It was simply there, hidden away like the bottle of whiskey one of his superiors kept in his desk drawer, ready when Daniel needed distraction or relaxation to be tasted. He had so much to learn and master that he was once again infatuated with work also. He felt at the height of his powers, fully committed and alert and engaged.

One reason he had been selected, he was sure, was because of his previous liaison work with William Friedman at the Army counterpart of OP-20-G. Now Daniel was no longer decoding, but rather going over masses of information that came in from other cryptanalytical sources for items of interest to the Navy, routing them where they must go.

When he had been in the process of being vetted for the job, his mother had called him. "Danny, what is it? Are you in some kind of trouble? The FBI, they come around to ask a lot of questions about you. I didn't tell them about Seymour."

Seymour was his Communist cousin. "No, Mama, no trouble. They just check you out sometimes. In fact, I guess I'm being promoted."

"Just so you're happy," his mother said plaintively. "When are you coming home?"

He sighed, closing his eyes and then opening them abruptly because he saw too vividly the discontented round face of his mother. They would make him feel guilty about not coming home often, when if they were truthful, they would admit his presence was an irritant. His sister with her baby meshed with his parents. Haskel was their pride. Both his sister and his older brother came and went in the gloomy family apartment in the Bronx weekly, almost daily. He arrived, claiming to be their son, but not belonging, not interested in the gossip about Haskel's patients or the local cousins or the latest exploits of Judy's baby.

He could not explain to his mother what he was doing, nor did she press him. She never did. He had sailed off the edge of the family charts when he went to

Harvard to study Japanese for the Navy. They lived by choice in a closet world, frightened by anything strange.

He himself was addicted to novelty, and the amount he had to learn in his new job only stimulated him. He relished an occasional encounter with Friedman, who was now presiding over an intelligence factory in Arlington, Virginia. Friedman looked thinner, balder but just as dapper and just as precise. He complained of the amount of administration he was stuck with. In addition to the Purple diplomatic codes, his office was handling the highly complex decodes of the Japanese army.

The winner of the most valuable Purple player trophy continued to be the Baron Oshima, Tokyo's representative to Berlin, who had just come through with a detailed report on his tour of the Atlantic Wall. He analyzed the German command in France, reported on the number of divisions, when they would be rotated and described the defenses. Contributions to the Allied effort on the part of Lieutenant Colonel Nishi, Japanese army attaché in Berlin, were running a close second, Friedman remarked. He looked over the German defenses with a professional soldier's eye, reviewing critically the placement of the artillery, the interesting use of the machine-gun emplacements to achieve interweaving cross fire. He analyzed the differing intensity of the defenses at various points on the coast of France.

Purple was still producing gold. Daniel would have little to do with what Friedman's factory, called by its employees the salt mines, was producing, except as Friedman or one of his top subordinates passed on some nugget directly relevant to Navy decoding and analysis. Nonetheless, he was flattered that Friedman remembered him and saw him personally, instead of turning his visit over to an assistant, which would have made more sense. Friedman was a man he would always approach with as much awe as curiosity.

Daniel was constantly involved with the information that came from the decodes of the German radio traffic, dubbed by the British Enigma codes, and the intelligence derived from them, which had been given the name Ultra. He was concerned with this material as it bore on submarine warfare and blockade-running between Germany and Japan. Once Germany had attacked the Soviet Union, the main route between Axis partners could not go overland, but weapons or matériel must go by water, susceptible to American submarine attack. He worked with a commander who conducted the higher level liaison and two assistants who did the fetching and carrying. It was a relatively quiet fiefdom within OP-20-G, offering a fascinating overview. Once he felt secure in his new job, he began to think more about Louise.

She had not replaced her French director with anyone else. Like Daniel, she seemed estranged from family—aside from her callow daughter—and to have made a family from friends. Of those, she had many, female and male, but he did not think any of the latter were her lovers. Often they came accompanied by wives or acquaintances. Her social life still revolved around her New York friends; she would never view Washington as other than temporary, in which she also resembled him.

Although Washington had provided him with the first work that had deeply engaged his brain and a new estimate of his own abilities, a new respect for himself, he would never feel it was completely real. His dreams centered on China and on Cambridge. The buildings of Washington seemed to him cold, dull and turned from molds. In spite of the history of the place, it did not strike him as having any. It made history, but did not seem to hold on to it. A historian was somebody who remembered how a senator had voted the year before.

Place interested Louise, and they compared notes endlessly on the various cities with which they were familiar. He realized by mid-March that she was no longer keeping him out of her life, but gradually allowing him to take more of her time. Still, he could not quite plot a way through her defenses of amusement, irony, wit. It was like living in a civilized comedy, he thought, this wooing of her, but how had Nick Charles ever persuaded Nora to stop raising her brows at him and making pointed remarks long enough to get her into bed?

That Sunday they rented a tandem bicycle and pedaled around the Tidal Basin, for fifty cents an hour, Daniel's treat. On the single-flowered cherry trees around the Basin, the buds were just swelling, a crack of pink showing. There were stumps where right after Pearl Harbor, an idiot with a strange sense of revenge had attacked some trees with an ax.

Louise rode in front of him, her auburn hair trailing from a pale gold silk kerchief tied around her head. The wind loosened from her a faint spicy perfume that blew back to him. If he leaned forward just right, sometimes a tendril of her blowing hair touched his chin. Pedaling a bicycle made him think about sex; lately he had noticed almost everything had that effect. Making his bed made him think about sex. Shaving made him think about sex. So did taking off his clothes or putting them on. Flowers resembled vaginas. Everywhere couples were embracing. There was more lust in the air than smog.

He was always seeing couples necking in the park, in hallways, on stoops, in bus and train stations, just standing on a corner. On some mauve evenings he felt as if everyone else were just about to go to bed with someone. Soon, he thought, watching the muscles in her neat buttocks flex. Louise was about the age of his first real romance in Shanghai, the wife of a doctor, but he was now ten years older than he had been and just as overwound sexually.

They stopped near the seawall, where old weeping willows chartreuse with spring bowed to the ground shuddering in the wind off the Basin. The golf courses nearby were busy, the two courses, the white and the Negro, for even at golf Washington was segregated.

"I'm a little out of breath," Louise said apologetically. "I'm not getting enough exercise here. At home—in New York—I walk miles every day. I don't try to, it just happens. Here I spend my time standing in trolleys. And sitting, sitting, sitting."

They were sitting on the grass, growing already although the ground felt chilly beneath them, leaning on the broad trunk of a huge grandmother willow. As if casually he put his arm around her. Watching some children playing follow the leader along the seawall, embarrassed by the fact that she was still catching her breath, Louise said nothing and did not move away. "We should be sure to come back when the blossoms are out," he said.

"And join the thousands?"

"I can promise you cherry blossoms without a crowd, if you have patience for a few weeks more."

"But the petals fall."

"In East Potomac Park along the drive, there are double blossoming trees—some light pink and some a deep intense color I prefer. The tourists will be gone before they start." He felt a little guilty offering this bouquet to Louise, because it had been one of the pleasures Ann had shared with him on a warm Sunday early in their affair. Among the graceful reddish black polish of the tree limbs and the clusters of blossoms and the petals underfoot like exotic pink snow, she had moved like a dancer, exquisite, shy, porcelain and silk.

Louise seemed made of hardier stuff. She knew how to dress and could emerge glamorous in mink and silk to her fancier evenings, but without makeup today under the sun, she looked younger, in fact, and healthy, sensual. Lately every time he touched her, however casually, his body went into instant arousal. He was always standing in odd positions to mask his erection.

He decided to follow up the success of his arm and try to kiss her, something he had occasionally attempted. She would turn her face and take his kiss on her cheek, then slip away. Oscar must have been a monster of persistence. He tried to think of a remark that would lead up to what he intended. A compliment on her beauty? The words stuck in his throat. In desperation, he brought his other hand up to her cheek so that she could not turn her face away. Her lips were soft and unresisting, surprised. He could almost feel her thinking, tensions flicking through the muscles of her back and arms. Then she kissed him back.

He had difficulty making himself proceed in that slow, measured inch at a time way he had learned. Perhaps she sensed that, because shortly, she wriggled free of him. "I don't have the temperament for this public passion." She smiled at him, getting to her feet. "We should pedal back."

He could not have said, pedaling furiously behind her, whether he felt more hope or more despair. It could take years at this rate. On her deathbed she would roll over and admit him to her sheets. He would die of extreme congestion. His sperm would boil, causing a stroke.

They returned the rental bike and headed home. He had intended to make a longer afternoon of it, then take her to supper, perhaps casually as she was, perhaps more elegantly after a change of clothes. Several fantasies had eddied about that possibility. Stuck zippers. Help me. Dress falling.

They chatted pleasantly all the way back, as they usually did. He had never had trouble making conversation with her or in fact found conversation something that had to be made, bricks manufactured without straw to fill that pit of silence. But he was nervous. In the hall, he expected her usual fast turn through her door, leaving him punished by this abrupt decapitation of their day for his boldness.

Instead she stood aside, waving him into her apartment. It had grown more and more hers as the months had gone by, until it no longer resembled the tentative and scruffy flat Susannah and Abra had shared and partied in. Many books had appeared and a great pile of newspapers and periodicals covered the coffee table that had formerly sported nothing heavier than highballs. Louise had the habit of reading half a dozen books at once, which lay opened where they had momentarily failed her interest, waiting for her curiosity to renew itself. Novels, poetry, plays, biographies, books on politics and economics, tomes on the woman question, sociology and history lay waiting on every chair arm and end table.

She obviously liked Klee and Miró, for lightness? wit? A few photographs in leather frames, mostly of her daughter but one with the President sitting behind his desk while Louise, Robert Sherwood and several people whom Daniel did not recognize posed around him. Art deco bookends, silvery metal, probably aluminum, in the shape of single-engined planes taking off and trailing behind them a pedestal of curved motion. Some painted peasant crockery that he knew was from Eastern Europe because his uncle Nat had pieces like that.

Usually she rushed him through so quickly he did not have time to look around, but she was standing in the doorway to the kitchen smiling rather tentatively at him. "Would you like some coffee? Or a drink?"

Perhaps it was her indecisive air. Perhaps it was simply her inviting him in without immediately setting limits. Perhaps it was her offering him a drink at four o'clock on Sunday afternoon in her apartment. Perhaps it was wishful thinking. It suddenly came to him as he was staring at a report by Edgar Snow on China, that she was a woman who did not yield by inches.

He had become accustomed since arriving in the States from China to a style of courtship such as he had pursued with Ann, where first came a kiss, then a tongue kiss, then the as-if-accidental caress of the breast through the cloth, and so on, at all stages protesting that stage was the last desired act. What he began to suspect as he put down the book and walked toward her was that Louise might be quite different.

Indeed she waited in the doorway, one hand on the frame, until he had come face-to-face with her and had bent his face to kiss her again. At that point she let go of the lintel and slid not backward this time but forward into his arms and kissed him vehemently back.

They stood kissing in the doorway until he could not contain himself further and tried to pick her up in his arms. "Dear Daniel," she said, her voice thick with silent laughter, "I'm heftier than you think and I can walk perfectly well. Come." She took his hand and led him into her bedroom.

He was not sure as he got hastily out of his clothes, while she got far more leisurely out of hers, whether she had not decided on this even before she had let him kiss her in the park, or if she had decided beneath the huge old willow. Since then, however, they had been delightfully of one mind.

Her body had not the tightness or the porcelain delicacy of Ann's. Her breasts were soft and full, not pointy buds; she had borne a child and her belly was full also. But she projected a sense of being at ease with her body and with his that was a tremendous aphrodisiac. She was active, passionate, easily aroused and clear in her demands. When he entered her, her vagina closed around him firm and gentle as her hand, intelligent, full of small conscious muscular responses. Prostitutes in China had used their muscles like that, but no one he had been with since. He could not control himself and came too quickly.

He was apologetic, mortified. He wanted to give her satisfaction that would wipe the French director and the mythologically endowed Oscar out of her mind. "Don't worry," she said, nuzzling his cheek. "If you touch me, I'll come that way too."

When she had, he said, "We can do it again if you want."

She laughed softly, more with pleasure than amusement, taking his newly risen prick between her firm warm palms. "So it seems. Why not?"

When the Postman Passes
at Noon, Twice

"Ma mere a un gros rhume. Ma mere a un gros rhume," the BBC said. It was half past nine and still the personal messages continued. Every week they seemed to get longer and longer, a clue that Resistance activity was building up everyplace in France and not just in their sector. Still Jeff found it tedious to sit through minute after minute of nonsense—my mother has a bad cold. My aunt has a fat goose. The barnacles turn blue. Christmas comes early. Christmas comes early.

Jacqueline was sitting on a leather car seat—pried from some fine wreck and set up near the desk in M. Faurier's garage—mending her coat. The atmosphere in the garage was heavy with Lev's smoke, from the cigarettes he managed to get on the black market, but heavier with leftover emotions from the early evening. Lev was in a foul temper—after all, he had known Gilles much longer than Jeff had. His cheek had stopped bleeding, but it had to hurt. Jeff too was badly shaken. He had only managed to have five private minutes with Jacqueline, and he could not judge her reaction by her face, as she was apparently intent on repairing the disintegrating coat that could not be replaced. The ritual of sitting through the messages on the BBC was one he could have dispensed with.

Then Jeff sat up. The BBC was talking to him. "Le facteur passera à midi, deux fois. Le facteur passera à midi, deux fois." The postman will come by at noon, twice.

He leaped up. "The stuff is coming!" he announced to Lev.

"You've been saying that for months," Lev said with a yawn.

"I've been saying that I wanted it, that I asked for it. This is an official message. They're sending two planes over at the next full moon. Tuesday, right? Weather permitting. Same spot as last time."

"The last drop was you. We haven't had a sou from them since, not a bullet, not a firecracker." Lev paced, his hands knotted behind his back.

"It sounds as if they're making up for the wasted time. Two planeloads could give us a decent amount of firepower."

"Unless they just drop some more wise guys," Lev muttered. He was not as friendly since Jacqueline had become Jeff's lover. Everyone disapproved at least a little, but mostly they minded that until now, no weapons had come, no explosives. He had had Raymond send message after message requesting, begging for arms, but until now, nothing.

Daniela came in with her arms full of newspapers. "*Quand Même* is out again," she announced jubilantly. "Fat new issue. I mean fat for a clandestine paper. . . . Lev!" Her voice rang out. "What happened?" She dropped the bundles, bolting forward.

His hand shot up to his face, as if surprised. "This? We took care of that double agent Gilles. We know he fingered Larousse for the SS. He's been running back and forth, back and forth between the railway workers and the Gestapo, playing both sides and selling us to keep himself in good."

Daniela touched Lev's slashed face with her fingertips, then ran for her bag to dress it. "But how could you be sure? Justice is not something to dispense like water when you turn on a tap."

Jeff intervened. "When he realized we had come to shoot him, he confessed. He said he could get us information. He tried to bargain."

Lev spat, then rubbed out the spot on the floor with his sabot. "The heart of a worm."

"Even when he was dying"—he turned to Jacqueline who was undoing the wire-binding bundles of the underground Jewish paper—"he was still trying to bargain. He still thought if he offered enough, he wouldn't have to die, even with the blood bubbling out of him."

Lev took a flask of marc from the cupboard and poured little cups for everyone, including Daniela who never drank anything stronger than wine. "If he hadn't been so greedy, turning in those peasants who were hiding the German boy, we wouldn't have suspected him. But he had gone there with us, and hardly anybody knew about them." The cut on his cheek where Gilles had slashed him was livid but looked worse than it was, bloody but shallow.

Jeff had then disarmed Gilles, as he had been taught, and felt a jolt of surprise when the knife dropped neatly from Gilles's broken hand to stand upright quivering in the floorboard. It had worked. Had he never really believed in the methods they had taught him in Washington and again in Kent and Sussex? Had he always suspected they were only playing? Indeed, he had felt primarily astonishment as he first disarmed Gilles and then knocked him down, with three precise blows of hand and foot.

Jeff saw the two boys again, Theo bounding like a goat in the dark, Alain exclaiming over the fireworks of the explosion. Dead? In a camp?

"I don't want that poison." Daniela waved it away. "Only the goyim drink that. You'll give yourself ulcers."

"Drink it." Lev pushed the old blue cup back across the table. "Listen to me, and drink it."

"Why? What's wrong?" She cleaned out the cut on his cheek, carefully.

"Drink it and I'll tell you."

Daniela stared into his face and drank off the cup like medicine, wincing. "So now tell me. What is it?"

"Now another one." Lev poured.

"Lev, no more. Tell me. Who's been deported? Who's dead? I see you, I see my Jacqueline. Who's missing?"

"Your brother was a brave man," Lev said. "We heard the news today."

"That was Daniela's brother?" No one had bothered to tell Jeff that; he felt like an outsider.

"Nathan was on a housetop in Neuilly. When a German patrol was passing underneath, he threw two grenades and got the officers. They surrounded the roof and he ran out of ammo. He had one grenade left. He blew himself up."

Obviously so that he would not talk under torture; the same reason OSS had given Jeff a cyanide pill in a false filling. He had not really listened to the story the courier had told. His mind had been fixed on the coming confrontation and his own desire to believe Gilles innocent in spite of the strong but circumstantial evidence convicting him. He found Gilles gentler, friendlier than Lev, and had preferred him. He did not want to give up the Gilles of his experience for the Gilles who sold people to the Germans to save his own skin, to protect his family and to provide them creature comforts. To Lev the shocker was that a Jew would turn in other Jews, that a resistant would hand in other resistants; to Jeff, the sticking point was how much he had liked Gilles. He did not want to be proved a poor judge of character. Therefore he had paid minimal attention to the courier and the news she had given Lev.

Daniela was sitting rigidly upright on the car seat beside Jacqueline, who held her. The blue cup lay broken at her feet. The raw smell of spilled liquor cut into the reek of gasoline and oil. Daniela stared ahead. She did not speak or move. Finally Jacqueline led her upstairs.

Lev slumped at the rolltop desk, scowling. "He was twenty. What kind of shitty world is it where a kid of twenty has to face a choice like that and die, torn into shreds on a rooftop? He should be thinking about going to school and getting laid."

"Yet it's kids who do the killing in wars, always."

"I don't mind the killing when I'm doing it. It's easy. You just forget they're human too."

"Like anything else," Jeff said. "The first time is hard and the next time less hard." He was not about to remark that he had never killed anyone. Lev had shot Gilles point-blank.

"You were fast," Lev said reluctantly and got to his feet. He came over and smote Jeff on the shoulder. "You saved my hide—or at least my beauty, nu? Maybe it hurt my pride, that I walked right into his knife, but pride heals faster than flesh. If I've been short tonight, I regret it. I didn't want to tell her."

"Lev, let me make you angry again. You're attracted to Daniela, she's attracted to you. What's holding you back?"

"I'm a married man, Vendôme. Daniela is engaged. Nothing is possible."

"How do either of you know the one you're waiting for is still alive or will want you back? Years have gone by."

"If Vera—that's my wife—can survive, I can wait," Lev said quietly with a dignity that impressed Jeff in spite of himself.

"Tomorrow we all may die quite hideously like Daniela's brother. What a waste, then."

"Look, copain, I'm myself till I die and then I'm just a stain on a wall. But while I'm myself, I control how I act. Sometimes I act well and sometimes I don't make it, but it's me, trying." There was a sound from overhead, a sharp cry and something falling. Lev reached for the bottle and filled their blue cups, Prussian blue, actually. "L'chaim."

Jeff raised his cup and they clinked them, elbows linked.

"Someday this will end," Lev said. "We'll have the bricks of our lives to pick up and fit together however we can."

"I met you as a fighter. I can't imagine your life before."

"Me, I'm a mason. I build. Now I just tear down. . . . My wife Vera's a doctor. I think sometimes even those assholes wouldn't be so stupid as to kill a doctor. It's the sort of little lie I like to believe day to day. You understand?"

"I try to."

A thin eerie cry came down through the floorboards, sustained, piercing as a note on a violin. Both men looked upwards. Lev poured another drink.

———————

"You can't protect me. It's absurd for you to try. I was in this long before I met you." She put her hand against his face palm out, a gesture of affection and re-proach at once.

"It's far more absurd for you to take chances as a courier. The Milice and the Gestapo have your description. Anybody can be a courier, ginger cat. You have no special skill at running errands."

"You're wrong." She let him pull her down on his lap. "It takes a trained alertness. I have that. It takes caution when caution is needed, boldness when boldness is needed, and the sensitivity to situation to guess which." She brought her face directly up to his, her eyes wide open staring into his. "Why can't I see into your brain through your eyes?"

"You'd see it sweating with anxiety." He often thought that Jacqueline had cooler nerves than he did. Mostly he acted by not allowing himself to consider the consequences, the dangers. She was conscious and finally braver. Yet he knew such comparisons would never arise for her. She did not consider herself brave, but living on borrowed time, time she had stolen, time she continued to steal, day by day.

Her hair had grown out, still lighter toward the ends, but with all its metallic colors and glinting hues back, running between his fingers. A pulse ticked in her throat. He thought of dragonflies, of hummingbirds for the glints in her, for her speed, her hovering, her pouncing, her fierce nature. Lily, he called her, for her skin, like the pinkish trumpet lilies his mother had grown with intoxicating perfume. She accepted his names without sentiment, without self-consciousness. She seemed to have few preconceptions about being in love. Her love was cool, crystalline, leaving her mind clear. She could be, she was, judgmental toward him. She held him to standards almost as high as she held herself.

She had not come to him, she had added him to her family, to the distant sisters, to the mother, even to the father she had not quite forgiven, to Daniela, her adopted sister. In bed she was surprisingly uncoy, direct. She liked her pleasure, she liked making love with him. If he came too soon, she would yell at him, as if he had dropped a plate on her toe. When he got drunk with Lev and could not achieve an erection, she scolded him as for any other small sin. She did not seem to divide off sex mentally from the rest of her life and to feel he needed to be handled in any particular way. He would have liked to have asked Zach if making love to boys was like that, because none of the other women he had ever been with had been so simply demanding and so lacking in manipulative behavior. Sometimes he missed being coddled, being handled, being arranged for, but he only grew crazier for her. Compulsively he sketched her, changeable as a field.

"You're not a woman," he told her as they lay bare flank to flank under the feather bed in his room. "You're an intelligent cat. You have a human intellect, but not a human soul."

"Is that a compliment or an insult?"

"Merely an observation."

"Tais-toi," she said gently, putting her hand over his mouth, and mounted him. He liked having her fuck him. He could control his erection better and watch her breasts bounce if she held herself up or feel them bounding against his chest if she lay more closely. He liked the luxurious feeling of making her do most of the work.

Sometimes he felt as if she were exploring her sexuality more than giving herself to him; sometimes he could even feel used. But he also felt her love, passionate, fiercely loyal. She never made him jealous; she never glanced at any other man with sexual interest. She never flirted, but seemed convinced he embodied sex for her. She pored over his body with minute attention. She caressed his inner elbows until he declared them a major erogenous zone. She discovered exquisitely sensitive spots between his asshole and his balls and on the inside of his ankles and between his big and second toes.

She scavenged food for him; she fed him and mended his clothes and darned his socks. Those female things she did with a concentration and zest that made him feel cherished. Yet she did the same for Daniela. If anything, she and Daniela had drawn closer. Daniela accepted him without enthusiasm but without rancor. Jacqueline shared her body with him and parts of her mind closed to him with Daniela, such as her problematic relationship with Judaism. Daniela and she had long involuted discussions of how their religion could be rendered more responsive to women. She was so rational a creature, she seemed to him quintessentially French, a female Voltaire, and yet she carried around her religion like a pet porcupine, he thought, caressing its quills and addressing it in passionate tones. It was a paradox he could not resolve.

She viewed his art as self-indulgence, and yet she was a decent critic. She looked at his sketches and pointed at once to a shoddy line or something superfluous or accidental. He would not lose her to another man, because she paid no attention to them as sexual beings, but he could lose her because he fucked up; he could lose her to the Gestapo. Every time she went off on a dangerous errand without him, he suffered excruciating images of her body bleeding, torn, impaled. He could not swallow. His stomach clenched to a metal fist. Only her safe return released him. In front of the others he managed to seem only normally concerned, but he knew that he was crazy while she was gone, and that any decisions he made then should be reexamined with the return of ease and sanity, when she reappeared.

The drop came on Tuesday, near the ruins of a château. It was supplies, the little parachutes opening, cartons and crates floating down in the light of the full moon but scattered over several miles. The pilot in the lead plane had been nervous and began to release before he was over their triangle of fires, so they were up all night collecting every last crate. In the nearby town of Vabre, a textile town with a fish hatchery, they opened the rubbish dump, steaming a little on the icy night air, to hide extra ammunition and plastique in the old trash.

"We won't be able to use that site again," Lev said. "We messed up the snow for two square miles. There's no way the Boches won't see it. They'll know we had a drop. They'll be looking for our weapons house to house. Your radioman Raymond had better move farther up into the mountains tomorrow."

Jacqueline volunteered to get up again after two hours' sleep and go to warn him in the little village where he was staying with a widow, about ten kilometers out of Vabre, and at the same time to deliver the latest reports for London. There were the railroad reports, the troop movements, the reports on outposts and guard movements in the Pyrénées. OSS was using that route heavily for their people and deliveries of information and money.

Jeff claimed he had a great need to talk to Raymond too, to send the coordinates of a new drop site for the next shipment. His greatest need was to keep an eye on Jacqueline, but he also considered Raymond felt a little too well protected and had been dragging his heels lately. Sometimes their people up in the mountains grew overconfident, since they weren't seeing the Germans or the Vichy collaborators every day, and the countryfolk around them gave them support that could fool them to the dangers of their situation. He had been shocked to learn that Raymond was where he had been the week before, staying in the house of a young widow who was reputed to be a first-class cook, able to make a fine ragoût out of a straw hat. It was time to build a small fire under Raymond.

The air was sharp as flint against their faces as they pedaled through the pale blue morning light along the gorge of the Agout, the road snaking among the grey and red rocks, the snow golden in the patches of sun, cobalt in the shadows. His sinuses ached. His ankle hurt in the cold. He dreamed of spring, of making love with her on a hillside that would smell of heather and broom. They turned onto a narrower road.

They were bicycling sharply uphill along a stream rattling under its ice, each thrust of the pedal an agony, when Jacqueline abruptly dismounted and motioned him to stop also, to come off the road. Leaving their bicycles hidden in a thicket, they scrambled up a rock over the stream. Icicles hung from its ledges. His feet and hands slipped in the holds he used. Ahead she wriggled up, crawled out on top and lay on her belly in the snow watching the village just below them. "What's wrong?" he whispered.

"I don't know . . . Listen."

He listened. "I don't hear anything." The village looked peaceful. The overlapping slates of the roofs in the mountain village resembled fish scales. Here they hung slate for siding, thin slabs. The effect was not pretty but grim, like stone tar paper. The villages in these mountains were small, stark, poor. Always there were many sheep and a few cows. The churches were small and bowed. Something in the grey rock, the sheep, the many boulders, the fast speckled streams aroused him as a painter. His Argenteuil, his Mont-St-Victoire, his Sacred Mountain was this landscape.

"Right. There's only one dog barking, and he's howling and has been. No other dogs. When have you ever come up on a village and the dogs haven't barked? And no children. Something's wrong." She frowned, shaking her head. Then she crept back to the bikes. "We can't go in."

"Jacqueline, I have to send that information to London."

"Something's wrong there," she said. "We must go back."

She was hardheaded. The village looked normal to him. He had the choice of going on alone, but without what he had come to do, because she was pedaling madly back toward Vabre with the packet of messages. Feeling greatly put upon, he pedaled after her, feeling the cold, his fatigue, the utter futility of having risen at six after going to bed at four, pedaled for two hours and now returning with the same information they had carried up. "Slow down!" he yelled at her. "My ankle is killing me. You're a stubborn self-righteous little bitch!"

It wasn't until they were getting ready to return to Toulouse that they heard that the village had been occupied by the SS, Raymond had been captured, the widow shot in her own yard and her body exposed in the town square. Twenty townspeople were taken as hostages and then machine-gunned as reprisal for the Resistance activities revealed by the presence of the radio. Had they entered the square, they would have seen the bodies, but by then they would have been trapped. The dogs had been shot too, except for the widow's spaniel. Some German liked spaniels and saved it.

Jacqueline took her premonition for granted, as did Daniela and Lev. "She can smell them," Lev said.

"God gives me that much," Jacqueline said. "It isn't what I'd ask for, but it's useful. It's necessary to be clear, that's all there is to it."

Was it a chess game they were playing with the Nazis, and if so, did the Germans and the Vichy collaborators ever lose any pieces? Yes, they had lost Gilles. On the Paris street they had lost the captain and his lieutenant whom Daniela's brother had shot before he blew himself up. And the war. That they were losing. He could smell the invasion coming, while the underground was sending out to the Allies precise and full information on all the German defenses, on their weapons, on their plans. It would come, and soon, he thought. When spring came, could the armies be far behind?

I belong here, he thought, with these people. It's right. I never belonged anyplace before, but here I belong. This is my landscape, my countryside, my light, my woman. I will sink roots here and flourish, like one of the mighty beeches. He had begun to cultivate a strong local accent, for he no longer wanted to sound like a Parisian. There had been painters in Toulouse always, but not landscape painters. Corot had painted around here briefly. The mountains in every direction were different: the Pyrénées, mighty, sharp peaks, long vistas bounded by glaciers, steep and lush on the lower slopes. The houses were built higher there, with sharply pitched roofs. The mountains of Lacaune were low and open, scrublands, sheep country full of outcroppings, abandoned stone sheds and farmhouses, small villages growing into the rock. Montagne Noire was covered with rich noble forests, hemlock and beech. He found himself constantly thinking of what land he would buy after the war. There was a country inn outside of Albi he discussed endlessly with Jacqueline. She would run the kitchen and he would run the hotel. That made her laugh, because she pointed out she knew nothing about food, except how to eat it, which she would gladly do on any occasion.

"We'll complain of the tourists and the foreigners," she said. "We'll talk about the difficulty of getting good help these days and rail at the petty thievery of the staff."

On all their errands and escapades and night excursions to sabotage the rail lines, a munitions dump on the Garonne, SS communications, he carried along his country inn, sometimes at Albi, sometimes at Salvetat, furnished it, planned menus, financed and refinanced his dream. Often they worked together, for Jacqueline proved to have the best touch with plastique in the group. On excursions into the countryside he felt as if he were secretly shopping for real estate, for after the war. He would never return to his old life, to the States, to failure. Here he would flourish. And paint. This was virgin landscape. Unlike Taos, where every rock he eyed had been painted ten ways before, who had ever taken an easel into the rock fields of the mountains of Lacaune? Whose eye had stroked the long flanks of these mountains? Who had caught the wild tulips? Who had captured the lichen-grey-green rocks among the rapids? This earth, this sky cried to him. It was his.

The Tear in Things

They would run through the cold, black morning, their salvaged cans clinking at where their waists used to be. The guards were all around them beating at them with their rifles. If a woman went down, that was it, Maman and she would not let each other fall.

Then they entered the din of the hollow mountain where they were building a factory, where at least it was warmer from the machinery. Hunger was all of the time, a howling from within the starved body slowly dying, slowly eating itself, the outrage of the body that it should be worked twelve hours a day at hard, fast labor dragging out carts loaded with broken rock, put into harness like horses, and given nothing but moldy bread of sawdust and watery soup of turnips or cabbage.

Love kept Rivka going, love for Maman like a hot coal in her, Maman who was the only warmth, the only good, the only softness and strength in the universe of acid sleet. Since they were two, one could always watch the other's few things, the can in which the watery soup was ladled, the scrap of rope, the leg wrappings, the clogs that could not be replaced: any of these stolen could mean death, so when they had to step into a real shower or be deloused, when they had to strip for a Selection, then the other would hold on and wait.

Sometimes Maman would insist on splitting her piece of daily bread and giving half to Rivka, because she said Rivka's need was more, for she was still growing, although she was not, she could not. Her bones ached. Her periods had never started; her breasts had never formed. She looked like a tall skeletal child, looming over her mother, when she saw herself reflected in standing water, in metal in the factory. Her hair was cropped so that her skull stood out grey. Her arms and legs were pitted with running sores.

In winter every day at roll call, as they stood in the dark and the air that was ice in their lungs and that squeezed even the pain out of their hands and feel and faces, women fell over. Sometimes they died on the spot. If they didn't, they were taken to be killed. Never fall. Keep standing, keep moving, and stay close to Maman.

When a prisoner threatened Maman, Rivka would bare her teeth like a rat and start swinging. When one of the guards or the kapos hit Maman or knocked her to the ground, of course she had to stand and look down. But she let nobody else touch Maman. Sundays and after the standing at attention in the evenings, sometimes Maman sang her Yiddish songs, "Schlaffen, mine yiddele, schlaffen," as they picked the lice from each other, the lice that gave them ulcers and brought typhus that killed. "Tumbalalaika" with its magic questions. What can burn, burn and not burn up? A heart. Yes. Then the women ghosts would climb onto the slats and shiver and try to sleep. In the morning someone would be dead and a neighbor would grab clothing, a hidden scrap of bread and their shoes, fast, because shoes could be traded for bread.

Naomi woke aching, aching. Her stomach seemed to be shriveled to a hard green potato in her chest. Every night she tried to stay awake, but finally she slept and then sometimes she dreamed about school or Alvin or pigeons or people shooting each other, but sometimes, she was there, in the place of death, locked into Rivka's body.

Sometimes she tried to bargain with G-d. Please, let them escape, let them out of the place of evil and I will be good. I won't let Alvin stick his tongue in my mouth. I won't let myself make up stories about Leib in bed at night. I won't think about Leib in that way ever again and I won't imagine that Trudi has an accident and dies suddenly, never once will I do it anymore. I won't help Sandy cheat on tests in English, G-d, and I won't feel superior to her and think how come I get A's when it isn't even my language. I won't steal from the dime store anymore, even if Sandy and Alvin and Four Eyes all beg me to. I won't even sneak any more looks at the gushy letters that Murray writes Ruthie, I promise.

If you just let me sleep and not know and not feel and not see anymore, please, I'll be good. She would help Aunt Rose meekly and zealously for several days, scrubbing and cleaning and shopping fervently, keeping track of the red and blue points with extra care, running around the same as Aunt Rose did to find a little bargain or a shop that actually had a quarter pound of butter or a little piece of lamb. Detroit was always undergoing meat famines, when nothing but offal could be found, and not much of that.

Maybe for several nights she wouldn't have the dreams, and she would try all of the time to be really good. She would even help Trudi with baby David, as if she didn't get too much of babies at home. She strove hard and then she had a dream and she felt like a fool. G-d was mocking her. G-d didn't care what lies she told him and so what if she was good for two whole days, big deal. G-d knew that inside she was no good, and that was all there was to it. To hell with it, which was a phrase she had taken to saying, although not at home. To hell with it. She affected a racy style and swore. Nobody knew what to make of Sandy and her at school. They did well in their classes. They were in college prep, but they were not middle class. Sandy had more clothes than Naomi, but they were both shabby in their washworn rayon blouses and skimpy cut skirts, next to the middle-class girls in powder blue sweaters and little pearl necklaces.

Sometimes Sandy and she wore oversized men's shirts. Naomi had helped herself to two of Duvey's last year, and lately she had persuaded Sharon to give her one of Arty's with frayed cuffs. She didn't care, because she rolled up the sleeves. Sandy and she had that shuffle all the fast girls used, and she could talk to guys out of the side of her mouth and pass comments with the glibbest. They watched the colored kids carefully and practiced jitterbug steps together, so they looked real tough out on the floor at the school dances after every scrap and paper drive. Mostly the girls danced together, but Naomi and Sandy frequently had partners. The Catholic girls passed rumors about them that they did it with all the boys, and the daughter of the Jewish dentist would not walk in the halls with them, for fear their reputation would rub off on her like greasy lipstick. The boys did not try any funny stuff with her, although out of respect for her or out of respect for Alvin, Naomi was not sure.

Clotilde asked her, How come you want to act like those V-girls? V-girls or Victory girls was what the girls who chased soldiers were called. Naomi couldn't answer. Maybe it was a style she could carry off. She didn't have the money to look like the popular girls who ran the clubs in school. Maybe if, like Clotilde, she had her maman, she would not need to act tough.

Sandy's mother, Mrs. Rosenthal, did not like the way Sandy was acting now that she did not have to drag her baby brother around with her. She did not approve of the way they hung out with the boys on the corner or of Sandy's wearing men's shirts. She said the way the girls walked together on the street, shuffling, arms linked, chewing gum and laughing loudly, looked cheap. Mrs. Rosenthal said Naomi was a poor motherless immigrant who didn't know any better and it was too bad that her aunt was too busy caring for other people's children to have time to watch over those under her own roof.

Mrs. Rosenthal said Naomi was a bad influence on Sandy, making her look cheap too. Mrs. Rosenthal tried to talk to Aunt Rose, but Aunt Rose laughed and said couldn't she remember what it was like to be that age? She said they were good girls and that was just the way they dressed. They'd grow out of it. Her own mother had thought she was wild because she went on political picnics with boys and girls together to hear Socialist speeches, and she could remember when parents thought it was immoral when boys and girls danced together instead of separately. Now parents thought jitterbugging was wild instead of the waltz or the two-step, but when those dances had come in, parents had considered them dangerous.

Mrs. Rosenthal got red in the face and said that maybe Aunt Rose didn't care to see to her niece's reputation, being too busy trying to make money off the neighborhood women, but she took being a mother more seriously and she was not going to let her beautiful daughter go to the dogs just because Aunt Rose didn't have a sense of responsibility to her own sister's child.

Aunt Rose said she had more of a sense of responsibility than Mrs. Rosenthal both to her neighbors who needed help and to her own sister's daughter, who was being raised with a sense of responsibility, not spoiled and taught to spend her days staring in a mirror. Naomi was a good girl and smart enough to get her own homework done and help Sandy with hers, and Mrs. Rosenthal ought to be grateful to Naomi for carrying Sandy on her back through high school. This was no time for Jews to take on airs and try to pull rank on each other, with the Nazis killing them every day and the rest of the world indifferent. They must stick together and recognize they were all Jews and equal in the face of trouble.

After that, Naomi wasn't welcome in the Rosenthal house, only thirty feet away from her own. They spent almost as much time together, with the gang and in school and coming and going. Sandy said her mother thought she was still a baby and was jealous because she had a true best friend. Her mother didn't want her to have any fun.

Trudi was worried about Leib who had been wounded and was on his way home. Ruthie was worried about Murray, going from one island to another. All that fighting was distant from where she cared about; it would be a long time before it helped her family. She wondered if she would grow up and they would still be fighting the war. Maybe by then they would have run out of men, and like the Soviet Union, they would let women fight too.

Maman was coughing. She had a fever and the bloody diarrhea. She could not eat the soup and she was weakening. On the way out of the mountain to the barracks, she fell down in the black snow and the guard beat her with his rifle butt on the head and on the back. Rivka yanked her to her feet and supported her, half dragging, back to the barracks. Rivka was terrified. It was unlike the fear that she always felt. They were all afraid all of the time, because they were not yet dead. They could still feel, and while you could feel in that place, you should be afraid.

Now each moment was the tooth of a saw blade cutting into her. Maman, you have to be well, Maman! Rivka begged inside her head.

In the morning she tried to get Maman up, tried to drag her, but Maman kept falling. Her fever was up. The kapo said she had to go into the Revere, the infirmary.

That morning Rivka stood at roll call alone for two hours, coatless, bareheaded in the iron air with rutted ice under her feet, and alone she marched into the dark hollow mountain roaring with machinery and echoing with blasting. Alone she worked, hauling broken stone out. Alone she stood in the line waiting and waiting, alone she ate the watery turnip soup.

She got permission from the kapo to run to the Revere, carrying her evening slice of bread she had saved, to pay Maman back for the half slices she had given Rivka of her daily slice. When she got to the Revere, a dirty barracks where the women lay on the bare earth, she could not find Maman. The nurse put her arms around Rivka. "Little one, they took her today. They said she was too sick to work anymore. They took her away."

Rivka screamed. She fell to the floor and screamed until the guards kicked her and the kapo beat her unconscious with a stool leg. Then she crawled back to the barracks. Already Maman's little scrap of blanket had been stolen. Rivka lay in her bed, hungry, hungry, for while she had been unconscious, someone had taken her slice of bread. Maman was gone and now she was truly and forever alone.

Naomi woke screaming. "Maman est morte," she cried out. "My mother is dead!"

Rose told her she had had a nightmare, but Naomi knew better. Rose brought her warm milk with a spoonful of honey and nutmeg in it and wiped her forehead and told her that everybody had bad dreams. Rose sat on the side of her bed and sang her a song in Yiddish about daisies and then a song of riddles, that one Maman always sang. Naomi turned her face to the wall. She was sleeping in Duvey's bed, and he was dead. He was down in the cold salt waters of the sea. Maman was dead. She herself deserved to die too.

JACQUELINE 8

Spring Mud, Spring Blood

30 mars 1944

Spring pricks at us, with its first soft airs stealing over the mud. The Garonne roars through Toulouse, fat with snowmelt. Every day the light grows longer and stronger, bloody at six o'clock on the bricks of our street. Danger and opportunity swell with the hard casings of the buds cracking open. Every day the Boches and the Milice pick off more of our people and every day more people join the Resistance. Eduardo, who is Spanish, says that people join when they think you are winning. He has just been among our maquis near Lacaune, helping to train new fighters. He is missing two fingers, but our best weapons instructor.

At nine each night, we listen to the oracle of the BBC, waiting for messages that give us specific targets to strike, railroad lines, factories, all in code, of course, and always waiting for that message that will propel us into the uprising that must come soon. From London the signal will be given to rise and attack, everywhere, at the same time that the Allies land their armies.

Being in love inside such a community of resistants is not the isolation I feared. I do not feel less close to Daniela or to any of the others; if anything, I believe I am more tolerant, more understanding of weakness. Physical satisfaction makes me better tempered, although Daniela laughs at me and says she doesn't think anybody else has noticed such an alteration! She says they are not about to change my name from ginger to honey.

More and more agents are coming over the Pyrénées or being dropped to other Resistance groups. Papa's group in Montagne Noire now has a British Jedburgh team, one of those three-person French-British-American teams they are sending us. Lev will not go to meet them. "The British are my enemies, the same as the Germans. The British put me in a rotten pisshole of a jail. Look." Lev ripped his shirt from his pants and hiked it up his back. "That was what the British did to me, in Haifa, to try to make me talk." His back is ridged with scars.

Jeff argued with him. "You have to take help from those willing to give it. I haven't noticed the Russians parachuting us any supplies."

"You think I'm a fool, I expect help from the Russians? Look, I trust the French Communists—up to a point—because like us they really want to fight. They aren't waiting for the Lord de Gaulle to lay on his hands and tell us we can fire our rifles. But who trusts? Listen, Vendôme, in Palestine the line changed and the party on high in Mother Russia decreed that the party in Palestine and in Persia was to be all Arabs and we were superfluous. In fact, anti-Semitism and attacks on Jews were a sign of proletarian struggle. You expect justice where Jews are concerned?"

For Jeff, the struggles between Left parties are obscure and fanatical, akin to the struggles of Christian sects in the second century C.E. Since I grew up with the political arguments of Papa and his copains ringing in my ears, I have trouble imagining Jeff's alienation from the frame of reference I take for granted. Americans seem to have a system where you belong to parties by where you live: if you live in Kansas, you are a Republican, and if you live in Georgia, a Democrat.

"Listen to me," Lev was saying. "The Communists recalled their best Jewish organizers—workers, good fighting men and women—from Palestine. They shipped them to Russia, where they shot them. So you tell me I look for help from Russia?" Lev spat. "We make our luck, and I don't forget all countries are against us. I never forget."

1ier avril 1944

Yesterday morning, a peasant told Roger about seeing the Germans execute five people in the woods after forcing them to dig a trench. At dawn we went south of the city where he showed us the spot and we dug up the bodies. One was a railroad worker in the Résistance-Fer, an engine driver from Montauban. One was a young man nobody could identify. Two of them were the prostitutes, Bibi and Paulette, from near the station, who gave the Resistance money and hid our people. The last was the body of Larousse. All had been tortured. Their naked bodies were pitted with open sores, with burns, with bruises. Bones were broken in their hands and feet. The nipples had been cut from the breasts of the younger woman, Paulette. Larousse was missing the nails of his right hand. Something large had been thrust into his ass until his intestines had ruptured.

Daniela and I laid out the bodies in a nearby dairy. I washed Larousse's body. Over Daniela's protests, Lev photographed them. He said we must keep a record because afterward people will say it was simply the way war was, and he did not want anyone to forget what had been done to Paulette and to Larousse. Then we reburied them under a cairn of stones. Daniela was very silent. Afterward, as we wept together, she said she understood her brother's decision, and finally she accepted it. It was better to die at once than to be tortured.

4 avril 1944

I keep dreaming about washing Larousse's body. He was thin and cold as water. His ribs stood out. His body hair was fine as corn silk and pale brown. In death, his penis was half engorged, like a pink flower. His eyes, glazed over, would not stay shut. I keep wondering and wondering. Had he, in the great pain he endured at the end, regretted the good we did together? Or had it sustained him, or were they never balanced in any equation, the good that Larousse did and the evil that was done to him?

He was the brother I never had, and now he is destroyed. Never will the love he lavished in perfect care on the children we saved find a more personal outlet. What does it mean, that one person can do to another what was done to him? Did they experience a sexual thrill when they drove that club through his rectum? Did they laugh? Did pain move them when nothing else could? Do they really think they are of some higher being? His body is the answer to questions that ask themselves in me all of the time, when I sleep, when I wake.

I think too of Bibi, who was perhaps thirty-five, and Paulette, no more than twenty-five, who lived together and made their living out of their bodies, who had probably been lovers. Bibi had been abandoned pregnant and poor, Paulette had come from Algeria—two Jews with dyed blond hair and garishly painted faces who were unfailingly polite and gentle with me. The railroad worker leaves a family of five. The young man was probably a British or American agent, but nobody knows. After the war, maybe he will be identified from the photograph. Now he is buried with the others, under the cairn.

Lev said that you could tell from the bodies that it was the Gestapo who tortured them, because they have certain practices they like to follow. He thought they learned torture from a manual, because they often did the same things in the same way. Of course, he said, there were individuals like Klaus Barbie who seemed to have some special passion for it, but by and large, they tortured by the book.

Jeff disappeared quietly when we were washing the bodies. Part of being in love is as if you have an extra eye or an extra heat-seeking sense such as pit vipers possess, so that you can track your lover. Whatever I am doing, I am aware with a little portion of my mind of Jeff. He said nothing, just quietly slipped off, but I knew he was being sick out back. I did not want to call attention, because if Jeff revealed his squeamishness, Lev would have one up on him. For all that they get along these days, there is still that male prickliness of place to consider. I felt sick with grief but not with nausea; the pain is what was manifest to me. Did the infinite pain of torture wipe out the life that led to it? Or does pain become finally meaningless, the weakness of the body caught in a place bodies cannot survive? I cannot seem to stop brooding on Larousse.

15 avril 1944

We have a new radioman, parachuted in. He is from Louisiana and he speaks a peculiar slurry French. He is called Achille, a devout Catholic who keeps aloof from the Jews he finds himself among. There is no difficulty getting him to move promptly when he completes a transmission. He is neat and keeps his gear together and ready to clear out the door within five minutes of finishing a broadcast. He will probably survive a lot longer than the more gregarious and comfort-loving Raymond. Jeff finds him efficient but complains he cannot establish the rapport he had with Raymond. I don't like the way he looks at me since he learned I am Jeff's lover. He views me as a whore, I believe. Achille is uncomfortable with us and therefore despises us. It was a great relief to place him in Cambon, in the mountains near Lacaune, and return to Toulouse without him.

18 avril 1944

I have just been reflecting how you are not supposed to say men are beautiful, and yet that contradicts my deepest experience, because Jeff is beautiful in his body and his face and his movements and his little gestures. He uses his hands more than most Americans I've observed, perhaps unconsciously adopting that custom from us. But he has a great stillness that I adore, when he sits and sits and stares and stares while his eyes devour the world.

When he wears that intent, amazed expression, I ask him what he is thinking about. Half the time he'll insist he wasn't thinking about anything, but if I persist, I find he was studying the light on the cypress needles or on the bricks, or the color of the shadow of a cloud or the particular green of the grass along the canal. Therefore I do not fall into the error I have often heard lovers make of saying, We are just the same, we are one. Jeff is not like me inside. Light and color move him the way words or ideas move me. Sometimes when he stares at a hill patchworked with vines and wheat, his hands move in his lap or in the air as if they are stroking something. He picks up an apple and turns it in his hands as if it were a small world; then he doesn't hear what the others are saying.

Usually I go home to Daniela every night, but if we are caught by curfew or out on an action together, then I sleep in Jeff's room overlooking the crowded cemetery. One way in which we are different always comes out then, because Jeff has a passion for making plans for after the war. He wants me to play let's pretend with him, but for me that is all it is, a game to pacify him. I think of Larousse's thin torn body, white as whey, and while I have never longed more fiercely to live and go on living, I cannot believe in plans.

Jeff needs to dwell on a future in which we will be together, here, a future in which he paints and we make a living in some pleasant way. Me, when I think about afterward, I imagine sitting in an easy chair in my own room safely reading a book while Bach plays. I remember certain dishes: veal in mustard sauce, challah, financier cake with almonds, butter on croissants, butter on beans, butter on potatoes. Real coffee thick with creamy milk. That is all I let myself imagine.

I do not love him any less than he loves me, but I cannot want the way he does—I don't believe in the world that much. No, I take what we have and cherish it and live it. If we should die together at once, suddenly, that would not be so bad as many likelier fates. A moment of painful surprise and then silence. Following all this joy.

20 avril 1944

We have never been busier, with more and more sabotage to be carried out. We do collect important information for Jeff to code and transmit through Achille to London, through the National Nitrogen Board, through the Résistance-Fer, through Thibaut in the mairie, through Margot in the Milice office. Sometimes the BBC broadcast specifically assigns us targets—shipments, troop movements, factories, bridges.

Tonight there were three different actions to be carried out. Lev was taking two men out of Toulouse to join the maquis at Cambon. Daniela was to coordinate the distribution of the new issue of *Quand Même*, the Jewish paper. Jeff and I, along with Roger, were going to sabotage a plaque tournante, an electrical turntable in a roundhouse. Locomotives are serviced in the roundhouse. Tonight there were twenty-four inside. The engine is driven onto a turntable until it balances on the pivot, then it turns around to the exit rails. Two charges placed just right on the pivots—taped there—will do damage quite neatly, injure no one and require replacement of the pivot—a job that can tie up all the engines in a roundhouse for a good long time.

I have proved quite tidy with explosives. Small deft hands are an advantage. I have learned how to place the charges so exactly that I require only a narrow beam flash. I handle the plastique almost casually now—never without caution, but no longer do my hands sweat themselves slippery. I must remark that I have noticed as soon as I began work with plastique, it lost its charisma. It became a tool, merely. The Sten guns remain the province of men and therefore potent, but plastique has been reduced by the touch of a woman to something like explosive dough. The men no longer compete to handle it.

When I kneel to wedge the half hour time pencils—they have to go off simultaneously—the night seems preternaturally quiet. Every movement of my fingers sounds abruptly magnified. My knees crack like castanets. Time feels elastic, stretched and stretched and about to snap back suddenly. Yet when I finish, I must force myself to leave. I want to hang around and watch, drawn back to the heavy machinery with its reek of oil and power.

In another existence, I would deal with these huge machines that are like dumb and amazingly strong dinosaurs, and lead them through their paces. I would be one of those women from Soviet posters who drive earthmoving equipment and build dams. Like Daniela's friend on the kibbutz, I would fight the men for the right to drive the tractor. Machines make us powerful, too. With a machine I can pick up a house. With a machine I can carry tons of coal. With a machine I can dig a hole through a mountain.

Tonight I sleep at Jeff's, and he is waiting impatiently for me now, so I will end. After an action, it is hard to go right to sleep.

21 avril 1944

This morning I was asleep when Lev burst in. "They caught Daniela last night. They've got her at the Milice barracks and this morning they're taking her to the prison. We're going to attack the truck."

I could not speak. I thrust on my clothes and checked my stolen Luger, slid it under my old blanket of a coat and stood waiting.

"Not you," Lev said.

"Yes, me," I said. "Daniela is my sister. You can't stop me from going. I have little enough family left."

Jeff was dressed now, that pointed foxy look he has before action. "Do you have a plan? Let's hear it."

Lev leaned over the rickety table by the window. "This is the prison truck." He moved a pencil along. "This is the gazogène truck. It pulls from a side street across. Blam. They collide. Here's the Renault coming up behind. We open fire and then we grab her. It's our only chance."

I tell the truth when I say I didn't care if it was a good plan or a bad one. I had to take Daniela back or die. That was all. I needed to be acting, doing. I wanted to strike Jeff and shake Lev hard, to get them moving. Jeff argued, "The truck hits the armored truck, okay, but you don't want them to come out firing. Jacqueline is in the truck, but she's pregnant. She's in labor. She's on her way to the hospital. She starts screaming and moaning and groaning. Roger is with her, he's the husband. You and I are behind in the Renault. Roger and Jacqueline create a diversion begging the police for help."

"As long as I have my weapon."

"No," Jeff said. "You have to look pregnant."

"I'll be pregnant. Look." I grabbed the cushion from the chair, but to myself I thought, Okay, but I'll give birth to a revolver.

At the moment in the street, actually bruised and shaken from the accident and with blood trickling from a cut in my forehead, I found myself proved right about the need for my weapon. The guards had smashed Roger against the steaming hood of the truck and were kicking him and searching him. Me they left lying on the street moaning, with the pillow giving me a vast whale belly. One of the policemen casually kicked me, but they had left me there like a pile of laundry while they beat Roger and then when he tried to argue with them, they smashed him over the head with the butt of a pistol. When I heard the first shots from the back of the prison truck, I fired on the guards as they turned, weapons in hand.

I think tonight of all the times Daniela and I have talked about violence and when it is justified and whether even then we could or we couldn't kill, and I am amazed, both proud and aghast at what has happened to me in this war, that I shot without thinking and accurately. It was decided by all sides long before, the police that they would capture and kill Jews and resistants, the resistants that we would fight back.

Roger was out cold from the blow to his head. The gazogène truck was wrecked. Pillow flopping out, I dragged Roger by the leg around to the Renault. They had Daniela, half carried between them. Lev slid in to drive. Another dead policeman lay half out of the prison truck, broken open like a can. Lev bent a fender backing out of the narrow street. Then he was off at full speed, while I held Daniela, shaking against me. We were jammed in, six in a car built for four adults.

"Hold me gently," Daniela said in a cracked voice, "I'm banged up. Do you have anything to drink?"

Lev passed back a flask. "Here."

Daniela shook her head. "Water, I mean."

"Drink this now," I ordered her, wondering what she would say when she found out it was me who shot the two Milice. I decided not to mention it. "How did they get you?"

"They busted the whole *Quand Même* staff. Everybody." Daniela sipped the brandy and gagged. "We can't go back to the garage. They have my address. Did they pick up the Fauriers?"

"No," Lev assured her, driving fast. "When you didn't come home, they packed up the kids and came to me. They should already be at Lacaune. We all better clear out of Toulouse. I've got the boys moving the weapons. We'll have to take to the brush just like Lapin. At least spring is here. Daniela . . . what did they do to you?"

"They roughed me up. They knew they had to hand me over to the Gestapo, so they were just amusing themselves."

"Did they rape you?"

"Is that all men can think of to ask? No. But I have a couple of broken ribs. With every breath, my side feels pierced. When the two trucks hit each other, I thought we'd gone over a mine. Could we get these chains off?"

"Soon," I promised, wanting to hold Daniela close but fearful of hurting her more.

"At least they didn't rape you," Lev repeated.

"Thank you for taking such an interest," Daniela said. "What's wrong with Roger?"

"He's coming to," Jeff said. "We'll have to get him looked at."

"Who's to look at him besides me?" Daniela said. "I'll give you instructions for taping my ribs as soon as we're where we're going. Soon. Please soon. I'm terrified the rib may pierce my lung."

I have to say that in spite of Daniela's condition. I felt as if my blood were fermenting with happiness, for Daniela had been taken from me and now we had taken her back. She lay against me, her eyes shutting, half unconscious in a trance of pain. At one point she opened her eyes, touched my face and murmured, "There's blood all over you."

I had forgotten that my forehead was cut where the Milice struck me when he knocked me down. I must say, I do not give a damn. If it leaves a scar, I can wear bangs. Daniela is taken back. I feel drugged with the poisons of fatigue and the ashy residue of excitement, but still happiness sings in me. She has been seized from death.

I don't even care that we had to go off and leave Toulouse with no notice and no preparation. By now I have no possessions except my journal, worn around my neck in a bag, and my Luger. Here the season is a month behind Toulouse. Sometimes they get thirty centimeters of snow in the winter. These mountains are not grand and snowcapped like the Pyrénées or as lush as the Montagne Noire. Jeff says it looks like Dartmoor in England.

This is real maquis country, scrub growth, with huge bushes of broom and gorse and many grey rocks scattered about. Good country for shepherds and the sheep I can smell roasting downstairs in this abandoned farmhouse where we have taken up residence, made of stone picked up on the hillsides. Daniela has fallen into exhausted sleep, properly taped up—she instructed me as I worked on her, so that I felt like a doctor operating on a patient according to verbal instructions given as the operation proceeded! From the southernmost of these mountains you can look across the valley at the Montagne Noire, but we are high up in the moors. It is extremely quiet. We can hear for a long way and see, from the mountaintops, for a long way too. Here we are nestled near a fast-moving mountain brook that tumbles down from rock to rock, grey and splotched yellow green with lichens, that look in the stream like huge frogs. From our room upstairs we can hear the sound of the water plummeting down. Although we are safe noplace, here we can talk in normal voices and stay together as a family, among the sheep, the river and the rocks.

Woman Is Born into Trouble as the Water Flows Downward

March was bitter and drab. The snows melted only to reveal the trash, the dog feces, the discarded orange rinds of winter, the sodden leaves of fall drained of color. Freezing rain fell, a phlegm of the air. Everyone was irritable and half the world had a hacking cough or the flu.

The war had gone on and gone on. Everybody was tired of Kate Smith singing "God Bless America" and bond drives every month. People bitched about wage and price controls and shortages. Everybody knew someone who had made a killing in the black market. Half the time when Rose and Sharon did have enough red points or blue points to buy meat or canned goods or sugar, what they wanted didn't exist. In March, already the union and the Democrats and Republicans were gearing up for the November election. The Russians were making a brave show, pushing the Germans back across the map, but in Italy, the front seemed stuck and casualties mounted.

Morris was attending a frenzy of meetings about the Jews of Hungary, who had survived the war until this spring but were now in grave danger, since the Germans, no longer trusting their allies the Hungarians, had taken over. Yet the State Department remained as hostile as ever toward intervening on behalf of Jews, and no government expressed interest in the negotiations to save that population. The British would not budge on refusing passage to Palestine. No country wanted more Jews, so they would go up the chimneys for lack of caring. Morris drafted letters, signed petitions, raised money, buttonholed his congressman. "The truth is," he complained, "the Democratic party is giving us the finger, because they know we're for Roosevelt and they don't have to bargain for our votes."

On the line at Briggs, Mary Lou was badly burned when a tank of oxygen exploded. Vivian and Ruthie decided to forgive her the anti-Semitic preacher and visit her in the hospital, but she was too doped up to know them. She kept saying, "It's so lucky my face didn't get burned," lying swaddled to the neck in white wrappings.

Ruthie liked welding, liked working in the mask and gloves so that no one could guess her sex, liked the sense of being wrapped up in the tools and accouterments of her new trade. She was good and fast, and so was Vivian. When they learned new tricks, they taught each other.

Vivian wanted to continue after the war; she liked welding and she was making good money. Her one ambition was to get on the day shift, so that she could work the same hours as her husband when he came back from the Army. She didn't worry as much about him as Ruthie did about Murray, because he was working in transportation. "They asked him what he did in civilian life. He said he built auto bodies. So they put him in the repair shop for jeeps and trucks. If he hadn't used to work on this old Nash," Vivian rapped the steering wheel, "I don't think he would have known the first thing. I figure he's okay if anybody is. He's in Palermo."

Murray sounded safe for the moment. He was back on Guadalcanal training. He said it was a different place, with movies and ice cream and real barracks. He talked a lot about his buddy Jack. He drew a picture of a land crab, which he said were like enormous cockroaches, got into everything and when they were crushed, stank of rotten fish. He did not mention his friend Harvey any longer, although she had asked about him.

Naomi had been having such bad nightmares that Ruthie had invited her to sleep in the upper bunk again. Naomi continued using Duvey's old room for doing her homework but seemed a little afraid of sleeping there, mumbling about a dead man's bed. Ruthie understood. At one point in her childhood, she would weep if she had to take the garbage out to the alley, because she developed a morbid fear of the rats scurrying there.

Naomi was asleep when she came in from work, so Ruthie undressed in the bathroom and slipped into her bunk. If she had studying to do or an exam the next morning, she could turn on a pinup lamp attached to the bedpost, prop her pillow against the wall and work without disturbing Naomi. Naomi moaned in her sleep and sometimes woke crying. Ruthie would stand beside the bunk brushing Naomi's curly hair to soothe her, rubbing her shoulders.

Leib had been sent back to the States, to the government hospital in Ann Arbor, where they were getting ready to fit him with an artificial right foot. Trudi, who went up to see him every weekend, said he was a real hero about his foot. He was supposed to be discharged within a month. She had not been permitted to bring baby David, but she gave Leib twenty photos: baby David eating, baby David with a rattle, baby David in the arms of every relative down to second cousin.

"What's a foot?" she said to Ruthie. "Wouldn't you trade a foot any day to have Murray safe at home?"

It was a barbaric idea, trading parts of the man you loved for safety. "Will he be able to walk?"

"So he'll walk with a limp. He can't run bases or play basketball, but he's a grown man, who needs that? He'll get disability, but it's not like he's a cripple. When I think what could have happened to him! His mother goes up there and cries. I think that's disgusting. I try to kid him around, so he knows he's still my husband and I'm crazy to get him home."

Trudi was working at the Henry Ford Hospital four nights a week. The hospitals were so short on help, they were glad to hire her back part time. She was toilet-training David in a hurry, as she had promised Leib. It made for a lot of yelling and crying, with Trudi's mother scolding her for abusing her son with her haste.

Trudi wanted to quit her job and she wanted to move out of her parents' house, but she recognized she could not expect to do both, at least not until Leib was completely well and settled in a job. She asked everybody she met about apartments. Detroit was tight. Apartments had been split and split again into tiny studios, and the smallest of those was rented too. Sometimes people slept in shifts in the same beds. No basement apartment squeezed in a former coalbin or wedged under dripping pipes was too dark or humid, and no room prized into an attic, barely heated and uninsulated, was too cold and drafty to rent.

Trudi was readying herself for Leib's homecoming. She had gone on a diet and had a permanent. She was even trying to remember to wear gloves when she washed dishes and baby clothes so that her hands would be soft, the way they said in the magazines, and so her nails would grow long. When Trudi got dressed up to see Leib in Ann Arbor, Ruthie felt very plain next to her, as if like Naomi she were a girl watching a woman. She did not own a dress like the ones Trudi put on for Leib, with peplums, flounces, draping that emphasized Trudi's curves. Trudi even wore perfume.

Ruthie had no desire to trick herself up the way Trudi did, and no one to get dressed up that way for. Dating had been mostly a source of anxiety, so she never missed it. Her idea of fun was to put her feet in a basin of hot water with Epsom salts and read a book that wasn't for school, to look at *Life* and drink hot cocoa, to sit with Naomi's head on her shoulder and listen to Jack Benny and Rochester, to go to a good double feature.

Nonetheless, sometimes when Trudi was getting ready, she missed that sense of doing something for your man, of having a man who was looking forward to seeing you, of that pleasurable ache of anticipation. She had had pitifully little time with Murray. They had made love three times in twenty-four hours, and that had been that. Trudi had a marriage, a baby, and now her husband back; Ruthie had only the blurring memory of hasty couplings in a backseat and on a blanket. Her favorite photo of Murray she had taken at the big fountain in the zoo, right after they had got off the little train that chugged around between stations marked Alaska and Africa. She remembered evenings spent in movie theaters and in coffee shops just before he left for boot camp. Sometimes she thought she was living on dreams too fragile to survive so much handling.

It had rained all Monday, all Tuesday, a hard pelting often horizontal rain that overflowed the clogged gutters and flooded the underpasses and the streets. Her galoshes had worn through and leaked, but could not be replaced because they were made of rubber. Her shoes stayed sodden. Her coat had that wet wool smell and so did her skirt. There was a lot of absenteeism at Briggs, blamed on the flu.

Finally Wednesday the rain stopped, but the sky did not clear. It hung a hundred feet in the air sagging like a fat belly and obliterating the tops of buildings. She had to wait a long time for a bus, since there had been some trouble on the line. The buses were wearing out and could not be replaced, like so much else.

When she got home, she walked into chaos. Sharon was crying and Rose was wringing her hands. "What's wrong?" Her heart seized.

"A lady from the welfare came." Rose rolled her hands in her apron. "She says we can't have the babies here and we're going to jail for it. It's a crime to take care of babies without a license like they charge for and inspect you. Anyway, we could never get a license, she said it herself."

"How did they find out?"

"Mrs. Rosenthal," Sharon said. "The dyed-blond bitch turned us in. What business is it of hers? Just because all she wants to do all day is lie on the sofa and listen to soap operas and then wax the floor, while her husband sells fish, she's got no call to stick her long bony nose in our lives!"

"We never hurt those little babies," Rose said. "How can they tell us we're not fit? I raised three babies of my own, and Sharon has two. I know ten times as much about babies as that dried-up prune."

Ruthie's second thought was whether Rose's brush with the law would come back to haunt her in social work, but she put that aside. "Mama, they may fine you, and they're probably going to close you down, but they can't put you in jail."

"She said what we're doing is against the law, and the state is going to persecute us."

"It's a minor offense, Mama. I'll get all the facts, don't worry, don't fuss."

"But what are we going to do for money?" Sharon wailed. "I can't live on those allotment checks. My rent is that much right off the top."

"Maybe I can get you into the plant," Ruthie said. "They're always hiring."

"With the children so young? Arty would never forgive me."

"Mama can take care of them. She's had a lot of experience." Ruthie tried to make them smile. "I'll see what all this means. Don't worry. If you have to go to court, I'll go to court with you. We'll get a lawyer. How about Mr. Untermeyer who's on Tata's immigration committee?"

"Laws, courts, police, this isn't good." Rose sat down heavily, twisting her hands in her apron. "This means tsuris, more tsuris. At least they didn't see Naomi. I don't want them getting interested in what she's doing here. That's all we need."

Ruthie wanted to go to bed and sleep for a week and wake with all problems solved and the house restored to calm, but she must eat swiftly and get ready for eight hours of welding. Tomorrow she would have to cut classes and go downtown. Whatever she could smooth over, the nursery was closed, permanently. The working mothers would have to make other arrangements and Mama and Sharon were unemployed.

That would mean less money coming in, especially for Sharon, who'd have to take a job. Ruthie's mind was juggling expenses and income and trying to make everything come out, as she changed for work and got herself together. No point worrying now. At work, she must concentrate, or she'd end up cooked in a hospital bed like Mary Lou. Troubles came down like the infernal and incessant cold rain, far more than anybody needed to make things grow.

BERNICE 7

Major Mischief

In April the WASPs at the Air Transport Command Base in Long Beach got their uniforms, although unfortunately for Bernice and her squadron, in winter wool and not yet in summer weight. When she first put on her uniform, she had an enormous desire to be photographed, as did Flo and everybody else. Loretta, one of the WASPs whose husband was overseas, took their pictures with a Brownie box camera. Bernice waited impatiently the week until the film was ready. Every one of them not off with a plane went along with Loretta to the Long Beach drugstore to pick up the prints.

The uniform was handsome, designed by Cochran herself: not khaki, not military drab or sickly green, but a deep, dark and vivid blue. Against it the gold of the wings and WASP insignia glinted handsomely. The women with curls had trouble with the caps, but Bernice just stuck hers on at a racy angle. She was also in luck because large sizes were plentiful. The uniform came with skirt and slacks: enormously practical, Bernice thought, and wished all women's suits would offer that choice. However, the Army still balked at outfitting women. Everything under the uniform was their problem, and they received no more ration stamps than other civilians for shoes, which they bought with their own money.

"Listen, don't complain," Flo said. "Imagine what the military's idea of a bra would look like. Probably come with thumbtacks to hold it on."

Bernice loved her snapshot, posed in front of a P-51 Mustang. She had a bunch of prints made and sent one to The Professor and his housekeeper. His letters came regularly but sounded disjointed. Bernice imagined her father sitting at his desk, asking his housekeeper, What shall I say next? and her prompting him, Tell her about the flood downtown. Say that the Narzisse are blooming. Bernice could hear her voice coming through in the occasional German words in the letters. The Professor did not know the English name of the bulbs Viola had planted almost twenty years ago, still faithfully poking up through the myrtle and among the evergreens. They had not existed as daffodils to him before his housekeeper labeled them Narzisse.

She had prints made for Jeff and for Zach and sent them off to the old addresses in London. She had last heard from Jeff in August. Zach wrote her occasionally, but she had not had a letter since early March. She did not take his silence personally.

Ferrying was going to be a lot easier when she was stuck in little towns that were violently suspicious of a woman alone, especially one who arrived flying a plane and claimed to be working for the Air Corps. A uniform, even when people didn't know what kind it was, provided a sort of license. A great many people thought badly of women in the military. A real woman wouldn't do that; they must be tarts or perverts. Nonetheless, the uniform guaranteed that she would not be arrested by some leering sheriff on loitering or soliciting charges immediately upon flying in, as had happened to two WASPs in Alabama. It meant not being hassled in restaurants or bars because she was wearing slacks and not a skirt. It meant a little more respect from the guys in airports. For her, looking in the mirror, it meant one more step toward being a professional.

Maybe when they were given ranks and accepted into the Air Forces, maybe she would stay on after the war. Her squadron commander thought that militarization would come any day, and then they would be regular officers. Bernice had no qualms. She knew she was serving herself and only secondarily serving her country, but she never refused an assignment, she got the planes there as fast as the weather permitted, and she flew in rough weather as in smooth. She did not care that the blue serge was ridiculously hot for California, she wore it and sweated gladly.

The next trip into Newark, there was a message waiting for her: a phone number and the initial Z. *Swiftly* was all it said. She called at once from a pay phone, feeding quarters, dimes and nickels in as it turned out to be a Washington number.

"Ah, you've blown in!" Zach trumpeted. "Top drawer. I should be able to tie things up here and toddle up on the eight o'clock train. I have a reservation at the Waldorf, so go check in as Mrs. Zachary Barrington Taylor."

"You're using your own name? Suppose your wife finds out?"

"We're in mutual pursuit of a divorce. She's marrying a lesser Du Pont, but still a Du Pont, and I'm at long last to be dispensed with. I'm trying to satisfy the lawyers' requirements and the government's too whilst I am briefly in God's country. You can nap while you wait, but be prepared to be rousted. Oh, and order some champagne before room service closes. Be seeing you."

She checked in with her duffle bag, in uniform. If the news got back she might be in trouble, but she did not expect it to. She kept her gloves on, nervous about the lack of wedding ring, and was shown up to a suite. She ran a hot deep bath, soaked in it, washed her hair, read the papers while eating a room service steak, then turned in early and slept.

She did not even hear Zach arrive. When she wakened he was kneeling on the edge of the bed naked and rosy from the shower, with the light on and a glass of champagne on the bedside table. "Wake up, drink up and let's get to it. Hello, how are you, take off those ridiculous pajamas. Does the government issue you those? I forbid them." He opened the window to a mild night and threw them out.

"Hello," she mumbled, rubbing her eyes. "I went to bed at nine. What time is it?"

"What do you care? Time for me. Really, my pussy, you have such nice big tits and such nice big muscles, if you only had even a little prick, I'd never look at another piece. I should have started fucking you years ago instead of wasting my time on your self-serving brother."

"Do you have any news of Jeff?" She was part anxious for knowledge and part temporizing. He made her feel like prey. Why did he excite her? That there was no courtship, no flattery, no gallantry, why did that make her want? The tension began to gather in her muscles, in her vagina, a sense of congestion, of pressure, an engorging urge. He had lost weight since they had been together last, but he would always be a big beefy large-boned man. It was a tension of physical challenge, as if she were about to take part in a wrestling match.

"Coming back through London I picked up some gossip. He's near Toulouse with some maquis. He's very wicked because he's supposed to be working for SI, that is, strictly intelligence work, but he's got it all messed up. He's sending through intelligence and running around the mountains blowing up trains and lately, I hear, a munitions dump."

"That sounds plenty dangerous to me."

"Oh, it's fun and games, believe me. He's flourishing."

"Where have you been? Can you tell me?"

"I always tell you all, don't I? Talk later, fuck now. I have been so tediously good and responsible and long-winded these four days I am fit to burst, I am ready to dissolve into hot fragments of flak." He raised himself on his elbow, looked her over and then fell upon her.

Love was not what they made. Fucking, she thought, that spadelike ugly blunt word was better. They grabbed each other and grappled. He was rough with her and often he hurt her, yet once she was excited, she liked that too, for the pain increased her excitement. They bit and twisted and mauled each other. Shortly he thrust into her, hard, driving himself in and in and in, exploding. Then he made her come with his hand. Why should it be more intense than when she touched herself? But it was. She came in deep convulsions that left her weak.

They both fell asleep. In the morning she woke to his weight and he was fucking her again, this time from behind, manipulating her as he pounded in. When they showered together, she saw that she had left bruises and scratches on him too. They ordered up an enormous breakfast and pots of coffee.

"I've been bringing the word, in vain, I'm sure, to Washington. Even Churchill, who will support any peabrained drooling dinosaur bitch who calls herself the King of Transylvania, understands that Tito is fighting the Germans and our man Mihajlović mainly fighting Tito. I've been with both parties, jaunting about the mountains of that misbegotten country where everybody speaks his own language. My dear, I'm something of a linguist, but a country the size of Pennsylvania with five different languages? It reduced your poor battered lover to pointing and grimacing like the duchess who sat on an anthill."

"Will you go back?"

"Not on your sweet ass. My usefulness there is exhausted. I'd get a bullet in the back of the neck. I'm off to muck about in France."

"Will you see Jeff?"

"Not right away. I'll be posted farther north. I won't get the particulars till I'm in Londontown. Let me tell you, the days of crossing the old grey A being jolly are vanished, indeed. I remember the Pan Am Clippers, beds, spotless linen, fresh flowers, dinners cooked to order. These are grim days. You sit in those bloody Liberators on bucket seats and for days and days while your life glides in front of your eyes like a movie in slow motion and you reflect on all the things you might be doing instead that would be more fun, like taking over again every exam you ever cheated at from kindergarten on. And the plane stops at every place it can jolt down where there's nothing but barbed wire and boobs getting drunk and trying to take money off each other at cards or craps. Dear heart, if there's anything amusing about little bone cubes or pieces of paper with numbers on them that you can't spend, I never figured it out."

"I've never been big on games either."

"Not even in high school? Didn't you ever go mad for your gym teacher or get lewd hanging out in the locker room?"

"I hated it. I was so much bigger than the other girls, I hated to take off my clothes in front of them. I was ashamed."

"Oh, pussy, that was silly. You're ravishing, and I'm sure some crooked soul there would have noticed ta beauté and done it justice. But the less for them, the more for me. Let's go stroll along Fifth and ogle the competition and work off breakfast, eh?"

As they walked, Zach would nudge her and direct her gaze to a sailor idling along with a wistful air. "Do you like him? Nice ass. But what a doggy air. No sauce."

Bernice enjoyed the license to stare, but she was unmoved by the men he was eyeing. She strolled at his side, looking in shop windows and enjoying their reflection side by side. Walking with him, she did not have to adjust her gait. Her uniform was a perfect weight for the day, overcast, fifties, a hint of fog in the air and the buds prizing open on the little caged trees on the side streets. She felt reeking with sex, on vacation, at the peak of her powers. This is it, she thought, I must remember this as long as I live, striding along Fifth Avenue with Zach, both of us dashing with our bodies like good horses well ridden, and I arrived in a Mustang fighter and I live in the sky as much as anyone can.

It was as if she stood on a mountain looking down on Bentham Center and on the house where she had spent so many lonely and boring years and could see herself typing away on professors' articles and students' papers, carting the baskets of laundry out to the yard to hang, making her father's meals and carrying her fantasies with her like a carpetbag of knitting, to be picked up moment to moment.

She stopped to glance into a bookstore window when, faintly aware that a woman was standing there also reading the titles, she turned to face her and found herself staring, her heart clutching and skipping in the astonishment of beauty that did move her and of a sort she had never considered.

The woman was even taller than she was, touching six feet in high-heeled boots, but leaner built, in an Army nurse's uniform, with skin of a deep ruddy satin black. Her features were a series of delicate but large ovals: long eyes with the white glittering almost blue around the mahogany iris, long mouth. Her hair was cropped to her skull and her neck was lean and elegant, like the hands. The face caught Bernice somewhere deep, the flare of the nostrils proud and haughty, the high brow, the mouth wide and shapely as a trumpet.

She was staring, when the woman gave her a quick hard look, not at all apologetic or demure. Normally, Bernice would have been deeply embarrassed and turned away, but she was wide open this morning to her feelings, to the world.

Instead of turning away, she smiled at the woman. The woman looked at her again, looked her over openly and tipped her a wink. Then she swirled haughtily and strode off.

Zach did not notice and Bernice, still jolted, said nothing. "I wouldn't half mind going back to Greece," Zach was saying. "I was shunting about the Aegean in early forty-one for the limeys on caiques in the Dodekanisa. I get positively drunk on Mediterranean light. Sexually for a woman it must be the pits, but for a man it's sumptuous."

Perhaps it was the both of them being in uniform: that for a woman felt like a bit of disguise, cross dressing. A uniform held you in. It was a kind of bondage but also a kind of power. The uniform was a license to do things that people out of uniform were not permitted. It said you were part of a large powerful armed group. It spoke of obedience to that group and immunity from punishment for doing what you were told. A true woman would not be in uniform but in frills and ruffles and flowery chiffon. Bernice was at once shaken and passionately intrigued. She had a set of liberal sentences in her head about Negroes, but never had she met one in any real way, face-to-face and honestly. The WASPs were all white, something she had thus far so taken for granted as not to have noticed.

"Sometimes, dear heart, I indulge in fantasies of retiring there for a life of healthy vice on an island where like the local British milord I would be a petty king, disregarded in important decisions but pandered to nicely. A lifetime supply of eager twelve-year-olds. The trouble is, I get bored on that diet. There's no edge. Not that I crave companions who may slit my throat, but if I was turned on by soft weakness, I'd be all for the ladies, right?"

She scarcely listened, her mind still on the woman and her wink. She had shared for a moment something new, something almost unimaginable. "Women have a great deal of unused physical strength and stamina."

"Do you feel unused, dear heart? Wait till we get back to the hotel. I have a horniness on me like the great unicorn himself. I never fuck in Washington."

"Why? Aren't there the same opportunities as elsewhere?" Opportunities, she thought. I have sex only when I am with him, common as eclipses of the moon.

"But I always have the feeling the FBI is taking notes. They keep sexual dossiers on everybody. No thanks. It isn't that you can't get away with the same things, it's that you'll get pegged and everybody knows. I prefer to be officially hetero in Washington, lest I bung up my chances."

This time he took her in the ass, but as he assaulted her clitoris at the same time, she liked it. It was a new way to be sore, anyhow. Then they ordered up a huge lunch. "I am sadly undernourished," he said. "Accompanying partisans is a healthy life if you don't get shot. Then it becomes rapidly unhealthy. When my divorce comes through, I am contemplating marrying a British female—I'm reliably informed that's the sex you have to marry, though I've never been able to figure out just why—eldest daughter of a viscount with no male heirs. White elephant of a country place dating back to the dark ages of nasty baronial architecture and no doubt costing as much to run as the duchy of Luxembourg, but also some nice factories in Birmingham which are doing quite well in the war. A widow. Husband bought it on the *Prince of Wales* off Singapore."

She realized he was watching her while eating heartily. Why? Then she realized he was checking her reaction to his announcement that he was contemplating marriage to another woman. Did he imagine she would mind? "Why are you in such a hurry to get married? I'd hate marriage, myself. I wouldn't do it for anything."

"It rolls the family off my back. It provides that veneer of respectability society demands. Now a British girl, she expects her husband to be buggering the butler and the footman. So much better training than my first wife. She didn't like sex all that much, but she was deeply offended by my little habits." He stood, abruptly. "So, you don't care if I marry the lady? Actually her name is Sylvia. She looks like a horse and she even whinnies, but she's not stupid. She likes plants. I think she fucks trees, actually, and her true emotional relationship is with the gardening staff. The war did not so much deprive her of her husband as of her head gardener. You won't get jealous?"

Bernice only smiled. She was mildly offended that he felt the need to check her out. "Zach, what earthly difference could it make to me whether you're married to your present wife or another one?"

"Quite so. Pass the wine. I have to take off at midnight tonight, but I have a ticket for you to California. The old boys network is intact, and I pulled a few strings. Unless they want you in Newark." He raised his glass to her. "To the best lay in the U. S. of A. I brought you a present." He pointed with his glass toward a chair in the corner.

She got up and wandered over to investigate. She found on the chair a coarsely woven woolen bag. In it was a black leather sheaf. From inside that, she drew out a steel dagger, about eight inches long and finely worked with intaglio decoration around the hilt. The hilt itself was fashioned of some hard wood bound over with leather and set with two stones on each side. "It's gorgeous. It looks old."

"I think it's Turkish, eighteenth century. Those are opals. Not first quality, but real. It's quite lethal, to defend your honor with, dear heart. I thought you'd enjoy it. One of Tito's chappies had it. I traded a BAR."

"You're right, I like it immensely." It felt ancient, decadent, powerful in her hand. It felt like eight inches of commandable death. She did like it. It seemed such an unlikely thing to have. My lover gave me a dagger. Very cautiously she fingered the edge and drew blood. She licked the blood from her finger and slid the knife into its sheath.

"If you ever have to use it, remember not to strike down but up. It's harder to defend against and it hits vital organs more easily," he said in a conversational tone, demonstrating with a butter knife against her belly. "Tonight I have procured us tickets to *La Traviata* with Licia Albanese. I adore opera. It's in such immensely bad taste and yet it's so thrilling—like life, pussy. Now let's go cruise the Village and sip some espresso and see if there's any decent cannoli left."

I Could Not Love Thee, Dear, So Much

D-Day and K-Day fell in the same week. Both were an equal surprise. The former was good news; not so, the latter.

K-Day began with a phone call from Kay Saturday afternoon. "Mother," Kay's voice sounded both distant and uncharacteristically timid. "I'm so glad you're home."

Louise experienced a flicker of guilt, because Daniel and she had just come in from bicycling and had taken a bath together, nuzzling like two large erotic babies. They had been about to slide into bed. She clutched her robe tighter. "Is anything wrong, Kay? Are you studying for finals?"

"Mommy," Kay said, her voice curdling with what sounded like suppressed giggles, "I got married this afternoon."

She had, it developed, married an air force bombardier about to go off to Europe. He had been training near Hadley, at Westover Air Force base. They had left school Thursday and driven south until they came to Alabama, where they could be married without parental consent.

"Don't feel left out, Mommy, it's just that you would have tried to persuade me not to, and that would have been no use. Robby and I just didn't have time to bother. We know we're right together, and tomorrow he has to go off to war!"

"Where are you?"

"In a little town in Alabama. Sweetheart, what's the name of this town? Anyhow, Robby has to report tomorrow. We're leaving and we have to drive all night, so please wire me some money at school because I borrowed fifty dollars."

When Louise got off the phone, she sat and cursed in a low fierce voice while Daniel watched her, amazed. He had never heard her say more than *damn* and had not had the opportunity to hear some of the more colorful epithets stored away from her street kid days in Cleveland. Afterward, she got drunk and he finally made supper and lots of black coffee.

Fuming, she wired the money. She could hardly bring herself to open the letter from Kay that arrived three days later, then read it over and over again, trying to find some shred of hope. When Robby returned, they would no doubt be divorced. She concentrated on persuading Kay that marriage did not mean she should abandon her course of study. Her daughter was now Mrs. Robert H. Dixon. He was not even Jewish. She didn't know what he was, and she doubted that Kay had any idea. She felt thoroughly defeated. What could she have done? Sat on Kay like a giant auk's egg? According to the laws of the enlightened state of Alabama, her daughter was old enough to marry, and that was what she had done.

———————

Louise was bored by Washington. She found the atmosphere male in the dullest staunchest way, rather like the federal architecture. She could not persuade herself she was having any impact on the policies of OWI either in regard to women or in regard to Jews in camps or as potential immigrants.

The men she worked with opened doors for her and offered her cigarettes, told her how sweet she was looking, begged her to pick out birthday presents for wives and girlfriends, asked her out to dine and made an occasional pro forma pass. They also ignored any suggestions she made as if she had not spoken. She imagined sometimes simply resigning and returning to her friends and her apartment and her secretary in New York; but she would have felt as if she were shirking. Daniel would have been hurt, and he could not abandon whatever he secretly did.

She loved him, surprisingly: not in the romantic way she had tried to love Claude, not in the all-encompassing way she had loved Oscar. At first she thought it was similar to how she loved Kay, with a wary eye, a lack of illusion, a focused caring, but she realized she was fooling herself. Loving Daniel had more joy in it than her daughter had given her since Kay had been twelve. With him, she was relatively carefree. She would not be spending her life with him, so she did not feel deeply implicated in his habits, his decisions, his deep structures of belief or disbelief.

How secret was the work Daniel did only became apparent to her when she was being vetted herself. One day she had a call from her agent Charley, asking her if she would like to take a leave of absence from OWI and go off as a war correspondent for *Collier's*. They felt the time was ripe for sending a woman over: The Luce publications had several, Clare Boothe Luce and the photographer Margaret Bourke-White. The *Herald Tribune* had sent Marguerite Higgins. With increasing numbers of women in uniform, they wanted her to report on the war to the folks at home, with a woman's eye for what their men were going through. Was she interested?

From the tremendous jolt of relief that brought her to her feet and started her pacing her cubicle in a sugar rush of energy, she knew how sick she had become of OWI. She was tired of sitting in committees with men who did not listen—hardly ever to each other and never to her—and who made the decisions they formed as if she were not present, increasingly selling propaganda to the public. Lately the Pentagon was pushing a line that blamed any shortages at the front on the unions, although from reports she knew that logistical failures of the Army, their own delivery system, were at fault. Still it looked as if OWI would not only fail to tell the truth, it would push a falsehood designed to divide the working class, those in the Army from those in the plants. Her enthusiasm for OWI had dried up.

She had to be investigated by the War Department before she could be accredited. She was questioned about her marriage, her trip to the Soviet Union, her relationship to Jewish organizations and, surprisingly, in great detail about Daniel and what she knew about what he was doing. Since she knew nothing, she told the questioners that repeatedly. Finally, it seemed to be Daniel who caused them the most concern. She almost wanted to beg him to tell her what he really did for the Navy, but at the same time, she wanted less than ever to be informed. Now she could honestly claim ignorance.

Finally the authorization came through. Daniel knew something was up, because he too had been questioned, but she had asked him to wait for an explanation. The day she got her Army credentials, she gave notice to OWI—where the news of her planned departure was greeted with thinly veiled relief—and took the train for New York to sit down to a discussion about exactly where she would go.

New York dazzled and stank under the flame that seemed to drip from the mid-June sun, the asphalt soft and tarry, sticking to the thin soles of her high-heeled sandals. What *Collier's* wanted was first a piece on the wounded and the medical corps in the European theater. *Collier's* thought that families back home would like to read about how their boys were being cared for. They also had in mind a real Annette Hollander Sinclair piece about the boys at the front, or as close to it as seemed reasonable. Pathos, heartbreak, rapture, loneliness, the iconography of home. They wanted her in France.

She had to be equipped fast. Back she went to Washington. The War Department, among its other duties, prescribed exactly what a war correspondent could wear: the blouse, field cap, jacket, pants of an officer but with little in-signia that said WAR CORRESPONDENT and, in her case, a skirt for more formal attire. With her new uniform ordered, fitted and in the works, she now had to tell Daniel.

She found herself stymied as to how to break the news. Although he said nothing about his work to her, she complained freely to him. He knew her dissatisfactions. Obviously he had been worried the post would not continue. When in doubt, she thought, make a meal. She roasted a chicken, using her last egg in the stuffing. She rarely did serious cooking, as the tiny kitchen was not designed for a lot of purposeful activity. The stove had only three burners and an oven smaller than her breadbox at home. Nonetheless, she made a supper she felt proud of.

He was late coming home. She held the meal and fussed, pacing. She even had candles and a bottle of local wine from Maryland, not good but red and wet. When he arrived, she escorted him straight to the table. "I was getting worried this might be one of your late nights, and I might have to sit down and toast myself."

He lifted one dark brow at her. "What brings this on?"

She thought, since they grilled him, he has been waiting. "I have good news and bad news."

He drained his glass, winced and poured more. "Let's hear the bad, first. You're leaving, aren't you?"

"For a while. I'm going over as a war correspondent, for *Collier's,* accredited to General Bradley's First Army."

His face went completely blank. She felt her stomach contract with empa-thetic pain. He said nothing at all for a while, and she could think of no words to mitigate the rupture. He said finally, "You'll get into action and I never will."

"They aren't going to make a soldier out of me—and I remain suspicious just how near the front I'll be permitted. Daniel, I don't have any desire to leave *you.* But I'm accomplishing nothing in Washington. This is an incredible chance. I have to seize it. It won't come again."

"Have you told your daughter?"

"Mrs. Robert Dixon? I'll write her. I did call my ex-mother-in-law. She's happy to rush into the breach. She's just remarried and she's feeling guilty—a retired dentist. She wants to fuss over Kay. She is, of course, appalled by the marriage, but determined to be cheery."

"If Kay hadn't eloped with that bombardier, you wouldn't have left the coun-try."

"I don't know," Louise said honestly. "But as it is, I feel too great a desire to wring her neck to be of much use." She got up and came around the table. "Eat your supper, Daniel, please. I wanted it to be nice tonight."

"Is this our last supper?"

"No, I don't go off for two more days. Come, you know you won't get rid of me so easily. When I return, I'll run to see you—if you still want. By then you'll be in love with somebody else."

"Are you going to see your ex-husband?"

"I don't expect to. But my comings and goings will no longer be under my control."

He started eating, although slowly, as if doing her a favor. She beamed at him. She could imagine someone quizzing her about Daniel and asking if he did not look like Oscar years before. The eyes were similar, the almost black eyes, the cheekbones, the black hair; but Oscar's was only slightly wavy and Daniel's was all tight curls, the pelt of a black lamb. Their bodily presence differed sharply. Daniel was tall and rangy, lightly built, agile, a little stooped as if he had grown tall too early and become self-conscious about the amount of space he took up. In China, he must have seemed even taller. He was gentler than Oscar, more vulnerable and less well defended. His emotions could spin him around.

This was the first time in her life she had left a relationship while it was good, and for reasons that had nothing to do with the man's infidelity. Daniel had been faithful and she would miss him keenly. The line of her work tugged her forward and away. She could not fool herself that anything was likely to bring them together again. She would not come back to Washington. Even if postwar events delivered him to New York, he was too young not to have fallen in love again long before then. She wished him nothing but well. She wished she could carry from her whole life only Daniel with her, Daniel and her typewriter. But she could not sacrifice for a relationship she did not believe could endure long regardless.

Surprisingly, Daniel announced that he wanted to take over her apartment. Certainly that simplified moving out. By July second she was sitting in the bucket seat of a Liberator facing a scowling major, who glowered at her, muttered and chewed his mustache all through the four days it took them to reach Casablanca. From there she caught a plane two days later to Scotland, and then to London at last, where she was to report in and receive her further travel orders.

ABRA 8

The Great Crusade

On May 30, Abra received a depressing letter from her brother Ready.

> *We took a bomb off Marcus Island. I collected a piece of flying metal.*
> *Just cut a few muscles rendering me stiff, a minor league injury. They*
> *made me a commander, as a consolation prize for missing some of the*
> *action. I'm fit now.*

He enclosed a photo. This leathery officer in a commander's braid was her favorite brother. His eyes squinting out of a face prematurely wrinkled were hers. They had conspired together summers, but now it was as if each were translating from a different inner language. She wasn't the world's best letter writer and he was close to the worst.

Then the letter got down to what it was aiming for:

> *Mother is very upset about your staying in England. With the renewed*
> *bombing, she's close to frantic. Mother believes you're involved with*
> *the man you're working for, some professor whom she describes as a*
> *German Jew. What in hell are you doing over there anyhow? It all*
> *sounds more than a little unsavory. I think you should hop the next*
> *available plane back to the States and show yourself to Mother, so that*
> *she stops having fits.*
>   *Abra, you know I'm on your side in the long run. You've got into*
> *some damn fool trouble in your life, but following some Jew professor to*
> *wartime London has to take the cake.*
>   *Unless you want to end up like Great-Aunt Josephine and keep*
> *canaries and coo baby talk to them all day, it's time to face the music*

and get back where you belong and shape up. I'm only saying this for
your own good.

Your loving brother,
Ready

Abra started to tear the letter into pieces, then stopped. He had been wounded. No matter how angry she was with him, the dangers were too real for her to destroy even so pompous and prejudiced an offering. Her mother's letters had been in this vein for some time, but Abra did not read them through, so the lamentations made little impression on her. Since college, she had always skipped what she called the noisome parts and simply read the sections with family news. She found that made her feel less hostile toward her mother and better able to write chatty letters home.

She took care to put her own rank on the letter back. She might be only a second lieutenant, but she shoved it at him, to end such family pressure. She did not bother telling him that it was at Oscar's finagling that she had been commissioned instead of becoming a private, like most of the other women researchers whom OSS had decided to militarize. He wanted to make sure they could eat together, and his boss considered that ample reason. She didn't think explaining the flippancy with which her contingent took militarization would commend them to Ready in his current righteous mode. At OSS they talked about cellophane commissions: you could see through them, but they kept the draft off. Oscar hated saluting and viewed military regulations as Fascist. Nonetheless as he said, without being incorporated in the Army, they would never cross the Channel. Oscar never stopped scheming to get to France.

She sat over her letter to Ready, writing each sentence slowly and tasting fatigue, for she had been up the night before fire watching—every two weeks she had to stand watch—and tasting too the vinegar of disappointment. She was not sure she could forgive Ready, but men on the eve of battle were strange. She had had some peculiar encounters with airmen, both RAF and American, and considered that perhaps war drove them all crazy. She wrote a brief icy letter saying that he might be in the Navy, but perhaps he might take notice she was in the Army, which did not consult families before posting officers. She said that the captain in question had been born in Pittsburgh. He was of a Jewish family, although not from Germany. She thought that his family had come from Russia, but that he was rather less Russian than they were Scottish, and she could not see what particular bearing that had on anything. She went on to say that she was involved in the war in London exactly as he was in the Pacific, and although

she expected a large measure of silliness from their mother, it was depressing
to receive it from him. What she would not deign to explain to her suddenly
Christian brother was that half a loaf of Oscar fed her far more than a whole loaf
of the Wonder Bread she had dined on before.

She shared a belief with Oscar that the invasion of France was imminent.
They were not cleared to know when or where, but that week, the city echoed to
the sound of big guns and bombers blasting the Pas-de-Calais. It felt as if the
guns were going off deep inside the earth and the bombs exploding miles below
her feet, vibrating in her small bones. Eisenhower's headquarters on Grosvenor
Square was throbbing with activity, but the bigwigs had gone elsewhere. The
London intelligence community felt jittery, on edge. The closer she passed to
the centers of power in her errands, the higher pitched everything became. In
the streets were rumors about German secret weapons which would make the
Wehrmacht invincible in Europe: jet-propelled airplanes, bacteriological warfare, death rays, glider bombs and missiles, rockets, bombs that would turn the
air itself to fire. Fortress Europe. Something seemed about to happen, then the
weather turned stormy. In the square men were coming and going in a great
hurry with grim expressions. People disappeared. Suddenly there were fewer
men at the big mess.

General Donovan was in London, everyplace at once. She heard that a great
many more of the Sussex teams—Anglo-American intelligence—were off for
France; certainly more Jedburgh teams were going. The loud arrogant major who
had been her pickup's roommate whizzed in to study some maps and then was
seen no more. He always said hello to Abra, looking slightly glassy, as if he
could never place where he had met her. Everywhere preparations for missions
in France were heating up. One afternoon when she was sent on an errand, she
entered a room where the floor was covered completely with French francs, to
the depth of several inches, like fallen leaves. Everyone was walking upon the
bills to give them an aged appearance, a secretary-corporal explained.

People kept starting conversations and breaking them off. General Donovan disappeared as rapidly as he appeared from Washington, but it was rumored that this time the head of London OSS, David Bruce, had disappeared
with him. The weather continued stormy, winds tearing the foliage from the
trees. On the old rubble, rosebay was blooming and frogs croaked from makeshift reservoirs for fighting fires, tanks in which the wan London children
sometimes drowned.

Briefly, she mentioned Ready's letter to Oscar as they ate in a French restaurant in Soho. It was to be a late night. After supper, they would resume work. She
made light of the letter but watched him.

"Too bad he's not around," Oscar said. "I think meeting me would somewhat deflate the family image of danger and deviousness."

"You'd be willing to meet him?"

"Why not?" Oscar motioned the waiter to bring more tea substitute. It was hot, anyhow.

Oscar was a family man; he would not be embarrassed. She felt a sense of relief, even though the meeting was only hypothetical for the duration. Oscar truly cared for her. He would not meet her brother unless he loved her; that proved his love. She felt really good for the first time since that letter had come.

"Have you heard from that Navy friend of yours recently?" Oscar wiped the last of the almost real sauce with some dry bread. "The one who lives in your old building?"

"I had a letter a couple of days ago."

"What did he say about Louise?"

"Nothing whatsoever, even though I asked." Daniel's letters were always full of the latest Washington jokes and gossip. Mail had been speeded up between London and Washington, until sometimes she had Daniel's letters in five days instead of the previous two to three weeks.

"It's odd he doesn't answer you," Oscar said. "Don't you think so?"

"If she had moved out, I'm sure he'd mention it. After all, it was my damned apartment she confiscated." Perhaps Daniel was avoiding offending her by mentioning Louise. Unlikely. He enjoyed teasing her. He was protecting Louise. From what? Her knowledge and thus Oscar's of what was going on back there. Was she being paranoid, or was something really happening?

Oscar was looking at her out of narrowed eyes. "You think his silence is significant?"

"Perhaps." She was not overjoyed at Oscar's persistence, but everybody wanted to know what was going on with their ex-spouses. The more she thought about Daniel's avoidance of the subject, the surer she was that Daniel was involved with Louise. Sometimes she thought that she understood Daniel a lot better than Oscar. Would he really have gotten involved with Oscar's ex-wife, who must be fifteen years older than Daniel himself? Yes, she rather thought that a young man who would get involved with a nisei in wartime probably had the independence of taste to seduce Louise Kahan.

Abra was visited with an extraordinarily vivid image of Louise in the restaurant, wearing that stunning green dress, her auburn hair in loose curls. On her oddly blunt strong hands an emerald ring flashed. Unlike Oscar, who never thought about clothes and who was getting more and more untidy as the war progressed, Louise had an elegant facade. Abra suddenly realized that Louise had selected Oscar's clothes; she was witnessing the decay of a once fine ward-robe. She did not think he had bought anything for himself in years. Not that it mattered, for their friends were equally shabby. Still, Abra considered that she was proving less able than Louise at the upkeep of Oscar, and that Louise might look over her ex-husband with a judgmental eye for her shortcomings.

Oscar was frowning. She thought he had come to the same conclusion about Louise and Daniel that she had. If so, he would revert to the subject later. In the meantime, they had to go back to work.

The next morning, she stopped in the basement to mimeograph a report for preliminary discussion, collating it and stapling it before she came upstairs. The machine clattered along, requiring constant attention to keep it moving. When she had a neat pile of their report on the German ball bearing industry, she car-ried it upstairs in a great stack to Oscar, to be glanced over and then forwarded for preliminary screening.

Nobody was in the outer offices and she caught a murmur from office after office as she climbed that reminded her of days in the States when everybody would have the ball game on. Yes, that was it, everyone was listening to the BBC. She glanced at her watch, but it did not seem the right time for news. Gradually she identified a voice as that of British General Montgomery, at a high pitch of rhetoric and some long-windedness. Oh, bother. What was he going on about?

Oscar's office was tuned to the radio too, everybody standing about or perched on desks listening, even the old radicals who analyzed the German-language pa-pers for them. Montgomery was still going on: "We have a great and a righteous cause."

"I believe that," Abra said. "Why do I bridle at hearing him say it?"

"Shhhhh!" said Oscar.

Montgomery rolled on: "Let us pray that the Lord mighty in battle will go forth with our armies and that his special Providence will aid us in the struggle. With stout hearts and with enthusiasm for the contest, let us go forward to vic-tory. And as we enter the battle, let us recall the words of a famous soldier spoken many years ago. 'He either fears his fate too much or his desserts are small / who dare not put it to the touch to win or lose it all.' Good luck to each one of you and good hunting on the mainland of Europe."

"What's all that?" Abra whispered, annoyed by the solemnity in the room. When generals called on God, she began to itch.

"It's begun," Oscar said. "What we need is champagne."

"A little premature to celebrate victories," Wilhelm the pipe fitter said. His scar was inflamed, for it reddened when he was excited. "Remember what happened to the British and Canadian lads at Dieppe," he said with his thick accent that made people glower in the Underground and the shops. He held his cigarette between his thumb and index finger, nodding at them. Oscar and Abra regularly passed on their cigarette ration to him.

The radio was speaking again. "We now repeat the historic communiqué Number One from Supreme Allied Headquarters. This was issued at 9:32 this morning, the first bulletin of the greatest invasion in the history of the world: 'Under the command of General Eisenhower, Allied naval forces, supported by strong air forces, began landing Allied armies this morning on the northern coast of France. The Allies have landed on two points of the Normandy Coast between Cherbourg and Le Havre.'"

People were running up and down the stairs shouting. She followed Oscar, Wilhelm and Beverly into the French desk office, where a big map on the wall had already attracted a crowd trying to figure out where the landings had occurred. Everywhere radios were tuned to the BBC. Just yesterday the liberation of Rome had been announced, but that had come as little surprise to them, as OSS Italy had been active in Rome for months.

"I bet that's where Wild Bill Donovan and Bruce disappeared," one of the French experts muttered. "Trust the general to get down belly to belly with the enemy," he quoted sarcastically. R & A had not been universally pleased by Donovan's graphic description of their allotted role.

Someone quieted the French expert. Abra was pleased that another besides herself remained irreverent, and that somebody else was being shushed. Oscar said, "They just said something about the Resistance."

Everyone waited. "According to the German Transoceanic News Agency, the 28th and 101st American Parachute Divisions have been dropped in the Normandy Peninsula of France. One question which now is going to cause a great deal of attention is the part which the French underground, the French patriots, may perform to help these paratroopers."

"Marshal Pétain appealed to the French people today not to aggravate misfortunes which will bring upon them tragic reprisals, but the voice to which they listened was General Eisenhower. A naval battle in the estuary of the Seine is now occurring according to German radio."

Cocking his head and looking at the French expert who had spoken earlier, Wilhelm said, "I heard there was a royal fracas, when de Gaulle learned that Eisenhower and the BBC were not going to let him speak to the French people, except as an appendage."

"Do you think we can keep him out? The field reports seem to think otherwise."

Oscar was not paying attention, staring at Paris on the map. "France," he muttered thoughtfully. "I wonder how soon we'll be going over?"

M19, the British intelligence service that ran escape routes for downed fliers and escaped military personnel, kept aloof from OSS as from MI6 and SOE, the British elder equivalent of the OSS Special Operations. They were thoroughly military and considered their security impeccable and everybody else's flimsy. They seemed to view liaison with underground groups as potential interference with their far more important endeavors.

However, among the intelligence community, as it called itself, of London, everybody loved R & A, Abra learned. Everybody patronized them as the sweet innocent buttercup of intelligence, but everybody wanted their reports. They gave more than they got, and so an aura of sanctity hung over their efforts. Although R & A was typified by internal catfights, vendettas of aroused vanity, plots in the toilet stalls and snubs on the stairs, it did not usually need to struggle for its life among the other intelligence organizations, who were constantly trying to prove that the others should be eaten by their group or otherwise cease to exist.

Thus Oscar's patience had been rewarded. He had established a relationship with a captain in MI9, who was pleased to have reports on the German economy and who knew that Oscar would appreciate news of Gloria. That news came in mid-June, when London was muggy and dank. With the aid of a double agent, the SD (the Nazi counterintelligence) had inserted a loop in her ratline, code-named Ivoire. Downed airmen had been passed on to a safe house, apparently like the others, where they were questioned as if to make sure of their stories, and the details of the ratline thus pieced together.

The Resistance had found out, but just as they sent warnings, the SD moved. That ratline was now out of operation. Most of the ratline operators had been taken by the Gestapo, but some had escaped. That was all MI9 knew. Oscar did not talk much but he also seemed to give up sleeping. He was looking gaunt.

June 18 Abra went to find out what had happened to Wilhelm, who had not come to work in two days. He had no phone. As an enemy resident alien, classified type C, benign, he was allowed to remain at large but could not own a bicycle or flashlight. She was always willing to run errands, because she enjoyed getting out of the office and seeing London. He lived in a row of attached houses in a mostly Jewish working-class area, renting a room from a leatherworker's family. She had been there before, as dealing with the exiles who helped OSS involved a certain amount of social work, since they were nearly destitute.

When she came out of the tube at Whitechapel, the broad road was half blocked with lorries flattened like tins and a rapidly running stream from a broken main, although the traffic edged through on one side, with a bobby directing. The sidewalk market was still going on, and she made up her mind after she checked Wilhelm and found out if he was sick or in trouble, she would give a quick cruise for something wearable or edible.

On Wilhelm's narrow street, the uneven row of squalid leaning row houses staggered along as it always had. Just in the middle of the block where several houses had stood including the leatherworker's where Wilhelm rented a room, a crater yawned, big as a pond. Windows were broken all along the street, stoops cracked, cornices toppled and objects pulverized, no longer identifiable. As she approached the gap, she waded through crushed and broken glass that jabbed through the thin soles of her worn shoes. As always there was a stench of sewage, of shit. Standing in midblock where perhaps twenty houses had been, she could plainly see a charred foundry still smoldering across the newly created field, two blocks away. In the field some lost chickens were idly pecking. Everybody with a yard around here had at least chickens and rabbits. What kind of bomb could have done all this damage? She had heard rumors of something called a doodlebug.

She imagined Wilhelm sitting over the table covered with German-language newspapers and commenting, half in English and half in German on the articles relevant to them, dictating to Beverly and claiming he could do anything, anything at all, except write, gesturing with his cigarette between the thumb and index finger.

She called to a woman futilely digging in the rubble in the next street. "I'm trying to find a friend. He was in Number Eighty-four in this street."

"They was all kilt," the woman said without looking up. "Twenty-three what lived on this street and two still missing. M'muvver among 'em. Made bloody mincemeat of 'em."

A phrase came to her out of the manual she had seen on agent recruitment, official OSS policy: "No agent should be recruited without serious thought being given to the means of disposing of him after his usefulness is ended." Now OSS wouldn't have to worry about the pipe fitter Wilhelm, Jew, member of a splinter left Communist group, creator of bad bilingual puns, admirer of the long-dead Rosa Luxemburg. He had been pulverized. She shuffled back and forth in the wreckage that covered the street and sidewalk to the depth of half a foot, staring at the crater. Gone. She supposed that Oscar or she would have to identify the body, if there was one. What could have made such a hole? Were these the vaunted secret weapons?

In the following days, rumor answered that question long before the government finally announced that rockets were falling on England. What they learned shortly was that the doodlebugs were pulse jet powered cruise missiles carrying a ton of high explosives at a maximum speed of four hundred miles an hour. The blast power was something new. Fashionable London began to empty again, evacuating to country homes; but working-class London felt more crowded than ever and cheap housing was being destroyed so fast, many families were again sleeping in the underground, as well as the barely tolerable shelters.

People seemed to feel it was a duty to try to remain cheerful, but their courage was wearing out like everything else. The scuttlebutt on the rockets was that they sounded like a locomotive when they came through the air above you, but that when they cut out, with a weird greenish flash, and the silence came, you were about to get it.

All the front windows in her flat were broken by bomb blast. She had them boarded up. It was like living in a cave. Her bed suddenly collapsed one night, the pegs having worked their way loose. None of her doors hung properly and none of the drawers would go all the way in. Bombing had warped the furniture. She no longer bothered to go to the shelters. A doodlebug that landed on a shelter would kill everyone inside anyhow. Better to stay home in bed. There was no warning they were coming, and they came as often in the daytime as at night.

The news from Normandy was all right, for the Allies were holding even if they had failed to advance much. Then Oscar got a letter from Louise saying his daughter had eloped with a bombardier. He exploded and pulled all the strings he could to try to call the States. A week passed and he was still trying vainly to reach Louise in Washington.

Monday while they were working on the final version of the ball bearing report, Oscar's phone rang. "Louise!" he barked into the phone. "I've been calling you every day. What are you doing about Kay?" He listened and then rose to his feet motioning her wildly out of the room.

Furious, she shut the door and sulked in the outer office until he appeared sometime later. "Louise is in town," he said mildly. "We're having supper with her. She specifically asked for you."

"Here? What's she doing here?" Abra was dismayed.

"She's a war correspondent, waiting to go to France."

"Her, a war correspondent? What qualifies her? Are they trying to turn the second front into a romance?"

Oscar gave her a look intended to wither. "Louise has been writing serious articles for ten years. Of course they won't send her into combat, but there's a lot of the war in London and behind the lines she can sink her teeth into."

She was never allowed to criticize Louise, who was supposed to be on some other plane than herself. It galled her. What happened to freedom of speech? Didn't Louise's carrying on with Daniel bring her stock down any?

They ate in the Grosvenor Hotel mess. Louise was an officer too. Oscar did not outrank her. Louise had, as she said with amusement, a theoretical rank of captain, in case she was captured. Abra was glad she was at least a second lieutenant. Louise looked radiant, Abra thought, and asked maliciously, "How's Daniel? Didn't he mind your coming over here?"

"Nobody enjoys all these wartime partings, do they?" Louise asked blandly. Oscar kept staring at her and asking far more questions about Louise than he did about Kay, who was the pretext for this get-together. Abra did not find the dinner a great success.

JEFF 8

The Die Is Cast

"I used to let myself be distracted," Jeff was explaining to Jacqueline as they lay curled into each other like nested S's in the old bed, upstairs in a farmhouse in the Lacaune Mountains. "I was always getting into affairs I didn't really want, because I wanted something. Do you understand?" The farmhouse had been deserted since an old woman had died the year before, her sons off in North Africa. They had fixed the roof and cleaned out animal debris. In their room, they could always hear the Agout, a white water stream plunging over the rocks outside.

"Half and half." Her cheek lay against his palm so that he could feel as well as hear her voice. A scent of roses seeped through the open window. Swallows nesting in the barn swooped by, madly twittering. Now that June was upon them, almost everybody took a siesta after lunch, but they were considered blatant, shocking, because he insisted they not bar the heavy plank shutters to the world. In the south in the daytime, houses looked blinded to him, sinister, mourning in darkness within, although he knew that habit enabled them to hold daytime meetings in Toulouse with perfect impunity behind closed shutters. She lifted her head to say, "I recognize the phenomenon. My friend Céleste used to get involved with men that way. . . ." She fell silent and he felt her muscles contract.

"Did you forget to do something?"

"I have so many friends who may be deported, who may be dead and I don't know." She shook herself, nestling closer into him. "Anyhow, the phenomenon is familiar to me, but not personally. I have more resisted than sought out connections. I feared losing myself."

"Your self is the one thing you can never lose, even when you want to."

"Observe the married women you meet!" She imitated an affected voice. "Oh, mon mari, my husband would never *permit* me to work. My husband would never let me go off by myself on a trip. Oh, we used to be friends, but that was before I married. . . . My own mother was never like that."

"Women give up less than you think. I always found them working hard to make me into the husband they wanted."

"You always speak as if you had had thousands of women." She poked him in the belly. "Like Don Juan in the opera, with his servant's lists, which of course he keeps to flatter the Don."

"Not thousands, but I imagine a good hundred."

"Ugh. And you loved all of them?" Her voice was round with scorn.

"I loved none of them." He held her tighter. "I loved some a little, but none enough. It was an enormous waste of time, all that energy finding a woman, making her love me and then getting rid of her."

"Ah, do you want to be rid of me? I could disappear in fifteen seconds." She made as if to sit up, naked as she was. They had not even a sheet over them, as the afternoon was warm. They had been up most of the night. Soon he had to drag himself from the cosy bed and go over the information he had collected from his agents that week, collate it, encapsulate and code it for transmission, a tedious job that took the better part of a day. Tomorrow he must go into Toulouse and pick up new reports. London was pushing him hard for fresh information.

"I want to hold on and on. I'm just explaining to you exactly why I am going to be a much better painter after this war ends than I ever was before. I wasted too much energy being bored. I moved every few months. Now I want to sink roots and never budge, oh, except maybe once in a while to see the shows in Paris and attend one of my own with a fancy opening."

"Bah, you're going to have to put up with Paris for a while. I have to get a degree. Unless I simply go on blowing things up. I prove to have talent for that."

"I think the prospects for advancement are limited." He sighed, sitting up on the bed's edge to lean out the window. "There's Lev, teaching the older Faurier girl how to shoot. Isn't she a little young?"

"They deport them younger than that and kill them younger."

The sunlight fell on her hair, grown out to its own color, bushy on her shoulders like a cloud of fine metallic yarn spun around her face. Her shoulders were delicate but strongly shaped, with little hollows just to the side of her full breasts with their purplish nipples. Ah, she was thin, small boned but wiry, amazingly strong for her size. Every day she walked or pedaled many kilometers, hauled heavy loads on her back. After the war, she would lose that cat's wariness, that sense of being about to bound off or change direction in midair at a strange sound. He found that nerviness attractive, but he could dispense with it.

They had an extensive garden up here. Several of the men hunted, including Lev who showed an aptitude for tracking. Trout lurked by the rocks in the river, where Daniela fished almost every day, saying the water soothed her. They had acquired two small but productive cows, three goats and a flock of darkly burnished chickens. They were healthier. They lived in less fear. They slept better and they were all in fine fettle and excellent humor: a good little group of maquis, seventeen strong scattered through the area, including six boys in a forest camp where many of their supplies were buried. For sabotage, they were a high-quality weapon. He did not count the older Faurier girl, Sophie, although Lev was training her. Of the seventeen, thirteen were men and four, women, all except for Mme Faurier at least as useful as the men.

Mme Faurier had her uses too: she cooked and foraged. Since she had revealed herself unable to refrain from wincing when she fired and thus misdirecting every shot, the possibility of turning her into a sniper had finally been abandoned even by Lev. She kept the books for them, and she was learning to process agent intelligence. Again Jeff was doing something unorthodox and contrary to procedure, but he did not see why he should remain the only operative in the group able to code and decode transmissions. If he were knocked out of action, how would they transmit to London or Algiers? Notions of security in London did not always prove out in the field. He felt he had to back up his expertise.

She wore her hair in braids wrapped around her head, perched on a short neck above a body that could be rendered by a stack of circles. She was gap-toothed and easy to provoke into laughter, but always wary, always with an ear or an eye alerted for her girls. Even while Lev was instructing Sophie, having her shoot at bottles set up on a stump, Mme Faurier was within view shelling peas.

Once he had disliked her, for no better reason than that she seemed to protect Jacqueline from him; now he liked her very much indeed, along with her husband who was their precious mechanic, fixer of all machines that could be fixed and cannibalizer of those hopelessly smashed.

He became aware Jacqueline was speaking. She was sitting in the middle of the bed with her legs crossed and her hands knotted together staring dreamily out into the blinding sunshine and talking about placing charges. "I like to use the smallest amount for doing the job and set it exactly at the point where it will do the most damage. Sometimes it's only a matter of timing so that we hit cars seven and eight, but let the earlier cars go through safely, since they have civilians on them. But with a turntable, with a bridge, placement is everything. . . . Sometimes I think of being an architect or a civil engineer."

He was not enthusiastic about her returning to school. However, it was pointless arguing now. He said only, "If you decide on either of those, Montpellier or Toulouse would do fine. No reason to return to Paris." He was perched on the window ledge. Right outside, the previous owner had planted a pink horse chestnut, the upright torches of its flowers swarming with bees. They bloomed later here than in London.

"Oh, I have to go back to Paris at least for a while." Her pupils were tiny, staring into the white light outside. Her eyes were pale green buds, the brown submerged for the moment.

"To trace your family?"

"To try."

Sometimes he felt behind her words an enormous force of the unspoken, as if they did not in spite of sharing bodies and danger quite share the same world. After all, falling in love with somebody from another country meant that only slowly would he come to understand what had formed her. His image of second grade or a holiday would be at odds with hers. Time together would give them a family history and culture mingling the nature of both tributaries. Their children would be bilingual.

He reached for his pants. Time to work on his agents' discoveries. Nowadays London was sending him long shopping lists of what they wanted, and his agents risked their lives trying to supply what was demanded of them. Every few weeks, one of them disappeared, and he had to recruit somebody else, revise drops.

That night, June 5, they listened to the BBC as always. The broadcast was long, nothing special for them, and Jeff found himself daydreaming as the maddeningly uninflected voice repeated each message: "The bears have a thick coat. The bears have a thick coat. I kiss you darling, three times. I kiss you darling, three times. Holiday greetings to Papa Noël. Holiday greetings to Papa Noël."

Then he came sharply awake, feeling as if cold water had rolled down his back. Surely he had heard wrong. "Shhhh!" he barked, although no one in the room had spoken. Mme Faurier was staring too: she had learned her codes well. "Il fait chaud dans le Suez," the bland voice repeated.

"Merde," he muttered, so used to operating in French he did not realize he swore in it now.

More messages. Perhaps it was not real. Then the radio said, plainly, "The die is cast." A bit of his schoolboy Latin came back to him. Alea iacta est. Caesar's phrase. He himself was only a barnyard general. That was the second code: the call for a general uprising. It was the signal to dig out the arms and give everything they had. He considered what they had, and it was pitiful. Fine for guerrilla ambushes but absurd for open war. For months he had been asking for mortars, heavier guns, antitank weapons, but only light arms had been dropped.

He was still mulling that over when another phrase came: "The arrow will not pierce." Then shortly after that, "Reeds must grow, leaves rustle," repeated in that maddeningly slow voice.

After the messages had finished, Jeff rose slowly to his feet. "We've been ordered to rise! They're activating Plan Vert: the sabotaging of railroad lines. We know our objectives. Plan Bleu also put in action: that's the hydroelectric power lines. Plan Violet: cutting the underground long-distance wires. We've got those targeted into Castres. Finally, Plan Bibendum. We're to try to slow down and if possible prevent German troop movement toward the field of battle."

"What field of battle?" Lev asked. "Are the Allies landing?"

"They wouldn't be pulling out all the stops if they weren't. It has to be now. It's come, finally, the signal for a general uprising."

Lev, who had been getting information from the cheminots, said, "They've been bombing the shit out of Pas-de-Calais. Think that's it?"

Everybody looked to Jeff who shrugged. "Sure, the Joint Chiefs call me nightly to chat about their plans. All I know is, they're coming and they want us to raise hell."

"About time," Lev said. "Let's maul the Boches!"

Special Forces Headquarters had allotted them certain targets two months ago, so that he had expected the invasion in May. The main objective was to prevent the Germans moving the southern divisions north in time to box up the beachhead and wipe out the Allied troops as the British and Canadians at Dieppe had been penned in and massacred. Especially important were the German Panzer units, but the Resistance had not been given good antitank weapons.

"The railroad men must be hearing the same messages," Lev said with satisfaction. "They're primed. They plan to carry out thirty-five cuts in the lines. Tomorrow is going to be a busy day. I suggest we go to bed now, try to sleep and meet at one. Don't we also have some bridges?"

"One rail bridge over the Agout, and one road bridge near Castres. That's ours."

"Do we have enough explosives for all our targets?" Lev turned to Jacqueline.

"We have enough if we're elegant, not if we're sloppy."

"Better do the Castres bridge first tonight," Lev said to Jacqueline.

Jacqueline preened herself, a ginger cat basking in the acknowledgment of her skill. He had an image of himself in the dining room at home, what remained after years of childhood dishwashing of Viola's good china in the breakfront, The Professor ensconced in his armchair at table's head under the electric chandelier. Jeff was presenting Jacqueline. "This is my fiancée. She can make a perfect om-

elette and she handles plastique and dynamite with a truly professional touch."
He smiled.

Lev noticed. "Yes, Vendôme, it is good, nu, to be unleashed at last to do what
we can to the bastards? Now that it's come, we can know there'll be an end. We
are only responsible now for how well we strike and how well we fight, hein?"

"Can we use the Renault?" Jacqueline asked. "We can get more done if we can
cover the ground fast tonight."

"We'll risk it," Lev decided. "We have a list of targets so long we'll be lucky
to hit half of them."

"Then why not start now?" M. Faurier asked. He looked ill with nerves.

"Too early. All right, suppose we start at midnight?" Lev rubbed his hands
together briskly. "Now, take a nap. A sho in gan eyden iz oych gut."

To which Mme Faurier said with a little girl's grin, "Az me hot a sach tsu ton,
leygt men zich schlofn."

Daniela glanced at Jacqueline and Jeff, smiling benignly as she translated:
"Even a short time in the Garden of Eden is good. And if you have much work
to do, go to sleep first."

"Mme Faurier, you must stay here to serve as message center," Jeff said. Her
face drooped. Lev however winked at him. Obviously he too considered Mme
Faurier might prove more dangerous to them than to the Germans. "Sophie
must hurry to the scouts, telling them the messages have come and they're to
travel to the Montagne Noire maquis to fight. Then both children should be sent
somewhere safe, if one of the families around here will hide them while things
are hot."

"If I am here, and you are all gone, they are safer with me."

The Jewish scouts had taken to the maquis life some months before, and now
all groups were closely allied with each other and under the command of the
local Armée Secrète, the military arm of the Resistance. At first the scouts had
trained with sticks, but at last drops had equipped them. Some of Lev's people
went to the scout encampment Friday evenings for services, as they had a rabbi
with them.

During the long night, they blew the bridges they had been assigned, cut the
cables underground and blew the tracks in two places, without casualties. The
night reminded Jeff of Halloween in Bentham Center, when he had run wild
with his friends setting bonfires, breaking windows, letting horses loose, Bernice
at his heels dressed in his clothes, which fit her. He thought too of escapades
with Zach, buzzing the town, landing on a frozen lake, stealing exam papers. He
felt the same sharp tang of excitement alerting the nerves, the same camaraderie,
the same pleasure at collective and individual boldness. It was reprehensible to

admit, but this was fun. His life had for too many years since been a long mid-western highway through stubble fields down which he crept with a dust bowl wind darkening the huge sky.

He thought, we will bring our kids back here in ten years to this bridge over the Agout, and say, look, children, your mother and I blew that bridge up the night the troops landed in France to drive the Germans out. The children—he imagined a boy and a girl almost the same age, as he and Bernice had been—would stare obediently at the bridge, long rebuilt bigger and more modern, and would not believe them.

At dawn they were standing on a treeless mountain with a view for miles and miles into the blue distance, over the long low ridges broken by cliffs. The culti-vated fields were russet, the rocks grey, clumps of trees dark green. Viperine and columbine glinted purple at the road's edge. Beside the path they were climbing up from the car hidden under a haystack, lizards were crawling out on the rocks to sun themselves. Wild roses were in bloom and among the grass he found a few last wild tulips, striped, and three-color violets. I am freeing this land and it will be mine, he thought: earned.

They got to bed finally at ten in the morning. When they woke, Mme Faurier had news. The Allies had landed in Normandy: both Vichy radio and the BBC agreed. "Normandy," Jacqueline said sadly, folding her arms across her chest. "That's so far away. I hoped they would land in the south."

They had targets for the day, although they had to move more circumspectly and under what cover they could contrive. They had a train to derail, a highway to block. When they returned, Captain Robert, their FFI representative, was waiting. "We want your troops in the Montagne Noire where we expect to be attacking the SS columns as they attempt to move toward Normandy. Get your people and weapons together and move out. It's the general uprising. The signal has come. We must strike to free France."

Jeff frowned. "All right, we'll get ready to move. I still think Mme Faurier should stay here. She can work on the information and encode it for Achille, and keep track of where he's hiding. But I have to make new arrangements with my informants before I shift locales."

"You're only moving a matter of sixty kilometers, Vendôme. We have orders to strike. Your soldiers should move."

"I have a meeting tomorrow with one of my people, and it's relevant."

Lev said, "No problem. We'll march and Vendôme can follow us after he sees his contacts."

Captain Robert grunted. "You're wearing too many hats, Vendôme. That makes for trouble."

"Lev knows these mountains better than I do. The next day, I'll rejoin everybody. What's the rendezvous point?"

"Gingembre took you to a village nearby, when you met Lapin. I will draw you a map now. Memorize it and then burn it, at once."

When Captain Robert had left them, Jacqueline announced, "If you risk going into Toulouse, I'm going with you. You would have walked into the trap they set when they took Raymond, if I had not been there. Who are you meeting?"

"Thibaut, from the mairie, and Margot, most important of all, who works for the Milice. Actually, I'm only meeting Thibaut face-to-face. Margot and I communicate through a drop. Safer for her, as well as us. I have one other drop to visit too, where I'm expecting information on the guards at a munitions dump."

———

The meeting with Thibaut was easy enough, a matter of both Jeff and Thibaut using a bistrot toilet and the packet changing hands. Then they headed for Jeff's old neighborhood, where he had a drop in the big cemetery, in a cornucopia showing off ceramic roses, mounted on a tomb. Under the flowers the cornucopia was hollow. It was also empty. Jeff frowned. What had gone wrong? He must try to find out what had happened to Guy, his spy at the dump.

Unfortunately they had a few hours to kill before they could expect anything from Margot at the next drop, outside the Cathédrale St-Etienne. They went to the movies and watched a story set safely in the days of Louis XIV, whom the groveling director had attempted to link with Hitler in an attempt to flatter.

They came out and argued about lunch. Jeff wanted to eat at a restaurant; Jacqueline felt the chances of being recognized if they sat about for two hours were great. Jeff slipped into a charcuterie and bought some ham, which Jacqueline would not eat. Very slowly he ate it, sitting on a bench, while she fidgeted. "That's ridiculous," he said. "Many Jews eat ham."

"I don't like it." Her lip curled.

"What does it really mean to you, rational as you otherwise are, to cling to a religion suitable for a desert people four thousand years ago?"

"I knew this would come out someday, I knew it!"

"What would come out? I'm an anti-Semite if I don't agree refusing to eat lobster or ham is intelligent? And you do eat lobster—I saw you."

"That was crayfish," she said irrelevantly. "So, I can't resist it. But I don't eat ham. That's symbolic."

"Of what? What has what you eat to do with your religion or with a belief in God, which you may or may not have, from what I can figure out." Why were they quarreling? Nervousness, perhaps. Probably he was also irritable because appetizing odors of the Toulouse cooking he adored filled the air from a nearby restaurant. Jacqueline ate so little, she did not understand he required a real lunch, and furthermore, she did not sympathize with his being a little tired of the Jewish cuisine of the camp. He longed for cassoulet, for ham, for sausages, whose presence the spicy wind from the restaurant advertised.

They looked at each other warily, neither wanting to quarrel but on the verge. Jacqueline finally permitted him to put his arm around her as they approached the cathedral. "I suppose I am touchy about the subject because I'm not consistent. Mme Faurier isn't touchy. She keeps kosher."

"You don't imagine your father does, up on Montagne Noire."

"Oh, my, we're going to see him tonight." Jacqueline moved closer, peering into his face. They sat on the rim of the fountain in the cobblestone square before St-Etienne. "Does he frighten you?"

"He did at first, bristling with weapons, that huge bodyguard shadowing him." Jeff stared upward. This was not the church he liked, St-Sernin, with its rose and cream simple soaring interior. St-Etienne was built of the same brick but strange and hybrid-looking, with a fortified tower lunging up massively beside the rose window. His drop was in the cathedral garden. "If Lev looks like a corsair, your father is the image of a maquisard. He gives the impression of being a big man. It wasn't until he embraced you that I saw that he's only a little taller than you are."

"The two of you seemed to like each other."

"I think we did. But that was only the preliminary inspection. No matter how hot the battle we may be heading into, I'll bet your father will have some attention left over to watch us."

"Then you must not tease me about ham."

"I so solemnly swear." He stopped her in her tracks. "In here."

"Already?" Jacqueline was startled and gave a quick glance around the square.

Jeff slipped into the garden, sitting on a bench. Just under the bench a brick was loose. Yes, Margot had left two leaves there. Between them, folded up and stuck to the upper leaf was a report written on very thin paper. Jeff had just detached it from the leaf and was slipping it into his pocket when a voice ordered him, in French, to surrender and raise his hands or be shot.

In a glance he picked out a marksman in the church tower, two Milice on either side, as he heard Jacqueline cry out. Someone struck him across the back of the neck and threw him down to be searched. They took his .38, went through his pockets and found the tiny wad of paper. They also found his sheath knife and the report from Thibaut. He was glad he had followed Captain Robert's instructions and burned the map as soon as he and Jacqueline had memorized it. As they pushed him ahead of them, he saw that one of their black sedans was already coming down the street. Jacqueline was thrust against the cathedral wall, held by two brutes of the political police. It had happened so fast he could not believe it. He had not even had time to swallow the wad of paper.

They had his hands cuffed behind his back, so he could not see his watch, but when they arrived at the commissariat of the Milice, a big old clock with Roman numerals ticked on the wall. Four-thirty. Why hadn't they taken them directly to the Gestapo headquarters on rue Alexandre Fourtanier? This was a leak inside the Milice; probably they would not turn them over to the Gestapo until they had questioned them and attempted to find out the extent of head-quarters penetration; with luck, they might not turn them over at all, but might tuck them away in a French prison. He realized as a high sign was exchanged and two officers marched out and then came back with Margot that they were only arresting her now. They had waited for the drop to be visited. At some point they must have followed her.

He had to think quickly. They had Margot. They probably knew nothing about him. He would claim to be an escaped American prisoner of war. He had met Mar-got only recently, asking for help getting back to England or Africa. What would she say? They would have no reason to believe he had contact with the maquis. Could he persuade them Jacqueline had no connection with him, that she was his cover? But they had her description, and her new papers were not the best kind.

The three of them were thrown into cells on the next floor up, at the back of the ancient building. There was nothing in the cell except a cot with a mattress perhaps a quarter of an inch thick, a high barred window and a can to piss in. He was left there for about an hour. They had taken his watch so he could only try to guess the time. The women were locked into cells some distance away, so that he could not communicate with them.

After a long time he heard the guards in the hall, opening a cell door. Margot or Jacqueline? Why not him? He cursed himself for allowing her to accompany him. He cursed himself for trying to run an intelligence network and work with the maquis at the same time. Vainglory. OSS was right. Each job got in the other's way. If he had not tried to do both, they would be safe with Jacqueline's father right now.

He heard the guards come and go another time before they came for him. Why was he last? As they hustled him down the hall he called out, "Cat. Are you all right?"

From one of the cells someone moaned. His stomach seized on itself, con-tracting. He imagined her raped, maimed. He saw her bleeding, torn open. A rage burned his vision almost blind and then subsided into cold fury.

They threw him into the interrogation room, where he lay on the floor. Each of the guards kicked him in the ribs, almost playfully. The door opened and boots came in. "This is no way to treat a prisoner, according to the laws and honor of Marshal Pétain," the boots said in a tone of gentle reproof. "Pick up the prisoner and put him in a chair, correctly."

The two guards muttered apologies and sat him in a chair as directed. "Now do remove the handcuffs. How am I to talk with the prisoner?" The voice of sweet reason belonged to a man in early middle age with brows darker than his greying hair, the same color as a small neat chevron mustache nestled under his arched nose. He offered his cigarette case to Jeff. "Now, then, you seem quite interested in the work of my department, M. Corrèze, although of course that is not your name. I suspect you're not French either, are you?"

"You have my identification." He declined the cigarette with a shake of his head.

"There's a little Jew in Toulouse, we caught her but then we lost her, although we'll pick her up again soon, no doubt, who makes very nice papers of identity."

"I am not a Jew," Jeff said coldly.

"You're not French either, are you?"

"Are you German?" Jeff asked.

His interrogator nodded in the direction of the portrait of Marshal Pétain on the wall. "I am French, of course, a veteran and a patriot."

"Then why do you do the Germans' work for them?"

"Here we support the marshal and the work we do is for our New France. You Jews who care only for money would never understand that." He must have touched a buzzer because a door opened and the two guards came in and lifted Jeff from his chair. "Our young friend says he is not a Jew. Take his pants down."

One of the cops took his pants down while the other grabbed his prick hard, turning it, and then reached under and grabbed hold of his balls, twisting them so that Jeff fell to the floor and writhed there, unable to speak. "A kike," the cop said, nodding to his superior, and went out with the other.

His interrogator drew on his cigarette and watched a perfect smoke ring drift up to the ceiling. When Jeff had finally pulled himself back into the chair and zipped up his pants, the interrogator spoke again, gently reproving. "Lying is such a waste of time."

He had trouble catching his breath to speak. He was still doubled forward in pain. He must speak clearly, though, must summon from whatever reserves he had a semblance of strength. "I am not lying. In the United States, all males born in the hospital are circumcised. It is believed that this is more sanitary."

His interrogator made a face of disgust. "First, I don't believe you. No people no matter how crude would do that to little babies, except the Jews. And the Muslims, of course. Are you going to tell me you're a Mohammedan?"

"You can check my statement with any doctor who knows the United States. Or anyone who has lived there long enough to know."

"Now you are saying you are an American spy?"

"I'm an American officer. I can give you my rank and my number. That is all."

"Oh, come now, even if you should happen to be an American officer, you are not in uniform and you are a spy, so the Geneva Convention does not apply to you."

"I escaped from a camp."

"What kind of camp?"

"A prisoner of war camp."

"And where is this mythical camp located?"

He tried to remember one he had heard of. "I don't want to go back there," he temporized. He was in pain and his eyes teared involuntarily. He could not find a position that did not hurt his balls. The pain reached high up into his belly. He kept wondering if they had torn something.

"And just where is it that we do not want to go back, American officer imaginary?"

"Chieti, in Italy," he said, hoping that even if the interrogator happened to know about Italian prisoner of war camps, that one would be long overrun by the Allies and the records hard to check.

"Oh, and you flew here on the wings of a little dove."

"I walked. I hitched rides in trucks. I took a train partway. Mostly I borrowed a bicycle and pedaled."

"Then why linger here? This story grows more and more inventive."

"I haven't been able to make contact with anyone who could help me to escape either by sea or over the mountains to Spain."

"Ah, you just happened to meet our secretary and get her to work for you and your other friend."

"That one's a girl I picked up today in Toulouse and took to the movies. I feel safer on the streets with a woman. Didn't she explain to you that she knows nothing about me?"

"Enough of this." Again he must have signaled, because the two men came back. They wasted little time, but began beating him, first slapping him around and then settling down to working over his solar plexus and belly. At some point he threw up the remains of the ham sandwich and they rubbed his face in it until he choked. At another point he wet himself, after one or more of them kicked him repeatedly in the kidneys. He passed out.

When he came to he was lying on the floor in an anteroom. One of the guards who had beaten him saw his eyelids fluttering and went off to announce he was ready for more. They flung him into the interrogation room again. Outside it was dark. "We had fun with your girlfriend," one of the guards said to him. "Nice pussy. We'll have to help ourselves to some more of that."

The interrogator was behind his desk, a few crumbs in his mustache that had not been there earlier. As he caressed it, he carefully removed them. Then he sighed. "You're less dashing now, that's certain. Now shall we have a truthful conversation? Where are you from?"

"The United States."

"OSS or M-2?"

"I'm a lieutenant in the American Army. I was captured in Tunisia and taken to the prison camp at Chieti. I escaped as the Germans were moving the prisoners to Germany."

"Lieutenant, if that's what you are, we want all the details of the spy ring you've been running. What kind of information was our little secretary giving you?"

"I only met her last month. What she was going to give me was information on how to get to Spain. What it said I don't know, because you read it, I didn't."

His interrogator nodded and the guards began again, smashing him in the face time after time until he could not help screaming. One of them kept pounding his ear until he thought the eardrum was burst. He could not hear anymore on that side. "I can't hear, I can't hear," he moaned, spitting blood and pieces of a tooth. His mouth hurt too much and the tongue was too injured for him to be able to tell what teeth were broken. He wished to pass out again, but he didn't. How long do I have to hold out, he asked himself, how long? Pain and pain and pain and pain. I don't get used to it. It is bigger than the world. It is a sea inside and outside. It's everywhere. I want to die. I want it to stop.

"Where do you say you're from? Where are your other spies? We want to hear all about how you send your messages out. Where's your radio?"

While they had him on the floor, one of them ground his boot into his belly and then his balls as the other stomped his right hand.

The phone rang. His interrogator picked it up. "I said no calls . . . Bah. All right. Good evening, Herr Sturmbansfuehrer. Yes, I was just interrogating . . . He says he is an American lieutenant. . . . We didn't think. Yes, Herr Sturmbansfuehrer, first thing in the morning. Of course. Thank you, Herr Sturmbansfuehrer, thank you. We'd be very pleased, thank you." He put the receiver back in its cradle and cursed for several minutes. "All right, pack him back into his cell. The SS wants him prettily packaged for them, after we did all the work. They want *all* of them in the morning. . . . Put him on ice and bring me Margot Foulac. We'll have another session with her and then I have further instructions."

As Jeff was dragged along the hall, his head banging freely on the floor, he cried out as he passed the women's cells, calling Jacqueline by name, although he could not speak clearly. There was no answer from within. After they had thrown him in his cell, he heard them opening a cell down the hall and he heard a woman's voice cry out as she was struck.

He lay on the floor where he had fallen. They had not bothered to put cuffs back on him. The Gestapo in the morning. He remembered with extraordinary clarity the corpses of Paulette and of Larousse, like a Grünewald crucifixion. Could he really hold out? How long before he would begin telling them about Jacqueline? About Lev? About the children hidden in the mountains? About exactly where the maquis were encamped in the Montagne Noire? How long? When they pulled his nails out one by one? When they attached wires to his genitals and burned them off? When they put him underwater and used the almost-drowning? When they forced the baton or broom or whatever it was straight up his ass and burst his intestines? When would he begin to say everything, everything, to stop the pain?

They would all die. Margot, Jacqueline and himself, who knew how many others they had caught, they were all going to die against a wall, but why wait, why play their game of endurance?

He did not talk, the Resistance said with pride about Jean Moulin and countless others. No, they let themselves be tortured to death. If very lucky, they finally were shot after digging their own graves. He would not play that role. He had always hated those games men played of who could be manlier, who was tougher. Zach played those games, not Jeff.

He had his own way out from the pain that never stopped, from his kidneys that hurt as they were burst, the teeth broken in his mouth, the terrible pain from some unknown organ ruptured in his midsection, the blood still trickling from a deep cut on the back of his head, the blood half choking him from his injured tongue. OSS had given him an exit visa.

They had at some point broken two of his fingers, stomping on his hand, but the two middle fingers only. He had the quick—and what he labeled at once irrelevant—thought that without the fingers being set soon, he would not be able to hold a brush. He could still reach back in his mouth and loosen the cap on the molar. Finally he held it in his hands, the L-pill they had equipped him with. Zach and he had used to make jokes about it, the capsule of potassium cyanide. They called it the doom cocktail, the little pill that will. He did not wait to think any longer. If he reconsidered he would not do it; then the pain would go on and on and on. He bit the pill, releasing a bitter metallic taste. A wave of nausea choked him but he swallowed the small pill along with a mouthful of saliva and blood. It would be fast, they had assured him back in London.

It was.

RUTHIE 8

Almost Mishpocheh

Life was tighter at home without the income from Rose and Sharon. The city had closed them down, although two neighbors, little Mrs. Entemann and Mrs. Rogovin, had come to court to swear they had given money only to cover the costs of feeding their babies. Finally the judge had levied a fine and a warning. It was a hardship to the neighborhood. Mrs. Entemann had to get up at five A.M. to take her children to her mother's on the streetcar and then hurry to work. Mrs. Rogovin quit her job; it was that or leave the baby alone.

Ruthie, always attuned to her mother and her father, noticed that Rose had lost some position in their relationship. No longer bringing in money, she catered more to Morris. She was humiliated at having been before the court. Although Morris insisted that the laws were made by the affluent to control the working class, and therefore no shame attached to trying to get round them, Rose was frightened. She had a record. She launched into heroics of household economy, making soap from fat and lye, walking miles to find what her family needed or wanted, waiting in line after line.

Sharon no longer had the rent for the upstairs apartment. Never having worked outside the home, she seemed frightened at the idea, half titillated and half offended. Ruthie, who had brought in money since she turned twelve and began baby-sitting, found Sharon's attitude exotic. Sharon seemed to view going to work in the five-and-dime or a factory as another woman might view the possibility of becoming a prostitute. In his letters, Arty took a similar line.

Rose snorted. "My own mother worked, I worked when I was younger, my bubeh was a button maker. Where does Arty get his fancy-schmancy ideas, his wife is a dollbaby? Sharon should get off her tuchis. She feels too sorry for herself, if you ask me."

"I can't pay the rent," Sharon moaned, sitting at Sunday dinner with her face in her hands. At once Clark set up a wailing in response. Sharon clutched him to her bosom, looking, Ruthie thought, quite manipulatively forlorn. "Whatever will I do?"

Ruthie said, "They're hiring at Briggs, on the night shift."

"You know I can't do that, with my little babies, and Arty would be furious. He says he's not risking his life fighting a war for me to go out and get a job like a man."

Only Morris smiled at her, pinching her cheek. "Don't worry, Sharonke, you can always move downstairs. We have plenty of room."

Rose looked at Ruthie, and Ruthie looked back at her mother. They did not think they had lots of room. They were enjoying the silence in the house these days. Naomi studied harder and her grades had recently improved. Rose's energy, no longer pouring over a houseful of her neighbor's little children, was focused on Naomi. She was fed like a heifer for a state fair. She was monitored as to the holes in her clothes, the stains, the seemliness of outfits. Her homework was watched over. Her nails were examined for cleanliness.

"Maybe we could sublet the apartment just till Arty comes home."

Naomi piped up. Ruthie had thought she wasn't listening, her eyes on her plate. "Trudi needs a place. Now that Leib's home, they're real crowded with baby David in that little room. Trudi and her mother are fighting every day."

"I'll talk to her," Sharon said. "I'll see if they'll agree to move out when Arty comes home. They say for sure the union will get him his old job back on the line."

Ruthie clasped her hands, suddenly cold, in her lap. "Don't you think you'd feel funny, somebody else using all your own things and breaking half of them?" She decided to be honest. "I'm not terribly eager to have Leib living upstairs."

"Shush," Rose said. "You had your chance at him, and now he's married to your friend, and you have your own young man. What's past should be bygones. Trudi needs a place of her own too, a mama with a baby and her husband home with a foot missing, poor boy."

Morris frowned at her. "It's not like you, Ruthie, to be so unfeeling for a friend in trouble. In misfortune, we find out who are our true friends."

Ruthie was blushing, her hands wringing invisibly in her lap. How could she explain that she did not trust Leib, did not want him close to her? She suspected her father and mother were right, that she was being mean. Maybe she envied Trudi her husband and baby. Maybe she did not want to witness her friend's happiness and taste even more bitterly her own loneliness. Maybe she was refusing to extend compassion to Leib. She felt she could say nothing more, but that she was always expected to make a sacrifice, were one called for; that her putting others first had come to be taken for granted, for everyone's convenience but her own.

Rose was saying, "This way, we can use Sharon's allotment for the family and hold on to the flat. Sharon, you get Leib to write the check to you and then you write the check to the landlord. When he comes around the last of the month, you be upstairs. That way he can't raise the rent and when Arty comes back, you can move right back in. With strangers, how could we make such a good arrangement for our boy?"

"Maybe they won't want to," Ruthie said softly, but she did not believe that. Trudi was fighting with her mother and Leib was goading her on, as he despised living in her parents' house. Trudi was still working at the hospital part time and Leib had his disability checks.

By July first, it was all arranged. Sharon moved downstairs into Duvey's old room and Naomi was shunted back to Ruthie's. The children would share Duvey's double bed with their mother, as once Arty and Duvey had shared it.

The first Sunday in July, Ruthie, Naomi and Morris helped them move in. Limping badly, Leib moved slowly, awkwardly. He lifted the boxes easily from the truck they had borrowed from a man who had been in the moving business with his father, Misha the Bear, but then he could not carry them up the steps. Ruthie knew how strong, how sure, how agile he had been, and her heart went out to him. A foot missing. She began to imagine what it would be like to have a piece of your own body permanently taken from you and a hunk of metal stuck there without feeling, without fine control.

The day was hot and muggy, overcast. For fear of rain, they worked as quickly as they could. Naomi was up in the truck pushing boxes forward toward Leib. When she came on something light, she ran upstairs with it. She was trying hard to make herself useful, Ruthie noticed. Naomi said to Leib, "I can baby-sit David for you, when you guys want to go out. I mean if you don't want to take him over to your mother's or Trudi's mother's house. I'm good with David, you ask Trudi."

"My mother moved in with my sister in Flint. She couldn't keep up the rent by herself," Leib said to Naomi. He was relaxed with Naomi, not speaking to her as if she was a silly child. Maybe war had changed him; maybe being wounded had changed him. Then he went on like the old Leib at once: "As for that witch Trudi calls her mother, I wouldn't let her change the bottom of a son of mine if she promised to lick it clean."

Naomi giggled. She turned to grab another box. It was light, so she slipped past and carried it up.

Leib leaned toward Ruthie. "So, we're to be neighbors, mishpocheh practically. Who would have guessed?"

"I think Trudi and Naomi cooked it up between them to escape Trudi's mother. They were fighting a lot, no?"

"A lot is no word for it. I wouldn't fight with her—I wouldn't stoop to that. This is pretty much a dump." He cast his eye over the rickety wooden house. "Although I've seen people living in caves, in holes in the earth, in little shacks you wouldn't keep rabbits in. I'll tell you all about it," he promised, putting his hand on her shoulder.

She ducked away at once, then felt as if she had overreacted. Maybe he just needed to lean on others sometimes. She had been told by women at work that when men came back from war, they could not talk about it. Sometimes, the women said, they were crazy. They woke up screaming. They couldn't make love anymore. They were mean and broke things and screamed at the children. They came back idiots or monsters. What they would never do is tell you what had made them that way. But Leib's tone was conversational. Maybe when Murray came back, he too would want to confide in her, to share experiences.

She hefted a box marked GLASS, BE CAREFUL!! Upstairs the baby was crying lustily and there was a thud of something falling. Ruthie hurried. Trudi was directing everyone where to put the boxes down, changing her mind every few minutes. Sweat rolled down Ruthie's back. Surreptitiously she glanced at her watch. She had a great deal of homework to do. Summer term had just begun, and although she had fewer classes, they were more concentrated. She could not help much longer. She wondered what could possibly be in all the boxes, and why some of them couldn't stay at Trudi's parents.

———

Leib and Trudi took a full week to unpack and settle in. When Rose and Ruthie were alone, Rose said, "How those two young people carry on! They yell and scream at each other and throw things. Then they're turtledoves half an hour later."

"Were you and Tata ever like that?"

"Never," Rose said with a shake of the head. "We screamed at the bosses, not at each other. What did we have to scream at each other about?"

"Well, what do they fight about?" Ruthie felt ashamed of her own curiosity, but it was as if she had a window into somebody else's marriage. She had that special wondering about Leib that came from the possibility that she might, in another life, have married him herself.

"I try not to listen. I mean, should I spy on them to gossip in the yards like a yente? They fight about money. They fight about where the sofa should stand. They fight about whether they ought to eat chicken or fish. They fight about who yelled and made the baby cry."

Ruthie smiled. "Well, it doesn't sound serious. I suppose it's just their way. Some people can't tell anyone else is really there if they don't pound on them."

"I'm sure." Rose made a gesture of washing her hands. "But I wouldn't care for all that noise myself, not in my bedroom, not in my kitchen. Enough trouble comes in from outside and down the street roaring."

The rest of the month went smoothly enough. They were all getting used to being in each other's hair. Ruthie dreamed of the small apartment where she would live, sometimes with Murray, and sometimes when he felt too far from her to be real, with just Naomi. It would be blessedly quiet. If Leib and Trudi worked on the line, they would not crave the excitement and noise of screaming at each other. They would crave silence pouring through the ears unctuous and healing as the warm oil Bubeh used for earaches. There would be room, space, light and silence. She could read without staving off fifty interruptions, without consciously blocking out sounds and crashes and childish tantrums.

Clark was becoming spoiled, she thought; Sharon favored him and sometimes made a scapegoat out of Marilyn, the older. Clark had a habit of wanting whatever Marilyn had, and Sharon's usual response was to order her to give it to her baby brother. Fortunately Marilyn would be starting kindergarten in the fall. Especially since Arty had gone to the Army, Sharon had made a pet out of Clark and carried him around, although he was four and big for his age.

The second week in July, she got the first letter from Murray after a gap of three weeks. He had been wounded and was writing from the hospital, but he said he would be out in a week or so, not to worry. In the meantime, he didn't mind at all having a rest and missing one invasion. She was upset by the letter. He'd been wounded while she had not even known. Several women in the factory told her they knew at once when something happened to their men, but she had been wrapped up in classes, work and her family, while across the world, he had almost died.

Ruthie decided she had been silly to worry about Leib upstairs; aside from the house being more crowded, Leib and Trudi's presence meant the entertainment for the family of overhearing their pitched battles and spending money for Naomi, who baby-sat for them regularly. Ruthie missed going over to Trudi's on

Sundays to talk and knit together. Leib was around most of the time. Besides his disability pension, he had a year's unemployment. The balloon company he had worked for was still out of business, so he couldn't return to his old job, and Ruthie did not know and thought it insensitive to ask whether he could still work on an assembly line at all.

Once a week, Leib had to go to a local hospital to have his prosthesis checked. On the whole he did not seem crushed. He was still a good-looking man, and limping down the street in his fatigues using a cane, he drew feminine glances as he always had.

Thus Ruthie had almost forgotten her nervousness on a Sunday when everybody in the family went off to a union picnic on Belle Isle: everyone except Ruthie, who had to study, and she found out, Leib, who was unwilling to go but had urged Trudi to take the baby and enjoy the respite from the heat. Ruthie discovered this when Leib appeared at the door of her room, where she lay on the bunk in a sundress, the fan trained on her, reading a government report on housing problems she was using in a paper.

Her first thought was relief she had not taken her dress off. Only lethargy had prevented her from undressing further, as she would have had to get down from Naomi's upper bunk, where she had fancied there was a little more air. Now she landed on her feet in thirty seconds, embarrassed to be caught on her back. "Leib, is something wrong?" She stood before him barefoot, still clutching the Government Printing Office tome, while he loomed over her. How enormous he was; she had never liked that feeling, a wall of male flesh hemming her in.

"What might be wrong, little Ruthie?" His voice was caressing, as it used to be when he wanted something. He continued to block her way. "We haven't had a chance to talk. You never came to see me in the hospital."

"Why, Trudi told us all about you. I have a job at Briggs, you know."

"Why didn't you come, even once?"

She could have honestly said that between working and school, Ann Arbor was out of the question, but it had never occurred to her to go. "That was Trudi's to do."

"Because you have your own boyfriend. Now you don't think of me at all, is that it?"

"I think of you as my friend's husband and our neighbor, Leib. How else would I think of you?"

He put his hands on her shoulders, hard. "The way I think of you. Always. Day and night. I've never forgotten you."

"You should have." She jerked away. She would have liked to force a passage out of the room, but she did not want to try to squeeze beside him. "Why are we having this conversation? I don't like it. I don't need it."

"I do, I need it. I need you." He tried to draw her closer, but she held up the book between them.

"Leib, those kind of tactics didn't work when we were going out. What makes you think you can strong-arm me now? I don't want you in my bedroom." Using the book as a wedge, she tried to slip past him.

"But him you wanted. That little fink."

"You have your wife and I have my fiancé."

"He's not your fiancé, he's your lover. Trudi told me. You let him do what you never let me do." His voice rose in genuine anger. "If you'd given me what you gave him, I wouldn't be married to Trudi. I'd be married to you!"

"I don't want to be married to you! What I do with myself is none of your business! Leave me alone, Leib. You keep bothering me, and I'll tell the whole family. You better believe me."

"I'll tell them about how you spread your legs for your college boy."

"Tell them. It's none of your business. You can't push me around."

"If you'd given that to me, I'd have married you. He didn't, he wouldn't." His face contorting with bitterness, his hands closed tightly on her back and hip. The warmth of his body burned at her. "What makes you think he's going to bother after the war?"

"I trust him. That's why I could do it with him. Because I trust him. I never trusted you and you know why. Because you'll try to force your wife's best friend when she's out of the house."

He stepped back, raising his hands from her ostentatiously. "Force you? Bullshit. I thought I'd show you what it's really like. I don't have to force anyone and I don't have to beg for it."

"Good." She marched past him out of the room and on through the house, clutching her book. She decided to trot out to the front porch and sit there, in full view of any neighbors around, where he could not molest her. "You stick to what's yours. That doesn't include me."

"If you tell Trudi, she won't believe you. She'll believe me," he said, grinning but still angry, limping heavily after her.

"I have no intention of telling Trudi, because there's nothing to say except you tried to make a fool of yourself and a whore of me." She marched on, reaching the living room. If he grabs me, I'll scream, but who'll hear?

He did not chase her, limping slowly and dramatically after. "You made yourself that for the college boy. I'm telling you, I'd have married you. Didn't I marry

Trudi? I come through. I'm the one you should have trusted. You'll turn to me, Ruthie. This foot hasn't finished me. I'm going to make it big. I'm not going back to the line. I'm not going to be a lousy working stiff, a loser. You'll end up turning to me, because you'll have to."

Sitting on the porch staring at the wavering lines of her text, her heart still beating too fast in her throat, she wondered how he could ever imagine she would come to him. Let him tell himself what nonsense he pleased, she would avoid ever being alone with him in the house again.

Return to Civilization

Saipan was a different sort of island than Murray had seen in the Pacific thus far. It was not a flattened bagel like Tarawa atoll. It was not jungle like Guadalcanal. It was more of a little country, a fair-sized island with a city and pleasant-looking villages. They had landed in an area of beautiful sandy beaches, lined with the usual coconut palms and adjoined by terraced sugarcane fields, but the civilized beauty of the place did not occupy his attention long. That first night they were shelled by artillery that commanded their shallow beachhead with maddening accuracy. All night long the shells came in among them, while from the quality of screaming, he tried to guess who had been wounded by the last shell but not blown to shreds.

Nothing, he thought, crouched in his shallow foxhole in fetal position, nothing made him feel as helpless as lying under an artillery barrage. When they came ashore, he felt naked crossing the reef, exposed, a target in the slow amphtrac lumbering along while shells and machine-gun bullets wiped them out. But then he was at least moving with some kind of chance to fight back or reach cover.

Under shelling, it was all luck, an ant trying to cross the kitchen floor before his mother stepped on it with a curse. He lay and heard the womp womp sound of incoming mail and prayed it wasn't aimed at him. Let me live, he wished, and sometimes wondered why. Maybe because the dismembered scraps of the men he had known turned his stomach. He and Jack were supposed to observe the system of each sleeping half the night and watching half the night while the other slept, but in their foxhole as the artillery shook the ground, neither slept. Phosphorous shells whooshed over and then somebody screamed. They fried men crisp. Howitzers with their up and down groan. Some bigger mail chugging through the air.

For some reason the brass had not figured out they were going to be taking civilian prisoners on this island, where a native population lived along with an estimated twenty thousand Japanese civilians, including families that had been on the island since Japan had taken it over in 1919. From the first day they were finding civilians and passing them back to rough stockades where there wasn't enough food or water.

There was heavy house-to-house fighting in the city, while they took villages and swung around to the north. Where the hell had all their planes gone? They had no air cover. It seemed like all the flying bastards had taken off and left them to their fate. By the fourth day of heavy fighting, the island was cut in two and then they got their new orders: the 8th Marines, along with an orphan battalion which had been stuck onto them until their numbers could be made up out of new marines from the States, were to take the fucking straight up and straight down mountain that dominated the landscape, the volcanic pillar called Mount Tapotchau. Take it? Murray didn't believe they could actually climb it. "What are we fucking supposed to do?" Jack asked. "Use ladders?"

Even the foothills were steep, rugged and covered with brush, with jagged canyons opening suddenly beneath their feet and caves offering perfect cover for the Japanese.

Gunny Reardon, who had recovered fast from his wound on Tarawa, nudged Jack with his elbow. "The gooks get up and down, don't they? Saddle up."

That was one of those Marine phrases, like calling floors decks, that Murray always winced at. Saddle up on what? One of those evil-looking land crabs? He was above them now, above all the flowering trees of the undulating south of Saipan. This was hand over hand climbing. Every so often Murray would almost black out in the afternoon when his old fever liked to start cooking. Jack would have to help him along.

They heard there'd been a big battle at sea between the Jap planes and the Americans, and the Navy pilots were calling it a turkey shoot. Certainly there didn't seem to be more than a handful of bombers left, hardly a nuisance. Big coastal guns from the neighboring island of Tinian lobbed shells at random, mostly blowing up buildings that were still by some accident standing after the heavy fighting down below, cratering the sugarcane fields or splintering some palms. They were slogging up the mountain inch by inch, handhold by handhold. Sometimes the beauty of the scene below them soothed him like an icy cloth on his forehead. Sometimes the green rolling hills and the sea cobalt out where the big ships lay, milky green over the reef, appalled him. The serene light, the flame trees brilliant with blossom, the brightly painted sea felt obscene.

"Sure," Jack said. "One of those Chamorros told me that Jap couples used to come here on their honeymoons. Like Niagara Falls. Watch it!"

A burst of machine-gun fire raked the slope, pinning them down in the lee of an outcropping. They looked at each other and decided silently to stay put. "Jap in a cave," Jack said, risking a quick squint up. "Let them bring up that kid with a flamethrower."

"He got it already."

They were taking heavy casualties, but Murray did not feel it the way he had on Tarawa. For one thing, often it was the guys who were new to combat who bought it in their first couple of days in action. In a way, he felt as if there was no point getting too thick with the replacements till they'd been on the line for a while. It seemed like a waste of time to get to know somebody who'd likely be dead before nightfall. Thus neither Jack nor he had bothered to learn the name of the kid with the flamethrower. The Japs liked to pick out guys with visible equipment; it attracted their attention. Some of the guys who'd been using equipment awhile were canny, but new operators tended to get blown away.

"Who's got it now?" Jack asked. He took a sip from his canteen. "We're getting low on water up here, you noticed?"

"Think I'm getting some private pipeline? You bet your ass I noticed."

That night Seabees brought them up water and chow and then got stuck spending the night during the usual after dark attack. The next day, the 29th Marines swung around the back under cover of a smoke screen while their group attacked frontally.

They were attacking across a small dip in the otherwise steady rise of the mountain when Murray moving in a low crouch stumbled and fell. When he saw what had tripped him up—the bloody intestines of a Japanese soldier wounded in both legs who had committed hara-kiri, and that he himself had slid into a puddle of blood and shit, he vomited.

When Jack edged back to help him, a shell hit spraying shrapnel for the most part harmlessly over the top of the dip. Murray was pressed into the ground with the breath knocked out of him. For a couple of minutes, he thought he was all right until he began to feel the pain in his left shoulder. One piece of shrapnel had torn into him. "I'm hit," feeling the blood soak out.

After a while, a corpsman came up to work on him. Jack waited with him. The corpsman said, "It's not bad at all. We'll get the bleeding stopped and dust it right now. But I can't pull you out of the line for this." The corpsman had him bandaged up in ten minutes and moved on.

He felt weak and what he wanted to do was sleep, but the gunny stood over them. "Get moving."

They took the peak. Then they stood on the top of the whole island and looked down on the fighting below. They were out of it now. The rest of the

2d and the 4th with a battalion of infantry from the Army between them had moved past and they were pinched out of the line. "Too fucking bad," everybody agreed and collapsed. Most of the 8th and the 29th were moved back behind the lines into reserve, but their companies and some others were left to hold the peak along with artillery observers. Murray's shoulder was stiff and sore but had not got infected, which he considered miraculous. On Guadalcanal, he would have had eight kinds of fungi growing in it by now.

They stank, all of them. Camping on the mountain, they looked like the worst hoboes he had seen come out of the freight yards to beg handouts in the depth of the Depression, scary gaunt filth-encrusted men his mother had warned him never to speak to. Her heart would not let her refuse them food, but their fierce need and their scabrous appearance terrified her. If she could see him, she would shrink from him. She would scream.

His shoulder throbbed, and it was hard not to flop over on it during his sleep and then wake. Jack was writing letters home, but Murray could not bring himself to move. He lay in the sun on a black rock just shaped to his body. The sounds of shelling rose, the sharp crackling fire of rifles, the roar of the BARs, the small percussions of grenades and the bangs and thuds of the different-sized shells. They had taken their mountain and now they rested on it, and he was glad and stripped to his physical existence, too worn to think, to worry. They chatted, they reminisced.

"I take a canoe up the river and it feels so good. No noise with a motor, I just glide sweet like a duck through the water, like the keel is greased I go. Then I find someplace on the bank and I haul out and just sit there happy as a turtle and I fish. I smoke and fish," Jack said.

How could Murray share in return his happy moments in the stacks of the library at Wayne? He dug into his childhood and brought out a river of his own. They decided together that Gisele and Ruthie were very special women, truer, gentler, harder working than any others. Murray shared his regret for not marrying when he had the chance.

When he had been hit, somehow he had lost his Zippo lighter, not the shiny ones guys had before the war, back when he didn't smoke, but the dark unpolished metal ones they were issued. He would have to get another, but in the meantime, they shared Jack's. The only bad part of being up on the mountain was that there was little shade and little water, but he'd rather be hot and dry and watching from the sidelines, a perfect balcony seat.

They heard that the Army and the Marines were almost at war down below. The Army hadn't advanced with the Marines, but had dug in and waited for the Marines to do all the work, leaving their flanks exposed forward, where the

Army in the middle was supposed to be. Marines called soldiers doggies and affected to despise them, just as the Army considered the Marines low-life. In this
operation, however, tough shit to the Army, for they were under the command
of a Marine general for once, Holland Smith.

That night a huge banzai was launched below. Thousands upon thousands of
Japs came streaming through the lines. General Smith had warned that a banzai
attack was imminent, but the doggies had not closed up their lines and the Japs
just blasted on through, cutting them to ribbons and sending stragglers storm-
ing into the hills. Up on Mount Tapotchau, they could tell the Japs had broken
through the lines below but they could only see exploding shells. Jack muttered,
"It sounds like the Japs have got back as far as the Tenth Marines Artillery—
looks like a bloody mess down there."

At dawn they watched through glasses trying to figure out what the hell was
happening. Their shared nightmare was that the Japs had many more troops
than they were supposed to have and had launched a major offensive. Even Sergeant Zeeland was edgy and remarked how few bodies they had found the first
days when they were advancing. The glasses went from hand to hand. Zeeland
grumbled, "Tell me what I'm seeing. I'm going crazy."

Jack looked astonished that the sergeant would admit there was anything he
didn't know backwards, but he lifted the glasses and searched where Zeeland was
pointing. "Marie nous sauve," he said. "It's the charge of the cripples!"

When Murray focused the glasses, he saw what everyone was looking at. A
line of wounded men, of amputees leaning on sticks, of men with arms in slings,
in tattered bandages, with heads completely bandaged so that they were blind
and had to be led by the hand, were coming to attack, some armed, some holding
bayonets mounted on sticks, some cradling what were probably grenades in arms
embedded in plaster casts. They were moving up as best they could to join the
banzai attack, which Murray could see had finally ended deep into Allied lines.

He had no time to appreciate the view, because they were given orders to
march down double time and join the mopping-up operations, back into the
line to replace the casualties of the charge, which had decimated companies.
When they finally got down the mountain, a matter of four hours instead of the
three days it had taken them to get up, Murray looked at the scene and could
not believe it. The field in front of the 10th Marines Artillery gun emplacements looked like raw hamburger. Exhausted marines had fallen asleep on piles
of corpses, because there was noplace free of maimed bodies and bloody slime.
The mangled dead were piled on the mangled dead. Few had been shot. Most
had been hit by shells directed flat along the ground like machine-gun fire, as
the artillerymen fought for their lives. He thought not even at Tarawa had he

seen so many bodies. There the bodies had floated in the surf and he realized in retrospect how clean a death that was, the blood draining out, the flesh washed. Here mud and blood and pulverized muscle and organs made a hellish stinking muck seething with flies. He closed his eyes for a moment and tried to imagine snow, nothing but snow. Then hearing a rifle bark nearby, he hit the bloody muck headlong.

For two days they cleaned up pockets of stragglers from the great banzai charge, but it became apparent that that pile of rotting meat that was being bulldozed into trenches had been the army of General Saito. The general's body was found near a cave that had been his headquarters by troops that were driving the few remaining Japanese soldiers into the extreme north of the island. After ordering the suicide of his army, General Saito had committed hara-kiri, then been finished off by an aide with a bullet to the brain.

They moved out to assist in the final mopping-up way in the north. That end of the island was rugged terrain. Now that the charge was over, marines were saying how lucky they were it had happened, because the Japs could have gone on fighting from defile to cave to flinty hill all the way to the cliffs that rose sharply above the sea, cliffs of limestone and coral, jagged and straight down: Marpi Point. As the marines converged, Murray guessed there were fewer soldiers than civilians left. Mostly civilians were milling around the point, a lot of them women with children and babies in arms. The marines took up positions on the edge of the plateau.

Some Marine nisei came up with bullhorns and called in Japanese for the civilians to surrender, that they would not be hurt. The Jap soldiers were yelling at them too from the caves where they were holed up. At least everyone didn't look terrified. Some kids were playing catch in a circle. From the brush, he watched them for a moment, there on the cliffs with the wind whipping the girls' black hair and the sea rising up the horizon so blue it hurt his eyes, and then one of the children missed. As the grenade exploded and the children were torn apart and their burst bodies hurled through the air, the men around him all groaned as one and Murray understood what game the children played.

A woman dressed in a sea green kimono looking like a big shiny butterfly ran with her baby in her arms to the cliff and hurled herself over, crying out something. A family group, father, mother, two little boys, went forward together holding hands and leaped off. Murray could hear more bullhorns from below the cliffs, where gunboats were circling. More and more people were running forward. He saw a man swing an infant through the air and dash its head against a stone. Then a woman took the corpse and shuffled slowly toward the cliff to walk off into space and fall.

An older woman unbound her long iron grey hair as if getting ready for bed and then stepped off the cliff, primly holding her skirts together as she fell straight down. A man grabbed up a baby and ran off, his legs still wheeling in the air as he seemed to hang a moment and then plummeted. The women's fall was slowed by their kimonos billowing around them, so there was a ghastly incongruous grace to their descent, as if they were large blossoms in lavender, in maroon, in pale gold, in sky blue floating.

As he stared, a woman carrying a little girl ran back and forth, back and forth, frantic as a trapped puppy with her ivory kimono glinting in the sun. She would run up to the edge of the cliff and then embrace the little girl she held and turn away. She did this over and over until finally she backed from the cliff, swung around and began running straight toward the brush where Murray's company was dug in. "Come on," the guys started yelling to her, "that-a-girl, come on!"

A machine gun sputtered from the caves. The woman jerked as the bullets tore through her, almost cutting her in half. She fell and lay crumpled, red soaking the ivory of the kimono. Neither she nor the child moved again.

"Bastards," Reardon said. "Killing their own women. They just ain't human. We've got to clean those yellow bellies out of there."

They did eventually clean the soldiers out of the caves, but it was too late. Hundreds of women, men and children leaped from the cliffs. The sea below was so choked that the propellers of the boats were blocked with flesh. Murray felt numb. Standing among the bodies that littered the grass at the cliff tops, he looked down into the sea of bodies below and again he vomited. How can we see all this and go on living?

A moment later he was following Jack uphill, where one of the new guys, called Tiny because he was six feet four and broad, was shouting that he had found a cache of booze in one of the caves. What all the men wanted more than anything else was to be dead drunk, and Murray felt at one with the guys around him. Never before in his life had that happened to him. Always he had been odd man out, the intellectual, the sensitive one, the Jew; but now he felt as if he were part of an animal bigger than himself, an ant in a colony who moved to the same chemical signals as the ant beside him and the ant before and behind. Sake called them. Sake promised numbness. If he would never forget the sight of that ivory kimono glistening as the woman ran toward them carrying her daughter and then the bullets tearing through her flesh, if he would never forget the green kimono floating like the wings of a Polyphemus moth as the woman turned and turned in the air plunging toward the sea and the rocks, if he would never forget the children in the sunlight tossing the dark ball between them until they all blossomed into fire and burning flesh, then the sake promised that soon, soon, he would remember but not feel.

They knew they were breaking regulations and did not give the faintest damn, as they uncorked the bottles, squatting in the cave where the corpses still lay in their blood puddled around their weapons. They knew that there were still hundreds of remnant soldiers sniping in the brush. They did not give a shit. I am one of them, Murray thought, drinking the sake down and feeling its warmth spread in his belly. I am no more, no less. The best is not to feel anything.

Wearily, Jack winked at him—contact less exhausting than speech—and he winked back. Some of the men were going through the pockets of the corpses, looking for souvenirs. The gunny, Reardon, stooped into the cave and shook his head at them. Then instead of giving them hell, he reached for a bottle and sagged against the far wall, shoving the remains of a kid whose legs had been blown off aside with his boot. "Aw shit," he said. "This is one asshole island."

JACQUELINE 9

An Honorable Death

9 juin 1944

I can scarcely write because two of my fingers are broken and splinted, and my left arm is in a sling, but here I am on Montagne Noire. Sometimes I think surviving is a duty; sometimes, a fate. Jeff has not arrived yet. I am awaiting news. It is a nuisance to be disabled at a time as busy and critical as this, as the battle for France goes on everyplace!

Two of the guards raped me. The third one didn't. The others said he was queer, but he said he was afraid of catching a disease, that I was probably a prostitute the American had picked up. I didn't believe his reason and neither did the other two, because they laughed at him. When they took me back to the cell, they were still making jokes while he opened a different cell. I knew from what he said that they had found out Jeff is American, which puts him in danger of being shot as a spy.

I knew the cell was different because, first, I had counted the doors going in, and second, this cell was on the right, not the left. I lay on the floor where they threw me. Then I crawled up on the straw mattress. Through the window I could see only pale lavender sky. I will admit I was crushed with despair and horror and I wept for a long time, until my eyes were sore and my sinuses blocked. I had nothing to wipe my nose on but my dress, already smeared with blood and their filthy semen, and my own urine, for I had wet myself when they tried to force me the first time.

I lay on the cot a long time like a stepped-on bug, blaming myself for our walking into their trap. I should have known. I berated myself bitterly for being distracted with our argument, with his presence. The presence of a man you love is a constant demand for attention, even when such attention is dangerous and inappropriate, and I am no more able to resist that demand than any other woman. I heard them taking someone out. They might come back again for me at any moment. I saw Maman and Rivka going hand in hand to the deportation train, and I had to act. I sat up and felt myself over. My face was covered with blood from my nose. It was sore and swollen but I did not think it was broken. Mostly I was bruised. My vagina was bleeding. I wished they had left me my underpants. They had been so busy raping me, they had not yet beaten me badly, although I was sure that would come later. I began examining my cell.

The door was firmly locked, solid wood set in a metal frame. The outer wall of the ancient building was made of stone. I scrambled up to hang on the bars and peer out. My cell overlooked a side street from one floor up. When I had looked out of the window of the cell I had been in before, I had looked into a courtyard. I began to wonder if the guard who had not taken part in the rape had perhaps done me a little favor, because the side street was much better than the courtyard, if I could get out. It was far to jump, but not suicidal. I could survive it, I knew I could.

I managed to scramble up and crouch on the narrow window ledge. A sentry passed below about every ten minutes, although not with regularity. Finally I figured out sometimes he just came to the corner and looked and did not bother walking the length of that side. Several times he stopped just around the corner on my side and smoked. I could smell his cigarette.

The glass had long since broken on that window in one of the many air raids that eliminated glass all over the city. Pressing my head cautiously against each gap in the bars, I found that the bar nearest the right hand had the largest gap between bar and wall, as if it had been pushed somewhat awry while the cement was still wet. The stone was not completely square. High up, the gap was even wider. It did not look large enough for a big cat to wriggle out, but I thought of the space a baby is born through, and I thought it was worth trying. But not yet. It was still the long pale mauve twilight. I was playing a game all this time of being perfectly still whenever the sentry was near and then working feverishly on the bars when he was around the corner.

I heard the gate at the end of the hall crash open and I flung myself down and ran to my cot. My heart began pounding so loudly my body shook. This time I listened to where they went. It was Margot they were bringing back, and then they took Jeff. He called out to me as he was taken down the hall, but I did not want to call the guards' attention to the fact that I was in a different cell than they had put me in originally, so I did not answer. Maybe the guard who had put me in here would also help Jeff. I felt bad at not answering Jeff, but I feared, irrationally but powerfully, that if I spoke and he heard my voice, he would instantly know I had been raped.

I took off my belt, with its brass buckle. I scrambled back up onto the narrow ledge and worked on the opening, taking care that no dust from my rubbing fell out the window. Whenever I saw or heard the guard approaching, I stopped. I knew that he could not see into the darkness where I was crouching, but nonetheless, when he was near I was afraid to move, afraid to breathe. I tried to forbid myself to think about what was going to happen to us and simply to focus all my energy, all my strength, on escaping. The sentry seemed so close as he passed, the top of his head only ten feet below me, I felt as if he could smell my fear. I thought that fear tasted just as my dry mouth tasted, of old blood and something tinny. I doubted first whether I could get through the narrow gap between stone and bar, and second, whether I could do it in under ten minutes. Otherwise he could hardly miss me hanging in midair over his head.

I made no impression on the rock, of course, but the mortar was weaker. I suppose altogether I scraped off about .7 centimeters. I felt every minute space gained made it more likely I would be able to wriggle through. My fingers were bleeding by now and I still had no idea if that narrow space would pass even my head.

It was finally dark when they came back with Jeff. I heard him cry out something in the hall, but I could not make out the words. They took Margot away again. I was sure my turn would come next, before I ever had a chance to try my plan. It did not seem like much of a plan, but it was all I could think of, and I had to try something. I had to. I crawled up on the ledge again. I realized that my clothes were only going to get in the way.

I hopped down and stripped, feeling more naked than I ever have in my life. I tied my dress and slip, my sabots into a bundle, which I placed carefully on the ledge so I would not drop it. I began trying to work my head through as soon as the sentry had passed. Then he called out something to another. When I heard shooting, I froze, but nothing more happened.

Then came my wonderful piece of luck. Planes arrived over Toulouse to bomb the railyards and the foundries. The ground was shaking and dust rising. The sentry disappeared. I forced my head through. It felt as if I had skinned myself and broken my jaw but there I was hanging over the street with my head through the bars and my clothing in a bundle on the ledge. I pulled it through so that it was on the outside with my head. I continued forcing myself through, wishing I were skinnier than I am. I wriggled and wriggled. Whenever I let myself panic, I got stuck. My own sweat helped lubricate me. I was sweating heavily, partly from exertion, for never have I worked so hard as I did to force my body through. My breasts hurt. They were bruised already from the guards. I thought my arms would rip from their sockets, but the hardest part was my hips. Finally I lunged and then fell, clutching the bundle. That was how I broke my arm. I lay stunned in the street while the sky bloomed with vast zinnias of flame, red and gold and incandescent white, the clusters of rockets from the antiaircraft batteries, the searchlights crisscrossing and wheeling in arcs, the rosy fall of a bomber and then the tower of flames where it went down in the city. I was dazed. My hip hurt so, I thought I had broken it too.

Lying there in the dirt and my blood, naked and filthy and torn, I felt like some small fierce creature of the night, a weasel, a stoat, something tiny and lithe and close to the ground with sharp teeth and an immense will to live. I had to get up in spite of the pain. I did not know how many bones I had broken but I could not care, I could not care. I pulled on the dress somehow, stepped into my sabots and crept along the building toward the street in front. I was afraid to head toward the back, as that was the direction the guard had run in when the raid started. I hobbled along the street, but no one was about except a fire truck going by.

I went straight to the house of a cheminot nearby. I could think of nowhere else to go, and I knew that once the raid was over, my chances of escaping in my bloody dress were slight. I felt ashamed, as if anyone looking at me could tell I had been raped. I could smell my stench, of their semen, of blood, of sweat, of urine. I banged on their door, but did not make too much noise as I did not want neighbors to hear. Then I realized because of the bombing, no one could hear me, no matter what I did. They live near the yards and all their windows were long ago smashed and the walls of the house itself cracked. I finally pushed on the old packing crate that serves as window curtains and fell into their kitchen with a great clatter, which brought the wife at once.

Now I am at the base in the Montagne Noire, with my people again. We are waiting word. Neither Jeff nor Margot seems to have been able to escape and I want to know where they are being held—the Milice barracks or Gestapo headquarters on rue Alexandre Fourtanier. Daniela set my arm and splinted my fingers. I am not much good. I couldn't shoot a gun to save my life, although it may come to that too. I am covered with hideous bruises and abrasions. My nose is swollen purple as a turnip. But I am proud that I escaped. Here in the high clean beech forest, I slowly recover.

I wish we would get news of Jeff. I fear for him. I am afraid they will beat and torture him. I have nightmares in which I am laying out his body, as I did Larousse, and each time I wake weeping. When I am wide awake, images of tortured flesh haunt me. I worry about Margot too, but I cannot pretend I feel her danger as keenly. I tell myself that Jeff was well trained and that if a civilian, a woman, can escape, surely he can too: not in the same way, of course, since he could never have wriggled through, but perhaps when they move him. One thing I dread is telling him about being raped, how he will take that.

10 juin 1944

The Milice shot Margot. That was the fusillade I heard from my cell. They did not want the Gestapo to know about their leak, to interrogate her about Milice headquarters, so after they had questioned and beat her for several hours, they shot her in the courtyard of the prison. We think the Gestapo has Jeff. We must find out.

They did not know who I was when they were raping me, but now they know I am the same organizer of the trips across the Pyrénées they were hunting earlier. My wanted poster has gone up everywhere, but I am told that they get torn down as fast as they go up. Like Papa, I have a price on my head. Papa is trying to find out where Jeff is being kept. I am impatient to know, so that we can make plans to break him out. Oh, Eduardo brought a new recruit to me, a construction worker who told me that the way I escaped is called the bar of freedom and was done wherever they could get away with it when the prisons were being revamped after the Nazis arrived. The workers would move one bar after it was inspected but before the cement hardened.

11 juin 1944

Papa came to our tent to tell me, while Daniela was changing the dressing on my hip. He is dead. The Milice killed him. There is nothing more to say, nothing. I cannot believe he is dead, but it is so, Papa insists. We cannot even recover the body.

21 juin 1944

Both Papa and Daniela gave me a talking to, that I must get myself together and set an example, that I cannot continue to give way to my feelings. Grief, Daniela says, is a luxury. Did I not urge her to think about the living when her brother killed himself with his own grenade? It seems to me I was insufficiently sympathetic then, but Daniela denies that. Papa orates somewhat more. He says we are at war and cannot pause to mourn or remember our dead until we have won. He asks me if I should have wished Jeff to collapse if I had been shot alongside Margot.

Papa said one thing is sure: Jeff did not talk before they killed him. No more arrests have followed. Mme Faurier has taken over running his agents from outside Lacaune, and the two operations are separate now as that know-it-all, the British radioman, keeps saying they should have been all along. Mme Faurier will continue to transmit through Achille. We will leave him hidden in the Lacaune Mountains. Here the maquis have that British radioman who communicates with London for them.

Many separate maquis groups have gathered here to fight the Germans, not only the Jewish Army and scouts but many local groups. There is some tension, but mostly we all get on. The Jewish squadron is actually admired for our discipline and our training: Lev is responsible for that. Every day one of our people says to me how much they miss Jeff's style and his energy. People have also been giving me drawings he left various places. I have been looking at them too much and I have decided I must hide them away. I know I am failing in my work. If I only escaped to weep and lie in my tent and walk on the mountains alone trying to imagine how he would have seen these landscapes, I should have died at the hands of the Milice too, as he did, as Margot did. The only time I feel some respite from his death is when I climb one of the old logging roads that rise steeply among the beech and holly. Purple columbine grows in the paths. Giant glistening diamond-backed black slugs slide everywhere, devouring the wildflowers. The world is peaceful noplace, but here it is whole. Cuckoos keep calling. I climb till I am exhausted.

I will try to see only the labor before me. That labor is hard, because I am frankly of little use, with one arm in a sling and the other hand partially splinted. Our groups have been attacking German convoys on the way toward Normandy with food or munitions, attacking too the concentrations of troops moving in that direction. We have gone a long way from practicing with sticks.

I forgot to say, in my personal craziness, that London called off the order for the general uprising. Too bad, folks, we changed our mind. Sorry about that. In the meantime maquis all over France went on the attack, expecting that mythical Force C to land by plane to reinforce us, and the Boches responded with tanks, planes, the full works, and wiped them out. They have also killed entire towns full of people as punishment. A woman arrived who may be the sole survivor of a little village in the Dordogne. She and I spent several days together, as we were both in the same state of torn-open crazy grieving.

I work with Daniela in our improvised field hospital, where every day's fighting brings casualties. We still have no doctor, but we have another nurse besides Daniela, and me, with my limited hospital experience. We had a drop of medical supplies and lots and lots more arms, food, gear. After all those years of shortages, suddenly they are dropping tons on our heads every week. Now everybody has at least one weapon. We feel rich.

26 juin 1944

I work in the hospital. My hand is out of its splint and I am doing exercises Daniela gave me to recover the full use. My arm in the cast itches terribly. I sleep badly and I can never tell when I will begin to cry, suddenly. Tears just start running from my eyes as if a faucet were turned on. It is completely out of my control, and mostly I ignore it, and try to get everyone else to do the same. I was pleased when my period started. The last thing I could endure is to be pregnant by one of those thugs. It was a week late, but at last it came.

Papa is a good leader, adored by his comrades. He and Lev get on well after a rocky start, but Papa is especially fond of Daniela. We have a lot more OSS and SOE people coming through here as if we were camped on a great highway of intelligence and guerrilla warfare: the former are American; the latter, British. I tend to be friendlier to the OSS. I ask them if they knew Jeff. One had met him in training, but none of them has turned out to be his friend. On the whole the Americans are warmer than the British, but they have dreadful or silly politics. I speak English very well now, but the British tell me I have an American accent.

We had horrible news of Vercors, which was the biggest maquis base in France. After they rose to attack the Germans on command, the Germans poured a whole army in there and wiped them out. Some of the maquis got away over the mountains, but whole villages were massacred down to the babies and even the pets, their bodies hung on hooks in the butcher shops. It is terrifying and leaves us unable to enjoy the news we hear from Normandy of the Allied advance. It seems they are really established now. The Resistance has been doing a good job of tying up German troops and preventing columns from reaching Normandy to join in the fighting. That is one reason the Germans are trying harder than usual to wipe us all out.

5 juillet 1944

Mme Faurier sent for me to come and talk to her. It broke my heart to see the farmhouse there, with the room upstairs under the steep pitch of slate roof where he and I used to sleep, with the sound always of water cascading over the frogsback rocks. Sometimes remembering happiness sticks in the chest like a knife. Everything I looked at—rocking chair, pitcher, plate, ticking clock—went off like little time bombs exploding memories, his face, his voice, his hands, the skin of his back, the way he would brood on a landscape as if it said and meant something entirely different to him than to anyone else.

Mme Faurier took my hands in hers, calloused and with the feeling they have always of being warm but worn. "We have learned several things. There has been a big shake-up at the Milice. The guards who assaulted you and the one you think helped you have all been sent to forced labor in Germany, and that captain has been demoted and sent to Pau. You see, the Gestapo got no one and the Milice had to be punished. In the general upheaval, we once again have someone inside now."

"What are you not yet telling me?" I asked none too politely, because I could feel her holding something back.

"The Milice did not kill Vendôme. He took his own life after torture."

I must have screamed, because she jumped up and put her arms around me, hugging me against her softness. She is shorter than me but plumper, softer-bodied. Normally I like to lean against her the way her daughters do, but I could not bear it then and yanked away.

"Jacqueline, he is a hero, like Daniela's brother. He knew too much. That's why OSS gives them poison capsules, so that if they feel they cannot take the torture, they have a way out. His is an honorable death."

I shook my head but did not answer. I could not speak.

"Jacqueline, they were torturing him already, don't you understand? They were watching him much more carefully than you. They hadn't figured out yet that you were involved. They knew he was a spy. In the morning, he was going to the Gestapo."

Like Larousse, I thought. I left at once—fled might be more like it—and headed back on foot to Murat, where the railway ends and the cheminots had promised to get me to Castres from which I was to be transported in a lumber wagon. I know these mountains pretty well from the time we spent here but I almost got lost twice. I had to force myself to concentrate because my thoughts and feelings were churning wildly until I felt the centrifugal pressure would tear me apart. When I did go astray, I had only to climb, because these mountains are denuded except for fragrant deep gold broom and heather and an occasional beech, and you can see very far. The ancients lived here, for the moors are full of upright monoliths, dolmens and burial sites, stones grey as the local sheep.

I had to face that I was furious with Jeff. I could not forgive him for choosing death. I felt that he should choose life at any cost of pain, because in life we had a chance to be together. I felt he had deserted me, and I did not forgive. I realized I could tell this to no one, least of all to Daniela, whose brother had killed himself.

I did not think my reaction to his suicide was justified or ethical, but I would not lie to myself. As I strode through the broom heavy with bees, I swore at him. I cursed him for choosing death. I cursed him for turning his face away from me.

Finally I threw myself down in the shade of a roofless stone shed, long abandoned, and lay there weeping until I fell asleep. I woke in the sun, feverish. When I opened my eyes, an eagle was circling over me. She was so close I could see the fiery glint of her amber eye. When I moved, she rowed heavily off and then soared on her powerful wings until she was invisible in the bright air. I went on lying there. I realized I have been humiliated to feel now and then a pang of sexual feeling, as if that had all died with him or should have. The sexual awakening that came to me with him was deep and beautiful, but highly dangerous while we are fighting for survival and fighting to win. If we had only been friends, comrades, he could not have distracted me so that we walked into that trap the Milice set for us. I was not alert. It was my fault. I was not paying sufficient attention; I lacked clarity.

So if my sexual feelings did not die with him, they should have. Now I must lock deep within my bones such a possibility, maybe for however short a time I may have to live, maybe until we break through into some other world. As I lay there, I swore to suppress all that. Around me mountain arnica was in flower. Mme Faurier uses it to make compresses for bruises and strains. I rose oddly relieved, although groggy, as if I had slept far longer than I could have, looking at how high the sun still stood. My anger was numb as a stone.

As I climbed the next ridge I felt for a moment as if I were in one of his paintings, a figure on one of those long dun or lavender hills he liked to paint. Then I simply concentrated on climbing steadily. I lived most of my life without him and I will lead the rest of it, whether it ends tomorrow or in forty years, without him. That is given. That and the need to be useful.

LOUISE 9

Rations in Kind

The file declared in big red letters: U.S. CONFIDENTIAL. Inside reposed Louise's orders with six carbons. It said:

SUBJECT: Travel Orders
TO: All concerned

1. Following will proceed by first available transportation from London to First Army Headquarters, then to proceed to such places within the Theater as may be necessary for the accomplishment of her mission, including entrance into the actual theater of war.

2. Travel by military aircraft is authorized. Rations in kind will be provided.

Mrs. Louise Kahan, Correspondent
By command of General Dwight D. Eisenhower

That was what the orders said, but that didn't mean that anything was about to happen. She was awaiting transportation to France. In the meantime, she was working on a piece about families living in the Underground. A lady from the Volunteer Services took her around, a little too genteel for Louise. She found a woman fire fighter who was a better guide.

The men she had been working with in OWI had been skeptical that she would actually go to France. "Louise, near the front lines? Not a chance."

Even if they turned out to be right, she could find plenty to write about in wartime London. She was still experiencing shock at her abrupt departure and total change of life, but she was as glad as she had been at first offer that she had seized the chance as it flashed before her. She felt brimming with energy and health and curiosity.

Ordinary people here did not complain of rationing as they did at home, but seemed to think it was only fair that everybody should have a crack at what was scarce. As for the rubble, nothing had prepared her for that. St. Paul's stood in classic splendor over surrounding ashes, absolutely alone. She understood that the worst of the bombing had been years before, but it had never entirely stopped and now rockets were landing. On her second day, she saw one in the air, lethal and insectlike, a wingless plane roaring and sputtering, canted down. An enormous explosion shook the earth. Although it was almost a mile from her, she felt the shock wave.

People looked shabby and pale, bedraggled by comparison with Americans. Her clothes stood out, even in well-to-do circles. She took to wearing her uniform most of the time. In the shops, there was little of anything, but PXs and American messes were abundantly supplied. So, too, were the restaurants where the well off ate.

Claude called her, and out of a mixture of curiosity and the desire to have some kind of coda to their truncated intimacy, she lunched with him. "How's the Marshal Zhukov epic? Are you on your way to the Soviet Union?"

Everything in his handsome face went a bit awry. "It doesn't really focus directly on Zhukov. Filming in the Soviet Union in the middle of the devastation of war is out of the question. We filmed it on the back lots and in Idaho—gorgeous scenery, very underused."

"I thought Kursk was in rather scrubby country, sandy, marshy. Some thick forests."

"It's not directly about Kursk. We decided to focus on the partisans. We have Tyrone Power playing the American flier and Hedy Lamarr as the Russian nurse."

Louise decided it would be better to change the subject, as the film obviously had. "So how long do you expect to be in London?" She felt a casual friendliness toward Claude. Hollywood was chewing him up, while she had escaped Washington.

———

She spent her third day running around to nurseries. In the evening, she had supper at the enormous Grosvenor mess with Oscar and his girlfriend Abra, whom she had insisted he bring.

She was pleased that he was still with the same woman; that had not happened since their divorce. Maybe he would marry Abra, if she hung in there long enough, and indeed, there she was visibly dangling, thinner, with a look somewhere between the American girl dazzle she had radiated at their last meeting and the worn, bled look of the Londoner.

Oscar was beginning to show middle age, she thought, oddly touched. He too was shabbier and markedly thinner. He was beginning to sprout an occasional glittering white hair over the ears. He had a looseness around his eyes as if he was not sleeping enough.

They finished a bottle of shipper Bordeaux. "As parents, we've been a disaster," she said. "I tried, but perhaps I lacked the talent."

"It's the times," he said. She thought that he looked at her far too much and should look at Abra oftener. Abra was depressed and sulking. "Families are torn apart everywhere. If the worst that happens to our daughter is a trek through divorce court, she's getting off lightly."

"Perhaps I consider divorce more traumatic than you do," Louise said acidly. "However, I imagine she'll have thousands of companions in that misery. Marriages between strangers living in a romance based on movies and pop songs are bound to shatter quickly."

"There's this to consider too," Oscar said with conscious malice, "his profession is high risk."

"And this to consider," Louise replied, "perhaps they'll both survive the war just fine and we'll be combusted. Then deprived of our ill will, they'll live happily ever after."

"I thought you'd be far more anguished about Kay," Oscar said, observing her carefully.

"I've resigned, in all senses. I am resigned and I have resigned. Kay will do what Kay must do. I have interfered and brooded and intervened, and to what end? Maybe if she feels free of me, she'll settle into being a person of her own."

Oscar seemed about to say something more, but as she observed Abra's lowered face, she changed the subject. "At least among the working-class people I've been interviewing here, I'd say the Soviet Union's stock is higher than ours."

"Remember, you've got a working class with less false consciousness about their class position, but a lot of illusions about Stalin and the Soviet Union—not unlike ours, before we went. Also, there are not several hundred thousand Soviet troops swarming over England. What they say about us is, overfed, overpaid, oversexed and over here. They resent how long we took to come into the war. The Soviets were almost as late, but they've suffered even more than the British."

"People also tell me that things have got more democratic here. That there's been a leveling, due to rationing and scarcity."

"The working class is doing better, unless they're in the armed forces, in which case their families live on air. Bevin's done a good job strengthening the unions and making conditions in the factories less sweat-shoppy—but basically, the rich stay rich. Many of the well heeled retired to the country estate before the first bomb fell on Stepney."

"At home everybody's doing well, but the rich are doing especially well. The bigger companies hog the contracts. After the war, there'll be an explosion of buying: houses, cars, refrigerators, every appliance that's been invented. It's going to be a very different place, I suspect."

She enjoyed herself, although she felt guilty when she glanced at Abra, who obviously did not feel the same. Nonetheless, when they had finished coffee and dessert, she excused herself and set off for Claridge's. She was not, however, immensely surprised when Oscar turned up there at eight the next morning. She was having breakfast in her room, and since they had the same name, the hotel announced him to her as her husband and sent him up. She did not dispute the assertion but ran to the bathroom to adjust her face and comb her hair. Fortunately bombing had caused the lift to malfunction, and he would have to climb four flights to her.

She would almost have time to dress. But did not. Louise! she reproached herself in the mirror, but the truth was, she loved the moss green dressing gown that set off her hair and her complexion, the peek of paler green silk from beneath it, and her keenest thought on the subject was, Let him see what he gave up. Besides, dressing gown and nightgown would have to stay in London with her extra baggage. She might as well get some use out of having dragged them across the ocean. If Oscar thought he could take her at a disadvantage by showing up without warning at eight A.M., let him discover her with her hair loose around her moderate but fetching décolletage. Tough, Oscar, just tough. She answered the door with sublime surprise. "Oscar, my goodness. At this hour. Is something wrong?" She did not for two minutes think anything was. He would have telephoned with bad news.

"Only us. I don't know why you insist on seeing me with Abra for chaperone, but it's no fun for her."

She motioned him to the couch and sat in the chair. "They have real tea here. Will you have some? Why don't you marry the girl, Oscar?"

"Whatever for?" He looked startled, accepting the tea.

"You're using up years of her life. I presume she'd like to have children relatively soon."

Oscar shook his head wearily. "She's an excellent assistant. She really is. Quick, bright, interested, hardworking but not ambitious for herself. That's how it all started. That's what I really wanted."

"My dear, that's never all you wanted from any woman, not for long."

"Moreover, we're in it together, OSS, the war." He finished his tea, sighing. "I presume you aren't about to marry your very young man."

She was startled. His narrow eyes were sharp as obsidian, watching. "What games we play. I imagine you know because either someone in Washington told you, or more likely, Daniel wrote Abra. He does write her. They have a long and durable flirtation going."

Oscar grinned but his teeth looked as if they would like to bite something, her perhaps. "To give that very young man credit, he said nothing, but that made Abra suspicious. What happened to your French director?"

"I like Daniel better. He has a more affectionate disposition. How can you justify referring to him as my very young man? I'd have thought Abra was the same age."

"I would never disagree that she's too young for me. It's a little wearing."

"And I thought it was austerity and the war effort!"

"Louise, you are not a bitch. Do not attempt to sound like one."

"I have that side too, Oscar. I have many sides."

Oscar got up lithely and came to stand directly in front of her. His knees touched hers. She found herself holding her breath. "Let's go to bed, Louise." He took her hands. "Let's have something nice from the chance of being together, here, now."

Her damned body was lapping like a fire at the underside of her skin. "Oscar, we can't. I can't hurt Abra that way."

"Oh, this time you aren't busy being faithful to somebody else?"

"It isn't that sort of situation. But I can't hurt Abra."

"Abra and I don't have an exclusive relationship. She hasn't asked for that or expected it, and I haven't either." He drew her to her feet. "Louie, Louie, come to me, be with me."

"Oh? Does she make much use of her freedom? Oscar, that situation's too depressingly familiar. I can't add to her woes." She pressed her hand firmly against his chest, keeping her elbows straight, holding him off. "I don't enjoy one-night stands, not even with an ex-husband."

He let her go and strolled to the little table, picking at the remains of her toast. "Denied even the barest crumbs," he said, but sounded amused. "Oh, Louie, we do strip off perhaps at least one coat of nonsense each time, don't we? Stay in London. You have plenty to write about here."

"As soon as they give me leave to go, I'm on my way."

"Hmmm. By the way, are we still expected to go on supporting Mrs. what's her name? Or is the flying goy picking up the tab now?"

"We're still supporting her, as I'm sure you can guess."

"I wish at least she'd married money," Oscar said, running his hand through his hair. "I'm making on paper just about my salary, but without speaking engagements and consulting and royalties, I'm hurting. I suppose everybody is during the war."

"Don't bet on that. A lot of people are doing just fine."

"With the paper shortages, all of my books but one have gone out of print."

"Oscar, I'm all right financially. Why don't I take over two thirds of her expenses, and you kick in one third?"

"Can you do that?"

She nodded. The size of printings was severely limited, hurting her last collection of stories, but her nonfiction book about women on the home front had been considered important and allowed a run that had made it a best-seller. Best-sellers were sprouting like radishes. People would read almost anything. As a correspondent, she was well paid. Her writing during the war had expanded her base of readers. She had the same readers for her fiction and a new set for her reportage. In England, she was still known almost entirely as a writer of romantic women's fiction, which sold well enough here, and her British colleagues appeared astonished she should wear the hat suddenly of a war correspondent. Nonetheless she was scheduled to be interviewed on the BBC that afternoon about women in the American war effort, on which she had been touted to them as an expert.

The conversation on economics dampened Oscar's ardor, as she had hoped, and he shortly departed, not however without saying he would be by that evening around nine to see her.

"Impossible," she said. "I'll be in the tubes. I'm doing interviews with people who've been living there for years. Imagine, keeping house in a subway station with your whole family, on the platform. I'm also supposed to visit one of those new super deep shelters."

"Tomorrow," he said firmly and grinned at her.

"Call first," she said, and saw him to the door, where he turned and quickly kissed her.

––––––––––––

She wrote up her stuff for cabling as she went. It would all have to pass British censorship and then American, but at least she intended to dispatch as much as she could and to remain caught up with her interviewing, so that if transportation and the go-ahead appeared, she would not lose the stories she had been pursuing in London. The truth was, if she had not been promised France and the Army, she would have been happy covering the scene in Britain for months.

Every day she discovered new material. She wanted to do something on women air raid wardens. Being a warden in London was a far cry from the easy job it was in the States. It meant being out in the raids and investigating each incident, beginning the rescue work, the recovery of bodies or fire fighting. She liked the fire fighter who had been acting as her guide, and wanted to focus on just such spunky women.

Her phone was ringing off the hook, because it seemed just about every journalist she knew and half her old friends from New York were coming through London on their way to France or back from Italy or off to North Africa. Everytime she left the hotel, she heard a male voice calling her name. Had she been in the mood for taking a lover, she would have had a wide choice, but she simply wanted to file her copy quickly.

She never got to write her story on women air raid wardens, because she was told to report to a field north of London. There, after only fourteen hours, she was fitted on a transport among piles of drugs and medical supplies and shipped to France, with her pack to sit on and her typewriter under her feet.

The air was turbulent over the Channel and at one point the plane dived straight down in a terrifying rush to avoid some obstacle or danger invisible in the blinded cabin. Even in July, it was cold in an unpressurized cargo plane, a version of the Liberator called the C-87. She was frightened and wondered sharply what the hell she was doing, transported with drums of sulfa dust and crates of bandages to the place where people were killing each other. She imagined herself back in Washington, curled in her bed with Daniel. She felt crazy to be here and not there. She even regretted that she had not fallen into Oscar's arms. He had been right when he said that that would have given them something to carry away. He had been right, she thought, pressing down on her typewriter to keep it from hitting her in the chin and trying to fend off rolling drums of sulfa.

————————

Louise crouched under the lee of a broken stone wall, plastered to the crotch of her baggy Army pants in rich Normandy mud. She was technically in the front—practically the whole lodgment area was so classified, but she had not yet got up to the real front. She was spending several days with the medical corps, covering their operation. She was sleeping in a tent with nurses, but now she had come forward from the field hospital to a battalion aid station.

The corpsmen stationed here responded to calls over the field telephones, to bring in the wounded on litters or occasionally by jeep. The wounded were taken from this shell-blasted farmyard to a collecting station, where they were moved by ambulance to the field hospital. If the wounded were not in shock or screaming, she interviewed them. She got the name and rank first, then the hometown. In the Army that was what officers tended to ask the men too. Where are you from, soldier? Then she asked them if they were married, or if not, did they have a girl at home?

Some of them were surprised to see a woman in the battalion aid station, but many were too dazed to notice, and some assumed she was a nurse. Usually they did not realize she was a woman unless she spoke to them. In her mud-encrusted boots and leggings, Army trousers, sodden trench coat and helmet, she looked like any other GI.

For the nurses themselves she developed enormous respect. They lived in the mud and worked around the clock. They were called officers but treated often like kitchen slaveys, viewed back home as being of dubious morals. When she finished her piece on the medical system as it carried along a typical soldier, she intended to focus on nurses. In the meantime, from her journeyings back and forth along the line from the wounding to final deposition, she was about to select a few soldiers to pursue through the process, the kind of personalized piece she had been sent over to write.

Her nose ran constantly and she had a sore throat. It was cold and wet here. She had put on her long underwear the first chance she had had to undress, although that had not happened till she had reached the field hospital. There the nurses had taught her how to wash herself in her helmet. The feet were the most important part of the body to wash and try to dry. Back at the field hospital, she had a cot to lie on, but here she had only her bedroll. With the ack-ack guns going off all night and the German planes coming over, the shelling that never let up, no place was quiet enough for prolonged sleep. After eight days in Normandy, she was already like the GIs in that her first desire was for sleep, even an hour of sleep curled up in a trench or now in the lee of a broken stone wall, waiting for wounded, and her second desire was to be dry and her third was for hot food. She ate the same K rations or C rations as everyone else.

The countryside was dark green rolling hills studded now with dead cows rotting, with high bushy hedges of hawthorn and sumac where snipers loved to lurk, apple and cherry orchards crossed by meandering narrow roads lined with high thick impenetrable hedges, the more important ones paved with asphalt, the lesser ones of gravel. Everywhere lay unburied corpses of people and animals, or hasty mounds where several bodies had been thrust under a coating of mud or sod. On every side stood roofless houses and wrecked machinery, exposing its scorched guts.

One of her uses to all the Americans was that she spoke reasonable French. That afternoon an old woman who had refused to leave her home gave Louise a wheel of Camembert and explained to her that the Boches had not mined the fields the way they were supposed to, because the local commanders, who had been having an extremely easy war in Normandy before the invasion, had been persuaded by the farmers that if they heeded Rommel's orders for mining the fields, the cows could not go to pasture and there would be no lovely Camembert for the Germans. The Germans had done quite enough mining in general, Louise thought, and thanked the local cows personally, although by now, most of them were dead. She brought the cheese to the battalion aid station where they ate it on the hard crackers that came in K rations, although two of the medics made faces and said it stank. Louise saved their share for her nurses.

The first night she slept in a dugout with the men in the field, she was frightened. She was afraid to seem friendly and took care where she placed her bedroll. By now she did not worry. They were too exhausted, too frightened, too battleworn to think of sex. They appreciated her presence. They wanted to be written up. They wanted people back home to know as much as she could tell. They liked her coming up to the action, and they gave her the driest spot to sleep in. She was developing a fine maternal air with them, for many were Kay's age or younger. The only times she was propositioned were by a correspondent and by an officer back in headquarters. The farther forward she went, the simpler became the thoughts and feelings: fear and survival and sometimes, anger. A persistent sniper could arouse hatred that Louise understood, after the first time she saw a soldier shot from a hedgerow as he was fixing a flat on a jeep.

It was a slow and sneaky war among these hedgerows. She did not think the entire area in Allied hands was more than twenty miles across. It seemed to her she had been there for months. She had always been chilled and wet through, she had always sniveled, she had always rejoiced when the sunshine dried them and the air was balmy and the grass made good bedding, she had always been so short of sleep that any quiet moment sucked her under, she had always dreamed of beds and hot water as the ultimate pleasure. Daniel? Oscar? They were in another universe. She was closer to the men coming off the line with their glazed eyes and rotting feet. She was closer to the stretcher-bearers who lay in the mud snoring like homeless dogs. She was closer to the nurses, with one of whom she stumbled to the latrine that night as shells lit the sky amber going over high, yeeeow, yeeeeow. The ground shook under them from shells landing closer. They both heard the two-noted mutter of a howitzer coming at them. They dove for cover and ended up in a pile of kitchen garbage mixed with human debris from the operating room. A stench of cordite and rotting meat filled her head. Louise threw up. They went back to their tent together and the nurse handed Louise a damp towel to wipe her face.

The Voice of the Turtledove

Rivka was under the earth. She was a slave in the cavern of the troll king. Rivka had been taken under the mountain where she worked in the dark making evil things that she spoiled as often as she dared. They were like huge metal insects that flew, but Rivka had only to check one tiny part with a micrometer. Naomi dreaded night when she slipped into Rivka's body in the noisy filthy cave under the mountain and worked while hunger tore at her and her fingers and toes bled. Rivka never saw the sun or the sky or trees. The walls of the cave were brown and wept. She thought of herself as being inside the belly of a huge reptile. Maman was dead, but Naomi was still joined to her twin who lived like a grub inside the cold dark earth, always gutted with hunger, shaking with cold, hollow with exhaustion, till sometimes the death always just under her feet seemed like a soft warm bed.

"It was all mud," Leib said. "Thick mud, dark as chocolate pudding. It got into everything, your bedding and your food and your teeth and your mess kit and your boots and your rifle. Every step you were fighting it. Everything turned the color of shit."

Sometimes Leib talked compulsively to her. The doctor had ordered him to walk every day, and when she could, she walked with him. He was supposed to be building up his muscles to control his new foot, but it hurt. When the pain started, he talked. When it got really bad, he shut up. His new artificial foot was heavy and awkward, so he could not move naturally. They walked block after block of Detroit with heavy full-bosomed elms meeting over the asphalt streets, roses blooming in yards, the little victory gardens on the sides of houses, glimpsed in back, in front where the square of lawn used to be. When Leib withdrew into silence, she passed the time looking into yards to see what people grew. As soon as Leib started talking again, she turned back to him.

He liked her company. Everybody said she was his favorite. She baby-sat David often but Trudi spent little time with her now. To save for a house, Leib encouraged Trudi to work full time at the hospital until he was better and could get a job.

"I'm never going back on the line," Leib told her, as they walked in the hot afternoon. Whenever they passed a sprinkler turning, she walked into the water so that its brief drops would cool her before they evaporated. "It's okay when you're drawing lots of overtime, but then what? You never get rich on the line. You just get old."

Naomi thought how tired Uncle Morris was when he got home, how exhausted Ruthie was. "It's hard," she said. "But I'd take it if I could get it, because it's good money."

"Good money, my ass," Leib said. He did not watch his language with her when they were alone together, but talked to her the way the kids talked to each other. She felt as if Leib alone of all the adults treated her as an equal. Of course they weren't really equal because he was years older and he had been to war and had a Purple Heart and a Bronze Star. He even told her how he had been wounded, stepping on a mine. She felt immensely proud as they strolled together through all the streets of the neighborhood and far beyond. He chose her as his friend, Leib, the best-looking man in the whole neighborhood in spite of his foot, and who cared about his foot anyhow? He was a hero, and he chose her. She wanted so passionately to please him that sometimes she felt as if she were burning up with that wish, her skin all prickling, her elbows and knees sticking out like spines with that sole desire, to please him.

When they walked together through all the green residential streets and the noisy business streets, she enjoyed his height looming over her, his size, his handsomeness. All reflected on her. It was a completely different feeling than sauntering with Alvin. Kids in the gang shuffled along, they shoved each other and the guys assumed postures to look tough. They were pretending, but Leib was real. With him, she was almost real too.

"We came into Naples like kings. Those little fuckers were starving. You never saw so many hungry people. I thought Detroit when Ruthie and me were in school was one sad place, but we would've looked like rich guys to these people. They didn't have holes to crawl into, just the dirty rags on their back. No water, no electricity, no gas, no food, not two walls standing together. Yet in three weeks, guys were minting money in the black market, hand over fist." Leib spoke rapidly, emptying himself out. "You could buy and sell everything from cigarettes, meat, women, booze, jeeps, trucks, drugs, you name it."

Sometimes she wished she could slow him down. She felt too young, too naive, to be as helpful to him as she wanted to be. He had suffered. He had been torn and wounded and used. Nobody but she saw what he had gone through. Trudi was too involved with plans, with little David and the house they would have. Ruthie was cold to Leib and scarcely looked at him. Naomi wanted to do nothing but look at him, his leonine head against the burning sulphur yellow sky of summer, his hair growing out to cover the scar in his scalp, for he had had a skull wound also. She wanted to look and look at him with her heart swelling in her as if it would fill up her body. She wanted to remember every word he said to repeat to herself later so that she would understand, she alone, and could help him.

"After Africa, we thought we'd be sent home. We had hard fighting. Nobody back here knows how bad Tunisia was. At first we didn't know what the fuck we were doing. They were slaughtering us, just running over us with their tanks. Then we learned or we got killed. We thought when we took Tunis finally they'd bring some other poor bastards over or call up some of those guys who had it easy way back behind the lines. We couldn't fucking believe it when they stuck us on the damned landing craft and we had to take Sicily. Now I think they'll make the same poor bastards fight all the way to Berlin. Okay, I saved my buddies when I came down on the mine, but I saved myself too. Better no foot than no body."

She hated when it rained and they could not walk. Every morning she took care of Mrs. Entemann's children, from seven till three-thirty. She was bringing in money. Half she gave to Aunt Rose and half she kept for herself. Uncle Morris took her to the bank to open an account. She had a passbook and they stamped what she put in every week. She got a quarter an hour for minding the babies, because neither of them was toilet-trained yet and she had to be changing them all the time. Naomi took her change out of its hiding place and carried it to the bank. America seemed to be rich enough to survive. That decision made her feel less a greenhorn. She was becoming very American. Often people could not tell she was an immigrant.

When she got off work, she ran to see if Leib wanted to take a walk. If he didn't, then she went to find her friends, but if he did, that crowned her day. She worried that when she returned to high school in the fall, he wouldn't wait for her till she got home. It was July, but at least once a day, she worried about what would happen in September. She did not want their time together, their precious intimate time, to lapse.

"Italy's all one fucking mountain after another, and the blonds—that's what we called the Germans—were always above us on the next mountain picking us off. One killing obstacle after another, one more fast muddy river with the bridges blown, one more mountain so steep you know they used to send mules up to bring us food and ammo? We had a whole bunch of mule skinners attached to our battalion, and damned if those mules weren't better fed and housed than us."

He took her arm often, tucking it against his warm body, so that she could feel his ribs, his flesh against her. Sometimes when he was tired he leaned on her, and although he was heavy, she was proud to help him. He did not ask her if she would help. He knew she would. He needs me, she told herself, taut with pride.

Sometimes his voice seemed like an eagle beating its wings against a lid put on its world. His wanting was fierce, but so far it was stymied. He did not know yet what he wanted, although he knew well what he didn't, to live and work like the people around him. He spoke of vague schemes but she did not doubt he would do something splendid soon.

"All my real buddies are in the Army, but Fatty Windsor is 4F. I might just ask him to give me a job tending bar. A lot of guys with good connections hang out in his old man's bar."

She listened passionately, every pore of her body absorbing his words.

"Now I'm finally of age, maybe he'll give me a job. You know, when they drafted me, I was too goddamn young to get drunk in a bar? Now I'm twenty-two, and already they took my foot and gave me this piece of metal, already I got a family like a millstone around my neck, which who needs by now, and I got no skills worth writing on a piece of toilet paper."

Often she grew weary of feeling guilty all the time because of her nightmares, because of her secret knowledge that Maman was dead and would never return to her, would never come and take her back home, and that her twin was a prisoner under the earth toiling and growing colder and farther away. The dreams came less vividly. She felt guilty too that she wanted them to fade away. She did not want to know. She did not want to be in Rivka's body any longer.

———————

It was the end of July and so hot that Detroit felt scorched, a pool of rancid oil. It had not rained in ten days and the air was used and thick. The grass was drying brown in Palmer Park. They had taken a bus today and walked in the park, because Leib hoped it would be cooler. He had been drinking beer, but said it just made him hotter. "Under the trees, it'll be cooler," he said, leading the way into the woods. His limp was pronounced. "I'm sick of the heat. I can't sleep at night. Have you been sleeping?"

"Last night, Ruthie and I took off our nighties and we both slept in our panties, it was so hot." She knew she shouldn't say that.

"That must have been a gorgeous sight. Wish I'd been there." He led her under a spruce and let himself down. "Ah, here it's halfway to cool."

The spruce made a dark tent under itself, as if they had entered a secret green room. She knew she should not be here with him. But why not? Nobody had said she could not walk with him. Trudi thought it was fine. When he did not walk the way he was supposed to, Trudi scolded him. Everybody felt sorry for him, crippled, but she did not think of him as a cripple. Her breath caught in her throat like the dry needles under them.

She sat stiffly beside him. He opened his eyes and looked at her and grinned. "Come here, Naomi, my Naomi. Come here." He put his hands on her shoulders and put his mouth on hers. It was not like being kissed by Alvin, although Leib too put his tongue in her mouth. He pushed her back on the needles to kiss her and her arms came around him. She loved him, she loved him with her whole life. The world rushed through her, wanting to offer itself in love to Leib, whose name was love, whose arms were around her, whose body pressed on hers like the world itself, heavy and inevitable.

He moved slightly off her and slid his hand up under her cotton blouse, closing over her breast. "I used to be in love with your aunt Ruth, do you know that?"

"Yes," Naomi said. She could hardly speak. Her voice sounded as if it were crushed in her throat.

"You're getting to look like her, the way she was when she was younger. You're getting prettier and prettier."

"I don't look like Ruthie."

"You look like you. I used to love Ruthie. Now I'm going to love you. Do you want me to love you?"

"I love you," she said, her throat hardly letting the words twist out.

"Yes, my dove, my precious, my baby. Let's see." He put his hand into her panties, between her legs. She cried out involuntarily. "You're a virgin, aren't you, little one? You haven't let any of the boys in yet."

"No." She could not stop him. She could not move. She sweated with terror. Where he thrust his finger into her, she hurt.

"Are you scared? Your heart is pounding. I'm not going to hurt you. I wouldn't take you here. But you'll love me, won't you?"

"I love you," she said in that throttled voice. She was glad when he took his hand away. He put it back on her breast, where it felt better.

"How old are you exactly?"

"Almost fifteen."

"Too bad," Leib said. "You're too young, Naomi, but you'll grow up and by then, it'll be even better. You're going to grow up for me, just for me, aren't you?"

She did not know what he meant but she said, "I am growing up. I'm old for my age."

"You're going to grow into my woman. You're going to be just what I want, aren't you?"

"You're married to Trudi."

"I had to marry somebody. I knew something would happen to me. I lost my foot, but I could have lost my life. I had to make a son. That's all right, Naomi, I'll make others with you. Trudi is a fucking bore. If she was home all the time, I'd strangle her."

She did not like what he was saying, for it frightened her. It opened a pit into which she was falling. She could not argue with his hand on her breast that was burning, his leg over hers, his mouth covering hers and kissing her. Surely that she had dreamed this so often had made it happen and she was the guilty one. She had made this wicked and dangerous thing happen by the magic of wishing it too many times.

"Take off your panties," he said, pulling back from her.

She did not move. "You said you wouldn't," she pleaded.

"Honey dove, I'm not going to fuck you. The last thing I need is to get you pregnant at fifteen. I had kids your age in Naples, you know that? I'm keeping you for the right time, because you're going to ripen just for me." He put her hand against something stumpy and she knew immediately it was what Sandy had called the man's thing. He pulled the panties off her and then he climbed on her and she found herself crying with fear, the tears rolling down her face. "Now put your legs tight together, that's right." He began thrusting back and forth between her thighs, rubbing against her hard, but he did not tear her, he did not come in. "Here, get your skirt up out of the way."

She stopped crying. "Trust me," he muttered in her ear, and she held him and waited. He was not going to tear her open. He was just rubbing against her. After a while, it began to feel good in a scary breathless way. Leib loved her. She was a bad girl who would be a bad woman, but he loved her. After he had finished all sticky between her thighs, he made her spread her legs wide and wiped her with his handkerchief. "When you go home, wash yourself carefully, always." He was smiling. "I thought you'd do anything I wanted, but I wasn't sure."

She put her panties back on and smoothed down her skirt. She did not know where to look, but finally, she could not help turning to him again, the dark beautiful sun that rose on her world.

"Don't say anything, not to Ruthie or to Rose. It's Ruthie you confide in, isn't it? If you say anything to her, everybody will blame you and call you a bad girl, and I'll have to move out. No more walks. You'll never again be my dove."

"I won't say anything. I promise."

"Not to your best girlfriend. Who's your best friend?"

"Sandy, but Aunt Rose and Mrs. Rosenthal don't speak to each other."

"You don't say anything to her. Nothing about how you know about men now, nothing. Promise?"

"Nothing," Naomi repeated solemnly. "I promise." It was like a ceremony, a vow with the dark tree bending with its green wings spread down to the ground, brooding over them.

DANIEL 7

Flutterings

It was a quiet shock Daniel felt, yet it reverberated through his life for weeks. A chill of depression lay on him in the sweltering August, as green leggy flies with iridescent wings and black flies and flies with the heads like jewels that drew blood when they bit, when mosquitoes and yellow moths and moths like scraps of paper bag all swirled in through the open windows and flittered around him as he worked. He wanted to exhaust himself at OP-20-G. He wanted to go out with the boys afterwards. What he didn't want was to go home.

Never had he lived with a woman before and therefore, he concluded, never had he missed anyone as he did Louise. He had a physical sense of severance. Furthermore every object released memories like static shocks. She had left in such a hurry that he was always finding her hairpins, her books, her lace-edged handkerchiefs, her fragrance for a time clinging to chairs, to pillowcases, to dresser drawers. He should not have moved down there, he knew it, but he could not endure Rodney any longer. He simply could not go from being with Louise, living with a daily sensual elegance, to sleeping in the living room on his mattress among Rodney's abandoned boxer shorts, beer bottles and chili cans.

The downstairs apartment was haunted by Louise. Was he angry with her? Yes. He could not forgive her for abandoning him. He was not used to women leaving him, yet the sense of being deserted was familiar. It made him remember how he had felt when his father had left them in the Bronx and gone off to China, left them to suppers of beans or oatmeal, to studying by candlelight because the electricity had been turned off for failure to pay the bill, of his feet always hurting because his socks were darned lumpy. The other kids had teased him because his father had run away, they said, run away to China.

That summer his mother had found a kitchen job in the Catskills and his older brother Haskel had gone along to work as a busboy, but he and Judy had been left with a neighbor. He had never spoken to Judy about that summer, but he had felt abandoned. Crying alone, he had decided nobody cared for him in his family, nobody, that they viewed him as an accident that had happened to them.

He was still stunned that Louise had left him. He had known, of course, how much she disliked her job at OWI and how frustrated she felt. Yet she was writing interesting articles, always, and she could have gone on doing that. Sometimes he blamed Kay. Louise always felt that whatever damn fool thing Kay did was Louise's own fault, issuing directly from a failure of upbringing. Daniel thought that after an early point, kids pretty much did what they felt like. The world the new generation lived in was different from their parents' world in its pressures, fantasies and standards, even its jokes and bywords. Kay experienced her war and Louise lived hers.

Why had she left him? Sometimes he was convinced it was to get back with her exhusband, who always loomed off there on the edge of Louise's mental landscape. Oscar was still her inner measure of male. She hadn't given him enough time to replace Oscar, and why not? That was the sore he returned to, licking and licking until it was infected.

Since he was fifteen, he had always been in love. Even during his chaste months at Harvard, he had been in love with his exacting mistress, the Japanese language, which he imagined as a courtesan with enameled face out of Hokusei, mocking him from behind a fan, body rippling under a silken kimono. Now he had bad dreams. Often he dreamed of Louise, leaving him again and again.

He had had two letters from her, letters from London, but he had not opened the first until the second had come. He had taken great pleasure in picking it up each day as he came home from work and then tossing it down again, forcing it to remain silent, dumb, rejected. Now that there were two, side by side, his curiosity overcame him.

She wrote him that the only thing she missed from Washington was him. The phrasing irritated him. She was supposed to be a writer, sensitive to language, yet she called him a thing. That was how she thought of him: a body, a convenience, a small pleasure to be put away after its season. I am Madame Butterfly, Daniel said to himself. He despised himself for his grief, but the world seemed to him full of shrill and gentle cries of pain.

The commander he had replaced had come out of the hospital and resumed his old post, so Daniel was back decoding and translating messages. Part of the American strategy in the Pacific was to bypass many strongly held Japanese islands, leaving them in isolation so that while they were unconquered, they were useless and in exile from the war. These ports and islands sent and received messages which OP-20-G had to monitor. The pathos of these little garrisons moved Daniel. They could not be resupplied or evacuated, but held out hundreds of miles behind enemy lines with their dwindling supplies and evaporating morale, radioing passionate devotion for the emperor and samurai sentiments to their superiors, who were writing them off as dead losses. They were bombed now and then, more for practice than for any military end, while leaflets urging surrender rained on them whenever any appropriate officer got around to ordering it done.

Although he wrote only brief formal notes, he went on receiving occasional letters from Louise. Then he began to see her articles. That is, he took to buying *Collier's* every week, because something from her was usually there. It was masochistic, yet he did it.

When the pieces on children growing up in subway stations gave way to stories about the daily life of artillery units and tank crews, he realized that she could be killed. Correspondents were shot, they were torpedoed, they were blown up by land mines or artillery shells or bombs that fell on them as on the troops. He was safe in Washington reading other people's mail while she was off sticking her nose into foxholes in France. Why? He could not quite put together Louise in the kitchen making gefilte fish or kasha varniskes with Louise kneeling behind a stone fence, as she was shown in an accompanying photo, her familiar face daubed with mud, the rest of her indistinguishable in its bulky khaki from the GI next to her. He stared at the photo on and off for the rest of the evening. Why? he asked himself, and he could not answer.

Abra had gone to London with her man, in vain pursuit of Oscar's undying love. If a woman was in love with a man and that man went to war, then if a woman could, she would go also, providing she had no children to hold her back. But Louise had gone off to war with the same motivations as any other war correspondent, for glory, for curiosity, for vague patriotism, for clear anti-Nazi motives but also as a shrewd career move. Finally that bothered him. He could not quite put that ambition together with the yielding body, the soft warm breasts and belly and the eagerly thrusting, welcoming hips. Why should those warm lips and those encircling arms and that body that smelled of a French perfume carefully dosed out each day, just one drop behind each ear and one drop behind each knee, why should that body so familiar to him under and over and twined with his own offer itself willingly to danger and discomfort? He accused Louise of concealing something hard and unwomanly in herself, an ambition complicated and functional as one of those rifles he had never learned to handle.

In June, Abra had written teasingly that she had figured out from his reti-

cence that he was having an affair with Louise, and she praised him as the last
gentleman, the noblest Victorian of them all, but by the time that letter arrived,
Louise had vanished. By the time Abra had his answer, she also had Louise
in London and Oscar panting after her. Her next letter was perhaps the most
naked she had ever written him.

*I don't know what I might have done in this war more useful than
what I am doing, but I doubt there would, honestly, be much. That has to
suffice, but it's cold comfort at the moment. One of the mistakes I've made
has been to let Oscar become my life. I see that clearly, how it happened,
why it happened, but it has meant that whereas in New York and even
in Washington, I swam in a school of friends, and other people's ideas
and perceptions inevitably jostled and changed my own, I have been
alone in an artificial semimarriage with Oscar since we left the States.
I have made no friends here. I have got into the habit of confiding in
no one, except you; and you had not till your last letter been particularly
open with me.*

*I have a strong sense how costly this mistake has been, but perhaps
I have shrunk from making friends for fear their observation would
throw light on my relationship with Oscar I have been at pains to
avoid. In some sense, I am still to Oscar what I was: his valued and
hardworking research assistant. I feel as if I am waking from a long
paralysis, but to what except despair I cannot imagine.*

*You tried to tell me what I was unwilling to hear. Sometimes when
people have been wiser than us, we become angry with them, but I don't
feel that. Instead I feel a tender gratitude for how hard you tried to be
honest with me about my folly, back in Washington when we lived as
neighbors in that funny little house.*

She signed the letter *love*. That was new. She had always signed flippantly
before—yours in potpourris of passion, leaping lizards of love, your humble and
obedient donna sirviente, and so on. Now, love. Perhaps she had merely run out
of flippancy. Yet he could not imagine Abra signing a letter without premedi-
tation.

If she were in Washington, he thought, musing on the letter in her sloping
hand, the loops below the line looking like paddles thrust out in a rush, he
thought he could go to her and finally resolve their long flirtation. I could have
her, he thought, but laughed at himself because the contention had to remain
unproved. The flirtation was heating up because they both needed something to

lighten their depression, that was the size of it, but he put considerable effort into his reply.

At work they had been monitoring the traffic from Saipan until the last cry of despair from the commander, the transmissions from Guam where fighting was fierce, ever nearer to Japan. Why didn't the Japanese give up, defeat after costly defeat? In what the American pilots called the Great Marianas Turkey Shoot, the Japanese had lost an enormous number of pilots and many ships. What did they expect could save them? Yet Japan had never yet been defeated. They kept using a phrase lately, *kamikaze,* which was the divine typhoon, the great punishing wind sent by the great goddess Amaterasu the Sun who had given birth to an ancestor of the emperor and thus must constantly protect him. When Kublai Khan had conquered all the rest of Asia and sent his fleet against Japan, Amaterasu had raised the divine wind, the kamikaze, and wiped out the invasion force. Such a miracle must come again, they believed. The war would continue.

He wondered sometimes if he would ever see the places that were so familiar to him in Japanese codes: Hollandia, about which they were translating dispatches daily until MacArthur's forces took it in April; Aitape; Biak, where the invasion had gone badly awry. MacArthur often disregarded the information, it was rumored, that the Magic decodes offered him. He trusted only his old intelligence buddies from the Philippines, the Bataan Gang. Magic was the field name for intelligence from their decrypts.

Nonetheless, the information went out and was often used. On 25 June, they had decoded a signal from the Japanese Eighteenth Army Commander General Adachi stating that he was planning a major attack in the vicinity of Aitape around 10 July. He sent on details of his three divisions involved, his battle plans and even where his command post would be located. This information was all bundled off to the intelligence officers who fed it to the commanders defending American positions on Aitape. What pleasure he found in his life at present issued from his sense of the precision and importance of the work they were doing.

Since he was spending his always limited social time with his co-workers, he began to put together a picture of how he seemed to them. Most seemed to have a high opinion of his work and his temperament. He was viewed as sweet-tempered, an image at odds with his own idea of himself as hotheaded, impetuous, adventuresome, a persona based more on his running wild in the streets of Shanghai than anything since. He considered himself anew. What he wanted most was a mixture of adventure and stability. He thought briefly of taking up again with Ann, but when he saw her, she gave out a high whine of anxiety like the cry of a hungry mosquito.

Then too his romanticism about her could not survive a lunch together. He began to remember the banality too, the pruned quality of her, stunted into passivity. If Louise had proved too ambitious for him to keep, Ann was too lacking in will to keep him. He was glad to touch fingers with her and feel she meant him well, although she could hardly maintain a focus on him even until the check arrived.

He had told Louise it was inevitable they should become involved, he remembered, and perhaps it was—too convenient for her to resist long; yet she had failed to consider him her equal or the equal of her ex-husband. That was her error, he muttered, wandering through the apartment that had seemed far more opulent when she had inhabited it, although she had left him almost all her things.

He began to wonder what would become of him after the war, although nobody in OP-20-G believed that Japan would collapse or the end come soon. Before the Navy had carried him off to this exotic occupation, he had served subpoenas on petty offenders. What was he equipped to do in a postwar world? What did he know? Cryptanalysis and Japanese. It did not sound promising. Maybe he should go back to school after the war and become a professor of Japanese, but would there be any call for them? He doubted there had been more than a handful in American universities before the war.

Surely the cryptanalytical branch would be closed down, because whose mail, whose signal intelligence, would America need to read? Perhaps he could get a job inventing puzzles for children's magazines or hobbyists?

Maybe he would go back to China and rejoin his uncle Nat, whom he never doubted would survive. His Chinese had lapsed, but he could renew it. Or maybe, he thought, with a sense of secretive and shameful ambition, maybe he would go to Japan. At least there a knowledge of Japanese would be useful.

JACQUELINE 10

Up on Black Mountain

15 juillet 1944

Yesterday the Americans dropped us, in the daylight, do you believe it, an enormous quantity of ammunition, guns and food, all decorated with little tricolors. They were B-17s escorted by Mustang P-47s, the long-range fighter the Americans and sometimes the British use to protect their bombers. We have been seeing many of them going over, but this time they came for us. They dropped us 12 containers holding 4 machine guns with 17,000 rounds, 44 rifles with over 60,000 rounds; 50 submachine guns with 16,000 rounds, 140 hand grenades, 100 kilos of plastic explosives with fuses and timing devices, 200 first aid kits, 40 kilos of packaged food and 40 kilos of clothing, blankets and shoes. None of the latter are for women and they are all much too big for me.

We are pleased to receive this bounty, finally, but lately they have been making even too many drops. This time four more of their own personnel parachuted down, too. Such a big drop in daylight so soon after the last is bound to attract German attention, so that while we are pleased with the outfitting, we are a little nervous, as befits Jews whose good fortune often calls down the envy and wrath of others, who select it to notice and remember. It is also the case that there were no mortars, which we desperately need, and nothing heavy enough to use against German armor.

Of course we were not singled out for this largesse, as it has been divided by all the maquis groups congregated in the Montagne Noire region—the Jewish Army, the Jewish scout maquis, local farmers and Communists and men who would not go to Germany on the labor draft from Toulouse, Mazamet, Castres and Carcassonne, Eduardo's Catalonians who have been fighting the Fascists since 1936. The other groups outnumber us. From this area of rocks and trees, we have been harassing the Germans nightly and sometimes daily. *We* did not include me until this week, but I finally bludgeoned Daniela into taking off my cast. Now I am trying to regain the full use of my arm. I have been practicing shooting—with live ammunition, we are so rich now. When I first learned to shoot, I had to practice without bullets, because we had too few to waste. Eduardo showed me some tricks about loading the Marlin submachine gun and using the parabellum.

I have been serving my turn at guard duty at the outpost on the Labrugières Road, near Fontbruno, a tiny village on the hillside. Last night Papa showed up to take guard duty with me. Now he does not normally waste his energies at this outpost, so I figured at once he wanted to talk to me.

"How is your arm?" he began, as if he had not seen me shooting perfectly well that afternoon, and had not anyhow asked me about my arm five times already since the cast came off.

"Fine. What is it, Papa? What's on your mind?"

"You ought to talk to the Americans who came. One of them is a major. He calls himself La Mangouste. Another animal, I said, I am the rabbit. He said he was pleased because he'd heard of me. We haven't had a major before. I think something is getting ready to happen—all these supplies, feasting after famine."

"Lev speaks English too. He can question them. He doesn't hate Americans the way he hates the British."

"You always get more out of them. Your English is the best in the camp."

"I'm tired of talking to Americans." I sat down on a rock, looking down the road into the darkness. I did not feel like explaining that the American officers remind me of Jeff a little—enough to hurt—but they are nothing like him, and that too is a disappointment.

"This one is not naive. He has been with the maquis in Bretagne, and long before that, he was with the Greek Resistance. He is older than the children they've been sending us, and of more use. He knows something about fighting. He parachuted into France before their invasion in Normandy. When the front overran him, he went back to London, and now he's here. I want you to find out what you can. He asks a lot of questions, but I don't notice he answers any."

"Tomorrow I'll talk to him. But, Papa, if he doesn't feel like talking, I can't turn him upside down and shake the words out."

"Oh, he talks. He talks like birds sing all day long, tweet tweet."

"So this is why you are standing guard duty tonight, because you want me to see what I can find out from your American major?"

"Well, it could be important. . . . No. It seems we can never sit down and talk. I cannot favor you too much, you being my daughter, but somehow it never happens that we communicate truly, except about munitions and plastique and couriers. By the way the men want to know if you think you have your cunning back with the plastique."

"Not yet. My fingers are still stiff. I do the exercises Daniela prescribed, and I improve. But I wouldn't trust me to do a delicate job." I do not want to try yet. I mistrust my own dexterity, first, and second, I do not want to go on night adventures as I used to do with Jeff, and everything will be the same except that he is gone. "I had better be a simple soldier for a while. The rifle and the machine gun I can handle nicely."

"Bigon is not as good as you were. He doesn't get the timing just right for the maximum damage."

"Eduardo is good, even with two fingers missing. Papa, I thought you wanted to speak to me about something besides plastique. So you said."

He cupped his hands carefully and lit a cigarette. Then as we heard a distant sound in the road, immediately he pinched it out and stowed it in his beret. We slid into the ditch and waited to see who was coming. It was a horse-drawn wagon, so we shone our light and challenged them. It turned out to be a farmer taking his sick child to the doctor, ignoring the German curfew. We wished him luck and let him pass.

Papa pulled at his beard and shuffled around for at least half an hour, before he finally got himself wound up to begin the conversation I presume he had taken guard duty to have with me. "Yakova, I'm very sorry for what happened to your young man, the American commandant."

"About that, I don't want to talk anymore, Papa. You and Daniela urged me to collect myself and press on. I have done that. Reopen the wounds, and I'll bleed again."

"I'm proud of you for escaping."

"If I had taken them with me, I'd be prouder."

"Nonsense. I should have made contact with you earlier, Yakova." Again he used my Hebrew name. The first time he did it, I thought it was unintentional. When he did it again, I knew it was not, and I waited to find out what was coming down the tracks, for something surely was. "It is a common way of thinking, that a daughter can't do what a son can, but my daughter has fought at least as well as anyone's son."

I paced to and fro. Half of me was pleased by his praise and moved, and half of me was angry. Finally I said, "You saved one daughter and one of your daughters has so far saved herself. But you had also a wife and another daughter, Rivka. What of them? Maybe they too could have fought."

He let himself down rather heavily on the rock I had sat on earlier. From the valley we heard an owl hunting, that hungry sad cry I had never heard before taking to the maquis and with which I am now so familiar I can tell that tawny owl from a barn owl. Much farther away two dogs were yapping back and forth at each other. He said, "You hold me responsible for what the Germans did. Is that fair? I saw my duty as fighting. I was trained as a fighting man, and I had the stomach to fight them."

"Close to eighty Jewish children I led across the mountains, but not my own sister. It was too late for her."

"Aren't they all your sisters? Or why risk your life to save them."

"Touché. And yes, I am a Jew now."

"Would you have married your American anyhow?"

"How do I know? I think so. My children would still be Jews. Would have been."

"Lev is a good man. I don't believe his wife Vera can have survived."

"Nor yours?"

"Vera was in the Resistance, and they had caught her before. With your mother, there is more hope."

"Lev doesn't move me, nor I him. Daniela cares about him. But she waits for her fiancé Ari and Lev for his wife."

"It's not a time for marrying," he said. "Still, deep within me, I would like to see you settled."

"You want me to set up housekeeping on the black mountain and sit on eggs like a mother raven? I mistrust dreaming."

"I have a dream. I want to beat the Germans and then I want to take the good comrades I have fought with and live in our own land. Eretz Yisroel. We had a seder here, such a seder. Next year in Jerusalem. The time is coming. Europe stinks of our blood, it stinks in my nostrils."

"Papa, you're French. You were born here, you're French through and through as I am. You think in French, you dream in French."

"From the days the Vichy government passed the laws stripping Jews of our rights, voluntarily passed those laws, leaped to pass them, I haven't felt French. I've felt like a stranger, always a stranger, where I was foolish enough to think I belonged as a tree grows out of the earth."

"You fight side by side with those who aren't Jews. We're all up on the same mountain trying to defeat the same enemy."

"I didn't say I hate those who aren't Jews. In a just world, a man can be any- thing he pleases in his faith and his friends and his politics and others can do as they please leaving him in peace. But if I survive, I want to live out my life in a world where if somebody accosts me on the street or turns me down for a job, I don't have to wonder if he's an anti-Semite."

"The British won't open Palestine to Jews."

Papa put his face close to mine. His teeth shone against his beard. "Then we'll fight them. We've got used to fighting, haven't we? What I'd like is to bring back Naomi and try to find Rivka and Chava and for you to come too. I'd like us all to go together."

"If Rivka and Maman come back from the dead, I won't break up the family. I'll go with you."

"Good." He took my hand in his. "That's enough for now."

20 juillet 1944

Today as I promised, I looked for the big blond American major who calls himself the mongoose. He had been off raiding a convoy and reappeared with the men in high spirits, a group of maquis from near Vabre whom I know little about, mostly Protestant farmers. Eduardo had gone out with them for the attack on the column, for the same reason I expect that Papa set me to talk to the major: to figure him out, assets and liabilities, as they impact on us, whom he has presumably come to lead.

Eduardo did not seem surprised to see me waiting around. He gave me his crooked grin. "You want a report before Lapin? He's good. He knows his stuff. In war there are cowards who are no good, men who fight because they must and men who like to fight. Now me, I have been at war for eight years already, but it's a business for mad dogs. The good life is a life when you can fall asleep under a tree without somebody dropping a bomb on you."

"And the mongoose?"

"He likes it. He gets very light, he shines in battle. I had a friend in Spain like him. We all die the same anyhow." Eduardo went to report to Papa and I to find the major, who seemed not at all reluctant to talk.

"The boys tell me there was another American around here, Vendôme, and that you can tell me what happened to him. He wouldn't be with the maquis. He'd be running an intelligence network. Where is he?"

"He was doing both. It worked out that way. He died at the Milice barracks, in the jail there, on your D-Day. I am told they beat him, but he did not talk."

He was watching me carefully. "They say he was your lover."

"What does that matter?"

"Did he tell you his name? His real name?"

"Of course. Jeffrey Coates. He came from America, Massachusetts, Bentham Center." I stopped because the major was cursing. He turned away, picked up a crude chair on which I had been sitting to pluck a chicken and smashed the chair to chunks of wood against a rock. Dalia, the sharpshooter, backed away with an exclamation and vanished into her tent, motioning for me to come after and leave the crazy American alone, but I understand anger in the face of death. I waited, asking, "You knew him?"

"I got him into this fucking business."

"You were not his keeper, any more than I could be. He chose what he chose."

He took my arm in a grip that hurt. "What didn't you tell me?"

"Much."

"How did he die? Did they shoot him? How?"

"He took that poison capsule I presume you too have handy in your tooth."

I thought he was going to break my arm in his reaction. Then he looked me in the eyes, his own grey as river ice. There is something in him I do not like, cold and hard, but just then we understood each other. "Goddamn him. He must have talked about me, about Zach."

"He talked about his sister, whom he loved. He talked about his father, whom he did not love." I saw I was going to have to lie to him. "And of course he talked with affection of you, of Zach."

"He never felt real affection for anybody in the world. He was lovable, wasn't he, our Jeff? He permitted himself to be loved but that was it. Even that bored him fast enough, didn't it?"

I didn't answer because frankly that seemed nonsense. This man is cold, not Jeff. We were all better friends to him, and that was why he wanted to stay with us. Finally I thought of something I could say. "He loved this landscape, especially around Lacaune. He planned to settle here after the war."

"If I'd been here, I could have covered his ass. He wasn't following procedures, obviously. He was taking suicidal chances."

"They only caught us because they had tailed one of his agents and were waiting for us to appear at the drop site."

His eyes were cold and still. "But they let you go."

"I escaped." I turned away. Suddenly I was sick of his suspicions and his ego. He seized my arm again. I said, "Let go of me. If you don't let go, I will defend myself."

"Don't imagine you could," he said, sneering at me, but as if doing me a great favor, he dropped my arm. I went into Dalia's tent immediately, where I did not think he would bother me.

When I was sure he had left, I went to the tent Daniela and I share. As I did so, a Messerschmitt came over, the second today. The men fired at it, but it simply rose a bit and circled back. I hoped Daniela would be here so I could talk to her about the arrogant American, but she was with our wounded. I'll go help, but I decided to make an entry in my journal to calm myself. I find myself furious and roiled up. I am sorry I lied to please him. Jeff did mention a rich friend of his who tried to control him, and I am sure this is that master manipulator in the cold flesh.

He speaks French correctly but his accent is hideous and— Some kind of explosion, finish later.

———

Thus ends the journal found by Lev Abel.

———

From *Le Journal de Marche*, Sergeant Lev Abel, leader, 1st platoon, 4th squadron, Montagne Noire Corps Franc:

On 20 juillet 1944, 10:30, we were attacked by a large German force. This force we later estimated to consist of five Panther tanks, four antitank guns, 1500 foot soldiers of four divisions, various artillery and armored vehicles, with air support. After the strafing runs by six Messerschmitts, a runner reported that a German column was advancing from the Arfons road.

In the initial bombing our commander was killed. Lieutenant Martin Lévy-Monot, known as Lapin, took command and led a group to a barricade, ordering the rest of us not to hold the peak but to infiltrate the German lines and regroup at a rallying point at Agoudet, 70 km distant. He would try to hold up the advance long enough to secure evacuation of the wounded and the retreat and regrouping of our badly outgunned forces. We had no antitank guns, no artillery, nothing with which we could stop armor. He took twenty-two men armed with grenades, machine guns, Sten guns and rifles.

I have found only one survivor of this force. By their heroism, they delayed the German advance long enough for many of our troops to get away, but we lost unknown numbers because of German barriers on the roads around Albine and Fontbruno. We cannot yet estimate our losses. We may never know what happened to some of our people in the scattered retreat. . . .

30 juillet 1944

Morale is low, but I am attempting to bring our forces together at the rallying point. We have been cut off from communication with London, but today a radioman turned up with the American major who calls himself La Mangouste.

He can get us more weapons, he says, but we must be ready to use them. I have begun intensive retraining. He says an Allied landing in the south is imminent, and we must whip our troops into shape to attack the Germans. I tell him if they do not give us antitank weapons, we are carrying out no frontal assaults. He says that harassing and sabotage are fine.

Every day a few more men trickle in, but we are not going to collect everybody in the same place this time, as we did on Montagne Noire.

8 août 1944

Today, we had a message as we listened to the BBC that another invasion is coming, this one in the south. La Mangouste confirms that this is true. We have seven days before 15 août when the invasion is scheduled. "This time they gave us more warning," I said to La Mangouste.

"They trust you more and they need you. You don't understand how long it's taken for those of us who understand shadow warfare to get the importance of the Resistance through the thick skulls of the regular military. If there's anything they hate, it's civilians with guns."

Our men are low in morale after the massacre on Montagne Noire and the loss of so many good people including Lapin, Dalia, our nurse, Eduardo and Gingembre, but we will whip them back into fighting shape. La Mangouste knows his weapons and he gives the men spirit. I said to him, "They are good soldiers, and only ask not to be forced to fight twentieth-century armor with nineteenth-century hand weapons."

"I have requested mortars for you, as I'm sure Vendôme did. But they aren't sending heavy weapons to the Resistance."

"There's a limit to how far they trust us, eh? Jews, exiles from Spain, escaped Russian prisoners, Communists, peasants."

La Mangouste agreed quite openly. "But also remember, what we send to you we take from the regular military, and they're fighting now in Normandy, in Brittany, in Italy and coming soon a big invasion here. Try to take weapons from a general sometime. I expect they'll want us to deal with the Wehrmacht in Castres, Mazamet and Carcassonne. From what your boys tell me, we can expect them to try to move out on Routes 112, 113 and 118. Not to forget railroads and bridges. We shall be as busy as ants at a picnic before long, so cheer up. Don't worry about the weapons lost on Black Mountain, because we're getting a fresh load."

The eleven-thirty broadcast had instructions for the drop, as La Mangouste had predicted, and also a list of targets. We are back in action.

Of the One and the Many

It was in Long Beach itself that the hostility toward WASPs that had been building in the newspapers and in the population came home to Bernice and to Flo, when men began yelling at them on the street. Bernice knew that they had been called all kinds of names and subjected to innuendo in the papers, glamour seekers, loafers, shirkers, women who just wanted to chase after pilots. Jacqueline Cochran had worked with Congress on a bill to militarize them, so that they would have the same benefits as other noncombat personnel, but the bill had run into extremely heavy opposition from the American Legion, from the civilian male flight instructors who were no longer needed and from the civil aviation community.

The first time Bernice and Flo were surrounded by a group of hostile men jostling them and calling them bitch and floozy and whore was at the base itself, where many of the civilian flight instructors from the flying schools that had lost contracts were trying to qualify as ferry pilots. Many of them failed the tests, and they hated the WASPs. From being invisible, they had passed to being far too visible. In Congress speeches were made about how they were spoiled women who were stealing the bread out of the mouths of men who needed jobs.

Congress was conservative, a product of the off-election of 1942 when rigid voting laws had prevented both the troops and the workers who had moved for defense jobs from registering. The Civil Service Committee said that there were already too many trained pilots who would be competing for scarce jobs as soon as peace came, when the Depression would immediately resume. They ought to be nurses or doing defense work or home with their families, like respectable girls. The general agreement seemed to be that WASPs, whatever they were, were not nice.

Bernice drew in. She felt most comfortable sticking to her own in the barracks. She stopped going to the bar pilots patronized. The pressure of the work did not lessen, for there were more and more planes to deliver. Around the Long Beach ferrying squadron, Douglas, Lockheed, North American and Vultee were belching out planes. Far away in a war of words they were forbidden to take part in, even to the extent of writing their congressmen, their fate was being decided. Bernice felt powerless—she who had felt enormously empowered.

Nevertheless at the controls of a fighter, she knew her skill, her competence, and she tasted the zest of flying fast and well. That remained to her, that and the company of other WASPs, especially Flo.

Flo had occasional flings, but they were not romantic, and perhaps understanding that gradually about each other drew them together. Bernice did not look to Zach for love or support. If she never went to bed with him again, she would be the same person, although with him she had discovered rooms in herself that would likely have remained shut up. She did not imagine there were many men who would turn to stare after her as a figure radiating sexuality. Men seldom seemed attracted to her, excluding drunks in bars or wolves who'd chase anything still breathing.

Flo had been in love and retained that burned air of somebody who has put everything into a man and lost. As she told Bernice, for her to wish to be in love would be like wishing to catch diphtheria again—which she had had as a young girl. It was wishing to be sick almost to death.

They were drinking in the barracks, now that they felt the atmosphere in the CAVU bar (pilot's jargon for ceiling and visibility unlimited) potentially stormy. Around the base, some kind of liquor could always be purchased. Sometimes they got ice from the mess and sometimes they didn't bother, in spite of the heat. They had a fan turned straight on them, to stir the turgid air. "Why should you feel grateful to this Zach?" Flo asked her, sprawled on her own cot.

"Because he taught me to fly. He gave me that chance. Because he gave me my body too in a new way. Because he doesn't make me put on dolly clothes for him and simper."

"Jesus, I think if I had to deal with anybody making up to me the greasy way that women have to do with men, I'd puke."

"Oh, I don't know." Bernice grinned at her. "Wouldn't it make you feel kind of important to have somebody fussing like that? The more fool she makes of herself, the more of a king you are."

"Do you reckon you'll marry him after all this is over?"

"Flo, don't think I'm some kind of an idiot. Rich guys don't marry women like us. He's got someone in mind, he told me. I think he wanted to see if I'd kick up a fuss."

"Did you holler and cry?"

"What for? I wouldn't like living with him, let alone running a house the way he'd want it. A house? An estate. I daydream of having a little shack somewhere it's not built up yet, near an airport."

"Desert's better for pilots than mountains. Every time I fly East, I look down on all that empty country. Should be room enough for a couple of battered fly-girls. You ever think about that? Running our own little service maybe. Getting a mail route for a stretch of wild country. Giving flying lessons."

"Ever since they wouldn't let us deliver the planes out of Romulus across Canada to Alaska, I've wanted to go north all the way. . . . You want to go up to Alaska and take a look, after the war?"

"I was thinking of desert, but it sure ought to be wide open up there. They say everything is done by dogsled or by planes. That if you call a doctor, he comes by plane."

Bernice sat up, reaching for the bottle. They had been talking each to the ceiling, but now she looked directly at Flo. "Will we promise that? Make a pact? That as soon as we can, once this war is over, we'll go to Alaska and give it a look. If we don't like it, we can work our way back here and try the desert."

Flo sat up too and faced her, knee to knee on their cots. "How do we seal a promise like that?"

Bernice realized they were both a little drunk. With the bottle between them they had helped themselves to twice what they would have in the bar. It was hot and they both felt thirsty and thus the level had slid down. "When I was a kid, my brother and I signed an oath in blood, but it flaked off when it was dry."

"We could swear on a Bible, if we had a Bible."

"Emma has a Bible, but I don't believe in it. I'm an agnostic."

"That's a kind of Protestant too, isn't it? I was brought up Pentecostal myself. But I don't believe anymore. I believed in hell long after I stopped believing in heaven. It seemed like the nasty kind of joke the bastard who designed women's bodies so you're always pregnant or on the rag for forty years would think up, you follow?"

"I believe this is it: this is the only life and the only chance we get. What we don't do is our own fault."

"What do I believe in?" Flo screwed up her face, considering. "I believe in my body, because if I bump on it, it hurts. I guess I believe in what hurts, because it makes you know it's there."

"If you believe in pain, you have to believe in pleasure too. You have to believe in what makes you feel good and strong and alive."

Big tears began to run out of Flo's eyes. She sat there shaking while tears ran over her cheeks and along the shallow grooves beside her mouth.

"Flo, what's wrong?" Bernice moved to sit beside her, putting her arm around Flo's shoulder.

"I don't know!" Flo moaned. "It was just what you said made me cry. I don't know nothing that makes me feel good and strong except flying and sometimes being with you, just talking and feeling like we're really friends. Ever since you picked me out when we were instrument flying, I've felt like you have more respect for me than anybody else ever did. Not that there's been a long list."

"I do care about you. You're my best friend."

"You mean that?" Flo stopped crying.

"Why wouldn't I? My brother used to be my best friend, but it wasn't ever equal. I was stuck taking care of our father, while he was painting and having adventures and love affairs. I envied him as much as I loved him."

"You aren't going back there after the war?"

"No!" Bernice said vehemently. "I wouldn't fit in that house. I can't be my father's servant any longer. He has a housekeeper now anyway."

"I can't go home. My family told me never to come back. They consider me a fallen woman. I said, hell no, Mama, I've risen and she told me I was damned."

Bernice tightened her arm around Flo's solid shoulder. Neither of them was fat but both carried ample flesh. Flo was shorter and lighter boned, but still a good size for a woman, stocky, tough, but soft and warm too under the grip of her hand. "Why shouldn't we make plans together, real plans? It isn't as if we owe anybody."

"Where would we get the money to buy a plane?"

"I own half a plane, back home. It's just a sixty-horsepower Piper Cub, but I have half interest in it. I've saved my wages."

"So have I. But we'd need a better plane."

"We'll get the money. Maybe Zach would lend us some. He'd act like a hard businessman and want to be persuaded we could make a go of it."

"Two women? Who'd let us."

"We will. We'll let us." Bernice hugged Flo, full of confidence, a flood of energy. She felt Flo's warm breast pressing against her own and in that instant she froze, catching her breath and aware suddenly that Flo was also sensing her sharply. Neither of them moved. Flo turned her face slowly toward her and stared, not with horror, she saw when finally she could meet Flo's gaze, but with some dawning question, a wild surmise of something improbable. They stared into each other's eyes, Flo's the pale grey of clouds caught on the shoulder of a mountain, the pale grey of a dove's feathers. Neither spoke, neither breathed, neither moved.

Then Flo jumped. Bernice heard it too, the laughter of women approaching, back from their evening out. At once she bolted from Flo's cot to her own. As she sat down, Flo reached forward and very lightly touched her knee. "We'll do it," Flo said. "We'll go to Alaska and live with polar bears. That'll be our secret."

Bernice sat dumbly on her bed as the women rolled in laughing and singing snatches of the ribald WASP songs. Emma sat down on the foot of Flo's bed. "Oh, you should have come with us. We saw this new Tyrone Power movie. He's an American flier and he comes down over German-held territory where there are these Russian partisans and Hedy Lamarr is a nurse with them. And Tyrone Power, he's shot in the shoulder, and she nurses him. So she falls in love with him. Then the Germans shoot her and she won't betray him and we all cried. But he steals a Focke-Wulf 190 and gets away."

Bernice could only nod feebly, jealous that Emma could make free of Flo's cot while she had to watch herself now. It was the woman on the street in New York again, but worse. She had not been shocked when Zach told her he and Jeff had been lovers. Perhaps she thought of sex as something men owned and controlled, so it was natural they should do it with each other as well as with women. But to lust after another woman, she did not even know the name for that. Lorraine had suspected her of that in Romulus, that was why everybody had been so pleased when Zach appeared and started fucking her. It had meant to the other women that she was normal. They were wrong.

For the next weeks Flo and she went on just as before, but paying more attention to each other, watching out for each other. Bernice carefully observed all the other women. Several of them were married, their husbands in the service. Loretta lived from letter to letter. Some had fiancés overseas. One was a widow, her husband killed at Pearl Harbor. Emma's boyfriend, a mechanic at Newark, was saving to buy her a ring. No, the other women were all thinking of men, looking for a man, engaged or married to a man, or recovering from the loss of a man. Of the single women on the base, only Flo and Bernice did not perk up when some lounging idiot whistled or when some Air Corps lieutenant on his way through made a pass. They had both opted out.

Bernice felt in no way superior. She was no better pilot, no more loyal or affectionate or understanding, no braver than the other women, only different in that secret way. Zach had sensed that difference and now Flo sensed it, but neither had run from her.

Over the next few weeks, she asked herself what might have happened if the three women who had been in town had not walked in, but she knew very well nothing could happen. She did not know how to approach another woman. She had never been a sexual aggressor. Her experience was confined to Zach, who had enough aggression to fit out a squadron. How could one woman suddenly seize another? It seemed impolite. If there were other women like herself, how did they get together? The violent grappling and great heaving and grunting with Zach had nothing in common with what she felt for Flo, except for that aching deep in the belly, that wanting.

The WASPs were under attack. They must be loyal. They were under discipline. Bernice told herself so long as she was a WASP and in uniform, she would not think more about Flo and what might happen and how. She found her vow impossible to keep. Very well, she would let herself occasionally puzzle, imagine, dream, but would do nothing. Thus their life together continued as they slept on cots four feet apart with the storage table between. Most of the time they were off separately flying the fighters that had to be delivered to the war.

However when they were together, Bernice knew that she looked at Flo far more often and far more intently than she used to. She noticed things that had escaped her, the perfect curve of Flo's ear against her hair, conventionally called strawberry blond, but closer to peach or to apricot, and then the sudden fleshiness of the lobe and the little dot that was a hole, for Flo's ears had been pierced and she wore tiny garnet studs.

Flo's hands were strong and firm but smaller than her own. Sometimes she wanted so badly to take Flo's hands in her own and just hold them, feeling the small sweet bones, that she had to crush her hands together behind her back to hold them in control. She also noticed that Flo looked often at her. I am in love, Bernice thought with terror, finally in love for the first time in my life, but with a woman. What will become of us? What can become of us? Finally she missed something from home: the library of St. Thomas, where she had been accustomed to taking out books in her father's name or going casually back into the stacks and reading whenever her curiosity was aroused about dolphins or Patagonia or Catherine of Russia. Surely in the library information lurked about what she had become secretly.

She watched herself with other women, but she did not feel the same desire to stare nor did their bodies carry that magnetic charge, so that sometimes when she was near Flo, the hair on her arms would rise. No, she refined her observation of herself, she did not want women, she wanted one woman. Maybe that was better; maybe that was worse. Love was supposed to be a miracle and it had come to her finally and late, but not so much as a great fulfillment as a great mystery and a great puzzle which, she felt, Flo looked to her to solve for both of them. Sometimes she asked herself why she just couldn't be content being friends with Flo. Wasn't friendship wonderful enough? No, something hungry in her said, No, not enough. Only everything is enough.

LOUISE 10

The Biggest Party of the Season

It was tankers' weather—clear and dry—and warm enough so that Louise could remember it was August. For several days she had been riding with the artillery, but the advance was too rapid for them to shell the enemy without hitting their own troops. The Germans were fleeing before the oncoming army.

As an indubitably well-equipped army, one of its excesses was correspondents. Everywhere she went she stumbled over thirty of her colleagues. However, she was not here as a military reporter. Human interest and the woman's angle, that was what they wanted, and so far they were thrilled with her. There was United Artists interest in her piece on the nurses as the basis for a vehicle for June Allyson, her agent Charley wrote her. The Army was pleased, *Collier's* was pleased, Charley was pleased, her publisher was pleased and contemplating a collection of her war pieces.

She could hardly recognize herself. I come from a long ragged line of adaptable people, she thought, riding on an antitank gun or plodding up the road between signs that indicated whether the shoulders had or had not yet been cleared of mines. My ancestors were always having to leave one country for another, one life for another. Sometimes they were only allowed to be peasants and sometimes they were only allowed to be merchants and sometimes they were only allowed to be moneylenders and sometimes they were only allowed to work in factories, in sweatshops, in tanneries. Yet her adaptability shocked her, for in her image of herself, she was married, living comfortably in a New York apartment with husband and daughter, planning dinner parties and attending rallies and plays. Now Oscar was with a younger woman, her daughter had married a bombardier, and she was almost accustomed to sleeping in ditches and barns.

She talked to the nurses and the WACs, she talked to the young soldiers around her. Everywhere they were welcomed and feted. In bombed villages, people brought them flowers. The hedge-to-hedge and house-to-house fighting had given way to a mad dash forward. Instead of settling in and housekeeping in the mud as soldiers will, they had new quarters every night. They might be digging foxholes in an orchard or they might be put up in a lycée, but they hardly had time to look around, when they were off.

Living in physical discomfort, grabbing food when she could and eating it standing, sleeping in her clothes on the ground, washing in a helmet, she found herself hardening. She was back in her childhood: walk-up cold water rooms, the toilet in the hall. All the years of comfort, of luxury, of warm running water and soft upholstery and clean fine linen and meals at a table with bone china, her secretary, her mink, her pastel suits, all that had only been lent her and under it she was the same street urchin who spat away from the wind and wiped her nose on her sleeve. Under all the manners and the love and the men and the perfume, there was this sturdy body that could walk all day through the mud. She ached. All of the time, something always hurt, yet she kept up.

She thought sometimes of her father, that stocky hard-muscled Hungarian Jew who had worked in a coalyard and died in a street car accident. Fortunately she had inherited some version of her father's stamina and strength. Every day she needed it. She felt ageless, sexless. Her twelve-year-old self felt closer than the woman who had loved Daniel.

They didn't even worry about strafing, because the Luftwaffe had fled. The biggest problem were snipers who waited in trees, in orchards, behind stone walls. She was walking along interviewing a PFC from Milwaukee when he fell before she even registered the crack and whine. As she bent toward him instinctively, as if to catch him, a bullet creased the top of her helmet, throwing her off her feet.

That made little impression on her, because she considered that shooting at her was a stupid mistake. What upset her was that her interviewing the soldier might have kept him from being alert for the sniper. Finally, she did not think so. Nobody stayed alert all of the time, and the boys were in a victory mood, observing few precautions.

They were just outside Chartres, settling for the night on the edge of a traffic jam of vehicles, near an unharvested field of very ripe wheat. One of the farmboys with the artillery was shocked, but a French girl told Louise the FFI—the army of the Resistance—had ordered them not to harvest until the Germans had gone. Louise had just got her C rations and perched on the hood of a burned-out truck to eat them. They had meatballs, dehydrated potatoes, canned peas poured together in the mess kit with stewed pears. If Louise had not been too hungry to refuse anything, she could not have eaten it. She imagined the food around them and sighed.

"It can't be. It can't be but it is. I'd heard you were around!" Claude was standing in front of her, peering into her face. "I can't believe they really let you come over!"

"I've been here three weeks, almost four. I'm not the only female correspondent." She had not seen him since London.

"Would you like some vin du pays with that slop?" He pulled a bottle out of his trench coat pocket.

"I'd love it! Do you want to eat with the guys? There might be extra. We had some casualties this morning."

"We've been foraging." He motioned behind him. He had a jeep piled high with equipment, a driver in uniform but not very military looking sprawled at the wheel eating a baguette smeared with cheese. "That's rather extraordinary, what you're eating."

She had another swig of the wine. "Better than K rations, no? I wonder if this generation will go home expecting to stir the cherry pie into the halibut."

"The military life seems to suit you, but really, if you hadn't had your hair loose, I'd never have recognized you. If you'll forgive my saying so, you look like any other GI." Claude seemed vaguely shocked and offended, as if she had let him down or fooled him.

"What are you doing here with a jeep full of movie equipment?"

"Making a doc for Time-Life. Want to know where we're going now?"

"Where?"

He moved closer and bent to her ear. "Paris," he whispered.

"Oh, eventually, you mean. Aren't we all?"

"No, I mean *now*. I'll have to be my own cameraman, but that's how I started."

"I know, you have a special invitation from General Heinrich von Stülpnagel, the military governor."

"You're out of date, Lulu. Stülpnagel's in prison, because he was implicated in that harebrained scheme to bump off Hitler, to use your American gangster phrase. No, it's von Choltitz."

"The butcher of Sevastopol."

"The FFI assures me I can get in. The Germans have lost control. For the last week, since the tenth of August, the railway workers have been on strike. On the thirteenth, von Choltitz tried to disarm the French police—he didn't trust them any longer. When the Germans came, the arms had simply disappeared."

"How do you know all this?"

"Lulu, Paris is a big sponge. The Germans can't control it any longer. Paris is rising, as Paris always has risen. I'm going to film it."

"May I come along?" Louise asked politely, but she was already determined she was going to seize this opportunity. The other correspondents were patronizing to her, but if she got into Paris ahead of all of them, that would end.

"There's going to be shooting. It will be highly dangerous. It would be a dreadful idea for you to come."

"Claude, where do you suppose I've been for the past month? I can't be in more danger in Paris than I was in Normandy, and I want desperately to go. You want your film. I want my story."

"Couriers go back and forth every day to Leclerc, de Gaulle's general, and to the FFI near Paris. They know Eisenhower means to bypass Paris, and the Resistance in Paris has been ordered by Allied Headquarters not to rise. But my friends tell me there's no way to keep the bread from rising. That's an old phrase from the commune, did you ever hear it?"

She looked at him carefully. He was ebullient, fizzing with excitement. He was going home, and he wanted to be there already. "I'm going with you," she announced. "That's the price of my silence." She spoke with a consciously flirtatious air, but she meant it, and she hoped that he might guess as much without her having to prove it. After all, her old association with Claude ought to be worth something, although she was quite sure he had no interest in renewing the affair. Like her, he just wanted to get to Paris in advance of everybody else.

She said good-bye to her artillerymen and climbed in the jeep, her pack and her portable typewriter and her bedroll ready to go. The driver, who greeted her in a Parisian accent, straightened himself up and they lurched off down the road. Louise assumed that they did not truly intend to drive through the lines in a jeep, but she was wrong. They stopped in every other village, where one or the other made frequent phone calls; accordingly, they wandered an erratic route, but after they left the Americans behind, they did not encounter the Germans.

"The post office is on strike," Claude told her. "The civil service is on strike. The police are on strike. There are wall posters all over Paris calling for an insurrection. I hope we get there in time."

It was raining but they were riding with the top down, so that they could roll out faster if they were attacked. She had no idea when they passed the actual front. They had essentially driven around it and the Germans were fleeing somewhere else. The scene resembled ordinary life far more than it resembled the previous fronts she had seen. When the Army had been pinned down near the coast, a company would really dig in. Near the front every piece of the topography took on great significance, every small irregularity representing either possible shelter or possible danger: an open field that exposed you to hostile fire, a culvert the enemy could ambush you from or infiltrate through. Every bush, every smashed tree, every ditch, every little meadow was known and sometimes named, as in the world of childhood.

The Normandy front had been packed with soldiers. Every hedgerow, every pile of rocks, every orchard, every dip in the ground, sheltered someone. Jeeps or half-tracks lurked where they could. Guns were mounted anyplace commanding a line of fire. Ack-ack guns took up positions in between. Shell holes pocked the ground. Between every little node of the front wires ran connecting gunners back to their command post and connecting observers to guns. The whole front was tied together with long telephone wires. Smashed and burned-out vehicles, roofless houses, fields with great craters among the ruined crops: that was the front.

Here they stopped in villages and the driver Ari had a chat with someone local. "Ari," Claude announced as if he were a proud parent, "is with General Leclerc but in touch with the FFI. There's already fighting in Paris and out in Neuilly. There's a general strike on, so we'd better bring in what food we can buy, which is what Ari's doing at the moment."

When Ari came back he brought another young man called Emile with him. Emile had a rifle slung casually on one shoulder and a string bag in which she could make out a ham and some cabbages and potatoes over the other. "We'll miss the fun, my children," Emile said in French, in which all conversation was from then on conducted. He climbed in beside Louise, put his arm around her and gave her a kiss. "A true American woman, peace must be back because we're getting tourists already."

Louise slid out from under his arm and put her pack and typewriter between them as they bounced along. "I'm a war correspondent for *Collier's*."

"Good, you will tell all the world how Paris is liberating herself. Are the Allies coming or not?" He poked Claude over the back of the seat. "Hey, where's de Gaulle? Is he waiting till we do all the work?"

Claude grinned over the seat. "I hear he's in France. The Americans don't want him here, the British don't want him here. Are you sure you do?"

"Ah, what can you say? He's the only leader everybody will accept. Just so long as he makes himself premier and not dictator, just so long as he respects the program of the Resistance. Better him than the Americans put Pétain back as soon as we knock him out. The Americans might even try to bring back the Bourbons, the way they tried to stick the king back in Italy. We didn't fight all these years for more of the same."

They entered into a furious argument about the power of the various forces in the Parisian Resistance and who would try to seize power and who had the best organization and soldiers. Louise, barricaded behind her typewriter and knapsack, kept quiet and listened, taking a few discreet notes. Besides what she sent back to *Collier's, The Nation* might appreciate a rundown of the political situation in Paris, even if writing it up had to wait till she got out of the battle zone.

She gathered that there was a truce between the Resistance and the Germans, due to run out the next afternoon. They were rushing to get to Paris before it expired. They reached a suburb where the local Resistance took over the jeep and handed them bicycles. They spent the night in a closed and looted factory before penetrating into the city. Emile went off with the jeep.

Ari brought her food and sat down beside her to eat. He was wiry and tanned, with floppy brown hair, dark snapping eyes, a full mouth and well-modeled features. He gave her the impression that his good looks meant little to him.

She began her questioning. "What's your name? Where are you from?"

He was, as she had guessed, from Paris, although he had actually been born in Berlin. His parents had fled as soon as Hitler came to power. They were both doctors, but could not practice in France and instead ran a little grocery in the Jewish section. He was extremely eager to find his parents and younger brother as he'd had no news since '41. He was also hoping to find his girlfriend, a nurse, Daniela Rubin. He said she was resourceful and he was convinced he would find her.

He had gone over the Pyrénées into Spain, where he had been put in a prison camp. He had escaped, managed in ways he declined to explain to reach North Africa by boat and had joined the Free French, although his intention had been to make his way to Palestine to join the Jewish Brigade.

As they talked, she questioning him and he as determinedly if less openly questioning her, they began to get a sense of each other. He was bright, this young man, although she doubted he had much education. At sixteen he had gone to Spain, he and two pals simply slipping over the mountains to fight the Germans there. Then he had been in the French army on the Maginot Line. This French army was much tougher than that one.

Neither of them wanted to sleep. They shared a bottle of wine and some bread and cheese. "It was in Normandy a couple of days ago. De Gaulle came to review us. For some reason he stopped in front of me. 'And how long have you been fighting, my son?' Maybe it was his manner, maybe calling me son. I said, 'Longer than you, my General.' Which is true, because I've been at it since 1937. I want to find my people! Daniela, my brother, my mother, my father, somebody. I can feel it: Daniela's here, in Paris, I know it. As soon as I find her, I'm done with fighting. The boys with the fancy tanks and the expensive airplanes can finish the job. I haven't lived with a roof over my head, a table, a chair, a bed, since I was a kid."

He was twenty-three. Sometimes he looked and sounded that; sometimes he sounded like a man in his forties. She thought that if Claude had selected Ari as a bodyguard as well as a driver, he could have done far worse. She suspected Ari could do more than take care of himself.

Very early they set out on the bicycles. Public transportation was on strike and nothing was working, neither the electricity nor the trains nor the apparatus by which food arrived and garbage departed. Finally even the overloaded phones had gone out. If you wanted news, you set off on foot or on bicycle to see what was happening.

Louise was pleased she had spent all those Sundays bicycling with Daniel, because she kept up with Ari far better than Claude did, who got off to a wobbly start and huffed along quite out of breath before they had gone ten blocks. Of course they were all pushing extra loads. She had her knapsack and her typewriter, although she had abandoned her bedroll because she could not balance any more on the bicycle; but Ari and Claude had the camera equipment to manage between them.

The streets were crowded. As many stores were open as were closed. The day was already heating up. She was dressed too warmly. She felt conspicuous pedaling down a Parisian street in her American uniform; it struck her as dangerous. At the bottom of the knapsack were rolled up a summer dress and a heavier one, bound by rubber bands. Her clothing was attracting too much attention. She slowed down and waited till Claude came alongside. "I had better change."

"When we arrive," Claude mumbled, red in the face and panting. He was pedaling doggedly, but several times Ari had to pull over to wait.

Obviously Ari was the person who knew where they were going, and Claude was only following him. When they came across the first of the barricades thrown up in a working-class district, Claude called to Ari to stop until he could shoot it. While he was occupied, Louise went into a café and changed in the toilet. The old lady sitting there asked her what the uniform was and when she said she was American, said she didn't have to pay for the toilet. That was good, as Louise had very few francs. She had been bartering soap and cigarettes. When she gave the woman a piece of chocolate, the woman stared at her with such an expression Louise thought she might burst into tears. She had always thought to work as a rest room attendant in France, it was a prerequisite to be impassive except for an aura of disapproval. Then the old lady very carefully divided the chocolate into three parts, each perhaps one inch across. "For each of my grandchildren," she said. "How excited they will be!"

When Louise emerged, Claude was still shooting, a group of children and adults around him in front of the barricade made out of a burnt car, paving stones, old signs, mattresses, an upright piano. Everyone wanted to pose with the dozen rifles they had, plus two elderly shotguns and a stockpile of Molotov cocktails. No one expected the truce to last. Raggedy improvised tricolors hung off the balconies and windows, along with red flags and occasionally the black flag of anarchism.

"Come, there will be plenty to shoot," Ari urged Claude. "Let's get going. You missed the siege of the Préfecture, with tanks. The Germans are still evacuating by the external boulevards. But the SS is staying and say they will fight to the death. Rol—the Communist chief—is down in the catacombs, where the phones still work."

They pedaled on. Claude and Ari decided to drop her at *Paris Soir,* the offices of a collaborationist paper which had been taken over on Sunday by the clandestine paper *Combat.* Ari said that all the underground papers had come up during the weekend and seized offices and printing plants. Most writers and editors who had been praising the Nazis fulsomely were evacuating with their masters or had gone into sudden retreat in the countryside. The offices were on the rue Réaumur near Les Halles, which the Resistance had taken over to set up soup kitchens.

She had a little trouble overcoming the skepticism of the *Combat* staff, but finally she hauled out her smelly uniform and threatened to put it back on. She showed her credentials to everyone until somebody who could actually read them turned up. Then they let her have a desk. She got to work at once. Fortunately the recently clandestine journalists were pleased to answer her questions. Von Choltitz had been ordered by Hitler to blow up Paris, but he was negotiating with the Resistance through the Swedish consul.

A courier arrived, reporting that heavy fighting had broken out at the Buttes-Chaumont train tunnel and at the Prince Eugène barracks near the place de la République. She wavered what to do, then decided to go along to Buttes-Chaumont. Everywhere barricades were going up out of sandbags, café chairs, broken furniture, manhole covers, dismantled signs. Sporadic gunfire sounded. Far from keeping off the streets, everyone in Paris seemed to be on the sidewalks or hanging out the windows. The whole population was too excited to remain inside. The paving stones had been dug up, pissoirs dismantled, some black Citroëns set afire. One of the men explained that black Citroëns were the favored car of the Gestapo, and nobody not in bed with the Nazis had a car any longer.

She followed the pack on her bicycle. Several times they were halted at barricades. At one, wounded were being treated from a recent shootout with armed collaborationists. Louise asked as many questions as she could, scribbled notes and pedaled off madly after the pack. When they did finally reach the park—the railroad tunnel ran under it—around six, the fighting was winding down. The Resistance had captured the trains that had been parked there and a load of ammunition from the tunnel. There was little to see besides corpses and burning cars.

The reporters invited her to have supper with them. Nearby one restaurant was still in business, and they all piled in. Louise realized she still had no money, so she bartered a pack of American cigarettes to the reporters to pay for her meal. They began to be a little friendly, full of questions about when the Americans were coming and what things were like in the United States and in England. Coffee was a dreadful broth made of toasted acorns, the wine rough and unready, her supper one fried egg and rutabaga soup. As they were eating, the manager announced that no one else could be served because he was out of food.

They were putting out their paper when Ari appeared around ten. "We'll go to Claude's," he announced. "We're all staying there."

"Claude still has an apartment?"

"His mother is Rumanian and they were Hitler's allies. She managed to get an Aryan card, so she hung on through the war and kept his boys. Simone, his wife, they let out Thursday, when the political prisoners were released—those the Boches didn't kill before they left." He made a slitting motion at his throat, grinning without mirth. "Even when the Boches were rushing out en masse Thursday, they shipped one last load from the concentration camp in Drancy. So recently! Even at the end, with the walls falling on them, they kill Jews. The Gestapo too cleaned house and now in all the cemeteries are little mounds of fresh earth and under them quicklime and bodies with no identification. People are digging them up trying to find their husbands, their wives, their children. Will we ever know for sure who lived and who died?"

Something in his voice made her ask, "Did you find your family or your girl-friend?"

"I found someone who saw my family deported. Let's go."

"Does Claude really want us to come visiting? He hasn't seen his wife in years."

"They have room." Ari winked. "Claude said you were his friend in America, so I told Simone that you're my friend. I'll take you there and then I have to look for Daniela. The Resistance took the Hôtel de Ville, the City Hall, already. I'm hoping someone there has information."

"Thank you for coming back for me."

"It's nothing. Tomorrow everything's going sky-high. I just hope we don't end up with a bloodbath like Oradour or the Vercors. But the more people pour out, the better. They can't shoot down five hundred thousand people, true?"

The apartment of Claude's mother was in the XVIe arrondissement, full of ornate heavy furniture that proclaimed its worth in tonnage, with an occasional spindly antique by contrast with more curves than comfort. Glass étagères displayed collections of snuffboxes and music boxes. The mother was a wrenlike woman in black, four feet ten and weighing perhaps eighty pounds who wore around her neck a lorgnette, the first Louise had seen outside a cartoon. She was taking the invasion in good spirits, pleased to have her son and daughter-in-law returned to her. In all the splendor, everyone was eating a watery cabbage soup and ersatz bread, one slice apiece, in a salon lit by three candles and three only, as there was a candle shortage in Paris and the power was out.

Louise felt her presence had to be intrusive, but she wasn't the only camper. Claude's wife, streaked as if her black hair had been painted white with a brush, her eyes enormous in her thin face, her hands covered with burns, had brought home from prison four other women equally gaunt and staring. Among the rotund mahogany pieces the size of sedan cars, they were drooping as if an enormous wave had cast them up here with the life beaten out of them. Claude seemed to settle down. He spoke differently here, softly and diffidently, almost cooing. His two teenage sons looked at him and looked away. They seemed not to know what to say.

Why did he let me come? she wondered, but realized he had no idea until they were actually in Paris where his wife was and whether she was alive or dead; similarly, he had no idea whether his mother had been shipped off to a camp. Maybe he had permitted her to come as padding between himself and the ugly realities he might encounter. Tomorrow she would find another place to stay. Claude seemed largely unaware of her presence, as of the four other released prisoners. His two sons stared at him and he at them. The younger, Roland, was fourteen and the older, Jules, sixteen. They seemed unsure what attitude to take toward their father. With their mother they were overjoyed but shy. She had been in prison two years.

Claude was appalled to discover both sons were armed and had already been involved in skirmishing. The older boy, Jules, paid no attention to his father's arguments but simply picked up his rifle, his grenades, some bread and a demi-bottle of red wine and went off to take up his duties for the night at a barricade. Roland did not so much entertain as terrify his father by describing how students at his lycée had made Molotov cocktails out of sulphuric acid and potassium chlorate from the chemistry lab. Simone did not seem to find her sons' activities unusual and confined herself to ordering them to be careful.

Claude was going to have trouble adjusting to his family. She stayed against the wall, invisible in the family turmoil, with one of the released prisoners slumped beside her, with tears appearing against her cheeks as if they were condensation on a stone wall, while her eyes remained shut.

The next day Louise was in the Hôtel de Ville interviewing the Resistance authorities when the Germans attacked. The telephone was working again, functional even into the American sector and beyond. She was able to file a story. She had just got it off when the first shell landed. Cautiously she peered out. Four Panther tanks were in the enormous plaza in front of the Hôtel de Ville that stretched from the rue de Rivoli to the Seine. They had just lobbed a shell to blow up the iron gates. From nearby windows people were firing at the tanks, doing no damage. Another shell hit the ornate facade and a ton of assorted statuary cascaded into the plaza. Below her, Louise heard screams and the sound of falling plaster and masonry. Under her feet the floor lurched. Was the building surrounded? Gunfire was general all about them but she could not tell who was shooting.

While she was peering down, a woman came running at the tanks. Her dead-on frantic rush was riveting, as if she meant to throw herself down and appeal to their mercy or fling herself in their path. From above, her wide scarlet skirt looked like a flower. She ran pell-mell all the way up to the one that had been firing and smashed a Molotov cocktail against the turret as she was cut down by machine-gun fire from the others. The tank burst into flames. Suddenly the other three Panthers turned and clanked out of the square. Louise could not believe that one woman, lying in a puddle of her own blood on the stone pavement, had saved the Hôtel de Ville, a formidable number of Resistance officials and Louise herself, but the tanks continued retreating. The woman's hair had been brown, her age perhaps seventeen or eighteen. Her face was intact, but her body had been torn like a paper sack. Another woman knelt over her, weeping. A life combusted in one act of bravery.

Just as if she were a tourist arriving in Paris, Louise went to the Left Bank hotel where Oscar and she used to stay. All the little Left Bank streets, too narrow for tanks to penetrate, were held by the Resistance. Whenever German tanks or personnel carriers passed on the Quai, they sprayed the streets with machine-gun fire. Medical teams were set up in every block and Resistance people directed pedestrian traffic between the bursts of firing. From the hotel, she called the baron, hoping she could find out where Gloria was. She asked for the baron, gave her name, and heard clearly through the phone the exclamation, "Impossible. C'est une espèce de tromperie."

The maid reported that the baron had gone on an extended trip.

"Actually it was the baronne that I desired to speak with. She's my sister-in-law."

Again the maid repeated clearly what she had said. Most certainly the maid was not covering the mouthpiece, so that Louise suspected she was the benefactor of a miniature uprising at the baron's. Indeed the maid said quite simply, "Excuse me, madame, but he says to hang up."

Gloria had a house in Maisons-Laffitte. She called there and got the cook. "Ah, madame, I remember you and your charming husband and your little girl who cried to ride the horses. The house is closed up except for me and the grooms. . . . Oh, madame, they took her away, the Boches. . . . The Gestapo, madame, they took her in March. Not a word since. But I pray for her."

———————

She continued to use the *Combat* offices as her base. She was their pet American, proof that the troops would arrive. It was ten at night when a phone call came that the first tanks of the French armor had entered the city through the Porte d'Orléans. The city sputtered with the crack of rifles, pistol shots, shells bursting, booming explosions and the grinding roar of tanks and half-tracks and trucks. It was hard to believe anyone in Paris was sleeping, for in spite of the fighting, sporadic everywhere and heavy in places, the city was pouring into the streets.

They could not get near the Porte d'Orléans, but soon the tanks approached as she stood in a crowd of people screaming for the best parade they had ever seen, three and only three Sherman tanks decorated with flowers, with tricolors, laden with women and children hanging off the turrets. People were singing the "Marseillaise" and embracing each other if they could not reach the tankmen. No more tanks appeared, although the soldiers assured the crowds there were lots more on the way, for they had outraced the others. They were headed for the Hôtel de Ville, followed by thousands of Parisians through the warm and smoky night.

The rest of the tanks did not arrive until early morning, when they entered Paris from three different directions. The streets had been crowded since she arrived in the city, but now they were mobbed. Even in hospitals, people were at the windows and up on the roofs. Armed resistants mingled with mothers pushing baby buggies and couples strolling arm in arm. Everywhere flowers rained down or were crushed on the pavement.

The French armor had broken their columns and tanks were rumbling down streets all over the city, heading to seize the railroad stations or ministries, and in many cases, finding them already occupied by the Resistance. She followed one half-brigade that trundled along accompanied by several thousand people toward the Quai d'Orsay across the Seine from Le Petit Palais. The Grand Palais was in ruins from a recent shelling. On the way, she saw Claude's older son Jules and his group marching along with a group of German prisoners. The French armor seized the German barracks at the Avenue de la Tour-Maubourg without opposition and then had a quick fierce battle outside the foreign office at the Quai d'Orsay. When the tanks rumbled up to ministries, the crowds erected barricades to prevent counterattacks and then stormed the buildings and took them over.

At the foreign office, after the initial battle, everyone thought the way was cleared and people started surging in. Shots rang out, sharply, and then automatic weapons fired on the crowd. A suicide squad of Germans lay in wait and opened up on people rushing the steps. All around Louise people fell. She rolled down the steps and took cover behind a tree. Then she crawled and ran back through the park, bullets whining around her. Beside her, an old woman fell on the tricolor she was carrying. Louise stooped over her. Shot through the head. Grey matter oozed with blood through the exit hole. She dodged on, taking refuge behind a stone wall that ran between the park in front of the Foreign Office and the street, the quai bordering the Seine.

She was pinned down by fire and lay in a stupor, realizing how exhausted her body was while her mind still raced. She felt foolish and naked, stomach to the sidewalk behind the stone wall in the summer dress she had put on so that she would not be so conspicuous in Paris. All round her vast spaces yawned, Les Invalides to the right, the Seine behind and across it open spaces stretching to the distant Louvre. She was protected unless a shell landed, as she watched the Resistance fighters storm the building until the street and the park were littered with bodies lying smashed in their blood.

Finally tanks began to shell the building. One of them was hit by mortar fire and burst into flames, the men inside screaming as they burned. She could hear equally fierce fighting from the rue de l'Université at the rear of the same ministry. She had followed a parade and fallen into a battle. Fragments of masonry fell around her and one struck her in the shoulder. At first she thought her arm broken, but it was only badly bruised. She crawled backwards away from the explosions, feeling the heat of a fire on her back. Behind her wall several wounded men and women had taken shelter. Louise crept over to help apply a tourniquet.

When the remains of the building were taken, she rose and crossed the Seine, feeling terribly exposed, trotting bent over behind the parapet like all the other pedestrians. The Place de la Concorde was studded with antitank stakes driven in. She realized she needed a rest room, badly. She ignored the bullets whizzing across and ran on. On the rue Royale, a restaurateur had broken out a keg of wine and was passing it around. The café was out of food but the toilets were functional and she could clean herself from her long crawl on the pavement. Then she took a seat at a table crowded with strangers who were all in love with each other. She felt dazed and disoriented. It was as if she were attending a huge unruly party where in certain back rooms, people were killing each other. Her left arm throbbed badly where a fragment of the Foreign Office had landed on her. She felt as if the front of her mind, her eyes, her senses were overpowered to bursting with images and sounds, but that her self had dropped away. At once numb and overstimulated, she found it hard to speak, but the noise level was such that no one would have heard her anyhow.

"De Gaulle is in Paris!" the restaurant owner shouted, climbing up on his own table. "He is going to the Gare Montparnasse to receive the German surrender. Paris is free!"

Everybody screamed and embraced and drank or spilled what was left of the wine. The "Marseillaise" was again sung and people began dancing to an accordion. Wearily she began worming her way through the mob toward the street. She was here at this vast dangerous party to do a job, and that included getting to the Gare Montparnasse to hear de Gaulle. Strange men grabbed her and kissed her wetly. She could not escape or wriggle free but must endure until let go. Her arm was hit so many times, she felt like bursting into tears or throwing up. She pressed on, suffering the hands of strangers, along the rue de Rivoli under the arcades.

Out in the street a big bonfire blazed with German signs and Fascist papers, while people capered around singing. A blind man sawed at a violin and a woman was standing on a barricade, singing. Children were squirming through playing soldier. Everywhere people were kissing or twirling around two by two or in large circles, hands clasped. On one street she heard a song of the Spanish Civil War she remembered, "Los Cuatro Generales." A Sherman tank was smoldering beside a Tiger.

By tomorrow the government would be in place no doubt, hundreds of other correspondents in town and everybody jostling for the same stories. She did not really mind. She had her stories and perhaps with other Americans, she might recover a sense of self again. She felt as if she had come to inhabit an eternal overwhelming present that had pressed out of her all personality. She recorded like a machine. Idly she wondered if Ari had found his Daniela as she pushed along under the arcades. In the Tuileries across the street people danced on the grass.

She passed the Hotel Meurice where the German commander von Choltitz had surrendered that afternoon after a short fierce exchange of fire. The bodies still lay in the street. At the far end of the block, a medical team was working with the wounded, carrying them into the former headquarters. Two young militants with FFI armbands lay where they had fallen, their gelid eyes open. One of them was Claude's fourteen-year-old son Roland.

The Grey Lady

Abra was relieved that the regular air raids had ended, but there was something new. Fewer buzz bombs had been getting through lately, since the antiaircraft people had got quite good at shooting them down at the Channel. With this new disaster, no planes were heard. No siren went off. Nothing gave warning until an immense explosion sounded, a shock wave traveled out breaking windows and toppling objects for a mile and a column of smoke and flames rose.

The government announced that another gas main had exploded, until people began making cracks about the flying gas mains. Finally Churchill spoke. They were officially called V-2s. Abra had not bothered to go to the shelters for a long time, and indeed, with the V-2s, there seemed little point. By the time you heard the explosion, you were still alive and they had missed you.

Frequently Americans just over mistook Abra for British. They said she looked like a Londoner. She understood what they meant, whenever she saw herself reflected in a mirror beside one of the newcomers. She had no mirror at home because hers had shattered in nearby concussions. There were no shop windows in which to catch a reflection, had not been in years. Abra was dependent on the still-intact mirror in the women's room at OSS to see herself in anything larger than a compact. When they said she looked like a Londoner, they meant she had no tan, looked pasty and thin. She wore her uniform almost always, because her other clothes had worn out and could not be replaced.

At work, they had never been busier. Most agents sent out by SO or SI had been overrun in the rapid advances. In Germany, the British confessed to having no agents, and while Allen Dulles out of OSS Bern was reputed to be running some, intelligence was stumped. Someone had hatched a scheme for recruiting through the Labor Branch, the only organ that maintained ties with members of the exile German community not in detention. The boilermakers and transport workers long scorned were now to be studied with an eye to what kind of agents they might make if dropped into Germany.

Since Oscar and Abra were among the resident experts on German labor, they were recruited. Sometimes Abra shepherded the exiles to be outfitted in the great underground rummage sale in Brook Street, where OSS had stockpiled items swapped in the prisoner of war cages, bought in Sweden and laundered into age or collected from exiles: underwear, belts, trousers, shirts, caps, uniforms, dresses, wallets, brassieres, cigarette cases, cuff links. Abra thought she recognized a jacket and a coat they had collected in New York.

Three times Abra was assigned to take German women to be outfitted. One was a nurse, Helga, four years older than Abra, who had been married to a Jew beaten to death in Cologne. She had been imprisoned for a year under the Nuremberg Laws, released because there was a shortage of nurses. Helga was a large soft-looking woman with round features making a series of o's in her round face, but she was both tough and shrewd. She had recently married the plumber in the project, Reiner, and they were to work as a team.

The second woman was a young Communist laundry-worker, Frieda. The third was Marlitt Becker Speyer, looking fit and eager, as elegant as ever. Abra recognized her at once, with a lurch of her heart; Marlitt remembered her after they had spoken for several minutes.

She shepherded the exiles through the BACH operation to work out cover stories and then to collect forged documents. Much of the time their trainer handled them, but she filled in. Besides an ID card and police registration, a German citizen would be expected to have labor registration, food and clothing ration stamps, travel permits, housing registration, plus draft exemption or military papers for the men. The cover story had to be as close to the truth as could be managed, to avoid snafus, in the new slang.

With tobacco scarce in Germany, the heavy smoker Reiner had to have the nicotine stains sanded off his fingers with pumice. Marlitt had the caps put on her teeth in New York replaced by caps in the German mode. All were unceasingly rehearsed on their stories. Oscar briefed the group on economic conditions in Germany, as far as they had been ascertained, and on what German citizens knew about the war from papers and radio.

The weather was wet and chilly. Every day for two weeks it rained. The bomb craters and the pools that had been dug into the ruins throughout the city to serve as reservoirs for dealing with incendiary bombs were overflowing their banks. Sometimes she came upon damage from the liquid-fuel rockets. A hole in London would gape big as a playing field.

The war in France was galloping forward, while Italy crept along. Her own inner war was one of attrition. Since Louise's visit, Abra felt she could no longer deceive herself. All evening she had been forced to compare how Oscar acted with her with how he acted with Louise. He was loving with her; he loved Louise. Now she was working on a gradual withdrawal, as from a drug. Tonight, she told herself, tonight you will not see him. You may see him Saturday, but not Friday, not Thursday. Had he noticed? She thought so, but she could not even be sure of that.

OSS was set up in Paris at the Couvent of Ste-Anne, a clinic and death house for the poor run by the Sisters of Agonie, and teams from R & A hurried off to the Balkan countries as they fell out of the war overrun by the Soviet armies, and then changed sides. Back in Washington, the main impetus seemed to be the war of the top echelon to survive the peace and continue as an organization. R & A was feverishly involved in research in anticipation of the victory over Germany, preparing studies on what must be done, ought to be done, should not be done in the occupation. All this felt premature in London with the V-2 rockets taking out blocks at a time, and eight thousand people living in each of the deep shelters.

Americans exclaiming over the good-natured long-suffering character of the British working class as represented by the homeless who lived in the tube stations or in the shelters, deep or shallow, gave her a bellyache. What did they expect? Total collapse? And what would happen to families then? Americans decided those who suffered were long suffering, an observation of high insight which she attributed to Louise. They did not see if people were bombed out, there was nothing to do but go to work the next day and camp out as best they could.

Almost every day she saw him at OSS. As they worked together, she remembered all the reasons she had fallen in love with him. Her abstinence often felt bizarre and demented. Why refrain from going home with him, why resist going to bed with him? After all, he was there and willing and here she was, wanting him. She did not always carry out her resolution. Frequently the impulse to hope veiled her grim certitude. How easy to follow him. How easy simply to go along. How laceratingly difficult it was to remember why she was resisting: only for her pride. Only to recover herself.

Did she secretly think she was reculant pour mieux sauter? She inspected her mental armament. Please, she begged herself, abandon hope. Hope has played you for a sucker all along. It is as it was the first night, a friendly fuck is all you can get out of him. Some nights nonetheless that seemed more than enough to wish for.

Oscar was no longer conniving to get into France, because Louise had written him from Paris that Gloria was in Germany, in a concentration camp for political prisoners. The work that Oscar and she were doing was far more important to the war than anything Louise could possibly take up. Louise was one of a swarm of reporters humanizing the war. Abra was not sure that war should be humanized. The side of it she had seen the past year and a half had consisted largely of poor people getting burnt in their houses or crushed under falling ceilings, the limp bodies of children being lifted from rubble, a headless woman in the road and the neighbors arguing who it was from what clues remained.

Yet Oscar seemed to have arrived at feeling guilty toward Louise, a tenderly swollen masochism he was nurturing like a rare cactus of the sort Professor Blumenthal had lining the south-facing windows of his apartment near Columbia, squat spiny things that occasionally belched out an unlikely flower. What did Oscar feel guilty about? Once Abra and he had talked about everything, or so she thought, but now there were volumes of silence between them. Oscar looked no more haggard than the other overworked denizens of the Labor Branch, but she resented that hidden sapping that came from an inner life sealed against her.

That he should feel guilty toward Louise infuriated her. Louise could probably have him back but did not care to. It was a bad farce, and she simply would not remain in her allotted role, the compliant mistress last on the list and taken for granted. She deserved more, she told herself. Her family would be delighted if they knew her resolve. She had no intention of passing on information that would give them that pleasure.

Yet at the base of her brain was a cache of hope, that at some point, realization would smite him and he would turn and see her. She imagined Ready scolding her for wasting her life, but she did not accept that. Becoming involved with Oscar, even at her grimmest she did not regret. Neither was she sorry she had come to London.

At parties, in pubs OSS personnel frequented, she ordered herself to flirt, but she could barely manage it. She seemed to have forgotten the moves. Men started the game with her, but nothing developed. Perhaps in attempting to give up Oscar, she was relinquishing her sexuality. What a joke if Ready and her mother in their fulminations about her becoming an old maid turned out to be correct. She saw herself finishing her degree at Columbia, and teaching political science in some midwestern grassland school. She would march to class in sensible tweeds toting a battered British briefcase, the same one she carried now. She would be well liked but viewed as eccentric, a character. Old Scotty. Lost her fiancé in the war. That would be the legend.

She was done with sex, a burnt-out case. If she could not have Oscar, no other man would do. The nagging annoyance was that she *could* have Oscar, on the same old basis. While she was indulging in fantasies of her life as a tweedy professor, another woman was probably eying Oscar and preparing a move into the space she had vacated.

———

One night a blast wakened her as the whole flat shook and large chunks of plaster fell. A rocket had obviously landed within half a mile. She did not think of it again until the next morning, when Oscar did not appear at work. She tried to call, but the phones were not functioning. No one seemed to know where he was, and then she heard someone talking about the rocket that had hit last night just a few blocks away.

She ran to his street, keyed up to terror. His side was standing, although damaged, but the other side of the street no longer existed. The door had been blown off his building and plaster littered the hall.

"Oh, Captain Kahan," a woman with a bandage around her head was picking through broken dishes, visible in the hall through the hole where the wall had been. "He was taken to hospital this morning. I have no idea, I was off getting my head seen to."

She was back at her desk frantically calling hospitals when Oscar appeared, moving stiffly. "I broke two ribs. That damned clock fell on me while I was putting out an electrical fire in the hall. Burnt my hand and cracked my ribs." He had lain under the clock for three hours. "Time hung heavy on me," he said, setting off a round of puns in the office in which Abra could not join. She had difficulty keeping herself from touching him, assuring herself of his presence. She had been terrified; at the same time, she was aware of being curious as to what her life would be like if Oscar had suddenly been killed. Why, she would continue working. After all, she too knew a great deal about their agents. She would do what she was doing, because that was what she had been trained for; that realization made her more tranquil.

She took him home with her that night and for the rest of the week. The dressing on his hand had to be changed and one on a cut in the small of his back. He was overtly cheerful about the accident. "It was what you might call a thought-provoking experience," he said. "To be helpless and dependent on somebody turning up to get that object off me. The flaws in my character seemed bigger than I'd ever observed them before. Do you suppose good behavior is dependent on an occasional scare?" He wanted to make love anyhow, but she had to climb on him, gently, slowly rocking.

———

Abra considered herself as accustomed to the blackout as anyone else. She never knew when she would see a colleague with a black eye or a sprained ankle from falling down a flight of steps. A code clerk had been run over in September while trying to cross the dark streets home. Never had she been as conscious of the moon and its phases. When the full moon gleamed down, the ruins and spires, St. Paul's dome, the palaces were bewitched silver and eerily beautiful.

Nonetheless she was not prepared for the countryside in blackout. "This is the world before electric lights," Oscar said. "We're standing in the past."

They were on a hill in Dartmoor, where no light shone as far as they could see. The waxing moon had not yet risen. The sky was clear except for low filmy clouds scudding over, beyond whose rapid passage the stars overawed. Oscar had his arm companionably about her shoulders. This was the last weekend in England for the first six agents, including the husband-wife team of Reiner and Helga, including Marlitt. Monday they would be flown to Paris, loaded into small planes there and dropped by night into Germany.

"The British think this is ridiculous," Oscar said, his head thrown back staring up at the stars. "They maintain you can't drop agents into a hostile country where there's no resistance to meet them and help them get started. I hope they don't fall right into a firing squad."

"Sometimes I wonder why they're doing it," she said, shivering as the wind tested her coat.

"They've been at war with the Nazis since thirty-two or thirty-three, some of them. And they're sick of exile. I only hope that the desire to find out what happened to people they knew doesn't betray them."

"Oscar, we didn't think up this scheme, and we didn't pick who got to go. More people were willing than they chose, by far."

Oscar was silent for a while. The wind whipped around them, while in the corner of her eye she saw some tiny nocturnal beast flash over a rock and disappear. "I volunteered, you know," he said at last, knowing perfectly well she had not known.

She felt sick. She said nothing.

"After all, I speak German and I've been using it almost daily. I spent a year in Frankfurt in twenty-eight. But they ruled me out right away. Nobody who wasn't born in Germany, nobody but exiles. They've begun combing more agents out of the POW cages."

"I think volunteering was one of your all-time silly acts," she said at last. "You have skills that are essential. I doubt if skulking about Germany pretending to be a Nazi is one of them."

"How would I know until I tried it?" He hugged her closer. "Never mind, they turned me down. So we send our Germans off and we stay."

"Oscar, they want to go. More than most soldiers do."

"No doubt." He led the way down, toward the sprawling manor house built in the local granite, where they were billeted. She did not tell him she had had a similar conversation with Marlitt the day before, and had said, "But you swore you'd never go back to Germany. Never."

"For this, I am gladly forsworn." Marlitt simmered with excitement under a veneer of calm. She was the oldest of the agents, the best educated, always a little aloof from the others, although friendly to Abra. "My husband would have been proud." She did not mean Mr. Speyer.

Oscar and she had been given adjoining rooms. Their liaison was so well established, they were treated as a couple. What would it take to release her? More strength than she had, perhaps. Oscar followed her into her room, not she thought from any strong intention but automatically, his mind still on the exiles, who had been tucked in bed early but who would be awakened by their trainer at odd intervals tonight, barking questions. "What is your name? Your address? Your birthplace? What color are the trolleys there? Where are your parents buried?"

She felt the flowering of a tender relief that they had not taken him, for they might have. They sent off less likely men than Oscar as liaison to guerrillas. That young man she had spent a night with in Chelsea had been killed in France with the maquisards. His roommate the arrogant major was considered an expert on resistance movements.

Receive what is given you, she thought, and got into bed with him without a word. They made love more fiercely, more passionately, than had been usual with them in a while. No matter what her head might decide, her body opened to him and imploded.

Afterwards nonetheless she wept, lying sleepless beside him hearing the wind try the casements and tweak at the blackout curtains. Oscar she assumed was asleep but after a while he said, "It makes you unhappy now. You need someone your own age, Abra. I'm not what you really want."

"Oh, yes you are," she said, trying to stop the flow of tears. "It's the other way round."

He was silent a long time. "I don't want to give you pain, Abra. Louise said I should marry you. Do you want that?"

"Do I want you to marry me because Louise says you ought to? You must be out of your mind!"

"But is she right? Would that make you happier?"

"What do you want?" she mumbled, her face half buried in the pillow.

"I want the war to end. I want to find Gloria. I imagine being home, but what home am I thinking of? Not the little apartment I had on West Fourth Street in the Village."

"What then? What do you want?" she insisted, muffled in the pillow.

"Everything's come apart, hasn't it, for all of us? My mother's remarried, my daughter's married, my wife is halfway to Berlin and my sister's in a concentration camp."

He didn't say his ex-wife; he said his wife. But he's never had another. Yet. Was he opening? Was this the miracle?

"Maybe we should get married. Would it please you, if not your family? I've seen you getting sadder and grimmer. Would that help?"

She could not answer. Six men had asked her to marry them before, and never had she been more than flattered and never had she hesitated to refuse. She doubted he was really bringing up the matter because Louise had sarcastically suggested he should. Perhaps he felt himself growing older and perhaps he did not want to end the war alone. Perhaps he did not want to return to New York and a little bachelor apartment to start all over again. His family had disintegrated, and he was preeminently a family man. He might be asking her to fill that vacuum.

"I'm thinking about it," she said, sitting up. Her tears had stopped. "I'm sorry I wept. I've never done that."

"Don't be ashamed. It's a draining time." He lay down carefully, propping his side with a pillow where his ribs were taped. "My ribs are still sore, even though they're healing, and it's hard to find a comfortable position. Still, I always sleep better with you."

———

When she got up, it was the day everything had to be gone over a last time, pockets turned out, wallets emptied, clothes pulled wrong side to, seams examined: the wrong button, matchbook, key, coin, receipt, or laundry mark that could lead to suspicion and arrest given a last thorough inspection. At noon, she found it hard to eat, for the tension in the room. The closer it came to time to drop these poor bastards into Germany, the more insane it felt to her. They were delivering them to hell.

Helga was in an expansive mood and kept proposing toasts. Her husband was more withdrawn, as was Marlitt, knitting at table's end on a blue scarf. For several months, all the OSS personnel in the room had been bending over the Germans, instructing them, correcting them, questioning them, creating an environment for them, dressing them. They had stood in loco parentis and now they were sending their little family off to probable disaster.

A whole apparatus had been created, called the Joan Eleanor system, whereby the agents inside Germany would use a new type of radio broadcasting a tight beam upwards, which they hoped would prove impossible to detect. A small plane would circle above with the equipment to pick up the message, so that long transmissions would be possible. Viewed now, not as a game but as something really about to happen in a hostile country, Abra began to feel as if she should jump to her feet and protest the patent absurdity. She kept quiet and drank more hard cider.

It was late afternoon before she got time to herself. Since they arrived, she had wanted to venture out on the moor. She had never been on a moor and associated it with the Brontë sisters, but they had lived in Yorkshire. There were horses remaining in the stables, and she asked if she could ride one. The groom hesitated, then seeing from the way she approached the horses that she knew what she was doing, suggested she take the grey gelding, a sweet-faced riding horse of middle age. Abra set off.

She had been warned against bogs, against fog, against attempting to penetrate far, against everything in fact except the Hound of the Baskervilles. The horse knew his way on the moor, so she let him take her where he thought she ought to go. It was obviously someone's customary ride, which the horse remembered after who knew how many months or even years? Where were the inhabitants of the sprawling house with its overgrown gardens offering last blowsy roses? Their furniture remained, stolid and unexceptional, their family portraits the same. Someone had been an avid fisherman. Someone had liked to read about naval battles and collect model ships.

She found Dartmoor starkly beautiful. There was no transition between the manor house and the moor. The gardens densely planted and thick with trees crowded around the stone house, its cottages, its pens and stables, its formal allée, and then beyond the stone fence, the vast moor began at once and stretched past the horizon. She passed nobody, although there were paths, bright green against the dark heather. In the distance she saw blackfaced sheep. Once two shaggy ponies whinnied and ran. A buzzard soared over her, hunting. The treeless hills were a deep rich brown, olive and purple, scarlet, densely furred with heather and bracken broken by outcroppings of granite, often piled up in the rough knobs they called tors. She passed an occasional brilliant and fervidly green bog, but stayed out as she had been warned. A kestrel stood in the air beating its wings blurry, as they had used to do long-ago summers in Maine. Everybody in the house had told her not to go out on the moor alone, but she had ridden by herself from age eleven on. Her uncle Woolrich kept horses. The sky was grey and low and might soon rain, yet did not.

The horse brought her eventually to a row of standing stones beneath a tor and there paused and began to graze. She slid down, experimentally dropped her reins and watched, but he did not move off. The time under the clock, yes, that had shaken Oscar more than he would let on. He had thought about his life and realized what a mistake he was making. It was the miracle she had hoped for, given now to her. He had turned to face her.

She passed inside the double row of stones, touching each as she went. Old, old. Time had ground them down like a horse's teeth. How confident she had been, the same at twelve as at twenty-two. The world was her birthday present, and she would want for nothing she set her heart on. The stone row mounted the hill and slowly she passed between them, a sense almost of fear gathering in her, a sense of strangeness, of power. This was not a New England pasture, not the stones of Fort Popham, where historic meant less than a hundred years old. From the top of the hill she could see circles of stone, pits and boundaries of something ancient. No one moved in the landscape, yet everywhere stood remnants of human will and desire.

Over the crest the row continued dipping to a massive stone that culminated it, grey-green and roughly shaped like a diamond with a hole through it. As she came closer, the hole looked almost polished, as if many hands had worn away at it. It would have been big enough to pass a package through, or a baby, or a head. She thought of stepping back out of the row before she came to the squat looming rock, but she did not.

She flung herself down on the heath and stared up until the standing stone seemed to sail across the sky carrying her forward, the earth turning faster under her bearing her toward night. I want to marry him, she thought. I want to. Once I marry him, I'll be the wife. I'll be the center. I will make him a home. I'll make him happy.

The stone loomed over her, squat, female, a wise woman mocking her folly. The sense of a presence was powerful. She did not feel so much alone as outnumbered. You'll never be the wife, the stone said, you'll always be the second wife, the imitation. Even if he doesn't say it, he'll always be thinking, Louise didn't do it that way.

But I'm flesh, she said to the stone. Flesh is stronger than memory.

Is it? the stone asked. Is flesh stronger than idea?

Why can't I have him, why? she asked the stone, half imploring, half demanding.

You can have him now if you want, but only the him you already have.

Tears began rolling down her face again, into the base of the great female stone. It was as it was, her life, hard as rock and it would take more tears than she could summon to soften it. She would return to Oscar's bed, because she would take the good that was offered her while not pretending it was the good she really craved. She lay with her head resting against the stone and oddly, as the tears dried, she smiled. Oscar was a rationalist through and through and he could never understand about the moor and the stone; but she had just discovered she was a pagan. Self-consciously, but with a pleasant sense of mischief and worship combined, she kissed the stone and pushed her head briefly through the hole.

The horse nickered softly, coming over the hill dragging its reins. She ought not to have left him that way. She rolled to her feet, whistling to the horse. Then she turned and saluted the stone. She caught the horse, mounted him and fled. When she reached the manor house on the moor's edge, the last supper was being prepared and Marlitt presented her with a beautiful wool scarf in shades of blue.

RUTHIE 9

Some Photo Opportunities and a Goose

Ruthie received her B.A. in a hasty and unimpressive ceremony at the end of August. Now she was enrolled in the graduate school of social work. Although layoff jitters ran through Detroit every month, the sole change had been that she was working a forty-five- rather than a forty-eight-hour week. Only the women whose men were in Europe were optimistic. Nobody looking at the map of the Pacific expected the boys home soon.

On the whole she found graduate school easier. She had only three classes. Compared to what she had been going through, her life seemed less harried. She did not have to wake until eight, which meant she got close to a full night's sleep. Often she had lunch with classmates, sparing her mother the need to stretch the points and scarce meat or cheese. She felt as if she had been bent over for years and now she could straighten up. In truth, whatever her fellow students said, graduate school was easier and she could afford to take time and do a better job on her papers. She liked the little projects, interviewing neighborhood women on their experiences with welfare for a term paper.

The cafeteria at school reminded her of Murray, of sitting with him in that intense staring before he had gone into the Marines. That brought him back to her, his gentleness, his warmth, his presence. She began to write him longer letters, improving on the automatic writing she had been dutifully turning out just before she got into bed. (I love you, I miss you, there was an accident at the factory Tuesday but we got an E for production again, it rained all week, Marilyn fell down the steps and cut her head.)

A letter arrived from Murray, complaining that he had lost his only picture of her. He said he had lost all his gear when he had been wounded off Tinian, so would she please immediately send him a new photo or preferably a whole bunch of them, as many as she has. How many more battles would he have to fight? Murray had been sick once and wounded twice, and still he did not come home. Wasn't there a point when a single marine would have been in enough battles to spare him? He still talked about Jack and now about Tiny and Slo Mo, but she thought he sounded lonely and sad.

Leib had not really changed, so maybe Murray wouldn't change either. Maybe he would return older, a little sadder, but the same gentle and intelligent and quietly strong man she had fallen in love with. She had to believe that. If only they were better at writing letters, so that they could conjure each other up on the page.

That Sunday, Rose and Morris went off with Naomi in the old Hudson that belonged to Trudi's parents, all five crammed in to look for a farmer who was reputed to have maybe a turkey or a goose. Rose had always roasted a goose for Thanksgiving, but this year she would settle for anything she could get, alive, dead or in between, so long as it had feathers. A crow maybe, was her parting comment as she pushed Naomi ahead of her to the rusting car.

Ruthie decided it was time to do something about new photos for Murray. She sat in a kitchen chair with a towel draped around her while Sharon cut her hair. "Ruthie, I just don't know what more I can do with you. I wish I could give you a nice finger wave, but your hair is kinky. I wonder sometimes if you shouldn't, you know, get one of those kits the coloreds use and straighten your hair."

"I should complain? I don't have to set it, I don't have to curl it."

Afterwards Sharon and Trudi laid out Ruthie's best dresses on the bed. They were not impressed. "You've been wearing this red taffeta number since we were in high school," Trudi said. "We have to take you shopping."

Ruthie insisted on her pink chiffon. "Just take a couple of pictures, please. I want to send him a picture of me in this dress."

"A summer dress when it's forty degrees out? He'll think you're crazy."

"No he won't, I promise. It's his favorite dress," she babbled. "Please, just take a couple of pictures of me in it and then I'll put on anything you tell me to. Okay?"

Trudi had a Brownie box camera that had been Leib's. With it he had taken a dozen pictures of Ruthie which she wished she could reclaim, if he still had them. She did not dare raise the subject with Trudi, who remained sensitive about Ruthie's having gone out with Leib.

"Where is Leib?" she asked cautiously, as Sharon zipped her into the pink chiffon. It was loose. Ruthie hoped she hadn't lost weight on her bust. She suddenly wanted to make Murray love her, because she was sure he had come as close to forgetting her as she had to forgetting him.

Trudi blew out her breath. "At a football game. Fatty got him two tickets to the Lions, and he took this guy Moose he met in Fatty's bar. He didn't even ask me if I wanted to go."

"Do you like football?"

"I hate it, and I'd freeze to death in the stands. But I feel like he should ask me if I want to go, instead of going right ahead and asking Moose without saying boo to me."

"Is Moose Jewish?" Sharon asked.

"Sure. But he's a crook." Trudi sighed heavily. "The doctor says Leib can't stand all day on the line. I wish he'd go to school like you, Ruthie. The government passed this new bill where they'll pay for it."

"Really?" Ruthie smoothed creases that came from the chiffon hanging undisturbed in her closet since that time with Murray. "I wonder if Murray knows? I'll write him about it."

"I'll show you the pamphlet the government sent Leib."

On the porch railing, Ruthie arranged herself with the coat open trying to smile at the camera as if it were Murray. She remembered the rich warm brown of his eyes with the little flecks of gold in the iris. Had she aged? Had she grown skinny, scrawny? It was as if her body had ceased to exist, and now she was trying to show it off.

She did not know if she was still attractive. The men at the factory had got used to working with women and they knew who was interested and who was not. It had been a long time since any of them had pestered her, more than pro forma. Her classes were ninety percent women. She wondered if Murray would find her withered into an old maid. That was what Leib kept saying about her. Why should she believe Leib? She kept away from him. She spent time at Wayne partially because with the house so crowded, it was hard to study, and partially because she did not like being around Leib, and she never knew when he was going to appear. Yet everybody else seemed to think they were one happy family.

Naomi spent a lot of time upstairs, baby-sitting. However, Ruthie was looking around for a better job for her. Child labor laws had been allowed to lapse for the duration, so kids were quitting school for factory jobs. She wanted to make sure that Naomi stayed in school, but she also thought it would be better if Naomi had a different job.

Now there was a real possibility of her being taken on in the bakery where the Fennimans were shorthanded, after school and Sundays. Naomi would make twice what she made baby-sitting and bring home leftover bread, on the occasions there was any. Ruthie's main aim, aside from thinking that an outside job would be good for Naomi, was to get her away from Leib. Leib had made a pet of the girl, who obviously worshiped him.

She did not really suspect Leib of anything concrete; after all, he had Trudi around and they went at it often enough, as everybody beneath them could testify. She felt he took advantage of Naomi's puppy love and drew her away from friends her own age. Naomi was growing up fast, filling out, shooting up. One day, Ruthie realized that Naomi was taller than everybody in the house except Leib.

Naomi's boyfriend Alvin was crazy about her. Naomi liked him, but that was about it. Ruthie could remember clearly that stage when a girl wanted a boyfriend but could not understand what all the fussing and deep breathing were about. Alvin seemed fine to Ruthie; she did not think he would lean too hard on Naomi, and she judged that Naomi could handle him. Of course she could understand Naomi having a crush on Leib, because romantic feelings for a man you could not have were easier to sustain—and far safer—than developing romantic feelings for Alvin, who after all was just a lumpy overgrown boy a little less smart than Naomi. Ultimately she did not believe in subjecting Leib to temptation. When they finished the picture taking, she would go to the bakery to see if the Fennimans had decided. Mrs. Fenniman particularly liked Naomi, whom she described as a brave girl, although Ruthie could not imagine why.

She tried the taffeta dress, but as Sharon and Trudi both pointed out, it had seen better days. Finally she put on the green velvet, bought on the layaway all through her last winter at Sam's. It needed brushing from hanging so long, but it still looked handsome. Trudi marched her out to the porch again. "That's good. Now smile. Get rid of the sour puss."

"Wait, I want to put on the earrings he gave me. There."

"Think about Rose coming home with a big fat goose," Sharon murmured seductively. "Think of the goose fat rendering, the way the whole house is perfumed. Think about the stuffing with the apples and the dried apricots. Think about how she makes the skin brown and crispy."

Boston Blackie, who loved the green dress, leaped up to sit in her slanted lap as she perched on the railing, holding on tight.

Rose did come back with a goose. It was a little over the hill, a little tough, but it was a real goose. When Ruthie got home from the swing shift, the goose was hung for the night, and Boston Blackie was in disgrace. He had climbed up the pantry door and bitten a mouthful of feathers. Now he was exiled to the basement. When everybody else had gone to bed, Ruthie called him to her room, where he climbed into bed with Naomi, who was moaning in her sleep. She had too many bad dreams, Ruthie thought, clucking over her, uncertain if she should wake her or let her sleep. Sleep had come to seem so precious to Ruthie during her years of always being short, that she let Naomi alone.

Thanksgiving, they had both the goose and a chicken, the latter for the children, for whom goose was considered too rich, and for Trudi who liked only white meat. Thanksgiving 1944, it seemed the democracies would survive and that the Fascists would finally be beaten. By next Thanksgiving, would Murray be with her? Would she be married?

Naomi had written to her mother in Paris at the old address, but the letter had come back two months later. Morris said he would begin inquiries through the Jewish agencies, now that France was almost liberated. The Germans held only pockets near the Swiss and Belgian borders. Morris went to the Joint and to the Emergency Committee and returned with some Paris addresses. He wrote a letter in Yiddish and Naomi wrote in French. When Naomi got home from school every day, the first thing she did, Rose said, was to check the mail and then look in the mailbox to make sure nothing had been missed. Letters from Europe, she kept saying, were very thin. They could easily get lost.

Secretly Morris said to Ruthie that he thought that it was probable all of the Lévy-Monot family had been killed. With France liberated, a letter would have come if there were anyone to write it. Ruthie agreed.

Ruthie too found her interest in the mail quickened. Murray had received the first of her letters stimulated by the revived hope she felt, and he responded in kind. His letters began to sound as if they came from the person she remembered. They were longer, full of anecdote. He had read *One World* and had an interesting conversation with Slo Mo about world government. What did she think of the idea?

He had also been reading *For Whom the Bell Tolls*.

> You wouldn't think I'd be reading a war novel, but I read whatever I can lay my hands on. It feels great to read again. My brain wakes up. That novel made me think about the differences between fighting a war in your own country, and in other people's. I wouldn't be nearly so lonely and we could see each other often. And my family too. But then it's your real estate and your civilians and ultimately your family that gets it.

Then the photos came. He said he remembered that dress, but that she should not look so sad when she wore it. She should look happy remembering him and thinking of when they would be together again. He said he liked best the one sitting on the porch railing with the cat, because she looked as if she was thinking about Murray and wanted to kiss him, and just looking at it made him want to fly right out through the barrack roof and rocket through the air like Superman, just to be with her for five minutes. I know what you were thinking about in that picture, he wrote. Ruthie smiled.

He said that the new legislation was good, and he'd go to school under it as soon as the war was over. No, he didn't want to live in an apartment. He didn't care if he had to commute. He wanted a house, a real house with a yard and just them, nobody else.

At that, Ruthie frowned, because she planned to take Naomi with her. She did not believe anyone in Naomi's family was left to claim her. She would not argue with Murray through the mails. She would worry about that when he was home.

He hardly knew Naomi, and Naomi hardly knew him. It would sort itself out. When Naomi spoke, most of the time she sounded like any other American teenager—a new word everyone was using and that Ruthie found herself adopting. Naomi had drawn back a little from her gang, although she still hung out with them. They did not seem to Ruthie as tough or menacing as they had. With Naomi's improved performance in school, Ruthie began to talk to her about college. She encountered in Naomi an unwillingness, almost a fear, of discussing the future.

"I don't know!" Naomi would say, turning her face away and tensing her shoulders. "Why talk about that now? What's the point?"

Trying to read through the official line of the newspaper stories, which week after week claimed that Peleliu was almost practically just about conquered, and yet the next day there was more fighting to report, she prayed that maybe the next island in the chain would not be so bloody or so hard. Murray wrote of training, and she wondered what the Marines planned to do with him next. His letters had become more emotional lately, desperate-sounding. One night she dreamed he was crying alone in a forest of tall dark trees. He was calling her, but she could not find him. She could see him very clearly sitting with his head in his hands crying as a woman would cry, but she could not reach him though she ran and ran.

JACQUELINE 11

Arbeitsjuden Verbraucht

They were still together, Daniela and she, and for that and that only Jacqueline could be glad. She was not sure yet, now that she understood the kapo's jokes about up the chimneys, that she should rejoice that Daniela and she had been selected as strong healthy specimens. Two thirds of their transport—two thirds that is of those who staggered from the cars still alive by the end of the fourth day without food or water and who had not been shot or clubbed to death in transit—had been sent by Dr. Mengele to the left. All the children, people above thirty-five, all women with small children, most of those wearing glasses or with a limp, had been sent to the left. For the first three weeks, while they were quarantined in barracks where they lay on filthy straw without room to stretch out a leg or an arm, Daniela and she had imagined that those spared what had been done to them must be better off. "Why didn't the cheminots sabotage the train?" Daniela kept asking. "Why? They know which trains are full of Jews and resistants. Why don't they attack?"

In herds of women lashed and beaten, she was stripped, tattooed, shaved of her head and body hair. She found in herself impassivity like a stone to be sucked in raging thirst and found outside Daniela, whom she set herself to keep always in her sight. What is done to her I can endure too. She found in herself intelligence sharp as a whetted knife. Why do they do this to us? First, they intend to treat us as beasts, so they try to make us beasts. We have no names, no clothing, nothing individual. We are forced to live in terror as if it were the air we take into our lungs. The skinnier, the uglier, the more scabrous, the filthier we are, the greater superiority they can feel. They rub our faces in our dirt so we may stink to them, and to ourselves.

Now they were out of quarantine. Those who had survived were routed out for morning appel, when they stood in thin grey shifts and outsized wooden clogs in the rain or with the sun burning their newly shaven heads for two to three hours, and again in the evening. Sometimes they were marched out for slave auctions, for entrepreneurs and businessmen to select workers. Rumors ran through the barracks, where sleep was always difficult in the stench and over-crowding and noise, of freedom, of punishment, of what was or wasn't going to happen to them or to others. Huge bold rats waddled around chewing on the corpses and attacking the living. Mice infested the straw. Some days they were marched out to carry huge stones they could barely lift from one end of camp to another, work without purpose or end, designed only to exhaust and punish and finally kill. To fall into the mud would be the end, to suffocate in mud.

Death surrounded them, women pulled out of line and beaten to death for some fancied tone of voice or look, women shot for stumbling, for stooping to pick up a potato peeling. Every morning corpses lay in the crowded bunks with the living, women who died during the night of starvation, of overwork, of a severe beating that had left internal injuries. Their bodies were rolled out like logs and stacked. Every dawn and every evening appel, more women dropped and were taken to be burned.

At first she tried to remember every beating, every kicking, every murder but what could she do with the rage that flooded her? Indignation took energy. Daniela must survive and she must survive. The SS men, the SS women, immaculate in their uniforms, well fed, shaved, perfumed, loomed over them like gods. Like demons they had not only their names but special secret names. The kicker. The hammerhead. The chozzer. Daniela and she must study them to outwit their malice. When the hammerhead shifted his gaze in a certain way, he was about to strike out. When the SS woman called the vampire smiled with her lips pursed, she was about to draw blood with her whip. The chozzer liked women to look down always. The kicker if you met his gaze would often pass you by. She hated having to study the idiosyncrasies of brutes as if they were laws of nature, that when the hammerhead whistled, you need not worry, but when he was silent, somebody would die soon.

"Remember reading Suetonius in school?" she asked Daniela. In the French school system, they had all read the same books at the same time. "I thought the Roman emperors were such monsters, that power enabled each of them to be-come hideous in a different and wilder way. But each SS man over us is his own Roman emperor. They are all crazy with power."

Never to be quiet, never to rest, never to be clean, never to sleep soundly, never to be full or have enough to drink so that the throat stopped burning and the belly was silent. Never free from terror. Never alone. Never out of the presence of the dying and the dead.

What manner of beings are they that feed their egos by reducing others to shit? Only the same as ordinary, but more so. Is that it? Ordinary hatred of the neighbor, ordinary anti-Semitism, ordinary despisal of women, ordinary acts of domestic and street violence, battering, beating, terrorizing, ordinary callousness shading into brutality given a license, a reward, a theatrical setting, a uniform, a credo. I kill therefore I am. I kill you, thus I am proven superior.

One Sunday afternoon as they were picking the lice from each other's seams, Jacqueline saw a woman who looked a little healthier than the others, with hair grown out a couple of inches, black with streaks of grey although her face was unwrinkled. She could not be a prisoner, because she wore a real sweater over the grey shift and real shoes on her feet. The woman barked some questions, then came toward the two of them. Jacqueline tried to sidle away into the crowd that jammed the fetid room. She had already learned that to stand out in any way was to die. Always attempt to avoid notice. That was not easy since she was one of the tallest women in the room, but she was beginning to stoop.

The woman stared at Daniela and then at her. "Which of you is Yakova Lévy-Monot?" she asked in Yiddish.

Jacqueline was terrified. First of all, it had already been beaten into her that she had no name, only her number. She was a haeftling, a piece only. No one had names here. She had been arrested under her own name, because at the last minute she had destroyed her false identification, since she was wanted under that name.

All the women looked away, as frightened as she was. But the woman who had entered held up her arm with the tattoo. "I'm just a Jew, like you, don't be afraid. Are you Yakova?" She had to repeat her question, as Jacqueline had little command of Yiddish.

Jacqueline nodded, waiting for the blow, the lash, the kick.

"I'm your aunt Esther—your mother's youngest sister. Come outside."

They both started to follow, but she turned sharply. "Who are you?"

"This is Daniela. Where I go, she goes, or I don't go," Jacqueline said, in a mixture of Yiddish and French. "We are sisters."

"What else are you?" the woman asked.

Jacqueline did not understand and looked at her blankly. The woman stared back, then came to a decision and motioned them both to follow her. They all squatted against the wall outside, where a drizzle black from the crematoria smoke pasted a layer of ash on their skin.

Out from under her sweater the woman who said she was Aunt Esther brought a pair of well-used but still good boots. "See if these fit. Now you can divide them if you want, each one apiece, but that won't do you much good," she said sarcastically.

They were big, but Jacqueline did not care. Real boots. "Maybe you could get some for Daniela too?"

"Do you know what they do to us if they catch us taking clothes?" She pointed at the chimneys. "Be careful that those boots don't get stolen. Listen to me, I'm an old number, I know. You're lucky if you can stick together, because you can watch for each other. Anything you leave will always be organized, stolen, because it's life or death, a scrap of sawdust bread, a slice of rotten turnip, a piece of cloth to bind your legs." As Esther spoke, Daniela translated. "I work in the office, because they found out I'm a good bookkeeper and I do sums in my head. So sometimes I have something I can trade to the women who work in Canada, where they sort clothing from the new transports. If you get sick, act well. Don't go to hospital, because Dr. Mengele will cut you up alive. It's a place where he plays with the dying as if they are violins of pain for him."

"Esther, my mother Chava, my sister Rivka, they were transported in December 1942. Are they here?"

"There are worse camps than this I've heard where everybody's killed, everybody, right away. There's hundreds of camps. People mostly don't last that long. I was in a factory in Lodz before. Listen to me, get into a factory if you can. Look lively. Straighten your spine and look strong and tall when they come to pick you. Pinch your cheeks. Otherwise they'll take you in a selection. Tell them you worked in a factory in France."

"Won't they find out we lied?" Daniela argued.

"The boss who picks you, he won't be there when they put you on the machines. They'll beat you anyhow."

"Esther, please see if you can find out about Maman and Rivka, please."

Esther shook her head. "What you don't know is better. Think of them as alive. Better not to know the truth. When I came, they took my son and my daughter. For the first four months, I survived believing they were in some other camp, a children's camp. I lived only to get them back." She paused for Daniela to translate.

"How old were they?" Daniela asked.

"Four and six. By the time I learned what happened to the little ones, I had become an animal, a beast that lives to live. You harden yourself. One of the women in Canada, she found her own baby's little dress. She killed herself on the electric wire. When we do that, the guards laugh. Always remember, if you die, they win."

"Ask her, has anyone escaped from here?"

"People escape, but they bring them back. Some Yugoslav partisan women got away. But as a Jew, nobody out there will help you. You have to make it on your own. Still, if you ever have a chance, seize it. They whip and hang you when they catch you, but the chance is worth it." She leaned toward them. "What of the war? What do you know?"

Esther had heard about the Normandy landings but had not yet heard about the August landings in the south of France. In the camp at Gurs the day before they were deported, Daniela and Jacqueline had heard that French troops had landed at Toulon. That was where she heard too how her father had died at the barricade.

"When we were being transported through Germany, we heard bombs falling. Germany is being heavily bombed, we could tell," Jacqueline said and Daniela translated.

"Why don't they bomb here? Why don't they bomb the gas chambers? Why don't they bomb the railroad lines here? Why?" Esther stood. "Get yourself chosen. You must."

"Aunt Esther, where are we exactly? We only know we're in Poland. If we ask the kapos anything, they just punch us."

"It's called Oświęcim, an old cavalry barracks, but now it's a city the Germans call Auschwitz. Women built it, in the winter. They gave them evening gowns to work in. None survived. This part is Brzezinka, what the Germans call Birkenau. Birchwood, like a nice resort." Esther grinned for the first time. They could see that her teeth were badly decayed and in front two were missing, broken. "How old do you think I am?"

Jacqueline felt a little embarrassed. She had always been told that her aunt Esther, the youngest of the girls, was only seven years older than she was, but that could not be. She shrugged.

"I'm thirty. And they sterilized me. My hair all fell out. The hair grew back, not like my womb. Have your periods stopped yet?"

Daniela and Jacqueline nodded.

"Everybody says it's drugs, bromide, but maybe it's just because you're starving." Esther motioned them back into the barracks and sidled off into the rain that made oily puddles on the ground.

Jacqueline put on the boots at once. She would barter the clogs for bread to someone whose clogs had been stolen. Maybe next Sunday Aunt Esther would come back with boots for Daniela.

Two days later—they were still keeping track of time then—they were among a group of women ordered to strip naked and march out before a group of the SS and men in business suits, who were joking together. Jacqueline had already adopted a technique to survive the stripping and the poking, the whipping and slashing. She imagined that her body was hidden inside an imitation body. The men could only see the imitation rubber body, but she was the bones hidden inside that they could not see or touch. At night in the bunk she had whispered that to Daniela, but one of the other women of the six who lay flesh to flesh in their narrow wooden bunk had heard and said, "Your bones? Ha, they can break them. And when they have burnt the flesh off, they grind them into bonemeal for fertilizer." Jacqueline told the woman to shut up or she would knock her out of the bunk. It wasn't for several weeks that she found out the story was true.

By that time they were working as slaves for Krupp, making grenades. Every morning they were wakened at four A.M. and stood on appel and every morning some women fell and were kicked to death or simply left on the field to be carted off in the trucks that daily took the dead, the dying to the crematoria. They did each wear one boot at appel. Daniela could not cram her foot all the way into the boot, but she could get it on enough to stand in it, to keep one foot warm.

Every day and every night the sky was red with flames, while heavy ash filtered down on them. The crematoria could not cope with all those gassed, for the Germans had grabbed the Jews of Hungary and were shipping them in the hundreds of thousands into the gas chambers. Every night large piles of bodies were burned in enormous pyres all around the camp, because the crematoria were overloaded. Ash fell from the sky like oily black snow. The stench of burned flesh hung in the air with the stench of decay. Sometimes half an inch of ash lay on everything.

In these barracks they slept only four to a bunk, Daniela and herself and two Hungarian Jews, a young girl named Rysia who spoke some French, and a young married woman Tovah who spoke only Hungarian and Yiddish. In the hour between the evening appel, the hours of standing in the square, and lights out, as the women were picking lice from each other, anyone who knew a poem recited it or they talked of food. It did not matter what language the poems were in, the women wanted them again and again. The women who knew the most recipes and could best describe them were in great demand. Rysia, who had helped her mother do the cooking for the inn and for her large family—of which only she remained—was particularly valued for her veal paprikash and her cherry strudel.

She can make you taste it, the women said. Mix the pastry again, Rysikela. Describe how the cherries smell. Rysia, who had done the same heavy labor all day as the rest of them and been marched to the factory seven kilometers through the increasing cold and back again, who had been fed only the same slice of adulterated bread and coffee imitation and worked a twelve-hour day on that, who had stood the appel for two hours that morning and two hours that night and been hit with a rifle butt four times on the trot back from the factory, who had for supper only a small bowl of watery turnip soup, put her last energy into creating for the other women fantasies of food. Rysia was only fifteen, but she had a woman's strength and stamina. Tovah had just turned twenty-one. Her family had owned a vineyard and made sweet red kosher wine. Her husband had come into the business and had just been learning how to graft vines. When she arrived, she was a dark plump woman. Now she was wan and lean.

Rysia looked like all the rest: gaunt, hollow-bodied, with a shaven head and huge staring eyes, a mangy ghost. Her hair had been red, she told them. Her mother had run a country inn, a restaurant with a few rooms upstairs, and her father operated a mill. Rysia spoke German, French and a little Russian as well as Hungarian and Yiddish. She considered herself uneducated, but she was quick. Daniela and Jacqueline had begun giving lessons, Daniela in Hebrew and Jacqueline in English. It was forbidden and they would be killed if anyone betrayed them, but the women loved the lessons. It took their minds off the hunger, off the terror, off the pain. "To learn," said one big rawboned woman who had been a laboratory technician, "it's to feel human briefly." Most of the women chose to study either English or Hebrew, but some insisted on learning both. Friday nights they tried to burn candles of rags or scraps stolen under pain of death from the factory. One woman led prayers for them in Yiddish, which Jacqueline was picking up more every day. Sometimes Daniela would pray in Hebrew as she lit the imitation candles, covering her eyes. Sometimes they had nothing to light at all, no little flame to ignite against death.

By now they knew that Tovah was pregnant. Mengele had not caught her on the way in. She would have gone straight to the gas, or else to his experiments. He liked to cut open pregnant women, or experiment with the effects of starvation on the fetus or the newborn child. It could take them quite a while to die, the mothers even longer.

Typhus, diphtheria, cholera were epidemic in the camp and killed hundreds daily. Sometimes marching to work they saw the men, who looked just like them, except that they wore pajamas instead of shifts. Starved, with shaven heads, they all looked the same, forced to run at the same SS trot, double time, carrying heavy loads, hundred-pound bags of cement. At the factory she could see no difference between the Krupp guards and the SS. When the women went once a day to the latrines, they were forced to run across the courtyard and if they moved too slowly, the factory people turned freezing water on them. Still they could mutter to each other. The slaves taught each other how to turn the heads on the grenades so they would misfire, and then to put the good ones on top. There were tens of thousands of women and men slaving for companies that clustered around the pool of labor in the camps, labor they paid nothing and could work to death.

One night Tovah gave birth. Daniela assisted her. Daniela held her hand across Tovah's mouth. If they were caught, they would all be sent to the gas chamber. It was a long birth. All the women who could endure to, watched, held her hand, wiped her brow with their filthy shifts. At last he was born, the little morsel, tiny but vibrantly alive. The kapo, who was going along with this, said, "Don't give him to her, or she'll never let go." That would mean death for both.

Daniela wrapped the baby in a torn rag from a woman who had died and the kapo put the little boy outside to die. A freezing rain fell. It should not take long. They tended Tovah as well as they could on the mud floor. Daniela slipped out into the night, where she would be shot if seen, and when she came back, she was plastered with mud. Jacqueline understood and kissed her. Daniela was shivering, but could not cry. They were kept raging with thirst and had no tears. Their ducts were inflamed and dry.

In the next selection Tovah was taken. The SS woman said she looked un-healthy. She went off with the women chosen to die without saying a word, without saying good-bye.

Rumors ran through the camp like disease. How can we go on? Jacqueline wondered, plodding through the freezing rain. This was a cold damp place, breeding chills and fevers, but if you could not work, you would be selected at once to die. She looked about her, cautiously, as they plodded in torn dirty rags down the road, always told to hurry, mach schnell, mach schnell, schwinehund. Random blows. Some days began with one or the other of them getting it in the head or the back or across the breasts when they marched out of the bar-racks, when they lined up for appel, when they lined up for their three minutes maximum in the wallow of the latrine, when they were marched to the factory through the fog that stank for miles of burning flesh. The grimy freezing grey rain was like universal pneumonia, a mucous discharge of the atmosphere.

Daniela was a bony witch with immense eyes under a grey shaved skull, nose and chin protruding like an old woman's. She could imagine what she herself looked like. Boils and open sores covered their arms and legs. They stank from diarrhea because they all had dysentery. The smells, nobody got used to them, the fearful stench of sick unwashed starving bodies and piled-up waste, of shit and blood and fear.

She could remember when they had first arrived in this place, this vast city of death and slave labor that the German SS men and women called Birkenau, she and Daniela had stared at the musselmen, at the apathetic creatures that had no flesh left, only ropy tendons and bones under the discolored greenish skin. They had felt revulsion. How could people let themselves become like that? Now she knew. Daniela and Rysia and she were still active, still moving, but they had become as frightful as those scarecrows they had turned from when they first arrived.

How long could they survive? She asked this of herself coldly as she worked at her machine. How long could they continue to work while starving? How long? One day when Daniela had been pulled from her machine and beaten by four Estonians who were working for the SS, because the machine had broken down and she had not made her quota, she collapsed in the column marching back. Jacqueline saw her start to fall and moved sideways, hissing at Rysia, who blocked Daniela's fall with her shoulder as they trotted on five abreast, as they were always made to march. The guard they called Slasher was amusing himself kicking a child who had fallen and missed Daniela's misstep. With Daniela between them, they shouldered her along until they were safe in the barracks.

That night Rysia cried. When Jacqueline, who had been trying to ease Daniela's welts and open wounds, asked her why, Rysia said, "You love each other so much. With my mother dead, nobody will ever love me like that."

Daniela raised her bruised head, her nostrils still caked with blood they had no water to wash off. "Rysia, we will make you our sister too. Yes, we will."

Jacqueline cupped the high-domed skull of the girl, encrusted as were all their scalps with running sores, and caressed what would have been her hair. "We'll be family."

"After the war, my darlings, my sweet ones, after the war," Daniela intoned through swollen lips.

"When we are liberated," Jacqueline said. "When we escape."

"Then we will eat enough, we will eat chicken roasted and gedempte flaisch and as much as we want until we are full," Rysia whispered. "We will have a warm bath and clean clothes and underwear and real shoes on our feet, with stockings. We will sleep on clean sheets in feather beds."

"After the war," Daniela intoned, "we will go to Eretz Yisroel and we will live together in a house and raise apricots, there, where the sun shines and it's warm. We will have chickens and sheep and a rosebush with red roses and one with yellow roses. No one will ever again call us dirty Jews. No one will make laws against us, ever again."

"Chickens! Eggs . . . real eggs . . ." Rysia intoned, cuddling up to Daniela as gently as she could in the narrow wooden bunk.

"Roast lamb," Jacqueline whispered, "and clean warm water and roses on the table." Why should she argue anymore? She had nothing to go back to. She had only Daniela and Rysia. She would agree to dream about Palestine. At least there it must be warm.

Every day she dragged herself from the crowded cage of plank bed, aching, feverish and thought she could not stand the stench, the noise, could not endure her own bag of bones wrapped in a foul scabby rag of skin, could not endure the pain in her vitals, could not endure working past the dropping point, the poison of permanent exhaustion that drained even the minerals from the bones, could not endure the fear jabbing their bellies, the hatred, the unending vicious petty and horizon-vast hatred.

To Daniela and Rysia she whispered, "I will not hate myself because I stink. I will not hate myself because I have no hair. I will not hate myself when they force me to run naked across the yard. I will not hate myself because diarrhea runs down my legs and they won't let us wash. I will live and tell the world about this. I will live and make them pay."

"Have you ever killed anyone?" Rysia mouthed back.

"Yes." She told her the story of rescuing Daniela, while Daniela herself listened with shock and dismay.

"You should not talk of that here," Daniela whispered, deeply upset.

"Here is precisely where I should talk about it. And remember."

"I will think about it all day," Rysia whispered. "Better than food."

On October 7, an explosion shook the camp and shots followed. In the morning they were kept standing at appel for hours. Word came through the grapevine, muttered without movement of lips. There had been a revolt of the Sonderkommando: the men who shoveled the corpses out of the gas chambers and loaded them in the crematoria. They were to be gassed, as happened to each batch finally, but this group revolted. Some women from the munitions factory had smuggled powder to them and they had made bombs. They had managed to kill some of the SS, nobody knew how many, but as they stood in the appel, Jacqueline looked sideways out of the corner of her eye at Daniela and blinked her pleasure and Daniela signaled back. They had to be extra careful because Slasher was prowling this morning and the SS female commandant was pacing before the rows, pulling out victims to kill. She had a way of wetting her lips when she was about to seize a victim, as if she could taste her. All the women of the Krupp factory were punished, randomly beaten, their food withheld, but four were taken away to torture.

They heard that the model ghetto Terezín in Czechoslovakia, often shown off to the Red Cross (who maintained Jews were simple criminal prisoners and not prisoners of war, and thus refused to help), had been largely emptied. The inhabitants were arriving but nobody got to meet them, because on October 28, which was the Czech equivalent of 14 juillet, they were gassed. The guards made jokes. The execution was arranged to celebrate Czech independence day.

The women who had been tortured from their factory had not broken and had given no names. One morning all the women were kept standing, soiling themselves as they could not help by the fifth hour, until the women from the munitions factory were marched in, mangled, bloody, to be hung before them. Nobody cheered because there had been an incident like that once and a machine gun had been turned on the whole block. Hanging is no worse than being gassed, she told herself. We'll find their names and remember.

The next day at appel it was snowing and they stood, many of them barefoot, on the frozen earth. Winter was coming. She began to understand that for all they had been through, the worst was yet to come. That night she asked the woman who had survived the longest, a woman who had been working first in the mines and now at Krupp since November of 1943, "Now that winter's coming, will they give us at least coats? Or stockings? Or blankets?" By now she could make herself understood in Yiddish.

The woman who was only twenty-four, she told them, just laughed. She opened her brown toothless gums and laughed.

MURRAY 4

The Agon

Landing on the beach at Tinian, Murray was hit with a .38 bullet that lacerated his shoulder and cut the artery. It was the same damned shoulder that had taken a piece of shrapnel on Saipan. He must lead with it. He missed the fighting on Tinian, but then his regiment joined him on Saipan.

The 8th Marines received replacements just drafted, kids of eighteen. They also got new officers and NCOs to replace those killed or badly wounded. Jack and Murray had both been made corporals and Reardon, promoted to sergeant major, encouraged them to snap in for sergeant. He liked them both, if only because they'd been through so much. They weren't regular marines, but they were old marines by present standards, and they could be counted on to help break in the kids. Zeeland was gunnery sergeant now.

Fox Company got a new second looey and a new sergeant. Sergeant Hickock had been with the outfit on Guadalcanal, before Murray had been assigned, then hospitalized with a leg wound. He had been with Baker Company that caught bad casualties on Tinian. Murray had seen Sergeant Hickock once or twice but had little impression of him except that he was regular marines, about thirty and a southerner, handsome, blond and square-jawed. He had a wife back in Columbia, South Carolina, and two boys, Lee and Jefferson.

He learned something else quickly about Sergeant Hickock. "Feldstein. What kind of name is that?"

"It's my father's name, sir."

"It's a Jew-name, that's what it is." The man was smiling thinly, looking around for support. What he mainly met was indifference. "Isn't it? You're a Jew-boy."

"You could see that on my dog tag. It's no secret. Sir." Murray felt himself heating, shame, anger, helplessness.

"I thought they kept Jews and niggers out of the Marines. How'd you sneak in?" He didn't seem to expect an answer, but he did. He repeated his question.

"I joined."

"Maybe they needed somebody to clean out the latrines, to lick them clean. We all know who started this war and who's too yellow to fight it."

He thought maybe that would satisfy Hickock, to have stirred up some of the new guys to pick on him along with Rostrovitz, a Pole from Chicago with whom he had never got along. Two days would pass and he would think Hickock had finally let him go. Jack stuck up for Murray and so did Tiny and Slo Mo Mazzini, a big kid who had been a replacement before Saipan, and he knew Reardon and Gunny Zeeland liked him. But in the Marines, an NCO could use any religious or ethnic or racial slur. That was the Marine way.

He tried to hold himself together. He had a deaf great-aunt on his father's side who wore a hearing aid. When she found conversation boring or inconvenient, she shut it off. Murray tried to pretend to himself that he had a hearing aid he could turn off. He tried to pretend he didn't understand, that that thin-lipped mouth was moving in some strange incomprehensible tongue. But he heard every word.

There was a lot of liquor on Saipan. There wasn't supposed to be, but the marines traded battleflags for it. Jack would sit around sewing up Japanese flags out of parachute silk and dipping them in iodine to look like blood and then they'd trade them to the Navy or the fliers for booze. There was also a hot market in Jap souvenirs, from canteens to swords to helmets and even skulls. Besides, every platoon had a still hidden. Murray didn't drink till he got drunk, but his fever had been coming back, and the booze helped. Otherwise sometimes he got the shakes. It was better not to stand out from the men in any way. Tiny drank too, against his upbringing, although he wouldn't gamble or shoot craps or visit whores.

A league of ball teams was set up, enlisted men versus officers in the various outfits. It passed the time. Murray had caught on his high school team, so he played catcher. Books were distributed in special armed forces editions. All the guys lined up for *Forever Amber* because it was supposed to be hot. He was reading *A Bell for Adano*. On Saipan they had movies regularly and shows every couple of weeks. In January they had the Andrews Sisters; in February, Joe E. Brown and Carmen Miranda.

He knew he was relatively lucky, because if he had come in as a replacement now, Hickock could have turned everybody against him. They could have driven him to despair and perhaps suicide, as had happened with a PFC a sergeant had decided was a fruit in Charlie Company.

As it was, he had more time with the company than Hickock did and he had his buddies. Hickock would drop fruit jokes on Jack and him and try to isolate him, but it did not take with enough guys to make life entirely miserable. Slo Mo was loyal to them because he thought Murray had saved his life on Saipan, which was debatable and if true, true of everyone of them. He was a big rangy kid of eighteen, deliberate in his movements, his thoughts, his words. You'd say something to him and maybe twenty minutes later when you were talking about something entirely different, he'd answer what you'd forgotten you said. That's what gave him the nickname. Murray decided he was not slow mentally but thoughtful, a decent kid who tried to understand what was put before him. Tiny stayed loyal too. He liked them, Murray suspected, because they did not make up sex exploits all the time and did not shoot craps constantly. Tiny had had a strict Protestant upbringing that had left him wary of sin but had not seemed, amazingly, to make him intolerant. He clung to them because they were quiet, Murray thought, and did not frighten him.

Murray was the oldest and played a casual father to Tiny and Slo Mo. They brought him their questions and their bruises and he gave advice, which was free. He was easily protective of them but he could not protect himself. Hickock was always after him, waiting to catch him in some minor infringement and put him on latrine duty or set him to scrubbing the camp stove every day for a week. He knew that regulations forbade that, but he knew nobody gave a damn for regulations when it was the sergeant doing it to a corporal. Sergeant Major Reardon might like Murray, but he would never interfere with what Sergeant Hickock, a regular marine like himself, felt like doing to one of the men.

One Saturday he came back from guard duty and Rostrovitz was hanging around grinning. On his cot was a picture of a fat lady, naked, with Ruthie's face stuck on her body. Rostrovitz or one of the other goons had cut up his photo, which made him angrier than the obscene picture. He ripped it up and set fire to it with his new Zippo.

"Hey, Prickstein. Jew-boy. Your girlfriend sent me that picture. Don't you like it better than the one she sent you?"

Murray stamped out the burning paper and wiped up the ashes. He wanted to push Rostrovitz's teeth down his throat. He wanted to squeeze his fat neck until he smashed his voice box. He made himself say, as he sat down on his cot, "Asshole, cutting up the pictures of pretty girls is the closest you'll ever get to one. Taking her face and sticking it on the body of some old whore like you're used to made you feel right at home, didn't it?"

"She's a whore too or she wouldn't fuck you. All Jew bitches are whores. They do it for fifty cents."

Murray wrote to Ruthie for new photos, telling her a story about losing them in battle. The 8th Marines could tell from the visible preparations that they were about to be sent into action again. They had been hearing scuttlebutt about Iwo Jima, so maybe they were going to be added to the carnage there. Some guys thought they were heading for Formosa. They'd be told when they were on board.

It was grade school again, he thought. Waiting for the bully to jump you, a big kid who is two years older and twenty pounds heavier and has it out for you, Christ killer. It's the Polish gang waiting to catch you when you have to cross the alley on the way home. If they actually slugged it out like a barroom brawl in the movies, he did not know what would happen. Hickock was four inches taller than him and had a longer reach, but he was lightly built, not a powerful man. Murray had watched him on the ball field and lifting loads. They both knew equally well how to fight dirty by now. The Marines will make a man of you: providing a man smelled like a pig and acted like a dog. He could never forget someone was out to get him, someone with power of life and death over him.

If there was a bad duty to be drawn, Murray drew it: something heavy to load, something filthy to clean, something sticky to wade through. He was Cinderella, but where was his fairy godmother to call out the ants to help him pick grains of rice from the ashes? Or rather, where were the elephants to help him carry crates of mortars he could scarcely drag? It went on and on. It smelled more and more like blood. How much could anybody take? How often could he bow his head and pretend not to hear, pretend he did not speak English, pretend he was standing in a snowstorm on Campus Martius, the big square in Detroit where rallies were held?

The precipitating incident was no different than twenty others. Maybe the effect had been cumulative. He swallowed his rage, he held it in and felt it become pain and cold fury, and he lowered his head and blindly persisted. It was a Saturday night and there was plenty of booze flowing. He went to a movie with Jack and Slo Mo. Tiny did not approve of most movies and did not go. When they were on their way back to the rough barracks that had been their home for the last months, Tiny was sitting outside waiting for them.

"Murray, they went in your stuff and took out your letters. They're reading them and laughing."

Jack tried to catch his arm but Murray pushed past him and flung open the screen door of the barracks. Sergeant Hickock was doing the reading, to Rostrovitz and about six of the kids, all laughing and too drunk at first to notice he had arrived. Hickock noticed at once and raised his voice, adopting a falsetto version of Molly Goldberg.

"Naomi is working in the Fennimans' bakery every day after school and all day Sunday, and the baker is pronging her with his kosher salami, and me too when I drop by, right on the counter in my big hot kosher oven."

He felt ripped open. He felt scalded all down his front. That they would even touch her letters was not something he could endure, that their fat dirty fingers should touch those letters drove him crazy, that they would read and make fun of her simple hardworking life and her gentle and loving nature, worrying about everybody but herself. He had punched Hickock before he even knew he had hit him. The sergeant flew back with the force of the blow and landed with a crash on the floor behind the cot. There was complete silence for a moment before everyone began punching and pushing each other and yelling, Jack rushing in with Tiny to pull Rostrovitz off Murray.

Then Hickock stood. "Calm down, boys," he said, wiping the blood from his mouth. "Hitting your superior is one fucking long time in stockade, Jew-boy. You're going to love stockade and I'm going to love knowing you're doing hard, hard time."

Sergeant Major Reardon intervened and finally there was no court-martial, no stockade. There was punishment detail, the work Hickock had been making him do anyhow. Reardon had persuaded Hickock that since they were going to sea in two days, they ought not to send Murray up. Murray was not sure Reardon had done him a favor. Stockade was hell, but Hickock was not going to forgive him for punching him in front of everybody.

He was demoted and lost his stripe, but about that he did not give a damn. What was bad was that he was under Hickock, going into action and helpless. His violent response had improved nothing. In fact Hickock hated him more and he had forfeited the tiny bit of Reardon's protection he had. Reardon told him he had the brains of a pile of dogshit and that if they were not shipping out and going into action, he would have spent the rest of the war in stockade and pulled a dishonorable discharge.

A dishonorable meant trouble getting jobs. It meant no GI Bill, no payments to finish college. He despised himself for striking Hickock. That was what Hickock had been goading him to do, and he had fallen into the trap. He would be in stockade now, except that Reardon had stood up for him and the new looey had backed up Reardon. The Marines were running short of men and the upcoming invasion was rumored to be tough. Reardon didn't want to lose one of his experienced marines just before the battle.

He despised himself above all for striking Hickock because it was the sort of John Wayne fisticuffs that were all show and push and shove and left him worse off than before. He had fought back out of weakness, not out of strength. Now Hickock had him just where he wanted him, a marked man who was not only expendable but slated to die on whatever stinking island awaited them. Jack and Tiny and Slo Mo all kept saying he sure was lucky, but he knew he had signed his death warrant with that stupid goyischer punch.

Taps

The tension about the WASP program that had built up during the spring continued all through the summer and into the fall. Congress did not approve their militarization; instead they lost in the House by nineteen votes. When Congress came back after summer recess, the mood seemed even less open to granting the WASPs military status, but still they waited. Every official notice about logbooks or attire was received with seething hope and fear, that it would be the news that would finally resolve their status.

In late August she found a telegram waiting for her when she arrived back in Long Beach. It was a Friday night and the chatter level in the barracks was high. "Did anybody else get one of these?"

Nobody had. She was up for officer training if the WASP militarization bill went through. She could not help wishing that this would turn out to be that notification.

It was not. The Army regrets to inform you. Jeff was dead. No date was given, and no information except that he had died under fire in France.

She sat on her cot with the telegram in her lap. She had to call her father, because Jeff had put her down as next of kin to be informed. Her father wouldn't even know. It had to be a mistake. It was so vague. People didn't die like this, on a piece of yellow paper, and simply disappear. Even with her mother, there had been a body. Where was the body?

She longed for Flo so fiercely that she stood and in one stride reached Flo's cot and lay on that instead. Flo was off ferrying a P-47 East. She would not be back for three days and Bernice would be long gone by then. She had to call her father. When it came to it, she found she could not. Her hand would not take the receiver down. She could not speak to the operator. No.

Finally she sent him a telegram and then she found herself driven to walk and walk, through the hot night trying to grasp her loss. Jeff had always been her male part. For all the years after Viola died until just recently, his had been the only affection in her life. He had been her foot in the world, her window into adventure. For those years of her confinement while Jeff was wandering around the country dissatisfied and footloose, neither had formed any lasting attachment beyond each other, halves of some unreconcilable whole.

War had severed them. She had not seen him since that summer weekend in Bentham Center. . . . Did Zach know? He was in France too. She could not bring herself to write about Jeff to that London address he had her use.

Flo will never meet Jeff, she thought, and he will never meet her. That seemed to her terribly wrong, a failing in the universe. For all of the rest of her life, she was going to miss him. Now there was only Flo. She had to find in herself the courage to take hold of Flo and hold on. To make her love real. If she lost Flo, she would kill herself. It was worth any risk to keep her.

It was early October when both Flo and Bernice, plus all the other WASPs stationed at Long Beach, got an official letter from AAF Headquarters in Washington. Nobody seemed in a hurry to read the letter. Either they had their commissions, or they were about to be washed out. Bernice could not open the envelope. The other women were standing around in a similar paralysis. Finally Flo ripped her envelope and read out loud:

To All WASP:

General Arnold has directed that the WASP program be deactivated on 20 December 1944. Attached is a letter from him to each of you. . . .

Flo stopped reading.

Everybody opened the damned envelopes and yanked out the mimeographed letters. It was true, they were being forced out. They were thanked briefly by Cochran and profusely by Arnold, and told to kiss off. They could apply to the Civil Aeronautics Administration for a civilian rating on a par with their military rating, and good luck in the future.

They were still delivering planes. Bernice tried to tell herself that Congress or General Arnold would realize it was a huge mistake and that they could not be thrown away before the war was over, pushed into idleness. Flo and Bernice, like most of the other women, ran around to every aircraft manufacturing plant in Southern California looking for jobs as test pilots, but no companies were hiring. They sent their résumés to airlines. The airlines did not bother replying.

A pall of depression hung over the barracks. A few of the women were not affected, those who had other plans and knew they could not have gone on flying indefinitely. The married women whose husbands were overseas took it best. One was planning to go into business with her husband crop dusting in California's Central Valley. They had been writing back and forth about their plans for two years. She got an early discharge and went off to start arrangements, sure the war must be over by Christmas with the good news in the papers and the WASPs being sent home.

Bernice heard Flo crying at night, but she did not know what to do. She felt helpless. They wouldn't even receive the veterans benefits being talked about, preferences for jobs or help starting businesses or getting an education. They had only the money they had saved from their pay. The women at Long Beach signed a petition offering to go on flying for nothing, for a dollar a year, because they were still fiendishly busy. One of the reasons that Bernice hoped was because the fighters kept coming in, and few pilots were qualified to fly them besides the WASPs.

They knew that the head of the West Coast ferrying division had put in a special plea to Arnold on their behalf, saying that he simply could not do without the WASP pursuit pilots. Then the news filtered down: Arnold absolutely refused to grant a reprieve. The pursuit pilots had most infuriated the American Legion and Congress, for that was considered a job with too much panache for a woman. After December twentieth, no women pilots were to remain with the Army Air Corps.

A WASP newsletter appeared with job information, but mostly it contained news of what was not open. TWA sent an interviewer, offering to hire WASPs as stewardesses. Schools offered jobs as counselors. Some of the women went for interviews as air controllers and were hired.

One night when fog kept her on the East Coast after she had delivered a Mustang to Newark, she wandered the streets of Greenwich Village, searching for something that she feared did not exist. Yet now and then she saw women on the streets who eyed her as the colored nurse had long ago, women who when she looked at them, looked right back.

It was eleven that night when she found a bar full of women, although at first she was not sure all of them were female. But they were, they were. She admired the style of some: jaunty, tough. She could look like that, if she tried. She had been drinking at the bar for half an hour, nursing a beer, when a woman her own height, a little thinner in a black turtleneck and overalls, leaned on the bar next to her and asked in a low-pitched voice, "Are you lonely, honey? I haven't seen you around here before. What's the uniform? Oh, you fly planes? That's exciting. I have a sweetheart who's a WAC, but she's overseas. . . . You can call me Frankie."

Bernice went home with Frankie, not because of any instant attraction but because she had to learn what she was and how to make love to Flo. She was terrified of making a mistake, of hurting Flo. It turned out to be easy to make love with a woman. That facility astonished her. She could have figured it out if she had not been so frightened, but maybe she needed the permission to be what she was from other women like herself—just knowing that women who loved women had lives and jobs and apartments. Went on living and did not combust with pleasure and joy. She also learned what to call herself: she was a lesbian.

"The poor bastards," Flo said. She was talking about the last class of Avenger Field, who were receiving their wings on December 7 and graduating into nothing. "At least we had the life for a while. They've knocked themselves out getting through training, and for what?"

"At least they don't know what they missed," Bernice said. "We're the poor bastards. We had it all, and now we don't have a thing."

Flo looked at her reproachfully and pointedly said nothing.

Bernice hastened to add, "Except our friendship. If we don't have a future, at least we don't have a future together." She had not told Flo about her adventure in New York. Privacy did not come easily in the barracks, and she could hardly drag Flo off to a tourist court.

She still could not believe the WASPs were ending. After all, she was on a schedule that barely offered her a day off between ferrying a P-47 out and getting her butt back to grab another. As December ground toward Christmas, it seemed clear the war had hit a snag. The lines on the maps representing Allied advances became stationary. Surely a reprieve would come. The Army could not be so crazy as to throw away all the time and money spent training them. The men clamoring for her job were not yet trained to do it. If they had been good enough, they would have made it as pilots and have gone overseas long ago. They were the also-rans, and they were going to take these fast and beautiful planes from her.

It could not happen. They had done a good job. They had excelled. They were efficient, they had a better record than the men at delivering the planes. They could not be punished like this. They could not be dismissed when the need for them was glaring. President Roosevelt would step in. General Arnold would finally refuse to buckle under to the pressure. General Marshall would intervene. Somebody would see the way to a sane decision, now, at the very end.

The next time back to base, a letter in the familiar handwriting of The Professor was waiting. Bernice hesitated to open it. The disbanding had been in all the papers, and even though she had written nothing about it, he must know by now. He was going to be expecting her back in her old position doing her old tasks. "No," she said aloud, glaring at the letter. Nobody paid any attention. They were all picking up bad news in the mail every day, and none of the women thought her standing there with a letter balled in her fist talking to it was unusual behavior.

Okay, get it over with. She walked outside. It was warm and the sun smote her across the face. Traveling back and forth across the country as she did, she was never used to the winter in the East or the summer in the West. She had a series of colds, and sometimes it was painful to take up the planes with her sinuses inflamed. A minor annoyance.

She sat on a crate and read the letter, preparing to remain calm before what was going to be The Professor's infuriating assumption that she would return to Bentham Center as his live-in maid.

Dear Daughter Bernice,

I know you are very busy out there and so Gertrud and I did not think it appropriate to bother you beforehand, since the Government urges us not to take unnecessary trips these days anyhow.

Nevertheless, Gertrud and I want you to hear our good news and rejoice with us. We were married last Saturday at the chapel in St. Thomas. It was a simple ceremony, as befits two middle-aged people such as ourselves, widower and widow.

Gertrud was raised a Lutheran, but she had no objection to the Episcopal ceremony, even though St. Thomas has always tended to be somewhat high for my simple tastes. The wedding should clear up Gertrud's visa problems and our difficulty with the neighbors.

Gertrud is a very fine woman and I know you will rejoice in our happiness when you meet her. She inquires if you are planning to come home for Christmas? I told her I don't imagine you can travel all that distance, but if you do plan to do so, let us know, and Gertrud will have your room ready. She is an excellent manager and a first-rate cook. I know your brother would also have liked her.

Included in the letter was an engraved announcement of the wedding.

Bernice wandered off to the barracks, amused with herself, amused with The Professor. She was astounded that he should have remarried, almost two decades after Viola's death; but that he should marry his housekeeper seemed wholly appropriate. What she had failed to anticipate was that not only did she not want to go home, she could not. The Professor had replaced her, as the Air Corps dismissed her.

The only item in the letter she resented was the sentimental reference to Jeff. She could not imagine Jeff having rejoiced in The Professor's marriage. She could not communicate with her father about Jeff, no more after his death than during his life. He was hers, all hers, not her father's.

She did not hear from Zach. Often there were gaps of months in their correspondence. He was at war, and when he had an interlude, he would write her. She assumed that if he had heard about Jeff, he would have written her.

December nineteenth, Bernice flew her last fighter out of Long Beach. A line of planes were sitting on the runway waiting for someone to deliver them, but as of the next morning, they would go on sitting there until more pursuit pilots materialized. In Newark, she delivered her plane. Then she handed over her pistol, her parachute, her flying jacket. Toting a suitcase, she walked out the gate to hitch a ride to the train station.

————

Flo and she were lucky: they found temporary jobs near Columbus, Ohio, delivering surplus trainers that the Army was getting rid of to people all over the States. It was a stopgap, but they would be paid decent wages and they would be flying.

The first time Bernice took up the little rickety Fairchild PT-19, with its open cockpit and its tiny 175-horsepower motor, she felt like weeping. It was like riding a bicycle after driving a Ferrari. The poor little thing was open to the elements just like a bike and seemed about as speedy. It was in middling shape, at a generous estimate. She wondered how cheap these planes were going for. It had better be pretty cheap.

That made her wonder if the Army might not be disposing of something a little more useful, like maybe the C-87 Skytrain, the military version of the DC-3. In the last few months, the WASPs at her base had been allowed to learn every plane around, to give them a better shot at jobs, and both Flo and she were checked out in all available two- and four-engine planes.

Flying this wobbly little trainer was a sharp and painful comedown. At the same time, she was aware that Flo and she were among the handful of ex-WASPs still flying anything. Even Jacqueline Cochran had been offered a desk job at an airline. After this, what?

The trainers were two-seaters, but they flew them alone. Most of the planes had seen hard use. They were glanced at by a mechanic and then they were hers to deliver.

They stayed in a tourist court for the first week and a half, before they found a rooming house that would take them, sharing a twin-bedded room up on the third floor under the eaves. The room was cold, drafty and of reasonable height only in the middle. Bernice had to approach her bed at a stoop; if she wakened suddenly and sat up, she would bang her head on the rafters. If it had been possible to get laundry done in Columbus, they would have used their own linens, as those provided by their landlady consisted of grey shrouds with holes in them and towels thin enough to use as mosquito netting, should the ice age ever end: but the war ground on and the few laundries that still existed took no new customers.

With some shyness, they set up their temporary housekeeping, assigning one of the wobbly and mismatched bureaus to each, neither overburdened with clothes. How quickly Bernice had got accustomed to wearing that handsome blue uniform, and how uncomfortable and fussy by comparison she found women's clothes. She was happiest in her flying gear of voluminous overalls. She owned few dresses or skirts and resented the thought of having to spend her wages acquiring some.

The first Saturday night, Bernice bought a bottle of an unknown bourbon which was as harsh as she had suspected. With the radio turned to dance music, they were sitting together on Flo's bed drinking. How do I make a pass at another woman? Her memory of the woman in the bar did not help. She could hardly ask Flo if she were lonely. Instead, she put her arm around Flo's shoulders. "Tired?"

"Worn out," Flo said. "I want to go back West when they lay us off."

"Consider it arranged . . . How's your back? Would you like a massage?"

"I'd love one." Flo turned away from her and took off her clothes, except for her panties, and then lay facedown on the bed. Bernice started out rubbing her shoulders, her middle back. She did that for a long time, straddling Flo's hips. Her own breath sounded loud as a steam locomotive in her ears. She could not rub Flo's back all night long, but this was her opening, if it was that. Was it?

Finally she dared let her hands move down to Flo's buttocks, kneading but also caressing. Flo made a little noise in her throat. Bernice let her hand brush the soft silky thigh. Flo said nothing. Bernice stared at her curly red brown pubic hair, just visible at the hem of her panties. She realized Flo was breathing hard also. She slowly brought her hand circling on the thigh, circling, circling, tracing up the inside. She was melting herself. Flo must know she was doing something besides a massage by now, she hoped, staring at the back that lay smooth and silky and silent and without expression. Finally she let her hand brush up to the curls. Flo moved then. She slid her thighs apart. She let Bernice's hand come home.

———————

It had been a bad trip. In late February, the weather was rough. When she had landed in Cairo, Illinois, the mechanic on the ground had teased her about flying a Popsicle, because of the ice on the wings. She asked him to check the engine, because it seemed to her that it was running hot. She didn't like the way it had been acting. He said he'd look at it. Still, she was supposed to push on. She delivered as fast as she could because she knew how easily Flo and she could be replaced. If it was this bad getting a job now, what was it going to be like when the thousands of overseas pilots came home? How many of them would be seeking jobs in aviation? These rickety crates might be the last planes she was ever paid to fly. Yet she could not bear to believe that.

In the meantime, deliver the goods and deliver it on time. That would keep her in the air; that was all that would.

The next afternoon, under a lowering sky and with a smart crosswind, she was beginning a slow power descent into Lawrence, Kansas—where the plane was to be turned over to its new owner—when suddenly the engine quit cold. She was at about five hundred feet, so she had neither the time nor the space to think twice. Glancing frantically down over the side with the wind tearing her face raw, she cursed the engine. It had not been running well. She had thought shortly after takeoff that the mechanic at Cairo had done nothing to fix the problem she had noticed the day before, but she continued on her way. Why hadn't she followed up on that conversation? Why hadn't she turned back when she felt the plane not responding as it ought?

She was coming in over small fenced fields, looking frantically for a long enough area to land. Fences everyplace. Cattle pens. Houses. She had only three hundred feet of altitude left. She had to stall in over the fence of the field right in front of her, no choice, no time. What can I do, she thought, slip and fishtail? Can that save me? She was almost at the end of the field and the wheels hadn't touched. Trees ahead. I'm not going to make it. There's not enough room.

She felt a shuddering crack through her body as the tail broke through the treetops. Then there was a deafening, splintering crash and the plane hit the ground nose first. She had a moment of blankness and then she felt more than heard the silence. She was aware she was alive. Something was terribly wrong. She felt broken. Automatically she pushed her hand toward the instrument board to cut the switch. Hot oil was soaking her feet. Burning hot oil. She hurt, sharply and dully all at once. Gas was pouring out of a broken fuel line, loud raw smell in her head, in her mouth.

Her legs would not work. She must undo her safety belt. She must use her hands and push herself out, get on top of the wing. Although the engine had shut itself off in flight, the hot manifolds could still explode the gas fumes, could still start a fire. Move. She associated the numbness in her legs and the way they would not move with the burning oil she could feel. With her arms and shoulders she dragged herself out and onto the wing. She could not move but lay dangling from it. Her face was covered with blood from a scalp wound. Blood in one eye partially blinded her.

Someone was running across the field she could see from her clear eye. She tried to call to them but she could not get a sound out. Flo is going to be furious with me, she thought, but I tried to bring it down safely, I tried. I did everything I could. I still can't think of any procedure I should have tried.

Everything went black. For a moment longer she heard a boy's voice yelling. Then she lost that too.

When she woke up, it was two days later and she was in a hospital bed in Lawrence, Kansas, with a broken back, multiple lacerations, ten stitches in her skull, four broken ribs and third-degree burns on her left foot. She was alive. That would be the end of that job. She lay in her casts and contemplated the future. To Alaska, somehow, with Flo. Her wife.

DANIEL 8

White for Carriers, Black for Battleships

What Daniel had lost with Louise was the ability to make up romance, to persuade himself of his genuine and passionate interest in a woman who moved him only physically. He worked hard, the feverish long hours of the hermetic discipline of OP-20-G. In the time he had free, he cooked for himself, he read, mostly in Japanese, always striving to perfect his knowledge of the language, to extend his grasp of nuance and his vocabulary, and for exercise he rode his bicycle.

When he saw her stories offered to him as to any casual passerby in the magazines, he felt her disloyalty sharply. It was almost like reading love letters written to someone else. That was what she was doing instead of being with him; that was what she had left him for. Her account of the liberation of Paris had caused a big splash, and since then, she had been writing less behind the lines color and more straight war reporting.

The newspapers showed General MacArthur wading ashore at Red Beach in Leyte, the Philippines, through ankle deep water. Over the net of their intelligence came word of a major Japanese naval offensive, a bold but baroque plan, involving attack from three sides at once in the seas around the landing force on Leyte.

The battle started about 0300 Philippine time. By the time he arrived, signals were flooding in. The plan, as they had figured it out from Japanese decrypts, involved using Admiral Ozawa's battleworn and fake carriers as a sacrifice to draw the American force north, away from their position covering the landing force and from guarding the San Bernardino Strait that protected the approach. In the meantime a pincer operation (one arm led by Kurita, one by Nishimura) would crack down on the helpless invasion forces to wipe them out.

On the big wall map two yeomen moved markers representing Japanese ships and removed those sunk, white for aircraft carriers, black for battleships, red for cruisers, green for destroyers, yellow for submarines. From the long table where he worked, Daniel stared at the pins. An enormous number of ships were involved. It was shaping up as a critical and overwhelming confrontation. As usual they were seeing the battle in reverse from every other American involved, because they were decoding only Japanese messages.

Something strange was happening as October twenty-fourth ended and the twenty-fifth began. Kurita's Japanese fleet sailed through San Bernardino Strait and nothing impeded them. The attacks on them had tapered off and stopped. Where was Halsey's Third Fleet? Then the reports coming in from hundreds of miles to the north, from Ozawa's decoy fleet, indicated they were under heavy attack. It was composed of battleships pretending to be aircraft carriers with new decks, old carriers and carriers without planes. In spite of intelligence warnings of the Japanese plan, Halsey seemed to have sailed off in pursuit.

Fortunately, as Kurita approached the landing beaches, he reported himself again in battle. Who then was fighting the Japanese to defend the landing forces? Daniel could not figure it out. The Japanese under Kurita thought they were fighting the Third Fleet, but the Third Fleet was hundreds of miles away, according to Ozawa, whose sacrifice ships were being picked off and sunk.

The only American force that seemed to be left to oppose Kurita's force in what was shaping up as a fierce battle could not be causing any problem to the Japanese—nothing but a handful of escort carriers, destroyers and destroyer escorts. They were not even armored. They had nothing to launch at the big battleships besides a few torpedoes. They had only weapons suitable for use against human bodies and small vessels. That could not be who was fighting.

Halsey had six new battleships. When he went in pursuit of the decoys, he must have split his force and left half of it, although why hadn't they been in the strait where they were supposed to be, instead of right off the landing beaches? The battle had ceased to make sense.

The Japanese were reporting many sinkings of American vessels, but they were getting hit also. Daniel felt frustrated, in common with everyone around him, because they could not comprehend what was happening. Losses on both sides continued to mount, but the names reported did not match the names of battleships or carriers in Halsey's group. Who were the Japanese fighting? Who was defending the soldiers and marines on the beaches, wide open and vulnerable to attack from the water?

Finally Kurita sent a message that he was withdrawing. The staff at OP-20-G were critical of Kurita, and with their inevitable confusion of viewpoints, muttered that he ought to be sacked. Yamamoto, shot down at a rendezvous they had established, would never have allowed a withdrawal at such a critical point, would never have faltered in sight of his objective. Of course Kurita was recovering from dengue fever, but nonetheless, they were all for firing him.

The battle made even less sense when it was over and the facts began to establish themselves. Halsey had taken his entire fleet with him. The strike force under Kurita had been fought off by that handful of unlikely light ships under Rear Admiral Sprague. They had borne loss after loss, planes from the escort carriers continuing to make mock bombing runs long after they had run out of anything to attack with.

Only afterward did Daniel notice that toward the end of the engagement, small Zeke planes with bombs strapped under their wings had dived straight into the *Santee* and the *St. Lo.* Gradually he began to understand that this was the secret weapon that the Japanese had been referring to in their signals. OP-20-G speculations had run to new types of bombs, a Japanese version of the German inventions of the late war, jet fighters, rockets, snorkel submarines.

Now he knew: the secret weapon was the willingness of young pilots to kill themselves if they could take a ship with them. They need not be well trained: all they had to do was fly once and crash once. The planes could be minimal: they were designed for one mission without return. It was most economical and unfortunately effective. They were flying in under the radar and then climbing briefly to dive on the ship of their choice. The American ships with their wooden decks proved especially vulnerable. They had a name, these suicide pilots. Of course, Daniel thought, kamikaze: the divine wind that had saved Japan from Kublai Khan's invasion fleet. Through the winter they heard more about the glorious suicides.

The New Year came and went in a wave of slush, while Bing Crosby crooned about a white Christmas and the papers were full of the Ardennes German offensive they were calling the Battle of the Bulge. Abra and he were writing regularly. They served as safe confidants for each other, for they were not only in different countries but knew the protagonists of each other's dramas. She was claiming to be finished with Oscar, but she had written that before, then returned to the affair.

Compulsively he read Louise's articles. Often he learned more from them than from her letters. She wrote as often as Abra did, but less honestly, he thought. They were short, rushed, often breathless letters.

I had a bath this morning, a whole real even somewhat warm bath.
I cannot recall the last bath I had. Oh, yes I can. It was in Rheims

*where I also shared a bottle of wonderful champagne with my fellow
scribblers. The champagne was cold, the bath was hot, the food was real
and I slept in a bed. That has, needless to say, hardly been the case since.
Usually the food is cold, the bed is wet ground, and the alarm clock is a
shell.*

  *The page just got crumpled because Sad Sack, the company dog, sat
on it in order to get my attention. So many of the GIs pick up pets,
you'd be surprised. Animals get the worst of war. Far more of them get
slaughtered than people . . .*

From *Collier's,* he learned she had been trapped in a German encirclement
for five days during the Battle of the Bulge. If the Germans captured her, what
would they have done with her? Raped her? Shot her? As a Jew, would she be
sent to a camp? Why did she need to place herself in danger? He was convinced
her frustration in OWI had led to this vindication through fire, but suppose she
got herself killed?

When he thought of her, it was in bed, her silky skin against him, heat and
softness. Lately other images intruded from the photographs accompanying the
stories: Louise, her body lost in vast male gear, smiling warmly but diffidently
from under the nozzle of a huge piece of artillery or straddling a ruined wall
or peering out of the turret of a tank. He looked at those bizarre images and
thought, she will never come back. He felt as if she were being processed by the
war into something else, if not a corpse then a being he did not know, perhaps
did not want to know.

Abra was frank about her terror at the rockets. Perhaps the growth he noticed
in her letters was one reason Oscar had asked her to marry him. Daniel wondered why after waiting so long, she had not instantly accepted. She wrote back:

  *What is offered so grudgingly after so long is not the same thing
that might have been offered originally, fresh and exciting and warm.
Let's just say the offer is a little stale by now and I have other ideas. I'm
working on establishing my freedom, and then enjoying it.*

Once her letters had been all shallow joking and flirting, but he thought they
had both come to appreciate having each other to confide in.

Daniel noticed a marked difference between the personnel who dealt primarily with the Enigma transcripts from the German forces and those who dealt
with the Japanese codes, which he thought reflected the different attitudes of the
bulk of the Navy, engaged westward, and the bulk of the Army, engaged east-

ward. The high spirits of those oriented toward the conflict in Europe had been depressed by the German offensive in December, but were again on the rise. They looked beyond the war, speculating, planning, politicking. They retooled old ambitions and designed new ones.

Those engaged with the Pacific war watched a rising curve of resistance and losses, longer and longer battles and fiercer and more lacerating refusals to yield an inch of terrain. There were no mass surrenders. As the war moved closer to Japan, every aspect grew bloodier and the costs mounted. No one looking toward the Pacific thought they would soon be demobilized. Daniel did not rush to make new plans or revise old ones. He saw the war stretching on and on, a year, a year and a half, two years. By then, Japan might be only barren mountains and burned towns, and the United States might be poorer by a million young men. He could not share the cheerful anticipation of those oriented toward Europe. To him the prospects looked grim indeed.

NAOMI 9

Belonging

During that winter the dreams began to weaken. Only once in a while did she enter the place under the mountain where the flying bombs were made, where hunger never stopped, where cold penetrated to the bones wrapped in loose papery skin. Seldom now did she look out through Rivka's eyes at the evil glistening walls of the cave pressing in on her.

She was working in Fenniman's bakery. She dropped her books at home, grabbed a bite of lunch and hurried off to the bakery, where she put on a white smock over her school clothes. It smelled sweet and hot and yeasty all through the winter when home was always cold and drafty, not enough coal to heat the house. There were always ends and broken pieces of dough to eat or bring back.

She felt important. She had a job, just like an adult. Every Thursday she received a paycheck. She took it straight to the bank and put it in her own private account. Then she drew out her own allowance for the week and the four dollars she paid Aunt Rose. She had an account in the same bank as Ruthie and Uncle Morris and Aunt Rose.

Mostly she sold behind the counter, but Sundays when she could come in early, she helped bake. That was her favorite day. When she baked, she felt as if she were a good person. Ruthie had got her this job, and at first she had not known what to think about it. Then she decided it was good that she was not in the flat upstairs all the time with Leib and the toddler David. The Fennimans had always liked her, since that hot June when Mrs. Fenniman, Alvin and she had helped Mr. Bates.

Trudi was pregnant again. Leib said it didn't matter and had nothing to do with what he felt for Naomi. In the Bible, he said, all the important men had more than one wife. A man like himself needed more than one woman, and he needed Trudi and Naomi both. Since the weather had turned cold, the things he did with her, he did upstairs, which made Naomi nervous.

She loved Leib, she could not help loving him because he felt to her as wide as the sky. Love for him was something she lay under as Rivka toiled under her mountain. Maybe that was why she had gradually stopped dreaming of Rivka, because she belonged now to Leib and not to Rivka. As much as she had hated the dreams, she missed them. She felt disconnected. Maybe Rivka was still trying to talk to her. Maybe Rivka was dead. She would have known a year ago, known instantly, but not any longer. She had put Leib in between Rivka and herself.

His body came around her like a fist and held her hot and tight. He had kept his word and he had not yet entered her, but that was all he had not done. Each time she imagined she would say no, but when he reached for her, she could not say anything. She was bad: that was all there was to it.

Sometimes she imagined him carrying her off to be together finally someplace else, anyplace else. Yet she liked Trudi. Trudi was friendly to her, while she was deceiving Trudi. She was Trudi's secret enemy. Ruthie had made her escape easier by arranging for the bakery job. Now she had no reason to be upstairs, and stayed away from Leib as much as she could. Yet from time to time, they would be alone in the house and he would call her and she would go to him.

Alvin had a job too, loading trucks at the *Detroit News*. Neither of them had much time to hang around with the gang. Even Four Eyes had a job, off the books for a numbers runner. Only Sandy did not work; her mother thought it unladylike. She was so bored, she hung around their house whenever she could escape her mother's surveillance. Sometimes Naomi worried that Leib would go after Sandy while she was working, but he claimed not to find her attractive. Leib was busy too, studying for his real estate license. Leib and his buddy Fats said there was going to be a real estate boom when the troops came home.

Alvin and she went to the movies every Saturday night and sometimes Sunday night too, because Alvin had money in his pocket.

"Sometimes I think I should quit school," Alvin said. "Why hang around getting a diploma nobody cares about? My uncle Barney, he went to college and he ended up in a shoe store and thought he was lucky. Now he's a clerk in the Quartermaster Corps. I could make more money than he ever earned, right now, tomorrow, if I quit school."

"What does your mother say?"

"What does she ever say? Go to college. Get learning. Don't be a goyisher kopf. She doesn't see there's opportunities."

"You wouldn't have time to spend with me."

"Suppose I quit and got a good job where I'm pulling down sixty bucks a week, regular. We could get married at sixteen with parental approval. So my mother will wail and raise her hands, but I can get her to agree. And you got no parents."

"I got parents. They're just not here."

"I suppose your aunt and uncle have to sign for you, but why wouldn't they? You're not their daughter, and they'd probably be glad to have somebody else picking up the tab."

"How come you want to get married, all of a sudden? You had a fight with your mother, or what?"

"We could have our own little place. Wouldn't it be sweet? I'd go off to work and you'd be waiting for me."

"I'm not quitting the bakery, Alvin. I like the Fennimans. They like both of us too, and you know why."

Alvin looked embarrassed. "Ah, they don't remember that time. It was almost two years ago."

"Sure they do. That's why they gave me the job, with me underaged."

"Everybody's hiring kids, that's what's so great for us now."

"Besides, what makes you think we could find a place of our own? We'd just have to live with my aunt and uncle or your mother."

"The war'll be over soon. They're already laying people off at Willow Run and all those hillbillies will go back where they came from and leave plenty of room around here."

"If they're laying off people at Willow Run, and if the troops are all going to come back looking for their old jobs, where are you going to be working in six months, Alvin?"

Grimacing, he raked his hands hard through his new crew cut. She had got to him. She was disappointed. She had hoped he would have an answer. Leib would. He would say he was going to get rich off those guys coming back. Sometimes with Alvin she felt as if he was matched against a giant, but he didn't even know he was fighting anyone. She wished he had not had his hair mowed to the roots in the new fashion, because he looked dreadful, victimized. Leib had grown his hair out again, combing it back. She hated crew cuts, for they made the men look strange, raw Frankenstein monsters. Walking down the street sometimes Sandy and she stared at men and giggled, because the ears stripped naked and sticking out from the new super-short hair looked like jug handles. She begged Alvin to let his hair grow, but he wanted to be in style. He wouldn't believe she didn't like it.

Always she was careful of his feelings, because she saw Alvin as like herself, vulnerable, half grown, not quite belonging. His very virtues worked against his being able to protect her, to keep her from Leib. He was big and tough in appearance. In the street, guys looked at him and looked away. Nobody bothered her with Alvin. Under his cropped hair and his hulking bones, he was sensitive, humane, considerate. He never pushed her too hard sexually. He was afraid of hurting her, afraid of causing bad consequences. Probably that was why he wanted to marry her, to go to bed with her without feeling guilty.

Once or twice she had considered doing it with Alvin to try to stave off Leib; she would say to him, I belong to Alvin. The thought of belonging to Alvin was faintly silly. They were friends who necked. He would caress her breast lightly, lightly, as if it were a bird he feared to crush. They kissed for twenty minutes at a time, but never did she melt into the hot liquid chocolate she became with Leib. No, Alvin and she were too alike for him to excite or overawe her.

Alvin was feeling flush. His mother's birthday came in March and he bought her a sweater. At the same time, he got a present for Naomi. That Sunday night, Alvin gave her a silver bracelet with a piece of blue stone called a turquoise set in it, like a piece of Mediterranean sky stuck in the silver. She put it on and brought it in the house to show everybody, Alvin behind her. The whole family plus Leib and Trudi were downstairs listening to Edgar Bergen and Charlie McCarthy. The radio upstairs no longer worked, and nobody had the parts to fix it, so Trudi and Leib came downstairs to hear their favorite programs.

Everybody admired the bracelet. Trudi said it was a perfect color for Naomi and her complexion, and that Alvin was really unusual to be able to pick out presents. Her father had always handed her mother a twenty-dollar bill on her birthday and told her to buy herself something.

Leib seized Naomi's arm in a tight grip. "Let's see. What did you pay for it, Alvin?"

Trudi shook her head. "What a thing to ask, darling. You can't ask him that in front of his girlfriend."

"I hope you didn't pay much," Leib said, "because see, it's flawed. Too bad."

She yanked her arm from him, furious. How dare he pick on Alvin? What had he ever given her? Alvin was looking down at the rug and she knew he would have liked to cry.

"I'm no jeweler," she said. "So what do I care? It's pretty and Alvin gave it to me, and that's just perfect," she said loudly, waving her wrist around.

———

The next time Leib caught her alone, which wasn't till Thursday night, he said, "What are you doing with that kid these days, that he's giving you bracelets from the jewelry store?"

"He's nice to me, that's all. He wants to marry me."

Leib laughed. "You'll be sixteen soon, and I guess that's old enough. But you'd be a fool to marry that kid. I'm going to take care of you in style so you can have turquoises big as bowling balls."

"Leib, I don't want to tonight. Trudi's pregnant, I don't feel good about it anymore. Please, Leib. It's not right."

"It feels just fine to me." He pulled her into the bedroom. "But you're right about one thing. I'm not going to fool around with you anymore."

"Then let me go. Please, Leib. Let me go downstairs."

"If you want to be downstairs, why did you come upstairs?" Laughing, he shoved her onto the bed.

"You called me."

"Damn right. And you better come when I call. If you hadn't, I'd have come downstairs after you. What do I care, upstairs or downstairs?"

He took all his clothes off. He had never done that. She tried to think if anyone might come in. Trudi and Ruthie were at work. Uncle Morris, Aunt Rose and Sharon were out at a rally about the camps and refugees, trying to make the government let survivors into the States. Uncle Morris hesitated to take her, because he thought she shouldn't look at the photographs. She was supposed to be studying. She had not known if Leib was going out; lately he was out so often Trudi complained. Naomi had been afraid of the meeting, afraid of seeing what she had seen in her dreams.

Now Leib was kneeling over her, pulling the clothes off her, turning her round and round on the bed to shuck off her clothes and dumping them on the floor. The air felt cold. She began to cry, softly.

"Cry before, cry afterward. It's time, babydoll. I'd be a fool to delay longer, for some kid to pick the cherry I'm waiting for. You know this is right, no matter what anybody else says. You're mine. I picked you out and I'm taking you with me wherever I go." He lifted her behind and put a towel under her. "Spread your legs. I said, spread your legs, Naomi."

Although he had been putting his fingers into her since the summer, when he pushed his thing in, it burned and tore her. She cried out and then bit on the pillow to be quiet. Every thrust felt as if it was tearing her again. She was glad when he finished, and begged him not to when he then started touching her. She was too sore to come.

He brought cigarettes back to the bed, passing his over to her in the way he had that she always found flattering. She was still crying but he was feeling expansive. He sat up against the headboard smoking and talking while he caressed her shoulders and hair. "All I need is a nut. A bit of capital to start with. Fats can get something out of his old man, but not enough. The time to buy land is now, right now, while nobody wants it. In six months, they'll be putting up little houses for vets so fast, the whole landscape will change. I see it coming, but if I can't get my hands on money, it won't do me one stinking piece of good."

Naomi lay uneasily beside him, chilled and lightly bleeding. Her vagina stung. She felt sticky, dirty. Tears continued to roll out of her eyes. Now she belonged to Leib, totally. But his wife was pregnant and she did not want to hurt Trudi and what did it all mean? There was no one to ask. No one to speak to. For her, only silence and fear. "Please, I'm cold. Can I put my clothes back on?"

———

A letter arrived for her, from a French Adjutant Lev Abel. In French it told her that her father had been a very brave man and a leader in the maquis. He had fought the Germans and killed many of them, the letter said, before they had killed him finally on 20 juillet 1944 in the Montagne Noire. Her father had stayed behind with a handful of fighters to hold off the Germans so that the rest of their forces could escape and regroup. He himself was alive because of her father.

He said that he was very sorry to tell her about the death of her father and to tell her so long afterward, but he had just found her address. A journal that had been written by her sister Jacqueline had been found after the battle in such a situation that they believed that her sister had been shot by the Germans, but an exact identification had not been possible because of the condition of the body. He wished he had better news for her, but he was sending her the journal. Under the circumstances of not knowing if Jacqueline were alive or dead, he had taken the liberty of reading the journal as far as he could. He explained that in 1943, she had begun writing in code, and that he had not been able to read it after that point. However, long before Jacqueline had begun using code, she had entered in her diary the address of her sister in the United States.

He hoped she would have good news of the rest of her family. He regretted again to give her the news of her father's death, but her father had been a great fighter in the Jewish Resistance, and it had taken a tank to bring him down. She should be proud of her father and honor his memory. He had had the pleasure of serving under his command. Further, he had worked with Jacqueline, and her bravery and intelligence in tight situations were sorely missed. She had saved the lives of at least eighty Jewish children.

He ended by saying that he hoped he would meet her someday after the war and that he had a photograph of her father taken when they were all in the maquis, which he had put in the package with the journal. He hoped she would like to have this photograph of her father in remembrance.

When she had finished reading the letter, she stood and then she fainted.

When she came to, she was lying on the living room floor with her head bleeding where she had banged it on the hot air register. Aunt Rose was kneeling over her with a washcloth soaked in cold water and vinegar. Naomi lay on the floor and began to weep and did not want to get up.

Always she had hoped that in the end, even if Maman was dead, even if Rivka had died, all alone with Naomi no longer listening, Papa would still come on his motorbike and take her back into a place where she belonged. Now there was no such place. There was only Jacqueline, far far away, maybe dead too, shot down as Papa had been. Even if she wasn't shot, she was only an older sister and could not help. Jacqueline was as weak as she was.

Naomi belonged to nobody now except Leib. Not even Ruthie was here to stop her tears, for Ruthie was at work. Now she was really an orphan, and she belonged no place good.

JACQUELINE 12

Whither Thou Goest

On January the eighteenth, Jacqueline and Daniela along with fifty thousand other haeftlings were still alive to stand appel. This day was different from all the others. They could hear the Soviet artillery as they had for two weeks, each day louder, a sound that rose from the earth up into their bones. They hoped, they longed for Soviet shells as they had used to long for the Allied bombers to come. The crematoria had been blown up and black greasy ashes no longer fell. However, the machinery of death had ceased without death itself ceasing. The dying were heaped in piles or shoved into barracks and locked inside. All week the SS had been burning papers and shooting inmates who knew too much.

To the accompaniment of the usual SS chorus of curses, blows with the butt of the rifle, kicks and random shootings, they were marched out and loaded into boxcars like those that had brought them to Auschwitz. Rysia was right behind, but with the arbitrary brutality that marked their lives, Slasher pulled Rysia from them and thrust her into the next car. Their car was as crowded, as filthy as on the previous voyage, but they were all in worse shape and began to die faster. There were no children, no old people, no babies this trip. Like the last time, they had no water, no food except for a tiny bit of bread Daniela and she had secreted under their ragged grey shifts. There was less suspense, she mused, for it was all death.

She had worried about rape, unnecessarily, on her way to the camp. Apparently when the SS had come into Poland, they had raped and immediately killed many women. But why would the SS bother with the stinking starving haeftlings when they had the overfed, overstimulated SS women and their own brothels handy? No, the sexual abuse had been sublimated into total violence. The SS men and women were always stripping them on some excuse or none, always beating them across the breasts. They did not need to rape to prove their power, as they had their rifles, their pistols, their clubs, their machine guns, their dogs sicced on the women to tear their flesh. Rape must seem pallid by comparison, she thought.

"So far we've come together, Daniela," she mumbled. "Whatever happens, we must stay together."

"I will never let you out of my sight." Daniela was wedged against her, both jammed against the wall of the unheated car.

"Listen to me, 'Whither thou goest I will go, where thou stayest, I will stay. Thy people shall be my people and thy gods my gods. Where thou diest, will I die, and there will I be buried. Let the Lord punish me so, if anything but death part us.'"

"Anyplace?" Daniela managed a skeletal grin.

"Even there." Yes. To Palestine or to death.

She could not think because of the hunger, the thirst. She was sunk into a state between sleep and waking, afraid to enter sleep fully for fear she would slide down into comfortable death. Her cheek was pushed against the rough cold side of the car. Through the cracks she watched the land. For months all she had seen was black, white and shades of grey: the grey clay underfoot, the grey sky overhead, the grey of their shifts, the grey of the bread and the soup, the black uniforms of the SS, the black flakes of human soot that drifted down, the ivory of bones. In her dreams a white fog choked her.

Whenever she emerged from her cocoon state, she pressed her face to the cracks and stared at the skies, glittery cobalt so bright she had forgotten such colors existed, the dark healing green of the pines, the blue of shadows on the snow, the vermilion of the slanting rays of the low foxy sun. Crows flapped away from the train as she gloated on their glossy wings. How miraculous, to fly. Why had she never stopped to marvel at birds, how perfect in their feathers with their bright eyes and beaks, able to lift themselves and ride on the wind? Blessed birds.

Daniela too was fighting the slope toward death, prodding with her bony elbow and giving her Hebrew verbs to conjugate. Jacqueline riposted with English verbs. Do, does, did, done. They stood leaning on each other, clasped. It was no longer like holding another woman, for neither had breasts or bellies or hips except for the jutting bones that bruised the other's sharp angles in the embrace of fleshless skeletons, devoid of sex.

They stuck their fingers through the cracks and scraped frost from the side of the car. It tasted of resin and evaporated at once in the mouth, relieving the pain for a moment. Every so often the train stopped and eventually the guards opened the door and shouted for the dead to be thrown out. By the third day half the women in the car had turned to bodies left in the snow. The first time the bodies had been rolled out, she had expected the SS men to order women out to bury them, in their meticulous way of disposing at once of the dead, but they did not seem to care any longer. All along the tracks corpses were strewn. Now there was room to sit in the boxcar, avoiding the mess on the floor.

Outside it was snowing and they kept putting their fingers through the cracks to catch the flakes and eat them. She wondered which had been worse, her trip in the burning summer heat in the first crowded boxcar to Auschwitz or this in the unheated car in the frozen winter. Then her head had been full of fantasies about what they would be facing. No imagining could equal it. All her worrying had been in vain. Would she ever again see Maman or Rivka? She had survived six months of Auschwitz. Could they have survived two years of camp life? Still, her aunt had made it and Maman might too. She had that endless energy to try to make things come out, to manage. If anybody could organize a little survival, it would be Maman.

In the bitter penetrating cold her arm ached where she had broken it, but she was used to that. She stared at the trees with their needles bowing under the snow, their roots wriggling deep into the hillside among the rocks drinking the clear cool deep sweet water, the sun falling on them till sugar brewed in their tissues and their sap sang. If she could become a tree, what a splendid life. To be a tall pine on a mountaintop, free, clean.

"If I had enough to eat," she murmured against Daniela. They were both sitting now, knees drawn up, heads propped. Their feet were blocked by women's bodies roughly stacked in the center. "Then I'd never again complain about anything. To think I used to worry if people gave me a nasty look or weren't fast enough to praise me."

"And I used to worry I was too fat. I'd love to be the fattest woman in the world. I used to stare in the mirror fiddling with my nose. I used to lie awake worrying if Ari was faithful to me. What would I care?"

It was hard to feel attachment to anybody out in the world, anybody free and still human. It was hard to worry much even about Rysia in the next car. That was a different universe where different people died as slowly or as rapidly as here. If she had a cyanide pill in her tooth the way Jeff had, would she take it? When? No. Because she could not leave Daniela. Never would she leave her.

It was the fifth day when the cars stopped, the last dead were thrown out and they were ordered to get down. They were in the middle of a tall beautiful woods. "They're going to shoot us all," Daniela muttered, eyes darting to seek cover. Instead they were marched, five abreast double time along a forest track away from the stinking cars. The air was crystalline and entered her lungs like shards of ice, but her head cleared. Ahead and behind they heard volleys of shots and to the side would lie bodies of women who had stepped out of line, walked too slowly, stumbled, fallen. She was stiff after so long in the boxcar. Twice she dared stoop to snatch a handful of snow. Daniela did the same. Finally ahead they saw Rysia. She had survived. Thus far.

Then they marched between stubbly fields. In the distance through a scraggy row of trees they saw many barracks, the familiar electrified wire fencing and guard towers, the SS men, the dogs, the smell of burning flesh. A small sign read Bergen-Belsen. They had arrived.

They trotted in between huge piles of logs with snow drifted over them. As they were marched from building to building, through icy showers, stripped, shaved, she kept tripping over logs in the path. "They must do a lot of lumbering here. Do you think we could get on a work detail?"

"Lumbering?" Daniela repeated, looking where Jacqueline's gaze pointed. "Those are bodies."

This place, they discovered, featured a different form of terror and death. There was none of the mad logic of Auschwitz, where everything was used, the last ounce of strength of the slaves, women and men, to produce rubber, ammunition, fuses, to sort clothes, to tailor, to remake out of old clothes fancy new clothes for Berlin; where every death was meticulously noted in columns and every recyclable part of the person ripped from the body, the gold teeth, the hair, the fat and bones.

Here there were the beatings, the shootings, the death on the wire, the dogs that tore the flesh, the hangings, but there was far more death by typhus, by starvation. There seemed to be no gas chambers. The bodies were stacked to be burned, but the system had broken down. Some days no food was distributed at all. Children ran through the camp, the first children she had seen since Dr. Mengele had motioned them into the poison fog in Auschwitz. She was moved to what would have been tears except that she could no longer cry, seeing the little ones covered with fleas and lice even worse than the adults, running in packs among the tents where they slept on straw together, forlorn rat children playing at appell, skeletal hairless beggars.

They were set to work building barracks. After a twelve-hour day, sometimes they had soup and sometimes there was none. Even Rysia looked an ancient crone now. Typhus and diphtheria were killing everyone.

When two SS guards came in with the blockalteste and a man in a business suit who held a handkerchief to his nose, they were asked how many wanted to volunteer to work in a factory. They looked at each other. The SS was always asking for volunteers, and half the time those were the ones marched to the chambers or shot. But sometimes it was work and a chance to get fed. "We'll die here," Daniela muttered. The three of them stepped forward.

The factory turned out to be one of many in Magdeburg. They slept in a barracks housing three hundred Jewish women. Every morning they marched from the barracks through the streets of the city to the factory, while the citizens watched, turned away, spat. Regular German workmen were employed alongside them, but many had recently been taken for the home defense forces, and they were to replace them. Working with them were Jewish men, the first they had been near. One man and two women were put on each machine making casings for shells. What they dared, they spoiled.

The man on their machine looked ancient, shriveled, with his yellow teeth. They could hardly communicate because he was an Italian Jew, who spoke only Italian and Ladino, but finally they managed by Jacqueline speaking her little Spanish slowly and the man, whose name was Paolo, answering slowly in Italian. He was twenty-six. He had been a civil engineer in Milan, active in the Resistance in a minor way passing on clandestine writings. He had been scooped up with the other Jews of Milan when the Germans took over. He did not even know if his wife, his child, his family, had been arrested.

He did not talk much. The camps seemed to have turned him simple. Sometimes he smiled at them with his loose yellow teeth, but mostly he worked, as they all did as slowly as they dared, as badly as they dared. They no longer believed that if they worked well they would be spared. At the barracks at least they got ersatz coffee and a piece of bread in the morning; turnip soup and a piece of bread at night; on Sunday, one slice of spoiled sausage.

There were French workers in the factory too, mechanics who fixed the machines when they broke down, as they constantly did. They were more protected and more uppity than the other slaves. One of them always said "Bonjour" when he passed Daniela and Jacqueline. They did not dare answer unless they could mouth the words without being seen, but always she looked into his eyes.

One afternoon he was replacing a flange on the next machine. As he left, he dropped into her lap something hard. She looked down. It was an apple. She almost fainted. She could scarcely hide it quickly enough. It seemed to her the luscious aroma filled the entire factory, but she brought it back to the barracks and with the knife they had manufactured from a tiny fragment of shell casing, Daniel divided it into three equal parts. Rysia, Daniela and she each had a third of an apple. It tasted like warm weather, like flowers, like sunshine, like promises. She cut it into smaller and smaller pieces, figuring out the smallest piece she could eat without losing the flavor. After it was gone, she licked her own hands again and again for the last of the savor.

In the factory it was less cold and there were no fleas, no lice and in the latrine, running water the times they were let to go. They could drink water until they felt full. They could wash themselves quickly. In the barracks, there was no running water and only a bucket that overflowed each night in which to relieve themselves from the terrible diarrhea that sucked their strength. Something in the food caused it, but if they did not eat, they starved. On the food, they starved more slowly.

In March bombs began falling on the factory. If it happened during the day, the Germans ran for the shelters, but they were locked in. After one such bombing, she saw the crushed body of the French mechanic who had given her the apple. They hid under the machines. Mostly the ceiling fell in and the slaves were killed, while iron machines stood hilled over with rubble but otherwise undamaged. They were forced to dig them free.

March 28 in the barracks, the women celebrated Pesach without food. Rysia asked the four questions, as the youngest woman still alive. Slaves telling the story of slaves who had risen up, who had escaped. At the close, at the words *next year in Jerusalem,* Jacqueline thought of Papa, whom she had had no time to mourn, but Daniela took her hand and Rysia's in a hard grip of promise. Part the sea of iron and blood for us! Let us go.

She enjoyed the bombing, because she loved the destruction, but it meant that they got killed, not the Germans, and still the machines survived. Then one night a tremendous raid pounded the town so the ground shuddered under the barracks. The plant was finally demolished. That day they did not march from the barracks. Their soup came that evening but otherwise they were let alone. Some of their guards disappeared. Daniela, Rysia and Jacqueline talked all day of escape, although in their camp shifts, they could not get far among the hostile population. They were stuck in Germany and did not know which way to run. Nonetheless, if they saw the chance, they would bolt.

The next morning the SS men came and called them out of the barracks, lining them up for a selection. They were made to take off their shifts in the cold wind, so they could be inspected. About half of them were pushed to the sides and machine-gunned against the wall, as the rest yanked back on their shifts to the usual measure of SS blows and curses.

After the remaining women had stacked the warm and bleeding naked bodies with the wounded, the SS poured gasoline over them and set them afire. They began marching out into the streets of the city as the pungent black smoke blew into their lungs. The women were herded to the railroad, but it had been bombed. Wrecked locomotives lay on their sides. The tracks were splintered and hung crazily over craters. They were kept standing there waiting for some SS miracle. Then they were marched back, faster than before, the guards shouting mach schnell, mach schnell, all through the city again so that by evening they had reached the far suburbs.

There they were herded into a deserted warehouse and locked in. No food came. During the night it rained and they were able to catch rusty water in the makeshift bowls they always carried, through the hundreds of leaks in the corrugated roof. They were wet to their fleshless bones and cold and hungry, but at least for a few hours, they were relieved of raging thirst. In the morning they were routed out to march double time.

The days soon began to blur, because their march was senseless, numbed, bloody. All day they marched. Women fell to the ground and were shot. Women ran into the woods and were shot. Women stumbled and were clubbed to death. Every other day they had soup, never enough. At night they were locked into barns. Daniela's feet were bleeding from broken infected blisters. Rysia had lost her shoes and walked barefoot leaving bloody tracks. Jacqueline had the boots that her aunt had given her. She tried to take a pair of boots from a corpse for Daniela or Rysia, but the SS guard they called Weasel knocked her down.

They were marching east, then west, then east again, then north, she could tell by the sun. Rumor said they were being marched hundreds of kilometers to Mauthausen, where all the camp inmates not yet dead would be collected and then blown up. Daniela thought Mauthausen was in Austria, near Linz. That would be south and east, but they were sure of nothing. They set one bloody foot after the other bloody foot.

Every day there were less of them. At night she slept on her boots to keep them from being stolen, and Daniela slept on the crude wooden clogs that cut her feet bloody, but were better than nothing. One night when they were locked into a bombed church, Rysia fought another girl for the shoes from a dying girl. They were big, but she tore off part of the shift on a corpse and made bindings around her feet. None of them were afraid to touch the scrap of bread or the clothing of the dying, because they were all dying. They all had fever and diarrhea. What there was to catch, they had. The bodies fell on the earth which no longer was covered with snow, which no longer was frozen but fresh and green. Little white flowers twinkled in the grass. The grass was coming up soft and sometimes they grabbed up quick handfuls to chew. Blossoms floated and lay soft, soft, on the earth.

At night in the barns, always someone was weeping. All day they marched with a break at noon, for the guards to eat. She began eating buds from the trees, scratching at the bark. She ate flowers and leaves. One day she had weak watery shit running down her thighs from something she had eaten, but she continued to eat whatever alive she could grab. One day there was no more bread. Every day more women were shot where they fell. Now they were a shorter line and only four abreast, the SS men with rifles prodding them. They were no longer counted at morning and evening.

Daniela could not walk without help. She was burning up with fever, her skin a dull purple, her mouth open, her tongue dark. She kept passing out. She kept begging to be allowed to rest and sleep and be quiet. "My head hurts so bad I just want it to stop. I'm on fire. I have to lie down. Just for a minute. I have to."

"Beloved, you must walk. You must continue. Hear the guns," Jacqueline begged. "The war is coming to us. The war will set us free. Live a little longer. Just a little longer, my darling, my Daniela." It went on and on. Women fell. Women were shot. Women lay down and died of fever, of starvation, of exhaustion, of old injuries.

"I'm too tired. It doesn't matter anymore."

"We can escape," she muttered to Daniela, but Daniela fell. Quickly Jacqueline picked her up, hissed at Rysia to bear her between them. Daniela's feet were infected and swollen horribly. She was delirious now. "Daniela, Daniela," she begged her, chafing her hands. "Listen to the artillery. Daniela, hold on."

Between them they managed to get her to the end of the day. They were exhausted and she was unconscious. Jacqueline lay with her arms around Daniela, who was hot, too hot. Her skin felt like sticky leather.

It was grey predawn. Daniela's eyes fluttered once. "I can't. Poor children. Shma yisroel, adonai elohenu, adonai echod." Her breath shuddered out and she was still.

Jacqueline let out a great cry that ripped her open. She fell on Daniela's body. She remained there weeping until Rysia pulled her off. They were being driven out onto the road again.

They had been on the death march on the roads for at least three weeks, maybe four, maybe forever. The sound of shelling got louder and louder. Several women SS guards disappeared that evening. The next morning, the remaining guards seemed furious and clubbed two women to death. Jacqueline said to Rysia, "I'm going to break when I can. Stay with me, watch me. Go when I go. They're going to kill us all."

She watched all the morning, praising with each step her good boots and her aunt whom she had not seen since Auschwitz. The guards were nastier than usual. Women faded into the woods, but they went after them and brought them back to shoot. Explosions sounded from ahead of them on the road as well as to their right. The SS bunched up arguing. The column of ghastly dying women staggered out of the woods by a farmhouse that had been struck by a bomb or a shell. It stood with its barn behind a chest-high fence. In the road an overturned army truck still burned. A corpse in uniform lay on his back in the ditch. As everyone was pushing toward it, Jacqueline turned, grabbed at the fence, dragged herself up slicing open her knee and flung herself over. She did not even bother to look. She fell to the ground with a hard bruising jolt and ran, bent over. She ran into the barn and plunged into a haystack. She felt as if she would suffocate. Her blood roared in her ears.

Rysia had not come after her. She was briefly furious. Then she slid into a faint. She came to again hearing the harsh voices of the SS men searching. Someone must have seen her go over. They fired into the haystack and a bullet tore through her arm. She bit through her lip but did not utter a sound. The hay would absorb the blood. She heard them leaving. Again she faded out.

When she came to she was covered with blood, a high dangerous whine in her ears. Slowly she kicked her way out of the stack, crawling forward. The shadows were long toward the west. The sun was just rising. She had been unconscious since the day before. She examined her arm. The bullet had passed through. The arm was red and throbbing, but she must ignore it. She crept to the barn door and listened. There was heavy traffic on the road. She must strike across land. She had lost so much blood she could not stand. She watched the house. There seemed to be nobody in it. She watched it until the sun had climbed about a foot. She was raging with thirst. She must move or die where she sat.

Still she could not make herself move. This would not be a bad place to die, quiet and alone and free of terror for a moment, with the spring sun mellowing the mud and the buds. All the chickens had obviously been stolen already, but there might be something left to eat in the house. She must make herself crawl to the bombed house.

Then she heard her name called, just once, hoarsely, and the door of the house opened a crack. She began creeping along, dragging herself. Rysia ran on all fours like a dog and dragged her inside. Rysia had taken off her shift and put on a man's shirt and wrapped an apron around herself. She was so thin it made a complete skirt. She had been eating a jar of jam she had found, her mouth bright red with berries. She pushed it quickly toward Jacqueline, exclaiming over her arm.

Everything was fallen down and dusty within, looted already. Drawers, dishes were tossed all around the burned area where the bomb had fallen. Rysia pumped water for them to drink and then washed Jacqueline's wound.

"I thought you were dead, my Jacqueline, I thought you were dead and I was all alone in the world to die like a mouse. I couldn't find you. I looked everyplace. Where were you? I didn't know what to do. I just sat here and looked for something to eat. There was a cabbage but I ate it all, it was a little one, I'm sorry. But here are some potatoes." Rysia started to slice them with a knife she had found. "A real knife," she pointed out.

"Find one for me too. But no, we do not eat them raw. We eat them cooked. Who's on the road?"

"People running. Families with carts and horses and sometimes a truck, all fleeing. It must be something good if the Boches run from it."

"We'll make a little fire and cook the potatoes and eat them with forks like human beings. We'll boil water, and I'll clean out my wound."

"Jacqueline, I want to live. If only the Russians or the Americans would come!"

"If they don't come to us, we must go to them. We must go carefully alongside the road and run toward them. Pack up a knife for each of us so we have something to protect ourselves and what food we can and something to carry water in, and we'll set out."

"Can you travel?"

"While there's life in me, I can go toward freedom."

About noon, they began to walk through the fields, keeping the road to their right. They carried with them the four last potatoes they had found in the farmhouse, roasted with a little salt. Rysia kept kneeling to touch the ground. She broke off a buttercup and put it behind her ear. Jacqueline smiled to see it. They looked like skeletons dragging across the plowed fields, both with hair close cropped and grey, with their skulls and huge eyes and open sores, Jacqueline with her arm wrapped in a bloody shirt, with a tablecloth around her shoulders for a shawl, her grey shift still on under it and a man's woolen cap jammed on her head.

People were fleeing along the road and after a while they walked near it, because they did not see any SS men and nobody was paying attention. Alongside the road lay the bodies of women from their group, with ravens feeding on them. Also scattered along the side of the road were things the evacuating Germans had thrown away, another jar of jam, a bottle of kirsch and knapsack full of silver spoons. They kept a spoon apiece, threw the rest back and put the jar of jam and the kirsch in the knapsack, which Rysia carried. Jacqueline drank some kirsch. It burned all the way down and then she felt better. She washed her wound with it.

Now there were corpses of German soldiers and occasional civilians. Rysia took a rifle from a dead soldier, but as she did not know how to shoot and Jacqueline could not use her arm, they threw it away. Instead they kept a grenade so they could kill some SS if they came back.

They heard the sound of engines, so they hid behind a stone wall. Jacqueline lay down, letting herself slide partway into the black red swamp of nothingness.

She hoped the SS was not about to appear. Maybe she would kill herself with the knife, after she armed the grenade for Rysia to throw. She must not faint.

"It's not the Boches," Rysia said. "Are they Russians?"

Jacqueline dragged herself up. A man crossing the field toward them raised his rifle. "Non, non," she shouted, trying to stand.

"It's two old women," the soldier said to the one behind him. He was speaking English.

"We're not old, we're haeftlings, we're prisoners, Jews. She is sixteen."

The men stared at them as if they were monsters. "You speak English," the first one said. "You sound like an American."

"I'm French. She's Hungarian. I've been shot." She sat down abruptly.

"Did we shoot you?"

"No, the SS."

"I speak English too," Rysia said and abruptly began to cry. The soldier gave her a chocolate bar.

"You were prisoners? What did you do?" the second man asked. He stood back from them, frowning. He did not like their smell, perhaps.

"We were Jews. That was enough. I was in the Resistance in France."

"You just stay here. Hey, Sarge, these two old women we found, one says she's sixteen and they speak English and escaped from one of those camps. One's been shot. What'll we do with them?"

"Just leave them for the time being. Somebody'll be along. The medics can deal with it. Let's go."

"Do you have bread?" Jacqueline asked the first man as he was turning to leave. "Anything, please! Even a bite!"

He gave her a piece of hardtack and then they were off. Jacqueline lay propped against the wall like a rag doll with stuffing leaking. They both chewed the hardtack slowly. She felt like laughing, for their liberators had not seemed thrilled with them. They were free and helpless. She slid into unconsciousness. When she came to, she was being lifted into a truck full of women who looked like herself.

"Who has us?" she muttered in various languages, randomly.

"The Americans are taking us to hospital," a voice answered in Yiddish. Jacqueline reflected as she passed out again that her Yiddish had markedly improved. Someone was holding her hand in a frantic grip, so she assumed Rysia was still with her. Oh, Daniela, she thought, I did not follow you into death, not into that country, even after I promised. But maybe I am coming along behind: slowly following after you along the red road of my blood flowing out.

ABRA 10

When the Lights Come On Again

Abra had grown used to sleeping with her coat and flashlight, which the British called a torch, just beside the bed in the event a rocket bomb hit nearby, knocking out the electricity, starting a fire or demolishing the ceiling. Sergeant Farrell in the office had been trapped for eighteen hours under a stairway—which was lucky, because everything else had been smashed. He told her the darkness had been the worst of it, not knowing if he had gone blind. That had led her to keep the flashlight nearby. The V-1s had not tended to knock the power off, but the V-2s did.

She was on American rations and thus ate well, but she froze in her rooms like everybody else and washed standing in the little kitchen. This was not as hard a winter, but it was a mean dispiriting season, ice, sleet, fog the color of old newspapers seeping through her cardboard and packing crate windows which had lost their glass from blast the spring before.

Nonetheless London was no longer a black pit after dark. They were on dim-out rather than blackout. People stopped having freak accidents plunging into areaways and breaking their necks. Of rubble they had plenty. She lived in a partially demolished city, to which each day added new ruins. Still many of the rocket launching sites had been overrun, and fewer V-2s were falling lately.

With the lights partially on, London looked shabby but had survived—as had she. All through the winter she had cast her web far and wide, politicking, making friends, cultivating acquaintances, putting in time at pubs and parties. She had never formally broken off with Oscar; sometimes she still slept with him. Rather she had made herself available. She picked up an RAF pilot; she allowed an Australian tankman to seduce her. She spent a Saturday night and a Sunday with a quartermaster from Harlem with whom she had reminisced about the prewar jazz scene.

What had she found? That in truth she had lost something of her taste for random adventure, but that enough of it remained to sweeten those hours. Each of them was a log dragged across the road back. Each of them brought her further from Oscar and her long fidelity. Having had something more, she no longer confused chatter and the odd confession with good communication, but she wasn't writing off the pleasures of occasional sex without complications. She liked going after what she wanted without truly caring what each of them thought of her.

She dressed and put coins in the meter to heat water for the real coffee the Americans got, although never enough to last. She was expecting her girlfriend Beverly, an OSS imitation corporal as she was an OSS imitation second lieutenant. Inside the organization, no one paid attention to those arbitrary ranks. Her doorbell had given up in a bombing raid that had brought down much of the ceiling. When Beverly arrived, she had to stand outside and yell, something she rather enjoyed doing in her flattened western tones. Beverly came from Moscow, Idaho.

This morning, Beverly, for once protective of British feelings, confined herself to tossing bits of rubble at the boarded-up window. Abra ran down to let her in. Beverly was perched on the steps smoking. "My daddy used to tell me, only fast women smoke in public and only whores smoke on the streets. But this war has gummed that up. All girls do it, like wearing pants and going off to hotels with men. What will they do with us back in Idaho?"

"Don't you think the same thing has been going on at home? Coffee's ready. I looked for you last night, but I didn't see you."

"We were at it till midnight." Beverly yawned, loudly. "Lots of goodies coming in from those tame Jerries you sent over. But we think they may have got one of the women."

"Helga?" Abra's hand closed tight around the cup.

"No. The other one. Marlitt."

The handle sheared off in her hand. "Damn. I broke the stupid cup." Cups with handles had not been manufactured in England for years. Her stomach began to hurt. She did not feel like asking more, but she was compelled. "What makes you think she's been caught?"

"She was giving us good stuff and now nothing, all week." Beverly shrugged condolence. She was tall, big-boned and fair, with a broad plain face, flaxen hair worn shoulder length, a broad gape-toothed smile and the manner of a good old girl, who likes men and expects them to like her. She was a widow, she had told Abra the first time they had talked intimately, without ever having been a wife. She had been engaged to a pilot lost in '43 on the ball bearing runs, when a third of the planes had gone down. Since then she had refused to form strong attachments to men. "Peace comes, I'll settle down," she predicted. "No point trying till then. Just get your ass kicked hard."

Abra thought that she herself had formed no close friendships with women during her first years in London because she had not wanted to expose her long pursuit of Oscar to anyone else's cool stare. She had not wanted to sound like Djika, indomitably pursuing a course up a dead end. Now that she was free, or almost, she wanted that other gaze, a woman who would double-check her decisions and keep her from fooling herself.

It was pleasant for both of them to go off to pubs together, comfortable in each other's company, but always giving the other the room to move off if she wanted to pursue something. Abra felt as if she was coming back into shape. Beverly and she went to movies and plays, plunged into the parties Oscar found boring. He was not a partygoer. He preferred one-on-one, or dinner parties where conversation was possible. Beverly could jitterbug and had learned the rowdier English dances; they practiced together and off they went every chance they had. Abra felt as if she had dropped five years. She wrote her mother begging her to send a dress she could go dancing in, but she doubted that her mother would come up with anything useful. She wrote the same letter to Karen Sue with more hope.

Beverly set down her cup meaningfully, although carefully, considering Abra's recent mishap. "All right, girl, what are you going to do? You have to make a move soon if you're ever going to."

Several people who had worked on the German agent project had been asked if they wanted to sign on to the U.S. Strategic Bombing Survey. Preliminary work had been going on in New York for months, but as the end of the war in Europe clearly approached, they were setting up offices in London and recruiting OSS people. Oscar had been approached also, before she was. He ruminated and said no. He was scheduled to go to Paris and then as occasion let him, to Germany. He had been processing materials from the German agents.

To Abra he said, "I have a pretty good idea what's real with the bombing. When our agents got into the Ruhr and Berlin, they found everybody eating fine and services scarcely disrupted. They complained we had given them clothes too shabby for the norm. Okay, now the cities are being leveled, but I doubt if this survey will be allowed to talk about how ineffective strategic bombing has been. I don't want to get involved in a whitewash."

Now Abra sighed, thinking of Marlitt. "I'm going to tell them I'm interested. . . . Do you think they'll take me without Oscar?"

"They're taking me. I bet we'll get to Europe finally." Beverly stuck out her lower lip. "Now tell me, are you going to get on board or dillydally around until all the berths are filled?"

"I'm seeing them today. I really am."

She did not believe it even after she had done it. They could not be interested in her without Oscar. What was she, except Oscar's assistant? Then she heard informally that they were taking her. They liked her background. She felt a stiffening of pride. She could make it on her own in this world, amazingly.

When the new orders finally came down, Oscar handed them to her without a comment.

"I won't be going with you to Paris," she said lamely. Even at this late moment, some part of her wanted him to beg her.

He nodded. "For me it'll be a loss, but for you, I suspect, a gain."

"Your appraisal's inadequate. This will be my great loss too." Are we really parting so formally? She could not believe it. She felt like someone in a stage play. Surely the curtain would drop and they would walk off together, as they had for so long.

She sat with Beverly over a doled-out glass of the weak war beer trying to explain why the exchange had let her down. Beverly said, "But what do you want? Him on his knees? Lover come back to me. You walk out the door, his balls fall off, and he says, clutching himself, wow I never knew."

The major who was now a lieutenant colonel passed them on his way out, a young British soldier at his heels. He paused, nodding at Abra and grunting hello with the same slightly puzzled air he always wore when he recognized her but failed to place her.

"How do you know Our Lord God Zachary Barrington Taylor?" Beverly asked, leaning forward, elbows on the tabletop.

"I spent a night with his roommate once. Who is the bastard, besides full of himself?"

"He's a gen-you-ine hero. Popped in and out of four resistance movements. A one-man army. They worship him at SO and tell tales that would do for a Superman comic. He's also queer as a five-leafed clover."

———

She was glad that the bombing survey was set up in another building, Eisenhower's old headquarters on the square, even though she was still within two blocks of Labor Branch. She began work there in late March, with the bulk of those recruited in the States arriving in April. She was assigned to a section studying the effect of the bombing on German morale. Back in the States a war was being waged over the future of OSS, and the hallways of her old unit were fraught and buzzing with the newest victories and defeats. A lot of the battle seemed to be fought in the newspapers, as well as in Congress. Abra observed that some of her colleagues viewed the approaching end of the war as a personal disaster. They longed to continue in intelligence and looked back on their collegiate or corporate careers with a shudder.

"Do you ever think about staying in intelligence?" she asked Beverly.

"No, by the time I'm safely home, I'll have enough pub crawling and working nine A.M. to midnight. I want to see the peaks and those rolling hills. I want to ride out in the early morning with the fog sitting down in the clefts. I want my horses and my own spread."

"I don't know what I want. I admit sometimes going back to Columbia and finishing a Ph.D. sounds exasperatingly dull. But I notice we are talking less about our Fascist enemies and more about the dangerous Communists lately, and this war isn't even over. It gives me pause."

"You know, it's guys like your Lieutenant Colonel Taylor who'll go bonkers. I hear he was in insurance before the war. He's been charging all over the landscape feeling like one hell of a dude. Now he's supposed to sit at a desk and worry about actuarial tables?"

"Maybe he should have got killed instead of his friend. His friend wasn't gung ho. He was some kind of artist."

"Taylor doesn't strike me as the type that gets killed. Other people around him may die like flies, but he'll walk through the bullets. War is hell for most people, but it's heaven on wheels for some of the weird ones, have you noticed?"

Abra drained her weak beer. "But what I'm trying to figure out is if I'm one of those weird types myself. If I haven't got used to this life, to being mobilized."

"We all have, girl. We'll have to get unused."

———

Oscar had long since left London for the Continent. Roosevelt died and the future yawned suddenly more uncertain. Abra had never voted for anybody else for president; she couldn't imagine how the government could continue with the center missing. Astonishingly, she received a promotion to first lieutenant and worked the usual six-day week on the bombing survey. There was talk they would be moved to Germany. No more rockets fell. More lights went on. Every two weeks, Oscar wrote her, chattily, affectionately. She responded in kind, for her sense of style demanded she be civil. A courier brought her a bottle of Chanel Number Five along with intelligence reports.

On May Day the news came that Hitler had killed himself. There was an impromptu party at the office. The next evening while they were returning from supper at the big mess in the Grosvenor House, they heard that the BBC had just announced the surrender of the German army in Italy. Rumors about that had been endemic in OSS for several days. It was understood that Allen Dulles of OSS Switzerland had a hand in arranging the surrender.

The radio was kept on that night. It was an addiction, to hear the good news repeated and hope for more. At ten-thirty, as they were closing up for the night, Stuart Hibberd came on and announced the fall of Berlin.

"It's over!" Abra heard herself screaming. "It's over!"

"That depends," Beverly said.

"On what?"

"First, whether the Bavarian Redoubt exists, and how well defended it is. If it's anything like we've heard, it might take months or a year to take it. Second, we know Himmler launched Werewolf, an underground of sabotage and clandestine warfare." Beverly did not want to be tricked into celebrating until she knew with absolute security no bad news was going to trickle in. Abra felt she herself was more like the general population, avid for something to feel good about. The tension of waiting just built over the weekend. It was all anyone was talking about. Is the war over? Is the war finally over?

Monday everybody seemed to be milling in the streets, hanging around outside Buckingham Palace. When she got into the office, she heard that Admiral Doenitz, the putative head of a state that seemed to be nonexistent, had finally accepted the surrender terms, but still no announcement came. She had a sick feeling that something was wrong. Perhaps the SS was holed up in the Bavarian Redoubt with rockets and new secret weapons. Nobody tried to work. People drifted from office to office and building to building exchanging news and rumors stirred together.

Why didn't the radio speak, why? At six came an announcement there would be no announcement by Churchill that night. What was wrong? She had no stomach for supper. She ate a sandwich at her desk, and tried again to read the materials spread about her. At seven-forty in the evening came another announcement: tomorrow would be celebrated as Victory in Europe Day and would be a national holiday, as would be the ninth. So was it peace? What a ridiculous wimpy way to end a war.

In the morning she woke in her dank bedroom groping for her coat and her flashlight, as the familiar sounds of yet another air raid broke over her. She was enraged with disappointment. Why doesn't the fucking war end already? Enough, too much, way past too much. I want my life! She was up, into her uniform and half into her shoes before she realized that it was not bombing but thunder. She made herself coffee with dried milk and saccharin, carrying it back to bed.

She lay in the cavelike darkness of her room, imagining the streets of New

York. At home, they would be celebrating, massed in Times Square. Sometimes she missed New York, but London had become her city too—and she found the survey work fascinating. Just lately she had been given more responsibility; one of her bosses had pronounced her reports literate, their highest compliment. She had a team under her. Soon they would be going over to Germany, which ought to be interesting. In some ways, it had been a disadvantage to her career to work with Oscar, because what she had done had become all his. Now she was on her own. Her work was visible.

The rain was over and the day warm and shining when Beverly appeared in the late morning, wearing not her uniform but a carefully saved linen frock, wrinkled but summery. Beverly had sandwiches and a thermos and a bottle of St. Emilion she had inveigled from somebody just returned from France. "I thought we'd go out in the streets with more people than you ever thought existed, and have a picnic. It's party day."

The crowds were jolly and well behaved, people with children and babies and even dogs decked out with red, white and blue ribbons and rosettes and streamers, with paper hats perched on their heads, with flags on their prams and borne overhead, carried cheerfully waving in the hand. Bunting hung from the buildings. There were street musicians with violins and accordions and people who carried a cornet or a drum or a mouth organ to make a joyful noise. Others were banging on dustbin lids or old petrol drums. Groups were singing or just cheering.

They milled around with everybody else slowly circulating toward the palace where an announcement was expected. Then they drifted away. After their feet tired, they found an unoccupied patch of ground in St. James's Park and sat down for their picnic. Bells were ringing from all the churches. They saw few people drunk and none violent. For one thing, the pubs had already run out and closed. There weren't enough spirits available to get drunk.

All of London seemed as the day wore on like a perfect children's Halloween party. People had put on fancy dress or funny hats. In a little street in Chelsea a piano had been dragged outside and a community sing was going on featuring at the moment "Knees Up, Mother Brown."

The bobbies looked on with polite approval as people tore down advertisements to build bonfires. Every street had one. In one street they were doing the Lambeth walk to a phonograph on a stoop. In another, children were leading a victory parade with drums and penny whistles. On the Thames tugs were blowing the V signal. As they wandered to Piccadilly, they came on a crowd of other Americans in a conga line and joined in, swung through the streets as she remembered holding on in the whip of childhood games.

She was happy and she was melancholy. She should have seen the end of this war with Oscar, at whose side she had gone through so much of it. Where was he? Would he think of her? The odds were that he was already in Germany, where she doubted they were celebrating. Her salvation was to put regrets aside and live in the present.

When the floodlights were turned on at Buckingham Palace, at the National Gallery, Whitehall, Big Ben, people cheered and little children oohed and aahed, for they had never seen city lighting. When Beverly and she were standing on the bridge near the tower of Big Ben watching it light up, a little girl next to them began to cry in fear. "It's burning," she moaned into her mother's shoulder. "It's burning."

She and Beverly rested on the embankment as the crowds swept past, moving in amiable eddies and quick good-natured charges. Everybody had their flags out, the few remaining French, the Belgians, the Poles, the Czechs, the Americans, the Australians, the Canadians. A woman in tweeds who ought to be wilting in the summery air stopped to tie her oxford and then marched off, waving a small Union Jack. Couples were kissing, standing tightly embraced as if to join right through their clothing.

Abra was reminded of her fantasy of the fall that she had dried up sexually. All day she had been in a vague state of sexual excitement, not really wishing to pick anyone up and comfortable in Beverly's partnership, but flush with health, with ripeness, with her own young and vigorous body. Her life seemed to her a great engineering work scarcely begun. Lately more excavation than construction had occurred. She had lost a sense of her own invincibility. In that way she was no longer archetypically American.

"Look!" Beverly cried, seizing her arm.

The fireworks were beginning, the first she had seen in four years, if she did not count the sometimes eerie beauty of the real thing. As each rosette of sparks and streamers burst upon the night sky, so much less black than it had been, a joy that was mostly youth and a sense of her own self swelled her chest.

RUTHIE 10

A Killing Frost

April twelfth was a Thursday. Ruthie delivered a paper in her Problems of Families seminar, dealing with changing patterns of child rearing in first- and second-generation immigrant families, which provoked far more controversy than she had imagined. It seemed evident to her that something was lost as well as gained when old patterns gave way to new ones. Therefore she found surprising the assumption on the part of most of her classmates and her professor that such alterations were always positive.

She defended her research and challenged their assumptions, but as she worked on the line, she was still vibrating internally from the debate. How dare those people think that everything done their way was superior? That foreign patterns meant stupidity? That everybody else in the world was always wrong? That those who dressed shabbily and lived in poverty were necessarily ignorant? That only not knowing better kept Italians actively Italian, and not proper white Protestants with Smith and Jones names?

They did think they were better, to the point where the lack of agreement on the part of anybody else astonished them. Oh, she had learned something about prejudice today. Maybe she had expected the vaunted neutrality of the social sciences to prove out. They had assumed that she was the one whose prejudices were clouding her vision, that she was engaged in special pleading. High up in the back of her head a wry voice proclaimed its lack of surprise and its savage amusement, but most of her was scandalized, scalded. She wanted to believe in goodwill—why? she asked herself, frowning behind the welder's mask. She loved the mask because it not only protected her eyes from sparks and hot metal, but because it protected her from other people's eyes. Did she have a need to believe in goodwill because she was a good person or because she was a lazy person and it was less work to assume others were well intentioned?

They could see nothing but superstition in family tales—bobbe-mysehs. The past was to be wiped away like dirt. Children were to have no notion where they sprang from, the histories that led to them, the people who had lived and died to make them.

When the public-address system announced an important message, everyone paused to listen. She had a moment of hope that the war in Europe at least was over. The troops had broken into Germany already. The newsreels were full of rapid advances. Maybe the Nazis had surrendered?

"Who's dead? What did he say?" Vivian pushed back her mask, frowning.

"He says the President is dead," Ruthie repeated, staring around her. "The President?" she repeated, realizing what she had just said.

"Is that some kind of joke?" Vivian glared. "What President?"

But there was only one.

It was almost silent in the shop. The line had stopped. Somewhere a warning bell was still clanging and some piece of equipment was still moving, probably a lift. A swirl of voices rose and quieted as the PA system sputtered and then repeated the announcement. "According to The Associated Press, President Roosevelt died of a cerebral hemorrhage this afternoon at 3:55 P.M. eastern war time. I repeat, the President is dead, of a cerebral hemorrhage. We picked up the news on the radio just a few moments ago, and we called WJR to confirm, but we couldn't get through. Then we called the *Free Press*. It's true." The voice trailed off.

Vivian covered her mouth, her hand pressing hard. Ruth felt that absurd desire to smile that sometimes came to her in the midst of calamity, as if to ward off further blows, a grimace of appeasement. What would happen now? Would the war go on? Would everything grind to a halt?

She knew rationally that such a question was ridiculous. Of course the war would continue. Of course the government would continue. Who would be president? It took her a moment to remember the vice president's name. It had been Wallace, but Roosevelt had dumped him and taken a senator from Missouri to appease southerners who considered Wallace too radical, too truculent. "President Truman," she said aloud. It sounded absurd. The President was Roosevelt. The President had always been Roosevelt except way back when she was a little girl and they were hungry all the time. His was the voice of government, that rich warm cocoa voice coming out of the radio and explaining how things would be and how they ought to be. Injustice meant the President didn't know, didn't have the facts, but always, you assumed he was on your side. If he knew, he would care, and he would try to make it better.

She remembered when Sharon had discovered that Marilyn thought that voice pouring like heat from the radio was G-d speaking. Sharon and she had tried to explain the difference between President Roosevelt and G-d, but she was not sure they had succeeded.

She looked around the shop, where men and women were openly weeping and others were smiling, those tight smiles of private pleasure. With a great lurch the line started and everybody rushed back to their positions. After all, there was still a war on.

———

The last Saturday in April, they all went to the movies to see *Since You Went Away* with Robert Walker and Jennifer Jones. Naomi was there with her boyfriend Alvin, sitting off to the side. After the Donald Duck cartoon about hoarding, the newsreels came on. It was the liberation of Bergen-Belsen, one of those camps she had read about. A terrible silence settled in the theater. Living skeletons stared from eyes as big in their gaunt heads as the eyes of nocturnal monkeys, of lemurs. Creatures of starvation and misery clutched their bones together staring without hope or recognition. Hills of bodies. Bodies heaped like garbage in a vast dump. Bulldozed graves. Mountains of worn shoes.

The Metro lion was roaring when out of the corner of her eye, Ruthie saw Naomi wandering up the aisle. Alvin looked after her, uncertain. Ruthie jumped up. As she had guessed, Naomi was not going to the women's room. She staggered from the theater and stood in the street, buffeted. Ruthie took her limp arm.

"I knew they were dead," Naomi said, tears streaming down her face. She stumbled and fell against a parked car. Two men began to laugh at them, assuming Naomi was drunk. "It's my fault. I let go of her."

Naomi wasn't making sense, but Ruthie could smell the guilt. "It isn't your fault. The Germans, they're the ones who did it, and they'd have done it to you if they caught you. If your mother died in a place like that, then her last thought must have been, at least one daughter of mine is safe, may The Name be praised."

Naomi sat down on the curb, head hanging over the gutter. In a thickened voice she asked, "Why me? I'm the wrong one. I don't deserve!"

"We all deserve life. Let's go home."

Alvin was standing uneasily behind them. "What's wrong? Why did she leave?"

"Her mother and sister were taken to such a camp."

Alvin whistled. "Holy cow."

Between them they bundled Naomi to her feet. Though it was only eight o'clock, the streets were already full of drunks, a couple screaming obscenities at each other, an aged colored man with a bottle muttering about blood, a clutch of prostitutes at each streetlamp. They got her around the corner and onto the residential street, but the sight of a bed of rotten tulips upset her freshly. Naomi slid from their hands and fell to the brown grass. A killer frost the week before had withered the spring flowers as they were opening, blasting the blossoms on the fruit trees. Alvin and she hoisted Naomi up between them again and bore her weight forward, her feet sometimes taking awkward steps, sometimes dragging. They had to stop frequently to rest, for she was dead weight. "Naomi, you're not alone," Ruthie said insistently. "You have us. We're your family."

"No, not alone," Naomi repeated and laughed wildly at the same time she was still weeping. Snot ran down her face with her tears and she breathed with open mouth, looking swollen, drowned. "I hate myself! I'm the wrong one, the bad one!"

"Naomele, the Nazis aren't G-d. They don't reward or punish, they just kill. The duty you have is to live your life and be happy for your sisters and your mother and your father, live out their lives too. See for them, learn for them, love for them, have babies for them."

Ruthie felt an odd pang as she spoke. Would Murray ever return? Would he come back to her real, not made of paper, of idle words, of strange dots on the blue bulge of the globe? Would she ever bear children of her own, or would G-d punish her for her fall, her trespass, by denying her fruitfulness? She was twenty-three. At her age, Rose had borne two children; at her age, Bubeh had already given birth to her own mother, Rose. But she had no babies, no husband. Only Naomi, who was growing up much too fast.

When they got Naomi to the house, she sent Alvin home and put her to bed. Somewhere in the cupboard must be the tea Grandma used to brew for nervous troubles and crises. Valerian she had grown with its rosy flowers on high stalks among the low thyme and parsley, boneset and mint. Ruthie sniffed at the old tea tins full of homemade remedies until she found the one she thought she remembered, then brewed up the tisane for Naomi. It should be made with honey, but they had none.

Naomi grimaced at the bitter taste but drank it obediently. The tears slowed. Ruthie sat with her until finally she fell into a troubled sleep.

Now that Ruthie was working only five days a week, she had been trying to spend more time with Naomi. At first it had seemed to her that she had lots of free time, working only a forty-hour week and taking three classes, but instantly everyone around her lunged forward to fill that time. Rose needed help. Clothes had to be mended, for they wore out much faster than they could be bought. The victory garden had to be replanted, although the hardiest crops, peas and coles, had survived the frost.

Sharon wanted to talk about Marilyn and Clark; Trudi wanted to talk about her pregnancy, little David's prodigies of understanding and what Leib thought he was doing, hanging around with Fatty from that bar and Moose, who had something to do with numbers. Morris wanted her involved with him in organizing pressure to permit more refugees into the country, in changing the laws so Jews could enter. Only Leib seemed as pleased to avoid her as she was to stay away from him. That ghastly summer day seemed to have exhausted his old lust.

She was pleased she had got Naomi into the bakery. The Fennimans liked Naomi, and it kept her out of the upstairs apartment. Yet Ruthie could sense something wrong in Naomi, ever since the arrival of the letter about the death of Naomi's father and sister. Yes, Naomi was in deep mourning for her family, and that would take years to work itself out. Ruthie understood mourning. Naomi was doing well in school, taking college prep plus typing courses, as Ruthie herself had done. Would things be any better for Jews after the war? Just lately, it had seemed to her as if the spurts of hate that splashed over her at work had lessened in intensity, but that might be because the worker-preachers who talked the most against Jews and Negroes were leaving as the war economy wound down. She was determined to put Naomi through college, although she herself would be laid off soon enough, she expected.

Vivian brought that up as she drove them to work. "Anybody else been noticing all the stuff in the papers about why we ought all to go back home and hang it up in the kitchen?"

Rena said, "Are you the girl he wants to come back to? Are you smelling good these days? Are your hands smooth? Are you looking like a movie star or are you looking like a truck driver? Ha. You think the union going to stand up for us?"

"Nuts," Vivian said. "They still address us Brothers and Sirs. All these years, they aint noticed we're ladies, they won't start helping now."

"So what's going to happen to us? I got my rating. Are they going to turn us out?" Rena asked.

Ruthie felt guilty listening to the other women. She would quit happily, because there was going to be a proliferation of social work jobs and she was going to walk right into one. Vivian and Rena needed the money.

"They just can't throw away all our skills. We good. They been telling us that. They think I'm going back to scrubbing floors for fifty cents an hour, they're crazy mad. I got two kids to support, and payments to make on the mortgage."

"I got the house to pay off, three kids and my mother. I'm dying for Jake to come home, but we never had it easy on his pay," Vivian said.

In the long silence broken only by the mutterings of the old engine, each of the women contemplated her deepest worries against the war's slow anguished ending.

V-E Day came midweek, an announcement, a postponement, a verification, a more detailed announcement amid the slow relinquishment of disbelief. Detroit smelled of new leaves, of sulphur, of rain, of lilacs, of smoke. Cars honked and people flooded into the streets, but Ruthie's heart was not in it. Her war was not over. Her man was not coming home, if he was still her man. His war was heating up.

They were all standing on the sidewalk watching the cars go by tooting and waving when Ruthie saw Leib put his hand on Naomi's shoulder and squeeze hard, a proprietary grip. Naomi winced but said nothing, standing under the weight of his hand with a look on her face of resignation, of a private oblivion. Ruthie frowned and something stirred in her, something coldly suspicious. Of course Leib touched women more than he should, being the grabby type. But that look, that resignation, she did not like at all.

She turned to Rose, but Rose was holding Clark up to see while he kicked and struggled. Sharon was bending over fussing with a broken heel. They were a shabby lot, her family, all except Trudi who had on a new maternity dress of a virulent hard pink Ruthie found she could not look at long without seeing green when she shut her eyes.

Trudi noticed. Trudi was watching, and her face grew hard.

Open, Sesame

Louise found herself in a wrecked dusty world where the wind carried ashes. The people were sullen and puzzled. They did not have the gnarled cheeriness of the London poor under attack. For years these wars had brought prosperity to the homeland. They had eaten well and dressed well and dreamed in Wagnerian myths when the rest of Europe lay down in the cold, hungry. They had had losses, but away, in the distant and heroic armies. Even in the bombed cities until the last two months of the war, the people had been well dressed, well fed; the milk was delivered, the butter came to the table and the trolleys ran more or less on time.

The center of Berlin was a wasteland of rubble, of dust every breeze lifted and dashed, gritty, into the eyes and mouth. Monumental architecture created an obstacle course of fallen columns and blocks of masonry, boulders dividing the stream of pedestrians. Fresh graves marked every plot of earth, where Russian and German soldiers had fallen and been buried, where civilians had been caught in crossfire. Behind the occasional intact facade on state buildings, nothing stretched but ruins. Papers, the work of a vast bureaucracy, blew everywhere, good for nothing but starting fires. The streets had to be trodden carefully, because broken glass drifted like fallen leaves, with small dagger sharp arrows borne on the sandpaper wind.

She could not encompass it, quite. She felt as if she had passed out of the twentieth century into a barbarous medieval dance of death. Barbarossa under the mountain had waked, put on his armor and summoned his people to the glory that was Valhalla. Smashed vehicles littered the streets pockmarked by shells. The real coinage was butts. Tips were left in butts, workmen were paid in butts, butts were bartered for food. Nobody she met had ever been a Nazi, not them. That was somebody else.

For months she had traveled with the troops of the First Army, under fire with them, trapped with them in the Ardennes, crossing the Rhine with them, sometimes back with the artillery and sometimes up in the front that was a meadow, a stream, a shattered street lined with what had been apartments. She had eaten their rations and slept in her bedroll on the ground, in barns, in an empty ammunition carrier, in headquarters in farmhouses and hotels, in nurses' tents and in crates that had shipped small planes. She had come to know many of them, and she had seen some of them wounded and some of them die.

Now that bond was broken. The war was finished here. Most of her colleagues had already scrounged transportation to the Pacific, to the battle raging on Okinawa and to the expected invasion of Japan that would follow, to the fighting that continued in the Philippines, in China and Burma and Southeast Asia.

She was unwilling to follow. This had become her war and she could not change her focus. Back in Hadley, Kay was pregnant. When the bombardier, her husband, had been transferred from England to Saipan, apparently there had been the opportunity during his furlough. Louise would be on hand for the birth, but the baby was not due till January.

She had informed her tenants that she would be in New York by August first. That gave them and her plenty of time to prepare for that return, the prospect of which made her queasy. She decided not to stay on for the war crime trials in Nuremberg, although at night when she lay in bed unable to sleep, she reconsidered her decision endlessly. Would that help her encompass what she could not yet grasp? Her imagination seemed to have seized up and halted abruptly.

She slept badly and could not remember her dreams. She felt bodiless, sexless, external to her own and other lives. Her job had been to report on the war; now what was she doing? Dawdling in the presence of a vast evil-smelling corpse. She lingered in Germany filing stories on the occupation, on the German underground Himmler had founded called Werewolf, on the only remaining shtetl in Europe—the community created by surviving Jews in the former SS barracks at Bergen-Belsen—on the survivors and their ill-treatment under the occupation of the Third Army. Patton was openly anti-Semitic and called the Jews animals. She was persona non grata in Patton's domain, but she was still going to Bavaria in the morning, because she had been tipped off about a strange cave there.

She was headed by jeep with George Monroney from AP, his photographer and hers toward Eisenach, the birthplace of Bach. She had little idea what they were supposed to see there, as the approach had been mysterious. Lately OSS, fighting for its postwar life under the hostile new President, had taken to planting stories about its exploits. Both George and she were suspicious of this jaunt, but they wanted to get out of Berlin. It was no doubt OSS propaganda, but might be of interest.

The autobahns were lined with pedestrians trudging east or west, carts pulled by women or men or scrawny farm animals, townspeople, peasants and displaced persons, slave laborers and camp victims like walking dead, grey skinned and skeletal, all pouring somewhere. Most of the corpses that had strewn the land-scape when she had arrived had been buried, but here and there, the decaying body of a horse gathered ravens. In some places that stench of death she had come to know far too well hung in the air. It was true that a dead man or a dead baby smelled no different than a dead pig. No trains ran and no postal delivery existed, no government to speak of, no newspapers, no radio, no phone.

In Eisenach an OSS sergeant met them, to shepherd them on to a little town, Merkers, where the Kaiseroda Salt Mine was located, apparently their goal. He seemed extremely nervous. They passed massed tanks, artillery, armored cars. "Was there a pocket of resistance here?" she asked.

"No," said the sergeant. "Please save your questions till we're inside."

The entrance to the mine was protected as if it were Allied Headquarters; they were passed through four different portals of scrutiny before they finally entered the mine itself. George wriggled his eyebrows at her. "This had better be good. What have we got, the real Hitler?"

At last they entered the metal gates to the mountain and were met by an OSS Captain North, who led them into a small office and lectured them before a map of the mines. The rumor of the existence of a cache of Reich gold here, the captain said, wielding his stick like a professor or one accustomed to giving briefings, was heard by an OSS emissary. The information had been passed on to the OSS detachment with Patton, but at first no one could find the mine or verify the rumors.

Finally a British prisoner of war turned up who had been used by the Germans to unload and store gold. He pointed out five entrances to the mine and said he had penetrated to the 1400-foot level.

When the Americans finally entered the mine, they found—and at this point they were motioned to their feet and marched to the first large room—half a billion reichsmarks. "At prewar evaluation," the captain said, not consulting any notes, "that is approximately $125 million, cold. This was, you understand, sim-ply dumped here in transit. Now we may proceed."

A quarter of a mile into the mine, they arrived at what had been a steel vault door, now blasted through. The Army Corps of Engineers had had to open the vault, the captain explained, turning on the lights. Everything seemed to work perfectly in the mine, the elevators, the lights, the ventilation. The air was dry and cold. They had entered a vast room, about half as wide as it was long. Captain North provided the statistics: 150 feet by 75 feet. The floor was hidden by rows of numbered bags. "Seven thousand four hundred and fifty-eight," the captain announced, pleased with his own memory.

As Louise gave a tentative kick to a bag and the photographers set off their flashes, the captain continued: "Each contains gold in the form of bars or coins. Bales of paper money are stacked along the right-hand wall, please notice. The paper money amounts to two hundred seventy-five million reichsmarks, approximately sixty-eight million, six hundred thousand dollars at the prewar exchange rate. We have counted eight thousand, one hundred ninety-eight gold bars, each weighing thirty-five pounds. We have inventoried one thousand seven hundred sixty-three bags of gold coins in single denominations and seven hundred eleven bags of gold coins in denominations of five and ten. Shall we move on, gentlemen?"

I am at last a gentleman, Louise thought. In the presence of so much gold I am gilded and desexed. She marched along while her cameraman recorded. She was experiencing mild claustrophobia as they penetrated deeper into the mine. She picked up a shard of crystal, salt to her tongue but clear as glass.

Next came precious stones, many still unevaluated. Captain North was apologetic. The stones would have to await the arrival of experts from Amsterdam. In fact, the entire treasure was about to be moved to what was considered a safer place. They looked at bags of platinum, of foreign currencies, boxes holding several millions pound sterling, dies for printing bank notes. They wandered rooms that were invisible picture galleries, full of paintings, properly stored the captain hastened to inform them, statues, vases, tapestries, engravings, etchings. They passed crated work by Van Dyck, by Raphael, by Rembrandt, by Dürer. A few paintings were carefully uncrated for the photographers by two privates under the direction of a lieutenant with a museum degree, while the party proceeded deeper.

"Ali Baba and the forty thieves had nothing on the Nazis," George said. He sounded as numbed as she felt.

"Was this to bankroll Werewolf?" she asked.

"The officials of the Reichsbank in Berlin who had all this transported here claim not, but I suppose we'll never know." Captain North seemed embarrassed to admit ignorance.

"Counting is easier than making sense of it," George said. "Could we have those dimensions again?"

The captain led them to another elevator and again they plummeted through the rock. Now she definitely felt claustrophobic. Pressing on her head, the mountains were about to shift and squeeze the breath from her.

On this lower level was one sizable chamber. Captain North stood with his hands locked behind his back. "We have here one hundred eighty-nine containers bearing the name Melmer and a shipping tag labeled Deutsche Reichsbank Hauptcasse 1, Berlin. This material is diverse. For instance, in this container, we have inventoried silver trays, candlesticks, Passover cups, flatwear, two hundred forty-one pounds. These three boxes hold watches, watch chains and cases. This one is powder puff cases, silver thimbles. These are all wedding rings . . ."

"All wedding rings?" The container stood as tall as she. "Concentration camp victims?"

Captain North nodded. "Another suitcase here, dental fillings. Everything seems to have been carefully inventoried, then packed in containers, including suitcases we assume were acquired in the same manner."

"How many shipments came here?"

"We've accounted for seventy-six." Captain North looked happy when he could say something concrete. His body drew inward as he stood among the boxes and suitcases. She began to like him a little. His discomfort was human and appropriate. The numbers were something to grasp.

He was reciting an inventory: "Watches, 6748.2 pounds; tableware, 29,147.5 pounds; precious and semiprecious stones, 691 pounds; gold rings, 1069.8 pounds; gold, silver dental fillings, 3101.3 pounds. . . ."

She stopped writing. She could not take it down.

"But it wasn't all precious metals and jewelry. Children's toys, 515.9 pounds. Drawing instruments, 104.4 pounds. Postage stamps, 89.5 pounds. Spectacle frames in bone, plastic, horn or metal, 691.1 pounds. Small hand tools, 311.7 pounds. Artificial limbs, 404.5 pounds."

Louise sat abruptly on one of the suitcases, a big strong one bound with a leather belt and marked with a name which had been crossed out, like the person to whom it had belonged, who had packed it for a journey to resettlement. She had to lower her head between her knees to keep from fainting. George, the two cameramen and Captain North looked embarrassed. She was behaving inappropriately, emotionally. Things, loot, objects. Surplus value: somebody's labor, somebody's thrift, somebody's hopes and fears. On a vast scale, here was displayed a hatred of flesh and a passion for metals, of which some were supposed to be base and others noble.

The men were discomforted. They joked and wrapped the loot in statistics. As one of those intended to be robbed of her life, she could not look away. She had no choice but to contemplate what passed understanding. That everything was inventoried and labeled and accounted for made the reek of blood more nauseating. She had entered Bergen-Belsen. She had visited Buchenwald and Dora/ Nordhausen. She knew how and where this loot had been gathered. She stood again and followed them out.

Somehow she was not surprised when they returned to the brilliant sunshine and moved out through the four guard points to encounter another captain standing by the outer ring, waiting. "Hello, Oscar," she said.

He peered at her and at first she thought he was about to act out surprise, and deep within the mountain of her shock, annoyance stirred, but in fact he was only making sure it was her. "I thought for a moment you hadn't come, that you'd been replaced by a man . . ." He was still staring at her intensely, grasping the arm of her overcoat.

"Did you arrange this?" she asked.

"More or less. Come. I have to talk to you. I'll get you back to Berlin."

She was too numb to care, the cold of the salt mine in her bones. In her pocket rode the chip of salt, tears turned to stone, a worthy souvenir. All those women whose rings had been taken from their hands, dead. All the children whose toys had been carefully preserved while the children were burned. She thought, he doesn't know me any longer, he's looking for someone no longer alive. She allowed him to drag her along by the sleeve of her GI overcoat to the jeep he was using, where a corporal sat smoking and reading the comics in the *Stars and Stripes*.

They drove up farther into the mountains. He was lodged with six other OSS personnel in what had probably been someone's rustic but comfortable country retreat, complete with the heads of stags mounted in moth-eaten melancholy in the high-raftered living room.

One of the others started to challenge him, but he said, waving them off, "It's my wife."

She felt too weary to speak the words she kept saying mentally as they went up the steps, his arm propelling her from behind as if he did not trust her to follow him. Not anymore, not anymore.

She sank into a high-backed chair and he knelt and drew off her boots, a gesture that startled her. She kept her overcoat on. "Where's Abra?"

He looked blank for just a moment. "Oh, she's near Frankfurt, with the bombing survey. She had sense enough to clear out. I imagine she'll be going back to Washington soon. We're all being mustered out. OSS is rapidly disintegrating, and so am I."

"Rapidly disintegrating?" She watched him warily.

He sat on the bed, kicking off his boots, and closed his eyes for a moment, then sat up as if forcing himself to remain awake, alert. "Gloria's dead. Have you been in any of the camps?"

"I went into Buchenwald with the American troops, April eleventh, the day they liberated it. I've been to Dora once and Bergen-Belsen often. Gloria's dead?"

"She was beheaded in February at Ravensbrueck."

"You're sure."

He nodded. "I've been in the Russian Zone several times, and they were helpful. I found a survivor who saw her beheading."

"Oh." It was as if a band across her forehead snapped. "In February! So near the end." She took off her coat. "Did you write Kay?"

He nodded. "Toward the end they killed more and more." He was rubbing his eyes. Wiry white hairs glinted among the black in the sunlight that poured in the high window.

Kay would be almost as upset as his mother. "I assume there's no way to get the body back."

"I sent home a box of ashes. I felt it didn't matter whose they really were, they were killed just as she was."

She stood beside the bed, wanting to comfort him but unable to touch him. "She was in the Resistance?"

"She was part of an MI9 ratline, caught when the Germans introduced a loop and rolled it up. Arrested March of forty-four. There's no sign that she gave them names under torture."

"Somewhere under that mountain, there're probably her rings and her jewelry."

"I'm sure her rings had ceased to mean anything to her. I just keep asking, why didn't she leave when she had the chance? Why didn't she escape down the line? She knew how."

"I suppose she thought she was accomplishing more by staying."

"So many bodies, how can I mourn one excessively? But in mourning one, you mourn them all too."

She began to notice things that she had been too exhausted, too self-involved to take in. He had slashed the right lapel of his Ike field jacket, probably with a razor. When his father had died, he had refused even the slashed ribbon. He thought it was silly, she recalled. On a table near the window was a pamphlet in Hebrew and English, the Aleinu, the mourner's Kaddish. "So, Oscar, what's happening to you? You're in mourning, really? You're suddenly a Jew?"

"What else am I?" He shrugged wearily. "How else do I know how to mourn, to really mourn?"

"I take that to be rhetorical, but also probably something you're undergoing, no?"

"I don't know what I know anymore. I want to go home."

"So do I, but to what?"

"You got mad when I said you were my wife."

"No, I got mad when you said I am your wife. I was your wife."

"Was, are, will be. I have no other wife than you."

"One wife and seven hundred mistresses. It's a bit much."

"Louise, our daughter's grown up, she's having a baby she writes me. Let's get old and die together. I need you. I fucked up, I know it, I fucked up everything that counted, I know it, listen to me, I know it. But you were proud too and you wouldn't let me come back. Let me now."

"Why now?"

"Because I'm afraid. Aren't you?"

"Afraid to be alone? I've been alone."

"I've been alone too. Don't mock, Louie. I'm unsuited to being with anyone except you. It's too much work to communicate, day after day and night after night, to someone who doesn't share the same premises, the same history. I'm afraid of what people are, really. I don't have the faith I had, in reason, in progress, in science, in Marx, in civilization. There's a darkness gathered over Europe that I can never forget or cease to deal with the rest of my life. My infidelities too were a matter of pride, Louise, and now it all seems not worth shit."

"Gloria's death shocked you, so now you think you're somebody else."

"Louise, I'm exhausted. I want to go home and you're home."

"I'm not home. I *am* somebody else."

"What we are separately is less than we are together."

She sat in the chair. "It's not that easy, Oscar. You can't just say, Whoops, I made a mistake in 1940 and let's just wish it all away."

He raised his head from his hands to stare at her. He looked weary, she thought. Something was wrong—not physical. He had the same strong peasant physique she shared; what was wrong with him was what was wrong with her, an angst she had to recognize. She said, "Partly we're suffering the release of the war. We've been geared up to it, living beyond our means, physically, emotionally. Partly we're suffering the attempted murder of our whole people, and its near success. It's a wound in us."

"It's a wound in the fabric of existence," he said.

"I'm not so cosmological, and I do not advise you to be." She found herself wryly smiling, a strange smile, one that twisted her face in a way it was not used to moving—not for a long time.

"But I want to start where I have to start to make things right. How can it be right when we're both wrong? Off course. French directors, brash young cryptanalysts—"

"What did you call him?"

"He's in the Japanese code reading section. Ah, he didn't tell you. What a closemouthed young man. I still have my sources. It's not quite as secret as they'd like it to be."

"Are you done retailing my adventures?"

"I only mention that it's time for both of us to go home," he was mumbling, his eyes half closed.

"Oscar, you don't understand. I have expanded to fill the entire apartment."

"I'll take Kay's room. She won't be needing it." He was slumping, exhausted.

"We have plenty of time to argue about all that later on." She had noticed a typewriter in the next room. She arranged his head on the pillow, pulled the feather bed over him before she went to work on her story. When he woke, she must return to Berlin. She paused to make sure he was sleeping, lying on his back as if he had fallen off a roof, his mouth slightly open and his hands at his sides, palms up. Supplication.

She smiled again, wryly. She was not sure she was willing to be exactly together, but they did not seem any longer exactly apart. Yet she was as she was, a woman harder and more difficult than he had known her to be. She could not guess what was going to happen, but she was not about to become a wife.

An Extra Death

On April Fools' Day, which Murray noticed sourly was also the Christian Easter, they were loaded onto amphtracs from the huge invasion armada lying off Okinawa. Then they were moved around to the eastern side of the island, but in fact they never landed. They were supposed to create a diversion, drawing Japanese firepower from the landings on the other shore. However, the Japanese did not contest that landing, and so they merely hung around offshore, then were taken back to the transports and climbed the nets to deck again. It seemed like a military April fool's joke to Murray and Jack, who had expected to land and fight. No one had told them they were only pretend, although he was sure if they had been needed for that diversion, the bullets and the KIAs and WIAs would have been real enough. You died just as dead in a feint as in a charge. In fact their ships were attacked by kamikaze pilots and two were hit, including a big transport, the *Hinsdale,* that burned for hours.

"Suppose the officers knew it wasn't for real?" Jack wondered aloud. "Not that Hickock would tell us anything."

Hickock had spoken to Murray privately. Hickock caught him in the passageway and said, his lean face two inches from his own, "Take a good look at this island, Jew-boy. When we land the landing force, you're going to die here."

"Aye, aye, sir," Murray said, according to regulations, and stared back. He did not doubt Hickock's word, nor did he doubt his ability. There were a lot of slots you put a man in where you figured the chances of his surviving were nil. It would just be a matter of putting him into those places till he was shot or blown up. His only hope was a Hollywood wound or even a maiming wound, because as long as Hickock was alive, he would not let up.

Everybody wondered where the Jap resistance was. The 2d Division had been spared Iwo Jima, after Tarawa and Saipan, but they had heard plenty. The casualties were beyond imagining. Whole companies ceased to exist before the fight was over. Some guys thought it was going to be a piece of cake here, because the marines of the 1st and 6th divisions were reporting a walkover. By the first evening, they were in positions they weren't supposed to take until D + 4. Some of the new guys thought that the Japs had given up, but neither Jack nor Murray agreed.

"The south end," Murray said. "That's mountainous. The other end is too flat and cultivated. Not good cover." Seen from the water, Okinawa was a green and pleasant land, hilly, well built up, with cities and towns and villages, roads and beaches, rice paddies, quaint-looking stone tombs. There seemed to be no jungle, fetid and fierce, like Guadalcanal, and it was not just a volcanic heap like Iwo, or a wreath of jagged coral flung down around a lagoon, like Tarawa. It was one of those attractive islands like Saipan, and that made him shudder. However, these people did not seem eager to jump off the cliffs to get away from Americans. Perhaps they should have. As the weeks went by, civilian casualties of the heavy shelling and the crossfire were at least as high as military casualties. Out of the loudspeakers on the ships came the news that the President had died. Murray was stunned, dizzied by a huge uneasiness, wondering what kind of country he would return to. If he did.

They were still being held in reserve, although fighting began to toughen on the island. The Army was still stuck before the first Japanese lines they had come against, while the Marines had fought a brisk engagement on the Motobu Peninsula, but still the 2d Division remained on its transports, waiting. Not that they were out of the line of fire.

Every couple of days, clouds of several hundred Japanese planes came at the huge armada, which was fifteen hundred ships strong: battleships, carriers, cruisers, destroyers, troop transports, ammunition carriers, supply ships, tankers, hospital ships, ships on radar picket. The heart of the raids were the suicide pilots in simple planes not designed to return, loaded with a five-hundred-pound bomb meant to explode when the little plane plowed into the big superstructure of the American ships or crashed into the flight deck of a carrier. Those kamikazes were surrounded by a swarm of everything the Japanese had to throw: Zeros, Bettys, Juds, Oscars, to protect them and inflict damage of their own.

The raids were constant and each time they sank at least a couple of ships and damaged many more. When they hit the ammo ships, the seamen on board never had a chance. You were lucky not to be nearby and get taken out by the exploding shells and rockets. "Fucking sitting ducks," Slo Mo said. Why couldn't the brass just unload them so they could be in reserve on land? They were taking more casualties as part of that huge floating shooting gallery than they would in the fighting, all the marines said, until they saw the wounded being brought out. It was beginning to look bad. Mostly the marines blamed the doggies. They never seemed to strike and move forward, but Murray noticed he saw a lot of doggie casualties coming out.

The kamikaze pilots hit everything: they knocked out carriers, they knocked out cruisers, destroyers, LSMs and LSTs. They hit the transports, the freighters, the tankers, the hospital ships. The ships fired back downing a lot of the bastards, but there were always more swarms coming. Twelve to twenty of them might attack the same ship at once, till at least one got through, and that ship was blown out of the water.

It was perfect hell being cooped up on the transport with Hickock always watching him, finding rotten details for him, trying to goad him into striking back again. He could not move or speak without looking around cautiously, trying to fade back among the men, trying to efface himself. He stuck as tight as he could to Jack and to Slo Mo and Tiny, the survivors from Saipan. Sometimes he half wished the ship would be hit and the waiting to die be over.

On the ship, he and Jack had got tighter with Slo Mo Mazzini. He came from Akron, which struck Murray as kind of a little Detroit. Slo Mo was just as thoughtful as he had been, but he moved faster now.

Murray's nickname was King. The newer guys in the outfit couldn't figure out why Murray was called King, because he wasn't the biggest or the meanest or the bossiest, and everybody saw how much Sergeant Hickock hated his guts. Maybe somebody would explain he'd been called King David ever since he poked Sergeant Hickock in the chin, because he wouldn't take no shit about the Jews. He was still the only Jew. Every time they got a fresh load of recruits he looked them over, hoping, but no luck. Jack was Frenchy, of course, just as Tiny was six feet four.

The men on board sharpened their knives and bayonets, took apart their rifles and cleaned them, did their laundry in the sea, wrote letters, gossiped, slept, played cards, read comic books, killed time. They were taken out of the armada and sailed toward Saipan. Then they were transported right back to Okinawa, only the 8th Marines of all their division. Tough luck.

Murray was standing by a bulkhead watching Hickock, himself in shadow and Hickock full in brief sunshine between the increasingly torrential rains. The sun fell on his close-cropped blond hair that looked white, his squared-off jaw and grey eyes squinted against the rare sun: tall, lean, careful of his appearance and affecting the swashbuckling Marine style, he looked like the minor lead in a Hollywood movie about the war. Why couldn't Hickock simply take the plateful of goodies life had put in front of him and let him live in peace?

Murray resented hating Hickock, like a parasite that hollowed him out from the inside. Life was hardly sweet, but it was his own, and he had not borne it through all these bloodbaths and stinking fetid jungles and jagged coral rocks pitted with fortified caves to spill it for one man's idiot prejudice. Sometimes in dreams Hickock suddenly turned and told him he was okay. Let up. In daily life Hickock was always there, watching him the way a farmer looks at a varmint he means to kill the first day of hunting season.

The 8th Marines were finally being used, to clean out some nearby islands thought to shelter Japanese troops and wanted in any case for a radar installation to take some of the heat off the radar picket ships the kamikazes kept blowing up. On one of those islands, Ie Shima, Murray heard that the correspondent Ernie Pyle had been killed by a sniper. Their battalion was being sent into Iheya, north of Okinawa, where a scout plane had reported a Japanese position. They were all so bloody sick of being on the transport, they were pleased to be landing on anything. They were standing so many general quarters they were getting no sleep anyhow, so they might as well be fighting with land under their feet and escape the exploding ships.

Murray felt less cheerful than Jack or Slo Mo, because several times he caught Hickock's gaze on him. Tiny was depressed too: he had been sleeping badly, tormented by violent nightmares. The order to land the landing force was given at dawn and the amphtracs started for shore. They were fine until they got to the narrow beach. Then shells started landing all around them, no cover, no defilade available, nothing but the shining flash of beach with shells throwing up sand and occasional fragments of coral or metal. Nothing but shells, no machine-gun fire, no mortars. Maybe the Japs were dug in somewhere inland, back with their artillery. Hickock ordered Murray out first as they grated on bottom.

He had Slo Mo on his right and Jack on his left. Still no machine-gun or riflery fire. Ah, now it began, to the left, sweeping over them. They hit the sand, but they were exposed. A shell knocked him unconscious. He wakened deafened and groggy. When he recovered a little from the concussion, he made a dead run for the fringe of trees, expecting the machine-gun fire to start and to feel himself torn apart. He saw the bottom half of Tiny upended from the shell hole. There was no upper half. He landed in the undergrowth, Jack beside him and then Slo Mo joined them, no longer virgin in combat and not slow under fire.

"Fucking monkeys," Murray said. "Those shells are coming from out there, not from in front of us."

"Friendly fire, you're just as dead," Jack said. "Is anybody going to let them know?"

"Dig in," Murray said, "or we'll get shot by our own people. Everybody's going crazy." Indeed, from their perspective among the trees, they could see that Easy Company was shooting not at any Japanese but at them, Fox. Murray saw Sergeant Hickock standing there yelling at the men back on the beach.

Without haste and feeling stone cold, he got Hickock in the sight of his rifle. He was on the rifle range perfecting the sighting that would give him the bull's-eye. God knows how many Japs I've killed who never did anything more than get drafted and try to stay alive. Now I'm going to kill one for me and mine. He took careful aim as if he were trying for a sharpshooting medal. The shells were landing on the beach. The screams of the dying came faintly to his injured ears. Only Jack lay with him in the shallow foxhole they had dug and only Jack saw what he was doing. Slo Mo was dug in ten feet over. Still he could not shoot. Hickock's face leaning into him. "Take a good look at this island, Jew-boy." His Molly Goldberg imitation reading Ruthie's letters. He looked at Jack.

Jack looked back at him steadily. Murray turned toward Hickock and pulled the trigger. Hickock dropped to his knees and then fell forward. Murray had hit the bull's-eye. "Come on," he said to Jack, "you and Slo Mo get the fuck inland. I'm going to find Sergeant Reardon and make sure he knows it's us and not the Japs. I got the dirty suspicion there's not two Japs on this island. Somebody's got to radio those ships."

In fact there were no enemies present. Except themselves.

The second week in June they were landed on Okinawa to relieve the 1st and 6th divisions, what was left of them. In some companies, there were three men surviving. They could smell the line as they came up to it. It was trench warfare Okinawa-style and the whole front stank like a backed-up toilet. It had been raining for weeks and the mud they slogged through was compounded of earth, of blood, of maggots, of bits of metal and burnt detritus, of shit and garbage. It was June but the trees were bare, stripped by the shelling.

The Japanese had an immense amount of artillery. Seventy thousand men on one side and fifty on the other had been bearing down on a strip of land about five miles wide, a barren but wet moon of rocks and mud, heavily cratered. Burnt tanks littered every hillside, for the tankmen had taken as bad a beating as the infantry.

When they collapsed for a rest, they were told that their provisions, their food, their water had been landed four miles overland on the beach, but that in between were the Japanese. They were told if they wanted their rations and their water, they had better start fighting.

The Marines always viewed the Army with a cold eye, for to them it looked fat, oversupplied, overcautious, with too many people behind the line in proportion to those on the line. The Army was rich in equipment, always hauling trucks, jeeps, half-tracks, vast tonnages of supplies and mechanics and subarmies of clerks with them. The Marines had a few tanks with them, some artillery, and that was about it.

"I'm glad they kept us out on the LST so long, getting crazy and playing poker, because I'm sure pleased that we missed Sugar Loaf and Chocolate Drop and all those fun places," Slo Mo said.

"You may be slow, but you aint stupid," Jack said. They saw the guys they were replacing, dazed and battered zombies. They looked as if they were cattle marching to the slaughterhouse instead of away from it. Life was not always sweet after a battle, Murray thought; if it was a bad enough battle and you lost enough people around you, close to you, living could seem pointless. Murray was now a corporal again; he had been given a stripe back, credited with figuring out the carnage on the islet was from their own side. He was promoted for making it through the rain of friendly fire to Reardon, before Easy and Fox finished each other off. He thought his stripe was a peculiar award for shooting his sergeant, but he was not about to complain.

They camped that night in a tomb. They had learned quickly to take cover in the tombs from the constant shelling and the equally constant rain. The Okinawans kept their ancestors in coral block huts built into the hillsides, with entrances shaped like vaginas, for the dead were returned to the womb of earth. Surrounded by little stone walls, they would not stand up to a direct hit, but offered protection from blast and shrapnel. In fact, the Okinawans used them as shelter from typhoons. The three of them moved the big blue urns of the dead outside and crawled in. It was close but the fresh air gradually filtered in, such as it was. Murray thought the polluted air on Okinawa could give a bad day in Detroit serious competition.

Jack lay near the door reading a Captain Marvel comic book. The captain was fighting the Nazis still—two months ago's comics. The day the war in Europe had ended, all the ships fired three rounds into the Jap positions to celebrate. It meant little to them.

"Maybe we'll get some help invading Japan, which is going to be like Iwo Jima and Saipan and Tarawa and this bloody muck all balled together," Murray speculated.

"Or maybe it means they'll let those guys go home and grab all the jobs and all the women while we keep doing this one foot at a time for the next five years." Slo Mo sounded depressed. "They say the Japs plan to arm women and babies, and everyone of them'll kill themselves trying to kill us."

How long does anybody have to do this? Murray asked himself. How long? Outside, not too near, there was a scream. Infiltrating Japs. Either a marine or a Japanese infantryman had just been knifed. Murray shifted to a more comfortable position. One reason he could not keep himself from hating the Japanese, no matter how hard he tried to tell himself that it was not the Japanese who were killing Jews, and that all armies fought dirty, and that they were amazingly brave and tough, was that they kept him from sleeping. They never seemed to lie down at night and go to sleep the way they ought to. No, all night they were infiltrating the lines, slitting marines' throats in their foxholes, sometimes drinking and working themselves up for a suicide charge. Why didn't they just lie down and sleep and fight tomorrow? If only they would leave the nights alone and let him sleep, every other night, even just one night in three.

He waited for Sergeant Hickock to rise before him, but Sergeant Hickock didn't put in his appearance. Instead when he was trying to sleep, he found himself haunted not by the man he had killed but by those he had been unable to save, the kids who had died beside him, the kids who had bled to death before they could be carried back to battalion aid, the kids instantly blown apart. He was haunted by Tiny and by Harvey, who died in his head again and again. Hickock was simply gone, and he could not find regret in himself. He had killed he had no idea how many hundred men including thirty-odd at once with a barrel of gasoline thrown into a cave on Saipan and lit; they had died horribly. He felt worse about them than about Hickock. He had killed countless men and one. It was a cosmic joke.

He realized he could probably kill anybody, except his buddies. The only emotions he seemed to feel any longer were loyalty to them, brute fear and sometimes anger, and then once in a while, relief. Relief that he was alive. Relief when they could eat something hot and sleep through a night. Relief when the shells finally, finally stopped for an hour. That shell on Iheya had left him with impaired hearing in the left ear. Would it ever come back? Relief that Hickock was gone. The Marines had taught him to kill well and efficiently and without thinking, and he had done so. If Jack thought the worse of him for it, he never said a word. Murray trusted Jack, he had trusted him with his life a thousand times and he would trust him a thousand more.

The incoming mail was heavy that night. They heard one coming, the swish and then a great thud that shook that tomb but no explosion. They looked at each other, waiting to die. Murray mumbled that maybe it was time delay, but nothing happened. Just at dawn they crawled out. There it was, a .90 millimeter, stuck in the mud halfway. The mud was so deep it hadn't exploded, or else it was a dud. Jack crossed himself. Murray could only stare at it. One of the clichés the movies liked was there were no atheists in foxholes, but he had completely lost his faith. Any world like this had no god, that much was clear. The only lord was death. Jack prayed for them, but Murray could not. His sky was empty except for kamikazes and fighters and lobbed shells.

They had flamethrowers, and each tank proceeded with a group of riflemen around it. The tank commander stuck his head out. "Okay, Mac, I'm set up for flamethrowing, but don't you go leaving me on my lonesome when the Japs pop out of their caves with satchel charges."

"Hang loose," Sergeant Zeeland said. "We're sticking to you like fleas to a fat puppy. We're your shadows." He put Murray on the BAR.

They passed the night's KIAs stacked up wrapped in their ponchos, only their boondockers sticking out, anonymous as any other parcels. Jack looked at him from his almost black eyes and he looked back with the same recognition. As they were lying behind the wall of a tomb shooting at another tomb, a runner checking on positions told them that General Buckner had been killed by coral fragments from a shell. Slo Mo was impressed. "Some battle, when generals get killed."

"You know, you're getting more talkative," Murray said to him.

"Is that bad?" Slo Mo already had that hollow-eyed half-dead staring look of too much combat. They all looked like that.

"Watch it." Shells coming in on them. The concussion struck them and Murray found blood on his face.

"I saw High Pockets rubbing dirt in his shrapnel wound to get it infected," Jack said. "That's one way out."

Murray thought of the stack of bodies, ponchos with boondockers stuck out. That was the other. He shrugged. "Hey, the tanker wants to move on up there."

"What's his hurry?" Jack asked, but he got ready to move out.

"When we get up by that smashed tree, watch to your right," Murray warned Slo Mo, and then he went out at a crouch. What he felt was scared, and what he felt was that Jack was to his right and Slo Mo was to his left and that was all there was to count on in the world.

JACQUELINE 13

Tunneling

It was the last day of April when Jacqueline came to and stayed conscious. She was in a clean high hospital bed in a ward with sunlight pouring in. When she asked about Rysia, the nurse did not know who she meant. All the patients in her ward were from one or another camp. Some had undergone amputations and many had contracted typhus. She had had a bad infection. "They almost took off your arm," the nurse said in a funny kind of American English Jacqueline had trouble understanding. It came out like, "Theyee most took off ya ahm."

She touched herself, counting, all there but weak, weak. The nurse told her she was in Bad Nauheim in Germany, which frightened her, but the hospital had been taken over by the Americans.

The nurse was rattling on: "But you responded real nice to the penicillin which I bet you never did hear of before, and that's what saved your arm and your life, so aren't you lucky? You weighed exactly seventy-one pounds when they brought you in here, honey, and you don't weigh a whole lot more now, but we're going to fatten you up."

Jacqueline had no idea how seventy-one pounds translated into kilograms—it sounded heavy—but she was still skeletal. With great effort she sat up, while the nurse, who she saw was redheaded and freckled, plumped up the pillows behind her and brought her milk to drink. Jacqueline had not tasted milk in four years. It was thick and rich like liquid ice cream. Sitting up made her heart pound.

"Oh, you had typhus too, but not as bad as most of them."

She began to look around the ward. Some women were raging with fever, some amputees and some just lying there, grey skeletons under sheets.

When the nurse had gone away, the woman in the next bed spoke to her in Yiddish. She said that she had been in Gross Rosen. She came from Austria and did not know how it would be to go back. The Austrian government would not give any help to Jews, because it said they had only been racially and not politically oppressed, and UNRRA (United Nations Relief and Rehabilitation Administration) would not help Austrian Jews because they were not citizens of any UN country. She felt afraid to go back, afraid of hatred, afraid that nothing was left of her home, her family. "I had a daughter three," she said, a shriveled woman of indeterminate age with great gaps in her teeth, "and I sent her into hiding with a farm family in forty-one. I want to find her, but I can't get any help."

A daughter of three. The woman might be in her twenties. Jacqueline wondered what she herself looked like. When the nurse came back, she asked for a mirror. "Honeybun, you been mighty sick. Is your hair brown?"

Jacqueline nodded.

"It's beginning to come back that way."

In the mirror she saw a skull. "Is that me?" she cried. A gaunt old man looked back, with grey hair three centimeters long and light brown in the last half centimeter. The eyes were enormous. The flesh was hung on the bones, blotchy with an odd purplish cast.

Jacqueline began to live from meal to meal. She was always hungry, although eating was hard work. She had an appetite that her body seemed fitted around, a cavernous demand to be fed. The nurse began surreptitiously bringing her leftovers that others had not finished, for in the ward many were still dying. She ate everything. There was chicken, dried beef in sauce, fried fish. Sometimes they had ice cream. Often they had canned fruit. She had not tasted anything sweet in a year, except for the jam just after she was shot. She felt a little ashamed, but she could not refuse anything. She felt as if her stomach were in her throat, voracious, screaming, a baby just reborn.

Every morning when she woke, she was back in the camp. Then she lay with her eyes shut tight feeling the sheets, and that reassured her. Here it was clean and no blockalteste screamed, beating on the sluggards, no shots rang out, no clubs drummed on flesh. She ate and she slept and she had nightmares, from which she woke soaked and shivering. She was sullen, she was angry, she was terrified. When she heard German voices in the hall, she tried to get out of the bed to run, but crashed to her knees, too weak.

She did not mind the American doctor, but when the German doctor came, she turned her face to the wall. The orderlies were German and played mean tricks on the patients. They would take the little mirror the nurse had given her and place it beyond her reach. They laughed at the woman who always wept. They pretended not to understand the German of the woman in the next bed. Then the orderly found a cache of bread she was hiding in her mattress and threw it out. Jacqueline was furious. That was her little food bank, bread she had saved from every day, in case the next day there was none. In the camp if you could save a little bread, you might live. That day the nurse came into the ward and yelled at the top of her lungs to all the patients that the war in Europe was over. Most of them lay and stared at her. Their war would never be over.

When she closed her eyes she saw women lined up for the winter appel in their grey shifts and ill-fitting clogs standing under the sleet while the SS counted them once, twice, again, again, while the woman beside her dropped and was clubbed to death in the snow. She smelled the burning flesh in her nostrils. She saw the open glazed eyes of those dead in the morning, worked to death, used up. She saw the smear on the wall that was the brains of a child dashed to death by a grinning guard. She saw the blood pouring from the severed breast of a woman with a dog set on her, tearing now at her throat. That was real. This was an unplace, among unpeople. The nurse had told Jacqueline her name many times, but she could not remember, for the nurse was a trick, a smile in the air like the Cheshire cat in *Alice*.

She began to stand. She wanted the mirror the orderly had hidden. She wanted to go to the bathroom alone, when *she* wanted to. She could only walk holding on to the side of the bed and then the next bed. Sometimes she fell. Soon she could go all the way past five beds to the bathroom. Once there she could use a toilet and flush it and then run the water and run it some more, drink as much water as she wanted and wash her face and sponge herself clean. Soon she was allowed to take a bath. She cried in the bath, her tears running into the warm water. She had little breasts again, like a twelve-year-old, the breasts of Rivka. That was why she was crying. Maybe Maman and Rivka were still alive. She had to get well and leave.

When she awoke the next morning, her stomach hurt. The pain wakened her and she had soiled herself. She had wet the bed. No, blood. For a moment she was frightened and then she realized she was getting the first period she had had since October. She wept again. Now she seemed to cry every few hours. The redheaded nurse carried a glass bottle into the ward with lilacs in it. Their scent made more tears flow. She had turned to salt water: a small spring behind a rock, that was her.

One day the redheaded nurse brought her a lipstick and powder to use. "Now, fix yourself up. You're getting a visitor. The night nurse tells me he came too late last night, and he said he'd come back this afternoon."

"A man?" For a moment she thought of Jeff, but he had died in Toulouse; then of her father, but he had been killed on the Montagne Noire. Who would be here trying to see her? Henri? That was another life; he had had quite enough of her before she had moved out and disappeared under a name he did not know. All the people she cared about were dead. Only she had incontinently survived.

Her face with the makeup was a woman's face, the face of an exotic terribly thin model under chopped hair, a little browner now, strange in its striation, tipped with silver like a fancy fur coat.

"Vous êtes Jacqueline Lévy-Monot?" the man boomed out, still several beds away. In French he went on: "You were with Daniela Rubin?"

Oh, she knew him now. How could she not? She had been looking at his picture for years. He had lost that sleepy schoolboy look he had worn in the picture, even though Daniela had told her that when it was taken, he had already fought in Spain. When he reached her bedside, the words jolted out of her, without forethought or volition. "She's dead! I couldn't save her, she's dead! All the way we came from Auschwitz to Bergen-Belsen to Magdeburg. Then she died on the road, in the death march. She would not get up. She had typhus. We carried her two days, Rysia and I, between us, but then she lay down and died before morning. It was so cold. Her feet were bleeding, infected. The clogs they gave us did that. We were used up, rags. We'd been starved too long."

He sat down by the side of the bed. "I'm Ari Katz. I was engaged to Daniela."

"I know, that's why I told you. I know from the photo of you she always had by her, until they took that too from her."

"When did she die?"

"Just before we escaped, Rysia and me. After she was dead, then I decided to escape. They were going to kill us all. They shot me then."

"I've been trying to find her. I couldn't stop hoping. Twice I saw someone who looked like her, once on the roadside, once in Bergen-Belsen."

"How did you get here? Daniela only knew you had gone over the mountains to Spain. . . . I used to take children over the Pyrénées. I was called Gingembre." It was hard to remember that she had had names and she had done things she chose to do, once.

"You were Gingembre?" He frowned with surprise. "You're sure?"

That seemed such a ridiculous thing to say that she laughed. It hurt. She did not know when she had last laughed. "Back when I was alive. Of course I'm sure."

He held out his hand to shake. "Everybody back in Toulouse thinks you are dead. They found your diary, your rifle and a body."

"I am," she said. "We all are."

"No," he said. "We're not dead. We're not even defeated. It is all only beginning."

She turned her face away from him and did not answer. How dare this man who was tanned and well fed and healthy and wearing clean clothes tell her she was not dead. She would not look at him or speak to him. After a while he said, "I'll see you tomorrow."

Still when he came the next day, she was sitting on the edge of her bed. She refused the nurse's cosmetics but would have dressed if she had anything to put on. "Bonjour, Jacqueline," he greeted her. "My name is Ari. Ari Katz." As if she seemed simpleminded to him and he must start over.

"What uniform is that?" He was some sort of sergeant.

"I was in the Second Armored Division, in reconnaissance, under General Leclerc. Oh, you mean—the French army. We get the uniforms from the Americans, and just stick our own caps on. Basically now I'm working with the JDC—trying to help Jews in the camps get into Palestine."

"Would you see what you can find out about my mother and sister? They were deported from Drancy in December of 1942. I'll write down their names for you. . . . I would like to get out of here, but I have no clothes."

He squinted at her. "I'm inept at estimating sizes. Do you know what you take?"

"Not anymore. I'm half the weight I was." She had an idea. "Let me see if the nurse has a measuring tape."

The redheaded nurse measured her and they wrote the numbers down for Ari. When he was leaving, he said, "I won't be able to get back for at least a week."

She decided she had presumed too much, asking him so many favors. She returned to her sulk, but the problem was that now she felt as if she were being wicked lying on the bed. After a day in fetal position, she got up and began walking to and fro. If only she had clothing. She spoke about her problem to the redheaded nurse, whose name was Betty Jo. Betty Jo said she would see what she could do. That day, Jacqueline forced herself to walk down a flight of steps, although she had to sit twice, and then back up, when she had to rest four times. An hour later, she tried it again.

Betty Jo collected a pink wool sweater with only two holes in it; a flowered blue scarf; a new slip in white satin that Betty Jo explained was a present sent one of the nurses and too small for her. Betty Jo also brought her a pair of drawers she had purchased, laid in tissue paper in a box. With her new little breasts, she could manage without a brassiere, if only she could get a skirt. Betty Jo brought her a torn blanket and a needle and thread and scissors. She sat on a chair at the end of the ward sewing herself a skirt. Soon it would be warm for the clothing she was producing, but it seemed to her the height of luxury to be too warm, to be overdressed, rather than shivering in the snow in a thin shift.

When she had finished, her skirt was scarcely elegant, for Jacqueline had never been handy with sewing, but it was wearable. She dressed herself, put the scarf over her hair and walked slowly but steadily to look at herself in the bathroom mirror. She could only see herself from the waist up, but she looked like a person. She liked the scarf because she had seen photographs of women shaved for sleeping with Germans and did not want anyone to think that was what had happened to her hair.

She would not let herself return to bed, except to rest between excursions, except to sleep. She slept badly, but she ate whatever she could get. It seemed to her she could go on eating all day, that she was never full, that she never would be full. Now she could walk down the two flights of steps to the ground floor, only resting between flights, and after she sat for five minutes, climb up. She still cringed when she heard German spoken. She pretended she did not understand it. In truth, her throat closed and she could not answer. Sometimes she found herself backed against the wall, trying to flatten herself out of existence. It was hard to overcome the habit of cowering, of never meeting a gaze. She had been a piece too long, a slave, a number.

She had given Ari up long before he returned. She was dressed and helping Betty Jo talk to patients, translating from Yiddish and French. Yiddish always made her think of Daniela, and somehow thinking of Daniela made Ari appear behind her.

"You look much better," he told her. "I have a present for you." He held out a box.

She did not equivocate but tore it open. It was a blue and white summer dress. Perhaps it was an ordinary dress, she told herself, but holding it in her hands, clean, crisp, fresh, dainty, she wanted to embrace it. She ran at once to put it on. Now she had enough strength to climb up on the toilet seat, so she could see more of herself in the mirror, headless with the dress hanging on her gauntness, but a woman, a person, a human being. She was wearing the slippers the hospital had given her, and she had still the boots from her aunt Esther. She lacked normal shoes, she lacked stockings, she had only one set of drawers and no brassiere, but she could escape if she had to. She could pass in the street.

She came back slowly toward the bed, uncertain why she felt suddenly frightened. Betty Jo and Ari fussed about her, but she stood stiffly inside her new dress. Then Ari took her arm. "Let's go out. The sun's shining, the day is beautiful. Let's walk in the hospital garden."

She went down the steps with him, carefully, slowly, but as they approached the door to the outside, she found herself pulling away. "No!" Her heart was racing in her chest, shaking her.

"Jacqueline, you must go out. You can't stay in the hospital much longer. If that nurse wasn't protecting you, you'd be thrown out."

He had his hand through her arm and he was tugging her relentlessly along. Now the door was opening and now she was passing out into the mild humid air. It was extremely bright and much too big, all around her from every direction attacking. It had no boundaries, no walls, only vast air over her head and space exploding outward. She drew in, clutched, unable to breathe. She shut her eyes and listened. Birds, traffic passing, someone shouting monotonously upstairs in the mental ward, the multitudinous busy rushing sound of leaves purling in a breeze.

She opened her eyes and followed him to a bench. The sun laid its hand on her face. She blinked and blinked. "Why did you come back? Why are you so good to me?" The leaves were two thirds opened, soft and vulnerable on the linden trees and the beeches. Along the wall a row of fat peonies were in bloom, white and pink.

"You were her best friend. You're all that's left of her."

"Daniela was nothing like me. She was a far better person. She was gentler and braver and she had real faith. She was a good Jew. I'm an indifferent Jew."

"I have one piece of bad news for you."

She covered her eyes. "They're dead?"

"Your mother died at Dora/Nordhausen. Your sister we haven't been able to trace yet. We know she was in the Tunnel at Dora, working on V-2 rockets. A huge underground factory there employed slave labor."

Maman gone, never another chance. For a long while she could not speak, grieving and also furious with him for telling her, for being there, for being so vivid and healthy. No, it was herself who should not be alive, with those she loved murdered. Yet not all were proven dead. Rivka might have survived, like her. She sat up. "I want to leave here. I have to find both my sisters. In the battle at Montagne Noire, Daniela and I were trying to slip through the Boche encirclement when they caught us. I threw away the ID I had, my Luger, my journal, with my other sister's address in America. . . . I'll need money. Is there work around here?"

"What languages do you speak?"

"Good English, fair Yiddish, scanty Hebrew, some Spanish and German."

"The Americans in Frankfurt will hire you, if your English is good enough."

"I'll go to them and try." She stood. "As soon as possible. Can you help me?"

Ari beamed, clasping her hand. "I'll try to get you an appointment tomorrow."

"Please!" It was time to act. Time to crawl outside. Yes.

DANIEL 9

Lost and Found

One activity at work that pleased Daniel was turning up two experts in seashells who knew so much about the beaches of Okinawa that the younger, in his late sixties, was flown out to the Pacific to help with invasion decisions. Everything else during the months of the fighting on Okinawa proved harrowing, for the casualties on both sides mounted until they were enormous, including the highest losses the Navy had ever sustained, and dreadful killing and maiming among the Army and Marine infantry. It left little reason to celebrate in OP-20-G, when the last of the major dug-in knots of Japanese soldiers were annihilated by flamethrowers and napalm or spent themselves in suicide charges, when the deaths finally dropped to a few a day from snipers and pockets of isolated resistance. It was a victory without pleasure, trailing intimations of disaster on an almost incomprehensible scale.

The mood grew grim among the codebreakers, because while Daniel was aware peace feelers and Japanese declarations of the necessity to end the war were coming in through the broken Purple diplomatic codes, the radio traffic of the Japanese army and navy revealed the same willingness to die by individual act and en masse, the same belief in the beauty and honor of flaming suicide. There would be three million troops defending Japan, besides the volunteers, the civilian brigades, the irregulars. Anticipated Allied casualties of a million were commonly predicted.

VE-Day had meant little to Daniel. Abra wrote him from Bad Nauheim in Germany every four or five days. He was amused by both of them, conducting their disguised courtship through the mails, writing not love letters but documents designed to demonstrate to the other how lovable each was, how warm, how witty, how knowing, how altogether irresistible. At the same time, he viewed her as entirely capable of keeping him on hold, then returning with a new lover in tow. After all, he was still writing Louise regularly, and if she did suddenly show up in Washington, he did not know what he would do.

July was sweltering. Several days the temperature rose in the high nineties and they were sent home, but mostly it rained. They decoded a telegram from a former Japanese prime minister to the Japanese ambassador in Moscow. "His Majesty is extremely anxious to terminate the war as soon as possible, being deeply concerned that further hostilities will only aggravate the untold miseries of the millions and millions of innocent men and women in the countries at war. Should, however, the United States and Great Britain insist on unconditional surrender, Japan would be forced to fight to the bitter end." The invasion preparations continued. "Unconditional surrender" had been repeated so many times that Truman must feel he could not relinquish it for fear of political repercussions.

July 28, a B-26 named "Old John Feather Merchant" left Bedford Air Force Base near Boston and crashed into the Empire State Building, hitting the seventy-seventh floor and killing twenty office workers and its crew on impact. The building caught fire, elevators plunged to the bottom of their shafts. Watching the newsreel, Daniel thought it a taste of bombing for New Yorkers.

The next day the radio reported a new kind of bomb had been dropped on Hiroshima and had wiped out the entire center of that city. OP-20-G seethed with speculation. The papers had mentioned the equivalent of twenty thousand tons of TNT. Nobody had the faintest notion what that entailed, but it was some big bomb and bound to bring home to the Japanese government that it was time to end the war while something was still standing. Daniel envisioned a struggle within that government between the forces of death and the forces for life, between idealized suicide, the cherry blossoms that lasted such a short time and represented to the Japanese the beauty of the samurai, and the sturdy peasant virtue of survival. In the meantime, the Soviet Union declared war on the Japanese, who had been begging the Soviets to make peace for Japan with the Western powers. Another atomic bomb was dropped on Nagasaki. On August 14, the Japanese government announced its surrender. The emperor spoke on radio for the first time to his people. The word "surrender" was never used, but the meaning was clear enough.

Daniel was on duty when the message came in. Everybody jumped up and ran to embrace each other. "It's over!" Daniel heard himself shouting. A yeoman threw a vast pile of decodes in the air, although they would have to be picked up. Within the hour, sirens were going off, bells tolling, cars leaning on their horns, a joyous raw cacophony. By his immense relief, Daniel could gauge how frightening he had found the prospect of invading a Japan bent on dying honorably in battle to the last possible casualty on both sides. The Japanese would learn to live under their first defeat and their culture would be the richer and earthier for it. Hundreds of thousands of young Americans would not die. He had never experienced peace as an adult: a life he could choose instead of a war that shaped or smashed.

OP-20-G could not take the time off to join in the mass orgy that shook Washington, because they had to monitor the communications to and from the Japanese troops. It was not certain that all commanders or all kamikaze pilots would obey the emperor. Indeed some flew to commit ritual suicide with their planes. An attempted military coup in Tokyo failed.

It was a time of too rapid decompression. Daniel wished he could join the excited people who stormed the White House fence and snake-danced on the grounds. Ann went into mourning and would not speak to anyone, for she had just had a telegram. When her father was released from camp and returned to his home, he was beaten to death by a mob. Ann submitted her resignation. Daniel went to the aunt's house, but Ann was gone, her aunt would not say where. He wondered if she had fled to her Japanese relatives, whenever they had gone from camp.

He got an infuriating letter from Louise. It contained not one word of love, not a word of plans for them together, but instead it presented him with a big fat problem.

Dearest Daniel,

Conditions in the refugee camps are dreadful. Generally the Americans vastly prefer the Germans, who after all are clean, tidy, efficient and wonderful at running things, including camps. In some cases, they have put the same guards back in charge, or others like them. On the other hand, they find the slave laborers and concentration camp inmates dirty, odd-looking, sick, disgusting and apt to whine. When they talk about Jewish DPs infiltrating Germany and Austria, they sound just like the Nazis.

Now, this is very important. I have located your aunt, Esther Balaban. She is only thirty-one, although she looks years older at the moment. Still, with a little flesh on her bones and the color coming back in her hair, she is looking better every day. She is an amazing woman, with immense powers of endurance—obviously, for she survived two years of Auschwitz and a year before that in the Lodz ghetto.

Esther wants to come to the United States. Her husband, your

uncle, was killed in the ghetto, shot down in the street. Her children
were gassed at Auschwitz. She alone has survived from your family
in Kozienice. This woman does not belong behind barbed wire. I am
enclosing a brief letter from her. She is learning English rapidly. Either
you yourself or your parents should immediately write to her and begin
the process of sponsoring her to enter.

The enabling legislation is . . .

Who the hell had asked Louise to go looking for obscure relatives? He groaned with vexation. He had a powerful urge to tear the letter into forty pieces, but he did not want to feel that guilty. That evening, he called his parents. He explained that Louise was a war correspondent he had met in Washington. He felt distant from her. His father remembered Esther only as a neighbor's child, but responded at once. "Eli's wife," he kept saying, "Eli's wife wants to come to us. How did he die? And the children? All dead? All the children dead?" His father would take over the process, obviously. Daniel wrote a brief note to Louise to that effect, wondering why she was still in Europe instead of returning swiftly as she had promised, hoping that she would read the words of his note as coldly as he intended them.

Abra was on her way back to the States. She had to decide whether to continue on to Japan with the reconstituted bombing survey. OP-20-G would be reduced to a minor operation soon. Those proficient in Japanese were invited to interview for the bombing survey in Japan. Daniel signed up.

Since he was eighteen, it had been in his mind to return to China when he could, and he had never quite abandoned that goal. By now, however, his Japanese was far better than his Chinese. The civil war in China appeared to be heating up, which could make travel difficult. In any event, Tokyo was a lot closer to Shanghai than Washington was.

His fellow workers gossiped over plans. Some decoders and translators went off to Colorado to study Russian. What they were training for was clear, but Daniel was not interested. Although he had proved to be an able cryptanalyst, he did not want to spend the rest of his life doing things he could mention to no one. No, the Japanese language was the route he was going to choose. There would be a desperate need for Americans who spoke, read and wrote Japanese. He suspected he had a career, although what it would be remained a mystery.

Perhaps he would end up in his uncle's soap business in Shanghai. Perhaps he would be the company representative in Japan. Perhaps he would work with the government of the Occupation. He would go along with the bombing survey and improvise his way from there. It should all prove fascinating.

As he went out to National to meet Abra's plane, he wondered where she figured in his plans. The night before he had dreamed about her. They had been walking and came to a hut, where they had immediately taken off their clothes and melted into bed. But when he lay over her, she had become Ann.

Did he fear disappointment? He had cared strongly for only one woman, Louise. As his correspondence with Abra had been growing longer and meatier, his letters to and from Louise had been trailing off. She had sent only a postcard in response to his last cold letter, from Exeter in England, saying that she expected to be heading back to the States next week. Probably she was in New York right now, but she had not called him. He would not forgive her.

Certainly he had no idea what there really was between Abra and himself, other than a lot of paper and ink. Her plane taxied in for a landing and now the stairs were wheeled out and passengers began to shuffle off. He saw her climbing down. She hurried along, talking with another young woman from the DC-4. He was standing on the observation platform, but Abra did not glance up. Both women seemed exhausted, sticking together, carrying duffle bags and parcels and wearing dusty and slept-in WAC uniforms. She looked older, certainly more angular, not quite as pretty as he had remembered, but that long-legged stride, at once colty and sexy, was good as ever. The other woman was also blond, broader faced and broader in the shoulders and beam than Abra.

He knew it would take her a while to get through the controls, so he ambled downstairs and found a bench facing the door she would have to exit. His lust was back, surprisingly. He had listened to reels of nonsense from her about Oscar, and he must not let that start again. He felt quite clearly that yes, he had been waiting for her these past months, but did she know that?

He yawned with boredom and vexation. The room was heavy with old smoke and stank of something rancid and mechanical. Finally Abra burst through the door with the other woman, and as Daniel stood, a white-haired man in a cowboy hat and fancy tooled boots rose from a nearby bench and bellowed, "Beverly!" He made a dead run at Abra, but it was the other woman he embraced, almost knocking Abra aside.

As a policy decision, Daniel seized Abra at the same time and kissed her, having decided while waiting to alter their relationship from the first instant. Caught off balance or off guard, she lurched against him, lay passive a moment and then kissed him back. The duffle bag fell against his leg. He did not intend to prolong a public scene, so he stood back while he was only beginning to realize that he was enormously enjoying touching her. She felt sparer than Louise, strong, wiry, but fleshy enough. He hoped, he prayed, there would be a taxi. There wasn't, but the white-haired man with Beverly in tow caught up with them outside. "My daughter tells me you're that Abra she kept writing us about." Introductions all around. "Yep, I was a dollar-a-year man, helping out with their problems around here, but I'm going back. Only waiting around this stinkhole to fetch my daughter home. Can we give you a ride?"

He had a limousine waiting. Daniel piled in beside the driver, while Abra got in back with Beverly and her father. Daniel gave his address. "My old apartment," Abra cried out. "Of course." He was sure she remembered it was his now, but perhaps she thought he meant to stay upstairs. Beverly was peering at him. She kept asking him questions about what he did. He gave his usual disengaging answers, dropping the fact that he might be joining the bombing survey as if it were still only a possibility.

"That's great," Abra said. "I've just about decided to do that myself. I can't think of anything else I'm dying to do. Look at how lush everything is. Look at all the people. Everybody's got new clothes. Have you noticed how fat people are? Everything seems so . . . obscenely untouched."

When he got her inside, she threw herself on Louise's couch. Her face looked suddenly blank. "I've been traveling for three days. For three days! My head is full of roaring, the floor is lurching under me. I have a bellyache, a headache, I'm filth and I don't know who or where or what I am or why."

"I'm going to run you a bath." He had procured a bottle of dreadful rum, which he mixed with cola to make it palatable. He put ice in from the little refrigerator Louise had finagled for the kitchen and handed it to Abra, sitting on the couch beside her while the bath filled.

"Don't touch me till I've had my bath," she warned, laughing. "I smell like an airplane people have used badly."

"Are you hungry?"

"I think *maybe*. I'm so confused I don't even know. I must be hungry. Mustn't I?" She shut herself into the bathroom to undress, taking her drink and her heavy duffle bag with her. Two days ago, he had removed the last vestiges of Louise's tenure from the bathroom, the bedroom, the kitchen—that is the last vestiges Abra might be able to identify. That morning, he had laid in a stock of edibles. Be prepared. He made sandwiches and put out potato salad and cole slaw from the delicatessen. He stood back, surveyed his table and admired the bronze and gold chrysanthemums he had bought. His mind told him that floating chrysanthemums was the term the Japanese used for a certain type of mass kamikaze attack. He sat down in the living room and waited.

When she came out of the bathroom wearing, not her uniform, not a fresh dress, but her old peach satin robe he remembered catching a glimpse of in the days when she had been his downstairs neighbor, he smiled with relief. Even though she was drying her hair in a towel and looking shy, standing on one foot in his living room, she would have got dressed if her intention was to keep him at bay. "My things are all so shabby," she murmured, looking down at herself. "My hair was filthy."

"Everything is shabby but you yourself." He rose and came toward her. "In Japan, we'll get you a beautiful silk kimono the color of the blue of your eyes." He put his hands on her shoulders and the robe slipped. "Are you very hungry? I've set out lunch."

"My hair is wet. You don't mind?"

"I don't care at all." He wondered if he should try to pick her up and carry her to the bedroom, but she was smiling and instead gave him her hand. She looked happy, relieved, a sudden shimmering of high spirits in her face that made her twice as attractive. She had not been sure of him either, he realized. She was naked under the robe and suddenly his clothes felt thick on him, suffocating. He had to tear them off, which he began to do as he stumbled beside her toward the bedroom and his bed.

Some Changes Made

Bernice and Flo were living in a tiny drafty house in San Francisco, near the wharfs where local fishing boats tied up. A spur for loading freight cars ran under their window. When the wind blew from the ocean, they smelled the chocolate factory in the next block. When the wind blew from the Bay, they smelled the tomato cannery to that side. When the wind blew from the north, they smelled fish. Their neighborhood was lively, housing Chinese, returned Japanese, Italians, colored people, Mexicans and queers, mostly male but a few like themselves. The little house wasn't cheap—nothing was.

After the fliers began to come back from the war, Flo had been laid off. They did not belong to the 52-20 club, which was what veterans called unemployment; they got no unemployment and no benefits. Bernice still limped a little, but her broken back had healed well and she did not care about the scars so long as Flo did not care. Before they had settled in San Francisco, she had taken a boat north and bummed around coastal Alaska in male dress, exploring the possibilities. She had found the land spectacular and the economy booming, a frontier. On her return, she got a job as a secretary in the offices of a small airline. Flo worked in a cannery. Friday and Saturday nights they went to Mona's, where they could dance together, at ease in the company of other women who were couples too. Bernice dressed butch then. She liked to. She felt as if she was handsomer in male drag than she had ever been in women's, and besides, it established who they were. It said she wasn't available to men, and that she had a right to Flo and could keep her.

One weekend after Bernice helped a male couple move, she borrowed their truck and took Flo out into the country, to Yosemite. The man in the office called her mister. "Evening, mister." Just for the hell of it, she signed them into the tourist cabin as man and wife. Then she lay in the rickety bed stewing. She had the credentials for a job, if only she were Mr. Coates and not Miss Coates, she had the experience. It would be so damned easy. Sometimes she imagined trying to pass herself off as her brother, pretending she was Jeffrey Coates.

It was not that she felt like a man, even in male clothes. With Flo, she sensed her own female power flowing out and returning to her. She felt her mother in herself, Viola's warm strength; she knew herself loved and gathered into female tenderness that she had missed and lacked and always, always wanted. She felt more of a woman, not less.

Neither of them was making much, although they saved whatever they could for their big ever receding plans. She saw old dyke couples in the bar, who both reassured and worried her. They gave her hope that two women could make a viable couple, flourish in their mutual love in spite of what society told them. Unless one or the other had money, she could also see long years of bare survival ahead of them, working-class dykes in marginal jobs who could playact at power and autonomy only in Mona's twilit world.

Maybe it was well the WASP had not been militarized. Lately some women had been coming by who had been open about their sexual relationships all through the war in the WAC and nobody had ever bothered them. Now with peace came witch hunts. Lesbians were called in for questioning, arrested, dishonorably discharged.

After Jeff's body was shipped back, Bernice went home for his reburial. She wanted passionately to take Flo along, but they did not dare. Bentham Center looked a little shabbier from lack of paint, although on the edge of town little pastel cupcakes of houses were being turned out in rows of tracts where there had been farms. The Garfinkle horse pasture was surveyed and staked for houses to come.

She slept in her old room, hung with Jeff's paintings. A French adjutant Lev Abel had written them a kind letter in French about what a hero Jeff had been and how he had died helping to liberate France. Lev Abel said he had known Jeff personally and that he had been very brave and had many friends among the resistance fighters, who all missed him sorely. He wrote too that Jeff had spoken often of settling near Toulouse after the war, and that he was sorry that Jeff should not enjoy the fruits of victory and the good life they all hoped would come with the peace.

Bernice had hoped that Zach would be at the reburial, but only a letter arrived. He sent condolences from Indochina. The OSS had awarded Jeff a posthumous medal. It was buried with him in the little cemetery about a third of the way up Jumpers Mountain.

Bernice was getting to know her new stepmother, a plump sandy-haired woman with a marked German accent and pale blue eyes, who looked Bernice over and over in a way Bernice did not find comfortable. She was glad to attach herself to Mrs. Augustine, who assumed her discomfort was due to her father's remarrying.

"He's going to leave her the house, he told me so." Mrs. Augustine clucked disapprovingly.

"I don't want it," Bernice said truthfully. She longed to tell Mrs. Augustine about Flo. Finally she did, after a fashion. She said, "Mrs. Augustine, I don't think I'm ever going to marry. I don't want to. I share a house with a wonderful woman in San Francisco. Her name is Florence. We were in the WASP together. I'd rather live with her than with any man."

"I can understand that," Mrs. Augustine said. "The best of them is all wrapped up in himself and they all expect to be waited on hand and foot. Who does the cooking?"

"We both do. We alternate. We know how to cook different things. Every Sunday, we eat out." To talk of their little habits and rituals made her feel less lonely.

Mrs. Augustine sighed. "It must be nice to come home and have somebody make supper for you, even just once."

She did not think Mrs. Augustine exactly understood her relationship with Flo, but in essence she understood. Bernice felt she had received a blessing from the only real friend she had in Bentham Center. The Professor asked few questions. He held forth on the returning GIs and the chance for St. Thomas to develop into a college with higher standards. He pontificated on Truman and the Marshall Plan and the reconstruction of Germany. His eyes mostly rested on his wife's face. Gertrud waited on him and bustled around him. Her new stepmother made Bernice nervous, but Gertrud seemed to find her new position engrossing. On the phone, she did not identify herself as Bernice could remember Viola saying, "This is Viola Coates," but rather, "This is Mrs. Professor Edward Coates."

Bernice was packing everything of hers that she still cared about, old books, pictures, Jeff's paintings, her bicycle, to ship railroad express to San Francisco. She also took some of Jeff's clothes, his good tweed jacket, some shirts and sweaters and flannel pants. In his old room she tried on his jacket and pants. She did not really look like him, but she looked like his brother. Nobody challenged her appropriation.

She bicycled to the airport every day to work on her plane, for she had finally bought out the lawyer. She was going to fly it back, because she could sell it in California. Finally the last day, Mrs. Augustine drove her out (she had shipped off her bicycle that morning) and she took her plane up and headed west. It was a trip she had made many times, always in a faster and bigger plane and usually in the opposite direction. Still, to fly again was to be thoroughly alive.

Making love to Flo was like flying. When she lay between Flo's thighs, she felt herself at the controls of a sumptuous machine, she felt empowered. She, only she, could give such pleasure as she drove carefully but at high speeds the beautiful body of her love. When Flo made love to her, she felt flown, pressed through the air in a high magnificent arc. Sex with Flo was tender, passionate, gentle. It was another class of event than the sex she had known with Zach, for whole being to whole being they embraced, given into each other's eager care.

She had written Zach with her new address, the details of her life, but she was not confident she would ever hear from him. She was surprised one fall Friday when he called her at work, summoning her to the Mark Hopkins for supper. She got out of work early pleading a headache, so that she could greet Flo at the door changed out of her work clothes and carrying a glass of wine. As soon as Flo stepped inside, she started kissing her, rubbing her hands in the small of Flo's back and then rubbing her mons through the cloth in a way that always made Flo crazy for it. She was assuming if she was dealing with a relaxed and satisfied Flo, she would get a weaker reaction to her news. To think she had ever imagined she would not know how to please her. Because she had caught her right at the door, Flo had a strong tomato smell, but as she ate her, Flo's own sweet sea scent rose. Afterward, she mentioned the phone call.

Halfway to the shower, Flo put her hands on her hips. "Oh, lover boy calls, and you go running."

"There's no love between Zach and me. Don't be jealous, sweet mama. I'm going to ask him for help."

"Why should he help two lesbians?"

"Because he's queer too. He just might. Because he loved Jeff. Because he enjoyed being with me, if only in place of Jeff. Because he has money and power and sometimes it amuses him to play god. He might think what I have in mind is funny."

"Alaska?"

Bernice pulled Flo into her arms, with Flo hanging back and turning her face away, refusing to look at Bernice. "You know it's okay here, but that's all it is. You working in the cannery all day, coming home with the last strength wrung out of you and with your hands all cut up. Someday you'll lose a finger. It's backbreaking work, and what do you make? Next to nothing. I hate being a secretary in a firm where I should be a pilot. I hate being grounded. We fly in bed, but everywhere else, we crawl on our bellies."

"He'll just use you. You just want an excuse to go to bed with him."

"If I have to fuck him, I will, but I don't want to. Believe me, I won't, if he doesn't make me."

"If you don't go, he can't make you."

"If I don't go, we have no chance, no chance at all."

Flo began to cry. "I don't want us to need *them*. Why can't we do it on our own?"

"We've applied for flying jobs everyplace people fly, every bloody place. Us and every other WASP. They won't let us fly. They want to push women out of the skies altogether—"

"Except that asshole who said I could be a stewardess, but you were too tall." Flo tied herself into her dressing gown, shaking back her strawberry blond hair.

"And not pretty enough." Bernice grinned. "Now don't cry, Flo baby. Don't cry. Likely I won't get anything out of him, but it's worth it to try, for us. For the two of us, I'll do anything in the world. You don't know the half of it yet. Now there's something you have to do before I go down there. Get the scissors. You're going to cut my hair all off, down to the skull."

"Bernice, you can't do that. They'll fire you from work!"

"Tomorrow morning, we'll buy a wig. They'll like that better. Listen to me, Flo, I'm going to see him in full male drag. I have to."

Flo wrung her hands. "Sometimes I want faith again. I grew up with hellfire and brimstone, and one day, it just wasn't there, the old guilt, the old glory. Now I wish I had it back, so I could spend the whole night on my knees praying. When I go around the house, when I'm worried sick about you, and I go saying, Oh, please, Oh please, don't let anything happen to my Bernice, I wonder who the hell I think I'm praying to, the doorknob?" Flo kissed her and sat her down with a towel draped around her shoulders. At the last moment, Bernice selected Jeff's tweed jacket, his woven tie.

———

Zach had given her his room number and told her to be there at seven. She was a little late and simply went on up. Her entrance was as startling as she had intended it to be. Zach stared, then flung up his hands. "I knew it, I knew it! Oh my prescient soul, if it isn't Mr. Bernard. Fascinating." He waved her to a seat and went on staring. He was darkly tanned, but what attracted her attention was the other person in the room. He was young, although probably not as young as he looked, slight, with golden brown skin and a high-foreheaded sweet face, Oriental but not Chinese, she thought, not Japanese.

Zach spoke to him in a language that had many vowels; however, while

Zach learned languages with ease, as he had boasted to her, he spoke them all with a strong American accent. The youth gracefully brought them a bottle and two glasses and then he put on his jacket and went out. Bernice stared after him.

"Just a little souvenir of my adventures in the creepy crawly Orient. He looks sweet, doesn't he? Oh, he is. But he's here partly because the French put a price on his head." Zach was standing, looking her over as he talked. "Tran fought the Japanese for years and now he has to fight the French. So boring. We were helping his brave band and they were helping us. The word we gave all the pilots who went down in Indochina was *Vietminh*—we'd tell them to keep asking for the Vietminh, because the guerrillas would pick up our flyboys and ferry them back to us. But under Truman—do you like ice? I can't remember—we are now on the side of the French. Excruciating stupidity. OSS is being dismantled. No more fun and games for a while. The bastards at State and War think they can do it for themselves."

She looked at his hand, but of course he was unlikely to wear a ring. "Are you married? Are congratulations in order?"

"I decided I don't care to live in London. It's threadbare. The smell of a second-rate power. More's doing here, and with our business raging into overseas expansion, I'd better base myself Stateside. I might marry into a San Francisco banking family. She's comely and well behaved and into redwood preservation. I'm also being courted by a richer and better-connected eastern family, although the lady in question would take more handling. Care to dispense advice?"

"Marry the redwood lady. You won't want to put the effort into the other."

"I've been thinking along the same lines myself. However, I have to balance all the various openings I see. This is a time empires are crumbling and empires are being built."

"If you do get heavily involved in business again, won't it seem tame after OSS?"

He sighed. "Still, it's all part of the same whole, I have to keep that in mind. Wild Bill Donovan himself is going corporate. I'll keep my hand in and wait for further developments, as they say. Well, dear heart, I'm sorry I couldn't make the ceremony. Was it touching and all that?"

She made her report. He had not commented on her costume after the first instant. She wondered if she had made a mistake, but remained careful how she sat, how she moved, how she stood. She was giving a performance, she must remember, a performance before an extremely critical audience. She made little attempt to alter her voice, just pitching it lower.

Finally he said, "You look like Jeff, and yet you don't. It's fascinating and sad.

That poor bastard. He couldn't face being queer and he preferred to rush off from me and die. By the way, he killed himself, did you know?"

"He killed himself?"

"Cyanide capsules. We were all issued them, in case of not being able to hold up under torture—which he was subjected to. Quite understandable but still, leaves me wondering."

She simply shook her head. She wanted to avoid arguing with him about Jeff, who was beyond their opinions. Zach was going on: "He was with a predominantly Jewish maquis, an odd lot, ill-armed but feisty. I worked with them for a couple of months myself and we were effective in harassing the Boches and raising merry hell. Liberated some towns, accepted the surrender of a garrison and other high times." Zach sighed again, deeply. "Those were the days, dear heart. I love a spot of guerrilla fighting. If you have decent weapons, you can have so much fun scoring off the other side. You know the best I ever met? Fiji Islanders. They melt into the jungle. I couldn't keep up with them—me! If I were setting up an intelligence agency, I'd send men to train with the Fijis."

"Jeff was dead before you got to France?"

"I was busy in Brittany till well after D-Day. I couldn't amble down to the south much before the Dragoon landings. When I got into the area, he'd been dead for a month. Frankly, he was running a sloppy operation. I could have saved his neck if we'd been together. I'm a professional and he never was."

"He was a professional painter."

"Even at that, a failure. However." He rose and pointed to a crate leaning against one wall. "I salvaged some of his work. I took the liberty of having a couple framed for you."

She had a pang of hot anger that he would keep what should be all hers and then dole out what he did not want, but then he had salvaged them as he said, and but for him, they would have been lost. She opened the box. In it were a study and two paintings of the same woman: one on a bicycle in a closely rendered landscape; another, three sketches of her face conversing; the third, her in bed, open shutters, open window, the bed table with a carafe and a gun, she on her side smiling like a cat with half-closed eyes, a long thin woman with rather large breasts for her weight, the landscape of stone and brush spread around her in a circle pressing in on the little room. "Who was she?"

"His local girlfriend. He was doing lots of portraits, which I think inferior to his landscapes."

"What happened to her?"

"She was killed in a German raid on the encampment. Just a kid he was pronging, the way he always had some woman taking care of him." Zach stood in front of her, hands on her shoulders. "The impersonation is passable but weak in minor points. You should make stronger eye contact and hold your chin up, not dipped."

She corrected her posture. "Better?"

"Better is if you're still doing it that way in fifteen minutes. This is not how you dress normally, I take it, and probably not designed to stir my gonads. What do you want, my cagey darling? I take it you want something. Everybody does, sooner or later, and you've been marvelously accommodating."

"I do want."

"What?"

"I want false ID. I want a male identity."

"My sainted aunt, why? Do you need a license to do whatever you've been doing in bed?"

"I have a license to fly but it won't do me any good as a woman. Zach, I love the woman I live with, but I need to fly. I want to go up to Alaska and start a bush airline. I can do it. I can fly anything, Zach, I'm checked out in everything the Army has. Now I can't get a job teaching beginners to circle the airport in a Piper Cub. Jeff made me his beneficiary and I saved money and so did Flo. But we need a man to run the operation, and that man has to be me. As a man, I could get a job tomorrow in Alaska."

He sat down on the couch and laughed, quietly. "It's so farfetched, it's amusing. We aren't entirely shut down. Probably I could give you what you want—an identity. But you can't go back on it. Once we've set you up as Bernard X with a particular war record, and so on, Bernice has simply disappeared and you can't turn back into her when you break up with Flo and decide you just laid eyes on Mr. Right and want to make little babies."

"Zach, I think it's fair to assume I will go to my grave with no more experience of men than you."

"I should think I might in some ways prove sufficient." He grinned and lifted a hand to silence her. "Someone at the door. Presumably our supper. Do let them in."

As they sat down to prime rib, Zach would hear no more of her desires and plans. He regaled her with tales of his exploits in France, Yugoslavia and Indochina until they had finished the meal and the bottle of French burgundy he had ordered with it. He made occasional corrections. "The smile is a little too . . . effusive? Propitiating? The voice should stay pitched lower. It's passable but could be better."

If he was giving her a critique to improve her performance, did that mean he would come through? Instinct warned her not to press him. Walk on through the evening, walk on.

After supper, he began to question her about Alaska. She had been studying maps, reading everything she could lay her hands on. She had a map with her she spread on the table. She also had brochures of used planes. The Army was divesting itself of large quantities of cargo and transport planes. She was careful not to ask him for money. She needed more, but with a new identity, she might be able to borrow. The false identity, the honorable discharge, the flying record, the accouterments of an alien male identity only he could give her.

"Think of my poor little friend, out there in the fog wandering. I think he was fooled by you. It's amusing, isn't it? But we won't give him cause for jealousy. It's too elegiac, isn't it? Are you disappointed?"

"Of course," she lied firmly, "but it will make it easier at home for me too. Flo was being very jealous."

"I must meet her sometime," he said languidly, grimacing at his watch. "Don't you think in a way he has something of Jeff's style? The litheness, the quick grace. Did you notice how he moves?"

Bernice produced an encouraging noise, unable to recall any resemblance.

"He's an artist too. Writes poetry in French and Vietnamese. All the cultured ones have that veneer of French culture." He looked at his watch again. "I told the little bugger to be back here in two hours, and it's close to three. I don't like that. Mommy must spank. Where would he take off to in a city he doesn't know, in a foreign country? I must have patience with him. The Oriental mind knows not of clock time."

As she left he was glaring at his wrist, peering down the corridor after her in the direction of the elevator.

It was a month later to the day when a package arrived registered mail from Overseas Enterprises Unlimited. In it was everything she needed to establish herself as Harry Edward Munster, formerly of Boston and the Army Air Corps, assigned to OSS during the war and honorably discharged as a captain with ratings up to four-engine planes. There was no note inside, but there was a letter of recommendation from Colonel Zachary Barrington Taylor who had been his commanding officer, and who said he could be relied upon at his new corporate address in Rockefeller Center for a more detailed reference.

Bernice held the package and smiled into the mirror as she took off the wig she had been wearing to work. It might work. It just might. It would be an adventure to try it together, at least for a couple of years. She could always kill off Harry in an accident in the Alaska wilderness. What other chance did they have? What other choice?

The Second Gift

In the three months since she had been brought to the dragon's treasure in the mountain by Oscar, she had seen him three times rather formally. They made appointments to spend a day walking in the countryside or touring with his jeep, eating at any country inn still functioning. They were not lovers, but amazingly they had resumed being friends. She imagined that would be the shape of their relationship, perhaps until one of them died.

She had been in flooded Holland, in Denmark covering their remarkable resistance and their marked success in protecting Jews, in Norway to view the burned northern areas, in Paris to cover what *Collier's* described as the rebirth of French fashion, and again and always back to the DP camps.

Thanks to her own reporting and that of others, a fact-finding mission on the treatment of displaced persons arrived in July. She had talked to the Harrison Commission about events she had witnessed, including Patton's use of German police and MPs to round up and beat Jews who had survived camps and were living in Munich and to force them into sealed boxcars for shipment to Poland, whence came tales of their murder. Thus she had rendered herself unwelcome as a correspondent. What was happening to the DPs in the camps, living on near starvation allotments of soup, bread, coffee and dehydrated food, behind barbed wire and guard towers, was the story she most wanted to cover; that was also the story in which magazines were least interested. Assignments were tapering off.

She had just gone to Bergen-Belsen again to visit the community the Jews had created there of impromptu schools and workshops. She was driven by her vision of these people who had been stripped of home, possessions, work, family, friends, community, country, everyone and everything they had loved, all connections now smashed, murdered, gone. How much loss could any human endure? They were that measure.

She had just finished interviewing a boy of fifteen who was frantic to find any surviving family when she was seized by cramps that doubled her over. She had dysentery from contaminated water. The doctor also told her she was suffering from total exhaustion, prescribing a month's bed rest. She shrugged that off, but Oscar, who turned up on the fourth day, did not.

The bug she had was stubborn or her resistance had been demolished by more than a year of living out of a duffle bag, no fresh food, catching what sleep she could on the ground, in barns, in empty ammunition trailers, in dripping tents, in bombed hotels where the plumbing had gone the way of the dinosaur. She was up and seated by the window in her hospital room reflecting to herself that her body was telling her something, perhaps that she was forty-two years old and not twenty-one and lacked an unfailing reservoir of strength to draw upon. Suddenly her body was charging her for the stress she had put it through. Then Oscar walked in carrying roses.

"I'm essentially done," he said. "OSS is being dismantled. R & A is going to the State Department, but not with me aboard. I leave for New York August twenty-eighth. *Collier's* has you booked on a flight two days later, via Lisbon. Will you go?"

She nodded. "If they let me out. I hate hospitals."

"The war's over. The announcement should come today, but we picked up the emperor Hirohito broadcasting his surrender to the Japanese people. It's done, Louise."

She lurched to her feet and stared out the window. In the courtyard a jeep was executing a smart turn. The day looked clay colored and dusty. "Is it really over? Those atomic bombs did it?"

"Perhaps they gave the peace party in the Japanese cabinet more leverage. Their sticking point was the emperor, and it seems that after insisting on unconditional surrender all the way, we will let them keep their divine emperor. It isn't clear whether we dropped those bombs on the Japanese or if they were actually aimed at impressing the Soviets." He steadied her. "They'll let you out of the hospital tomorrow. But only if you behave."

"What does that mean?"

"If I could have got you passage sooner, I'd have done it. It's time to go home. You look like death in life, by the way."

Louise sighed. "I hate the idea of hanging around here. If I'm to be unemployed, I'd rather be unemployed at home." She could do nothing more for the camp victims here; any political pressure would have to be applied back in the States.

"I have a place we can go. Peaceful. No ruins. That is, no contemporary ruins. No camps. Quiet. We can have it for two weeks, starting tomorrow. It's in Devon. Have you ever been?"

She shook her head no, sinking into her chair. "I think the bug is stubborn because it isn't just a bug. Reality made me sick, not a microbe."

"Will you go to Devon with me? We're both finished over here."

"It seems decadent and uncaring to take a vacation."

"Consider it a convalescence. Or you can stay in the hospital, if discomfort sits better with you. It won't be luxurious. It's just a cottage on a big estate we've used."

A decision felt too difficult. It was simpler to acquiesce.

———

"It's a little more rustic than I'd realized," Oscar said ruefully, surveying the cottage. In the big house where he had stayed before, an archives division of R & A was packing the war for shipment to Washington. By the end of August, OSS would be out of here, and its owners reinstalled.

The cottage was built of stone under a thatched roof, picturesque as he had described it to her, but with only a peat stove for chilly evenings and to heat water for a bath or dishes. The kitchen had another stove, fortunately with some gas left in a cylinder. It lit with a match and a great whoosh. There was only one bed, an observation which caused her a moment's suspicion until she saw how woebegone he was looking.

"It's beautiful, Oscar. Just be glad it isn't more authentic. Have you ever seen the figures on how much of rural England lacks indoor plumbing? Besides, I'm the invalid. You're the cook and housekeeper on this trip, right?"

"You'll be amazed how I've learned to take care of myself."

"Abra didn't take good care of you?"

"Abra didn't take any kind of care of me. She's not a berrieh, Louie, but it was educational. I have new skills. I can cook, I can clean, I can iron my own shirts, although I confess I look forward to New York laundries."

"You can cook, you can clean, and I have no housekeeper any longer. Maybe I should marry you?"

"That's my idea," he said. "If we can manage between us to do one good thing. Now I'm taking that ancient bicycle to town for provisions. Will you be all right?"

"I'll be fine." And she was, bundled in a quilt to watch the afternoon fog creeping over the lavender and maroon moor. Oscar had borrowed several books from the library of the big house, and she had Joyce Cary's amusing new novel *The Horse's Mouth* in her lap. Much of the time she just watched the fog stealing toward the cottage, built on the edge of the manor park with only a low stone wall keeping them from the vast treeless spaces that beckoned. Inside she was rebuilding her sense of self.

Clotted cream seemed to be the medicine her dysentery required to quiet it. The food here was more plentiful than anyplace she had been since Normandy, with smoked trout, salmon and Dover sole. The fishing boats were going out regularly and they bought local runner beans, gooseberries and plums. Dining in town the third night, they had lamb. Her strength came seeping back. Every day they walked farther out on the moors.

As she grew stronger they wandered from hut circle to menhir to stone row to stone circle and up on a tor for the long view, which always led on to more hut circles, more menhirs, more stone rows and other high rocky tors. Fortunately Oscar had a good map. Maps, he explained, had not been sold in England since the invasion scare in 1940 and had only just become legal again. however, they had always had maps in the big house, to guard against adventurous OSS personnel falling into bogs. Each morning it did not pour, they set out for a clapper bridge, a tor, a particular circle. The half-wild ponies began to recognize them and only moved a modest distance away.

He looked handsome and vigorous with the exercise, the fresh food, but she knew he was not sleeping well in his bag on the floor of the central room. She was up in the loft bedroom with a view out on the moor. Downstairs was the kitchen and the other room and a toilet. They bathed in a washtub in the kitchen. She thought that on the whole Oscar probably found it rougher camping than she did, after her months with the Army. For her it was a welcome halfway house between utter discomfort and utter comfort.

Letters from New York came for him via London OSS. "I'm fondly awaited back at Columbia. I have three classes, a graduate seminar. I don't know how I'll do it—bluff through with my old notes in a box somewhere. They say they're expecting a lot of vets to enroll. That should be interesting, don't you think? A different kind of student body. Not so naive. My publishers want me to spruce up my book on the Weimar Republic and the roots of Fascism, bring it up to date. That should keep me busy and off the streets all winter."

"I don't know what I want to do. I don't see much scope for myself as a correspondent any longer."

He wrote replies and went to town to post them. As the sun shone brightly, she dragged a chair outside. She half dozed, musing in the overgrown garden. Small fuzzy lavender daisies in busy clumps stuck up above the matt of weeds drawing bees. Something smelled sweet but she could not track it down. She had never had a garden, so she had never learned the names of plants. She had reference works at home that contained plates of garden flowers. When she needed to be accurate for one of her stories, she looked up an appropriate name, then forgot it five minutes later.

Reunion stories would be big. The man has been at war, but the parting had occurred earlier, perhaps the year war broke out. Were they divorced? No, too racy. Safer to have them engaged and ruptured. They break apart from selfish immaturity on both their parts. In this story, she has to have sinned against him (out of pride? immaturity?) as well as he against her. Is he maimed, wounded, like Rochester? Not this one.

She felt him standing behind her. He had returned from town and in her story trance, she had not heard him. She spoke without turning, her eyes on a raven passing over the long slope, "Love, I wonder if there's a typewriter ribbon in the big house I could have? Mine's so worn I can hardly use it."

"I'll check it out. Are you filing a story from here?"

"Not that kind of story. I've just had my first fictional idea in more than a year. I thought my mind had stopped working that way. That I'd lost my vein of fantasy that brings in the good dollars."

"Perhaps I inspire you." He sauntered around and stood with his back to the low stone wall that marked the end of the weedy garden and the beginning of the moor. "To fantasy if nothing else. Do you know what you just called me?"

"Called you?"

"Love, you said."

"I did?"

"Even our unintentional utterances, according to Freud, are indicative of our real desires."

She laughed, clasping her hands behind her head. "Do you consider my real desire general or specific?"

"Louise, only you know by now if you want me or your young Navy man. If you want me, I'm yours. I can change my habits. I'm older, Lord knows. I can try to be wiser."

Alas, poor Daniel, she thought, it's no contest. My life is my life, of a piece. "I'm here with you, not with him. No?"

"Partly, partly." He had pushed himself off the wall to stretch. The sun tipped his dark curls with copper. As he came toward her, his eyes had that hot molten expression she remembered, oh she remembered, down in her body she remembered.

She sighed noisily. "Is it all starting again?"

"Living? Yes, it's starting again. Loving? Let me show you how it can be. Please, come to me." He put his hands tentatively on her shoulders and then under her arms to lift her. Where his hands touched, her breasts ached, as if they filled suddenly with milk. Her body betrayed her, her body delivered her to him. Oh, nonsense, she scolded herself, letting him draw her up out of the chair. Why else did I come here? But for this, to heal into this. She tilted back her face and he kissed her. Honey in the belly, honey in the veins, honey in the womb. Someday, she thought, I'll write about sex how it really is for women, not for the magazines but maybe a publisher would touch it. How everything thickens and quickens at once.

To say how, she thought, as they were in bed naked and tangled together, mouths joined and hips twisting to press and squirm closer, it is at its best impossible to tell where one body starts and the other begins. Animal magic. Choice made flesh.

"I won't leave you again, I won't! It was the stupidest thing I ever did in my life. I was a putz, a schmuck. I had an attitude that anything that was offered to me, I should try."

He would be more faithful than he had been, he would be mostly faithful. She thought that he would try and maybe succeed. It would be the two of them alone together as it had not been for twenty years, and that would be in itself an adventure.

After they had made love, she fetched a bottle of the local hard cider for them to drink in bed, the quilt gathered around them. "It's going to be interesting politically," Oscar said. "We seem to have come out of the war feeling invincible. Prepared to pick up the White Man's Burden with a vengeance. But things have been happening among the colored populations at home and everywhere, a new militancy that could continue demanding changes."

"I visited an all-Negro tank outfit. They were fantastically decorated, given that they had to do five times as much to get any recognition. And they were deeply angry about how they'd been treated by the Army. All that's going home too. But *Collier's* wouldn't let me write about it, saying nobody was interested in some Negro tankers."

They settled down to filling each other in on what they had been noticing and thinking. Suddenly it was six-thirty and she was starving. They had talked for two hours without pausing. That moved her more than the lovemaking. She had a sense of roots deep in soil groping together. She was being healed to their common history, her life was coming back together. Her long anger was almost gone. Oh, in fights it would try to seep out in bitterness, but she would be wary. Miracles came seldom and rebirth more rarely yet and for countless and uncountable and never to be counted women like herself, her age, her body type, death had come from a machine gun, from blows of the butt end of a rifle, from poison gas, from poison injections, from starvation and typhus and neglect, from all the nasty ways to die warped minds in a violent and relentless system could devise. They had died of a lack of common respect and common love. They cried out to her, take him back and go live in peace as husband and wife and as Jews. Go make a home again and give thanks. Life is the first gift, love is the second, and understanding the third.

After they spent their first night sharing the bed, Oscar woke at dawn, shaken. "I was with the Army. We were pursuing the Nazis into Bavaria. We kept talking about Werewolf, the underground Himmler set up but never finished connecting." He flinched, scrubbing at his eyes. "You probably guessed I was involved in counterintelligence work in Germany, seeking out Nazi cells. That's what I was doing in Bavaria, when we met at the hunting lodge. But this was an absurd dream."

"I don't require you to dream in good taste, Oscar. Tell me about it."

"The American colonel I was with, he was tall and blond and midwestern, brave and naive. We kept pursuing an SS officer. There were chase scenes, in and out of ruins. Finally we had him cornered. Then the SS turned into a real wolf and he leaped through the air and as his teeth sank into the American colonel's throat, he disappeared into him."

"'What happened to the Nazi?' I asked the colonel.

"'What Nazi?' The colonel just stared at me. 'There's no Nazi here.' That's all there was to it." Oscar sat up, a dew of sweat on his forehead. "Silly dream. How are you feeling this morning?"

"Not silly. Witty, rather, in the sense that indeed where have they all gone? Every German was anti-Hitler. But he disappeared into the American?"

"Louise, I was for intervention. We had to fight Germany. There was no choice. It would have been better to do it in Spain than in North Africa, and better to do it in 1937 than in 1942, but we had to. But I do fear what the war has done to us. I do fear what I am beginning to understand of the bottom side of what we call progress and civilization."

"We've both lost our certainties. Great gaping holes where they used to be." She touched his cheek on which the tough dark hairs had grown during the night, an occasional white one gleaming. We shall grow old, she thought, and was oddly comforted. "To answer your question, I feel fine. From what was wrong with me physically, I am recovering. And we've begun to recover something as precious as health."

"Our love?"

"That too. I was thinking of communication."

The Harvest

In July, Ruthie was laid off from Briggs. By that time most of the women had already gone, Rena first. Since Vivian had been let go, it had been increasingly hard for Ruthie to get to the factory, way on the east side, so she was not sorry. Vivian and Rena were trying to get jobs as welder and riveter respectively.

Not only were women being laid off en masse, but entry jobs were being redefined to involve heavy lifting, to exclude women from the factories. In a Flint auto plant, all the women were put on the graveyard shift in violation of seniority, and the UAW, which continued to address members as sirs and brothers, refused to fight for its women members. The auto plants were reconverting, preparing to roll out cars and trucks. When the women went to the unemployment office, officials told them that if they applied as welders or riveters, they could have their unemployment compensation terminated because they were unfairly limiting their employability. The U.S. Employment Service would only refer Vivian to what they called women's jobs, and they kept trying to force Rena into being a maid or a cleaning lady.

Ruthie received unemployment as she was interviewing for social work. She was surprised how many of the agencies were reluctant to hire a woman except as a secretary. Once she would have been happy to get a secretarial job, but no more. She kept looking. She did well on the Civil Service exam. Detroit was shaken by a polio epidemic. Even on the hottest days, mothers feared letting their children go swimming in the parks or the river. People thought that was how it was transmitted.

The gas shortage had eased a little so that Morris could take his car out of storage. Leib worked on it with him until they had it running again. It was understood they would share it, since Leib had put so much time into running around for replacement parts. Leib volunteered to teach Naomi to drive, so Ruthie invited herself along to learn at the same time and to keep an eye on Leib. Trudi knew how to drive, but she was getting too big to slip behind the wheel.

Ruthie was astonished to find out she liked to drive, and by early August, she had her license and so did Naomi. One sunny Saturday in August, they took turns driving into the country, taking the new expressway to Willow Run. It was a ghost town out there, the dormitories deserted, the little huts empty. She wondered if that was the sort of place Murray and she would have to live, if he still wanted her when he came back.

"Will you marry him when he comes home?" Naomi asked, as if she could read her mind.

"How do I know what will happen? What he'll want? We haven't laid eyes on each other for three years!"

"But if you do marry him, I'll hardly ever see you."

"Why won't you see me, unless you go blind? And don't marry me off before it happens. The war isn't even over, kine-ahora, so let's not talk about his coming home."

Ruthie parked by a small lake where some colored people were fishing, a woman and two men, with a baby lying on a little rug in the grass. "Catch anything?" she called.

The woman answered her, a little wary but neither hostile nor friendly, "A couple of bullheads. No white folks' fish."

Ruthie left the car and wandered with Naomi along a path under the pines that grew down almost to the water's weedy edge, with blue green reeds standing up like thick grass, water lilies in a cove, then a stretch where the waves lapped on a crescent of gravelly sand.

"I wish I could read the whole journal," Naomi said. "It's all I have left. Of any of them."

"I know you were working on breaking the code. I saw all those lists."

"I can't do it. All I can figure out is a word or two. Sometimes I get furious at her, frustrated, because I can read it right up to the point where they leave Paris and go down to Toulouse, and she starts taking the children through the mountains. Then it becomes just nonsense, pages and pages of craziness where half the words make sense and the other half are just stuck in, like, I saw Daniela chair the red book outside the city."

"Why did she do that?"

"She was scared she'd be captured and the Nazis would read her journal and learn too much."

"You sound as if you feel very close to her."

"How can you feel close to a dead person? Everybody in my family is dead. Why did they make me live if they were all going to die?"

"They could only save one. Why not you? You're very precious."

"She used to hate us—the twins. Then she got all sentimental about us when she was underground. She even started calling us by our Jewish names, Naomi, Rivka. She forgot what we were really like—brats."

Ruthie hugged her cousin, who stood unresponsive, staring off: her cousin who was four inches taller than she was and at least as full-figured suddenly, startlingly. "You're a very special person, a sweet and good and smart young woman, Naomi. Your parents would be proud of you, your mother, your father, your sister too."

"Ha!" Naomi pulled sullenly away. "They'd hate me!" She started walking fast toward the car. "I want to drive now. It's my turn."

On August 14, Morris came home from the factory at eleven in the morning, saying that the plant had closed to celebrate the end of the war. Rose was in the yard washing clothes with a scrubbing board and a brush. His work clothes were boiling in soapy water on the stove. She yanked off her soaked apron, although her faded cotton dress under it was just as wet across her full belly. Ruthie threw down the want ads to hurry after them into the street. A car passed honking its horn, the windows open and guys leaning out. "The war's over! The war's over!" Ta ta ta tum went the horn.

Sandy Rosenthal came running down the steps of the front house. "Is it true? Is it real this time?"

Everybody milled around. Ruthie felt as if she were going to fly apart. People were leaning out their windows shouting to each other. Around the end of the block came the sound of a drum. A ragged procession of neighborhood kids paraded down the sidewalk and then into the street, wagons, bikes, tricycles, a scooter, two dogs, one with a flag in his collar, a baby buggy decked with bunting. In the buggy was a struggling tabby stuffed into a baby dress. The children were blowing horns, banging on pot lids and trash can covers.

Everybody was kissing and hugging. Bells were ringing in the Polish Catholic church and in the African Methodist church nearby. A siren began to wail and from the through streets came a rising cacophony of honking and tooting. Detroit was preparing to party, from one end to the other. Everybody who could stand upright was getting ready to take to the streets.

Ruthie hugged Sharon. Then she ran off to Fenniman's bakery to fetch Naomi. She wanted to sing and dance, she wanted to run through the streets with everybody else. The end of dying, the end of killing, was that not a true holiday under the sun? A new world, the United Nations Morris kept talking about. Freedom from want, freedom from fear, freedom from persecution.

Right after Labor Day, Ruthie was hired by Aid to Dependent Children, which was undergoing a great expansion of caseload as women were being laid off or pushed into poorly paid jobs. She was hired to start the following Monday, and she did. Murray wrote he had high points and should be among the first marines home. Then the last week in September a wire came from San Francisco. He would be on a train arriving 7:54 Tuesday evening and she should come and meet him along with his parents.

Ruthie dreaded calling Murray's parents. None of her early fantasies that they would treat her as their daughter-in-law-to-be had worked out. She waited a day, sure he had wired them also, but no call came. She had to call them.

"They don't know how to act," Rose pronounced, folding her arms across her breasts. She shook her head. "German Jews are more Germans than Jews, even after this war I tell you that. They are born with rulers stuck up their behind."

Ruthie picked up the phone, put down the phone, picked up the phone, put it down. She could not continue being cowardly. She dialed, praying they were not home. His mother answered, a woman who had never told her to call her anything but Mrs. Feldstein. "This is Ruthie."

"Ruthie?" Mrs. Feldstein repeated dubiously, as if she knew either too many Ruthies to guess which one, or none at all, and could not possibly be expected to know any.

"Ruthie Siegal," she said dryly. "Murray sent me a telegram to meet the train with you tomorrow."

"Oh. We had thought we would only be family at such a moment. We weren't planning to make it a social occasion."

"Mrs. Feldstein, whether you like me or not, Murray asked me to be there, and I'll be there." Ruthie quietly but firmly put the phone down. She sat there, tense with anger and humiliation. Her postwar life was getting off to a splendid start. The first thing she had done to celebrate Murray's homecoming was to tell off his mother.

She did not even know if she wanted to see him that quickly. Who was he anyhow? A stranger in a uniform who had spent time with her when they were both much younger, a man who had seduced her in a parked Dodge on Belle Isle in summer 1942. He had sent her photographs of himself, the most recent in his uniform by a little Japanese teahouse with a Japanese woman on either side in kimonos. She had frowned at that picture, on the back of which he had written, Me with two guides. Guides?

That whole next day, she suffered about what to wear. She had time only to go home on the trolley, eat quickly and change even faster. The good wishes of her family were ringing in her ears as she maneuvered the car she had borrowed for the evening out of its tight place at the curb and drove carefully to the station, her hands wet and clammy on the wheel. She had considered wearing the pink dress of that evening, but it seemed pitiful and out of place. Finally she had selected a maroon dress she had bought for work, tailored and with the new longer hemline. She thought she looked almost sophisticated. *That* to his mother.

The station was hung with banners welcoming the troops. As she was worming her way through the crowd, the gate to a track opened and a mass of people stampeded toward a departing train. She was carried along helplessly to the gate to the platform, which stood partially ajar. There she managed to pry herself out of the mob and cling to a bar until they swept past her. She was bruised and queasy. She wondered if Murray had neglected to tell his parents he had asked her to come to the station—perhaps his own feelings were ambivalent. In letters to his mother, had he expressed doubts about her? Finally she arrived at the right gate, but the train was late, expected at eight-fifteen.

In the press, she did not even see his parents until nine o'clock, when the gate finally opened and the first travelers began to pour through, a mix of servicemen with bags over their shoulders, families and the usual business travelers. As the first friends and relatives glimpsed the voyagers they were awaiting, they shrieked and ran forward. Then she saw his father, whose hair was now more grey than brown, with his mother just behind bobbing back and forth to crane at the discharging passengers.

Finally she saw him, tan and fit but with an expression that she would not have called a Murray look, borne along in the procession with a dazed, sleepy, glazed-over face. He looked handsomer than she remembered, as if a subcutaneous layer of fat had burned off, paring his face to more mature, tauter lines, but he looked also . . . less alive? He must be exhausted.

She was still staring at him when his mother rushed forward to embrace him, followed by his father. His parents looked so pallid, so flabby and beige next to him, they might have been his grandparents. It was typical of the lack of connection between his parents and her that at Thanksgiving, she realized, she had not even considered calling Murray's family for a bird. She was still watching, unable or unwilling to move, when Murray's gaze brushed across her, then instantly jarred back.

She came forward then, buffeted by the crowd, but before she had taken four

steps he had surged forward to grab her. When he kissed her, he tasted of tobacco. It was like being kissed hard by a stranger. She found herself weeping, and
the rest of the evening was played out in short bursts of confusion.

On Friday she went to work as usual and Murray slept all day, so it was not
until the next evening that they saw each other alone. He arrived at six-thirty
with his parents' old Dodge. The sight of it gave her flutters of misgiving. He
took her out to Chinese. The restaurant where they had eaten when they had
been dating was still open, with the same old woman at the cash register nodding them in, another willowy teenager waiting tables.

Murray seemed alert, jumpy even. As soon as they took a booth, he lit a cigarette.

"You smoke now."

"Didn't I used to?" He was staring down, his mouth tight. He had nothing
to say until their orders were taken and finally the wonton soup arrived. "Wasn't
that your old boyfriend Leib I saw on the porch?"

"He's married to Trudi and living upstairs with his wife and two children. He
lost a foot in Italy."

"That's cosy. Your old boyfriend upstairs."

She felt icy. "No, it isn't cosy. It's rather nasty, but nobody would listen to me.
Sharon couldn't keep the upstairs place on her allotment check, and Arty didn't
want her to work. Murray, I wrote you all this."

"I don't remember." He passed his hand over his forehead, as if he were sweating heavily.

"Murray, I don't like Leib. One time he caught me alone in the house and he
made a pass at me—"

"Oh? Did you fuck him?"

She winced at his tone and language. "No. Why would I? Or because I gave
in to you, do you think I'm a whore?"

"What happened?" He had a habit of turning his head partly away from her
when she spoke, evasive, frightening.

"Nothing happened, except bad words. And I have to be careful all the time
in my own home so I'm never alone with him. You understand with seven people
living in our apartment, that isn't difficult. My whole last year in school, I could
hardly study at home. Now I'm afraid he's after Naomi."

"Naomi? That little French kid?"

"You haven't seen her. She's not little and she doesn't sound French anymore,
although the kids still call her Frenchie."

"Working in the factory, you were surrounded by guys."

"Working on the line, I was surrounded by noise. Murray, during most of the time you've been gone, I have been working six days a week, going to school full time and doing my sleeping Sundays. If you don't feel like picking up things again, that's your choice, but don't invent excuses. I haven't had time for another guy, and if I'd had the time, I wasn't interested. Whatever your family may say, as if they ever saw me, I've been faithful one hundred percent. Maybe it's yourself you're talking about?"

He looked up and into her eyes. "I believe you. It's a nightmare, living in an all-male world where women are just what they have between their legs. You start believing anything. There's something in you, Ruthie, I almost forgot, that's a center. Everything else swirls around it, but there it is, something I can rest on."

He began to talk compulsively about Jack who had gone home to his wife, a certain Schlomo. He did not try to get her to make love, but brought her home when the restaurant closed, leaving a huge tip for tying up the table. He told her he had trouble hearing in his left ear, which is why he kept turning his head.

The next day he brought her presents: a fine pale green kimono with chrysanthemum blossoms, a heavier silk in dark maroon, a sake set, two fans, lacquerware, a serving bowl with cranes embossed. Then he told her to pack a picnic lunch and took her out into the country. He had a blanket that he carried into the woods. When she saw that, she knew they would make love. She was afraid. She hardly knew what she felt, because the quiet room of her mind felt as overcrowded as the train station had been. She did not know if she felt love or if she felt fear.

The first time was as painful as the very first time had been, but by the next afternoon, it was easier. "It's the middle of October. How long can we go on outside? And the car is like making it in a phone booth. Do you realize we've never had a damned bed to ourselves?" Murray was dressed again, propped against a tree smoking. The taste of the tobacco disgusted her. Either she would have to start, or she would have to get him to stop. With a deep sigh, she asked him for a cigarette.

He was quarreling with his parents by the end of the week. She understood; they wanted the son who had left. He alternated between fierce ambition (Wayne would not do at all, a streetcar school. Perhaps he would go to Ann Arbor) and being unable to organize himself to go down to the government office to get in the 52-20 club, as returning soldiers called unemployment. Every night he called Jack or Jack called him. Schlomo called in the middle of the night, drunk, and woke Murray's parents.

Schlomo was not Schlomo but Slo Mo and Italian, dark skinned, lightly but strongly built. He turned up at Murray's doorstep. His parents had called him a drunkard and he had left home after two weeks. He couldn't live in Akron anymore, he said. He thought he'd look for a job in Detroit, where his pal was. As far as

Ruthie could tell, he did not look for any job. Instead Murray and Slo Mo rented a tiny apartment farther downtown, in an area mostly colored. Murray said he liked it because it had a bedroom door that shut. Within a few days, it stank. Beer bottles piled up, chicken and pork bones from local rib joint takeout, newspapers.

Ruthie was in despair. She felt as if Murray had turned into a pile of unwashed laundry. She hated to go back with him to his filthy apartment and climb into the bed, while Slo Mo listened to loud music on the radio right outside the door. All he seemed to want to do was eat trayf, drink beer, make love and sleep. He slept half the day. Finally she asked him to take a walk with her and talk to her, seriously.

"Murray, I can't go on like this. I love you, but I don't know what you want. I can't go on sleeping with you, the way we are. I feel guilty about it. I hate going to your apartment. It's filthy. I want to help you get yourself together, but I don't know if that's what you want."

He was silent a long time, his hands knotted at his sides. "I didn't think it would be like this. On the ship, it all seemed so clear."

"I can't help you if we don't want the same things."

"Let's get married. Tomorrow."

"We can't get married tomorrow. We have to have a license. We have to get a rabbi."

He shrugged. "If you want a rabbi, sure. I guess if you get married at the courthouse, they talk about God down there too. Let's get it moving."

She seized him by the arms and turned him to face her. "But is that what you want?"

"I want you. I know that much. Yes, it's what I want. If Jack was here, we'd be okay, but he's with his wife. He's having troubles too, but he's doing better than me and Slo Mo. I need to be married. Jack keeps telling me that, and he knows me."

Jack might know this Murray, but she did not. However, if he was her duty to make whole again, then it became her to get started on it. As he kissed her, she clung to him. They would get married and she would work and he would go to school. There he would find himself again as a Jew, as a man, as a scholar, as a thinking being. She would start sending away for applications tomorrow, order his transcript from Wayne, get his papers in order.

She read in desperate search for information, late at night when everybody else was asleep, at breakfast, at lunch, on the trolley, everything she could about returning servicemen and their problems. Articles said it was her responsibility to make good. He had suffered. The woman must submit, but she must be maternal. She must be strong but conceal her strength, she must be sweet and giving and think only of him, and he would heal. Murray would again be Murray. That was her real task. All the articles talked about how she must be entirely feminine. Freud was suddenly being quoted with approval in even the popular women's magazines.

They were married the second week of November, just after Ruthie found a four-room apartment on Dexter Boulevard, far from the two-man slum Slo Mo and Murray had created. Slo Mo's mother was calling him up every day, so that Ruthie hoped he would soon get tired of waiting around Detroit and go back to Akron. Dexter Boulevard was lined with brick apartment houses that had always seemed to her the height of middle-class comfort. With the good money she was earning and Murray's unemployment, they could carry it easily. Suddenly she was a different person, Mrs. Feldstein. At work she had to fill out tax forms and they made up another nameplate for her, as if she had just been hired. She sent away for a new driver's license.

Murray liked the apartment, but it wasn't his dream. He was beginning to remember his ideas. They bought a bedroom set, very modern. They felt proud of it, with a Hollywood oak bedboard and matching dressers, his and hers. Their other purchase was a Formica table for the kitchen with chrome chairs. Murray wanted everything modern, nothing fussy. He was taking an interest in the furniture. From Trudi he borrowed books of house plans.

Ruthie was resigned to saving Murray first, and then bringing up the subject of Naomi. For the moment while Naomi was in high school and they were getting settled in their apartment, she could stay put with Rose and Morris. When Murray looked at his house plans and sketched houses, she mentally included a room for Naomi.

They had been married for two weeks when Murray began to talk after they got into bed, about Saipan, about a Sergeant Hickock, about Jack, about Tiny and Harvey, about Rostrovitz who had cut up her picture, about Okinawa. Gradually she began to understand what he was telling her.

Finally she said, holding his heavy head against her breast, "You had a right! You did what you had to. Nobody else needs to know."

"Don't you hate me? Are you disgusted? I murdered a man."

"You killed many men. That's what they made you a marine for. So one of them hated you personally," she said firmly. Make him strong. Make him clear again. "About that one you can feel good, because he meant to have you killed. Right? You wouldn't be here with me, ever."

He fell asleep clutching her in the middle of the new bed. She lay awake, staring at the ceiling. A killer, she thought, feeling fear solidify in her belly. That's what they took him and trained him to do. Now I lie with a man who killed and killed and who weeps about it. Always in him will be this old blood reeking. It should not have happened to him, it should not have happened. But to whom, then? Who deserves this burden? To whom should this blood come home?

L'Chaim

While working for the Americans in Frankfurt, Jacqueline moved into a house where survivors who had managed to buy or scrape together enough papers to escape the DP camps were living. It had been part of a row of brick houses that a bomb had sheared off, so that rooms and corridors opened into rubble, but they boarded up those false entrances and lived in the rest. Oddly, the plumbing worked, although they had no heat or any way to cook but an iron camp stove they set up. It was an improvised existence, full of stratagems and scavenged objects.

One of the women, a Polish Jew named Mindele, asked her why she didn't go back to France. "It's safe there," she said. "You must be crazy to stay around here."

"I'm trying to find my sister, who was in Dora."

"Ah." The woman nodded. They understood the search for relatives. Now she was comprehensible to them, but they all urged her to marry the handsome soldier who was working for the JDC.

"You don't understand. He was the chassen of my best friend."

"So you should marry him for her. Were you sterilized?"

"No."

"Then you're blessed. They did that to me. You must marry your friend's chassen and make children for her, for all of us."

"We don't love each other."

"That kind of love." The woman shrugged. "You were in Auschwitz. You know what counts. To eat, to live, to be free. And to make children to replace the dead. To bring joy back into the world."

The survivors knew much about each other that nobody else could. She translated for the Americans and tried to help other survivors, to protect them from contempt and bureaucracy and the continuing brutality of the German police and the occupation MPs. The Americans liked her because she spoke English with an American accent and they thought she was pretty. They were fooled by little devices that hid the skull underneath. They were a people who went much by surfaces, which is why they liked the Germans, who had mostly had a comfortable war until the last few months, and why they despised the survivors from hell as quarrelsome, ill-dressed, ugly ingrates, whose very existence caused them problems.

The Americans put in requests to locate people that she had to give priority, while the survivors, called Displaced Persons and lumped with those who had voluntarily come to Germany to work for the Nazis, could not get out of the camps to find if their parents, their children, their spouses were alive. A young American woman came from Bad Nauheim asking about a German Jew who had been an OSS agent. Jacqueline could see that the woman felt concerned through her brusque veneer. She traced the agent Marlitt Speyer to Mauthausen but there she disappeared, probably into a common bulldozed grave. The woman did not want to accept that answer. Frankfurt was full of people trying to find spouses, family, friends, full of people trying to organize (in the camp jargon she thought in still) papers, a job, a deal, emigration, people trying to reclaim or bury their past and seize a new future, mostly elsewhere.

Ari continued to see her regularly until he went off on a mission he did not explain, the first of August. That relieved her of the awkward position of having a gentleman caller who was not. The night before he left, they walked by the river together. "You've put yourself back together remarkably," he said. "I have to say, when I found you in the hospital, I thought you were a mental defective. You sounded retarded. You looked like a middle-aged child and you talked like one."

"What a sweet and flattering tongue you have. Daniela said you were blunt."

"When I get back, we should get married and go to Israel together."

She laughed. "You and the women in the house. Why? Losing your fiancée and my best friend is no reason. I'm not for marrying. I may have begun to look like a woman, but I am not. I'm a revenant. A ghost."

"You may have been a ghost two months ago, but you're a woman now. I finagled a look at your hospital records, so I know they didn't sterilize you."

"Ari, you're good-looking and you'll find plenty of women who'll want to make babies for you."

"But not Gingembre. Not a beautiful woman who fought with the maquis and saved eighty children from death and has the best hands for plastique. I've been annealed myself, Jacqueline. I've been turned into a soldier. That's what I know how to do. We've learned a set of peculiar skills, but where I'm going, there'll be a use for them. In another life, I would have been the scholar I set out to be. In this life, I know more about how to kill than how to dispute Halakah, but I choose who and why I kill."

"You're attracted to me because of my connection with Daniela. Yes, we have that in common, but you draw the wrong conclusions!"

"Jacqueline, listen. I was engaged to Daniela when I was nineteen. The last time I saw her was in 1942. I came back for her. I would have married her, but she's far more real to you than she is to me. That's not my fault. What I found was you."

"I understand. From twenty to twenty-four makes a lot of changes in a normal life, when they used to have those. I'm twenty-three going on seventy myself."

"You're young, you need a real life. We're both alone. Desperately alone. Let's save each other."

"I stay here because I'm still hoping to find my sister. Working in the DP office for the Americans, I have access to the maximum information. If she's alive, I'll find her. And maybe get a valid address for Naomi."

Not all the Americans were naive and easily fooled. One woman who was a journalist, an American Jew, would ask her sharp questions and publish the answers, so she soon got herself into trouble with the occupation authorities. Jacqueline did not think she would last long. She wore a captain's uniform, but she explained she was not really in the Army. She arranged for Jacqueline to give testimony to a fact-finding mission of the new American president. Jacqueline called her Louise La Rouge, for she had auburn hair and a temper too, though used, Jacqueline noted, not to blow off steam but to effect changes. La Rouge ran herself into the ground trying to improve conditions in the detention camps.

La Rouge knew what Jacqueline was looking for. One day in August she sent to Jacqueline a woman who had been at Dora, in the Tunnel, who remembered Rivka. "It was on the march. They marched us on foot with no food, guarding us with machine guns."

Jacqueline could only nod. She felt frozen. All this time, like Ari, she had known but she had hoped.

"She and another little girl tried to escape. They ran into the forest, but the SS tracked them with dogs."

Jacqueline took the woman by the shoulders, restraining herself from shaking her as if she could force a different truth out. "Are you sure they caught her? Are you sure she's dead? In the confusion she could have slipped away. One body looks like another."

The woman only nodded, her eyes asking Jacqueline not to insist on the details. "Yes. But she died quickly."

"Since July 1942? No, she died very slowly."

They embraced each other. Jacqueline carefully wrote down the woman's name, she did not know why. She had begun a new journal, but there was little in it besides vocabulary in her different languages and notes for people to interview, contacts, names, addresses.

La Rouge came to see her briefly, looking pale and worn. "I was in the hospital. Really, I'm all right now." Outside in the street, a captain was waiting for her in a jeep. "I know you want to look for your sister in the U.S. Here's my New York address. I'll be there in two weeks. I may be able to help you come over."

Jacqueline knew La Rouge was carrying a hundred requests, messages, dossiers, promises. "Soon it will be time for me too to leave here." Jacqueline kissed La Rouge on both silky cheeks. Always she smelled of perfume. La Rouge gave her a raincoat, as if offhandedly, and then picked her way through the rubble to the waiting jeep. The raincoat fit her, so could not ever have fit La Rouge, who was shorter than Jacqueline. It was a good trench coat with a wool lining.

Lev came to see her at the office just after an American holiday they had in early September. She was astonished how absolutely delighted and moved she was to see him. He felt like family, a brother she had often quarreled with but her own blood. He brought with him a frail woman who walked on a crutch. She had lost her toes to frostbite. "This is my wife, Vera. I found her in the camp near Linz in the Austrian zone. We're on our way back to France. Why don't you come with us?"

"I don't know where I want to go. I don't belong anyplace."

"We're going to Palestine as soon as we can," Vera said. Her voice was extremely soft, as if something were wrong in her throat.

"I must testify in some trials. We have a bit of cleanup work in Toulouse. I can't tell you how astounded I am that you're alive. We buried somebody as you." Lev shook his head wonderingly, fingering his beard. "A body torn apart by grenade. We found your journal."

"My journal? Did you keep it?"

"I sent it to your sister in Detroit. I told her you were dead."

"But you have her address?" She hugged Lev and wept. She managed to get off for the rest of the day and they went back to her house where no one would bother them when they talked of the living and of the dead. Among the requests Lev had received that awaited his attention back in Toulouse was locating the grave of Lieutenant Jeffrey Coates, late of the OSS. His body was to be shipped back to his family in the States. Would Jacqueline object? Should he perhaps neglect to locate the grave?

She shook her head. "It was so long ago, Lev. He belongs to his family, not to me. If I could have Daniela's body, I would take that with me, but I don't know where I'd take it."

He seized her hands in a strong grasp. "You're a survivor. You know how to fight and some nursing too. You'll be needed in Palestine. The British forbid us entrance. But we're getting in, the aliyah bet. You have no other place to go, Jacqueline, unless you want to go to America."

"I've been working with the Americans. They don't understand. They know nothing about politics. They confuse Socialists and Communists. They think Zionists are Communists. They like the Nazi industrialists because they're clean shaven and efficient. They don't understand the Russians at all, because they've never been hungry or invaded or bombed. . . . The women in my house, they want me to marry Daniela's fiancé in her place. Maybe instead I'll take her place in Eretz Yisroel. Maybe I will. But I have to see my sister first. I have to get a visa from the Americans to let me go find her and then I'll decide. Naomi's the only family I have left."

"We're all your family. If you go to America, you think about what I've said. If your heart moves you, come with us. We won't be going until I finish in Toulouse, maybe by the Gentile New Year."

After Lev and Vera left for France, she waited for him to send her Naomi's address and she considered what he had suggested. She should follow them to Toulouse. Where else did she have to go?

She was walking through the rain back to her house one evening wearing the raincoat La Rouge had given her. She was crossing a rubble field grown high in weeds between two rows of standing houses, when she saw a big burly woman seize a child. A pack of the wild grubby youths who infested the town ran taunting and screaming away. Jacqueline did not like the way the woman was shaking the waif, and stepped nearer. She had to speak German nowadays often enough, and she barked out a query.

"A thief!" The burly woman held up a cabbage. "I'm calling the police right off. These damned thieving foreign trash!"

"I'll pay for the cabbage," Jacqueline said in that same loud harsh voice. A cabbage. Once she would have killed for that. She was back in the camp among the slave laborers and as they lay three to a bunk, they murmured recipes in the dark. "And this is how I make my own gefilte fish. First I buy a live carp and I bring him home from market, one with bright eyes and a sharp nasty look that shows he is strong . . ." "In making the strudel, touch is everything. I use only a slab that has been in my family for generations, marble and hollow in the center with use." Why was she thinking of that? The way the girl stared at her, her spiky red hair soaked with rain, mouth opened, tears forming in her eyes.

Weeping now. Jacqueline's gaze dropped to the shoes bound on with rags, and then she knew Rysia. Those were the shoes Rysia had pulled off a dying woman and fought another slave to keep.

In front of the woman neither of them spoke to each other, not until Jacqueline had paid for the cabbage and drawn Rysia away by the elbow. Jacqueline asked in Yiddish, "Where have you been? Nobody in the hospital knew. Why didn't you find me sooner?"

"I didn't know you at first. You look so different! It is you?" Rysia was dragging on her arm, staring at her. "Let's find someplace dry and eat the cabbage."

"I have a house. We'll go there. You can eat with us."

"I've looked and looked for you! All I knew was that you were in Frankfurt working for the Americans. They told me that at the hospital. I've looked for you in all the camps, everyplace! I've been here for weeks and weeks looking for you! I thought they lied and you were dead."

Only after Rysia had gobbled a whole pan of soup and a loaf of bread could she settle herself to talk. She propped her hands on the packing crate table, water heating on the camp stove for a little real coffee Jacqueline got from her American bosses, and stared at Jacqueline.

"I went with you, but they let me go in a week. You weren't conscious and I was afraid to stay in Germany. Slowly I made my way home to my village Ceppany, near the Rába River. When I got there, the war was over. In the village, other people, Gentiles, were living in my parents' inn and running the mill. They didn't welcome me. They claimed they'd bought it and it was theirs. There were no Jews left! An old teacher of mine told me to go to the Soviet soldiers and demand the mill back. She said they would do justice."

"Did you go?"

"I thought, what do I know about running a mill, and I was frightened of the people. I heard of another Jew who had come back in the next village and then just disappeared. I didn't want to be the only Jew in Ceppany. I hung around, but nobody wanted me there. Some Russian soldiers gave me food and tried to make me go to bed with them, but I told them I was only eleven. I think everybody was mad they didn't rape me, because they had raped others. Finally I decided I couldn't stay, so I started back to look for you. It was hard. Everything now is cut into zones with border police. The Russian commandant had given me papers, but I discovered that if I showed them at the entrance to the American zone, the Russians wouldn't let me out or else the Americans wouldn't let me in. I kept trying for two weeks along the border. Finally I threw away all my papers and went through in a load of potatoes."

"You know what tomorrow is? It's Erev Rosh Hashanah, Rysia. L'shanah tovah tikatayvou. May we be inscribed for a good year." She put her arm around Rysia. "Don't worry, we'll organize what we need. Now, come meet my housemates. They've all been in the camps, you're safe here."

When they went to bed that night, Rysia lay in her arms clutching her, shuddering with fear and fatigue. "I was so afraid you had died in hospital, died like everyone else. Then I was afraid I'd never find you, that you'd gone back to France. I looked for you for so long, in every street. Every day I looked for you. I gave up hope but I had nothing else to do. I'm afraid I'll be arrested. Jacqueline, I have no papers."

"We'll fix that. Daniela was the best counterfeiter, but I'm not useless myself. I know every little racket going here. Once we get you papers, I'm going to take you to Toulouse, where Daniela and I were in the Resistance. We have friends there. I have to get a temporary visa from the Americans to go find my sister Naomi in the U.S."

"When you get your real sister back, you won't want me."

"I have lost my other sister, my mother, my father, my best friend, my lover. How can only one sister make all that up?"

"I'll go where you say, but don't leave me there alone. I can't stand being alone."

"We'll make a family. We know who each other really is. Only you and I are alive to tell what we've been through and the mountains of the dead behind us."

"Do you think I'll ever grow up? Ever be a woman like other women?"

"You'll be a better woman than other women. We've been each other's mother, we've been each other's baby, we've shared the last scrap of bread."

"And that apple, remember that apple," Rysia said. "A whole orchard inside it."

Beside her Rysia fell asleep, still holding tight. She could not extract herself to find a more comfortable position, but she did not mind lying awake. It would be the New Year. Rysia and she would go to the river and perform tashlich, throwing the crumbs in and throwing the sins away. Her sin had been quietude and despair. Her sin had been emptiness. L'chaim, life, was the toast they would drink tomorrow. She knew the worth of her friends, how strong they were, how utterly to be trusted with death and with life and rebirth. She would follow them into the war they were entering. She had no other family, no other land or loyalty, no other home.

She had no choice, finally. Rysia was stateless, but so was she. She had delayed returning to France, in part because she would never forget the way she had lost her country and her citizenship under Vichy as under the Germans. No, she was as stateless as Rysia. She belonged to no one but the friends who had survived and who were going, as Jews, to make a place where Jews could never be stateless. Into her head came no images beyond Daniela's fantasy of the apricot trees in bloom. It did not matter. Europe stank of blood. She knew she was not so much going toward as going away from, but she was going in the only company she cherished. The war had taken from her everyone she loved, but it had given her Rysia back for the New Year, it had preserved Lev and Vera alive. It had cast up Ari, whoever he would be to them.

But first, she must find her only living sister—who perhaps no longer spoke French. Who perhaps would resent her, remembering only childish antagonisms. Who perhaps liked living with a rich American family and would resent any effort to haul her off into danger and poverty. She did not know, but she had to go face-to-face and find out. At the least, she would recover her journal, which had so much of her old life stored in it. Memory had become a religious function to Jacqueline, and she studied how to keep it intact and powerful.

The love she found in herself was not the love that Ari sought but deeper and more primitive, tribal, familial, sisterly, motherly. That she could give. That she would give. She would give her strength, her love, her knowledge, her history, her self. They would cobble a family together out of refuse and rubble; they would scavenge their debris into a life.

The View from Tokyo

They had married in haste and informed the two families at their leisure, which, as the letters arrived whose anguished shrieks distance comfortably diminished, seemed wiser and wiser to Daniel and to her. They were installed in the Frank Lloyd Wright Imperial Hotel in Tokyo, middle-level members of the bombing survey, civilians again. The hotel had stood through the bombing as well as the earthquakes it had been designed to survive. Tokyo was a ruined city. Whole residential areas consisted of squatters' huts of refuse patched together. Charred safes that had held valuables still stood with no house remaining above them.

Daniel's family back in the Bronx was sitting shivah on him. Abra's mother wrote that her father had almost had a heart attack and that she was disinherited. She also heard from Ready, who had married Karen Sue and was not inclined to indignation, and Roger, who was. "You will find to your rue," he wrote in his flourishy script, "that doors will be closed to you that formerly swung wide, that hearths that welcomed you in will turn you cold away. Formerly your name on a card could admit you to the best clubs and secure you courteous attention. What kind of attention can you expect with a name such as Balaban?"

Daniel's uncle in Shanghai sent a present of exquisite silks and a sweet letter, along with a photograph of his family. It seemed that during the war years, Daniel's aunt had died and his uncle had married a Chinese woman. In addition to the stalwart older Balaban children, he posed with a new set of toddler offspring. He was not about to lecture Daniel on his marriage. "The Balabans have always been adventurous," Daniel said. "I suspect we took in some Tartars on the way. Do you mind being disinherited?"

That made her laugh. "I'm not my father's heir, and we're not the wealthy side of the family. I have a trust fund from Grandfather Scott, and one from Grandmother Woolrich. I came into that this year. It's invested in blue-chip stocks and produces a steady eight thousand a year. It won't make us rich, but it gives us a base we don't have to worry about."

"Every day I learn new things about my wife. Do you have any other hidden assets?"

"Lots," she said, "but they're not generally regarded as negotiable."

Daniel and she did not suffer as much as many people would have, she felt, from the disapproval and rejection of their families. They believed that time would bring the parents round. Both had left home early and definitively. She felt they were already far more important to each other than their families had been to either of them since puberty. Both of them had had the sense for years that their families did not really like them as they were, and that the less about their lives that was known in the old home, the better it was for domestic tranquillity.

They had just spent two days in Kyoto, which had never been bombed and was just as beautiful as Daniel had anticipated. Traveling with him was perfect. He spoke the language, he understood, he rapidly picked up the proper forms of behavior. He was interested in seeing everything, but what interested him most was their mutual experience. It was not the pool, the garden, the rock, the temple, but that he and she were seeing and knowing together with exchanged comments the pool, the garden, the rock, the temple.

How lucky she was that he had been hidden away in cryptanalysis all through the war, or someone would have grabbed him. She had married him because she loved him, but what shallow love that had been she already understood. Now that they were together she was falling in love with him in a new way that made her feel as if everything before had been practicing scales, exercises to develop the hands, the eye, the mind. Partly what she loved was how much he loved her.

Daniel was affectionate and passionate; and hers. He was not sloppy or uxorious in public, but unfailingly courteous and attuned. They were a team. They did not hold hands and coo, but worked together efficiently, excitingly, enjoying their competence, their intelligent communication and complementary skills. Abra had learned a great deal about munitions and the economy of war; Daniel knew a vast amount of and about the Japanese.

But his affection was novel, a man who cared warmly, who expressed that caring readily and without forethought or rationing. At first she had silently but constantly compared him with Oscar. Indeed Karen Sue had remarked to her that she obviously had a thing for Jewish men; perhaps she did. Or perhaps what she had wanted in Oscar and never gotten was exactly what was supremely haveable in Daniel. Now she rarely thought of Oscar except in connection with London during the war. He had ceased to exist as a force in her psyche. He was superannuated.

When Oscar sent them a fine camera as a wedding present, she was pleased merely. She had no trouble writing him an honest thank-you. Daniel was briefly suspicious, but she made him understand that Oscar liked to make family of everyone.

Theirs was, she thought, a relationship of equals at last, at last, and having had this, what woman would settle for a rationed dependency? Daniel knew far more about food and art; she handled their finances and began to take a greater interest in money in general. She was astounded daily upon waking, upon reflecting during the workday, upon retiring beside him at night, to discover how actively happy she was. Not that she thought him perfect. He had no taste in clothes, no sense of how to dress himself to display his charms and to give clues to others that would inculcate respect. He broke the back of books he read. He failed to clean the basin after he shaved, and frequently left the toilet seat up so that when she rose in the night to pee, she fell in. He sang, abominably, in the bath, the shower and while brushing his shoes. These small flaws reassured her. A whole warring sector of life had come to peace and was planted over in roses and wheat. Mine, she thought frankly, when she looked at his handsome head, his slender remarkable hands, his crisp hair. Mine. Me. Us. She would take on any enemy with him and for him, she was sure of that.

An air letter came from New York:

My dear nephew Daniel,

I hope you don't be angry that I write you. I know how it is with you and your parents but I am so grateful for your help in coming to this great and beautiful and safe country I want you should know how I feel. You should keep in the mind too that I am here and seeing your parents and can let you know how they are and let them know how you are because you shouldn't forget they care about you in spite of present quarrels and troubles.

I got a job as bookkeeper in the diamond district and I am studying English in the night school to become citizen and speak and write better. I thank you a hundred times for your help and I will be a good friend to your parents. When you have grandchildren for them, then they will soften. In the meantime mazel tov to you and your lovely bride. Your sister just had a baby boy they named Sherman. I never heard of such a name except for a tank. Be well and come back well.

I wish I could send you a wedding present, but I am saving to bring

over other people who need help. But when you come back to this country,
I will celebrate with you and give you a present then.

> *Your loving and grateful aunt,*
> *Esther Balaban*

"We should send *her* a present," she suggested. "What would she like?"

"I never met her." Daniel stuck his lip out. "I didn't exactly move heaven and earth to bring her over. I'm feeling mildly guilty. My parents did the whole thing. We'll send her a kimono. They fit anybody."

The next day they were scheduled again for Hiroshima. It had been set up three times before, and each time canceled. They couldn't figure out what the fuss was about. After all, Abra had been looking at bomb ruins for years, first unofficially and then in an official capacity. But this time finally the cars arrived and off they went, with the rest of their party of eight. It was a crisp clean November day when Mount Fuji was clearly visible with fresh snow farther down each week and the leaves displaying fine ancient-looking washed-out tints on the ground, the last chrysanthemums still raising golden and bronze withered manes.

They lay in the bed side by side, untouching and silent. They stared at the ceiling that moonlight whitened to bone.

"No, besides the enormity of it, it is different," she said. "What you'd see with what I suppose we'll have to call old-fashioned bombs is that it's so arbitrary, fate with a nasty sense of humor. A baby is thrown through the air and lands on a mattress. A young man is decapitated by flying glass. A grandmother hides under the stairway, and that's the last thing standing. In a row of houses, one is missing like an extracted molar. It's a capricious evil, do you see?"

"Death on the human scale. Death you can grasp." Daniel's voice was a croak.

"There nothing's left. Not an ant. Not a weed. Not a butterfly. Not a mouse. Nobody was lucky. It's flat as a pane of glass. It didn't matter who took shelter and who didn't."

"I can't get my head around it," he said. "The void. A force that turns people from breathing flesh into an image on stone, like a photograph."

"It is different, isn't it? Whole families, whole communities, wiped out. Not some, not half, all. It's something new under the sun, Daniel."

"They kept saying it was like the sun. The sun came down. We can't live inside the sun. . . ." His voice died away. They lay in silence.

She fell into a jumpy reverie, images of the day flashing before her, frozen, stark. Had he fallen asleep? His breathing was too shallow. Finally she could not endure the silence, in which their love, their life, all lives felt acutely fragile. "People in that hospital are still dying. Not just burns. I was talking to the nurses. Some kind of death rays go on killing people."

"Radiation," he croaked.

"Madame Curie!" she said, sitting up.

"That's right. She discovered radiation."

"Handling the radium. It killed her, slowly."

"Will they all die, everybody from Hiroshima? Everybody?" He sat up too.

"Does anybody know? I don't think anybody knows anything." The moonlight floated on the air like ash. "I remember when the bomb was dropped, I was glad, because I figured that would end the war, hooray."

"This isn't what I thought it would be like after the war. After Fascism." He lay down again. After a long silence, he said, "No wonder they kept putting us off. I can't sleep."

"I feel as if I'll never sleep again. Imagine the fireball, the moment of blast. Do you think they really knew what they were doing when they dropped that thing? Another at Nagasaki still to be seen."

"You said *they*, not *we*."

"Nobody asked me for permission."

"O brave new world, that has such creatures in it. Moloch in person. The angel of death appeared in the sky too bright to gaze upon." Daniel flung himself from side to side. "I took a sleeping pill. Should I take another?"

"It won't work."

"I have such a strange feeling, Abra, as if God's finger is on me, and I'm an agnostic through and through."

She leaned on her elbow over him. She laid her head softly on his chest, feeling his heart beat. "God's finger? We *are* getting Biblical."

"We have to do something about it. I feel as if I looked out through a vast eye and saw the future of the world in a plain of ashes, of sand turned to glass, flesh vaporized, time itself burned up."

"What can we do?"

"First, put our opinions in the report if we can."

"It might be a matter of politics," she said. "I used to be good at that. When we're back in the States. If we do go back."

"If we do." He sighed.

"People back home don't know anything about the bomb. It's just a matter of making them see. Nobody knew."

In spite of the sleeping pills, they lay awake all night. They watched dawn

spread over Tokyo, already beginning to rebuild amid the rubble. Abra wondered about his uncle in Shanghai. Surely when their work here was finished,
they could manage a visit. They had been invited to a Japanese home for the
first time the coming weekend, and that should prove interesting too. They were
both stunned by what they had seen, and she did not think they would forget.
Nonetheless, between them they drew on enormous energy, and the world was
noisy with invitations like birdsongs that filled the remaining trees of Tokyo. At
Hiroshima, there had been no birds.

Flee as a Bird to Your Mountain

The telegram was there when Naomi arrived home from school. Her over-crowded high school was still on half sessions, so she was always home by one-thirty. Normally she got to the bakery by two and worked till they shut at six-thirty. Then she ran home, where they were waiting dinner for her. But today that part of her day, the least fraught, the simplest, was cleft through. She sat in a kitchen chair to read the telegram while Aunt Rose and Sharon in their aprons pulled up chairs to face her expectantly.

The telegram was in garbled French from Jacqueline from Toulouse in south-ern France and said that she was coming to Detroit via New York, leaving Mar-seille on the first of December, the earliest she could book passage.

"My sister's alive," she said.

"Your twin?" Aunt Rose asked, beaming. She let out a long gusty sigh.

"No." She did not explain that she never called Rivka her sister. Rivka was, had been, part of herself. The better part. The good half, or the half she was only good with. "My older sister Jacqueline."

"I thought the Germans had shot her?"

In answer Naomi lifted the telegram. "She's coming here. I can't make it all out."

"Where will we put her?" Sharon asked, frowning. Arty was still in Europe in the occupation forces, and after Ruthie got married, Sharon had moved Marilyn into Naomi's room. She was six, attending kindergarten in Naomi's old school. Marilyn was thin for her age, prone to sinusitis and sore throats, a sharply obser-vant but reticent child whom Boston Blackie had adopted as his own.

Rose rubbed her hands together, considering. "There's always room. We'll put Marilyn in your room, and Jacqueline can share her sister's room."

"Maybe she doesn't want to stay here," Naomi said weakly.

"Why wouldn't she want to stay with mishpocheh? Is she rich?"

"I don't even know where she's getting the money to come," Naomi said.

"Ketsale," Aunt Rose said. "This is big news for you but we can talk at dinner. You'll be late to work, you don't hurry."

For the first time Naomi burned an ovenload of bread. Then stuttering, she explained to the Fennimans. They rejoiced with her, thinking her tears excitement, joy. Naomi felt guilty, for she knew better. She was terrified. Her period had not come last month. There was no one she could talk to, no one she could tell. Ruthie was the only one she thought of confiding in, but Ruthie had disappeared into Murray. She came to the house several times a week, every Friday with Murray whom her eyes would scarcely leave; when she was there without him, it was only a little better, because he was all she talked about. Trudi and she chatted endlessly about how men were changed by war and the trouble they had adjusting to civilian life, while Sharon worried whether Arty would be the same way.

She did not tell Leib, because she had got in the habit of trying to stay out of his way. She no longer felt that mesmerizing love like a mountain over her. What did she feel? She felt bound to him, powerless. She felt used. She felt anger, sometimes a cold sour fury, something spoiled inside her. She knew she must tell him eventually, but that telegram had given eventually a deadline. She had no idea how long it would take Jacqueline to reach Detroit from Marseille, but December first was only two weeks away.

Still she let the two weeks pass, always hoping, always praying, running to the bathroom twice as often, staring at her cotton panties and demanding that a spot of blood appear. She begged G-d to give her her period as a birthday present. Instead she was given a new coat, a warm winter coat in red wool of which the family was enormously proud. She began to have morning sickness. Everyone complained about how long she was taking in the bathroom, how vain she was becoming. Twice she could not make it to the bathroom. Once she ran into the alley. Another time she vomited in her room and cleaned it up with Marilyn watching with big eyes. Then she had to pretend to spill part of her bottle of Evening in Paris from Woolworth's to cover the sour smell.

Sandy talked of nothing lately but, After we graduate. What colleges are you going to apply to? Naomi always said she didn't know. She wasn't going to go to college, because she wasn't going to finish high school, but she did not tell Sandy that. She was going to bear a bastard and die in childbirth, in her bed or in the alley where she had thrown up. They would all say what a bad girl she had been, but they would feel sorry for her. If only she could get the dying over before Jacqueline arrived and learned what kind of sister she was crossing oceans to find.

Everyone was speculating on what would happen when Jacqueline arrived. The general assumption was that she would be staying in Detroit, looking for work. Naomi did not think so. She thought that Jacqueline meant to take her back to Paris, but she also must want her journal. What Jacqueline meant to do mattered little, Naomi thought, because what Jacqueline expected to find was a sweet little invented sister who was still twelve years old, still French, still good, still virginal. She knew from the journals that Jacqueline had slept with Henri, and that gave her some hope; but that had been for food and Henri had not been a married man with two babies already borne by his wife, David and the new baby Linda.

Sometimes she told herself that she had loved Leib, but if so, it had dissolved in her misery like chalk in water. All she could remember of what she had called love was the feeling of being held in place, transfixed. She did not know if she had lost something precious or awakened from a fantasy, but what she had wakened to was worse. Sometimes she imagined drawing her savings out of the bank and running away with her baby hidden inside.

She sounded out Sandy. "Do you ever think of doing it with a boy?"

"Sure, I think about it, but my mother would break my neck. Every time I go on a date, she waits up with the porch light on and she has to know every single minute."

"Do you tell her everything?"

"Most of it. Who wants to tell their mother about necking?"

"But what happens to girls who do it? Do they all have babies?"

"If all the girls who do it had babies, half our class wouldn't graduate," Sandy said smugly. "Or one third, anyhow. That's what condoms are for. I explained them to you years ago."

"But if they get pregnant anyhow, do they always have babies?"

"Some have operations and some have babies. Mostly they go away to homes and the babies get adopted. But sometimes, like Magda Revitch and that colored girl with the braids, they keep their babies and raise them. Then they've really had it." Sandy mimicked slitting her own throat.

That was the sum of the information Sandy knew: nothing about abortions other than that some fast girls who got caught had them. It seemed hopeless. If a girl had a baby, then obviously she hadn't gone, so it was no use asking her; if the girl had an abortion instead of a baby, nobody would know, so you couldn't ask her either. Finally as December first passed, she had to speak to Leib. After weeks of avoiding him, she found it impossible to catch him alone. Leib had passed his real estate license and gone into business with Fats and Moose and some silent partners whom Trudi said were crooks, with money from numbers and prostitution. Trudi was angry with Leib because he was always out. She had quit the hospital again to stay home with the baby. Now she said it was worse than when he was in the Army, when he had written her twice a week. At least if he wrote letters, she'd be more in touch than feeling him climb into bed two hours after she'd gotten in, observing him eat his eggs in the mornings and watching him rush out the door when Fats tooted the horn on his De Soto. Trudi was not as friendly to Naomi as she had been. Lately she always asked Sandy to babysit.

Finally Naomi got a chance. Leib came downstairs one evening saying he'd run out of cigarettes and was off to the drugstore that stayed open till ten. The guy there usually had some under the counter at a high price. "Anybody want something from the drugstore?"

"I'll go with you," she said. "There's some shampoo I want."

"So you can stay even longer in the bathroom?" Sharon asked. "What's wrong with the Halo I use?"

"My hair's too curly for it," she said. Any nonsense to get out. She had already put on her coat and stood by the door.

"Let her come along," Leib said. "I like company."

"Okay, get me some corn plasters." Rose counted out the change.

When they were walking down the street, Leib said, "So after playing hard to get for a month, you decide to throw yourself at me when it's freezing down to hell. What do you think, we can do it in the park tonight?" He put his hand heavily on her arm. He still limped but he could move more rapidly than he had in the summer.

"I have to talk to you. Leib, I'm pregnant."

"Impossible."

"It's true."

"By that lumpy kid?"

"You know I never did it with him."

"Maybe you better start."

"That's not possible," she said angrily. "No."

"How do you know you're pregnant? Have you seen a doctor?"

"What doctor could I trust? I've missed two periods, I have morning sickness and my breasts are sore. I looked up all the symptoms in Aunt Rose's doctor book." That was an encyclopedia of information about illnesses and parts of the body. Coming on Naomi looking at it, Ruthie had confessed to her that she had tried to find out about sex from it when she was thirteen, but while the doctor book was strong on inner organs, it stopped there. Naomi wished she had to look through books to learn about sex.

"The first step is to get you to a doctor. Lots of girls think they're caught when it's nothing. Then I'll figure what to do." He gave her a slap on the buttocks. "Seems like every time I touch a woman, I knock her up."

Naomi began to cry. He took hold of her by the shoulders, shaking her. "Stop that. You want to walk in the house weeping? Quit worrying. I'll take care of you. I got a sense of responsibility toward you. What I have to figure out is the timing, whether I'll have enough money coming in by the time the baby's due to set you up."

"Leib, how do women get abortions?"

"Don't worry. I have connections for whatever we need." He paused as they passed an alley, then drew her into the darkness to kiss her. "Your breasts are growing. If it wasn't so cold, I'd do it right here, but my pecker would get frost-bite. Listen, Sunday I'm looking at lots. Afterwards, I leave her at her parents. We're eating with them." He took her face between his gloved hands, cold leather against her cheeks. "I say I forgot something, so I have to pass by the house. About five-thirty."

"I'm still at the bakery."

"Seven then. You be upstairs. Now I get it, why you've been playing cold. You're scared, but there's nothing to be scared about. It's copacetic. What belongs to me, I take good care of. Either I'll set you up in a cosy little apartment right off or we'll drop this baby and go that route when you finish high school."

"But Uncle Morris and Aunt Rose won't let me do that."

"You're sixteen. You can just walk out one day and if they don't know where you went, then they don't know where to look for you. They're just poor Jews anyhow, they've got nothing to offer you. The future is formula houses by the thousands out where the land is cheap. I see that and I'm going to make a killing. Little saps like Ruthie and that schlemiel she married, Sharon and Arty, they're all going to be looking for six-, seven-thousand-dollar houses with a VA mort-gage. They're going to be lining up. I'm moving Trudi and the kids out there." He pulled her hard against him. "See you Sunday, seven P.M. upstairs."

"They'll hear us."

"Sunday night Morris always has a meeting."

She lay awake with her hands clasped on her belly. He would help, but he would make her do whatever he wanted. She did not exist any longer. She was a vehicle to bear or not to bear Leib's child as he chose. She had lost one family, and now she was going to lose her second. As angry as she was with Ruthie, and she realized that night as she lay in bed that she was very angry, she did not want to be cut off. Nevertheless, maybe the kindness she could pay to all of them was to disappear as if she too were dead, like all the rest of her family. But the baby was not Leib's, it was all hers and she called it Rivka. Rivka was hers and hers alone and she knew it. Rivka was Rivka returned, to grow up again and be loved.

All dead except Jacqueline, who was coming. Leib knew that, but clearly it had not registered on him. What difference could it make, finally? A wasted trip. Unless Morris and Rose were right, and Jacqueline did mean to live in the United States?

She lay under Leib again and by the end of the week, he took her to a doctor, a real doctor with a waiting room out by Seven Mile Road. The doctor took a urine sample, but remarked that he thought she was pregnant. Leib gave her a dime store wedding ring for the visit. She imagined herself alone in an apartment with the baby, waiting endlessly for Leib as Trudi waited in the new suburb. It would be better to die.

Maybe she should kill herself, but she could not until Jacqueline came. It would be wrong to add one more death to the pile. She owed it to her sister to wait and to tell the truth, so that Jacqueline would be released from whatever false caring was dragging her thousands of miles. Naomi ought to die, but Rivka ought to live, little Rivka hiding in her belly smiling.

A phone call came from New York. Aunt Rose was speaking Yiddish on the phone. Then she called Naomi, who was listening to "The Green Hornet" while she did her American history. The voice was familiar yet different. "Naomi, ma soeur, Naomi, je viendrai te voir jeudi. J'arriverai à six heures du soir, j'ai tout expliqué à notre tante. Pendant ces trois jours, je donne encore cinq conférences au sujet des juifs après l'Holocauste. C'est Joint qui paie mon passage, tu comprends? Mais je me dépêche le plus possible, ma soeur. Tu es en bonne santé? Je t'embrasse. J'ai un désir fou de te voir à l'instant même."

She tried to catch Leib the next morning, but he was not up. That evening she tried again. He was briefly in the living room getting the car keys from Morris. Behind Morris's back, he nodded at her, winking. Meaning she was pregnant, as if she hadn't known already. She tried to signal to him that she had to talk, but he was out the door with the keys.

Thursday arrived. Rose and Morris went to the train station with her. In spite of the afternoon's snow, which had stopped, leaving the night stark and bitter, the train was on time. Morris made a big sign with Siegal on it. He said, that way nobody would be embarrassed if they couldn't recognize each other after all these years. Naomi's heart pounded. She had to run to the bathroom to throw up. When she got back, she saw a woman with Morris and Rose, a tall woman, very thin and very beautiful in an army greatcoat and a beret. Naomi moved forwward slowly, slowly, as the station spun around her and voices rose into babble.

Sweat broke out on her face. It was and it wasn't her sister. Naomi slid to the floor as Morris bounded forward to try to catch her.

When she came to in a ring of staring faces, she was ashamed. They were not the only people meeting Jacqueline, for there was a formal delegation from the local Jewish group handling her visit and a photographer shooting off flashbulbs at Naomi fainting before she could be pulled to her feet. "For shame," Rose was saying, "this is a private thing, she should meet her sister come back from the dead without light bulbs in her face."

Jacqueline was handling the reporters in English. There would be a formal meeting with the press tomorrow at eleven. She would be glad to answer any questions then. She had a presentation for them and press packets. Now she was tired and wanted to see her sister.

Jacqueline was not staying with them, but at the Statler. "I had them book a double room." She was holding Naomi's hand and staring into her face. Her eyes were the same hazel. "I wanted you to stay with me, at least tonight. We have so much to talk about. Will you come?"

Naomi was crying. She only nodded. At least that way she could tell her what she had to right away, tonight.

Finally they were in the room with Jacqueline's suitcase and briefcase bulging with papers, charts, mimeographed statements in four languages. "You're so big, so blooming, so gorgeous, Naomi!" Jacqueline said to her in French. "To see you again, I can hardly keep my hands off you. I hope I didn't shock you, appearing suddenly. They thought I was dead, but I was among the living dead, in a camp."

"Jacqueline, there are things I have to tell you too."

"Don't cry, my darling, don't cry. Sit. Please, sit down as if you mean to stay a little while with me anyhow. I know you have a life here. I know that."

"You wasted your time coming for me."

"To see you is not a waste of time. If you want to stay here, I'll understand, but don't make up your mind till we discuss all possibilities."

"You don't want me. I'm of a bad character. I am pregnant."

"Pregnant?"

Naomi could only nod, tears flooding from her eyes. Now two people knew her shame and Jacqueline would thrust her out, send her home and scream at Morris and Rose for letting her be ruined, when it had been only her own fault. She tried to say that, but she could not speak for sobbing.

Jacqueline came to her in two long strides and sat her down on the edge of the twin bed that was to be hers. "Baby sister, my only, my dear, why do you cry? Do you think I care whether you went to bed with some boy? You're young to

have a baby, but you're strong. You have the baby or you don't have the baby—
how far along are you?"

"Two months and a couple of weeks."

"If you don't want to have the baby, we should act soon. I think in New York
I could fix it. If you want to, that's fine too. What about the father? Do you love
him?"

"I thought so, but I don't." She stopped crying. Pressed against her lean sister
who had taken off the greatcoat and wore a sweater and skirt, she slowly relaxed
and talked. The tears began again but not spasmodically. Slowly, slowly, like the
blood she had hoped for every day, warm slow tears were trickling onto Jacqueline's sweater where Jacqueline held her to her breasts, smaller than Naomi's.

"I think I may cut his balls off," Jacqueline said cheerfully. "I'm going to take
you away for sure. I don't want you in the same city, on the same continent, with
this bastard. What's wrong with Aunt Rose that she can't keep him off you?"

"But it was my fault! I wanted him. Not what happened. I didn't know what I
wanted. I thought he was a big hero and I had a crush on him from his wedding day."

"It's not your fault, little one." Jacqueline was stroking her shoulders. "It's not
a big bad sin. I've seen too much death and not enough life. Everyone's on my
back to make babies. You want a baby, I'm telling you it'll be just fine. The father's
Jewish, even if he's a momzer."

Naomi had cried herself out. Her eyes were swollen and sore. She lay against
her sister, touching her hair, her arm. "What's that?"

"My number. From Auschwitz."

"Was it bad there? I saw pictures, in the Yiddish papers. Piles of bodies. Was
that where Maman and Rivka died?"

Jacqueline began to shake against her, and now Naomi was holding her big
sister and comforting her. Jacqueline shook and could not speak, while slow tears
slid from her eyes. Finally she uttered in a choked voice, "I can't talk about it to
you. Not yet. I shouldn't be alive."

Jacqueline needed her too, Naomi realized, and sat up straight on the bed.
Jacqueline needed love, needed holding and coddling and looking out for. She
stroked her sister's tight hard body, racked with convulsions of grief. "Will we go
back to the apartment in Paris?"

"I don't think I could bear Paris. I went to the apartment. There're French
people living in it, and they acted as if I was impossible. I saw Maman's lace
tablecloth and they denied it. The Germans took half the things anyhow. I got a
few keepsakes from the butcher downstairs who saved them for us and put them
with his things when he went into hiding. Maman's candlesticks. Her brooch."

"Are you going to stay here, the way Uncle Morris and Aunt Rose expect?"

"Here? No!" Jacqueline laughed, touching Naomi's face again. "How precious to see you. I have friends in Toulouse, they'll be your friends. Don't frown with worry, they're not bourgeois. They're crazy like me, friends from the Resistance and the camps. I'll tell you all about them, my sister, my darling, my baby, and they'll be family for you too."

"Will we live in Toulouse?"

"That will be our base. We're going to Israel. In the meantime I'm raising money and making speeches. I turn out to be good at that. I have an odd set of talents." Jacqueline laughed, more sharply. "Would you like a little schnapps? I have a bottle in my suitcase. Just a little, not to make the baby drunk."

"I can have the baby?"

"If you really want to. You're young to have a baby, but if you want it, it would make the others happy."

"Why should they be happy if I have a bastard?"

"Vera was sterilized in Ravensbrueck." Jacqueline poured the brandy for both of them and lay back against the pillow to talk about the people she said were waiting for them in Toulouse. Rysia who was a year older than Naomi she talked about, who had red hair and was Hungarian; Vera and Lev who were married she talked about; and Ari she talked about the most.

"Is he your boyfriend?" Naomi asked, wondering if she had got back her sister just to lose her as she had lost Ruthie.

"No, I don't love him. I can't love any man yet."

"Me neither."

Jacqueline kissed her. "You have already loved enough for a while! You're so big and gorgeous and healthy, everybody will fall in love with you, you'll have to get used to it."

Her sister seemed to her mysterious, more powerful than Leib, crackling with a hard energy. "But if Ari is so nice, won't you change your mind and love him? It may happen anyhow even if you don't want to."

"I was in love, little sister. With a man I fought with in the Resistance. He didn't want to survive as much as I did. Or maybe that's the wrong way to look at it, to confuse luck with will. To survive is no sign of good or bad character, but a gift. Something I must earn every day."

"Do you have a picture of him?"

"No. And a portrait he painted of me has disappeared. He was American."

"Is that why you don't want to love anyone?"

"Not that way. I have my own agenda, as they say in organizations. But Ari needs someone to love, he needs that a lot." Jacqueline smiled, her eyes half shut like a cat. She described how things would be.

"I can have the baby for Vera and Lev," Naomi said, sitting up.

"You can't have a baby for somebody else. You aren't a cow."

"Why can't I do something good and important for somebody else, just once? Why was I saved when Rivka and Maman and Papa all were killed, if not to pay back my life somehow?"

"To be killed is wrong. To live is good, a given right. You don't have to pay for living. They should only have to pay for killing. But they won't. Nobody but us gives a damn finally. The Americans are already in bed with the Nazis getting ready to fight the Soviets, who are buggering the Poles and the Czechs and the Hungarians."

"But if I want to do something good, once, just once!"

"Besides, when we go to Israel, we'll be starting a kibbutz. All the babies will be in the crèche, mixed up."

"Jacqueline, you always laughed at Papa when he talked Zionism. Why are we going to Israel instead of staying in France?"

"If the French officials hadn't cooperated with the Nazis, had not handed over records, if French bureaucrats and French cops hadn't helped round up Jews, if Vichy hadn't rushed to pass anti-Semitic legislation and deport Jews as fast as the Nazis, then the French would have saved as many of their Jews as the Danes did. Now in the Resistance there were anti-Semitic parts, but in most of the Resistance, we got along. There were heroes, like the village of Le Chambon, where the whole village saved Jews and never turned one in. But unless we go live there, I can't live in France. On the street I turn and I expect a raffle—that's what we called the roundups. On the Métro, in shops, I stare into faces and I wonder, what did you do? Whose side were you on? I can't live my life that way."

"We could live here."

"I couldn't get an immigration visa. I have an arrest record. I only got a visitor's visa because the Jewish agencies moved mountains to get me in for a month. The Americans don't care that the Nazis arrested me for Allied activity. An arrest record in their eyes is an arrest record."

"What were you arrested for?"

"Are you tired, baby sister? We can talk tomorrow."

"I have to go to school."

"Fuck school." Jacqueline laughed. "I have gotten coarse, Naomi, I'm hardened, how I hope you never know. My bones are made of steel hammered thin. But I still know how to love my family and my friends." She rose on her knees to hug Naomi again. Then she began to cry slowly into Naomi's hair. "Ah, dear one, we have stories to tell. Now if you don't want them to know you're pregnant, they don't have to know, your aunt and uncle. He's making money, this momzer? Good, I'll talk to him."

They did not go to sleep until two in the morning and then they slept till nine, when Jacqueline, who still had trouble with American phones, had Naomi order up breakfast. Naomi watched her sister eat. "You eat more than Uncle Morris does."

"I'm always hungry," Jacqueline said, grinning.

Naomi looked and looked at her sister who was the same and different, who was still her sister but altogether somebody else. She was falling in love with her own sister. Her heart felt stretched wide open, pierced with love. "Maman would be so proud of you."

"Naomi, we all have our guilts. Mine is that I quarreled with Maman over that silly boy and she was taken without me."

"What could you have done?"

"At that point, maybe nothing. I was an idiot then. I had no skills, no knowledge how to behave. I could neither kill nor save."

"I can't do either one. But I can have a baby."

"Sixteen is so young, Naomi. We have time for an operation."

"Sixteen is not so young. They say Bubeh was seventeen when she had her first baby."

"Time to get ready for my press conference. I'm doing things for the Joint and some for the Jewish Agency for Palestine. Then I have to pay a visit. Do you know where Leib's office is?"

Naomi nodded. "What are you going to do?" Her stomach clenched.

"Why, he's going to pay your passage to Marseille, and then he's going to make a generous contribution to our organization. Isn't that nice of him? Then I'll take you with me to California and Chicago and Texas and then we go back to New York and you make your final decision on having or not having. Then I take a quick trip to someplace that sounds like Lalala." She squinted at a printed sheet. "Savannah. Then we go to Marseille and you meet our gang."

It all exploded Friday. "Back to Europe? But why? Why should she take you back into ruins and trouble." Aunt Rose twisted her hands in her apron. "You should talk to my baby sister Esther, she'll tell you what it's like and how much better it is here."

Morris was frowning. "Palestine's even worse. The fighting is just starting there. Violence every day. Bombing, shooting. The British are sinking the boats full of Jews fleeing Europe."

Naomi looked at Jacqueline, sure she would answer them. Jacqueline wore a blue wool dress, dark and bright at once. Her aureole of hair was quelled into braids. She sat very still in the middle of the far side of the table from Naomi, her hands crouching on the table on either side of the plate Rose had been about to clear. "You don't get anything good without fighting for it. She belongs with me and I belong there."

Naomi thought, She thinks they make a great fuss about danger. For her it's given, like the air. My sister, the lioness. Jacqueline's hair was lion colored. Naomi liked best when it was loose and wild. She liked to brush Jacqueline's hair. They were finding little rituals and habits to say their love to each other. The argument raged around her. She felt calm within, calm around the hidden child who smiled at the uproar. The child who would be born in the Land. They were already traveling, Jacqueline, herself and Rivka. Nobody else understood.

Ruthie stood, her chair falling back. "You can't do this! She has a life here, she has a family! I'm planning to put her through college. She has a future here. She can make something of herself."

"She is something," Jacqueline said guardedly. "Herself. My sister."

Murray stared at Ruthie as if she had gone crazy, but Ruthie for once was paying him no attention. "We're her legal guardians. We could stop this nonsense. We can't permit you to take her into danger."

Morris made a face. "I'm not going to use the law against sisters."

"Tata! We can't let it happen. She's ours too! We have to use any means to protect her. She belongs with us! We love her at least as much."

"You're married," Jacqueline said. "How much of yourself do you have to give her? Ask her what she wants."

Ruthie ran around the table and grabbed her hands. "Naomi, you're throwing your life away. You can't turn history back. You have a life here, a future!"

She could not help seeing herself for a moment with Ruthie's eyes, and suddenly going to Eretz Yisroel became something out of a child's picture book. Reality was America, college, a good job. People did not suddenly start countries. In Ruthie's eyes she was sailing off the edge of the world into a silly and dangerous fantasy. How could she hurt Ruthie? Then she looked at Jacqueline, whose eyes were the eyes too of their papa, looking now not at her or any of them but into inner space with that cold stare they took on sometimes, cold as the wind off a field of graves. She squeezed Ruthie's hands back and then pulled her own free. "You have Murray. You have your mother and father and your brother and sister-in-law and your nephew and niece. She has only me." She felt as if she were tearing loose from her own flesh. She wanted to beg Ruthie to let her go willingly.

"She's not entitled to your life!" Ruthie cried, clutching her hands across her breasts. Her eyes welled over.

My lives, Naomi thought. "You'll come and see us, when the Land is won. You'll come too." She stood and put her arms around Ruthie, who began to weep. I won't have to tell her the truth to get away, Naomi thought with enormous relief. Jacqueline and I can keep Rivka secret.

"Many people are waiting for her and for me, people to whom she'll be as dear as she is to you. Naomi brings a blessing to them." Jacqueline rose also, her hands turned palms upward at her sides. "She brings love."

———

That was the way it happened. In the New Year of 1946, which is to say the month Tevet of the year 5707, there disembarked at Marseille on a choppy day Jacqueline Lévy-Monot, who had a French passport, and Naomi Siegal, who had an American passport, and invisibly, Rivka, who had no passport yet at all but claim to three different nationalities, one of them not yet issuing passports. They were met by Ari Katz, Naomi's future husband, for although Naomi and Ari did not as yet know this to be true, Jacqueline Lévy-Monot, aka Gingembre, had already decided that matter.

The End of One Set of Troubles Is But the Beginning of Another

After Words: Acknowledgments, a complaint or two and many thanks

I conceived of this novel soon after finishing *Woman on the Edge of Time* in 1976. At that time I began accumulating books, clippings, bibliographical references and queries and began slowly to evolve the characters. The magnitude of the task was apparent early and daunting to me. I actually intended it to be a third longer than it is and to include the Soviet Union, but the inability to get a grant to cover that research made me alter my scheme. Basically my only financial acknowledgments are to all the colleges and universities at which I did readings, workshops, lectures and everything but a fan dance to support me as I wrote the book over the past seven years. I am especially grateful to the University of Cincinnati, where I served as Elliston Poet as I was putting the penultimate form of the manuscript together.

I owe a debt to a number of people who helped me, to Howard Zinn and Roslyn Zinn for checking my forties details; to Regine Barshak, one of the few survivors of Drancy, for sharing her experiences; to my friend Ruth Linden of Brandeis and the Women's Holocaust Media Project, for going over my chapters about the camps and sharing her interviews and her research with me; to Adrienne Rogers for checking my French, and for remembering her student after all these years; to Rabbi Debra Hachen for giving me many dates and Nancy Passmore of *The Lunar Calendar* for helping with dates also; to my assistant Kathy Shorr for her hard work, intelligence and almost unfailing good spirits; to Claire Beswick of heroic enterprise and my dear friend Elaine McIlroy, both of the Wellfleet Public Library, who sought out for me well over a thousand books on interlibrary loans, who ran down obscure World War II pamphlets, yellowing government documents, out of print memoirs; to my equally dear friend Stephen Russell of Twice Sold Tales, who found the books I needed to own even when we were assured by everyone they didn't exist, and who, while wearing his other hats as musician and disc jockey for public radio station WOMR, researched dates on songs, as did Janice Gray of WGBH Boston. I also apologize to and thank all the other people who endured my endless questions about what they did or had done to them in the war. I am grateful to Ruthann Robson for reading the third draft and giving me useful comments; thanks to Professor Eleanor Kuydendall of SUNY New Paltz and Jacqueline Lapidus for helping with assorted facts on France of 1939–45, to Professor Kormel Huvos of the University of Cincinnati for correcting my geography at a critical point and to Marilyn Sweet, formerly of the CIO in Detroit, for giving me some information about Briggs; and I celebrate the bibliography and the answers to occasional queries that Valerie Miner and I exchanged, good vital networking. I also want to express my full and ongoing gratitude toward my agent Lois Wallace for her belief in this work.

Since this is a novel and not a scholarly work, I don't intend to append a list of sources. I read so many memoirs, biographies and histories of government officials, of OSS and SOE personnel, of camp survivors, of American generals and would-be generals, of marines and those who covered their war, of the French Resistance, of the race riots in Detroit, of the decoding operations in Washington, Hawaii and England, that acknowledgment even of the finest is pointless. However, there were certain books I want to mention because of their importance to me. *Those Wonderful Women in Their Flying Machines* by Sally Van Wagenen Keil was simply the best single source of information about the WASP I found, and a fascinating job of recovering forgotten history. Amy Latour's *The Jewish Resistance in France* was invaluable to me in locating exact sites I used in the novel and imagining my way into those times, as was Vera Laska's *Women in the Resistance and in the Holocaust.* Serge Klarsfeld's *Memorial to the Jews Deported from France 1942–1944* is a tremendous monument. The military histories I leaned on most heavily were John Costello's *The Pacific War 1941–1945* and Liddell Hart's histories (although I read far more naval history than I needed, as I discovered within myself another alternate self, as I always do in writing novels, this one an armchair naval strategist). Karen Anderson's *Wartime Women* was very useful. *Proceedings of the Conference, Women Surviving the Holocaust,* edited by Esther Katz and Joan Miriam Ringelheim, was important to me in confirming observations I had incorporated from my own readings of memoirs and interviews and putting it all together. I would also like to point out the importance of the Holocaust Library in keeping that history alive by publishing important sources. Similarly, I found a number of books published by Calmann-Lévy extremely useful, containing material unavailable in English. Anybody interested in cryptanalysis owes a debt to Ronald Lewin's books; memoirs by men like W.J.

Holmes and Edward Van Der Rhoer and Ronald Clark's biography of William Friedman, *The Man Who Broke Purple*, helped me a great deal in creating Daniel Balaban's milieu.

I could never have written this novel in the time I did without working on a computer, and I could never have managed the research and been able to have access at once to just what I needed without a powerful data base oriented toward words and text. I used Superfile (FYI) and used it hard. The data base if printed out would be eight times longer than this novel—all on floppies! This is a novel conceived in the imagination, but I wanted nothing to happen in it that had not happened somewhere in the time and place I was working with. I have also relied heavily on my own memory and on the memories of my family and of families I have known well. At times I have slightly altered events, for instance making the *Ohio* not only an American built tanker, as it was, but under American rather than British command, since otherwise Duvey would not have been aboard her. I have also sometimes used one consistent name for entities (Hypo, FFI) that changed their names frequently, using one term before or after its actual application for the convenience of the reader, who will swim in enough alphabet soup anyhow. I am also sure I have gotten facts wrong, and sometimes even primary sources were contradictory.

Finally I thank my husband Ira Wood. Perhaps nobody should ever have to read an 1100-page manuscript six times in all its drafts, but he did, and was unfailingly clear-sighted and penetrating. He also gave up his own work for a month to help me with the research abroad, which was sometimes fun and sometimes drudgery and occasionally quite unpleasant. This is one more adventure we have shared. Finally I thank Colette, Dinah, Jim Beam and Oboe for taking turns sitting on the computer and making it work, and for going along to dreary motels and lonesome cities to earn their kibble.